ULYSSES

ULYSSES

A Biographical Novel of
—‹‹‹— U. S. GRANT —›››—

ROBERT SKIMIN

St. Martin's Press   New York

Production Editor: David Stanford Burr
Design: Judith A. Stagnitto

Library of Congress Cataloging-in-Publication Data

Skimin, Robert.
   Ulysses : a novel / Robert Skimin.
     p. cm.
   "A Thomas Dunne book."
   ISBN 0-312-11360-9
   1. Grant, Ulysses S. (Ulysses Simpson),
1822–1885—Fiction. 2. United States—
History—Civil War, 1861–1865—Fiction.
3. Generals—United States—Fiction.
I. Title.
PS3569.K49U45 1994
813'.54—dc20   94-19812
             CIP

First Edition: October 1994

10 9 8 7 6 5 4 3 2 1

To Claudia

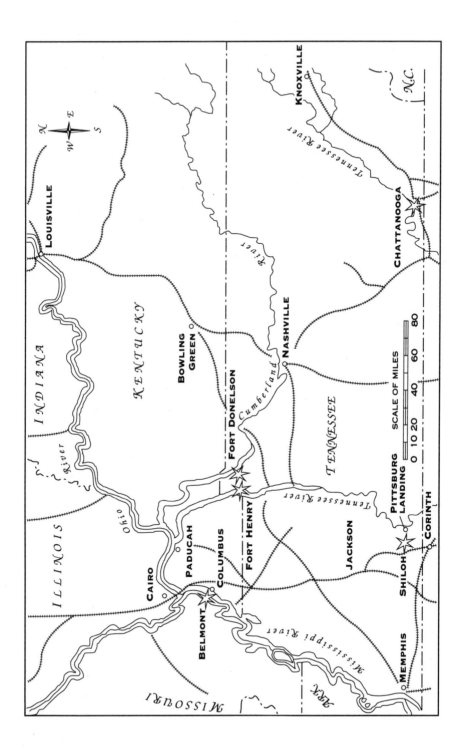

Author's Note

I n 1977 I became interested in Grant. I don't recall what propelled me in his direction—a desire to learn about the Civil War (I knew very little about that conflict then) or a compulsion to write about a drunk who came out of the boozy fog to do it all. We had parallels: I had completed a twenty-year career as an army officer, and I had also climbed out of the bottle. Both of us were from Ohio, we were the same size, and I hated to retrace my steps, as he did. *Something* pushed me. I spent three years researching and writing the novel.

And just as I finished it, William S. McFeely's excellent biography *Grant* came out and won the Pulitzer Prize. My *Grant* went on a shelf. I was crushed. I turned my Civil War knowledge to another work, *Gray Victory* (St. Martin's Press, 1988), an alternative history in which the South won the war. It was acclaimed and I decided *it* was the reason for my writing the Grant book in the first place.

Then, in January 1992, I was diagnosed with throat cancer. I was sixty-two, exactly the same age as Grant when his cancer appeared. Following heavy radiation at M. D. Anderson Cancer Center in Houston, I was quite ill. Because so much had been done on the Grant book, and I could work on it in my weak condition—or perhaps for some unknown fateful reason—I decided to drop progress on another book and rewrite it with a fresh look.

I'm glad I did.

To thank everyone who has helped over the years would take pages. John Y. Simon, the executive director of the Ulysses S. Grant Association, has been a willing source since my first research efforts. Dozens of cheerful librarians have helped immeasurably, most notably Linda Gant. I'm also indebted to all of those authors, from U. S. Grant (his excellent *Memoirs*) and Julia Grant, through Bruce Catton and Lloyd Lewis, and finally McFeely, who have provided such rich data on this remarkable man.

—Robert Skimin
El Paso, Texas 1994

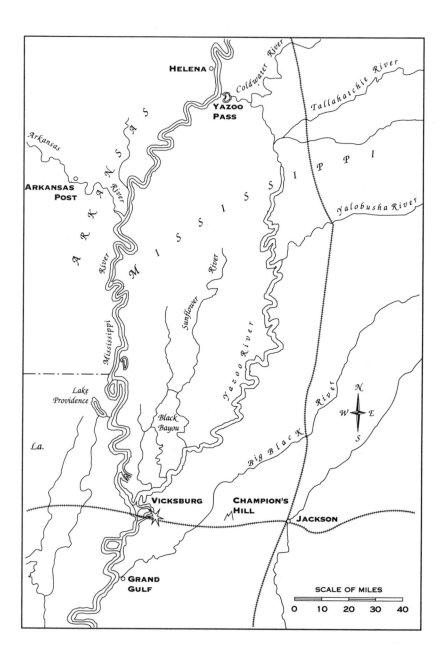

"Grant is a mystery, even unto himself."

—GENERAL WILLIAM TECUMSEH SHERMAN

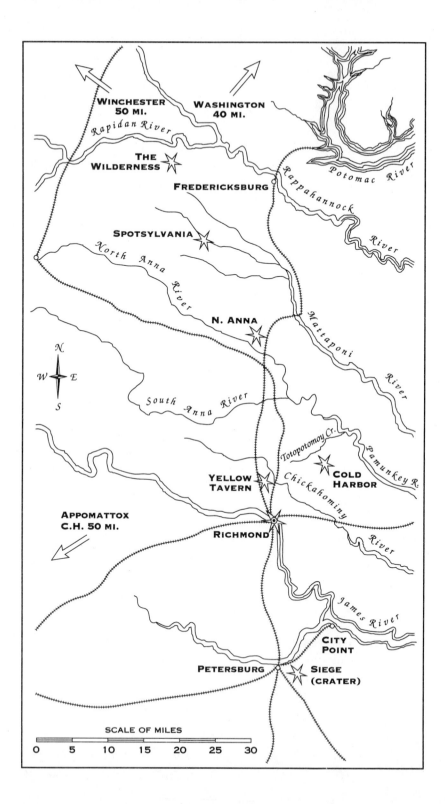

PROLOGUE

As he looked blearily into the cracked mirror, Grant tried to recall his foray, but only glimpses returned. His hands shook, his eyes were blood red, and his filthy uniform reeked of whiskey and vomitus. He moved unsteadily to the washstand, leaning over the dirty, cracked basin. Pouring the entire contents of the porcelain water pitcher over his head didn't even dent the fuzziness. How had he gotten back to the hotel? How long had he been gone? Bits and pieces flashed back—sailors, soldiers, miners, dance hall girls, blasting music, a fistfight, a shrieking monkey . . . raucous laughter. And always the nearly empty glass, demanding to be refilled.

But mostly darkness.

Darkness pierced by leering faces, screeching noise, and rowdy color.

He touched the bit of caked brown mud on his beard, and remembered falling on the bespattered wooden sidewalk and looking up at a bearded sergeant who laughed through missing teeth and saluted him!

He'd disgraced the uniform—

His money!

His thirty-three dollars. Quickly he reached for his wallet. Empty! His pockets yielded seventeen cents. Just seventeen cents left of the entire, carefully saved stake on which he was to get to New York. How could he have been so insanely stupid? What was he to do now, go begging? Sherman had offered. But he couldn't, simply *couldn't* go to him like this.

The nausea swept over him, sending him back to the basin. He retched, heaving only a bitter yellow fluid, then stood, shaking. He reached the stinking bed, sank down and closed his eyes, trying to still the quivering, jumping nerve ends. He had to get himself together, clean himself up so he could find Tripler. Tripler was a doctor—he'd help him. Old friend, friend of Julia.

Julia! Dear Lord, how could he have forgotten her in his insanity?

And he didn't have one single excuse.

He loathed himself, felt utter repugnance. How could what was supposed to be an army officer be every bit as bad as the worst, most abhorrent bum? He was no better than the most disgusting thief on the street. And that was just what he was, a thief. Hadn't he stolen their money—poured it down his gullet and puked it away?

Oh, my dearest Julia, how could I do this to you?

He went to the window and looked out. Three stories should be enough to break his neck . . .

Was this what the Mexican called *hora de verdad,* his hour of truth? Moment of truth? What was the difference? One thing was certain—just as with the army, he was finished with alcohol, absolutely, indisputably finished. He would never touch another drop for the rest of his worthless life.

Never.

PART ONE

CHAPTER 1

He had made up his mind when it came time to put the initials on his new valise. There was simply no way he was going to set himself up for ridicule with "H.U.G." There had been a controversy following his birth over naming him, and in the end he had become Hiram Ulysses Grant. But immediately everyone had started calling him by his middle name.

Actually, they had called him Ulys, pronounced You-liss.

Well, he'd heard all about how the poor plebes got ridiculed, and he wasn't about to give them HUG as a starter. Nosiree, Ulysses Hiram it would be. It was bad enough to be five feet one inch tall and weigh just 117 pounds, without adding an opportunity for more nonsense. He spoke softly as he placed his bag before the receptionist's desk. "Ulysses H. Grant reporting for enrollment."

The clerk, a corporal, glanced at him with disdain and turned to a roster. Several moments later he looked up. "Haven't got any Ulysses H. Grants coming in from Ohio. Got a Ulysses S."

Misprint? No matter, it had to be him. "I guess somebody made a mistake. But I'm from Ohio and the rest of the name's right, so it has to be me."

"Then you're Ulysses S. Sign in here."

"But my real name is Hiram." The S could possibly stand for Simpson, his mother's family name, he thought. But it didn't matter; it was still wrong.

The adjutant walked up. "What's the problem?"

"This Animal doesn't know his own name, sir."

He looked into the lieutenant's bored gaze. The officer said, "Sign in according to your orders. If there's a mistake, you can apply to the War Department for a change."

Grant picked up the pen. "All right, uh, all right, *sir.*"

The next few days were the most confusing of his life. Gone were the quiet, nonthreatening days of life in a small Ohio town. He was now in a snarling, shouting muddle of depravity, designed surely to remove every vestige of his privacy and self-respect. "All right," the figure in gray, a third classman named Rosecrans, shouted from in front of the formation, "You are all Animals. No, you will be Animals if you learn *how!* At the present you are *Things!* That's right, you're not worthy of a name. You are civilian *Things.* In civilian *rags,* because you are not yet fit, not worthy of wearing a uniform. For those of you who manage to learn which foot is your left, there is a slim possibility that you might be around until Judgment Day on July first.

"In the meantime, since you have the simple minds of civilians, you will continue to wear that attire. You will also learn that everything down to a pile of cow dung is addressed as *sir!* You'll be on a dead run from five in the morning until ten at night. And in between steps you'll be trying to accumulate enough knowledge to pass the Judgment Day test. Yes, you primeval, shabby *Things,* you will learn the ways of the cadet corps, even if you don't make it beyond Judgment Day. And sixty per cent of you won't.

"You'll hear drumbeats and bugle calls, the brains the Academy has provided for Things that are incapable of thinking. I advise you to closely heed their messages. They'll summon you to parade, to drill, to mess, to study, to inspection, and to roll call. And when you Things are so tired you can't lift your private parts, they'll tell you when to go to sleep."

Rosecrans scowled, pausing momentarily before going on, "There are seven grades of crimes for which you can receive black marks, or demerits. If one of your silly civilian hairs is out of place, you'll get demerits. And as soon as you accumulate two hundred of these, you will be gone, Things. You will be gone back to your civilian mama. That's how easy it is, so . . ."

Grant was unable to comprehend much of the whirlwind, but his peers were in the same boat. At the end of the third day he was standing in the late afternoon sunshine by the bulletin board near his barracks when he saw his name listed as "U. S. Grant." And he wasn't the only one who noticed. "Hey, look who's with us—*Uncle Sam* Grant!" a voice exclaimed.

Following a titter from the crowd, another voice proclaimed, "Naw, that's *United States* Grant!"

Grant winced inwardly. Would this name thing ever quit? He looked up into the mirthful brown eyes of another newcomer who was several inches taller and a couple of years older. "Why so downcast?" the other young man asked, "or are you Uncle Sam?"

Grant shook his head. "I'm afraid that's me, but it's—"

"Uncle Sam." A friendly hand was extended. "My name's Rufe Ingalls, Sam. I didn't know they were giving us a mascot." He laughed out loud.

More ridicule, Grant thought. Why had he ever given in to his father about coming to this fool place? He didn't want any part of the army, of West Point, nor certainly any of this nonsense. And now he was honor-bound to stick it out. Four years! How could he ever make it?

"What's the matter, Uncle Sam, cat got your tongue?"

"No, I'm glad to meet you."

"Good. Now, we'd better hurry if we're gonna make it to supper."

4

* * *

His posture had never been too good. And now he was the continued butt of barking orders to pull in his gut, thrust his shoulders back, tuck in his chin for the required number of skin wrinkles. What had such silly requirements to do with winning wars? And saluting, saluting everything—animal, vegetable, or mineral, but mostly anything in a gray uniform. The constant drill; he'd never master the movements. How could he, when his feet and legs were more used to controlling a horse than to walking?

Out of bed on a dead run before the sun broke the cool Hudson morning. So tired he could drop before its last glow hung on the western horizon. Eat on the run, go to the toilet on the run, bathe on the run. Some of the Animals stopped running only to pack their bags and depart.

Why had he ever grown that last two inches? Four feet eleven would have kept him out. Mascot! Well, he'd show them. He'd be around when some of these Eastern smart alecks were long gone. Just keep his mouth shut, as usual, and play everything straight. Listen in class. Once over lightly would be sufficient with the books from what he'd seen. Arithmetic—because that was all most of the so-called mathematics boiled down to—looked easy and was one of the most important subjects. He couldn't spell too well, but that wouldn't show up in orals—and that was the way they gave the Judgment Day test.

Of course, he could throw the exam and get on back to his peaceful life in Ohio. Lie on the sunny banks of the river, ride a fine horse, be his own man. People didn't call you names there. Yes, that was a tempting way out of this silly thing.

No, his father would be mortified. He'd pass.

If he didn't die of lack of sleep first.

Grant was too busy just trying to survive to even contemplate the physical aspects of the Academy. He knew a smattering of its history since the Revolutionary War, such as its importance as a powerful defensive location on the Hudson River, and the traitorous action of Benedict Arnold in that conflict. He knew that middle America, but not exclusively, sent its small-town boys there for a free scientific education, and that many of its graduates went on to become America's leading engineers, as well as some of its foremost scientific professors at other colleges such as Harvard and Yale; that they built railroads and bridges, as well as other harbor defenses and the few forts the young country was acquiring.

Aesthetically, he also missed most of West Point's beauty. Two years after Grant's arrival, Charles Dickens would visit the Academy and write in his *American Notes:*

> *In this beautiful place, the fairest among the fair and lovely highlands of the North River, shut in by deep green heights and ruined forts . . . along a glittering path of sunlit water, with here and there a skiff, whose white*

sail often bends on some new tack as sudden flaws of wind come down upon her from the gullies in the hills; hemmed in, besides, all around with memories of Washington, and events of the revolutionary war, is the Military School of America.

It could not stand on more appropriate ground, and any ground more beautiful can hardly be. . . . The beauty and freshness of this calm retreat, in the very dawn and greenness of summer—it was then the beginning of June—were exquisite indeed.

The one place that did impress Grant was the green promontory overlooking the broad sweep of the Hudson as it wound grandly around the upriver bend from below the famous Plain where most of the notorious drilling occurred. Now and then he was able to steal a few private moments of solitude there. He would sit in silence, off to the side so other cadets wouldn't infringe on his moments of welcome peace. Here he could shut everything out, go back to pleasant boyhood times with the horses. He could look up the wide river to the north and imagine Iroquois war canoes rapidly approaching, their oars flashing, sunlight glinting on tomahawks and beads. Bright colors and sweaty bodies, war paint and resolute faces, narrow shocks of hair. Resolute warriors off to battle.

But mostly the quiet place offered serenity.

Somehow, the last week of June was reached and it was time for the entrance exams. The physical tests were quite easy, at least for a farm boy like himself with surprising strength for his size. His deportment had been adequate throughout, with only his drill ratings being low. But it was his academic marks that counted most, so that the business of his "having two left feet" didn't matter so much. And finally it was over. He erased his blackboard scribblings and saluted the last of the examining board of professors. He hadn't broken any records, but he had passed and that was all that counted. While he still wasn't excited about making it, there was a touch of inner pride that he couldn't ignore.

Then it was on to the tailor and the fitting of major items of uniform. Foremost was the swallow-tailed coat of sheep's gray, with its high, uncomfortable collar. Other items of issue were a gigtop hat, tight white pantaloons by the dozen, other upper-torso wear—always adorned by dozens of buttons that had to continually be shined to a high luster—and the kit that included the heavy saber. It was a good thing he was strong because that saber required special manhandling by one his size.

Now he was faced with the remainder of summer encampment, prior to the beginning of the regular curriculum in September. H. U., or U. H., or U. S. Grant from Georgetown, Ohio, was a plebe, a member of the Class of '43 of the United States Military Academy. He would still be on probation until January, but he was in. For better or worse.

He fared quite well as the days passed, garnering only enough demerits to place him in the middle of his class. He casually became acclimated to the jeers about his size, even accepting the name "Uncle Sam" in stride. And his peers started getting used to his quiet ways. He seldom wasted words, and never revealed his thoughts.

A highly unpopular plebe who seemed to think he had special privileges was a heavy, hulking son of an army colonel. Jack Lindsay was the typical bully, tormenting his smaller and less confident peers whenever he could get away with it. Grant paid little attention to him until one day at squad drill when he fell into formation next to Lindsay, only to find an elbow pushing him off balance. Grant edged over, ever so slightly, but the elbow followed. Standing at attention, Grant whispered, "Cut it out, or we'll both be in for it."

Lindsay sneered, pushing so firmly that Grant nearly fell on his face. As he caught his balance, a cadet sergeant moved quickly in front of him. "What's the matter, Mr. Grant, can't you even *stand* at attention?"

Grant stared straight ahead, stifling his anger. When the formation ended, he looked into Lindsay's jeering smile. His powerful overhand right caught the colonel's son in the middle of the forehead, knocking him to the ground, stunned. Grant looked down coolly. "Don't mess with me anymore, Lindsay."

The bully picked himself up, glanced from Grant to the onlookers, mumbled an oath, and stumbled off. Fortunately no cadet officers witnessed the incident, or there would have been trouble. Fighting was a major offense in this world of young gentlemen. From that moment on, Grant was regarded with new respect and his name was permanently changed to the more affectionate "Sam."

Usually.

One night shortly before nine P.M., three lordly first classmen paid Grant a visit in the barracks. They were escorted by Cadet Corporal "Rosey" Rosecrans. Grant jumped to attention as Rosecrans said, "This is the Animal you inquired about, gentlemen. You'll have to forgive him for not growing up yet."

Their leader was slender, his rust-colored hair a trifle unruly. He had a mischievous look. "Oh, that's all right. He may command a brigade of midgets some day." The senior walked around Grant, inspecting him. Then he barked, "Are you the United States, or Uncle Sam Grant we've been hearing about?"

Grant tucked his chin in tightly, but spoke calmly, "Possibly, sir. I'm U. S. Grant."

The slender first classman smiled, extending his hand. "I'm Sherman, Mr. Grant, and these gentlemen with me are both Virginians. This old one with the bulky body is solemn George Thomas, and his tobacco-spitting friend is Dick Ewell."

Grant stood at ease, eyeing his visitors warily. He'd heard about all of them. Thomas, the quiet old man of the Corps at twenty-four; the sarcastic Ewell, who was known as "the eagle with a lisp"; and the free-spirited "Cump" Sherman, one of the most popular cadets in the Corps. "How do you do, sirs?" he asked cautiously.

"Do you come from Indian country, Mr. Grant?" Ewell asked.

"No, sir, Ohio."

"Same thing, isn't it?"

"No, sir."

"Are you going to be the father of our country, Mr. Grant?" asked the smiling Sherman, "or will you settle for being commanding general of the Lilliputians?"

"C'mon, Cump," the soft-spoken Thomas said. "You've seen the oddity and had your fun. Let's move on and quit taking up the poor lad's time."

Sherman stuck out his hand. "By the way, I'm from Ohio too. So don't let these country boys give you too much trouble. If you need anything, Mr. Grant, come and see me."

And as suddenly as they had popped in they were gone. Grant heaved a sigh of relief and shook his head. Now the upperclassmen were treating him as a freak, although he had to admit it hadn't been too unpleasant. And Sherman's gesture had been kind, whether he meant it or not.

But he'd never need any help—if he couldn't make it on his own, he just wouldn't be around. One thing was for sure, he'd just met some of the biggest names in the Corps. Not that it meant anything to him. Or did it? The Corps. More and more the term was beginning to be significant to him, in spite of himself. It was sort of sneaky, the way it crept up on you like that. But whether he wanted to accept it or not, it was the glue that held West Point together . . .

The West Point in which Grant found himself in the summer of 1839 had known a short but stormy history as a military school. The Academy was born in March 1802 as sort of a stepchild of the Corps of Engineers. The first superintendent, a brilliant nephew of Benjamin Franklin, had side-stepped the traditional curriculum of the day and emphasized the physical sciences, mathematics, French—in which most of the world's advanced military theory was being taught—and military drafting, or drawing, as it was called. The New World needed professional men in all walks of life and particularly to lead its military. When the War of 1812 came along this requirement was particularly noticeable. Prior to that time the entrance requirements were so lax that the cadets at one time included a twelve-year-old, a man who brought his wife, and a one-armed man. That would change drastically.

With the war, Captain Alden Partridge arrived to fill the superintendent's chair with his autocratic regime of strict military discipline. The two stone barracks he built set the tone for the Academy's future appearance, and it was he who adapted the cadet uniform that gave birth to "the long gray line." But Partridge couldn't keep his hands off anything and morale among the faculty eventually became so bad that he was court-martialed for insubordination by order of President James Monroe. Major Sylvanus Thayer assumed command in 1817. Within a short time, Thayer's organizational genius enabled him to make West Point one of the top scientific institutions in America—for a time the only college in the country with an engineering course. His faculty achieved worldwide fame and the Academy became fashionable for young men of high social standing. A man of broad vision, Thayer rightfully earned the title of "Father of the United States Military Academy."

Although the primary mission of the Academy was to produce army officers, many West Point graduates went on to high civilian achievement building important bridges, harbors, and railroads. A second lieutenant by the name of Robert E. Lee saved St. Louis as an important port on the Mississippi by developing its dredging process. But now and then there was another side to the coin: Edgar Allan Poe detested the Academy and got himself dismissed a few months after entering the Class of '34. He went on to quote the raven evermore.

Shortly before Grant's arrival at West Point, Richard Delafield took the reins and assumed the continuing struggle to keep the Academy out of the hands of the army's chief engineer. Described as a "pudgy man with heavy, sandy eyebrows, an abundant thatch of hair, and nose that would have made any eagle jealous," Delafield was the fussy type, whose method of ridicule earned him the nickname "Dicky the Punster." His mark remains today in the martial English Tudor flavor of the Academy's architecture. Heavy arches, crenelated towers, and slit windows, all set in forbidding gray stone, were incorporated in the new library, the stables, barracks, riding hall, and a new mess hall.

But most of this was lost on young Grant. Cadets seldom saw the superintendent, or wanted to. The man who had the most impact on their lives was the commandant. That officer was in direct charge of all military training of the Corps and was usually around somewhere—observing, inspecting, checking. Captain C. F. Smith was the commandant. A grand, handsome man—tall, ramrod straight, magnificently mustached—the Pennsylvanian was the epitome of leadership and Grant thought him one of the two most envied men in the nation. The other was "Old Fuss and Feathers," General Winfield Scott.

It was at the end of summer encampment, during the parade for President Van Buren and General Scott, when Grant was struck by the most ridiculous presentiment. As his company was passing the reviewing stand at "eyes right" his gaze locked on the magnificent figure of the general. Six feet four and resplendent in his fancy dress uniform, the hero of the War of 1812 seemed the most striking officer he'd ever seen. That was when the crazy notion flashed through his head that someday he, Ulys Grant, might be standing on that same stand being honored.

He chuckled to himself.

Ridiculous!

Absolutely absurd that an Animal who had four long, struggling years as a cadet ahead of him should—ludicrous. Here he was, getting hallucinations about being a general when all he could do was think about getting out, out of the doggone army forever. He chuckled again. Still, the thought *had* been warming.

He was tempted to tell his new roommate about it, but he knew the story would be too juicy to keep quiet: the runt imagining himself a Fuss and Feathers someday! No, Rufe Ingalls would never be able to keep it quiet. He still couldn't believe they'd been teamed up to share a fourth-story room in the corner of North Barracks. Well, at least the tedium would be broken, since it seemed as if Rufe was trying to set a record on how fast he could break all the rules of the place.

CHAPTER 2

"Hey, Sam, you heard about the horses?"

Grant looked up from his belly position in front of the fireplace as Rufe slipped back into the room from his late-hour poker game. It seemed like his roommate was just asking to get caught. "What horses?"

"Word's out that Dicky the Punster got approval to include horsemanship in next year's curriculum and he'll be bringing in a whole stable of horseflesh for us."

Grant jerked to a sitting position. Could it be possible? "Which toilet seat did you get that rumor from?"

"Heard it from Thompson in the poker game. And Talbot confirmed it."

Horses! Could it really be true? He pictured himself riding leisurely about the reservation, galloping, jumping a rail fence . . . brushing, petting, currying, speaking softly in the language a horse knew so well. West Point could be a whole new world! He blew out a deep breath. "I sure hope it's true, Rufe."

"Uh-huh. From the way you talk about horses all the time, you might even begin to like this place."

"Aw, I like it okay."

"You're a stick-in-the-mud, Sam my boy. Can't even get you to tag along to Benny Havens with me."

Benny Havens was the off-limits place that had attracted cadets for years, the nearby tavern that had defied superintendents back through Thayer's time—the infamous Benny Havens, where the boring, plain table fare of the Academy was replaced by Benny's roast turkey, oysters, and special buckwheat cakes, usually washed down by a mug of hot flip or some other alcoholic drink. Going there was strictly against the rules, worth tons of demerits and possibly grounds for expulsion. But cadets would never cease to take the chance. Rufe was right, he'd never even been tempted. It simply wasn't worth it.

But horses! "Tell you what, Rufe old boy, if the story about horses is true, I'll go to Benny's with you to celebrate."

Rufe grinned. "I'm gonna hold you to that."

* * *

It was eleven days after graduation of the Class of '40. Cump Sherman, who had followed up on his proffered friendship and gone out of his way to be nice to Grant, had left with a commission in the Artillery, although he could have chosen the prized Corps of Engineers had he so desired. The loquacious and brilliant Sherman had stood fourth in his class academically, but his mischievous ways had produced enough demerits in four years to set him back a couple of notches. Besides, he thought going into the Artillery might get him directly involved in the ongoing Seminole War.

Another summer encampment had begun. Grant watched the new plebes straggling in, relieved that he wasn't one of them. He was briefly posted as a corporal, but soon lost his stripes. How could he be a drillmaster when he could barely execute the maneuvers himself? He'd be satisfied to remain a private for his entire stay, just as Cump Sherman had. Besides, he no more enjoyed railing at Things than he did making a dumb animal suffer.

This was an exciting day for Grant; the horses had arrived and were being unloaded down at the river landing. He saw them being hurried to the stable area—confused, mostly frightened. What friends would he find in that assorted pack? Rumor was that Dicky the Punster hadn't wasted any money on fine mounts, that many were unbroken. All the better for him.

The dragoon sergeant who had been appointed riding master was Sergeant Herschberger. A thickset, bowlegged man with deep lines around his eyes and a voice raspy enough to smooth barbed wire, Herschberger looked up that evening when Grant approached him at the stable. "What do you want, mister?"

Grant walked to a stall and nuzzled the nose of a bay mare. "I just want to say hello to some of your new mounts, if that's all right."

The sergeant's grim visage softened. "You like horses?"

"More than I do a lot of people."

"Know how to ride?"

"Some. But I'm looking forward to what I can learn from you."

Herschberger watched as Grant opened the stall. "Watch out! That one ain't broken yet."

Grant smiled as he petted the bay. "She won't hurt me."

The mare stood perfectly still, relaxed.

Sergeant Herschberger stroked his chin. "I'd say you've been around a horse or two, mister."

Moments later, Rufe Ingalls walked up. "Looks like you're enjoying your new friends."

Grant grinned as he came out of the stall. "Sure am."

Ingalls glanced dubiously at a young stallion. "Well, you can have my share of that pleasure until somone civilizes them. By the way, we'll slip out a little before eight."

Grant shot him a questioning look. "What do you mean?"

"Your introduction to Benny Havens, remember? Aren't these beasts known as horses?"

"Oh, that."

"You aren't backing out, are you?"

Grant wished he could. "Of course not. How long will we stay?"

"Until a little before lights out. Just in time to get back in. You're going to have a grand time."

"I'll be ready." Why had he made such a doggone promise?

The hole in the fence was not far from North Barracks, but the devious route necessary to get to Benny Havens took nearly thirty minutes. Grant kept expecting a tactical officer to jump out of every bush. Why had he let himself get talked into such stupidity?

Finally they were there, at the most famous—or infamous—institution in the history of the Academy. To Grant's surprise, it was quite clean and pleasant, a little dark for obvious reasons, its candlelit walls decorated with all sorts of military paraphernalia. A pike here, a sword there; muskets, all kinds of pistols, parts of uniforms, bayonets, rich old paintings by obscure artists. And even though it was midsummer, a small blaze flickered in the large fireplace. Grant took it all in, wondering how many cadet plots had been hatched in this place.

A buxom girl with a low-cut blouse, a bit plump but pretty, met them with menus. "Your usual table, Mr. Ingalls?"

"Certainly, and this is Mr. Grant, the mole roommate I've told you about. Sam, this is Purity, the darling of the Corps."

Purity made a slight curtsy, showing her dimples and more. "Only part of the Corps, Mr. Grant," she said.

Ulys blinked into the chasm between her full breasts and felt a stirring. It had been a long time since he'd been near a girl, let alone one so provocative. In fact, he'd *never* been near one *this* provocative. He was glad the light was low because he knew for sure he was blushing. He'd been squeezing in a few of those French novels when he was supposed to be studying, reading about love, yet never experiencing its flavors, or favors . . . or, oh, he didn't know. He'd never been with a girl, not even close to all the way.

He looked away from those breasts.

Rufe ordered drinks and the famous oysters. Oysters of any kind would be a new experience to him. He'd tried alcohol on occasion when he and some other boys back home had gotten into his father's wine. He had also imbibed a couple of times in the past year when there had been a celebration of some kind in the barracks and someone had sneaked the stuff in.

He looked around, feeling as if the whole Corps were watching him, but in reality there weren't more than a dozen cadets in the place. Still, that was a lot. He shrugged to himself. The honor code certainly couldn't include Benny Havens, or there wouldn't be much of a Corps—what with everyone being bound to report violations. Nope, didn't count here.

Those flips sure made him feel good.

Good thing Rufe was picking up the tab; he sure couldn't afford any kind of an outing like this. The oysters didn't do too much for him—a bit too salty. But at least they were well done. He couldn't stand anything not cooked, especially meat. It all went back to his father's slaughterhouse.

He sure wished Purity would come back and lean over like she did the last time. Now they were singing, with everyone joining in. He couldn't even carry a tune, but he'd heard the words before—to the tune of "The Wearin' of the Green."

"Come fill your glasses, fellows, and stand up in a row,
To sing sentimentally, we're going for to go;
In the army there's sobriety, promotions very slow.
So we'll sing our reminiscences of Benny Havens, oh!
Oh! Benny Havens, oh—oh! Benny . . ."

Rufe slapped his shoulder. "Ain't this something, Sam? An army doctor, off fighting Indians in the far, far West dreamed up those lyrics. Some song, huh?"

Grant nodded, but then he pictured himself trying to explain to his father why he'd been kicked out of West Point for going to a tavern. And not even another good look into Purity's blouse was worth that. "I guess it beats sitting back in our room all right. Aren't we supposed to head back pretty soon?"

Rufe pulled out his big pocket watch. "Only nine-fifteen, Sam my boy. Lots of time. You've got to learn one thing about sin, son. You don't *do* it and worry about it at the same time. Relax! Besides, I told you we always have a lookout."

It was a good thing. No more than two minutes later, a cadet burst into the great room shouting, *"Officer coming! Officer coming!"*

Rufe grabbed Grant's arm. "C'mon, follow me!"

They ran to a back door that was jammed with other cadets. Rufe pulled him out of the entanglement, leading him on a dead run around a small barn. Grant tripped, falling flat, then stumbled to his feet, following the blur of white pants ahead of him. Suddenly Rufe stepped out from behind a bush. "Whoa, take it easy."

"But what about—"

Rufe laughed. "The raiding officers don't know about our little escape route. Nobody's ever been caught on it yet."

"Stand fast there, you cadets!" an officer shouted.

Rufe jerked his arm, starting to run. "Until now!"

They fled headlong along a doubtful trail until at last they fell into some bushes, panting. Their breath sounded like elephants exhaling as they listened for footsteps. Finally Rufe whispered, "I think we lost him."

Grant was shaking, half from fright, half from anger at himself. What a stupid game he'd been talked into. Here, he sweated out demerits every day, struggled with senseless marching, battled French, and he was chancing it all for a drink, a song, and a glimpse at a bare bosom.

"C'mon," Rufe said, "We can just make lights out."

Grant's new roommate in his second year was George "the Dragon" Deshon, a solemn, studious lad from Connecticut. Rooming with Deshon was a pleasant relief. Although he would never lose his fondness for Ingalls, the more stable life with a top student should hold fewer perils—or so Grant thought. However, underneath Deshon's strait-laced demeanor lay a paradox. Although deeply spiritual, he had an insatiable desire for tasty food—preferably late at night.

Since it was virtually impossible to purchase, even steal, food from the local farmers because of Delafield's tight rein, Deshon calmly turned to the only other source. He stole from Delafield. Not much and not often, some apples here, a pie there, he was quite careful and quite guiltless about the crimes. Now and then he said, "Maybe God didn't mean for me to be a soldier, maybe He did, but He certainly didn't intend for me to always live on the sinful fare of the mess hall."

When the Dragon "happened upon" a liberated fowl, he knew just what to do with it. One of the prized, illegal possessions of their room was the carefully whittled spit for the fireplace had its special hiding place when not in use. Naturally, Grant enjoyed partaking of the forbidden fruit, even though it took a while to quell his qualms about his roommate's obsession.

One evening about eight, the Dragon sauntered into the room smirking. "It's not Thanksgiving yet," he declared, pulling a small, cleaned turkey from his coat, "but I do believe we should have a bit of the repast."

Grant shook his head, chuckling and reaching for the spit. "Where did you ever—"

"Tut, tut, my boy. Count thy blessings—and throw some wood on yon fire."

Before long, the juicy bird was impaled over the leaping blaze, blessing the stark little room with its promising scents. At 11:15, Deshon stuck a fork into the crisp skin of the bird's breast. "Ah, I do believe it's ready, Sam. Would you care for a leg, or—"

"*Ten-shut!*"

The door of the room banged open to admit the cadet officer of the day and Lieutenant Grier, the real officer of the day. Grant and Deshon jumped to attention in front of the fireplace, moving imperceptibly sideways to keep the spit out of view as the inspecting party moved around the room. Grant was sure his heart could be heard beating out on the Plain. Finally Grier stopped in front of them, asking, "Aren't you fellows up a bit late?"

They answered in unison, "Yes, sir."

The lieutenant's eyes avoided the fireplace. "Yes, the studying does require late hours, doesn't it? I'm glad to see such commitment." He turned to leave, but stopped by the door. "By the way, I once received twenty demerits for cooking in quarters. But that was when I was a second classman, back in 'thirty-four."

The two criminals slumped in relief as he left. Grant shook his head, blowing out a big sigh. "I'll bet you can smell that bird clear down to the end of the hall."

Deshon nodded. "May God bless his beneficient soul. And may we never forget, no matter what rank we ever attain—he who eats forbidden turkey is to be forgiven."

"Amen."

Grant was now Sergeant Herschberger's favorite cadet. His ease and talent with horses tugged at the old cavalryman's heart. Shortly after Christmas some new mounts arrived, some only partially broken and the rest completely unbroken. Grant finally confided to the riding master that he had been breaking horses as long as he could remember, and asked that he be permitted to help with the new ones.

"I shoulda known, ya little devil," the sergeant said. "I think you're part horse. Certainly, you kin help, but I don't want you getting hurt."

Grant smiled. "Pick out the toughest one and let me try."

He had the big sorrel eating out of his hands within days. And by now, more and more cadets were coming to the riding barn, stealing a few moments to watch him ride. One day he noticed a broad-shouldered, rough-looking cadet observing him. He recognized him as the junior from South Carolina, James "Pete" Longstreet, a leader in competitive sports and field exercises.

When he stopped to unsaddle, the burly Southerner drawled, "Your name's Grant, isn't it, tyke?"

"Yes, sir. And you're Longstreet, right?"

"Yup. I've been watching you work for some time. Don't think I've ever seen anyone as smooth, sorta like you were part of the animal. You must love horses as much as I do."

"I grew up with them."

Longstreet grinned. "Then I guess you and I oughta get to know each other a little better."

Grant began rubbing down the sorrel. "Fine with me."

It was the beginning of a friendship that would bring him into a circle of juniors that included Rosey Rosecrans, Don Carlos Buell from Ohio, the fiery Southerner Earl Van Dorn, and John Pope, who had gained fame by bringing about a uniform change earlier in the year.

Returning from his sophomore leave in Illinois, Pope had sported a change in pants styling. Instead of the multiple buttons on the side, his mother had installed a buttoned slit down the center, covered by a flap he called a "fly." He was called before the superintendent. With a straight face, Pope asked Major Delafield if he desired a demonstration of the ease with which he could get his member out in case of need. Dicky the Punster declined and dismissed the cadet. The next day, the post tailor shop was busy modifying trousers, and Mrs. Delafield was busy haranguing her husband about the new indecency.

More content with the horses and in the company of the many friends he was making, Grant barely noticed the months slide into May and the advancing end of his second year. The long-desired leave was approaching and his anticipation mounted. How long had it been since those hazy days back in Ohio? He'd departed as a hick kid, which he still was, but, by lightning, he'd go home with two years of service and four more inches on his slender frame. And he didn't have to be ashamed of anything. He was certainly a far cry from the perfect cadet who'd gone through without a single demerit—the fabled Robert E. Lee, back in the Class of '29—but he was in the solid middle of his class: 24th in rank, with sixty-nine demerits, he stood 144th out of 219 in the Corps. Although position didn't matter much to him, it wasn't all that bad for a cadet who couldn't march, was considered sloppy, and didn't study much.

CHAPTER 3

Grant thoroughly enjoyed his summer. He had a couple of flirtations, but nothing serious and no enticements like Purity. In far too short a time, it was up the Hudson and back to the long gray line. Walking up to the Plain from the landing, he was surprised to feel a touch of warmth, of belonging. He was back where Dicky the Punster reigned and where the Dragon would have new culinary schemes. But this trek up the hill was different. No confusion over names, no waiting harassment, just a job to do for two years. The system was firmly under his belt—just keep his nose clean and get by. No responsibility, horses to enjoy, even short leaves once in a while.

And he was right; his junior year was uneventful, leaving him still in the middle of his class. As usual, there were minor embarrassments like a dancing lesson debacle. He simply couldn't do anything to music—had, in fact, begun to dislike it intensely. However, his solid poise and fame in the riding barn gave him status, although he really didn't give much of a hoot about having it. His enjoyment of the Dragon's evening snacks ended when he headed into his senior year and gained a new roommate.

Frederick Dent, Jr. looked lazily up from his bunk, drawling, "I hope you didn't track too much horse dung into the room. I don't mind rooming with a Yankee all that much, but I *am* sensitive about certain odors."

Grant tossed his hat on his desk, chuckling. "Quit trying to talk like Longstreet. St. Louis is in the North."

"You see, what you don't understand is gentility, Sam. We Southerners who are landed gentry are responsible for maintaining the rapidly eroding quality of America."

"You mean the quality of your slaves."

"Tut, tut. Never try to discuss something you know nothing about."

Grant opened a book. For some reason, the humor was fading tonight.

"C'mon, Sam," Dent persisted, "admit you don't know a damn thing about slavery. Just like the rest of you so-called abolitionists."

Grant sighed. He should never have mentioned his father's political views. "Okay, Fred, I guess slavery is your business and none of mine. But that still doesn't make it right."

"That's just what I've been trying to tell you, boy. Right is in the eye of the perceiver. Our nigras never had it so good. Why, without what we've given them, they'd still be undressed slaves to their African masters. That's who sold them to us, you know—their chiefs."

"They're people, aren't they?"

"No, they're nigras—property. And as soon as you interlopers realize the fact, the less trouble there'll be."

Grant put his book aside. "All men are created equal."

Dent moved to the fireplace. "You just don't understand. You know that's just bunk. *Nobody* is equal. That's the kind of tripe you nigra-lovers spew to cause trouble."

Grant frowned. "What is your doggone problem tonight, Fred?"

"I just read another holier-than-thou tirade in the paper and it bothers me, that's all. You damned Unionists are so ignorant of reality that I can't believe it."

"Now, just a minute. Don't run the Union down just because some writer made you mad. The Union is forever and that's why we're here going to this school."

Dent was too worked up to stop. "To *hell* with your Union, nigra-lover!"

Grant jumped up, knocking a chair aside and raising his fists. They squared off, glaring.

Quickly, the absurdity of the situation hit Grant. Two friends all heated up over nothing. Their argument hadn't even developed into anything juicy yet. He dropped his hands and began to laugh. Dent tried to swing at him, but the effort lacked resolve. In a moment, both were roaring with laughter.

The weeks were flying by as they had in his third year, and graduation began to loom hazily on the horizon. In March Grant tried once more to have his name changed officially, but it was a lost cause. He would be commissioned Ulysses S. Grant and so be it. And it really didn't matter to him. By then, every cadet was considering the branch in which he'd like to get his commission.

"But Sam," Fred Dent said, "it would be absolutely ridiculous for you to go anywhere but in the dragoons. With your talent with horses, you're a natural." He chuckled. "And since the Corps of Engineers isn't exactly stalking you, why not give it a try?"

Huh, Grant thought, the snobbish and highly touted Engineers weren't after *any* of the Class of '43, not with *their* grades. And he was plumb in the middle. Couldn't even get into the Artillery or the Ordnance Corps. It was strictly the dragoons or infantry, because the Cavalry regiments were full of brevet second lieutenants. He'd decided to request the dragoons, with the Fourth Infantry in St. Louis as his second choice. "I *am* giving it a try, Fred," he replied, "but I haven't got a prayer. I just hope I get the Fourth. Then I can sponge off of your family and meet those beautiful sisters you're always bragging about."

"What would they see in a runt like you? What'd you say the old grippe brought you down to—a hundred and seventeen pounds? Hell, around St. Louis, we throw 'em back your size."

Yes, the cough from "Tyler's Grippe" had cost him some weight, but he'd grown six inches at the Academy. He wasn't worried about it. Any more than he was worried about his future billet. His new plan nullified any extended regimental service anyway. Yessir, a couple of years in the line, then back to the Academy to teach math. Not a bad profession, a quiet job on the faculty. And if he didn't want to stay, he could probably resign and get on with one of the several colleges that were springing up all over.

"Did you hear what I said, Sam? You'd be just a minnow around St. Louis. Why don't you go see Delafield and ask him to pull some weight about the Dragoons. Hell, he knows you're the best horseman to ever fill a West Point saddle."

"No, sir. I haven't been in that office in four years, and I sure don't want to start now. Besides, I believe in settling for what comes my way."

"Oh, don't give me that noble bull."

Grant smiled. There wasn't anything noble about such an attitude, it just happened to be the way he felt. Play the hand the way it was dealt, and if it didn't work out, it wasn't your fault. "The only thing I want to do is set that riding mark before I leave these hallowed grounds."

Dent shrugged. "Oh, don't worry. You will. All I want to do is *leave* these hallowed grounds."

Graduation week was a blur, a combination of nostalgia and impatience. On Wednesday Grant would have his one chance to stand out from the undistinguishable center of thirty-nine graduates. He had arrived at the stable early, wanting York to be as well-groomed as he would ever be. For this would be the last time the big cantankerous sorrel would be ridden by the only person who'd ever mastered him.

Grant stood quietly waiting for the final event of the riding show, patting York, gentling him, asking him to give his best when the time came—in a language only the two of them knew. York was warm from an earlier workout, and a bit nervous before the large crowd of spectators. His eyes were wary, defiant, just what Grant wanted.

The riding hall with its high ceiling was packed with faculty, visiting dignitaries, and cadets. Even the tall commandant, Captain C. F. Smith, was there. The smell of fresh sawdust and hay mingled with that of the long tanbark-covered floor, and the chatter of the spectators was a buzz in the background. Finally it was time. A hush fell. Sergeant Herschberger, resplendent in his blue dress uniform, moved purposefully to the jumping bar and placed it even with his eyes. With a slight smile on his weatherbeaten face, the old dragoon announced, "Ladies and gentlemen, Cadet Grant will now attempt to break the Academy record for the high jump, which is five feet, four inches. His first jump will be at that point."

A buzz went through the audience.

The sergeant's voice rose. "Cadet Grant!"

Grant inhaled deeply, easing the big horse to the starting point. "Okay, big fella," he said softly, "we're on center stage. Let's *go!*"

They were off at a trot, quickly reaching the far end of the hall where they wheeled, a small young man and a powerful animal welded together. The pounding hoofbeats became the only sound in the hushed hall as they flew toward the waiting bar. All eyes strained. Then Grant urged York up and over! As he reined in, the riding master announced, "Cadet Grant has just *tied* the Academy record! I will now raise the bar one inch."

Once more horse and rider trotted to the end of the hall and turned. And once more the huge sorrel rose gracefully and cleared the bar. The record was broken! Applause filled the large building, but it wasn't enough for the cadet from Ohio. Grant pulled up beside Herschberger, speaking softly. "Give me six feet."

The sergeant started to demur, but Grant was already trotting to the end of the hall. The riding master cleared his throat and announced, "Ladies and gentlemen, Cadet Grant will now try, at his own request, the amazing height of *six feet!*"

Grant slowed at the turning point, waiting. His voice was low, but urgent. "All right, partner, this will be the greatest moment of our lives. Let's go down in history."

He touched his heels to York's flanks and they were off, gliding, finally thundering toward the high obstacle. York's takeoff was perfect, the greatest burst of power Grant had ever experienced astride a horse. They must have cleared the bar by at least two inches. As he pulled up, pandemonium broke loose. Rufe Ingalls was the first to throw his hat in the air. It was the first time the hall had ever experienced cheers. As the applause continued, Grant trotted impassively to the superintendent's box, where he saluted. The big grin had to wait.

And finally, at long last, it was graduation day. He'd made the rounds the night before, starting with several contemplative minutes at the promontory that overlooked the sweeping Hudson—the place with the marvelous view that had given him his only comfort when he was a plebe. Then it was the gruff goodbye to Sergeant Herschberger while he petted York. And then back down the Plain that had been the scene of so many formations, so many parades, so many miseries. The drums and music had been quiet, but he had felt the pride, had almost heard the muffled sound of the marching feet of the hundreds who'd gone before. The Corps. He had felt the swelling in his breast, the momentary brimming in his eyes. He might not ever be a good soldier, but he'd known then that he finally belonged to a proud fraternity that he would never forget. The Corps.

He'd thought of the line from Tennyson's poem: *"And thro' the field the road runs by to many-tower'd Camelot."*

Now, standing at ease in the second rank, barely listening to the final words of the speaker, he thought back to when General Scott had stood on that same reviewing stand. Nearly four years earlier, but it seemed like yesterday. He remembered the foolish thought that had gone through his boyish mind—that someday he might be up there. What an absurdity! The magnificent Captain Smith was there again, two places from the speaker. Impeccable, solid as granite. What a soldier. Would that he could serve under such an officer in the confusing days ahead, whatever they might bring. Was there any destiny for him in the uniform of his country, as his father so foolishly insisted? Doubtful. But again he felt the pride . . .

The band struck up "America," the popular anthem adapted to the music of "God Save the King." Out of the corner of his eye he caught a glimpse of the national flag waving slowly in the light breeze. He came to attention for the last time as a cadet at West Point.

He was a brevet second lieutenant.

CHAPTER 4

It was quite probable that many of Grant's traits came from his mother. Hannah Simpson, a Pennsylvania girl, was a pious Methodist—undemonstrative, confident, and self-absorbed. At times she was almost mystical in her matter-of-fact approach to life, as if she were satisfied with some inner secret. She seldom smiled, never wept, and guarded her conversation as if she had only a limited number of words to use in her lifetime. To some it appeared that she treated each of her six children with indifference, seldom showing concern for their foibles or their temporary dangers.

Perhaps her chemistry was ideal for the excitable, often emotional, and sometimes impassioned man she married. Jesse Root Grant was a seventh-generation product of a Connecticut Yankee family, the son of Captain Noah Grant. The captain had been a Revolutionary War veteran and itinerant cobbler whose propensity for fathering children and consuming distilled spirits had been his strongest suits. Noah was also an adventurous soul whose desire for new land had brought him west to the Ohio River country. When the captain's home broke up for good, Jesse wound up on a farm near Youngstown where he was exposed to the joy of books and the fervency of a foster father who was immersed in politics. Following this, he apprenticed himself to his half brother, Peter, who owned a prosperous tannery in Marysville, Kentucky, not far from Cincinnati. He later worked in a northeastern Ohio tannery owned by Owen Brown, whose teenage son, John, was already becoming an ardent abolitionist.

At twenty-nine, Jesse was slender, his six-foot frame slumping a little, and his serious eyes seeing life from behind gold-rimmed eyeglasses. But he was never boring. Following a bout of malaria, or ague as it was called, that disabled him for nearly a year, he found himself deeply in debt. He moved to Point Pleasant, a hamlet on the Ohio side where a new tannery had opened.

He was candidly in search of a wife and upon meeting the slender, chiseled Hannah—one of three heirs to a six-hundred-acre farm—he quickly decided she was the woman. At twenty-three, she was already bordering on "old maidhood." Ignoring Jesse's opinionated, disputatious fanaticism on politics and slavery, she accepted his offer of marriage in the summer of 1821. They moved into a modest house next to the tannery, and ten months later she gave birth to an attractive son with large blue eyes and reddish-brown hair.

After finally getting a name, the little boy became Hannah's "Lyss" and eventually "Ulys" to nearly everyone else.

It took a year for the ambitious and industrious Jessee to get out of debt and arrange sufficient funds to open his own tannery in Georgetown, the county seat of Brown County, twenty-five miles east of Point Pleasant. Soon his two-story brick house was completed and Jesse moved his family into their new home.

Ulysses was a quiet child, undoubtedly inheriting his mother's reticence. One trait he didn't acquire from Hannah was her prim neatness, for wearing apparel would never be one of his considerations. As it would be later at West Point, the only place where he stood out was with horses. He was fascinated by them and was often alert near the tannery, so that he might hold the teams of visiting drivers. When he was six, he broke a horse to collar and harness in one day, and was already a good rider. He purchased his first horse at the age of eight and never forgot the experience.

Not far from Georgetown, a farmer named Ralston had a colt which Ulys greatly admired. By now doing the work of a much older lad, he felt justified in asking his father to purchase the colt for him. "Well now," Jesse said, "what makes you think you should have a colt of your own?"

"Because it's important to me, Papa."

The twinkle in Jesse's eyes was barely perceptible. "That's a sound answer. And how much do you propose we pay Mr. Ralston for this special piece of horseflesh, young man?"

"I don't know, Papa. But he's worth whatever it costs."

"You don't sound like much of a Yankee horse trader."

"I don't know what that is, Papa." He watched his toe draw a circle in the dust. "Can I have him?"

Jesse smiled fondly. "Well, we can *try* to get him."

The boy looked up. "Try?"

"That's right. I don't know what you see that's so all-fired exceptional about the animal, and he's probably not worth over twenty dollars—but here's what you do. Offer Mr. Ralston that price. If he doesn't take it, offer him twenty-two fifty, and if he won't take it, go to twenty-five. But that's positively all I'll pay."

Ulys's eyes sparkled. "Oh, thank you, Papa!"

When the boy showed up to strike his bargain, he was carrying a bridle. A knowing Ralston smiled. "And how much is your father offering, boy?"

Ulys looked up with wide eyes. In a brave voice he replied, "My father said to offer you twenty, and if you wouldn't take it, to offer twenty-two fifty. And if you don't take that, to go to twenty-five."

Ralston shook his head. "Well, I just can't take twenty, or twenty-two fifty, so I guess it's twenty-five or nothing."

When the story spread around the village, Ulys became a laughingstock among the other boys. He never forgot the chagrin it caused him. But he had his colt. Additionally, he acquired one more nickname: "Useless."

Jesse's industry paid off. By the time Ulys was ten, his father had acquired two farms and various other land holdings. The tannery, with its sideline butchery, was quite successful. A livery stable added to the income, with Ulys doing most of the driving. Throughout his teens, the boy worked hard at the required farm chores, but held a deep aversion to the tannery. He simply couldn't stand seeing animals killed—which led to his being the only growing boy in Georgetown who disdained hunting.

When he was sixteen, Jesse came up with the West Point plan, and although Ulys was honest and told his father he had no interest in attending the Academy, the die was cast.

Now, with his graduation leave in Ohio finished, he was ready to report to the Fourth United States Infantry at Jefferson Barracks. It was his first step into manhood.

CHAPTER 5

SEPTEMBER 30, 1843

"Lieutenant Grant reporting, sir."

The Virginian, Lieutenant Colonel Garland, returned the salute and motioned to a chair. "Sit down, please. It's my policy, Mister Grant, to brief all new officers personally. Now, as you probably know, Colonel Josiah Vose is the regimental commander. But since his health has troubled him of late, you probably won't be seeing much of him. Colonel Kearny is the senior officer here at Jefferson Barracks and, therefore, the post commander. The Barracks is the largest permanent army installation in the country . . . a busy place, Lieutenant, but still run in a manner that can afford you maximum time off for your own pleasures when you complete your daily duties.

"The Fourth is joined here by the Third Infantry, each with eight companies. You are entering a proud regiment. It is composed of somewhere under five hundred enlisted men, and your arrival makes twenty-one officers. As is usual these days, many officers of higher rank are away on staff duty, so junior officers are often required to command in positions above their respective ranks. You, for instance, could well be a company commander very soon.

"You've taken on a challenging career, and you will be carefully observed in your earlier duties. I personally believe there will be trying days in the near future, possibly even a conflict. So it will behoove you to learn as much as possible in the next few months." Colonel Garland stood, smiling warmly and extending his hand. "Welcome to the Fourth."

Outside the headquarters building, Grant squinted into the pleasant morning sun. Pete Longstreet was waiting with an extended hand. He mimicked Garland. "Why, Lieutenant, it sho' is a pleasure to welcome you to the proud Fourth. Course, if you're lucky, you may die as a captain in this here proud regiment, but son, you sho' are welcome."

Grant grinned. "Oh, I thought it was nice of him. He's the first lieutenant colonel I've ever spoken to."

They walked toward Officer's Row. "He's a fine man," Longstreet said. "I'm even considering him for a father-in-law, that is, if Louise ever gets old enough. That's his second daughter, son. A real beauty."

Grant nodded his head. "Do you think he's right about upcoming trouble?"

"Oh, hell, yes. We'll be fighting those damned Mexicans before you can learn to spell Santa Anna. We'll kick their asses a thousand miles from Texas and maybe chase them all the way to Panama. And we'll all come out colonels."

"That's a long way from brevet second lieutenant."

"Especially one as dumb as you. Oh, let me warn you about something, Sam. The presiding officer in the officers' mess is usually Captain Buck Buchanan, a real martinet. He's got two records—one for bravery against the Indians, the other for eating young lieutenants for breakfast. Don't cross him."

"I don't want to cross anyone, Pete."

"Where have they assigned you?"

"Company One."

"Huh, that's interesting. The company commander is a mathematics fanatic. You two should get on well."

Riding in the feeble February sun on the handsome black mare his father had given him as a graduation present, Grant felt as if he was going to meet some kind of a ghost or illusion. The *real* Julia Dent was finally coming home to White Haven. It had all begun back in the first week of his final year at West Point when Fred Dent had started raving about his favorite sister. Seldom did a day go by without his saying something about her. His description had been appealing: clear bright complexion, dark shiny hair usually drawn back in a chignon; strong and athletic; large, dark eyes that showed her wit and compassion. Bright, compelling. Outstanding horse-woman.

It went on and on.

Pete Longstreet, too, was one of her admirers. He'd taken her to society balls in St. Louis, as had other dashing young officers. "There are more beautiful, even prettier young women around," Pete said, "but Julia Dent has *charm,* boy. She can twist you right around any finger on her delicate little hands."

Her St. Louis connection was the wealthy O'Fallon family, to whom she was kin. They were the cream of the city's society. In fact, she had been staying with them to attend school in the city since early October. Well, Grant had decided, if she was all that keen on dancing, she sure wouldn't be interested in him—not with his two left feet.

Fred had asked him to pay his respects to the Dent family at White Haven, so he had done so shortly after arriving at the Barracks. He had been coming to the stately place in the country once or twice a week ever since. You couldn't call it a plantation exactly, he'd decided, it was more like an elegant farm. To him it was a welcome comfort and respite from the military bustle of the Barracks. Situated on nearly a thousand acres five miles from the city, the rambling two-story white farmhouse with its tall pillars was set in a surrounding of locust trees and accentuated by thick branches of honeysuckle vines. To the rear of the house were the barns, stables, and slave quarters. Mrs. Ellen Dent, a slender, lovely woman in her late forties who had given birth to eight children, had liked Grant from the start, and had continued to make him welcome.

Mrs. Dent seemed to take pleasure in the respectful manner in which he stood up to Colonel Dent in the political discussions. In his midfifties and obviously quite the lazy Southern planter, Frederick Dent had purchased White Haven more than thirty years earlier. He was a Marylander who had moved west after making money in Pittsburgh for a few years. No one had ever asked him about the source of his "colonelcy." Irascible and unforgiving, he was an unrelenting enemy of anyone who disagreed with Senator Hart Benton, or Andrew Jackson, or slaveholding, or himself. One of the reasons that Grant knew how to handle Dent was obvious: he'd grown up under Jesse Root Grant.

But it was Julia that Grant was so keen to meet. Reining his horse through the turnstile that led to the house, he felt excited about finally meeting this seventeen-year-old girl he'd heard so much about . . .

Julia watched through an upstairs front window as Grant rode in. So at last she was going to see this young lieutenant everyone was raving about. One would think he was the greatest thing to ever come out of West Point, to hear her family talk. Fred had always mentioned him in letters from the Academy, always bragging on his horsemanship. Her mother smiled quietly when she spoke of him, as if she knew some kind of a secret. And her sisters, the silly things—they thought he was Sir Lancelot!

Especially little Emma. Only eight, she was positively, madly, in love with this young man from Ohio—whom she described as having a porcelain complexion and a face as pretty as a China doll. How could any army officer be so described?

As a matter of fact, it was silly to even give him this much thought. Weren't lieutenants a dime a dozen? Still, there must be *something* about him, or he wouldn't have made such an impression on the family. And what was a girl's life all about if she couldn't get a slight flutter at the prospect of meeting a handsome young man?

My, how smoothly he dismounted from the elegant horse he was riding. And there goes shameless Emma, rushing to him wantonly, holding his hand and towing him into the house. Hmmm, how the sun seemed to cast a copperish tone on his russet-colored hair. And where was the ramrod-straight spine with which every young officer walked? Well, best she go downstairs and get the introduction over with.

"Miss Julia Dent, may I introduce Lieutenant Ulysses S. Grant?"

As she curtsied, she heard the soft low voice. "My pleasure, ma'am."

The jaw was square, the mouth strong, and the eyes bluer than she'd have guessed. He seemed shy, none of the flair of Pete Longstreet or the others. Yet there was something more, something perhaps *solid* about him. Yes, that was a good word—solid. She'd find out when they went riding together. Riding was always a good way to get to know someone . . .

And ride they did in the next few weeks, sharing their love for horses, the woods, the streams, the animals, and the land. He was highly interested in all phases of the farming at White Haven, and she had a good grasp of it. She loved to fish, and now and then they touched when he baited her hook or removed a wriggling bass from her line. His tales of duty were skimpy, although he did mention being fined a bottle of wine by Captain Buchanan for being late returning to mess following a long afternoon's ride with her. He began to spend more and more time at White Haven, and while she was gaining the animosity of little sister Emma, she found herself looking forward to his visits. She didn't even mind going to a ball with him, even though he struggled through only two dances.

For the first time in his life, Grant wrote a poem. "It isn't much," he said, shifting his weight from one foot to another as he handed it to her. They were resting the horses on a little grassy knoll that was showing off the year's first wildflowers. "I don't know anything about writing."

She read it aloud:

We have a long ride ahead,
*   You and I.*
The sun is just rising,
*   For you and I.*
The storms haven't gathered,
*   The rain hasn't fallen.*
Nor have we yet seen
*   The sky so blue,*
Nor heard the birds
*   All atwitter.*
Before the purple twilight,
*   And the bright evening star,*
We have a long ride ahead,
*   You and I.*

She smiled, her eyes brimming, and kissed him on the cheek. "That's so sweet, so gentle," she said. Holding it to her breast, she added, "I'll keep it forever."

He just shrugged, but he was highly pleased.

One day late in March he arrived with a flush of excitement. "Look at this, Julia," he exclaimed, handing her a letter. "Remember, I told you I wrote to that professor at West Point about a position as an instructor? Read this!"

She quickly unfolded the letter:

West Point, New York
March 10, 1844

Second Lieutenant Ulysses S. Grant
Company I, Fourth United States Infantry
Jefferson Barracks, Missouri

Dear Lieutenant Grant:
I am in receipt of your last letter requesting assignment as an assistant professor of mathematics here at the Military Academy. Since I considered you one of my most apt students, I believe you would perform commendably in such an assignment. Unfortunately, no vacancy exists at the present. I will place the matter before the superintendent to initiate action for a fu-

ture assignment in this capacity. A vacancy may occur within a year, certainly within two. In the interim, Sir, I implore you to enjoy your duties with the Fourth.

I am very respectfully,

Y. Obt. Svt.
William Church
Captain, U.S. Army
Professor of Mathematics

Julia smiled at his pleasure. "Oh, Ulys, I'm so happy for you. It's the answer to your dreams."

He replaced the letter in his jacket pocket, trying not to show his excitement. "Well, a lot of things can happen in that amount of time. There's that Mexican talk, you know."

"Oh, Colonel O'Fallon thinks that'll all blow over. Besides, let's not talk about such things when you're about to become a professor. How do professors live at West Point?"

"They have small houses for quarters. A nice social life, quiet, secluded, respectable. The ones without outside income don't live too high."

"How long would you stay there?"

"Probably as long as I wanted, if some major war didn't come along."

She smiled, teasing. "Professor Grant, huh?"

He blushed slightly. "Not yet. C'mon, let's go for that ride."

But larger events *were* looming. Although the Senate disapproved President Tyler's move for annexation of Texas, it appeared the Democrats would jam the measure through in the next session of Congress. The country broiled in the controversy, while the War Department began to move troops into position should there be a need in the Southwest. The Third Infantry departed Jefferson Barracks on April 20 for Fort Jessup near the Texas border in western Louisiana, and the rumor was out that the Fourth wouldn't be far behind.

Not wishing to get caught up in a tide of unknown duration, Grant applied for twenty days' leave to visit his family, now living in Bethel, Ohio, another small town east of Cincinnati. He departed by steamer on May 1, just missing the regimental alert. Shortly after arriving home, he received a note from a friend announcing that the Fourth was departing for Louisiana within days—that he shouldn't open any other mail from the Barracks if he wished to finish his leave. He received nothing, but the time dragged. Being with his family was inadequate and he knew why. One day he straddled a chair in the kitchen where his mother was baking bread. As usual, Hannah acknowledged his presence with a nod of her head. After several moments he blurted, "Mama, I told you some about Julia Dent when I first came home . . . well I . . . that is, I think I love her."

Hannah continued to knead the dough, saying nothing.

"What do you think I should do, Mama?"

"Does she know?"

"I'm not sure."

"Why don't you tell her?"

"Oh, Mama, she's such a lady and all. I—" He shrugged.

Hannah picked up a towel, wiping her hands. She moved close, looking directly into his eyes. "Lyss, you may not understand this, but nice young ladies fall in love too. Speak your mind to Miss Dent."

He watched his mother fondly, relishing the longest bit of conversation she'd ever afforded him. And she was right about telling Julia. By gum, his leave had just come to an abrupt end—he was White Haven bound!

Grant hurried into the office of the regimental rear detachment at the Barracks to find Lieutenant Dick Ewell—"the eagle with a lisp"—in command. He saluted and sat down. "Dick, I need a favor. I know I'm many days behind the regiment, but I have an important matter to clean up here before I depart. Can you authorize me a few more days' leave?"

Ewell smiled. "Wouldn't have anything to do with that charming Miss Dent, would it?"

"Something like that."

"Okay, take six. That ought to be enough for anything."

Grant jumped up. "Thanks, Dick. I owe you one."

He couldn't remember the mad ride to White Haven—or at least to the Gravois. The quiet creek didn't normally have enough water in it "to run a coffee mill" as he would one day describe it. Now it was a churning, broiling torrent overflowing its banks. No matter—he'd swim it. He plunged the horse into the rushing current, going under briefly until the strong animal began to swim. Minutes later, they scrambled up the opposite bank and headed off at a gallop. A fine-looking suitor he'd make, soaked to the skin with muddy water!

But it didn't matter. All he could see was Julia. Julia, Julia, Julia! Why hadn't he come to his senses before he left? What if she'd found someone else? How would he ever tell her? And even if she *possibly* felt the same way, there was her father to contend with. Certainly the colonel didn't want his daughter getting married off to a lowly brevet second lieutenant making his kind of pay. But he could wait . . . wait forever if that's what it would take.

Trotting up to the veranda of White Haven, he found most of the family sitting around enjoying the pleasant evening. Little Emmy dashed out to meet him, laughing. "Land of goodness, Lieutenant, you been swimming with your clothes on?"

Grant jumped down, hugging her. "My horse got dry." He looked up to see the pleased Julia coming toward him. "Can a wet traveler stay a spell?" he asked.

Her dark eyes were soft in a gentle smile. "Long as you like. In fact, we might even be able to find you some dry clothes."

Later, sitting on the veranda following dinner, Julia touched his hand. "I'm glad you're back, Ulys. And I'm glad you missed the departure of the regiment. I, well, I guess I missed you more than I thought."

He looked at her gently, taking her hand, then dropping his gaze. Now was the time to tell her, but . . . "I know," he managed. "My leave was, well, it wasn't what I expected. After being with you so much the last few months, I . . . well, you know."

Darn it, why couldn't he say it? But she might laugh. He got up and walked to the steps, trying to put some new words together. The night was muggy, his collar tight. He turned. "I mean, well, it would have been nice if you'd been there with me."

Her voice was low. "Yes, I think so."

An awkward silence. *Why couldn't he say it?* "I, uh, guess the regiment will be in Louisiana for some time."

"Yes, I suppose so."

"And maybe we'll be going on into Texas, maybe Mexico."

"Probably."

He moved close to her. "Julia, I . . . well, it's good to be here for a few days. I guess I'd better be getting on back to the post tonight. I'll be back out in the morning, if it's all right."

Her hand touched his arm. "Ulys," she whispered, touching his cheek, "is there something else you want to say?"

He looked into the dark shadows of her eyes. "I . . . yes, I love you." Then the words came in a torrent. "In fact, I've loved you from the start. I *know* I have. Why do you think I came out all the time, why I got more leave? I love you, I love you. There, that's it. I love you so much I can't stand it."

She stretched up and brushed his cheek with her lips. "Oh, you darling, beautiful, quiet young man. How I've wanted to hear those words. You have no idea how I've hoped, because you see, I feel the same. Probably have from the day I took you away from Emma."

He smiled at the thought, taking her in his arms and holding her tightly. "I love you so much. Do you think you could be the wife of a poor army officer . . . I mean someday?"

She laughed softly.

"What is it? Does that amuse you?"

She kissed his cheek again. "Darling, I'll follow you anywhere—if you'll find someone to dance with me."

CHAPTER 6

Immediately after reporting to regimental headquarters, Grant sought out Pete Longstreet. They shook hands warmly, the burly South Carolinian asking, "And how's the fair Julia?"

"Oh, she's all right."

"All right? You didn't spend an extra week in St. Louis for nothing. Is anything set between you two?"

"No, not with this Mexican thing hanging over our heads."

Longstreet slapped him on the back. "Same old reserved Sam Grant. You wouldn't tell me anyway. Okay, let me brief you. As you know, the nearest point of civilization—if you can call it that—is Natchitoches. This present Garden of Eden where we're living was named Camp Salubrity because it's above the mosquito level. The tents are well-ventilated—particularly when it rains.

"And you don't have to worry about your old friend Buchanan. He doesn't preside over the mess anymore. Far as social life goes, there just ain't much. Some of the wealthy planters have pimply-faced daughters they'd like to marry off, so they invite us young officers around for shindigs. They have some pretty handsome horseflesh, so you oughta get popular. And your old friend Rufe Ingalls is over in the Third at Fort Jessup. Said you're the worst poker player in the army because you trust everyone who ever sat down around a deck of cards."

Grant chuckled. "I'll ride over to see him soon as I get a chance."

They went into Longstreet's tent where he poured them a drink of bourbon whiskey. "Best typhus medicine there is," he said, sipping. "Have you changed your mind about Mexico, Sam?"

"Nope. She's a weak nation and if we were to attack her, we wouldn't be any better than those greedy European monarchies gobbling up additional territory."

"Well, you'd better get used to the idea. I heard old Zach Taylor is on his way to command our Army of Observation. And you know he's a warrior, not some fancy martinet. You won't refuse to fight if there's war, will you?"

Grant shook his head. "I have a commitment to the army and my country, but that doesn't make it right."

The letters between Grant and Julia flew, professing their love for each other, but it took him a while to screw up his courage to write to her father. Finally one night he reached for his pen and forced the words onto paper:

Dear Colonel Dent,

Sir, I feel that I should appraise you of my situation here at Camp Salubrity and speak to you of other matters.

When I write to Julia, I discuss life here. Now it's no secret to mention that we may be moving shortly. It all depends on the election and whether Texas is annexed. As you may know, some are calling this the "Army of Provocation."

Certainly, having Brevet Brigadier Zachary Taylor in command means battle is probable. I'm sure you recall his heroics in the last war with the British and his exploits with the Indians.

Old Zach, as he's known to the men, is my kind of general. He's probably the most casual officer in the army. He never seems to wear a uniform, just old sloppy clothes that might include a loose linen coat and a big palmetto hat. He looks and talks like a visiting planter, which he actually is, because he owns a big plantation here in Louisiana. He has a funny way of sitting sidesaddle on his magnificent horse, "Old Whitey." And he always has time to speak to the younger officers and the enlisted men. He spoke to me briefly just yesterday, asking what I knew about cotton. All I could do was mumble something about his horse!

I heard he encountered much sadness a few years ago, about 1835, I think. His daughter eloped with a young officer named Jefferson Davis and died of typhoid a few months later. But I'm sure in your worldliness that you know about that tragedy.

Although that's a melancholy way to broach the subject, I, too, wish to speak of marriage. Upon my departure from your lovely White Haven, both your charming daughter, Julia, and myself discovered our love for each other. Since there was no time then to speak of it, I now wish to ask for your daughter's hand in marriage.

I realize I haven't much to offer materially, and that an army officer doesn't make much in the way of pay. But, sir, I promise to always provide for your gentle Julia to the utmost of my ability. If need be, I will resign from the army to do so.

Please pardon the abruptness of this request, Sir, but I humbly seek your permission to pursue this suit. Thank you.

> *Respectfully and always*
>
> *Your Obt. Svt.*
> *U. S. Grant*

Grant threw himself into activity, knowing the wait for an answer would be unnerving. Shortly he was given temporary command of A Company, personally taking over a majority of the drill supervision. He became interested in the problems of the new replacements, mostly immigrants who spoke little English. Drill was the key, the only solution to the communication problem. If they could learn to react simultaneously to any given order in formation, they could survive a fight. For one who had so despised drill at the Academy, he now saw it as the basic element of discipline and performance.

He also saw his chance of teaching mathematics eroding. Following his earlier letter from Professor Church, he had studied in earnest during much of his time off. Now he knew his dream was practically useless, so he turned his interest to the intricacies of the army's supply procedure.

He heard nothing from Colonel Dent.

Julia, not as frequent a letter writer as Grant, wrote that her father objected to the lack of resources, but that "he's just a good, stubborn man who is mere clay in my hands. Time will solve the problem."

As the year moved on with the verdant countryside taking on fall hues, a letter arrived from Grant's father. Nothing had softened his Whig views:

> *I worry about the slavery influence on you, having friends like this Longstreet and being involved with that family outside of St. Louis. How much do they corrupt your mind? Do you know that by bringing Texas into the Union, they hope to form four slaveholding states from the republic? That would mean eight new Southern senators! William Lloyd Garrison has called upon the Northern States to secede from the Union if Texas is permitted to enter. And William E. Channing has stated, "I ask whether we are prepared to take Texas on for serving slavery. I ask whether as a nation we can stand forth in the sight of God and other nations and adopt this atrocious policy." This Democratic pretender, Polk, is shouting "Manifest Destiny" and all that other bunk. But he's just a puppet of the slavers. He's nothing but a Whig deserter who is riding this Texas thing into the White House as part of a massive Jacksonian plot. Tell your brother officers the truth, son.*

Soon the news circulated that England would surely grab Texas as a cotton-producing colony if the shaky, debt-ridden republic was not protected. And who, Northerner *or* Southerner, wanted that? Polk's argument that New Mexico and California would open great new vistas of American growth without slavery turned the tide; the electorate voted him in as the eleventh president of the United States. His election was greeted with cheers amidst the Army of Observation in western Louisiana. Action couldn't be far away now! Grant took it in stride.

A lonely Christmas passed for him, then on March 1, annexation of Texas was finally passed by Congress—and would be effective by July 4. Time was drawing short. Grant simply had to get things at White Haven resolved, so he applied for a leave.

Colonel Dent pulled on his gray mustache, scowling. "Julia is a lady, Mr. Grant, accustomed to the finer things in life. What have you to offer her? Twenty years from now you'll still be a damned captain, suffering along on nothing. Is that what you want for her—for a gentle, educated woman who can have her pick of position and wealth?"

Grant kept his composure, but he wasn't going to let the old devil get away with that kind of blackmail. He looked at him soberly, his blue eyes steady. "Sir, I realize my prospects don't appear to be much at the present, but after my tour of duty is up there'll be many roads open. Don't you see that I want only the best for Julia, just like you?"

The colonel looked off toward the road, not replying.

"Sir, I'll do my very best by her. The important thing is that we love each other."

"Hmph, love is it? That's the only word you youngsters know these days. Love will solve everything, won't it? Well, let me tell you, young man, it doesn't put food on the table, doesn't make influential friends, and doesn't buy beautiful gowns." A mask of pleasantry slipped over the colonel's face. "Let's look at it realistically. You aren't the pick of the litter, are you?"

"No, sir, never pretended to be."

"Then what gives you the arrogance to pretend you're good enough for her?"

Grant walked to the edge of the veranda, turning. "I just believe I am."

"Well, I'm leaving for Washington in a few minutes and I have things to do. Let's say I'll think about it."

Stubborn old man—just like his own father. "Then I'll assume I have your permission, sir?"

Dent turned to enter the house. "I'll think about it, Mr. Grant."

Ten minutes later, as the colonel's carriage drew away, Julia took his arm. "Was it difficult?"

Grant nodded. "He doesn't want me as a son-in-law."

Her lips brushed his cheek. "But *I* want you as his son-in-law. And that's what matters, sir. I intend to be Mrs. Lieutenant Grant, and that hard-headed old man won't stand in my way." She held up her little finger. "I'll twist him around this so tightly he'll be begging for a wedding!"

Mrs. Dent turned from where she was waving goodbye. "And *I* want you in the family, Ulysses. So he hasn't got a chance."

Chapter 7

Corpus Christi, Texas

On December 8, Grant looked at the orders promoting him to regular second lieutenant with a date of rank of September 30. In spite of his shrug, he was quite pleased. Five of his classmates had been promoted earlier and four others were on the same orders. But twenty-eight of thirty-eight were still brevets. "Not too bad for the cadet who never worried about class standings," remarked Fred Dent, who wasn't one of those favored.

Taylor's army was now the Army of Occupation. It had moved to New Orleans and then President Polk had ordered it down to the sleepy little fishing village of Corpus Christi, an act designed to make the Mexicans give up an area known as the Nueces Strip. The Fourth Infantry's aged commander, Colonel Vose, had died of a heart attack supervising battalion drill and the new commander, Colonel William Whistler, had a drinking problem. In fact, Grant was sent into town one day to find him. Eventually the colonel was located in police court. Released, drunk, into Grant's custody, the old colonel showed him a picture his eleven-year-old son had sent him. Ulys, himself no slouch at drawing, was highly impressed.

In his letter to Julia that night, he had written, "It's a shame that old officers have to stay in because there is no pension. Take Colonel Whistler, who was once a legend. Among other feats, he won a five-mile footrace with a fleet and powerful young Potawatomi chief and later killed him in a knife duel. But now, after forty-five years in the army, he's just hanging on."

With rain nearly every day, the dreary months on the Texas coast passed slowly. Taylor's army was strengthened by the arrival of volunteer regiments, such as the First Ohio and the Mississippi Rifles—commanded by now-Colonel of Volunteers Jefferson Davis. Grant, who had been the regimental quartermaster for the past several months, hadn't heard a word from Colonel Dent. His letters outnumbered Julia's almost three to one, but she'd told him in the beginning it would be that way. She had a minor eye problem that made writing a chore. Besides, she was working on her sewing, and he'd decided that task was hard enough on her beautiful eyes. He missed her terribly.

"Did you see Captain C. F. Smith, the former commandant of cadets, yet?" Pete Longstreet asked. Longstreet, now with the Eighth Infantry, and Fred Dent with the Fifth, were sharing the usual evening bottle of wine with Grant.

Grant's eyebrow shot up. "No. When did he get in?"

"Couple of days ago. Are you still one of his worshipers, Sam?"

"I'll take him over all these old colonels any day."

"Me too," Dent chimed in. "He's a damn sight more officer than Brigadier Worth, our good old drunk Whistler, or Twiggs, or that foul-mouthed Georgian, Mintosh . . . even Garland. By the way, Pete, do you know how that Jeff Davis is getting along with Taylor?"

Longstreet shrugged. "They're Southerners. I heard the old man affords him gruff respect, in spite of his daughter and all. Trouble is, they're cut from different bolts. You know how the general is—common as an old sock with a hole in it. Well, Davis comes from a cultured background with the opinionated scorn of his class. Bottom line, though, we know who the boss is."

Dent changed the subject. "What are you going to do when the shooting starts, Sam?"

Longstreet snorted. "What *can* he do? The regimental drudge will be so far back he'll have to read about battles in the newspaper."

"What about you, Pete?" Fred asked. "How do you think you'll react when the lead starts flying?"

"Who knows? Do you? Does anyone?"

Dent sipped and stared into his wineglass. "I was just thinking—wouldn't it be a shame to go all the way through the Academy, do all this training, and then flunk out in battle."

"Surely some cowards have graduated."

Longstreet agreed. "I don't suppose anyone can be truly certain."

Grant shook his head. "I guess we'll just all have to find out in our own way, won't we?"

The battles of Palo Alto and Resaca de la Palma were the first contact with the enemy. At the time they were considered battles because they were the first of the war. But in retrospect, they seemed to be only skirmishes. However, when the American press—hungry for juicy stories to print back home—finished embellishing their telling, they were more like Waterloos. They began so casually that Grant had neither the time nor the need to build up any worry about how he would react. He felt no particular fear, more a sense of excitement. Although many of the Mexican officers were European trained, the lower ranks were filled with ignorant, low-paid, unmotivated peasants. Thus, defeating their superior numbers hadn't been too difficult. He'd come through a few cannonballs—although most of the solid shot had come slowly rolling through the American ranks, and a soldier had only to step aside to avoid them. And there had been musket fire that caused a number of casualties. But all in all, those two battles had served only to whet Grant's whistle for an active part in what was coming. He reread the answer to his request for return to company duty:

> *Lieutenant Grant is respectfully informed that his protest can not be considered. He was assigned to duty as Quartermaster & Commissary because of his observed ability, skill, and persistency in the line of duty. The commanding officer is confident that Lieutenant Grant can best serve his country in the present emergency under this assignment, and will continue to perform his assigned duties.*
>
> Lt. Col. Garland, 4th Inft. Comdg. Brigade

He'd done his share as quartermaster and commissary long enough. And he'd done it well, he had to admit. But he was a line officer. He didn't want anything special, but they were handing out brevet promotions already. To Braxton Bragg, the brilliant artilleryman, now a brevet captain. To some of the colonels. If he could distinguish himself—possibly be mentioned in a dispatch, get one brevet—then maybe Colonel Dent would look on him more favorably. So Garland had turned down his transfer. Well, he'd just have to find another way.

*　　*　　*

Even though the two battles had already taken place, Congress didn't declare war until May 13, 1846. The American plan included a threefold campaign: northern Mexico would be invaded by Taylor, an army under Colonel Stephen W. Kearny would occupy the territories of New Mexico and California, and naval forces would blockade both Mexican coasts. Taylor's occupation of Matamoros took place on May 18 and the road to Monterrey lay ahead. Although many volunteers poured into the city, the enlistment system was so inept that it seemed as if more soldiers were going home than were arriving. Grant wondered aloud if Matamoros was one huge replacement center for *home!*

And it seemed that no politician came in as a *private.* Seven of them were brigadiers and one a major general. Now just what was a brevet brigadier like Taylor to do with a "good Democrat two-star" like Butler? As a starter, one could give him an outstanding volunteer colonel like Albert Sidney Johnston from Texas, Class of '26, as chief of staff.

Another political arrival was Brigadier Tom Hamer, member of Congress from Georgetown, Ohio—the old friend of Grant's father who had secured Ulys's appointment to the Academy. They'd wanted to elect him colonel of the regiment back home, but he'd enlisted as a private, then accepted major's leaves. Now a one-star general, Hamer was trusted by Taylor as the only politician general who could hold volunteers in check—including the rowdy Texans. In fact, Old Zach gave him as chief of staff Lieutenant Joe Hooker, on loan from the First Artillery and one of the army's fair-haired young officers.

General Hamer was sitting outside his tent, smoking. Hooker was reading nearby in the fading light. Grant saluted. "Evening, sir. Hello, Joe."

The general smiled, rising. "Ah, Ulys, pull up a stool and have some brandy. How are you tonight, ready to resume your tutorial duties?"

"Yes, sir." Shortly after Hamer's arrival, he'd come around to see Grant, speaking of home and the tanner's family. Incredibly, the congressman had asked him for a private education in military basics—drill, formation, and tactics. Grant had been taken aback. Tactics? A lowly second lieutenant teaching tactics to a *brigadier?* Hamer had told him he was just collecting a debt, that the young man he had sent to West Point had just been an investment—a means of one day getting a summarized education for himself. They had met several times since.

Grant protested that he knew little about tactics, and he was not alone. Captain Sam Hardee, only two years senior to Grant, and the man who'd risen so fast because of his brilliant studies on the subject, had been captured in a *tactical* blunder back in April! "In my opinion," Grant had told Hamer, "science is surely a game for European generals, while success in these Mexican battles would be dictated by decisions of the moment, based upon the expeditious, and common sense."

Joe Hooker handed Grant a glass of brandy and excused himself, saying he had an appointment. As he walked away, General Hamer said, "In addition to being brilliant, my young Hooker has the thirsts of a satyr."

"Sir?"

Hamer smiled with indulgence. "Oh, that's right. Joe told me you're one of the innocents. I was, uh, referring to his appetite for the young señoritas. You don't indulge, do you, Ulys?"

"No, sir. I'm engaged. Remember?" Grant sipped the brandy.

"Sorry I brought it up. Isn't it beautiful this evening? There's something about this country, the semitropical without the proliferation of foliage, I guess."

Grant knew the rumors about Joe Hooker, also that most of the other officers shared the charms of the beautiful young Mexican girls. Put those dancing black eyes, flashing white teeth, full breasts, good wine, and the ever-present guitar music together with lonesome men and it was inevitable. But Julia was waiting. "Yes, sir," he replied. "When it cools off the nights are lovely."

"How is your Julia, by the way?"

"Fine. She's thinks I'll be home soon."

"Maybe you will. When we take Monterrey, the Mexicans should think twice about continuing this silly war. Didn't you tell me her father is creating some kind of a problem?"

"He just doesn't think I can provide properly for her."

"I imagine every father feels the same. And I'm sure he knows what young officers are paid."

"I was hoping maybe when the war's over I might be able to go back to the Academy to teach. I heard my old roommate, Deshon, is an instructor there. Then, too, maybe I'll be lucky enough to get promoted before this is over."

Hamer sipped his brandy. "I wish I could help, have you transferred to me. But you're a regular and have to stay with your regiment. Maybe I can write to the old gentleman in St. Louis, tell him how fine I think your prospects are. Coming from a general officer and a former member of Congress wouldn't hurt, would it?"

Grant felt a surge of excitement. Sure wouldn't. "Sir, I would be greatly in your debt. But that would be such a bother—"

"Nonsense, I'll write tomorrow. Does he have anything against Democrats?"

Grant laughed. "He hates Whigs."

The general suddenly groaned and a look of pain crossed his face. "Damned dysentery." He'd suffered from it ever since arriving in Mexico. Moments later the wave of discomfort passed and he said, "I'm going to tell you something I've kept to myself around here." He looked steadily into Grant's eyes for seveal more moments before saying, "I've received feelers about being the Democratic nominee for the presidency in 'fifty-two."

Grant nearly spilled his brandy. His patron, president of the United

States? Astounding! He stared back at Hamer. "Sir, I, I don't know what to say."

The brigadier smiled. "Does sound kind of farfetched for a country boy from Ohio, doesn't it?"

Grant's mind raced. So much would be possible! Maybe Colonel Dent had heard something. Now that letter would *really* be meaningful! He just shook his head, saying nothing.

Hamer sipped from his brandy glass again. "If such a ridiculous thing were to happen, I guess I'd have to take care of the officer who taught me how to be a general, now wouldn't I?"

Another surge of excitement. A solid future for Julia. It smacked of favoritism, something he strongly resented . . . Still, if it meant a good life for Julia . . . and the deck was so stacked against him anyway. "I wouldn't want anything I didn't deserve," he said quietly.

"You wouldn't be getting anything you don't deserve, Ulys. I happen to think you belong on at least a division or corps staff. Who knows, with your commissary experience, maybe in the paymaster department."

Tantalizing! A sure route to major, maybe even lieutenant colonel . . . Good locations with a rich social life for Julia . . . proper surroundings for the children. Marvelous. "I wouldn't be able to thank you enough, sir. But there's still a war to be fought."

The dying light flickered off the general's red hair. "Old Zach'll get us through in short order, son. Then we'll talk about the future. In the meantime, I'd appreciate your secrecy about what I just told you. Political generals have enough problems as it is."

"But you aren't the normal political general."

"I'm close enough."

CHAPTER 8

Ulysses also wished to go among the host of Trojans, for he was ever full of daring.

—HOMER, THE *ILIAD*

Colonel Garland stood staring down from the outcrop of moss-covered walnut trees at the objective. Monterrey, the Jewel of the North, home of fifteen thousand residents of Spanish and Indian blood. The beauty of its orderly, verdant courtyards and rich orange groves beckoned peacefully as the hot September sun began to flee behind the Sierra Madres rising so sternly to the west. Soon and ever so briefly that light would be a soft scarlet, perhaps forecasting the blood that would bathe the city on the morrow.

Garland turned slowly, looking into the faces of his waiting commanders and staff officers. His voice was calm, "That's it, gentlemen—what we've come so far to vanquish. Don't let the quiet aura of her beauty deceive you though. Behind her fortifications, General Ampudia has upward of ten thousand men, pitched for death, ready for us. Fortunately, they are the usual poorly trained Mexican peasants and local citizenry. By this time tomorrow night, the city will be ours and most of those rascals will be dead or gone.

"As you can see, the city is guarded to the south by that mountain stream—the San Juan de Monterrey. Those two forts which guard the east—one of which is named Diablo for the devil—will be avoided until taken from the rear. Our problem lies in the black fort you see between us and the city and the Bishop's Palace to the west. Their heaviest guns are supposed to be in those two places. A smaller fort, Soldado, supports the palace. These forts are on high ground and surrounded by extensive earthworks.

"Old Zach sent the Texans down today to look the place over. They tried to pick a fight to avenge their Alamo, but Ampudia ignored them. They say the streets are barricaded to the hilt, so it looks like we'll have our work cut out for us."

Garland looked around again, pausing. "Tonight Worth's division will circle around to the west and camp just out of range of their guns. First thing in the morning, he'll attack. To divert some attention from them, this brigade—consisting of the Fourth, the Maryland company, and Bragg's battery—will charge down the slope, taking what fortifications we can on our way into the city. With good fortune, we'll be in there by noon, and the war may be over by nightfall. Get your men to sleep early. That's all, gentlemen."

As the murmuring group of officers broke up, heading for their units, Grant stared at the darkening city. What had Garland said—that the war could be over the following night? He still didn't think the war was right, but he didn't want to be left out of it. He'd gotten in on the briefing only because he was a staff officer. Glory for everyone but the regimental drudge. He frowned and headed for the quartermaster tent.

Shortly after dawn everyone heard the roar of Worth's guns. Grant, finishing his skimpy breakfast, looked around at the other officers in the mess tent. Tension and excitement marked their faces. Colonel Garland took a final sip of his coffee and got to his feet. Saying nothing, he hurried outside. Grant wanted to follow, grab his arm, and make one final request to be a part of it. No, Garland would have too much on his mind. The brigade had to move shortly. Maybe, he thought, he could go over and see his friend Sam French in Bragg's battery. No, he'd only be in the way. Go see to your mules, stable boy, he growled to himself. That's your heroic role. But doggone it, he was a regular, not just a bean provider!

He walked outside into the quiet bustle of prebattle.

As the six understrength companies of the Fourth began to form up, he walked over to the regimental corral. "Bolding," he called out to a private, "saddle up my big stallion."

"Going somewhere, Lieutenant?"

"Maybe. Just do as I say—quickly!"

Something might come up, or . . .

He'd find some excuse, making sure the ammunition was getting where it belonged, something. They'd need him somewhere down there, he just *knew* it.

The bugle call rang clearly through the fresh morning air.

They were moving out. He hurried to help Bolding with the cinches. "Sergeant Gordon," he shouted, "I'm going for a little ride. You're in charge here until I return."

The skinny old quartermaster sergeant started to protest, but Grant stopped him. "Just do as you're told. You know how to handle things. Keep the ammunition moving and be ready to get food and water up to the city this afternoon."

Gordon shrugged. "Yessir."

Grant still didn't know what he was going to do. Just keep watching from the outcrop for a while, see what might develop. The brigade was far below now, moving like so many bugs in the slanting gold of the early sun. They reminded him of maggots, inching slowly toward the city. Too bad he didn't have a glass to see better, or those newfangled field glasses some of the officers had. There, the tiny puffs from the enemy's guns, followed by the soft thumps trailing along a few seconds later. Last night's raindrops created millions of reflective beads, a shimmering brightness that belied the darkening danger descending on his regiment.

He simply had to get down there!

With a quick urging, the big wild stallion he'd broken and trained was carrying him swiftly down the slope. He felt the pounding of his heartbeat. Soon! This was what it was all about, this was what an army officer was meant to do. His long-barreled pistol was primed at his waist, his saber ready. Soon . . .

Now he was in the flat, galloping toward the maggots who were quickly growing into soldiers, soldiers fumbling forward amid the crash of battle sounds. How abstract those noises of battle had been from above, yet so *real* now, not far ahead. He reined in as he reached the rear ranks. Must be Garland's reserve. On through. No time to respond to the startled, questioning looks; the battle lay ahead. Where should he go? No matter, from the sound of things, an officer coud be used anywhere.

Now, as he slowed the big horse, the first signs of reality. A private screaming in pain, his arm hanging in scarlet shreds. Another with blood streaming into his eyes. A young lad looking up in pain from his dead friend's remains. The crashing echoes of cannonballs, musket fire all around. The answering roar of Bragg's guns. The too-bright sun, hazy in the stinging smoke. A young corporal dazed, staring blankly. Men down, frightened, stunned.

Garland had been stopped!

"Sam!" Grant whirled to see Lieutenant Charlie Hoskins, the Fourth's adjutant, slumped beside a bush. Poor Charlie had been sick for a week. "Sam, I'm about done in with this damned dysentery. Had the shits for days. I lost my horse. Can you let me have yours?"

An adjutant was always on the run in battle, relaying commands. What an affliction to have when he was most needed. Grant quickly dismounted, handing Hoskins the reins. "Sure, Charlie. What can I do to help?"

Hoskins pulled himself to his feet and swung up into the addle. "We're getting blasted from that damned tannery, that eastern fort you can see. Somebody didn't know what the hell he was talking about. A bunch of our people are pinned down in a small vale, just ahead. They can probably use you there."

As Hoskins wheeled away on the stallion, Grant moved off at a fast trot. The bombardment was getting worse. *Those gunners must have all the guns in Mexico!* Quickly he was among the Marylanders, whose ranks had been badly hit. A lieutenant, wounded in the throat, was making gurgling sounds, probably dying. Death and fear were everywhere.

Grant saw a blinded soldier staggering around, crying. He took the boy's hand, leading him to the shelter of a nearby rock. He should stay and provide some kind of assistance, but he would be just as badly needed by his own troops. Picking his way into the edge of the vale, he found the familiar uniforms of the Fourth stretched out in every direction, blood again the common denominator. He was greeted by the body of a lieutenant who had been with the regiment for only a month. Four years of the Academy for a few weeks of wearing gold bars, he thought.

He edged up to the gnarled tree that was serving as the command post. Colonel Garland spotted him immediately. Breaking off a conversation with a captain, he waved. "Ah, Grant, I see you couldn't stay back. Good thing. Hoskins just took a ball in the hand, so I need a new adjutant. How fresh are you?"

At last! "Like I just got up, sir. What can I do?"

The brigade commander's face was drawn. "As you can see, things are in a bad way and we're behind schedule. I'm going to move out of this draw in fifteen minutes and attack that tannery. Get a message off to General Taylor asking for reinforcement, and one to Bragg telling him to get those guns up here. The infantry commanders have already been notified."

"Yes, sir."

Garland's route of approach to the fort took the brigade through a cane field. The Mexican artillerymen spotted them almost immediately and concentrated a withering hail of fire on the sugar cane. Once more the brigade was pinned down, receiving terrible casualties. Grant hurriedly calculated that approximately one third of the officers were dead or wounded. The same was true of the sergeants.

The rage of futility was upon Garland. "Where are those goddamn Volunteers Taylor has been pampering? Grant! Tell Bragg we're getting the hell out of this cane with or without them!"

As Grant scribbled the message to the artilleryman, a courier arrived with a message from Taylor. Grant opened it, reading before handing it to Garland. "Butler's division of Volunteers coming. First Tennessee and Mississippi Rifles to provide flank support in direct assualt.—Taylor."

Garland read quickly. "About time. This goddamn canister is tearing us to pieces."

Another runner panted to a halt, saluting and asking for the colonel. He had a message from Colonel Jefferson Davis stating that they were approaching the fort. Garland turned to Grant. "Move 'em out!"

Although the Fourth never made it to the tannery, the Tennesseans and boys from Mississippi roared over its walls twenty minutes later. Both Davis and Campbell, the commander of the rowdy lads from Tennessee, would argue for years over who took the objective with knives.

Garland, seeing he could achieve nothing at the tannery, moved three companies into the edge of the city. Grant knew the colonel was trying to save face, but he was too busy relaying commands to dwell on the thought. Having no runners left, he went to Captain Bragg himself. The arrogant artilleryman snorted when Grant gave him new orders. "Hell, we should've blasted right in to begin with. Stick around a few minutes, Lieutenant, and you'll see how some real soldiers fight." Bragg turned, shouting, "French, we're gonna move right into the city. You stay here with two sections, giving them hell as I move up a hundred yards, then we'll leapfrog!"

Grant was amazed at how smoothly Bragg's men moved the guns without their dead horses. In less than ten minutes, Bragg had two sections in position, firing. Then, throwing Grant a wave, Sam French moved his sections quickly forward. Grant turned to get back to Garland, but was stopped by a familiar figure. General Hamer reined in his horse. "What are you doing here, Quartermaster?"

Grant couldn't suppress a grin. "I'm Garland's adjutant, sir."

The general dismounted, watching the gunners. "Tell him General Butler's been wounded, and that I'm in command. The First Ohio will be here in a few minutes."

Grant nodded. "How do you feel, sir?"

Hamer pulled out a thin cigar and lit it. "I'm all right. You get on back to your boss."

Garland's brigade had been able to penetrate only a few blocks into the heavily fortified streets. The Ohioans had been able to do no better. Taylor soon pulled them all out, sending Garland to occupy the tannery. Just after dusk the rain began to fall, making the grisly task of recovering the dead and wounded difficult. It was the duty of the adjutant to tally the information and render a strength report to the commander. At midnight he reported to Garland in the captured fort. Although unscratched, Grant had tended to several of the wounded and was covered with blood. "Sir," he said softly, "I'm afraid our day was quite costly. Near as I can figure it, we suffered one hundred sixteen killed and wounded, nine of them officers. And God only knows how many of the wounded will die."

Garland was slumped in a huge red chair that probably had belonged to the Mexican commander. His face was drawn and weary in the low light of the kerosene lamp. He nodded, expressionless. "Thank you, Mr. Grant. Sounds like a pretty high price for what little we accomplished."

Grant felt sorry for him, remembering the colonel's confident speech from the night before. They were far from drinking the wine of victory on this tragic night. And the smell, the tannery smell he'd hated so much in childhood, offended him. "We'll finish them off tomorrow. If you have nothing further for me, sir, I'll check the guard and get some sleep outside."

Garland nodded. "I wish they'd quit ringing those damned church bells. You'd think we lost the battle."

The bells had been pealing since dusk, but had barely registered with the busy Grant. The Mexicans had held off a powerful American army for their first success. Let them sound their pride. They might not get another chance.

Aside from Worth's storming and taking of the Bishop's Palace on the west side of town, the next day was one of rest—except for the burial parties. Grant stood sadly by the hole that accepted the body of Bob Hazlitt, tall and cheerful Bob Hazlitt, his ex-tentmate, who had been one of the regulars at the Dent parties so long ago in St. Louis.

Ah, Julia, dearest Julia, how do I tell you about this dreadful day . . . this carnage that some men revel in . . . this slaughter of brave boys . . . yes, and women and children within a city of innocence? I must spare you, but how do I write, when only this sadness is on my mind? And we haven't even scratched the city, the inner fortress. May God help us tomorrow.

A sunlit morning brought little to cheer about; the fierce fighting continued unabated. Noon passed. Garland's tone was tired as he stood in a doorway looking toward the heavily barricaded central plaza. "God, if those devils only knew how short of ammunition we are, they'd jump over those defenses and wipe us out. And the Third is just as bad off. Grant, get a volunteer to ride back to headquarters for ammunition." He handed him a message form. "And you'd better get somebody who's good on a horse. Those intersections will be deadly."

"I'll go, sir."

The colonel sighed. "Well, if we don't get the ammunition, I guess I won't need an adjutant. Good luck."

Grant tightened the saddle cinch. His stallion had also been killed with Hoskins. "Well, Nellie," he said softly to the gray mare, "we haven't known each other long, but we're going to make the most important ride of our lives. And you're going to take the brunt of it, pretty girl, because I'm going to be on your side like a scared Indian. You just give it all you've got and we'll get through."

Moments later he urged Nellie forward. Gunfire was everywhere, with soldiers fighting house to house. The din was terrible in the narrow streets. The mare's speed surprised Grant. As they flashed through the first intersection, a bullet tore through his right boot. He'd have to get down lower on the left side. Another intersection rushed by, and another. *"Move, Nellie! Atta girl!"* He caught the blur of faces as he roared through intersection after intersection, each a stream of lead that miraculously missed. But soon the firing subsided. They were out of it.

He swung into Taylor's command post, jumped out of the saddle, and practically landed on a lieutenant colonel. It was Old Zach's chief of staff. "Sir," he panted, "Grant from the Fourth. I have a request from Colonel Garland for immediate resupply of ammunition for both the Third and Fourth. The situation is desperate!"

The colonel nodded. "We know. Orders have just been issued for them to withdraw."

"But, sir," Grant pleaded, "they can hold with firepower. And those street intersections will wipe them out if they withdraw."

"We'll cover them, son. Now, you just catch your breath and take it easy for a while."

"But I'm the Fourth's adjutant. I have to get back!"

"They won't need an adjutant for a direct withdrawal. You've done enough for now."

Grant started to argue, but stopped. "How are we doing, sir?"

"Pretty good. We've reduced all their forts and are working toward the plaza. We received an encouraging sign from General Ampudia just thirty minutes ago. He wants us to hold up the fighting so the women and children can be evacuated."

"Are we going to do it?"

"No. General Taylor told him we'd cease firing when he surrendered."

Grant managed to find a small telescope with which to observe the ceremony the next morning. He rode Nellie up to a knoll some two hundred yards from where the American officers were meeting the Mexican contingent with the white flag. Amazing, he thought, how bright and commanding that symbol of truce appeared. A flash of hope, of reason. And how common, how drab the American leaders looked, compared with the gaudy Mexicans. And now to the terms; rumor had it that Old Zach would be lenient. After some thirty minutes of discussion, the Mexicans saluted and headed their mounts back to the city.

The battle of Monterrey was over.

The word flashed through the American camp. Victory! Ampudia had capitulated! And a great victory it was, against a heavily armed and entrenched enemy that outnumbered the attackers by nearly two to one. Although there was some grumbling about Taylor's magnanimous terms—particularly among the Texans—Grant was pleased. The general had considered the fact that hundreds of civilians would have been slaughtered—to say nothing of American troops—if it had been necessary to storm the plaza. And he felt the Mexicans had fought with dignity. Still, Grant knew that Taylor would be severely criticized for his leniency.

All Mexican military, with arms and full equipment, including six field guns, were permitted to march out of the city with full honors of war, thence to repair to a line seventy miles to the south. They were not to cross north of this line for a period of eight weeks—plenty of time, it appeared, for the two governments to solve their differences.

Taylor had opened the door for peace.

CHAPTER 9

A untie" Robinson was the closest thing to a mammy Julia ever had. But the tall, intelligent black woman was no house slave, brought in from the fields. She enjoyed the special status of her freedom in the Dent household. She was literate, had been married briefly, and was capable of the sound judgment necessary to be a steadying influence on the sometimes willful girl whom she so dearly loved.

They were seated under a stately elm, not far from the big house, enjoying the mild fall sun. Auntie was crocheting a pillowcase for the future household of her charge, listening as Julia read from Grant's latest letter:

The criticism of General Taylor's lenience with the Mexicans continues. No doubt you've read in the papers that even President Polk thinks he was too soft. And General Quitman, the rich sugar planter from Natchez, is constantly critical of Old Zach's actions. He's the firebrand who wants to make all of nothern Mexico a part of the Union, the slaveholding part. I don't know why he doesn't get shipped home, but I suppose it's politics again.

Auntie held the crochet ring at arm's length, examining her handiwork. "Huh, Mr. Grant's too gentle to be mixed up with such as them big mouths. I know'd that the first time he ever came to White Haven. Good thing he's got old General Taylor running things down there."

"Yes," Julia said wistfully. "Listen to how tender he can be in the midst of describing those awful things . . . 'hillsides covered with tall palms whose waving leaves toss to and fro in the wind like plumes on a helmet, their deep green glistening in the sunshine or glittering in the moonbeams in the most beautiful way.' He's much too sensitive to be a warrior, Auntie."

"Amen, child. I've always known that."

Julia lay back on the brown grass, closing her eyes. "Oh, Auntie, if he has to go on another long campaign, I just don't know what in the world I'll do. I wrote and told him about Papa's financial problems, told him he'd be getting next to a pauper for a wife, and that he was free to break the engagement."

"I know, child. And he wouldn't hear of it. What'd you expect from him? Money don't mean nothin' to him. Just you, honey."

Julia heaved a deep sigh. "Oh, I hope so. I truly do. I'd follow him anywhere, eating beans." She sat up quickly. "And here he talks about Fred. 'One of the nice things about our quiet period is being able to eat with Fred and Pete Longstreet whenever we want. And how we talk. Or at least they do, because I mostly listen. It doesn't pay for me to express my real thoughts about this unholy war with them, because they don't agree with me and I think too much of them to struggle, at least with my future brother-in-law.' " She smiled, shaking her head. "Isn't that just like him?"

"Uh-huh, but I'll bet he tells 'em what when he does speak up."

"I s'pose. Oh, Auntie, am I engaged to a myth? Is there really a gentle, handsome lieutenant down there in Mexico who loves me, who never looks at those pretty señoritas? Or is it a silly dream? It's been so dreadfully long now, I wonder if it ever happened."

"He happened, honey, that's for sure. Did you get another flower?"

Julia gently spread the envelope so Auntie could see. "Oh, yes. A yellow rose, all pressed and still pretty. See it?"

"Sho' do. You don't never have to worry about a young man that's thoughtful enough to add touches like that. Uh-huh, that boy loves you so much his big heart must be busting all over."

Julia felt warm clear to her toes as she lay back again and closed her eyes. It was a rose from a jewel. Oh, Ulys, my beautiful Ulys, my hero, my love. Come home safely, darling, come home to me soon.

Grant stood beside the graveside of General Hamer, mourning as deeply as he could ever remember. The dysentery had reached so deeply into Hamer's vital organs, poisoning him, destroying his resistance, that he had finally succumbed. Grant watched in detachment, not hearing the chaplain's words, struck more deeply by the great man's death than by any of the battle losses. During these many months in Mexico, the former congressman had become a father figure to him, a man of wisdom and temperance, of humility.

Even as he had nursed the general, night after night near the end, he had felt that the illness was an untruth—that so strong a man, so prime in his early middle age, so unusually clear in his resolve, would recover and someday lead the nation to sanity and fairness.

Such a man of vision, a man of dreams for the great Union, dreams based on the common sense that a lowly lieutenant could grasp. No pretensions, just constant wonder that such responsibilities could be thrust upon him. And now this talented, honest man, enclosed in that flag-draped pine box, was being lowered into the soil of a country where he should never have been in the first place . . . lost to a country that so dearly needed him, but would never even hold his remains.

The clear, lonely sound from the single bugle split the silence, sounding a finale known to no other kind of funeral. Never before had those notes stirred him so, conveyed such emotion, such loss. How could anyone who cared so little for music be so moved, so permeated with sadness, by the lingering notes of one horn?

It was over. He stood, even after Hooker departed, staring at the fresh brown soil in the alien sunlight, gazing blankly at the dust to which Hamer had returned. His patron was gone. No, his friend! Probably the first truly mature man he'd ever really known. He'd felt instant and terrible guilt when the thoughts of what Hamer could have done for him crossed his mind. Not future positions, not even a wedge against Julia's father, mattered when one had lost such a friend.

Grant slowly lifted his head, coming to attention. He raised his hand in a salute he held for several moments. A patriot was dead, a man he would never forget.

And the first tear he could remember since childhood slowly made its way down his cheek.

It was the first letter Grant had received from his father in some time. And as usual it was an outpouring of Jesse's political fires. Grant reread the contents, trying to sort out the real implications from the bias:

Bethel, Ohio
April 2, 1847

My dear son,

I hope this finds you in good health on your way to the City of Mexico. I knew the Mexicans would never let the war end after Monterrey. I wonder what that God-forsaken Polk will do now. As you know, the only reason he managed to get that one-legged Santa Anna back into the country was so he could take over and give us what he wanted. But instead that renegade raised a huge army to beat us. Polk's face should've been red! And then, when Santa Anna headed north to ambush the weakened Taylor army, Polk should've finally decided he wasn't much of an armchair general—or much of a president!

You know the only reason he sent General Scott to command the main body of troops in Mexico was so the Democrats could kill Taylor's chances of becoming president. After his Monterrey popularity, they had to do something. That's also why they took your regiment and those others away from him. Polk figured he'd have to sit out the rest of the war without further glory.

Old Zach really gave it to that Mexican at Buena Vista, didn't he? I read where he had only 4,600 men to go against Santa Anna's 15,000. What a general! What a president he'll be! The Whig party, from one end of this blessed land to the other, can't stop rejoicing. He just can't miss being our next man in the White House.

It's just a rotten shame that Polk won't let him command the whole army to finish off the Mexicans. But I guess he still hopes Scott will get enough glory to counteract Old Zach. It just isn't possible, son. The Whigs are going to save this country with a "Rough and Ready" president. And those slaveholding Democrats be damned!

Speaking of that, I assume you are still engaged to that slaveholding girl from St. Louis. That is, if she hasn't married a rich Democrat by now. I really wish you'd wake up about that, son. Sooner or later, we're going to have to fight those Democrats (and I know what I'm talking about) and we Grants just can't have a slaver amongst us. Think on it.

Your mother and all your little brothers and sisters send their love along with mine, and pray for your safe return from that ridiculous war.

Your loving father,
Jesse

Grant shook his head as he put down the letter. His father would always be the same old hardheaded man, always black-and-white political, always defiantly Whig and an abolitionist. Well, it was great news that Taylor might be president. He was much like Hamer, a patriot of common sense. General Scott would always be the great man he saw on parade back at West Point, the most magnificent, impressive officer he'd ever encountered. And he was proud that the Fourth was serving under him. Yet his familiarity with Taylor, the man's easy simplicity, was another thing. He would always hold the deepest respect for the man who differed in so many ways from "Old Fuss and Feathers."

He picked the letter up again, frowning. His father would just have to accept Julia when the time came.

CHAPTER 10

AUGUST 17, 1847

Having returned the night before from a big supply trip, Grant had excused himself and ridden ahead shortly after dawn. Now, stopping at a parapet on the mountain rim, he gazed in awe at the spectacle below. Through the breaks in the mist, he saw stretching ahead what looked like a huge inland sea—the Valley of Mexico, the final destination of a two-year journey. The fog below gave him the impression of an immense floating island, with the surrounding mountains standing a serene but vigilant guard.

He didn't know how long he sat there in the saddle, enchanted by the spectacle, remembering the battles and events along the way. His mount, Nellie, was quiet, as if she too were in awe, pondering the coming events. He patted her neck. Was she also wondering how an army of some seven thousand effectives could defeat three times their number in fortified positions in the capital shrine of a desperate people? Although Santa Anna had less than half his force in regulars, and the conscripts were just a step away from the pitchfork, emotion would be a mighty factor.

He turned at the sound. The mustached officer rode up slowly, taking in the sweep of grandeur. As he stopped a few feet away, Grant noticed his major's leaves and the flash of his engineer insignia. Grant saluted. "Morning, sir."

The major touched the brim of his hat. "Morning, Lieutenant. Quite a view, isn't it?"

"Like a wonderland."

At just that moment, the sun broke through in dazzling brilliance, illuminating each tiny drop of moisture like a minuscule diamond. The valley fog began to rapidly dissipate, revealing glimpses of the lush valley below. Softly, the major said, "One would hardly believe the sorrow that awaits in such sublime splendor. Look! The spires of the village churches are emerging, the lakes, the emerald fields, the olive groves. And there to the south, the majestic Popocatepetl, almost near enough to touch. What majesty we're soon to disturb!"

Grant heaved a sigh. "Certainly is something I'll never see again."

"Nor myself. And I must find a way through it."

Something about the major had been picking away at Grant. He'd seen him twice before at a distance. He must be . . . of course! He edged Nellie closer, extending his hand. "Name's Grant, sir, from the Fourth."

The major turned, accepting the handshake. "Lee, staff engineer." He turned for one last look, then turned his gray horse around. "Well, that's enough of the aesthetic. Take care of yourself, Lieutenant."

Grant stared at the departing form. Lee! Scott's chief engineer, the hero of Cerro Gordo. The perfect cadet he'd heard about since his first day at the Academy. Captain Robert E. Lee, now brevet major; Captain Lee, a name that often popped up in discussions in an officers' mess. The fairest of the fair-haired in the army.

Lee.

The next few days would wipe out the aesthetic side of the Valley of Mexico for Grant. The Fourth Infantry, still in Garland's brigade and Worth's division, fought difficult battles for San Antonio and the heavily fortified convent of Churubusco. The latter battle proved to be the most costly of the war, partly due to General Worth's arrogance. Again Grant deserted his supply wagons to get into the thick of it. When the last enemy shot was fired, some 1,050 Americans had been killed or wounded, though Grant had once more again escaped injury.

The following day, August 21, General Scott arranged an armistice with Santa Anna, providing a period during which neither side could improve its positions or receive reinforcements. It would be a period for treaty, leading to an end to the hostilities. Nicholas Trist, the United States Commissioner, would negotiate.

A week later, Grant and Fred Dent rode over to the Fifth Infantry's mess for a reunion called by Pete Longstreet. It was a rainy evening, but the moisture wasn't limited to the outdoors; a prodigious supply of alcoholic beverages had been assembled inside the large tent. And Grant, of late getting used to his evening's drinks, was quite prepared to down his share. As they dismounted, he said, "You may have to carry your future brother-in-law home tonight."

Dent laughed as he tied his horse. "Or vice versa."

Longstreet greeted them effusively as they entered the mess. "Welcome, lowly officers of the ever-in-trouble Fourth Infantry. As soon as you have a glass in hand, we successful warriors will tell you about battle, battle from the heights, from where noble victory can be tasted."

Longstreet's left arm was in a sling, a result of the minor wound he had received while raising the flag above Churubusco. "Allow me to introduce George Pickett," he said, "who stole the flag from me and claims credit for planting it atop the enemy convent. And this boy of twenty, wearing first lieutenant's bars, is the famous George McClellan, Scott's diapered engineer. And this scrawny, horse-faced captain is Tom Jackson, the infamous, sometime artilleryman and hero pretender. As a matter of fact, all present are hero pretenders, having gambled life and limb to be mentioned in dispatches and get promotions."

Grant noticed Longstreet's new captain's bars as the Southerner raised his glass, shouting, "Here's to the heroes!"

As they shook hands around, amid the laughter, Grant couldn't help a slight feeling of envy. Don Carlos Buell and Earl Van Dorn were wearing major's leaves, Dick Ewell, captain's bars. Even Dent was a first lieutenant. Cump Sherman, out in the California campaign under Frémont, was a captain. Buchanan, his old nemesis from the officers' mess at Jefferson Barracks, was about to be breveted lieutenant colonel. The vaunted Lee, in just the short time since their meeting, was sporting silver leaves and would probably get eagles. Garland had been recommended for his long overdue brevet star. And here he was, still—

"Gentlemen!" Longstreet loudly began. "Another toast . . . to the only second lieutenant in our august midst, a man who desires neither fame nor glory, a man who deplores battle but always manages to find himself in its eye . . . a great horseman who feels someone should *always* wear a gold bar . . . From the canefields of the Fourth, I give you Sam Grant!"

He could merely chuckle at the absurdity. After sixteen months of campaigning in enemy country, handling every dirty job to the best of his ability, of being involved in nearly every battle, he was still the goat. Oh, well, someone had to sweep up. He emptied his glass, smiled, and announced, "My congratulations to all of you. It seems that my station in this war is to watch only my *juniors* get shot down."

It was one of Grant's longer speeches.

A cheer followed.

By the night of September 6, it was obvious to General Scott that Santa Anna was not honoring the conditions of the armistice, had in fact been building up his force and defenses during the entire period. And Trist had gotten nowhere with his treaty proposals. Scott knew that the only answer was a final, total assault on the City of Mexico. He called his commanders together at his headquarters four miles south of the city on the evening of the 7th.

The major Mexican fortress was Chapultepec, a hill some two hundred feet in height just southwest of the city. From this heavily barricaded position, two major causeways led to the city—one to Belen *Garita* (Gate) on the southwest, the other to San Cosme Garita on the northwest. Down the middle of each causeway ran an aqueduct; on the sides of the road were deep, mostly impassable marshes. Molina del Rey—the King's Mill—an imposing group of stone buildings that were fortified to the hilt, stood at the foot of Chapultepec.

Before Chapultepec could be taken, Molina del Ray would have to be neutralized. The mission was given to Worth's division, the means of taking it fully entrusted by Scott to his feisty general. Garland's brigade was in position two hours before dawn. Since the Fourth had a new adjutant, Grant was going to act as a troubleshooting extra staff officer. The colonel had just nodded in agreement when Grant requested an active role, replying, "I don't know why you ask, you never stay back anyway." He grinned. "All right, act as my liaison with Smith's battalion as a starter."

Grant nodded. "Yes, sir." Smith's battalion was a hard-fighting bunch of soldiers commanded by the former commandant of cadets at West Point—the stalwart captain that Grant had so admired. The heroic Smith was a brevet lieutenant colonel now, about to get his eagles. His separate, highly regarded battalion was in support of Worth's division.

Grant wondered just what Worth's plan really was. Did he honestly think Molina del Rey was a soft touch? Did he think he could roar through it, rush on over Chapultepec and into the city—be the final grand hero? Already the Fourth and Fifth had been badly mangled by grapeshot and accurate musket fire on their first assault on the mill. Only the timely arrival of a battery of horse artillery, firing at close range, permitted the Fourth to reorganize.

In the confusion of the second attack, Grant was startled to see Fred Dent lead a charge at a Mexican battery positioned in front of the main mill building. He watched in wonder as Dent led a small group to the top of a building, saber swinging, pistol belching fire. A half-dozen men were pinned down with Grant behind a small rock wall. He wanted to help Dent, but the musket fire was murderous. He watched fearfully as he saw Fred and one remaining soldier alone in the midst of the Mexicans. *Fall back, Fred! Fall back!* But it was the enemy who broke, running to the far end of the roof. Then, as though playacting, he saw Dent slowly collapse.

"Follow me!" Grant shouted to the nearby men, dashing out of the shelter. God, he thought, if Fred were dead, killed while he'd sat and done nothing, he'd never be able to face Julia. Never. Moments later, he bent over the grimacing Dent. Blood was beginning to soak his left leg from a wound in the thigh. "It's only a musket ball," Dent barked. "Go after them. Don't let them get away!"

"They'll wait," Grant replied, twisting a kerchief around the lieutenant's wound. "Here, keep this tight, while I put you up where a surgeon can find you."

"No, dammit, leave me!"

"Shut up," Grant said, lifting him to a narrow ledge. "Now, just lie still until a medico arrives. We'll win the battle without you. Besides, you're already the hero of the day."

But Dent wasn't listening; he'd passed out.

Grant still faced three hours of stiff fighting before Molina del Rey would fall expensively to Worth's command. And expensively for Scott, who lost eight hundred effectives and still faced Chapultepec.

Both sides licked their wounds for a day, then the costly assault on the hill fortress was renewed. Charge after charge from all sides was repelled. Finally, on the night of the 11th, Scott massed his artillery to blast Chapultepec to a point where the infantry had a chance. The bombardment lasted throughout the 12th and until dawn on the 13th, when the foot soldiers again threw their ladders against the entrenchments. Garland's brigade was ordered to circle north, clear of Chapultepec, to hold the San Cosme causeway against reinforcements, and to bottle up the fortress defenders.

By eight o'clock, Mexicans began streaming out, many of them trying to get back to the city by the route occupied by Garland. Small battles raged in several directions, but now it was the *yanquis* who held the upper hand as they mopped up the disorganized, fleeing Mexicans. At this point, General Worth decided to begin his race for the city, for the Halls of the Montezumas—the government buildings the marines would later make famous. Garland received an order to proceed as rapidly as possible to San Cosme Garita.

Out on the causeway, in the vanguard of the brigade, Grant was fighting his own little campaign by the seat of his pants. Some six hundred yards from the heavily defended gate, he and his handful of men ran into heavy canister fire, accompanied by musketry from the rooftops of the outlying suburb buildings. There was also a sandbagged barricade across the road.

They quickly took shelter in the grotto of a huge aqueduct. Corporal Bolding, from the quartermaster section, had tagged along. He asked, "Whatta we gonna do, Lieutenant, hang around here all day?"

"No, but you are going to sit tight while I look around. Keep everybody down."

Grant hadn't the slightest idea of what he'd find. Maybe there was a way to flank the strongpoint. He slid down the deep ditch slowly, listening for a pattern in the cannon fire. When he thought he had it figured, he peered cautiously through a small bush. Yes, if he could make it across the road to the left . . . He jumped up, hitting full stride, dodging and diving into the ditch on the other side, then rolling quickly to his feet, running Indian-fashion around the last buildings. Stopping beside the small wall, he found that his arrival had gone undetected. The defenders must have their attention riveted elsewhere. Now, if he could get back . . .

Moments later he slid into the grotto, out of breath and sweaty, noticing that some thirty men and three officers had joined his makeshift unit. He nodded to Captain John Gore and quickly described the situation. "If I can have a dozen volunteers, we can go back the same way and hit them from the rear. That is, if it's all right with you, Captain."

"Sounds good to me, Sam. Meanwhile, the rest of us will get ready to charge the barricade."

Grant turned to Bolding. "Get me some volunteers."

"Yessir!"

Shortly, Grant led his party stealthily back along his previous route. Again, for some unexplainable reason, their move was undetected. Catching their breath, the men checked their firearms and listened to Grant. "As soon as you hear a commotion out front, we're gonna hit them from the rear. And make all the noise you can muster. They'll think there's a whole regiment back here."

A minute later, Gore and his party opened fire.

"Now!" Grant shouted, jumping to his feet. "Give it to them!"

By the time he reached the rear of the sandbagged barricade, his five-shooter was empty and the Mexicans who hadn't been caught in the crossfire were running wildly toward the garita. Grant turned to give chase, but was stopped by Gore. "The colonel just sent word to hold up until he gets some guns forward to soften up the gate. He thinks Santa Anna will concentrate a main effort there."

Two hours went by and nothing happened. Grant was again impatient. Maybe he could flank the gate itself. Once more telling Bolding to sit tight, he started another solo reconnaissance. Some fifteen minutes later, he spotted a small church close to and just south of the garita. Hmmm, he thought, noting that its belfry was about twenty feet higher than the surrounding houses, offering interesting possibilities. Very interesting. Now, if he just had some firepower . . .

Working his way back to his men, he ran into a young artillery officer who had a one-gun mountain howitzer section—a small artillery piece that could be quickly dismantled and put back together in minutes. "Lieutenant," he said with a faint smile, "How would you like to help me win the war?"

"Sounds great, but how?"

"Just bring your gun and all the shells your men can carry and follow me. We're going to church."

"To *what?*"

"Let's get moving."

Back into the ditches, sometimes waist-deep in stagnant water, Grant led his little command. Quickly, furtively, they crept southward, eventually climbing out of the water and skirting the outlying houses until he spotted an apparently safe route to the church. Telling the gunners to lie low, he strode boldly up to the front door of the church. After what seemed an eternity of pounding, the door opened a crack. A middle-aged priest peered out in alarm.

Grant's Spanish was limited, but he found the word. *"Abra!"* he commanded.

Wide-eyed, the priest shook his head and tried to slam the door. But Grant's boot was already inside. Sticking his pistol in the clergyman's face, he said, "Abra—open, or I'll have to kill you."

The priest tried to close the door.

Grant slammed his shoulder into the heavy wooden portal, throwing the man back against the entry wall. Pointing his five-shooter at the cowering padre, he turned, shouting to the gunners to join him. By the time his eyes had adjusted to the dark interior, the artillery officer was leading his men into the foyer. "Here!" Grant shouted from the steps to the belfry. "Get that gun up to the top and put it together as fast as you can."

Within minutes, the small howitzer was in action and enemy officers were glancing uneasily around as its shells began to fall in their midst. But with the overpowering noise of the major attack to the front of the garita, they couldn't detect the source. In the cramped area of the belfry, Grant was reveling in his gunner's role, picking targets, adjusting range, shuddering with each roar of the little gun, and noting the effective results.

Suddenly a face appeared at the small entrance to the belfry. Grant recognized him: Lieutenant Pemberton, Worth's aide-de-camp. "Who's in charge here?" Pemberton shouted.

Ulys wiped some of the black grime off his face and answered, "U. S. Grant, Fourth Infantry."

"You're to come with me, Lieutenant. General Worth wants to talk to you."

"But I'm busy."

"He knows that."

Grant nodded, turning to the artillery officer. "Keep pumping it into the same area. I'll be back as soon as I can. And get some more rounds somewhere." He picked his way down the steps behind Pemberton.

Five minutes later, he saluted the division commander. Garland was at his side, nodding approvingly. Grant knew he was undoubtedly the most bedraggled, dirtiest officer Worth had ever seen. The general eyed him closely before speaking. "Quite a job you're doing in that church steeple,

Lieutenant, raising all that hell. Good ingenuity. When this is over, I want a full report as to how you arranged it. In the meantime, I'm grateful. The whole division owes you thanks. I'll send another gun to you shortly."

Grant murmured, "Thank you, sir." No sense in telling him there's only room for one gun in that belfry. Generals don't often listen to second lieutenants.

"And Colonel Garland will join me in reporting your actions."

Grant saluted again and hurried away.

Grant kept his gun in action until the fall of San Cosme Garita, moving forward in other independent actions until the fighting died out. That night he stayed with Worth's division near the gate, helping dig passageways from one house to another as the command crept toward the city center. But Santa Anna had had enough. He pulled his troops out of the city during the hours of darkness, leaving the capitulation of the city to its councilmen. Officially, the City of Mexico surrendered at one A.M. on the 14th of September, 1847, and with its fall, the end of hostilities between the two nations approached.

Fred Dent, left by Grant atop a ledge at Molina del Rey to be found by the medicos, had rolled off and broken two bones. He later good-naturedly chided Grant. "Thanks, Sam, for putting me up there. I was hurt much more by the fall than the wound." He was breveted to captain for his courageous action at the mill.

Now it was Sam Grant's turn.

Suddenly, after being a second lieutenant throughout the war, he was showered with promotions at regimental headquarters in the suburb of Tacubaya. He received a brevet first lieutenancy for bravery as of September 8, a brevet captaincy as of the 13th for his actions at San Cosme, and a permanent first lieutenancy dated the 16th.

Of those who won three brevets and wound up as colonels were C. F. Smith, Robert E. Lee, Joseph Hooker, and Braxton Bragg—all prominent officers who, in another time, would play an important part in the life of the quiet young brevet captain from the Fourth Infantry. But as September drew to a close it was obvious that the peace negotiations would take time. It was also true that an occupation force would have to remain in the conquered territory for a period. It would be nearly another year before the young officer from Ohio, the reluctant cadet and adventurous quarter-master, would see his beloved Julia.

Early on the night of his promotion to brevet captain, he slipped into a back pew of the magnificent Cathedral of Mexico, even though the closest he had come to Catholicism had been attending Episcopal services at West Point. There, he closed his eyes and said a fervent, silent prayer for General Hamer, ending with, "Sir, I wish you could be here today to lend order. With all of the politics being played, you're going to be sorely needed."

As he rose to go, his eyes brimmed, and he wondered if he would ever get over the congressman's death.

CHAPTER 11

There is music in the forest leaves,
When summer winds are there,
And in the laugh of forest girls,
That braid their sunny hair.
—FROM THE *PERSONAL*
MEMOIRS OF JULIA DENT
GRANT

E mma was now twelve, but just as vivacious and mischievous as ever. She had been keeping watch for two days, insistent on being the first to see him. Now, late in the afternoon on this hot July day, she saw the gray horse with its tanned rider approaching the house. "Oh, how handsome he is!" she exclaimed to no one in particular. She turned from the veranda, shouting, *"He's here! He's here!"*

Julia, sewing in her room to kill time, jumped to her feet and dashed to the mirror for last-second adjustments. Giving her glossy black chignon a final pat, she turned to the stairs. She had barely slept for two nights, but she didn't feel a bit tired. Suddenly she seemed to be floating on air, in some kind of a dreamland.

Was he really here? Had those horrible, endless four years of loving a ghost, a vague vision of masculine beauty, a memory who wrote simple but beautiful letters that she held to her lips and breast—had they actually come to an end? Dear Lord, have you answered my thousands of prayers and actually brought my beloved home safely to me?

As she ran down the stairs, Grant swung down from the saddle, enjoying to the hilt the scene he had lived so many times. How often had he coaxed himself to sleep picturing such a sunny day and riding a handsome animal up to the front of this charming old house? Of dismounting to catch the rush of her warm beauty in his arms, to crush her to his chest and wipe away the fears that he would never again see his beloved, his—

Julia ran to him, stopping for a fleeting moment in hesitation. "Ulys?"

He could only stare.

"Is it really you, my darling?"

She rushed into his arms, kissing his cheek, his lips. He felt her warm tears as she held him tightly. "Yes, my dearest," he replied softly, "I think so."

He continued to hold her, absorbing her sweet scent, feeling her warmth, her breathing. It was all real, real! Within seconds he was surrounded by the Dent household, Emma kissing him, a hug from Nellie, another hug from the brimming Mrs. Dent, who said, "Welcome home, son."

Son! That was a welcome sign. Colonel Dent came out of the house and stood on the veranda. Was there a smile, just a trace? The older man came forward, extending his hand. "I'm pleased for your safe return, Captain."

With everyone talking at once, Grant couldn't manage an intelligent answer. It seemed he was in the midst of a group of magpies as he was swept up on the veranda. Julia hung on his arm, wiping away her happy tears. "How long do you have?" she managed.

"Two months, two whole months of leave," he replied.

"What did you bring me from Mexico, what did you bring me?" Emma persisted.

Mrs. Dent's voice was firm. "Come inside for some lemonade, and you girls hush. Poor Captain Grant can't talk to us all at once. And besides, your father wishes to speak to him first. Captain—Ulys—I believe you'd best see him now, in his study."

"Yes, ma'am." He smiled again at Julia, raising his eyebrows quizzically. She nodded reassuringly.

Colonel Frederick Dent stood by the lone window of the small but comfortable room. He turned as Grant entered. "Well, young man, it appears you've done quite well by yourself in your Mexican adventures, and I must admit I'm proud to have you as a friend of the family. Please sit down."

The huge mahogany desk took up much of the room, but Grant barely noticed it as he dropped into an overstuffed chair. He felt a tightening in his chest, his mouth was suddenly dry. What was the colonel up to? Would he dare, at this point, to stop everything?

Dent sat behind his desk, lighting a long cigar. "First of all, I wish to thank you for aiding young Fred when he was wounded. His mother would have me believe you saved his life."

Grant shook his head. "Nothing of the kind, sir."

"Well, be that as it may, we are in your debt." The colonel frowned. "But that has nothing to do with your proposed marriage to my daughter. I believe a stronger campaign has been mounted against me on this subject than on Chapultepec. Julia is quite willful, you know, and—" He sighed. "Unrelenting. I had hoped her ardor for you would dim with the passing years, but she hasn't changed at all. Now, I'm going to appeal to your common sense. Just what do you have to offer the gentle, somewhat spoiled daughter of a Southern planter?"

"I—"

"—A girl who has been exposed to no hardship, is used to servants, and is proud of her heritage. And, Captain, a somewhat frail girl who may quite possibly be physically incapable of the rigors of army life. God only knows what dangers she might be exposed to. Would you demand that this girl join your, at best, questionable future?"

Grant looked into Dent's stern expression. The old devil had been polishing this speech for four years, never intending to give in! Well, he could talk forever and it wouldn't make a whit of difference. "Sir," he replied in a measured tone, "Julia is stronger than you think, capable of handling almost any piece of horseflesh. As you know, I love her and respect her. That will overcome many problems."

The colonel snorted. "Love! I'm not interested in any romantic dreams. This isn't a novel. I'm talking about *reality,* boy! What kind of a future do you think you have in the army?"

"Frankly, I—"

"If you're lucky, you'll make major someday. You'll never have any money or property. You're a hero now, but that sort of thing dies out with time, leaving only a skimpy salary and a bunch of debts. What would you ever have to leave to your children—memories?"

"I'll take care of that when the time comes."

Another snort. "Sure, you'll rise to the occasion, won't you? Just invent money whenever you need it. Well, sir, that isn't good enough for me— or my daughter."

Grant's blue eyes iced as he stood, controlling his tone. "Sir, preferably *with* your permission, I'm going to marry Julia. And you will never have to worry about her welfare. I must respectfully state that the matter has been decided between us."

Dent stood, exhaling a large cloud of cigar smoke. His gaze locked with Grant. Finally, he nodded his head and extended his hand. "Then I'm afraid I have no choice but to welcome you into the family. I'll tell the womenfolk to start planning the wedding."

Grant drew in a deep breath and slowly let it out. *He'd won!*

It had been so long since they ridden together, and now as they walked to the house from the stables, Grant stopped and took Julia in his arms. The warm purple evening was settling in on them and he didn't care who might be watching. He kissed her, then smiled. "You look so lovely in the first light of the moon."

She sighed and leaned her head against his chest, then suddenly pulled her head back. "Did I tell you that I've been looking forward to being an army officer's wife?"

"Not exactly."

"I'm not the sheltered little girl Daddy likes to picture. I can make do with whatever we have, darling. I know that whatever you undertake will be successful, and I told your mother so in my letter of invitation to the wedding."

He shrugged. "The army has its own way. And speaking of the wedding, I doubt they'll come down for it. Mama is quite a recluse, and Papa is almost as set against my marrying into what he considers a decadent Southern family, as your pa is against having me. 'Course they'll come around once they meet you."

She scowled. "Oh, I *hope* they'll come. We don't need any squabbling on our relatives' part." Her eyes blazed momentarily. "But it's *our* life, Ulys, and we'll live in a cocoon if we have to!"

The wedding was set for eight in the evening on August 22 in the Dents' small house in the city. Uniform-conscious St. Louis would have yet another high-society affair to read about in the morning paper, or at least as high society as Caroline O'Fallon, of the philanthropic O'Fallons, could make it. After all, Miss Julia Dent of White Haven and Gravois Creek was like family. Caroline had been almost as busy in the preparations as Mrs. Ellen Dent herself, influencing the selection of the masses of fragrant flowers that filled the comfortably unpretentious Dent house. Mrs. O'Fallon had insisted on ordering the one hundred candles to ensure the quality of their soft glow and long life.

Her crowning achievement, however, was the bridal gown, which she had ordered direct from Paris many weeks before the bridegroom had even left Mexico. Of watered silk, touched off by cascades of fragile lace, it was set off by a veil of white tulle with a lovely wide fringe. The bride's corsage was a bouquet of white cape jasmine. The gown was thought to be the finest to arrive in the city for some time. It was whispered that Mrs. O'Fallon had even ordered the first rain shower in weeks, to ensure the bride and groom a fresh start in their marriage.

When Julia appeared at the top of the narrow, paneled staircase with her father, Grant felt a tiny catch in his breath. Surely, she must be the loveliest young woman he'd ever seen. Her petite form with its tiny waist billowed out into what seemed a sea of white mist, above which, framed under the diaphanous veil, her soft smile radiated happiness. His eyes were riveted to her slow, gliding descent. His beloved lady, his sweet, gentle beauty, was inching slowly toward him. In just a few minutes, she would belong to him forever.

The string trio did well on the Wedding March, he guessed.

Beside him, he heard a low whistle from Major Pete Longstreet, his best man. In moments she was beside him before the minister, whose words drifted over them like a litany in a foreign language. He managed the "I do" at the proper time without being conscious of speaking, and, at last, placed the tiny gold ring on her finger. His kiss was light and quick, as if his touch would break the charm and the dream would end.

It seemed an eternity before all the guests and family were gone, but finally they were alone in the bedroom designated as the honeymoon chamber by Emma. In fact, Grant wasn't sure that the little pixie wasn't hiding somewhere, in the closet or under the bed. Julia turned down the lamp and came to him. Her lips brushed his cheek as she embraced him. "Oh, darling, is it really true? Am I really Mrs. Ulysses S. Grant? Are you no longer my distant dream?"

He pushed her back gently, nodding so slightly, smiling into her warm dark eyes. He had never seen her without her chignon, hadn't realized how long her inky tresses were. Smiling gently, he was completely lost for words. Slowly, he pulled her wrist to his lips, then remembered with a start that he hadn't given her his wedding gift.

"What is it, darling?" she asked, sensing his alarm.

He went quickly to his jacket, finding the small box. Handing it to her, he said softly, "I couldn't afford the beautiful jewel you deserve, so I'm afraid this token will have to do. It may be presumptuous, perhaps vain, but it's all I could think of."

She took the box from his outstretched hand, quickly tearing loose the wrappings. Reaching into the soft tissue, she extracted a narrow black velvet strap that held a chased gold locket. Her eyes widened, "Oh, darling, it's lovely, so—"

"Open it."

Carefully, she picked at the catch. Inside was a miniature daguerreotype of himself. A soft sigh escaped her lips as she looked closer. After a moment, smiling up at him, her eyes brimmed. "Oh, Ulys, how could you know this would be the most precious gift I could ever receive?" Happily, she fastened the strap to her wrist. "I'll wear it forever, my dearest."

Moments later, the bridegroom turned down the lamp until the wick flickered out, conquered his qualms, and stepped out of his robe. Slipping into bed, he nervously drew his sweet-scented bride into his arms. "I'm afraid I'm not very experienced. I haven't—"

Her eager lips stilled the unnecessary words.

CHAPTER 12

It was impossible to get it through his father's head that his brevet captaincy was only a wartime rank. Civilians seldom understood peacetime manning levels, just as some officers had trouble facing the actuality of returning to lesser rank. It was a certainty that Jesse Root Grant would always make sure that the good people of Bethel, Ohio, would hear proud reports of his son, the captain. If there was anything to report . . .

Grant had hoped life and duty in Detroit would be interesting; instead it was the epitome of boredom. They had first been assigned to the cold little Lake Erie town of Sackets Harbor, near Watertown, New York. But Grant had decided he wanted his quartermaster's job back, and the regimental headquarters was in Detroit. Old Colonel Whistler was back in command of the regiment, with a favorite in the drudge's job. But a letter to General Scott returned the position to Grant after the winter had passed.

He had taken two more months of leave before reporting to duty, spending much of it with his parents in Bethel. It had been an idyllic interlude with Julia, in which their lovemaking grew even more zestful and became a beautiful part of the close relationship that would mark their marriage.

Although his parents hadn't greeted Julia with whoops and hollers, it had been only a few days before her bubbling warmth rubbed off on them. She reported that even Hannah had grown somewhat communicative before their stay was over. Jesse, ever opinionated and argumentative, proved no problem for Julia; she'd spent her entire life handling just such a man. So it wasn't long before the older Grant became attached to her, even offering their home at any time she might wish to stay with them. His brothers and sisters became her ardent admirers.

Old Zach had won the presidential election just before their departure for Sackets Harbor, delighting Jesse to the point that he got babbling drunk. Grant never could understand his father's glee in seeing Taylor elected. The general was a Southerner and the owner of many slaves—the person-ification of what Jesse hated with unbending passion. But he was a Whig, and that was all that mattered.

Politics! Grant would never understand it.

With little to do as a peacetime quartermaster, Grant had to remind himself that he could be with some other part of the regiment in one of those remote little posts along the Canadian border where Julia couldn't be with him. Detroit was a growing city of more than twenty thousand, so they weren't confined to the army social life. But that was mostly what Julia engaged in. She had Eunice Tripler and John Gore's wife, Lucinda, as companions and co-culprits in planning parties and other entertainments.

He'd first met Doctor Charles Tripler when he was a plebe at the Academy, later encountering the surgeon in Mexico, where he was the medical director for Twigg's division. And he also knew Gore quite well from the war.

Julia dragged him to almost every dance, often to the weekly cotillions in the Michigan Exchange Hotel. With her lightness of foot and natural gaiety, she was a popular dance partner with most of the officers. He was content to just escort her and sit quietly smoking his faithful pipe while the musicians did their best to torment him. Once in a while there would be someone to talk to, or he'd slip out with the boys to have a nip on the veranda. He didn't mind, as long as she enjoyed herself.

After a few months of hotel living, they'd found a decent little cottage on Fort Street East. It wasn't in one of the better parts of town, by a long shot, but close to the post. However, even its low rental of $250 per year chopped up a quarter of Grant's income. What a pleasure she made of their hours together, always dreaming up ideas to brighten his time at home. She knew, though he tried to keep it from her, how discontented he was with the lack of military activity. *Drudge* was really an appropriate word in peacetime.

Thank heaven for the departmental sutler's store on Jefferson Avenue, where several of the retired officers and some of the more interesting sportsmen in town often met. Having a ready whiskey barrel made the sutler the most popular man in town. It was a good place to play cards and listen to some pretty interesting discussions. Sure, he imbibed a bit heavily at times, but his beloved Julia didn't object, or at least she pretended never to notice. So he wasn't hurting anyone, was he? He'd hate to even think about putting up with this stale duty without a drink or two.

And *stale* was another appropriate word.

Except for this particular afternoon. His new trotting mare, the one he had recently bought from that politician, was going to win him some money. This fellow, Kibbee, who hung around the sutler's store now and then, refused to believe his mare could do that mile of straightaway down Jefferson Avenue in less than three minutes in a buggy with an extra passenger. Now here was a little excitement.

Grant drew back lightly on the reins and pulled up in front of the store, tying the mare to the hitching rail. He'd put new grease in the buggy's wheels just the night before, so everything was ready. Entering the sutler's, he saw that the usual crowd was there, plus several new faces. John Gore met him, handing out a mug of whiskey. "Here, Sam, wet your whistle before Kibbee starts blowing off. I think he's invited everyone he knows to watch you go down the drain."

Grant sipped, enjoying the harsh taste. "Thanks, John. I hope they brought money."

"Oh, they did. You sure you can do it?"

"I'm sure *she* can do it, so get some money down."

"I brought about fourteen dollars."

"Good. I've got about fifty."

"Where'd you get fifty dollars?"

"I won some on those races last week, and raided our savings."

"Does Julia know?"

"No, but this is a sure thing, and the only way I know to make some extra money without stealing it."

After a half-hour of drinking and loud discussion, the bets were down. Grant nodded at the tall Kibbee. "You ready?"

Kibbee always spoke as if everyone was hard of hearing. "Damn right, Grant. I hope you don't mind being a laughingstock. Under three minutes with me along—ha! Like taking candy from a baby."

Grant just nodded. Kibbee had no idea he'd already made the run in the wee hours on a couple of mornings—without an extra passenger, but with plenty of time to spare. The mare didn't know her new name was Bonnie yet, but she knew the tone of his voice and touch. Another of his long line of four-footed friends. "Just get in the buggy and we'll find out."

As soon as they were settled in their seats, Grant trotted Bonnie toward the starting point up Jefferson. Stopping there, he pulled out his large pocket watch. He handed it to Kibbee, saying, "I know this watch is accurate, but I'll be so busy driving, you'll have to keep track—along with those others back there in front of the sutler's. You'll have to be the starter, so let me know when we come up on the next minute."

He knew Bonnie sensed what was coming and was ready. He tensed, waiting for the signal. "Go! shouted Kibbee.

And they were off, the little mare's feet moving immediately into her soft, fluid rhythm, stretching her flying hooves, blurring down the smooth dirt street. "C'mon, baby, c'mon, girl . . . *go, Bonnie, go,"* he urged, as the buildings began to flash by. They quickly reached the first quarter, then the halfway point. Couldn't be more than a minute and three-quarters gone, and the stretch would go faster. They were going to make some money! "Go, baby, go!"

Reaching the last eighth of a mile, he slapped her gently with the reins and felt a slight response. The beat of her hooves was the only music he enjoyed, his song. Now a hundred yards to go. There was Gore, cheering and waving his hat. They flashed by the street corner that marked the finish. As he reined in, Grant turned to his watch. Kibbee held it out to him in glum silence. The second hand was just coming up on the minute. "I make it two forty-seven, Grant. You've got some horse here."

He was elated as they drove up to the store amid cheers. A smile touched his lips. Too bad there couldn't be more moments like this. Well, at least it would be nice to buy drinks for a change.

Grant didn't know why he suddenly felt a twinge of guilt; perhaps it was the whiskey. After all, he'd won, hadn't he? And it really wasn't a gamble, no risk to it. No risk at all. But supposing, just supposing something had been wrong with Bonnie today? Supposing she'd stumbled, pulled up lame, or any one of a dozen other things?

That fifty dollars had comprised most of their money. What would he have done if— And Julia trusted him so, leaving all financial responsibility up to him, and running the house on a stringent budget and all. How could he have faced her?

And just to be a hero among the boys.

He finished removing Bonnie's harness, petting her, uttering the gentle things an animal lover showers on a possession and friend. Even after buying all those drinks, he would be over forty-five dollars ahead, money they could well use. Still . . .

Julia had fixed a particularly appealing meal with roast beef, even using her fine china. Her mood was light and gay, radiant, in fact. She was wearing a new dress she'd just finished, of light wool for the autumn chill. After a few sips of afterdinner coffee, she said, "I think I'll let the table wait, dear. Can we go out on the porch for a bit? It isn't too cold."

Grant finished lighting his pipe. He was still troubled by his afternoon folly. He'd decided a confession would only confuse her, and besides, she'd probably laugh anyway. She had such faith in him, such blind, trusting faith. "Certainly," he replied.

Many summer nights had been spent on the top step of their back porch, a place where they could hold hands and discuss the day's trivialities, share the comfort they afforded each other. Tonight, she took his hand and leaned her head against his shoulder. The bright new moon was just beginning to announce its arrival over the board fence. She sighed, saying, "Oh, Ulys, how I love you. I dearly love being your wife."

"I'm glad."

She chuckled. "I didn't hear you say anything about supper tonight."

"Good, delicious, as usual."

"But it wasn't usual. Didn't you notice I made a special occasion out of it?"

"Uh-huh, the good china and your new dress."

"You *did* notice."

"What are you celebrating?" Had she heard about the race?

"Oh, just the most wonderful thing that's happened to us since our wedding night. It was stage setting for a great announcement."

"Which is?"

She stretched up and kissed his cheek. "Early next summer, you're going to be a father."

He stared at her silently for a moment, dumbfounded. "You're . . . you're *expecting?*"

"Isn't that the normal way?"

"Are you sure?"

"Doctor Tripler is."

He took her in his arms, not knowing what to say.

Moments later, she pulled back, giving him a sweet smile. "But if you don't trust him, I can put the dishes in the sink and we can make sure."

He shook his head. At times, she could be downright wanton. He stared down at her tiny midriff. "But we can't do that for some time now, right?"

She laughed, coming to him. "Oh, only for another four months or so."

Julia had promised her father that she would come home to White Haven for the birth of their first baby, so she departed in early May. Putting her on the train was painful to both, but more trying for Grant. After all those years of waiting, this would be their first separation since his return from Mexico. Two months would be a long time. Moving in with the Gores would alleviate some of the loneliness, though, and he would have everything ready when she returned. There would be plenty of room in the large Gore house for both families, enabling them to save money all the way around.

A healthy, lusty Frederick Dent Grant was born on May 30, a naming that pleased the colonel considerably. It also gave Grant a good reason to buy a lot of whiskey from the sutler's barrel—and to consume a big share of it himself. Upon their return to Detroit, Julia also brought along a deed to sixty acres of White Haven—Dent's belated wedding present. "There, you farmer," she laughed as she handed the paper to him. "You're a land-owner now."

Two days after her return, word flashed across the country that President Taylor had died of illness after only sixteen months in office. Grant felt an immense sadness, recalling vividly the death of Tom Hamer. He pictured sharply the lackadaisical dress and often sidesaddle appearance of Old Zach, and the solid trust he always evoked in his command. Now what would the country do under this Millard Fillmore, a New Yorker who was rumored to support the Fugitive Slave Law? But that didn't matter as much to Grant as it would have a few years earlier. After his continued relationship with the Dent family, he was more indifferent to the slavery argument.

The Triplers came over that evening after dinner, and the conversation naturally dwelt on the dead president. The three officers had had personal relationships with Taylor, so the reminiscences were somber and vivid. Eventually the talk turned to the political situation.

"Well," said Tripler, "look what he inherited. Polk stole New Mexico, Arizona, and California for fifteen million dollars and many thousand lives. Taylor rides into office on his reputation as a hero, unqualified for the job. He was an unpolitical Southerner all the way, with three hundred slaves. Yet the antislavery people got his ear and the new territories entered the Union as Free States."

"Wait," Gore interjected. "California made itself a Free State."

"Yes, but Washington had a say in it."

"And the South got upset."

"But," Gore replied, "none of those territories were adaptable to slavery, anyway. All three were full of free Mexicans who worked the big haciendas and land grants for a pittance. Why should the rich landowners take on the problems of supporting a new peon system of Negroes?"

"Besides," the doctor said, "I think the slavery issue is like the early morning fog. It obscures the real issue, which is money. The North has factories and a huge industrial potential. The South is growing decadent and refuses to mechanize. It has King Cotton, but has to buy everything from the North. But the Southerners sell much of their cotton in Europe, where they can get more for it, while the rich Northerners keep legislation in effect that ensures high tariffs, keeping European goods out of the country. It's all about money."

"I think you're right, Charles," John Gore said, "but you can't discount the slavery issue so simply. There's too much rhetoric and impassioned feeling about it. What do you say, Sam?"

Grant sucked on his pipe, shaking his head. "I think most of the everyday people don't care, because it doesn't affect them."

Gore smiled. "Same old pragmatic Sam."

"I wonder how the historians will treat our honest Old Zach?" Grant asked.

Tripler sighed. "I think he was used and that's how it'll be written when the eulogies are long over. In the meantime, the Democrats will desecrate him, and the Whigs will let him take the blame for all their problems."

Grant nodded his head in agreement. A shame a great general could get caught in such a trap.

CHAPTER 13

In June, the regimental headquarters moved back to Sackets Harbor, and with it, the Grants. Julia again made do with an uncomfortable little house provided for married lieutenants, painting and brightening it with touches of color. She made new curtains, and bought a framed oil painting for the small parlor. When Grant groused about being there, she carefully told him how pleasant the post was the second time around. He found another place to while away the hours in card games and listen to cracker-barrel politics, a tavern in the nearby village of Watertown. And he began to drink more.

Shortly after Thanksgiving, she told him they were going to have another child, and a few days later, she brought up his drinking for the first time. "Darling, I hate to even mention this, but you know our church has a temperance drive on. I've heard the Sons of Temperance have over a hundred thousand members associated with Presbyterian churches around the country." She came to where he'd dozed off in a chair after the evening meal and stroked his hair. "I wish you'd think about taking the pledge."

He looked into her dark eyes. "Do you think I need to?"

She couldn't hide the pain it caused her to discuss the matter. "I think if I were you and didn't have little Fred to care for, I'd be drinking too. Probably a lot more than you do. But, darling, it worries me a little. I know all the officers drink—it's part of the life—but I don't like to think people are talking about you. Not when they don't understand you."

He felt guilty because she had brought it up, but his drinking really didn't present a problem. It was only a means of escape. And with whiskey so cheap, he actually spent little money on it. Never got into trouble. "I'll think about it," he replied.

He'd just have to slow down a bit. He'd be all right.

Why, he could quit any time he wanted to.

But he wasn't all right when he came home at sunset two days before New Year's. He was staggering and he tripped coming into the house. Crashing into the kitchen table, he looked up sheepishly as Julia rushed to him. "Are you all right, darling?" she asked, her eyes wide with fright.

"Sure am, dear. Just got my feet tangled up."

She helped him up and into a chair. "You sure?"

"Yes. I, uh, just had a couple too many. I'm fine. What's for supper?"

Her voice was cool. "Some venison I fixed with that new recipe."

She filled his plate in silence, taking her time. When she finally came back to the table, tears were streaming down her cheeks. She quickly blotted them, turning away with a barely audible sob. He watched helplessly as she slumped, hanging on to the edge of the cupboard. He got up, knocking the chair over, and went to her. They'd never had a fight, not even an argument. And the only tears he'd ever seen were those of happiness, except the time when she left for White Haven to have little Fred. He circled her tiny form with his clumsy arms, turning her to his chest. "There, there, darling, I'm sorry."

The words sounded hollow.

She sobbed, not looking up, then cried uncontrollably. He couldn't think of a thing to say, nothing intelligent or comforting. Finally, she pushed away, pointing to little Fred, who had been watching quietly from his high chair. "Just look there, Ulys, look at your confused son. Do you know what he's wondering? He wants to know who this stranger is who comes staggering, no falling, into our kitchen. He's wondering because I tell him every day how wonderful his father is. That's you, Ulys, the drunk who staggered in, the man who's supposed to be his great father."

Grant stared first at little Fred, then at Julia. "I'm truly sorry."

Lifting her son from the chair, she said, "I'm going over to the Gores' for a while. I hope you can sober up before we get home."

He watched them leave, feeling an unaccustomed sense of shame. He poured a cup of coffee and sat at the table. Well, he'd done it now. The part about young Fred had cut through the haze; in fact, her words had chilled him. He'd never considered the infant—really never considered Julia, in his fruitless trips into oblivion. Her words echoed. *That's you, Ulys, the drunk who staggered in.*

Surely she wouldn't be talking about it at the Gores' house, she had too much quality for that. But they knew; probably everyone knew. The regimental drunk. He'd never cared what anybody thought about him, that was their privilege. But now it reflected on his loved ones. Here he was, almost thirty years old and he was nothing but a sot of a loser. How low can you sink, Grant?

She found him asleep in the chair when she returned. After putting Fred in his crib, she sat down beside him, watching, feeling compassion, reaching for the dear, torn, overlooked, beautiful man she loved so dearly. She shouldn't have railed at him so. She'd never do it again, no matter what. He was too good, this strong, tormented man whom God in His grace had given her. And now, in his pain, he was overdoing his antidote. Darned demon rum!

She kissed his cheek, brushing her lips against the evening stubble. Taking his hand, she watched his azure eyes flicker open, his alertness struggling back. "Darling," she pleaded softly, "will you forgive me?"

His senses collected themselves. What was she doing, kneeling, asking for forgiveness? He shook his head. "For what?" he managed.

"For my terrible words."

He stood, pulling her into his arms. "Don't apologize for the truth. I've been blind in my selfishness. I, well, maybe I can find a way for you to forgive *me*."

In the morning, he joined the Sons of Temperance.

CHAPTER 14

FORT VANCOUVER
SEPTEMBER 22, 1852

"Sam! Sam Grant!"

Ulysses S. Grant looked down from the rail of the coastal steamer as the little ship edged its way into the timbers of the wharf. Shouting at him and waving exuberantly was an unmistakable figure in an army officer's uniform. It was Rufe Ingalls, his former roommate at the Academy and one of the two members of his West Point Class of '43 who had been promoted to captain in the regular army. They hadn't seen each other in seven years.

"Hello, Rufe!" he hollered back.

As soon as the gangplank was lowered, Grant hurried down. Ingalls shook his hand warmly. "You sure are a sight for these sore old eyes, Sam. I've been going mad waiting for you to arrive."

Grant returned the grin. "How are you, old friend?" The headquarters of the Fourth Infantry had been assigned to this new post in the still-raw Washington Territory, close to the end of nowhere, and he had been pleasantly surprised when he heard that Rufe was stationed here.

"Bored stiff. I've been in this godforsaken place for three years now and I haven't been in one good poker game the entire time. C'mon, you'll be billeted with me in that two-story frame mansion you see up there on that bluff—the one with the balcony and the long piazza. I've got a welcome bottle waiting."

As they walked away from the wharf, Grant looked around in wonder at the unspoiled beauty of the place. Even in September, everything seemed green and fresh. The trees were so tall and majestic, the air pure and still. Magestic, snow-capped Mount Hood rose in the distance. He had been impressed with the abounding natural beauty of the area ever since the little steamer had turned into the mouth of the great Columbia River. After the long cruise from New York—which included a hazardous and difficult crossing of the Isthmus of Panama, and the sudden death of John Gore from cholera—the cool tranquillity of the Northwest was more than welcome.

"We call my house the Quartermaster Ranch and Colonel Bonneville has given his approval for you to move right in, if you wish. We supply officers gotta stick together, you know."

Grant nodded his head in agreement. "Sounds good to me. Did you really build this fort yourself?"

Rufe grinned again. "Of course not. These delicate hands of mine were meant only for shuffling a deck of good cards and fondling the silken flesh of beautiful women. My underlings did all the work."

Grant took in the well-constructed stockade, its cannon tower, storehouses, and rough-hewn barracks. By contrast, the framed wood officers' quarters looked like mansions. "I guess your engineer training finally came in handy."

"Right," Rufe replied as they entered the piazza. "C'mon, let's have that drink."

Grant shook his head. "I'll pass on the drink, unless you have some coffee warming. I, uh, took the pledge at Sackets Harbor last year."

Ingalls raised an eyebrow as he looked at his friend. "You mean you don't drink anything at *all?*"

"That's right."

Rufe shook his head. "I don't know how you'll make it here in the wilderness. Things get pretty bad without something to ease the doldrums. You mean nothing at all, *period?* Well, I'll be damned. First, two of our classmates become preachers and now that two-fisted drinker, Sam Grant, says he has quit the bottle. What's next, a revelation?"

Grant chuckled. "Just get me some coffee."

"The whole world's going to Heaven in a handbasket. I hope you're not going to tell me you've sworn off cards too."

"No, but I can't afford to gamble much. I've got a family back home that I want to bring out here as soon as possible, and that costs money."

"Probably more than you'll be able to save, Sam. The cost of living's pretty high here, even with your West Coast differential. Whiskey's dirt cheap, and I make a few dollars a month at the poker table, but I spend all I make, just as a single man. You can't even hire a cook for captain's pay."

Grant felt a sinking. He'd seen the exorbitant cost of everything on his brief stop in San Francisco, but he hadn't thought it would extend all the way up here to the wilderness.

Ingalls went on, "Anything we don't grow or make up here costs a damned fortune."

"Then I guess I'll have to turn back into a farmer," Grant replied.

Rufe reached into his pocket. "Oh, I almost forgot. Here's a letter from your wife that came a week ago."

Grant snatched the letter from him. Julia! He'd heard nothing in all the weeks since leaving Ohio, not one word. Excitedly he tore open the envelope, the familiar handwriting swimming before his eyes:

My dearest Ulys,

I hope this finds you somewhere in good health and spirits. Knowing that no mail would reach you on your long journey, I waited until I had the big news. Three days ago, on July 22nd, with little trouble at all, I gave birth to Ulysses S. Grant, Jr., a beautiful, healthy, blue-eyed copy of my handsome husband. He has a lusty voice that cries for his mommy's milk every minute he's awake, so I just know we have a little general on our hands. . . .

The rest of the words melted away; they could wait! *"Hallelujah!"* he shouted. "You can pour that drink, old man, I've got a new son!"

SPRING, 1853

Grant poured another "four fingers" of whiskey, as Rufe had named his usual drink. He stared at the glass, thinking how sad it would make Julia to see that he'd backed out on the pledge. But then drinking back East had been different, had created a family problem, had made him less of a father and husband. Here, in this forlorn wilderness, where there was so little to do, everyone drank.

At least during the fall and winter the zestful Rufe had been around to perk things up with his lively humor, long horseback rides, and card games. Now, with him gone, the insidious boredom had set back in. And with it, the old Sam Grant had returned—the Sam Grant of Sackets Harbor and Detroit, the bored one who drank too much. He despised himself for it, but it seemed the only answer. He was so incredibly lonely, missed Julia and the boys so much—and he hadn't even *seen* one of his sons.

He was as blue as a whetstone.

He had tried so hard to raise the money to bring them out to the Coast, but it seemed that everywhere he turned he ran smack into a brick wall. He and Rufe and another captain by the name of Wallen had tried selling ice to San Francisco, but the price had fallen before their shipment arrived. That was their first financial failure. Next came the livestock venture—cows and pigs for shipment to the San Francisco market. Now that had been right in his line, having been a farmer so much of his life. He and Wallen had borrowed the money from the aloof Colonel Bonneville for a crippling two percent per month. When Wallen took them to San Francisco, some of the animals had died aboard ship, the market had dropped, and they had lost money. He'd be paying the colonel back for several months yet.

Still the intrepid farmer, he'd then decided to pluck some money from the ground. Certainly that rich black dirt the Columbia provided would treat a son of the soil favorably. He'd leased a hundred acres, bought a couple of scarecrow horses, which he soon fattened up for the plow, and planted oats and potatoes. Potatoes had been a scarce and expensive commodity in San Francisco, except that by the time the crop came in everyone and his brother had turned into potato sellers.

It seemed he was doomed as a farmer.

Like everything else.

And especially in the eyes of "Little Mac," who had been acting quite superior since his arrival. McClellan—Brevet Captain George B., to be exact—was in charge of an engineer survey party that was to explore the passes of the Cascade Range and present a report for a railroad route to the East. The engineer officer had first gained fame on General Scott's staff in the Mexican War, then had added to it with skillful surveys in Texas.

McClellan was about twenty when Grant first met him in Mexico City, a fuzz-faced boy out of the Class of '46. Got into the Academy by exception at the age of fifteen because he'd already had two years at the University of Pennsylvania. The runty scion of Philadelphia aristocracy had arrived at West Point already the prodigy that legends were made of. He had been of no interest to Sam Grant then, and he wasn't now.

The McClellans could have the glory; all he wanted was his Julia.

Grant walked out on the piazza with a fresh drink, sinking into a rocking chair and relighting his pipe. A voice behind the red ash of a cigar identified the engineer. It was tinged with superiority. "Well, if it isn't our drinking quartermaster. Are you sober tonight, Grant?"

"Unfortunately, yes."

"I'm sure you can fix that."

Grant ignored him, sipping the whiskey.

"Now that I've leaving in the morning, do you mind if I ask you a personal question?"

Grant watched McClellan's handsome features in the dim moonlight. He said, "Doesn't bother me a bit, Captain."

"You've done a bang-up job for me overall, helping fit me out and all. But I'm damned sure that you weren't sober all the time. I'm curious about how good you'd be without liquor, of if you ever try it. Why does someone with your capabilities have to turn into a drunk?"

Grant took a long pull on his pipe. He ought to tell the boy wonder to go jump. The reply came out softly, "I don't suppose you'd understand if I tried to tell you."

"Can't you take it out here without the whiskey?"

Grant didn't reply.

"Others do." McClellan actually softened for a moment. "What about your future?"

"The only future I can see is hanging up this uniform and getting behind a plow where I belong."

"But that's stupid! You're an army officer!"

Grant just stared off into the inky shadows. He ought to get up and go inside. He didn't need some young miracle worker meddling in his unhappiness. "Look, McClellan, why don't you just stick to your surveys and let me handle my own problems? You won't even remember me in your arrogant march to glory, so don't trouble yourself now."

McClellan sniffed, chewing his cigar. "I'll forget you said that, Lieutenant."

Grant turned quietly back to his whiskey as the boy wonder stomped away.

*   *   *

71

The little spot where he'd spilled some booze on the paper showed on the upper left of the second page, but he wasn't going to rewrite it. And it was like everything else—he hated to do anything over, whether retracking because he forgot something, or because he didn't get something exactly right the first time. He simply hated to back up and repeat anything. He reread the letter and decided it said what he wanted to convey, whiskey spot or no whiskey spot . . .

Fort Vancouver
Sept. 21, 1853

My Dearest Wife,

I purposely left my rank off the return address because I wanted to surprise you, darling. Today I finally received a letter from the War Dept. telling me I'm promoted to captain with a date of rank of August 6th. I suppose I should feel elated over this permanent promotion but that's not the case, I'm afraid. It took the death of Captain W. W. S. Bliss for the vacancy to occur, which I consider a pretty sorry means of getting promoted. And he hadn't even been on active duty with the regiment for many years.

So instead of joy, I write of gloom, part of my discomforture with the army, and being away from you and the dear little ones. When I think of never having seen Ulysses, Jr., whom you call Buck, I'm deeply saddened. A little boy should know his father, just as his older brother should. And such a dear wife as you should have her husband at her side.

I'm pleased that you are home among your loved ones at White Haven. I know my family loves you, but they can be trying—particularly Father.

I'll soon be leaving for my new assignment at Fort Humboldt, a post in the lumber country not too far from San Francisco. As a line captain, I'm finally getting out of the quartermaster business, which is a big relief. I'm to command F Company. The bad news is that the post commander is Brevet Lt. Col. Robert C. Buchanan, who hasn't liked me since way back at St. Louis. He's really still a captain, so you see what I mean about anybody's future in the army.

A thousand kisses for you, my dear, dear Julia. Adieu from your affectionate husband.

Ulys.

P.S. My increase in pay isn't much, but I'll send along a little more money. Maybe I'll go into the lumber business in California.

U.

CHAPTER 15

rant stood before the highly polished desk, wondering how such an exquisite piece of furniture had reached such bleak surroundings. He slowly raised his right hand in a salute. "Sir, Captain Grant reporting."

Robert Christie Buchanan, known as "Old Buck" throughout the army, looked his old spit-and-polish self as he briskly returned the salute. "Well, yes, Grant. I've been looking forward to your arrival. I trust you've had a pleasant journey and stayed out of trouble in Frisco."

"Yes, sir."

There wasn't an iota of warmth in the post commander's expression. "Fort Humboldt may not look like too much, but I'm quite proud of these log cabins that I've hewn out of this forest. Your stay here will be as pleasant as you wish to make it." He looked disdainfully at Grant's attire. "You look like you've slept in that damned uniform, which may be the case. At any rate, as a company commander, you will be expected to adhere to a dress code probably more exacting than what you were used to at Fort Vancouver. I believe an officer's appearance bespeaks his attitude."

Buchanan rose, walking to the window and looking out. "The Fourth Infantry has suffered a heavy desertion rate from the day its troops set foot in California. As you undoubtedly know, a lot of these soldiers enlisted just so the army would ship them out here to be near the gold fields, and then disappeared into the get-rich-quick flotsam on arrival. We've been able to refill these vacancies only partially with new recruits, and your company has been particularly depleted."

Old Buck turned. "How about your personal discipline, Grant?"

"Sir?"

"I've heard you have a drinking problem. Had it back at Sackets Harbor and at Vancouver. Have you gotten yourself under control?"

"Sir, I'm always under control."

"Well, see to it that you stay that way here at Humboldt. I expect my officers to conduct themselves in an exemplary manner at all times. We all drink, but do it off duty and with judgment. Is that clearly understood?"

"Yes, sir."

"Very well, report to F Company and assume command at once. Welcome to Fort Humboldt, Grant."

Grant saluted again and turned to the door. He'd known Old Buck wouldn't kiss him on arrival, but the lecture had been galling. Oh, well, commanding a company might be a challenge, at least interesting enough to hold off the decision for a time . . .

*　　*　　*

It wasn't. Grant's duties required little time and it wasn't long before the local activities grew boring. Since none of the five other officers at Humboldt were interested in card games, even that pastime was denied him. In fact, there was literally no social life. He drank more in privacy, and at times in quantity. But nothing could erase the longing for Julia or the wretched discontent deep within him. His love for her had taken a long time to develop into this intensity and it was not something that could be swept under the rug and postponed for a prolonged period. In his extensive leisure time he often rode the white mare he called Winter on excursions to local settlements and the larger towns of the area, such as nearby Eureka. Now and then he visited San Francisco. On one such excursion he heard that Cump Sherman had resigned from the Third Artillery and had gone into banking.

The following morning at eleven he arrived at the small bank, wondering what kind of a reception he'd receive. Thirteen years was a long time. But Sherman welcomed him with open arms. "Sam! You old son-of-a-gun. I heard you were up at Vancouver with the Fourth. What are you doing here—on leave?"

Grant looked up into the intense brown eyes under the prominent forehead. The redheaded Sherman hadn't changed much from the homely cadet he remembered seeing graduate so long ago. "No," Grant replied warmly, "just a few days off from Humboldt, where I'm stationed now. I've been out of touch up there. Didn't even know you were out of the army until yesterday. And rich enough to be a banker, too."

William Tecumseh Sherman grinned. "A few good investments at the right time, Sam. That's all. A lot of us have done pretty well out here, and have turned in the blue suit. But let's not talk here. I know a pretty good eatery where we can lift a couple and do some catching up."

The long lunch session was stimulating to Grant. Being with Sherman was the most enjoyable time he'd had in a long time. They traded cadet and wartime stories, talked of their wives—Sherman had recently married the daughter of Senator Ewing from his home state of Ohio. They also wandered into politics, where they were on common ground. Then it was back to the future.

"I tell you, Sam, there are thousands of opportunities here in California. Halleck, with whom I served here during the war, is out of the army and doing very well as a lawyer and real estate baron. You should meet him. And Joe Hooker, weren't you and he together in a campaign in Mexico?"

Grant nodded his head. "Uh-huh. He was one of the handful that went from lieutenant to full colonel. I knew him briefly before he got all that fame. Quite a rounder and ladies' man, if I recall. Is he out too?"

"Yes, made quite a killing on firewood and land. He took two years' leave of absence, then resigned. He's in seventh heaven with the wild way of life here." Sherman ordered another round of drinks. "How about you,

Sam? You thinking about hanging up your uniform and getting in on things?"

"Yes. Trouble is, I don't know if I'm cut out to be much of an entrepreneur. Every little money-making venture I've tried has flopped."

"Want me to look around and see what I can find for you?"

"I appreciate the thought, Cump, I really do. But if I call it quits, I want to get back home to Julia as soon as possible."

Sherman shrugged. "This is the place of the future."

Grant took a big sip of his second drink. "And the army isn't. It doesn't matter how you perform in the peacetime army, only who dies."

"I know, it's an unholy damned system."

Too soon the reunion was over. Sherman invited him to dinner, but he had to get back to Humboldt . . . to the real world of nothing, to his private and public demons. As he watched the erect figure walk away, the sadness set in: success departing, failure watching. Two separate universes, as sharply different as day and night, connected only by a slim association of the long past. And divided abruptly by the stark realism of truth.

He really shouldn't have had so much to drink the night before, knowing he had to pay the troops the next morning. It had just been one of those nights when everything was at its darkest, and he'd wanted to obliterate it all. Grind out the pain, slip away into the land of nothing, the void . . .

But he had awakened at five when the effect wore off. It was the bad time, getting up, the time when he often gagged, coughed, and felt the queasiness. It was also when his hands shook with that tremor that made coffee hard to drink, that caused the contents of a spoonful of sugar to spill before he could get it to the cup.

It was just after he relieved himself that he reached for the partially empty bottle sitting there on the dresser. Couldn't count out money in that condition, not with those distrustful hands betraying him. A little of the hair of the dog always settled them down. He picked up the bottle and removed the cork, spilling a little of the whiskey as he tried to pour it into the dirty cup. He quaffed it down like medicine, shaking his head with a shudder at its taste. But the second drink was a little easier. And before long, the queasiness passed. The third one invited the fourth, and by the time he arrived at the orderly room, everything was better, *much* better. He'd just get pay call over with, sign a couple of routine things, and saddle up. Head for the woods, the silent, nonaccusing, beautiful, friendly woods where he could open another bottle and lose himself again. He even made a clever little remark to the first sergeant.

There was no problem, at least not until Old Buck showed up and stood off to the side of the pay table, glowering. Probably going to get on him about his sloppy appearance again. He recounted another tiny pile of money. God, what an infinitesimal amount of money a private made each month. And he couldn't even hold it together as a captain. "Here you go, Torrence," he said to the soldier in front of the table. "With your accounts paid up, you get seven dollars and ninety-one cents." He chuckled, adding the age-old joke, "Don't spend it all in one place."

He looked up at the handful of soldiers left in the pay line. Why was he trying to be funny? It really wasn't funny at all. Besides, he seldom joked with the men. Wasn't his way. But then, the whole thing was a joke, wasn't it? No wonder the kids ran away to the gold fields. No, they didn't have a right to do that—they'd committed themselves to a period of enlistment and they had an obligation.

But *he* didn't have any obligations. Not after ten years, no sir! He counted out the next pitiful little stack of money.

Buchanan's icy words penetrated his wandering thoughts. "Captain Grant, I want to see you in my office just as soon as you finish."

He glanced up. "Sir?"

"That is, if you *can* finish."

"Yessir."

Grant tossed off a casual salute as he approached Buchanan's desk. "Reporting as ordered, sir."

The post commander's eyes were hard, his scowl cold. He bit out his words. "Captain Grant, you are under quarters arrest for being inebriated on duty. Or are you too damned drunk to understand?"

"No, sir, I understand your words, but not your meaning. I'm not—"

Buchanan exploded, "Goddamn it, don't argue with me! Your words are slurred and I can smell you a mile away. You're drunk as a hoot owl and I'm not going to put up with it! Go to your quarters and sober up. You are not to have another drop of spirits, on or *off* duty, until further notice. That is a direct order, Captain!"

"Yessir." Grant saluted and departed. He went directly back to his cabin, polished off four fingers of whiskey and went to sleep.

Although his hands were shaking badly the next morning, he drank nothing. Remorse over the previous day's events had settled over him, and he was worried that he might be punished and bring disgrace on his family. He reported as calmly as possible to Buchanan after breakfast. Old Buck ignored him for several moments before looking up and speaking abruptly. "I've prepared the papers for your court-martial, Captain. But based on your heroic service in Mexico, I'm going to sit on them and see if you straighten out. One slip, if I just *think* you've had a single drink during duty hours, and you're finished. Do you understand?"

Grant didn't blink an eye. "It won't happen again, sir."

Grant sat staring at the document. Although he'd been promoted several months earlier, his official commission as a captain had just caught up with him. How different it was from the one granting him his brevet captaincy at the peak of his wartime fulfillment, how hollow. He reached for the whiskey bottle and poured his first drink in ten days. He stared at the commission, seeing it blur into the personification of everything he'd disliked for so long, his chains, his misery, his loneliness. It was the symbol of his imprisonment.

But no more.

No more.

He stared back at the commission. It doesn't matter, Julia, I'm coming home. I'm through, finished. I don't care what I have to do to feed the little ones, how many ditches I have to dig. I'll do it outside this stifling army.

Moving to the desk, he dipped the pen and began the first of two brief letters to the Adjutant General of the army. The first was his acceptance of his captain's commission, the second an announcement of his resignation, effective the 31st of July—three months hence.

He'd give them to Buchanan the following morning.

He wasn't sure why he bought the bottle of rye whiskey, but then he never was. It was primarily the wait in the cheap, dingy little hotel. He was killing time until he could get free passage on the Pacific Mail Steamship Company boat to New York, a matter of several days. He should see Sherman again, possibly Hooker and a few others he knew in San Francisco, but he was sure the story of the pay table had gotten around, and he didn't particularly want to explain it.

No, he certainly hadn't *intended* to buy the bottle. It was the waiting, and that shabby, bare-walled hotel room. Besides, what could it hurt? And now that it was finished, how could a good, carefree look at sinful Frisco hurt him? He didn't weave as he stepped out into the moist early evening, in fact, he thought he was quite steady. Slipping once in the mud that oozed through the cracks of the battered wooden sidewalk, he plodded along with the deliberate, wide-spaced steps that often mark a drunk's course. What a polyglot of mankind, he thought as he moved through the noisy, crowded streets. A gaudily colored parrot shouted something unintelligible, a monkey on a sailor's shoulder shrieked at some irritant. Bearded miners, English and French dandies, freed Negroes, stolid Germans, excitable Mexicans, the ever-present long-queued Chinese—all a sea of faces pushing their way through the throng.

The second saloon was a busy place. He edged his way to the bar and ordered a drink, and then another. The bright-cheeked singer's soprano was lost amid the babble of dirty men's boasts and fantasies, which in turn were in loud competition with a small but vigorous brass band that forced him back into the mud and slimy water of the street. He'd always had trouble with loud music.

Finally he wound up in yet another strident place where a ratty little miner tried to sell him an interest in a "million dollar" claim for fifty dollars. Two drinks more brought a proposal of half interest in the same claim if Grant would stand him a visit in a local sporting house—one with "Chinee girls, exotic Polynesians, tight-lipped Frenchies, and some good hot-pussied nigras from New Orleans."

Grant pushed the pleading man aside and forced his way back into the raucous street. One moment he was stifled, the next he felt strangely alone. In one place a buxom little prostitute had eyes like Julia, and saddened him deeply. The hours wore on as saloon after saloon turned into the biggest spree of his life—a kaleidoscopic drunk that lasted two incoherent days and finally, somehow, expired back where he had started.

As he looked blearily into the cracked mirror, he tried to recall his foray, but only glimpses returned. His hands shook, his eyes were blood-red, and his filthy uniform reeked of whiskey and vomitus. He moved unsteadily to the washstand, leaning over the dirty basin. Pouring the entire contents of the water pitcher over his head didn't even dent the fuzziness. He looked back into the mirror, watching the water drip down over his face. How had he gotten back to the hotel? How long had he been gone? Bits and pieces flashed back—sailors, soldiers, miners, dance hall girls, blasting music, a fistfight, a shrieking monkey . . . raucous laughter. And always the nearly empty glass, demanding to be refilled.

But mostly darkness.

And *mud!* Seemed like it had rained the whole time. His shoes and trousers were covered with mud.

But a drunk got wet only when he weaved from saloon to saloon.

He watched a bug crawling up the stained wallpaper beside the cracked mirror. Some kind of water bug. He oughta squash it, but he didn't know if his stomach could stand the sight.

He turned, glancing at the nightstand. The sunshine from the open window reflected off the water glass, colorful, bright—too bright. Hurt his runny eyes. He went to the glass, picked it up. Just enough water to give his head another dousing. Why wasn't it raining now?

Suddenly, Tom Hamer's face floated in front of him. What would the congressman turned general think of him now? He was a disgrace to the great man's memory.

Oh God, how can I do this to myself?

His money!

His thirty-three dollars. Quickly he reached for his wallet. Empty! His pockets yielded seventeen cents. Just seventeen cents left of the entire, carefully saved stake on which he was to get to New York. How could he have been so insanely stupid? What was he to do now, go begging? Sherman had offered. But he couldn't, simply couldn't go to him like this.

The nausea swept over him, sending him back to the basin. He retched, heaving only a bitter fluid, then stood, shaking, his eyes bloody slots. He reached the stinking bed, sank down and closed his eyes, trying to still the quivering, jumping nerve ends. He had to get himself together, clean himself up so he could find Tripler. His old friend from Detroit was stationed in the city, and to make ends meet was practicing medicine on the side. He couldn't ask the doctor for money, but maybe Tripler could help him medically.

Julia! Dear Lord, how could he have forgotten her in his insanity? And he didn't have one single excuse.

He loathed himself, felt utter repugnance. How could what was supposed to be a man be every bit as bad as the worst, most abhorrent bum? He was no better than the most disgusting thief on the street. And that was just what he was, a thief. Hadn't he stolen their money—poured it down his gullet and puked it away?

Oh, my dearest Julia, how could I do this to you?

He went to the window and looked out. Three stories should be enough to break his neck . . .

The simple way, the ultimate ignominy.

Was this what the Mexican called his *hora de verdad,* his hour of truth? Moment of truth? What was the difference? One thing was certain—just as with the army, he was finished with alcohol, absolutely, indisputably finished. He would never touch another drop for the rest of his worthless life.

Never.

Ever.

Somehow he managed to get back to a fitful sleep. And when he shook his way back to the basin two hours later, he found some fresh water down the hall. After washing his sticky body, he did what he could for his uniform and went down to the lobby, only to find that he was overdue checking out. He'd paid only through the previous night. He went back to the room and threw his belongings into the scuffed old leather suitcase. In his sheaf of papers he found the certificate he'd been saving for New York—the voucher for $41.20 per diem, which was due him for the court-martial over which he'd presided in February. Allen could cash it for him, good old Allen, the quartermaster.

But Major Allen had gone out of the city for a few days, so Grant presented his claim to the quartermaster's chief clerk, a man named Ogden. After examining the certificate, Ogden shook his head. "This form was drawn up incorrectly, Captain. I can't authorize payment."

"But the fact that I have it proves the money is due."

"Sorry, sir, it'll have to be returned to the originator for change."

Grant slumped into a chair. Now it seemed the fates were playing tricks. He spoke softly, "But you don't understand. I'm flat broke."

"I'm sorry, sir, I really am."

Grant's gaze centered on the worn couch across the room. "Do you suppose I might be able to spend the night here? I'm slightly ill and had to move out of my hotel. Perhaps I'll be able to think of something tomorrow."

Ogden shrugged. "I suppose it'll be all right."

"Thank you. I'm sure Major Allen would approve."

Picking up his hat to depart for the day, the chief clerk withdrew a dollar from his pocket. "Here's something to get you some food, sir."

Now it was charity from clerks, Grant thought. He accepted the money, murmuring "Thanks."

Ogden nodded his head. "Maybe I can find a way to pay you for the certificate in the morning and get the error straightened out later."

Grant shook his hand, replying "You're very kind."

Dr. Tripler lit a cigar and leaned back in his big leather chair. The sound of the rain falling leaden on the brick street outside the window added to the somber tone of his words. "I don't have the answer, Sam," he said. "No physician does. Spirits have varying effects on different people. Some can swill down gallons, others get drunk on a couple of swallows. All I know is a lot of lives are ruined by it. You, for instance—I saw you drinking too much back in Detroit and in Sackets Harbor before you took the pledge.

"With you, it's an escape tool, a means of being able to bear the discomfort of having to do something you're really not sold on. It works like a balm on a sore, except that some balms heal, while whiskey creates new problems. And what's so bad about it all, Sam, is that so much drinking is going on around you—with your peers—that you don't realize how much of a slave you're becoming. It's insidious. You become addicted to it just as surely as if it were morphine or opium."

"I can take it or leave it, Doc."

"Then you'd better leave it. Your main sources of unhappiness will soon be ended—both being in the army and your absence from your family. If you continue to drink too much, you'll have only yourself to blame. Use this last spree of yours as a memory jog, anytime you get so inclined again. Recall how much you were disgusted with yourself. Personally, Sam, I think you're too much of a man to be crippled like this anymore."

The words were soothing to Grant's tormented conscience. How could he possibly ever forget his terrible guilt and degradation of the day before? *Ever!* He heaved a sigh and nodded his head. "I've already made up my mind. I'll simply stop drinking completely."

"Well, I wouldn't make any harsh promises to myself. Breaking them can be quite destructive. Just watch it. If it seems to be taking over again, be careful."

Grant's blue eyes looked straight at the doctor. "It will *never* take over again."

CHAPTER 16

S ir, you must either settle your bill, or we will take legal action."

Grant frowned in response to the hotel manager's ultimatum.

"And, of course, you will have to give up your room."

"But, sir," Grant replied in his quiet voice, "I will soon be getting money from my father in Ohio."

The manager, a plump little man with a waxed mustache, shook his head. "The Astor House does not provide charitable lodgings for army officers, Captain."

"I'll have money for you by this evening, sir." Grant turned from the desk and headed for the front doors.

"You have until tomorrow morning," the manager rejoined.

Grant went outside into the hot busy street. He very much disliked the island of Manhattan at this moment, and wished only that he could clear up his local debts and be rid of the place. Julia and his sons were in Missouri, not New York, and the more he thought about them, the more he wanted to jump on the next train and head for White Haven.

But he didn't even have enough money for the train ticket.

He had spent the last of the money Buckner had loaned him going up to Sackets Harbor. When he had first arrived in San Francisco, a young man named Hunt, who had been a sutler at the Fourth Infantry post, had borrowed several hundred dollars from him to start a business. When that failed, Hunt returned to Sackets Harbor, promising to repay the debt. But not one red cent had been repaid, and Grant had been unable to locate the scoundrel on his recent trip to his former post.

Crossing the street behind a huge beer wagon, he headed east toward the river where he could catch the ferryboat.

Captain Simon Bolivar Buckner had been a year behind Grant at the Academy, but their friendship had begun there. They had seen each other at times during the Mexican War, where Buckner had also received two brevets to captain. During the postwar period they had spent some time together, including being part of a party that climbed the volcano Popocatepetl. Now a regular captain in the commissary corps on Governor's Island, Bolivar was still the handsome six-footer with an imposing physique. The only difference Grant had noticed when he first looked him up after arriving in New York was that he now wore a bushy dark mustache. "Good morning, Sam," the Kentuckian said, as Grant entered his airy office. "How was your trip to Sackets Harbor?"

Grant dropped onto a worn leather sofa. "Fruitless. The bird has flown."

"What will you do now?"

Grant shrugged. "What can I do? I wrote to my father for money."

"Will he send it?

"I hope so."

"Do you have anything left?"

"Two dollars and twenty-two cents, after the ferry." He told Buckner about the hotel manager.

"How'd you get so broke getting here?"

Grant shrugged again. "Coming across the Isthmus, I encountered a down-and-out soldier I knew from the Fourth Infantry and loaned him twenty dollars."

Buckner shook his head. "That wasn't too sensible."

"Well, I couldn't ignore him. Can you loan me some more money until my father comes through? I hate to ask, but—"

"Gladly," Buckner replied, reaching into his desk drawer and extracting a couple of bills. "Here's ten dollars to eat on, and I'm coming back with you to the hotel to guarantee your room rent."

Grant knew what his friend might be thinking—that he wasn't sure Grant wouldn't take the hotel money to the nearest bar. He sighed. "I don't know how to thank you, Si." Emotion caught in his throat as he took the bills. "I hope someday I can find a way to repay you."

"I'm not worried about the money."

"I mean for helping me out of this predicament."

Buckner put his hand on Grant's shoulder. "Friends don't need repayment. You know that, Sam."

WASHINGTON, JUNE 28, 1854

SIR. In reply to your letter of the 21st inst. asking that the acceptance of the resignation of your son, Captain U. S. Grant, may be withdrawn and he be allowed six months of absence, I have to inform you that Captain Grant tendered his resignation but assigned no reasons why he desired to quit the service and the motives that influenced him are not know to the Department. He only asked that his resignation should take effect on the 31st July next and it was accepted accordingly on the 2nd instant and the same day announced to the army. The acceptance is therefore complete and cannot be reconsidered.

Very Respectfully,
Yr. Obt. Svt.
JEFFERSON DAVIS
Secretary of War

Jesse Grant reread the letter and threw it down on his desk. Stupid War Department! Stupid Jefferson Davis. He was nothing but a slaver himself. How could he know Ulysses didn't mean to actually resign. The boy was just distraught over his prolonged absence from his wife and little ones. Treat a homesick boy that way, and he's liable to do *anything* irrational.

Jesse shook his head. He still couldn't figure out why his son went that far, though. Why, he was a huge success, having just got his permanent captaincy and all. Big war hero, big future. Must have gotten drunk or something. No, he probably didn't drink much—not like those other sots in the army. No, Ulysses couldn't have been in his right mind when he applied for resignation.

Maybe a letter to the president . . . no, he was a Democrat.

Ulysses just hadn't taken into consideration what this meant to his father, or the pride he had in his son's accomplishments in the service. He should have known that a man, sixty, who was comfortably well-off from a lot of hard work and a successful business, ought to be asked about such a serious move. Why, resigning from his country's army was a disgrace to a patriotic father who had gotten his son into West Point!

What was the world coming to?

What in the name of Heaven was wrong with Ulysses?

Jesse turned back to the other letter that had come in the same mail, the one from Ulysses asking for a loan. Had to settle up some debts in New York, and needed some money to get home on. What had he done with his salary, gambled it away? Why, he must be making over twelve hundred a year now. Huh, that was a fortune when Ulysses was born. Never knew he was such a spendthrift.

Shouldn't send it to him, but he did want to see the boy and get him straightened out. What would Ulysses do? He'd never liked the tannery business, and besides, his other sons were in the management positions. But he couldn't leave the boy stranded with those wolves in New York . . .

Grant looked through the slanting rays of the sun at the familiar sights along the road. Though thickly foliated trees had grown some, it was almost 1847 again. Seven years earlier, he had ridden up to this always lovely big house at White Haven with the anticipation of a young man bursting with romantic love—a returning hero, proudly wearing his brevet captain's bars, eager to claim his bride-to-be, on top of the world. But it wasn't '47. Now, instead of riding a fine horse, he was on this old rented plug, he was in debt, had no occupation, had incurred his father's wrath, and was, by most standards, a failure.

He had dealt with his remorse about the drinking, and his chagrin had lessened; and he felt absolutely no guilt about resigning from the army. He wished he had something to show for his years on the Coast, but he didn't, and that was that.

What had he told a couple of people in California? When they next saw him he'd be a rich Missouri farmer. Well, it might take a while, but that's just what he'd be. Maybe not rich—money wasn't that important— but comfortable enough to afford his family the good life they so much deserved.

His *family:* what a solid, warm word. Julia. He could feel the excitement building, the anticipation of seeing, hearing, touching her. And the two boys—Freddy and Bucky, as little Ulysses was called. A son he remembered only as a baby, and one he'd never seen. Four years old and two.

And there it was! The house, set so beautifully in those magnificent trees, the scene that had danced so vividly through his mind for the past two years. There was the darky running out to meet him, the other one shouting at the house, announcing his arrival. Figures began to swarm out, waving, smiling, and in their midst, running down the steps, was his beloved Julia.

She nearly bowled him over, running into his arms as he dismounted. Showering him with kisses and words of love, she squeezed him tight and put her head on his chest. After a moment, she said softly, "Oh, Ulys, my darling, I'm so glad to have you back."

CHAPTER 17

Colonel Dent leaned over the crib, watching his sleeping granddaughter. "What is she, seven weeks old now?"

"Eight," Julia answered, smiling beside him.

"She seems healthy enough."

"Like a bear cub, Papa."

Dent pulled out a cigar as he took a chair. Frowning, as he struck a match to it, he asked, "What are you going to do about him, Julia?"

"About whom?"

"That husband of yours. I can't stand the thought of you living in that cabin he's building. Why, that's what white trash and nigras live in."

"But, Papa, it's more than just a cabin. It'll have two large rooms downstairs—dining and sitting—and three bedrooms up, and a kitchen and servants' quarters out back."

"Huh, he can't even afford to feed his own family, let alone servants."

"We never go hungry."

"If I hadn't given you those sixty acres, you would."

"Now, Papa, don't go into that. Ulys is doing the best he can, clearing and selling wood like he does. I've never known anyone to work as hard as he does. Do you know he slaves on the house until dark almost every night? That's right. He wants it to be perfectly tight against all kinds of weather. And when I finish decorating the inside, it'll be the most homey, comfortable place around. You'll see."

"Well, when you get tired of playing pioneer, you know where you can live. Even staying here in your brother's house is stupid." The Grants were living in Louis Dent's house, Wish-ton-wish, a place Julia liked to describe as "a beautiful English villa set in majestic oaks." It had been necessary for her brother to go to California, and he had been glad for them to stay there. The trouble was that it was quite a way to their own place, where her husband had to go every day to cut wood and farm the land.

"Now, Papa, let's not go into that again. We needed to be by ourselves for several reasons." She smiled as she looked toward the crib. Her little Ellen—or Nellie, as everyone called her—had been born here. "Besides, Hardscrabble will be all ours."

"That's another thing. Just what the hell's he trying to prove, naming it that? *Hardscrabble!* Sounds like that useless husband of yours is making fun of me."

Julia's expression hardened. "Now, Papa, you know I won't put up with such talk. Ulys had to start from scratch and has a long way to go, but I'm married to a great man, and I won't have you criticizing him."

The colonel shook his head. "He's a laughingstock to a lot of people around here, what with paying nigras to work for him when you've got title to three of your own. And paying them too much, to boot."

"He does what he thinks is right."

Dent sniffed. "Yes, and you make shirts for the boys out of your old dresses. What kind of reasoning is that?"

"Doesn't hurt them or me one bit."

"And that thing about the mule. I heard he bought a fellow's mule at auction, fellow by the name of Tergle, just so's the man wouldn't lose it for not paying his just debts. Then your captain gave it back to him. And when the constable took the mule again, he bought it right back. And Tergle's still got the mule. I just don't see how a pauper can be a philanthropist!"

"You just don't understand him. He can't bear to see anyone in worse straits then he is."

The colonel walked over to take another look at the sleeping little Nellie. "All I know is he turned in a steady job in the army to be a wood-cutter. And he doesn't seem to care."

Julia kissed her father's cheek. "He cares, Papa. He's just a private person."

Grant did care, particularly when he delivered wood to Jefferson Barracks, as he was now doing. Word of his trouble at Fort Humboldt had trickled down from the Northwest, so he was sure there was plenty of back-door gossip. He could hear them now: "There goes Grant, that woebegone figure in the old blue army coat, driving his wagon full of wood. Shame that a West Point officer could fall on such straits because of drinking. He's probably going to sell that load and head straight to the nearest tavern."

Well, let them think and say what they wanted, he was doing the best he could. 'Fifty-six had been a difficult year, with only some twenty-five acres under cultivation. Couldn't raise crops on land that hadn't been cleared of trees. But wood continued to bring four dollars a cord, and he expected to cut another hundred cords or more this year. Now, if he only had money for seed . . . He'd tried his father again, much as he hated the thought. Old Jesse had promised, even in his hurt, to help, but the money hadn't been forthcoming.

Maybe he should remind him.

But this was a bad time, what with the Whigs headed for oblivion, to ask Jesse for anything.

Remnants of the Whigs had joined hands with the new Know-Nothings, an offshoot of the United Americans. The Democrats were splitting, owing to the Northern and Southern animosity over slavery. And in the chaos, the new Republican party was gaining strength. He'd joined the United Americans briefly, but couldn't swallow their anti-immigrant stance. After all, didn't everyone spring from foreign stock at one time or another?

The presidential race had boiled down to three candidates. The Know-Nothings ran Millard Fillmore; the Democrats, James Buchanan; and the Republicans nominated John C. Frémont, the army officer of exploring fame. Frémont, the son-in-law and political opponent of Senator Benton, Colonel Dent's friend, had a flamboyant, egotistical reputation in the army, and was militant about saving the Union. Under him, secession would have been inevitable. Fillmore didn't have a chance, and Buchanan—in spite of being proslavery—had denounced Southern agitation, and had sworn to preserve the Union at all costs.

He'd never voted before. In the army, he didn't feel that his vote was important. This time, as he'd told Colonel Dent, he'd decided to "vote for Buchanan because I don't know him, and against Frémont because I do."

Now, in January, Buchanan was being inaugurated.

And Ellen, the lovely and charming colonel's wife, the woman who had befriended him from the first day he visited White Haven, the mother-in-law who had never ceased to believe there was something special about him, died following a month's illness. She was only forty-eight.

"There's two hundred and fifty acres of good pasture and over two hundred acres of plowed ground," Colonel Dent told Grant. "Julia's nigras can handle the house and keep it up, and I'll make an outright gift of William Jones to you. He's a good field hand, you know. The rest of the nigras, except for one house servant to help Emma with the house in town, will be sold."

Dent paused, then went on. "In addition, I'll advance you seven hundred dollars for seed and other such things as you might need. At the end of each year, you can pay me fifty percent of the profits. I can't think of a more handsome offer, can you?"

Grant shook his head. No, he couldn't. Julia's father had been lonesome ever since his wife died, and he wanted Julia and the kids back in the big house. He intended to spend quite a bit of time in the city, as well. Just eking by at Hardscrabble had been too hard on Julia, and this was a fine opportunity. "Sir," he replied, "I'm honored by the opportunity. I'm sure we'll prosper from it."

He wasn't too pleased about having a slave given to him—and he certainly wouldn't write home about it—but he'd need all the help he could get. And just as soon as things were rolling smoothly, he'd give William his freedom. Yes, things would be better now . . . though he would be sorry to move out of Hardscrabble. After all, he'd built it with his own rough hands, and it *belonged* to Julia and him.

But Ulysses S. Grant didn't bargain for the Panic of '57 that came along later in the year and devastated the country. Nor did he bargain for the low crop yield at Hardscrabble, or that he would have to sell his gold-hunting detached lever watch and chain at Christmas in order to have money to buy gifts for his family.

Shortly after the birth of his third son, Jesse Root Grant II in February of the following year, Grant drove the wagon through a particularly heavy snowstorm to deliver a load of wood to a tavern with the unlikely name of The Feathered Nest. It was located a mile outside St. Louis and was frequented by a number of sergeants from Jefferson Barracks, as well as some of the local farmers. When he finished unloading the wagon, he went inside to warm up and get paid. Nodding to the half-dozen patrons who were standing at the bar, he stomped his feet, went to the potbellied stove, and rubbed his hands. It was one of those iron stoves that had a little red-hot spot about a foot square when it was stoked up and doing its job, and it felt good. He waited for the proprietor, Charlie Norton, to finish waiting on a customer. A tall man with thick glassses and a receding chin, Norton wiped his hands on his dirty white apron and ambled down the bar to where he was close to Grant. "Colder'n hell out there, ain't it, Cap'n."

Grant nodded. "Must be about fifteen above."

"I got some hot rum over here. I'll stand you a glass."

"No thanks. I just want to warm up a little and get on back home before it gets any worse out there."

"How much I owe you?"

"I piled up a little over a cord. Five dollars'll do."

Norton nodded, reaching into the cash box and withdrawing some bills. At that moment, a burly man at the bar wearing three stripes on his blue uniform sleeve stepped over to the stove. "Say," he said, "ain'tcha Lieutenant Grant from the Fourth Infantry down in Mexico?"

"I was," Grant replied quietly.

The sergeant had a big, drooping mustache and a booming voice. He stuck out his hand. "I'm O'Leary from Bragg's battery in those days, Lieutenant." As Grant shook hands, the sergeant stared at the faded blue overcoat. "How come you're deliverin' wood these days?"

"I have a farm not too far from here."

"Well, I'll be damned. Let me buy you a drink, Lieutenant."

"He's a captain now," Norton said.

"All the more reason. Give him one of those hot rums to warm him up."

Grant shook his head. "No thanks. I'm going to be running along in a minute."

"Can't do that without one little drink to Mexico, Cap'n," O'Leary boomed. He held out the steaming cup of rum.

Grant looked up at the others at the bar. They were all watching him. One drink wouldn't hurt—it'd be cold driving back. No, he couldn't. "I'd better pass," he replied.

The sergeant's big grin was close, beaming down at him. The mug of rum was right in front of his face. It was suddenly quiet as everyone continued to watch. *One* wouldn't hurt.

"I think it would be downright impolite not to accept one drink, Cap'n."

He nodded his head and took the cup. The hot rum burned its way down, but felt and tasted good. It had been a long time. He raised the cup as O'Leary said, "Here's to General Taylor!"

Everyone, including Norton, drank to the dead president.

"And to General Scott."

Grant raised his cup, then took a hefty drink.

"And to a general named Hamer," Grant said, surprising himself. "The best civilian general the army ever had."

They all chimed in, "To General Hamer."

After three more toasts the cup was empty. Norton refilled it.

Following twenty more minutes of zestful recollections about Mexico, Grant bought a round of drinks. By lightning, he hadn't enjoyed himself this much in a long, long time!

He awakened, sitting on the floor, propped up against the wall by the tavern stove. An oil lamp on the end of the bar was turned down low, creating strange light and shadows that mixed eerily against the wall. It took him over a minute to remember where he was. His mouth was dry and sour, his head ached. He got slowly to his feet as the memory of O'Leary and the others flooded over him. The rum! *He'd gotten drunk!* All of those promises . . . all of those good intentions—broken. What time was it? He reached for his watch, but he no longer had one. There was a clock behind the bar. What did it say? He moved close and stared. Four thirty-three! Julia would be worried to death! He put his hands to his head. *How could he have done it?* He turned, found his army overcoat hanging over a chair and got into it.

Why?

Talking about old times with a sergeant wasn't reason enough.

What would he tell Julia?

He went through his pockets. He had one dollar and five cents left out of the wood money. Shaking his head, he pulled on his gloves and headed for the back door.

Julia was dozing in the front parlor when he stomped the snow off his boots and entered the nearly dark house. A lamp burned low on an end table. Outside, the sky was turning a damp gray over the white countryside as dawn brought in the new day. She stirred under her robe, rocking the chair where she waited. "Is that you, Ulys?"

"Yes, darling, it is."

"Where in the world have you been? I've been worried silly."

He went to her, taking her hand. His voice was low. "I made a grave mistake. At the tavern I got involved with an old soldier from the war and I had a hot rum. One drink led to another, and I guess I fell asleep."

Her eyes were wide. "You smell terrible."

"I'm sorry."

She frowned. "You don't need to apologize to me."

He nodded. "I broke my pledge."

She came into his arms. "I was so worried."

"I guess I can't take even one drink."

She brushed his lips with hers. "I'm just glad you're all right. Now come, let me make some hot coffee and some breakfast for you."

He shook his head. It was the only time he'd ever really broken his word. The first time hadn't actually counted. Taking the Presbyterian pledge way back at Sackets Harbor had been sort of the thing to do back then. And the West Coast duty could be blamed.

Now, only he could be blamed.

He saw himself in that cracked mirror in that dirty hotel room in San Francisco. A bug was climbing up the wall. A sorry man with vomitus in his beard and blood in his eyes was staring back at him. The man was a weakling, and he lied to himself.

Could he ever change?

Three weeks later, Ulysses was driving his wagon through downtown St. Louis when he heard a voice say, "Grant, is that you?"

He looked up to see a tall, red-haired figure standing on the street corner, staring at him quizzically. "I'm afraid so, Sherman," he replied, hauling back on the reins.

William Tecumseh Sherman took in Grant's scraggly beard, his nearly shapeless hat, the old, faded blue overcoat, the mud-spattered boots, and said, "What in blazes are you doing?"

"Why, it appears I'm hauling wood."

Sherman shook his head slowly, then threw his head back in a hearty laugh. " 'Pears so. What in the hell are you doing that for?"

"Solving the poverty problem."

"Well, I'll be damned. C'mon, park that thing and let's go somewhere where we can have a drink and talk."

There was a place for the wagon and team just across the intersection. After tying the horses to the rail, Grant replied, "The talk will be welcome, but I'll pass on the drink. What's a rich San Francisco banker doing here?"

"Huh, that's history. The only difference between you and me is that you have a wagon and some wood."

They went into a small nearby tavern where Grant had a sarsaparilla and listened to Sherman's story. "I'm a dead cock in the pit," he said, his long face sad. "It was the panic last year. The St. Louis bank, Lucas and Turner, closed my California branch, and by the time I got to New York, they'd closed that one as well. In fact, as you may know, they're suspending here too. I've come here to turn in my records and square my accounts with the home office. Tell me about your adventures."

Grant shrugged. "Maybe you should say *mis*adventures." He gave the fellow Ohioan a brief summary of his struggle at White Haven.

Eventually Sherman said, "Not only am I out of a job, but I'm deeply in debt. Some brother officers, a few of whom you probably know, entrusted me with funds to invest wisely for them. I thought I had done so until the roof caved in. I feel honor-bound to make good their losses, so somehow I have to make some money."

"But you're not legally responsible, are you?"

"No, but they trusted me."

Grant nodded his head. "I understand."

"Fortunately, I bought quite a bit of property when I was stationed here at the commissary after the war. In fact, I speculated rather wildly, because St. Louis was supposed to be the land of opportunity. If I can dispose of these lots and parcels, I'll be able to pay everyone back. I'll still be broke, but that'll be off my head."

"What then?"

"My father-in-law, Senator Ewing, has offered me a position back in Lancaster, Ohio." Sherman paused, adding contemptuously, "Managing a saltworks."

Grant raised an eyebrow. "With a good salary?"

Sherman shrugged. "Enough to live on. He's rich and wouldn't want his daughter and grandchildren to go hungry. It's a long way from the thrill of California banking." He laughed. "Banking and gambling are synonymous, you know. I once wrote to my wife, Ellen, that of all lives on earth, a banker's is the worst. No wonder they are specially debarred all chances of heaven."

They talked on, getting into politics, with Grant greatly enjoying the voluble Sherman. An hour later, they shook hands and Sherman walked out of Grant's wearisome life, little knowing how much they would one day mean to each other.

CHAPTER 18

It was one of the coldest springs ever recorded, with the crippling June freeze destroying crops throughout the Midwest. Although White Haven escaped the worst of it, the lingering cold weather wrecked Grant's crops. Then disaster struck in the form of the ague, the malarial fever he had experienced his last year at West Point. He lost weight and energy as stiffness and muscular pain added to his miseries. Julia suffered, watching his body bend and his face grow haggard as the weeks passed. Although he dragged himself to the fields daily, there was little he could do physically and his meager work force was unable to nurse the crippled crops back to a decent production level.

One day in early October, he returned from a trip to town totally dejected. Sitting down to a cup of hot tea with Julia, he announced, "I'm afraid I'm not the farmer I thought I was. It's time to call it quits."

Julia gazed into the tragic look of her man's dismal defeat. "Oh, darling, it'll work out next year. No one, not even a man in superb health, could have made it in all this dreadful weather we've had. You're a *good* farmer. It just seems that you get one bad break after another." She came to him, holding his head against her breast. "Next year we'll—"

"There won't be a next year, not here. Your father and I had a long talk, and we're going to sell. He's going to get rid of four hundred acres of the north end, and we're going to sell Hardscrabble."

Julia slumped into a chair, feeling a tear slip down her cheek. "But darling, Hardscrabble is such a special place, something that's all ours."

"I know, but I'm so deeply in debt, with no prospect of getting out. It's the only way."

"What will you do?"

"Your father put in a word for me with your cousin, Harry Boggs, who has that real estate and rent collection business in town. Well, I went to see Boggs, and he's willing to take me in. There may be a real estate boom in St. Louis soon, you know. And he gave me a minor partnership. I doubt that I'm much of a salesman, but I'll give it a try."

She patted his hand. "If that's what you think is best, I'm all for it."

His new business cards read "Boggs & Grant, General Agents, Collect Rents, Negotiate Loans, Buy & Sell Real Estate, Etc." With him as a partner, he knew without being told that Boggs thought Colonel Dent would help them drum up business. He didn't particularly like that idea, but he had to do something.

The Boggses provided a room for him in their home, so he could stay in town during the week. He spent the weekends at White Haven. Although the chills and periodic shakiness of his illness lingered, he threw himself into the strange world of sales and collection. He was suited for neither. He was too prone to expand on the faults of a property, and he was a sympathetic believer of every sad story a delinquent renter related. A typical example was the time a woman told him such a miserable tale that, instead of collecting the rent, he gave her his last fifty cents.

He moved the family into a small rented house in the city in March, the same month he freed William, the slave. Colonel Dent berated him for not selling the valuable field hand to ease his financial pinch, but Grant would have it no other way. His real estate activity did produce a buyer for Hardscrabble, though. He took in trade a comfortable house at Ninth and Barton streets, plus a $1,000 note, due in five years. The only catch was the buyer still owed $1,500 on the house mortgage. Grant covered himself by keeping a deed of trust against Hardscrabble.

Near the end of the summer, he heard that the position of engineer for St. Louis County would be opening up. The position with Boggs was simply not producing enough money, so the $1,500-a-year job sounded very good. "I should be able to handle it with one hand," he told Julia the night he heard of the upcoming vacancy. "I'm a West Point–trained engineer, and the position requires only supervision of wagon roads and bridges. This could be our chance."

Julia quickly shared his enthusiasm. "How do you get appointed?"

"A five-member board of commissioners will make the selection."

"Is anyone else in the running?"

"Yes, a German fellow who's supposed to be some kind of an engineer, but I think I can get some letters of recommendation and stand an excellent chance."

"You could start with John O'Fallon, and Papa will help."

He took her hand. "Yes, darling, I really think this is our break."

But Grant didn't take into consideration the fervent politics of St. Louis. The city was strongly divided into two camps, the Free Soilers and the pro-Southerners. In fact, each side had its own paramilitary organization, the pro-South Minute Men, and the pro-North Wide Awakes. And three of the commissioners were Republicans. Nevertheless, Grant acquired thirty-four signatures to letters of recommendation in the next ten days and presented his formal application.

A week later, Colonel A. R. Easton, a commissioner whom Grant had known in Mexico, summoned him. "Sam," he said, "you've been outflanked, three to two. Your connection with the Dent family was probably the main factor, and the fact that you were purported to have voted Democratic didn't help. Also, your opponent is a German in the midst of a large German population that is almost totally Republican.

"These are hectic times, Sam. A man's qualifications don't matter as much as where he stands politically. Now, I know you keep a low profile. I've even heard that your father-in-law makes disparaging remarks about you being a dyed-in-the-wool Northerner. But still, you have slaves."

"I have no slaves."

"Your wife does, I'm told. And that's enough to cook your goose with the Republicans. Looks like you're damned if you do and damned if you don't."

He stared at the floor. What now? Out of the army five years and he had absolutely nothing to show for it. Even the Hardscrabble deal was sour, with long litigation in front of him. He was a failure as a farmer, as a businessman, and now in politics—of which he really had none.

". . . But there may be another position opening for you shortly—the assistant superintendent's position at the customs house. It'll pay only about twelve hundred a year, but it'll be steady and better than nothing. Remember, being a Democrat helps on a federal job, so I've got some pull. Think you'd be interested?"

Grant shook his head. "I don't have to think about it. I'll take it."

The government job lasted almost two months before the superintendent died and his replacement brought in his own staff.

Now even death was working against Grant.

He was thirty-eight years old, and the avenues were running out.

Much as he hated it, he'd have to go plead with his father to find a place for him in the tanning business, the always abhorred tanning business.

It had taken him all these years to reach a point where he'd have to beg for something he'd sworn he'd never do . . .

CHAPTER 19

So strong you thump O terrible drums—
so loud you bugles blow.
—WALT WHITMAN

FEBRUARY 9, 1861
GALENA, ILLINOIS

Grant looked up in surprise as John Rawlins burst through the door to his small office in the back of the store. His intense black eyes glowing with excitement, the city attorney shouted, *"They gone and done it!"*

Grant turned up the kerosene lamp. "Done what? Who?"

At twenty-nine his neighbor, the black-bearded Rawlins, was well-known in Galena for his fiery political passion, his aggressiveness, and his proficient profanity. He was Grant's only friend, outside of his brothers, in this still-prosperous Mississippi River trading center in the northwest corner of Illinois. He replied, "Those sonsabitches down in Montgomery, those traitorous delegates from the seceding states, have set up a separate government. They're calling it the Confederate States of America, and have picked our perfidious former secretary of war as their goddamned president!"

"You mean Jeff Davis? Where'd you hear that?"

"Just came in on the telegraph."

Grant felt a chill. This was the beginning; it had actually happened. Now the blood would flow. He shook his head. "I guess the handwriting was on the wall, but I thought they'd have more sense."

Rawlins paced. "It just makes me sick!"

The attorney had come to Grant soon after his arrival in Galena. An ardent buff of the Mexican War, Rawlins had heard that the new member of the J. R. Grant firm had been a heroic captain in that conflict, and had quickly gone to the store to introduce himself. It had been pleasant for Grant to find someone who looked up to him and was also an eager listener to tales about Mexico—the only successful period of his adult life. Dedicated to the hope that Douglas could save the Union, an ardent Free Soil Democrat and anti-Republican, John Rawlins had made his months in Galena interesting. Grant sighed. "One thing's for sure—they'll fight. They may not last long, but they'll fight like the devil while they do."

"If only they'd had the sense to back Douglas, the Democrats could have presented a solid front, and we'd have a strong man in the White House. There'd have been no secession and sure as hell no Confederate States. Damn them to hell!"

Grant stroked his scraggly beard. The Confederate States of America—sounded like a joke. But it certainly wasn't.

Rawlins dropped into a chair. "I wonder what our rail-splitting local boy is going to do when he gets in office?"

"You know what he said when he was running—'A house divided cannot stand.' He'll have to fight to uphold the Constitution."

"You make it sound simple. When and how?"

"When he gets pushed into something. Those hotheads down there will take care of it. They're already taking over federal installations. He'll probably start calling up volunteers."

"What are you going to do when the war starts, Ulys?"

Grant shrugged. "I'm a trained regular officer. I'm sure there'll be a place for me. I might write to the adjutant general and ask for a colonelcy. I don't know yet. Besides, the first shot hasn't been fired."

Grant took a roundabout way home, ambling along, stopping here and there, trying to piece things together in the cold early evening moonlight. Galena had been good for him and his family, the first solid position he'd had since getting out of the army. Since his brother, Simpson, who managed the quite successful J. R. Grant leather goods store, was suffering from consumption, he had recommended that Ulysses come to work there. He could handle the books and help with the general clerking. Jesse had agreed. So the U. S. Grants had packed up and taken a boat up the Mississippi to their new life.

Though the salary wasn't too good yet, a partnership was in the offing sometime in the future. And keeping the accounts was simple for a former commissary officer who liked arithmetic.

He'd stayed out of the local political situation as much as possible. His youngest brother, Orvil, who also worked in the store, was the fanatic—an arch-Republican.

He'd hoped sanity would prevail nationally, but deep down, he knew it wouldn't. Now this development in Montgomery. Other things, like John Brown's raid on Harpers Ferry in '59, had stoked the fire. But still, it was oratory and fiery words. Abolition. States' rights. Politics. South Carolina had upset the applecart in December, being the first to thumb its nose at the Union. Then in January came Mississippi, Florida, Alabama, and Georgia. Texas joined the exodus over old Sam Houston's angry protest.

He walked up the final steep steps to their rented two-story brick house and went through the front door. "Darling, the rebels have joined hands," he told Julia as she embraced him. "I don't think our lives are ever going to be the same."

* * *

On April 12, all speculation ended.

This time it was Orvil who burst into the store, with a wild look in his eye, shouting, *"The bastards have done it, they've fired on the flag!"*

Two customers and the clerk on duty turned in unison. "What? Who?"

"The Secesh traitors are bombarding Fort Sumter! Just came in on the telegraph." Orvil slammed a fist onto the counter.

"Now take it easy," Grant said. "Tell us the whole thing."

Orvil went to a drawer and pulled out a bottle of whiskey. Taking a swig, he said, "General Beauregard's batteries are pounding the hell out of Sumter, and they can't hold out. It's war for sure now!" He took another drink from the bottle, then handed it to the nearest customer. "Have a drink to celebrate, 'cause we're going to kick their asses *now!*"

Grant watched the excitement take over their faces as they all began to talk at once. All he felt was sadness. He'd read about Lincoln refusing to give up Sumter in Charleston Harbor. And he'd read about Beauregard giving up his position as superintendent at West Point to be appointed a brigadier in the new Confederate Army—and commander at Charleston. What a shame; the flamboyant engineer, whom Scott credited with being the primary factor in taking Vera Cruz, becoming a traitor to the country that had given him so much.

And there were many others.

He thought about Pete Longstreet, about Simon Bolivar Buckner, the arrogant Bragg. There'd be dozens he had known who would side with the rebs. What would his brother-in-law, Fred, do? For some reason, he suddenly recalled an engineer major with whom he'd shared a few early morning minutes above the City of Mexico; a Virginian, what would Lee do? And he'd heard that Cump Sherman was superintendent of a new military academy down in Louisiana—Sherman had made a couple of remarks that day they were together in St. Louis, something about not disturbing the slavery situation. Would he disregard his Ohio heritage and stay in the South?

Huh, he hated to think of the good officers he knew who would join the rebellion.

Two of Orvil's cronies came whooping into the store. The way they acted, one would think a war had been won, instead of just started. He felt detached, an observer of a black play. What caused normally rational people to go crazy in anticipation of a tragedy? But these young people didn't know anything about the maiming and death of war. Could this be happening all over the country? Most assuredly it was in the South.

Madness. He felt ill.

Orvil waved the bottle at him. "Here, Ulys, surely you'll drink to *this!*"

Grant pushed his arm away. "Most definitely not to this."

History relates that minor incidents, lesser in magnitude than perhaps one day of battle, create wars. Fort Sumter was not such. As Grant saw in the weeks that followed, it was a calculated move to trigger the laggards into joining the Confederacy, to get the great Southern states involved to seek a quick rebel victory. The hotheads wanted war. And it worked. In short order, Virginia—and her reluctant western counties—North Carolina, Arkansas, and Tennessee seceded. Kentucky and Missouri teetered. Ohio led Indiana, Illinois, and Iowa in demanding war. And the rest of the North loudly waved flags as Lincoln asked for seventy-five thousand militiamen to volunteer for ninety days.

But Grant knew it would take a lot more men for a much longer period to put down the issue that had been joined. "Rawlins," he said to his friend, "this will be the most devastating conflict this country has ever seen."

The flag-waving, cheering, and shouting were as boisterous in Galena as anywhere. Grant attended the vocal town meeting in the courthouse three nights later. He sat off in a corner, quietly listening. Congressman Elihu Washburne, an energetic ex-Whig who was now an ardent Republican, made a rousing speech asking for full support of the war effort. Other dignitaries followed, building to the climactic and impassioned exhortation of John Rawlins: "I speak to you tonight as one who has been a Democrat all his life, yet now feels party lines should be erased. We, as a great and growing nation, are threatened in a manner that can lead to our very extinction.

"And I'm an avowed Douglas man, who believes that great senator will quickly throw his full support behind President Lincoln, as I do now. Our flag and our Constitution have been sullied, not only by those who rate slaveholding above unity, but by the so-called chivalrous minority of landowners who see their feudal way of life threatened . . ."

Grant, like all the other listeners in the jammed courtroom, sat entranced as his friend raced on, black eyes glowing, his resonant voice claiming silence between the frequent cheers. He'd never been aware that the young city attorney, who had drunk so eagerly from his cup of Mexican War stories, was capable of such eloquence and persuasion.

A half-hour later, Rawlins's voice dropped almost to a whisper in the silent room. "As I said, this is no longer a question of politics. It is simply a country, or no country. Only one course is left open to us." He paused, gathering for the crescendo. *"We will stand by the flag of our country, knowing God will look over us in battle!"*

Grant was swept up in the ovation, truly moved by Rawlins's words.

When things finally quieted down, he and the excited Orvil left together. They walked three blocks through the milling, stimulated crowd before Grant caught his younger brother's sleeve. Over the music of a nearby brass band, he asked, "Orvil, we both know Simp isn't going to live too long. Do you think you can run the business without both of us?"

"Why—you thinking of going back in the army?"

"Maybe."

"Yes, I think so. When would you leave?"

"Don't know."

Orvil grinned and clapped him on the back. "Go to it, big brother."

Two days later, Grant was called to a meeting with Congressman Washburne, Rawlins, the mayor, and a few other officials. The subject was the raising of a company of militia from Galena. Governor Yates had announced that Illinois's quota of the president's call-up would be six regiments. After some twenty minutes of discussion, Washburne, a thin man with a surprisingly ample belly, looked at Grant and said, "Captain Grant, I don't know anything about you except what John Rawlins has told me, but you've had extensive service and we'd like to have you command our proud company."

Grant had guessed this was coming, had mulled it over at length, and had discussed it with Julia. He simply had too much experience to go back in as a captain. His organizational and command capabilities suited him for a colonelcy, or at least a lieutenant colonelcy on some major staff. Besides, he still retained some of the army regulars' contempt for the "cornstalk militia" and its system of electing officers. Make 'em toe the line with a little discipline and they could vote you right out.

He got to his feet, clearing his throat. "Thank you, sir, for the honor. But I'm afraid I must decline. I feel I might be better utilized in another capacity later on. I'll assist wherever I can in recruiting, and later to some extent in training the boys, but I cannot accept the captaincy."

He couldn't help but notice the disappointment on the faces of Rawlins and Washburne. "Very well," the congressman replied, "we'll look elsewhere."

When the meeting broke up, Elihu Washburne approached Grant, saying, "Captain, I'm sorry I put you on the spot in there. I guess, in our fervor, we forgot that you might be more valuable in a higher position. I know very well Governor Yates is going to be hard put to assemble his regiments and get their training started. Would you consider helping along that line?"

"Why, yes, I suppose so."

"Excellent. I'm going to Springfield for the opening of the legislature next Tuesday. Why don't you come along?"

Governor Yates shifted in the chair behind his huge desk, listening to Washburne tell of Grant's West Point training, his many years of service and experience as a quartermaster, adjutant, and commander, and of his Mexican War reputation. Grant, attired as usual in his baggy civilian clothes, felt like a piece of leather goods being sold to a client. He glanced uneasily at Colonel Mather, the state adjutant general, who was watching him intently.

The governor twiddled with a pencil for a moment before asking, "What do you think, Mather?"

The colonel shrugged. "I don't have any appointments for someone of his experience at the present, but I can use some clerical help in my office—someone who can read and understand army orders and regulations."

"Good. We can start there, Captain. Sort of a civilian assistant for the time being. Then I'll need some assistance in mustering in companies to form regiments. After the first six, I'll be authorized ten more, and getting them into service will be quite a chore. Captain Pope may need some help."

"I've never done it before, sir," Grant replied quietly, "but I'll see what I can do."

"Good. You take him in tow, Mather."

John Pope, the elegant son of one of Illinois's prominent pioneer families, and now the federal mustering officer in Springfield, looked up in surprise as Grant approached his desk. "Well, Sam Grant, you old son-of-a-gun! I heard a rumor that you were here. Sit down, man, and tell me about yourself. I heard you got out of the army and went into the lumber business or something. Would you like a drink?"

It was hard to realize that the confident captain was the same cadet who'd come back from leave and introduced the pants fly to a shocked West Point community. "No thanks, John."

"I heard you liked your whiskey out West, so I thought I'd offer. What are you doing over at Mather's office, watching the amateurs bungle things?"

"No, I'm just shuffling papers."

"Damn shame. A West Pointer who knows more than twenty of these civilian officers put together. But I shouldn't criticize them too severely— I expect to be commanding a brigade of civilians shortly."

"Yes, I heard you were on loan from departmental headquarters, and in the meantime looking for a star with the Volunteers." Even though Pope had graduated from the Academy a year ahead of him, the dashing officer had been two years his junior as a captain. But he had stayed in, so he was ready for a big jump in rank.

"That's right. Gotta move up for the big action. That damned George McClellan is a major general of Ohio Volunteers already. Can't let that kid get too far ahead." He lit a cigar. "I'd like to get a division once the real fighting starts. Why aren't you back in uniform?"

"I'm trying, John. I just can't find anything at the moment."

Pope looked disdainfully at his attire. "I don't wonder, the way you dress. You aren't too imposing, Sam."

"Clothes don't make a soldier. I learned that from Old Zach down in Mexico. You remember." Pope had gotten one brevet there.

"But Zach's long gone, along with a lot of others. Did you hear that Joe Johnston resigned as quartermaster general to accept a star in Virginia? Damn, I never thought he'd be one of the turncoats."

Grant shrugged, struck a match and held it to his long-stemmed meerschaum.

"What do you want, Sam, a regiment?"

"If I can get one. I think I could handle it."

The handsome Pope snorted. "Huh! You'd be a hell of a lot better than these local politicians that get elected to command by the farm boys who owe them for favors. Or the plowboy who wins the popularity contest. Some of these days, Sam, this country's got to learn that the army isn't a democracy. Can't be and never will be, if battles are to be won. That's the only thing that worries me about getting a brigade. And particularly when they're going to be in for only ninety days."

They chatted on for another hour, with Pope offering to teach Grant the ropes of mustering. He also offered to keep his eyes peeled for a command vacancy. Then Grant returned to his office, filled with mixed exhilaration and despondency. McClellan wearing two stars already? Maybe he ought to bend his principle about accepting political patronage. But wasn't he already on the perimeter with Washburne and Yates? On the perimeter and shuffling papers.

Pope would have to wait for his jump to the rank of general. Benjamin Prentiss, a colonel commanding the Tenth Regiment, was elected brigadier. Prentiss had been one of the first Volunteer officers to get going, having led the first companies to the river ports and capturing contraband munitions. Pope was angry, declaring as he left that a regular officer didn't stand a chance against windy political officers. But he wouldn't have to wait long to get his star.

The next day, Colonel Mather called Grant into his office. "The governor has decided to put you in command at Camp Yates and make you mustering officer. Actually, I guess the term is 'in charge,' rather than in command, since you are still a civilian. This ninety-day enlistment will make it difficult for you, but I suspect it'll soon change to three years, or the duration. Do you think you can teach these lads to stand at a semblance of attention?"

"Probably."

"Good, and your pay will double to four-twenty a day."

His mustering work was soon finished, and there was still no billet in sight for him. On May 24, he collected the pay due him and headed home to Galena—still an ex-captain looking for a way to get in the moving stream. He awakened about four the following morning and couldn't get back to sleep. Going out to the porch, he lit a long-stemmed clay pipe and started reminiscing from a tired old rocking chair.

He relived some of his West Point days and several of his Mexican adventures, particularly the whirlwind of some of the battles—and recalled some of the senior officers he'd known. General Tom Hamer came back to him vividly, saying, *"You belong on a division or corps staff, Ulys."*

The sadness touched him—what a great man.

Hadn't thought about Hamer in ages.

Well, he might get there, if someone would just find a way to get him started. But he was still in the little eddies that drift around close to the bank, well out of the current. Surely God, in His infinite wisdom, could find a place for him in the terrible events to come . . .

PART TWO

CHAPTER 20

COVINGTON, KENTUCKY
JUNE 12, 1861

Grant turned the corner, four blocks from his father's house. He'd been sure the trip would be worthwhile. Oh well, at least his conscience was clear as far as his family went. He'd done his best to talk his father into moving back to Ohio, to get out of this state that didn't know which side of the fence it was on, a place where an outspoken abolitionist might not be too welcome. Right across the river from Cincinnati, but slave country.

But Jesse wouldn't listen. No, he'd said, "By God, I'll stay and say any darned thing I please for as long as I want!"

So be it for that part of his coming here.

The other had been for naught as well—the visits to McClellan's headquarters in Cincinnati. Two days he sat there, being told the general wasn't in, when he knew for sure he was. Two days of humiliating putoff by the boy wonder. Two days of being ignored, of watching the bustle of a busy headquarters from a bench by a wall. He had gone not only unnoticed, but unwanted. He'd made up his mind to accept any rank down to a majority.

But McClellan didn't even have the decency to see him. Certainly, the new general wasn't holding their minor differences back in Vancouver against him. Surely he'd be interested in knowing that the drunken captain he'd criticized then had changed—that a different man awaited his crumbs, one willing to provide service to the utmost of his ability. But the snub was there, openly. And he hadn't done any better otherwise; letters to Ohio and Indiana, asking for commands, were unanswered. Best go back to Springfield and see what develops.

Head bent, he turned into the yard, climbed the steps, and entered the house. It was to be his last moment of total dejection for many months.

"Ulysses!" his father said more loudly than usual from the vestibule, "I went ahead and opened this telegram from Governor Yates. You're going to be a *colonel!*"

The bold words danced around as Grant read:

In that a vacancy has occurred in the 21st Regiment you are hereby offered the position of commanding officer with the rank of Colonel of Volunteers. Should you accept this appointment please report immediately.

> *Yates*
> *Governor of Illinois*

His hand shook as he reread the exciting words, afraid to trust them. He would have a chance! And not from any popular election, but by choice—the way he wanted it. He nodded, smiling. "Well, I guess I'm in the war, Pa."

Grant quietly walked into the headquarters tent, quickly spotting the adjutant. The captain looked up, taking in Grant's shabby clothes and unkempt beard. "May I help you, mister?"

Grant handed over his orders. "I, uh, guess I'll take command of this regiment, Captain."

The adjutant glanced at the orders, gave him another searching look, and jumped to his feet. "Yessir! What can I do for you?"

"Not much for the time being. I'd like to see the executive officer."

"Yessir, that's him, Lieutenant Colonel Alexander, over there in the corner."

Alexander stood at his approach, remembering the stocky, shoddy figure from the mustering. He extended his hand. "Welcome to the Twenty-first, Colonel Grant. It's good to have you here."

"Thank you, Colonel. I understand there've been a few problems."

"That's an understatement, sir. If the officers hadn't gone to the governor, we'd've had a mutiny on our hands, or total desertion."

"What seems to be the main problem?"

"Total lack of discipline. Your predecessor was a worthless drunk."

Grant knew the term. "Then we'll have to turn them around, won't we?"

"Hard-core regular army discipline, Colonel?"

"No, I don't think that'll work. We'll be firm and use our guardhouse once in a while, but I don't want it filled up. In the beginning, I'll handle each punishment myself—and it won't be by the book. Later, I'll return that responsibility to the company commanders, where it belongs. What's your background, Colonel?"

"I'm a lawyer and not much of a soldier."

"Well, you will be."

"How do you plan to get started?"

"Drill. The soldier learns to drill in his squad, the squad in the company, and the company within a regiment for all battle movements. So we're going to run their butts ragged on drill. I want it scheduled all day long. They'll learn and they'll get so tired doing it, they'll forget about going over the fence. And I'll be out there with them. But first, I want you to dispense with those eighty club-wielding guards you've got watching them."

"Aren't you taking on quite a bit for yourself, sir?"

"That's what they gave me these eagles for. And I'm sure you're wondering why I'm not in uniform. Fact is, I'm too broke to buy one. As soon as everything starts rolling here, I'm going home to borrow some money to get properly outfitted. Till then, you'll have to stand all the regimental ceremonies in my place."

"Yes, sir." Alexander's voice had a respectful tone in it.

"Also, you've got a lieutenant down in one of the companies named Vance. Went to West Point for a couple of years, so he should know basic drill. Appoint him temporary drillmaster."

"Yes, sir, Vance is a good man."

Grant nodded. "Now, let's you and me go for a little walk so you can introduce me to some of the officers and sergeants." A slight smile touched Grant's lips as he added, "And one thing we have to remember is that these farm boys have a lot of imagination of their own."

Grant made himself known in the next few days, not just through simple orders that the lowest soldier could understand, but by personally mingling with the men. He appeared at drill with every company, quietly watching, making mental notes for Lieutenant Vance, sometimes personally drawing an officer aside for instruction. The men responded to the hard work and the removal of the guards by staying in camp at night, or at least the majority did so. The few who still climbed the fence and headed for the joys of Springfield, were confined, but let off easily. Within a few days, the short colonel, in his old slouch hat and worn clothes, had become known in the regiment as "the quiet man." And favorable results began to show throughout the organization. But early morning was never a time of good cheer.

Soldiers, since well before Hannibal's time, hated getting up. Normally, in a large camp the bugle sounded *Reveille* at brigade headquarters. One favorite response, originated by a private was, "Gabr'el blow your trump! I don't want this world to last any longer." At regimental headquarters, Reveille was announced by fife and drum. A popular wording was:

> *Wake ye lazy soldier, rouse up and be killed,*
> *Hard tack and salt horse, git your gizzard filled:*
> *Then go to fighting, fire yer forty round;*
> *God dead and lay there, buried under the ground.*

After being measured for uniforms by a Springfield tailor, Grant made a quick trip home to Galena to see his family and raise the three hundred dollars necessary for some horses and the other costs of outfitting himself as an army colonel. He found a cream-colored gelding named Jack that pleased him, his only concession to vanity. But then, he'd always had a weakness for good horses.

Upon his return to camp, he was quite pleased with the improvement in the regiment. Now his major problem lay in getting most of the remaining six hundred men to reenlist for the three-year or duration-of-the-war period. In spite of the remarkable change in attitude, he was sure many of the boys were thinking about going home. And June 28, just two days away, was the deadline.

A message arrived from Springfield the next morning. John Rawlins had arranged for two Democratic congressmen to give reenlistment speeches to his men, if he wished. Grant asked his executive officer about them.

"McClernand," Alexander replied, "is about forty-eight, Logan probably a dozen or so years younger. Logan's a black-haired, black-eyed fire-eater and McClernand's quite the same—except he has a longer nose. The people in Logan's southern district think he's a god, giving him quite a constituency. He split from Douglas, supporting the South, but he's a loyal Union man. I think if anyone can help keep our lads in, it's those two. How'd you get them involved?"

Grant's smile was faint. "Friends."

Both congressmen came to have lunch with Grant in his meager officers' mess. He found them both stimulating, feeling more inclination toward Logan than McClernand, who seemed to be less genuine for some reason. Following the meal, the regiment was drawn up on parade, then assembled around a huge crate to listen to the illustrious guests. John McClernand spoke first, eloquently and straightforwardly. He spoke of Illinois sending a president to Washington, adding, "Surely this great state can be counted on to provide the *best* volunteer soldiers." He finished to cheers and quickly introduced the fiery Logan.

Grant was slightly worried about John Logan's Southern sympathies, but his fears were quickly silenced. The swarthy thirty-five-year-old congressman began quietly, quickly building his tempo. With flashing eyes and powerful phrasing he said, "There is no greater glory than defending this proud flag that means you are an American! And that means you're not just someone who puts on a uniform for ninety cheap days and never gets outside the state, never hears a shot fired in anger.

"Boys, you can't fall out now. You can't leave your country in the lurch, pretending you did anything for her . . . because you haven't. If you go home now to Mary, she's going to ask, "Why, Tom, are you home from the war so soon?' And you're going to say, 'Yes.' And she's going to ask, 'How far did you get, Tom?' And you're going to reply, 'Springfield.' "

Grant joined in the loud laughter, finding hope in the proud cheers that followed. Of the 612 men assembled, 603 reenlisted by nightfall. And he had met two influential men.

Grant couldn't understand it. His hands were actually shaking.

He had been ordered to lead the Twenty-first Illinois to a leafy creekbed near Florida, Missouri, where a marauder named Tom Harris, who called himself "Colonel," was camped with his band of irregulars. Now, as his column was deploying for the attack, he suddenly felt a sense of panic, of gripping apprehension that something would go wrong, that he would fail in command. He felt short of breath and his hands shook on the reins. *He was afraid!* Ridiculous! He'd been through all those battles in Mexico, and had never felt any real fear.

But this was different. How many men would be lose?' How easy it would be if he were the lieutenant colonel . . . it wouldn't be his fault if something went wrong. He'd wanted command and now it was paralyzing him.

His heart felt like it was in his throat. His eyeballs were like hot stones, burning his blinking lids. He *must* get hold of himself! But it seemed as if he'd been poisoned and the stuff had permeated his whole being. His legs were weak, his mouth dry and bitter. This is nonsense, he told himself. I'm a soldier, trained and tested.

He looked at his quivering hands and closed his eyes.

This can't be happening!

The sun seemed too bright, the air too still, oppressive.

He had to shake off this vise that had clamped on him . . .

He wiped sweat from his brow, tugged the campaign hat lower.

Activity! That's what he needed. Ride around to the rear, check things, get busy, shake it off. Fear—he'd once discussed it in Mexico with his friends. It would never happen to *him*. But it *was* happening!

He blew out deep breaths as he rode, and felt some relief. In moments, he was considerably better. Shortly, Lieutenant Vance, who had led a patrol to reconnoiter the enemy position, galloped up. *"Sir, they're gone!* The stream bed's as empty as last year's whiskey bottle. The rebs must've seen us coming and tucked their tails between their legs!"

Grant couldn't believe his ears. His mortal enemy had fled? He shook his head. All that fright for nothing. Whom did he think he was coming to do battle with—Napoleon? No—just a ragtag bunch of irregulars led by some malcontent who didn't know how to drill a squad.

Tom Harris had fled.

He laughed to himself.

He had just learned a lesson.

Never would he forget this incident. Never would he forget that his enemy possessed the same fears or worse. From this moment on, he would always assume that those fears exceeded any of his.

He thanked Vance and turned to Alexander with a steady voice. "Colonel, the Twenty-first just won its first battle by marching well. Scared 'em to death."

CHAPTER 21

Yes, we'll rally round the flag, boys,
We'll rally once again—
—GEORGE F. ROOT,
The Battle Cry of Freedom

AROUND BULL RUN, IN VIRGINIA
JULY 21, 1861

"Form up! Form up!"

The hoarse shouts of the officers and noncommissioned officers who were trying to create some kind of order among the demoralized recruits went unnoticed as Sherman's men broke under the vicious rebel charge. Dust and smoke all but obliterated anything that was happening more than twenty yards in any direction, while the hot July sun sifted through and further parched lips already dry from fear and heat. Musket fire peppered the air between the crash of artillery and the shouts of the attackers. Limp regimental and national colors added surreal brightness as they fell and were picked up again. Other splashes of color, from the Sixty-ninth's red trousers, fezzes, and bright green flag, added to the rainbow of the battle. Confederate troops in blue, and Sherman's Second Wisconsin in their militia gray, had confused everyone and had been fired upon indiscriminately. The wounded cried out, and the dead littered the ground in scarlet pools. Horses ran about, riderless and wild-eyed, blood spraying from their flaring nostrils.

Sherman grabbed the reins of one, a black mare, and swung up into the saddle. His horse had been hit in a foreleg and had gone down. The redhead touched his knee where a shell fragment had drawn blood; a Minié ball had creased his shoulder as well, but had done little damage.

"Pull back!" he shouted to a captain from the Thirteenth New York. *"Get back over Stone Bridge!"* They were on the north slope of Henry Hill, and their position was untenable under the force of the counterattack. He brought his revolver up and shot a rebel officer on a huge brown stallion point-blank.

They had been under fire for well over three hours, and his entire brigade had encountered devastating waves of shot and shell. The Seventy-ninth New York Highlanders and the regular battery from Sherman's old Third Artillery constituted the rest of his command. Sherman's Brigade was a part of McDowell's army of thirty thousand that had engaged General P. G. T. Beauregard's rebel army, which had been encamped near Manassas.

Early on, McDowell had nearly driven the little Frenchman and his equally raw troops from the field, but just as the battle should have been won, Jackson and Joe Johnston had arrived and thrown their rebel commands into the Federal army, and the tide had swiftly turned. Now Sherman, sickened by the sight of so many corpses, was doing everything possible to extricate his brigade with some semblance of order. The Thirteenth New York streamed over the bridge. Some fell into Bull Run and swam across; some drowned.

And everywhere the yellow dust and black smoke saturated the air.

But there was little order anywhere. Across Bull Run, fleeing soldiers encountered enemy fire as it crashed into their midst. Wagon drivers panicked and wheeled toward Washington—twenty miles away. The mass of camp followers and spectators who had come out from the capital to watch the fun joined in the growing mob as it rushed wild-eyed and hellbent toward the city.

And Sherman's men would quickly become part of it.

He had never been so disgusted in his life.

The words danced as Grant read the *Daily Missouri Democrat:* "THOUSANDS OF FEDERAL TROOPS FLEE BACK TO THE SAFETY OF WASHINGTON . . . The Confederate Army, commanded by General P. G. T. Beauregard and supported by General Joseph E. Johnston, crushed the attack of General Irvin McDowell's Union Army . . . severe losses on both sides . . . large numbers of Union artillery and other weapons captured . . . fear for the safety of the nation's capital . . . President calls for more troops . . . General in Chief Scott reevaluates Washington's defenses . . . McDowell's follow-up questioned . . ."

Grant shook his head as he wondered about the battle they were calling Bull Run. Was the command too much for McDowell, a new brigadier, up from major? Was his intelligence about the rebel force faulty? Most probably he'd been outgeneraled, and no wonder—he'd faced Beauregard and Joe Johnston, two of the army's most brilliant senior officers before they defected.

He read on about the enemy: Tom Jackson, now a colonel with a new nickname from the battle—a "stonewall"? The "eagle with a lisp" Dick Ewell a brigade commander, and *Brigadier General* James Longstreet!

No wonder.

Of the other Union commanders involved, the names meant nothing to him, except Colonel William Tecumseh Sherman, who led a brigade. Old Cump. He wondered what Sherman had felt when the battle began to disintegrate. Surely, he hadn't failed as a commander.

Well, this Bull Run—or Manassas—certainly proved one thing that should have been obvious all along: the rebs could fight major battles and win. It positively wouldn't be a short war.

*   *   *

Grant's next big news from a newspaper was different.

The evening of August 3 was hot and muggy, with thunderstorm build-ups threatening off to the west. He had enjoyed a supper of well-done beefsteak, just the way he liked it, and had just completed a letter to Julia. He was also thinking about one last conciliatory gesture to Colonel Dent. He hated the thought of kissing the old man's behind much more, but he knew how uncomfortable the situation was for Julia. He glanced up in surprise at the chaplain's excited interruption. "Have you seen today's paper, Colonel?"

He adjusted his eyes to the small print under the headline ILLINOIS TO GET FOUR GENERALS. It went on: *"Washington,* August 2nd. President Lincoln today announced the nomination of seven major generals and thirty-four brigadier generals. Of the brigadiers, four are citizens of Illinois. Leading the list is the West Point graduate Ulysses S. Grant of Galena, who served conspicuously in the Mexican War. The others—"

He couldn't believe it!

There had to be some mistake. Only two months earlier, he'd been almost ready to beg for a majority from McClellan. How? Must have been Yates, or Washburne. Yes, Congressman Washburne; he was in with the Republican clique in Washington, probably had Lincoln's ear. A friend of Rawlins; maybe his friend, the city attorney, had his finger in it as well. It smacked of politics, but one thing obviated that smirch—he knew he could do a good job as a general, was absolutely certain of it. And that was the bottom line.

Tom Hamer's rank had been all political, but he'd delivered.

He'd have to accept a double standard about it.

A star!

Regardless of the political ploys involved, he was innocent of involvement; it had come—or would, with the confirmation of Congress—from above, from the Federal government. It had been a long time since they pinned the captain's bars on him in Mexico.

He reread the article, still not believing, and found that Prentiss—this time not an elected rank—and John A. McClernand were also to be brigadiers. He doubted that it would ever matter, but at least he ranked them by a fine line of being first on the list. He wondered how McClernand, the congressman, would do.

But he had his own responsibilities to worry about. He hadn't paid back the debt for his colonel's uniforms yet—how could he obtain the sash, sword, and all the uniforms befitting his new rank? He'd just go without for the time being. Appearance had never mattered before, why should it now?

He looked into the chaplain's beaming smile. "Well, General," the clergyman said, "What's it feel like?"

Grant had to smile. "I was just thinking that I can't afford a sword."

The chaplain laughed. "Well, I guess the regiment could find a rusty old blade to give to its former commander."

John A. Rawlins, Esq.
Sheean & Rawlins Law Office
Galena, Ill.

Dear John:

    It was with great sorrow that I received the news from Julia of your beloved Elly's untimely death. I know it leaves you with an aching void, and my heart goes out to you.

    I received my official appointment a couple of weeks ago, with date of rank of May 17th. I think you had something to do with this gratuitous promotion, and I thank you. I'll try to measure up as a general officer.

    As you probably know, I turned the 21st over to the capable Col. Alexander. Tomorrow I report to General Frémont for further assignment. I think the rebs are going to make a move on Kentucky, so I hope I can do something about it.

    And now, John, I know you have three small children, but I need you. I have practically no staff and I need a reliable adjutant—someone I can trust to get my orders out and take some of the administrative weight off me. (I've never been much good with paperwork anyway, and stuff too many notes in my pocket.) All I can offer you is a captaincy for now. I know you've never been a soldier, but I feel a confidence in you I can't explain.

    Seems I'm talking too much about myself. Please come.

Respectfully yrs.
Ulys

Grant had been sitting in the dark hallway for nearly two hours, waiting to see the famous Major General John C. Frémont, the "Pathfinder" of fame, infamy, and fortune. He'd heard most of the stories about the ambitious Frémont who'd conquered the West. As a lieutenant of engineers, he'd explored, surveyed, and mapped the Oregon Territory, and the rest of the Oregon Trail with the famous scout Kit Carson. Sherman had served with him in California during the Mexican War, where Frémont had been promoted to major. Again he had made a name for himself, being appointed military governor of California—until his arrest and court-martial for insubordination by General Kearny. To beat dismissal, he resigned his commission, only to have gold discovered on his vast California estate—and to become immensely wealthy. One of the first two senators from that state, he ran for president on the new Republican ticket against Buchanan. That was when Grant voted against him. An ardent abolitionist, Frémont had come back on active duty as a two-star by the grace of the Republican administration.

    Now here he was commanding the Department of the West, with rumor having it that he did so with pompous incompetence. It was also bandied about that his wife, Bessie, the daughter of old Senator Thomas Hart Benton, fancied herself the deputy-commanding general and issued orders in his absence.

The Pathfinder was set up in grand style in St. Louis, with all the glitter a rich general who possessed a huge, mostly foreign staff and bodyguard could muster. One newspaper article had described him as "a military emperor lost in his own magnificence." He was also so well-insulated by his staff that a lowly new brigadier had to cool his heels and hope the great man would get around to him.

It reminded him of his wait on McClellan.

Seemed waiting was becoming a way of life. He'd thought about going to see Colonel Dent, but he didn't want an argument.

"General Grant, will you please come this way?"

The major's French accent just didn't seem to fit in Missouri.

He was ushered into the general's sumptuous office, which was filled with ornate western artifacts, flags, paintings, and a massive desk. One huge painting of Frémont climbing a mountain peak held sway on the wall across from his desk. Slowly Frémont turned from the window, right hand in his uniform coat, Napoleon-like. He observed Grant critically, not speaking for several moments. Finally he said, "Please be seated, General."

As Grant took a chair, Frémont added, "I thought you might be more imposing, considering your Mexican War feats. And I thought surely you'd report in uniform."

"I'm waiting for my uniforms to arrive from New York, sir."

"Couldn't you get a local tailor to put something together?"

"I couldn't afford both."

Frémont sniffed. "I see. Well, Grant, I'm trying to make up my mind. I've heard some rather disconcerting things about your conduct on the West Coast—that you were a drunk, and were forced to resign."

"Not so, sir. I drank rather heavily at times, but resigned for personal reasons. There was no court-martial pending."

Frémont scowled. "Are you referring to my unfortunate circumstance in California?"

"No, sir."

"I was innocent, you know. But that isn't the point. How are your personal habits now?

"I almost never drink."

"Do you think you can continue in your abstinence?"

"General, nothing—and that includes drinking—will interfere with my performance of whatever duties I'm assigned."

Frémont watched him for several seconds, then offered him a cigar. As Grant lit up, his new commander asked, "What course do you think the war here in the West will take?"

Grant paused a few moments before replying. "The Mississippi's one of the major keys to the war. Whoever commands it will rule the West. There are also other navigable rivers here that we should consider. And I believe we should take the initiative before the enemy does. Also, we should move into Kentucky as soon as possible."

"I think you're right about the rivers, but it would be a bold move to go into neutral Kentucky. I don't know if Lincoln would be pleased. It might tip them off the fence in the wrong direction."

"Doesn't bother the enemy."

Frémont licked his cigar. "Do you know I'm planning an excursion in that direction?"

"No, sir." Grant didn't know if the general was planning anything except the next military ball.

Frémont moved to a large wall map of the area. "Come here so I can show you what I've outlined to the president in a letter. Not that he is smart enough to grasp it, but . . ."

Grant listened for the next forty minutes as the Pathfinder skimmed around the same basic plan that had been going through his own head. But Frémont's concept was vague. He complained too much about the lack of cooperation from Washington, and what he considered to be a severe shortage of men and supplies.

"Well then, Grant, I'm giving you command of the District of Southeast Missouri, which includes all of Missouri south of St. Louis, plus all of southern Illinois. Proceed to Cairo and remove all traitorous opposition from your district. We'll have the Missouri slaves freed in short order." He picked up an Indian statuette and rubbed it, adding pompously, "I will then free all the slaves in Arkansas, Kentucky, and Tennessee by next summer."

Grant wasn't interested in freeing slaves, only in ending the insurrection. "Is that all, sir?"

"I'll have your orders written immediately—and, Grant, get into uniform."

But uniforms would have to wait if he were to get to Cairo—pronounced Kay-ro—the muddy, fever-ridden, rat-infested, mosquito-plagued site of the district headquarters. Cairo, Illinois, in spite of its malaria and daily discomforts, was the energetic junction of two mighty rivers—the busy Ohio and the mighty Mississippi. It was also the frenzied hub of military buildup of a rapidly growing Federal army. Grant wandered around for two hours after his arrival, observing the hectic scene, then walked into the bank building that had been requisitioned for district headquarters.

He entered the large room that served as the commander's office, where at least a dozen men were babbling around a table where a portly colonel was checking papers and trying to converse. Grant watched and waited for a few minutes before spotting a piece of blank paper on the table. He leaned over and scrawled, "Ulysses S. Grant, Brig. Gen., Army of the U.S., hereby assumes command of the District of Southeastern Missouri on this date, September 4th, 1861."

Colonel Richard Oglesby glanced at the note and back at the short man who had handed it to him. "You're Grant?" he asked quizzically.

"That's right, Colonel. Now if you'll dismiss these people, we'll sit down and talk."

In spite of his pressing administrative requirements, Grant was eager to seek out the enemy and start fighting. The next morning a small man named Gibbs, carrying credentials as a scout for Frémont, came to him with alarming news. Gibbs had just returned from downriver, where he'd been observing the movement of Confederate troops while posing as a traveling salesman. "General," the scout said, "The Bishop sent old General Pillow to those high bluffs at Columbus several days ago. They're digging in to build a fort that will control the river for the range of their guns."

"Hmmm," Grant replied, eying the spy. Columbus was about twenty miles south of Cairo. He'd read earlier that the arrogant and cowardly Gideon Pillow had accepted a star in the Confederate Army. He remembered that the former law partner of President Polk had been a disgraceful political general in the Mexican War, that he'd fled with a minor arm scratch at Cerro Gordo, that his own troops and the rest of Scott's army had held him in contempt as a troublemaker with no interest other than himself. And the "Bishop" the spy had referred to was Leonidas Polk, who'd graduated from West Point in 1827 only to resign six months later and become a clergyman in the Episcopal Church. He had become a bishop, but had turned in his miter for a uniform of gray, and was now a major general commanding Confederate forces in the West.

"How strong is Pillow?" Grant asked.

"He has at least a brigade."

"So it looks like he'll be there for a while."

"No, General, that's the bad part. He's about to march on Paducah. Could be on the way right now. I guess the rebs think they can have all of Kentucky without a struggle."

"You're sure of this, Gibbs?"

"I ain't been sticking my neck out to bring you any guesses."

As soon as Gibbs left, Grant went to his maps. As he'd known all along, Paducah, about forty miles due east of Cairo, was vitally located where the wide Tennessee River joined the Ohio, just ten miles below where the Cumberland did the same. Each of those rivers led into the Confederate heartland—the Cumberland to important Nashville, and the Tennessee all the way down to Mississippi and Alabama, liquid highways down which a resourceful army could utilize gunboats and be resupplied.

Paducah had to be denied to the enemy!

He called in Oglesby and his adjutant, telling them he intended to move on Paducah with two infantry regiments and a battery of artillery. He asked the colonel to round up some of the idle steamboats that were tied up nearby, to be used as transports, then to alert the subordinate commanders. He then dictated a message to Frémont: "Based on information received from your scout, Gibbs, enemy forces under Pillow are en route to Paducah. Urgent that they not be permitted to occupy this strategic point. Am preparing to embark by river early this morning for Paducah with 9th and 12th Illinois, plus supporting units, unless notified otherwise by you. Acknowledge."

He felt keyed up. Action seemed to do things to him, to stimulate something deep inside. But he'd have to stay out of the way, see how well these people executed orders before he meddled. They were all strangers. If only Rawlins were here, or anyone he knew he could trust. He wished he could give Julia a commission. His new aide, Lieutenant Laglow from the twenty-first, hadn't arrived with his horses and personal belongings yet. He wasn't too sure he'd made the right choice on Laglow either. He'd wanted Vance, but felt the officer was simply too vital to his green regiment.

By three P.M. the transports were arranged and coaled up with no hitches. No problems had been reported from the regimental commanders either. He assumed all troop units would be ready to embark on time. He didn't want to enter Paducah before daybreak, but likewise didn't want any delays on the forty-five-mile trip upriver. He wanted to be anchored outside of the town well before first light. Frémont should have gotten his message by now.

At eight P.M. he again telegraphed Frémont. "Confederate column reported fifty miles southwest of Paducah, heading north on foot. Unless further orders are received, I move on Paducah tonight. I now believe Pillow will be no more than six to eight hours behind me."

If all went well now, Pillow would be met at his destination by an Ohio farmer in a battered old slouch hat and a long pipe.

Grant glanced at his watch for the twentieth time. Ten minutes after eleven! And still no word from Frémont. Nothing. Then all at once he knew: it was the old army game. If Frémont acknowledged, giving consent, the responsibility for the action was his. If not, and the mission failed, he wasn't responsible and could have his subordinate's head to hand upstairs. If the mission succeeded, he could claim the glory without ever mentioning that his underling had taken all the risk.

Well, the game could just forget him in this war, even if he stayed a brigadier forever. Give 'em an answer—right or wrong. That was what responsibility was all about. But if he didn't take Paducah, he'd never have to worry. He looked at his watch again. If he was going to depart by midnight, he'd better get started. He turned to his aide, Lieutenant Laglow, who'd arrived with his horses and other things just before supper. "Let's go to Paducah, young man."

Grant watched from the bridge of his command steamer as the troops completed an orderly disembarkation at the Paducah waterfront in the gray, fresh dawn. It was obvious when they arrived just before sunup that the local citizenry had been expecting a different bunch of strangers. Confederate flags, probably sewn by local matrons, abounded throughout the town. The ensigns, however, quickly disappeared as Union uniforms began quietly streaming off the boats.

This part of Kentucky was known to be in full sympathy with the Southern cause, so the Federal commander here would have to stay on his toes. He'd leave a couple of gunboats, make sure all roads and bridges were secured, then send an extra regiment along to beef up the garrison.

He wasn't worried about Pillow, even if the old coward had two or three brigades. The artillery battery would fire salute blanks throughout the day, and the cavalry troop would patrol in plain sight continuously. The timid rebel general would think a whole Union army was in the town. Leaving a screening force, he'd probably hightail it back to the Chalk Bluffs at Columbus without delay.

With the rebel force gone, he'd send a note to the Kentucky legislature explaining the need to bring Federal troops to their soil.

Twenty-two hours after departing for Paducah, Grant was back at Cairo to begin the difficult task of building an army of sorts to move into the Confederacy. As he stretched out in bed, he allowed the fatigue to catch up. He'd earned his pay these last two days.

CHAPTER 22

Grant stared at the message from Frémont: "Occupation of Paducah well executed. Your prerogative was exceeded when you contacted the state legislature. Such communications are in the sole realm of my office. You will refrain from any such contacts in the future. Paducah will be removed from your command and a suitable general officer assigned to that area."

Grant blinked. One line about the Paducah enterprise, and the rest a chastisement about prerogative? He'd stepped on Frémont's tender toes, but that was no reason to make Paducah a separate command. What if he sends a political general over there?

The man who would command Paducah would be the least worry Grant would ever have. Two days later, he looked up in complete awe to receive a magnificent brigadier. It was General C. F. Smith, his former commandant of cadets, the soldier's soldier! Still ramrod stiff, lean and erect, the once-splendid mustaches now white and drooping a bit, Smith was as imposing as Grant had perceived him that first time when he was a plebe, and again in Mexico.

Smith's voice was deep and precise. "General, I thought I should stop in to say hello before going on to Paducah. I frankly don't know why Frémont's making it a separate command, but that's none of my business."

Grant shook his hand, fumbling for words. "I'm glad you did, sir. I, well, I can't tell you how pleased and surprised I am to see you. I was afraid the general might send one of his hangers-on."

Smith took the proffered chair. "No, I don't think he's *that* dumb. And I was available, having just gotten my star ten days ago."

Grant shook his head. "I feel embarrassed by this situation, General. I still feel, well, like a cadet in your presence. There's no rhyme or reason in my ranking you."

Smith was cool, but casual. "Breaks of the game. I've never been one to get involved in politics. I don't believe in moral issues and never make statements about where I stand. Just try to do my job."

"Where were you before this?"

"Commanding the Department of Utah when the war broke out. Then they sent me to New York as the recruiting officer."

"What a waste. And to think they took a major like McDowell and gave him command of the eastern army. What's wrong with General Scott?"

"He's old and sick, and was vulnerable to those who questioned my loyalty because I didn't speak out about the terrible wrong of the South."

Again Grant shook his head. This majestic warrior should have been offered the top command, over every officer in the army. "Stupid. Well, sir, would you mind having lunch with one of your admiring former cadets?"

Smith's expression softened. "I'd like that."

Rawlins was due in five minutes. Too bad he hadn't arrived in Cairo in time for supper, but hopefully there would be hundreds of other suppers. Grant rubbed his beard, where he'd shortened it. Why was he so sure Rawlins was his man, the one on whom he could lean, the one who would take the paperwork off his hands? What was there about the young lawyer that so impressed him? Why did he inspire such an inherent sense of trust?

John Rawlins of the melancholy, aesthetic face, the lustrous coal-black, expressive eyes; of deep, fervent passions that so quickly rose to the surface and burst upon whomever was present . . . the incredibly patriotic and adept man who was so vivid in speech, yet so intensely spiritual within. Could this volatile mixture of a man harness his drives into soldiering?

Rawlins was the second son of a lazy, happy-go-lucky, hard-drinking Scots-Irish farmer, whose 320 acres of land had joyfully resisted the minor attempt of their owner to be harnessed into a productive farm—that is, until John Aaron, at age fifteen, took over. Very close to his evangelistic Methodist mother, Rawlins later headed for the ministry. But after a year of seminary, at twenty-two, he threw in the cloth for the law. Supposedly, he had been hauling a load of charcoal to Galena when the stubborn team of oxen refused to go up a steep hill. The angry, decisive Rawlins reportedly stormed off to a nearby lumber company where he sold the team, wagon, and charcoal on the spot. He then went directly to town and asked a prominent lawyer to let him be his assistant while he studied for the bar.

It was also rumored that the experience with the oxen had a strong effect on his considerable command of profanity.

Now that his beloved wife Emma was dead, it was only natural that he should respond to Grant's letter and throw himself into the war with the same headlong fervor that had marked most of his thirty years.

Grant answered the knock and admitted his friend. After warm greetings and talk of home, Grant shifted into a briefing for his new adjutant. " . . . And I'm also in command of what little navy we have out here. Presently that consists of three gunboats that are really converted steamers. They're supposed to be pretty vulnerable, with only some patched-on oak planks for armor. Some new ones are being built in St. Louis, though. And if this is indeed to be a river war, they'll be extremely important. I'll expect you to get to know the naval officers commanding.

"And I want you to stay on top of the hospital situation. Our new surgeon, Dr. Joe Brinton, impresses me as a dedicated man, but the facilities are terrible. And many of the contract surgeons come from questionable origins. There are few medical supplies and a shortage of nurses. Back to the surgeons—I suspect they are letting too many soldiers get medical discharges for minor problems. Same thing happened in Mexico. When you get your feet on the ground, I want you to personally approve all such discharges."

Rawlins's eyes lit up. "Think they're buying their way out?"

"Possibly."

"I'll stop *that* in a goddamned hurry!"

"Just wait until you know your way around a bit. I'm counting on you too much to have you jumping into any crusades just yet. We have a massive job ahead of us. I just heard that General Albert Sidney Johnston has taken over the entire Western command for the rebels. He's one of the best they've got. He came back in the army from Texas during the Mexican War and did a whale of a job there. Any army he commands will be hard to beat, and his Kentucky line extends generally from Columbus over to Bowling Green, where my old friend, Simon Bolivar Buckner, is in command.

"I was quite sorry to hear that he went with the South. Do you know, Rawlins, that he loaned me money and watched over me like an anxious parent when I was in New York, trying to get home after California? He knew I'd been drinking too much out on the Coast, and was afraid I'd squander everything."

Rawlins edged close. "I've got to ask you about that, Ulys—uh, General. I promised Washburne that I'd keep an eye on you and make sure you stayed away from the bottle. He considers you his private general and he has heard the old army rumors same as everyone else. Are you still staying away from the demon rum?"

Grant chuckled. Rawlins's intense hatred for alcohol was supposed to stem from his father's excesses with the bottle. He was famous back in Galena for his temperance stand. "Yes," he replied, "I'm still dry."

Rawlins scowled, his black brows knitting together like a band of coal. "I happen to think you have greatness in you, that you're going to be an outstanding general in this stupid war. And by God, I'm not going to let any worthless drinking get in the way."

Grant smiled. "So you're going to be my savior too?"

"That's right. And any son-of-a-bitch that puts temptation in your way is going to have his ass kicked!" Rawlins relaxed, smiled. "You've got the preacher here now, and he hasn't even got a uniform."

"We can take care of that tomorrow. I just received mine from New York, but a captain won't be too hard to outfit. By the way, what do your political contacts think about McClellan taking over that new Army of the Potomac?"

"Washburne thinks the little son of a bitch is a power-mad fake. His big victory in western Virginia was overrated, certainly not enough to warrant his new command. Fact is, a story is circulating that if he hadn't had Rosecrans, he wouldn't even have won it."

Grant thought back to the first hard time he'd had as a plebe. Cadet Rosecrans, on a dusty plain . . . when McClellan was what—thirteen or so. And now . . .

"Did you ever know McClellan?" Rawlins asked.

"Slightly."

"He's quite a promoter, so I don't trust him. I hope Mr. Lincoln isn't wearing blinders, because I also heard that General Scott is too ill to continue and wants to retire."

"I hope not. If we ever needed a general in chief with his organizational capability, it's now. He's a great soldier."

Rawlins shrugged. "Everyone gets old."

"Yes, and some of us have a lot to learn while we're still young. *You* are going to take a rush course on how to be an officer. You have the qualities, but you need to learn the procedure. You'd best start with military courtesy and protocol, since both will be extremely essential. So I'll be your mentor, beginning right now. This is how you salute . . ."

Cairo, Illinois
October 27, 1861

My Dearest Julia,

How my heart reaches out to you and the children in Galena. I wish so very much that I could spend even a couple of days with you and hold you close, or just hold your hand as I've done so much. But I can't justify any kind of leave for myself.

I'm impatient to strike at Columbus, but I know the enemy is too intrenched to take the place without a siege. Waiting, however, does give the troops of this command further chance to train. I find myself working from dawn to midnight most days.

John Rawlins has adapted superbly, as I guessed he might. I don't know how I could keep up without him. You'd think he was a West Pointer with many years' service. And it's rather humorous the way he protects me. He's just like a mother hen—you'd think he's ten years older than me, instead of the other way around.

Cump Sherman's now a brigadier. He was given command east of

*Paducah, but got into some kind of a twist with Secretary of War Cam-
eron. He was promptly relieved, as you may have read in the paper, and
Don Carlos Buell replaced him. Isn't that strange—Buell and Buckner
opposing each other in Kentucky? Both of them are friends of mine, were
classmates at the Academy, and are friends of each other (I guess).*

*I think Frémont's in trouble with Lincoln about freeing the slaves in
Missouri. Gen. John McClernand is here at Cairo as my post commander.
He's the congressman who helped with the 21st Illinois.*

*But enough army talk. Maybe in a few weeks it'll be possible for you
to come see me and spend some time here. All depends on the situation, but
you might do some planning in that direction. Sorry I write so seldom, but
you understand. I miss you terribly, darling.*

> *Your loving husband,*
> *Ulys*

On November 2, word was announced that General Scott's resignation and
retirement were official. Major General George B. McClellan was now
wearing two hats—those of general in chief of the army and of field commander of the Army of the Potomac. At thirty-four, the prodigy had risen
all the way to the top. Grant shrugged and Rawlins cursed.

On the same day, the opportunity for Grant to get after the enemy
arrived in the form of a rather confusing order from Frémont. A force was
to be dispatched to chase Jeff Thompson, a rebel brigand, into Arkansas,
and a demonstration was to be made toward Columbus, where Polk now
commanded. It would be a wonderful opportunity for Grant to get his
bored troops into something besides drill.

He'd been eying a tract of riverfront farmland called Belmont for some
time. It was only a three-shack hamlet with a makeshift rebel fortification,
but it was just across the river from Columbus and would be vital to any
Federal force striking the rebel stronghold. Grant decided to demonstrate
there, and hope for resistance from his spectators on the other side of the
river. On November 3, he dispatched Colonel Oglesby with a strong brigade
to chase Thompson.

On the 6th, when a Confederate force was reported to be moving out
of Columbus to intercept Oglesby, Grant's "demonstration" took on new
meaning. He was excited as he called his adjutant into his office.

"Rawlins, we're going to turn our demonstration into a major raid on
Belmont. But we won't be able to stay, so we'll use steamers for the round
trip. The gunboats *Tyler* and *Lexington* will support. Our force will consist
of two brigades, one commanded by General McClernand, the other by
the senior regimental commander. We'll move downstream tonight to a
point a few miles above Columbus, then debark and attack just after daybreak on the Missouri side. When the rebs spot us, it should be a lively
day."

Rawlins frowned. "Does Frémont know about this?"

"He told me to demonstrate toward Columbus."

"But this sounds like more than a demonstration. What will you gain?"

"Intangibles, Rawlins, intangibles."

"Will you be writing the orders as usual?"

"Yes, but you can send out a general alert now. And I hope you've been practicing with that revolver of yours."

Rawlins grinned. "I could hit Jeff Davis in the left eye from a hundred yards."

Grant watched the cool first light begin its work on the river bank, and then glanced at the glassy little waves from the prow of the steamer as they disrupted the dark, mirrored surface of the river, creating strange images. He clutched the rail of his flag steamer and smiled inwardly. The tiny flotilla with over three thousand men had silently drifted the last few miles downstream in the past two hours, and was ready to disgorge its lethal cargo on command. Strange how he felt such rich exhilaration with battle pending, this sense of power, of anticipation—like a child on Christmas morning. Remembering his baseless fears on the fruitless march to meet Harris, he felt absolutely no timidity . . . only excitement in the morning stillness.

Would he ever quit being a second lieutenant?

Silence. Only the gurgles of water from the prow disrupted the quiet.

As he expected, the land above the riverbank was low and marshy, with some cleared fields interrupting the solitude created by stretches of timber. A fairly broad cornfield, with spent stalks clinging to the last of their barren dignity, offered the most solid-looking landing site. "Can you get us in there, Captain?" he asked the steamer skipper at his elbow. "And leave room for the other transports?"

"Yes, sir, General, wherever you want."

"Good. Proceed." Grant turned to Rawlins. "Looks like a good place to start a day's work. Pass the word to disembark and form up for the two-mile march to Belmont."

Riding with Rawlins beside him and Lieutenant Laglow slightly to the rear, Grant mixed in and out of the column, observing march discipline, stopping here and there. Periodically a passing soldier waved to him. Forty minutes after the march began, he heard the sharp crack of musket fire. The advance skirmishers had engaged the enemy! *These were the first angry shots fired at any major force he'd ever commanded.* Everything up to now was history.

He nodded to his adjutant, whose eyes were bright. "Here's your war, Rawlins. No more listening to Mexican War veterans for you. C'mon, *let's go!*"

Grant urged the big black, Cinders, into a trot, and was soon up with the skirmishers from the lead regiment, the Seventh Iowa. The men appeared to be cool and well-controlled under the intense enemy fire. Better than he expected. Bullets were snapping into the trees around him. They'd have to keep moving. A shell crashed off to his right. Screams of battle echoed through the woods. A nervous Laglow pleaded that it was too dangerous for a commanding general. Suddenly Cinders screamed and stumbled. Grant jumped clear as the beautiful black went down.

Scrambling to his feet, Grant hoped that what he knew wasn't true. But the animal had taken a slug in the upper part of his right foreleg. Cinders thrashed with wild eyes as he tried to quiet him, but blood was spurting from the ugly wound. Grant's heart wrenched, knowing what he had to do.

He'd seen many wounded animals shot, but had never had to do it himself. Slowly he raised the revolver and ended the misery. He loved these simple, faithful animals far too much. Besides, men—*human beings*—were being maimed and killed all around him. What was a horse? Ignoring his aide, he bounded onto Laglow's mount and rode toward McClernand.

All at once, with loud eerie yells, a determined rebel force smashed into the Twenty-seventh Illinois, forcing its center back for over ten minutes. But just as it looked as if the break was coming, the regiment gathered itself and held fast. McClernand threw a quick counterattack in from the Seventh Iowa and the threat was over. The move toward Belmont picked up, edging along, gaining momentum through the next two hours. At 11:20, the first shouting Federal troops bounded over the slight earthworks of the Confederate camp. Disorganized rebel soldiers panicked and headed wildly for the river. From their vantage point, Grant turned to Rawlins. "I think we're winning a battle today."

Rawlins flashed an excited grin. "Yes, sir. The good Lord has smiled on us all right. What do you want me to do now?"

"Go tell McClernand to drive on the river. Looks like a rout, but we must follow up. Make prisoners of all who don't swim away. Maybe as many as a thousand of them."

"Yes, sir!"

Grant rode slowly into the camp area, at first sharing in the raucous glee of his victorious soldiers. They were shouting and dancing around, throwing possessions and clothes the enemy had just left behind high in the air. Nothing like a little victory to shoot their spirits up, he thought. And it hadn't been easily won; although heavy casualties had been inflicted on the enemy, his troops had taken their share of Confederate lead.

But his warmth faded quickly as he realized that the men—and some officers—were so busy celebrating and looting that nothing was being done about the enemy at the river. Then, to add to the bedlam, a regimental band came marching in, playing "Yankee Doodle" as loud as it could. He looked around the jubilant crowd for McClernand. Finally spotting his adjutant with some Illinois officers, he shouted, *"Captain Rawlins!"*

An enemy shell crashed into the far end of the encampment area, hitting a handful of men. Grant jerked around. Polk knew his rebel troops were at the river and he could shell this place at will! Rawlins poked through the revelers. "Did you call me, General?"

Grant's blue eyes were ice. "Where's McClernand?"

"I gave him your message, but it was too late. The party had already started."

"Find him and have him report to me at once. Then put these enemy tents to the torch. Maybe that'll get these lads' attention! I—"

Heavy musket fire interrupted, both from the river area and from the north. Grant looked around in alarm. Of course! Polk had seen, and had sent reinforcements who rallied the troops at the river bank. *The rebs may have cut them off from the steamers too!* "Rawlins. I want you to get all the officers to me immediately. And I don't care if you do it at gunpoint."

As shells continued to rain down, the soldiers scrambled for what little cover they could find. A shout of *"We're surrounded!"* was taken up and repeated by the suddenly frightened victors. Within two minutes most of the officers had reached Grant, including McClernand. They were sheepish, frightened. "We're surrounded, cut off. What do we do now, General?"

"We're not totally surrounded," Grant said firmly. "We cut our way in here and that's how we'll get out. Get your units together and prepare to march with skirmishers out front. Smartly! More enemy reinforcements will be coming across that river at any time." He looked sternly at the brigade commander. "General, you handle this evacuation while I go on ahead. That is, if you can."

He told Rawlins to stay with McClernand.

The fight back to the transports should have been easier, since the rebs hadn't landed as many reinforcements as Grant had thought. But his troops had gone from the elation of victory to what looked like the depths of defeat, and they didn't fight well. He rode on ahead to check on the steamers and the regiment he had left to guard them.

Riding out of the trees nearest the anchored steamers, he was relieved to find no gray uniforms. In fact, he found no troops at all. He rode quickly to the sloughs where he'd instructed the regimental commander to remain, and again found nothing. Where in the name of heaven was his regiment? He looked at the steamer decks. *They had already embarked!* He felt a surge of fury, but quickly realized how lucky he was that the rebs hadn't come between him and the transports. It was too late to pull the troops off now, with the first of his onrushing soldiers nearing the boats. He'd get around to *that* colonel later! He was certainly learning about Volunteer command the hard way.

Heading back through part of the returning Seventh Iowa, he ran into Rawlins. "McClernand is kicking asses in the rear, General. Everyone should be here within thirty minutes."

"Good. Now, Rawlins, I want those boats loaded as soon as possible."

"Yes, sir, I'll move them. Where're you going?"

"To look for stragglers. I don't want to leave any able-bodied men here. Oh, and I think Doctor Brinton's got some wounded up in those farmhouses. Be sure and get them on the boats."

A short while later, Grant rode down through a cornfield to see what was going on by the river. He found a point that afforded a fair field of vision, and pulled his meerschaum out. *Why hadn't Polk hit the landing site?*

Or was he gone and the ineffective Pillow in command? Or maybe it was the strong demonstration General Smith was making over on the other side of Columbus. Maybe Smith had taken the heat off.

He shook his head. They should be down at the riverbank by Belmont taking prisoners instead of scurrying aboard the steamers like rats fleeing a sinking ship. But then, he *was* lucky. He was sure he'd been heavily outnumbered, counting the garrison across the river. If the enemy had sealed him off from the transports, things would be mighty messy. He could see the headlines now: GRANT'S COMMAND CAPTURED IN ITS FIRST BATTLE!

Suddenly the unmistakable noises of moving soldiers startled him. No Federal troops could be down here! Holding his breath, he heard them drawing nearer. *Rebs?* Yes! How did they get here? No matter. Was he still to be captured, off daydreaming by himself? Leading his horse, he began to slip away. Twenty yards, thirty—quietly. After another ten yards, he got up on the side of the saddle, Indian-fashion, urging the animal into a gliding run. Finally, he swung up, spurring the horse into a full gallop, ignoring the lashing cornstalks and the flying bullets.

He took in the situation at the landing point in a glance. He must have been gone longer than he thought because the transports were pulling away from the bank, pouring out black smoke. Only one remained. He had about a hundred yards. Shouting, he reined in just a few feet from the steamer. Someone on the crowded deck must have recognized him because a plank came flopping down to the water's edge. As musket fire popped behind him, his horse slid down the muddy bank and trotted over the heavy board onto the deck of the transport.

The commanding general was the last to leave the Battle of Belmont!

CHAPTER 23

Rawlins handed Grant a cup of steaming coffee. "Have you read the St. Louis paper, General?"

Grant looked up from the pile of paperwork that had accumulated during his absence.

"Seems everyone thinks we were defeated at Belmont," Rawlins said.

"They're entitled to their opinion."

"What about you—now that you've had time to absorb the losses and all?"

"I don't think so."

"Those intangibles of yours, huh?"

"Yes. The troops got their baptism of fire and learned a lot. So did I. We met an enemy force of more than equal strength, well-rested on their home ground, and routed them. If follow-up to the river had been accomplished, we would have marched out in total victory."

"The rebs are claiming they thrashed a force of eight thousand."

Grant shrugged. "Still no word from Frémont?"

Rawlins grinned, handing over a message. "No, and there won't be. They finally relieved the son of a bitch."

Grant read the dispatch quickly. Major General Henry W. Halleck would assume command of what was now called the Army of the Missouri, and Frémont was to get a future assignment.

"What do you think about that?" Rawlins asked.

"Oh, I guess I never cared much for Fancy Dans or emancipators. I suppose Frémont believed in what he was doing, but I guess the man just wanted too much to be in the White House."

"Aren't you being a little too kind to him?"

Grant raised an eyebrow. "Who am I? Let's think about Halleck. I heard he did a good job in California during the Mexican War. Then he resigned and went into law practice in San Francisco. And got pretty rich, I guess. You know anything about him?"

"Yep. I found one of his former staff officers and got some lowdown on him back when I figured Lincoln would fire Frémont, and I guessed Halleck might be a replacement. As you know, he's a West Pointer, Class of '39—some four years older than you. He's also a consummate politician."

Grant produced a slight smile. "Like me."

Rawlins snorted and went back to his notebook. "Halleck is quite the student of modern warfare by the book, and can discuss it intelligently. His own battle record consists only of skirmishes in California. He's bright, petulant at times, and always seems to cover his ass."

"Why do you say that?"

"If anything goes wrong in his command, the files will never place the blame on General Halleck. You might keep that in mind."

"I don't worry about such things."

"I know. And Belmont is a glaring example. You should have tried someone over those mistakes and documented it all fully."

"That would have gained nothing. What else do you know about Halleck?"

"That's about it, except that his prewar nickname was 'Old Brains.' He may be difficult for us country boys to get along with."

"Not for me. He has *two* stars."

Cump Sherman ground his teeth as he read the front-page story in the December 11 *Cincinnati Commercial:*

GENERAL WILLIAM T. SHERMAN INSANE

The painful intelligence reaches us, in such form that we are not at liberty to disclose it, that Gen. William T. Sherman, late commander of the Dept. of the Cumberland, is insane. It appears that he was at the time, while commanding in Kentucky, stark mad. We learn that he at one time telegraphed to the War Dept. three times in one day for permission to evacuate Kentucky

*and retreat into Indiana. He also, on several occasions, frightened leading
Union men of Louisville out of their wits by vastly exaggerating Buckner's
force, and the assertion that the city could not be defended. The retreat from
Cumberland Gap was one of his mad freaks. When relieved of the Kentucky
command he was sent to Missouri and placed at the head of a brigade in
Sedalia, when the shocking fact that he was a madman was developed by
orders that his subordinates knew to be preposterous and refused to obey. He
has of course been relieved altogether from command. The harsh criticisms
that have been lavished on this gentleman, provoked by his strange conduct,
will now give way to feelings of greatest sympathy for him in his great
calamity. It seems providential that the country has not to mourn the loss of
an army through the loss of mind of a general into whose hands was committed
the vast responsibility of the command of Kentucky.*

Sherman stared at the terrible words—"insane, stark mad, mad freaks,
madman, loss of mind." He flung the newspaper away and smashed his fist
into his palm. "Those *bastards!* Those dirty *bastards!*"

He got up from the kitchen table and leaned his head against the wall.
Closing his eyes, he wished every damned newspaperman, every worthless
reporter, and every single son-of-a-bitching editor in the world would die
by fire. It had all started when he began his private war on the press. Early
on he had seen the danger of permitting reporters full access to information.
They would print anything in any way they saw fit, and had no respect for
secrecy or military dispositions. He regarded many of them as spies, giving
information to the enemy via their stories. That was why he imposed cen-
sorship in Kentucky and barred the bastards from his camps. Once, when
a reporter disobeyed, he had him clapped in prison.

And the press retaliated, attacking him at first in little ways, then growing more aggressive. They began the rumors of his having a mental problem,
and wrote copiously of his slightest habit or practice. They recorded his
not eating or sleeping, of his chain-smoking—calling his cigar butts
"Sherman's old soldiers." They hounded him and used innuendo to per-
fection.

After the debacle at Bull Run, he was promoted to brigadier with date
of rank of May 17, and was sent to Kentucky as second-in-command to
Robert Anderson, who had commanded Fort Sumter at its fall. When Anderson departed soon after, he was elevated to command with insufficient
troops and equipment to mount a campaign. It wasn't long before he began
to run afoul of the War Department and the administration. Then, when
McClellan took over, his problems with the higher-ups increased. Even with
help from his powerful father-in-law and the other U.S. senator, his brother,
he couldn't get what he needed.

He'd been criticized for being afraid to move against the enemy.

And perhaps he *had* overestimated the rebel strength. Maybe Buckner
had fed false information to his spies.

It was just that he knew how well the enemy troops were led and motivated. He'd learned a great deal about Southerners when he was down in Louisiana running the military academy just before the war. He knew what kind of units he'd have to face.

Oh, he had to admit that he hadn't been totally well, unable to sleep, writing a couple of rash letters, but he wasn't *crazy*. Sure—he'd stated that it would take two hundred thousand troops to win, but he meant the whole Mississippi, not in Kentucky, as he'd been quoted as saying. He just wasn't a war dog, sniffing the scent of battle without the means to win it.

Goddamned press!

He went to the stove and poured himself another cup of coffee. Sitting here at home in Lancaster, cooling his heels, wasn't doing him that much good. They called it "getting a rest." Exile, that's what it was. It was nice to be with Ellen and the kids, but damn it, he belonged back in the war. Maybe Halleck would find something for him to do again. He turned and picked up the note from the kitchen table. From Grant, it read, "Be of good cheer. I don't believe anything I read about you. You will do big things in this war once you get your real chance."

How kind of the man.

His glance fell on the newspaper. This kind of poison wouldn't get him back in the war.

Goddamned press!

Grant lay back in bed, momentarily spent. As always, their lovemaking had been completely satisfying. His sweet, calm Julia was always a vibrantly passionate partner, and their not having been together for so long had merely stimulated their coupling. She was so warm and smooth, with her unbundled tresses flooding over his arm like black silk. Her scent was, as always, delicate. His heart was full of her, his darling Julia.

She propped up on one elbow, running a tiny finger through the reddish curls of his ample chest hair. "How long are you going to let me stay, Ulys?"

He smiled. "The rest of the night, honey. Just like the other girls."

She stabbed a fingernail into his chest. "Other girls, huh! Seriously, darling, how long can the kids and I stay here in Cairo?"

As long as he was here, he wished. His reply was measured. "You know how it worries me. We aren't too secure here yet, what with unknown enemy strength so close and all."

"But you have so many troops here."

"Not enough to stave off a heavy surprise attack."

"How long?"

"I guess a week will be okay."

"How about a month?"

He stroked her hand. "Right now, you could talk me into a decade, but in the morning it'll return to a week. That's all for now."

She kissed his ear. "Can I be a camp follower later on?"

"Of course."

It had been marvelous having Julia and the kids in Cairo, but there was so much to be done that any distraction—let alone four zestful children—was severely detrimental. His command was growing daily, encumbered by the constant entanglements of military immaturity and its famous administrative snares. Plus the horrendous supply troubles. Small arms in particular were a major problem, being outdated and of too many variations for the available ammunition. Filthy, muddy Cairo was becoming a vast, unwieldy glut of instant soldiers, mismatched equipment, and civilians trying to cash in on the war.

No, with his demanding twelve-hour days, the family would be far better off up in St. Louis with Colonel Dent. He might be able to make a quick trip up there for a Christmas visit.

If it hadn't been for all of his quartermaster duty, he would be having an even more difficult time of it. Colonel Joe Webster, his chief of staff, was not yet capable of taking too much of a load off his shoulders. On the other hand, John Rawlins was adapting more every day. But much to Rawlins's violent distaste, many of his staff officers were drinking rather heavily, and Grant simply could not find it within himself to play the reformed drunk and tell them to stop. Not as long as they could perform their duties. The Lord knew he'd like to have a drink once in a while himself, but he couldn't. Besides, Rawlins watched him like a hawk, a situation he found amusing.

His adjutant's overactive concern about alcohol was a boon, though. The scabrous gossip about his drinking was still out there. "Old Grant is pouring it down again, drinking on duty, befuddled by whiskey." Rawlins had heard from Washburne that the president had received such a report. Immediately, the adjutant had taken it upon himself to write a strong answer—after first showing it to him—swearing to his general's abstinence. Rawlins hadn't even permitted him a sip of wine on the prisoner exchange with General Polk. Wasn't that a strange twist—an infantry general not being able to drink a bishop's spirits!

Shortly after the Belmont expedition, he'd had a heart-to-heart talk with McClernand—first about the extensive battle report the former congressman had sent *directly* to Lincoln. He realized the two men from Illinois were friends, but channels had to be observed. Then he discussed the battle itself, and McClernand's failure to follow up. "I hope a lesson has been learned, General. I know I've learned from Belmont. Regarding your heroic action as we headed back to the steamers, I'm told you had three horses shot out from under you, and I commend you for your personal bravery." But McClernand, whom he ranked only by total service, had been a bit peevish about the soft reprimand.

Fortunately, Dr. Joe Brinton provided stimulating company. Too bad the surgeon couldn't do more about the terrible sanitary conditions and the resulting high sick rate. He had a strong opinion that disease and death from wounds would be the biggest killers in the conflict, and he never quit harping on the subject. Grant's relationship with the doctor was one of mutual respect. Once, while Grant was away for a short period, McClernand had countermanded a rule Brinton had instituted governing military hospitals within the command. The doctor had told his medical people to ignore the general, and related the incident to Grant upon his return. When he finished, Grant replied, "Doctor, take care of my sick and wounded to the best of your ability, and don't worry about regulations." He then signed the written report of the incident, adding, "The reason for having a medical director is that he shall be supreme in his department. The decision of Surgeon Brinton is sustained." A copy was sent to McClernand.

There was no fully reliable intelligence about enemy concentration. The last estimate placed rebel strength in the Columbus complex at somewhere between thirty-six and fifty regiments, with supporting cavalry and artillery. Over to the east in Bowling Green, General Albert Sidney Johnston, the senior Confederate commander in the West, stood pat with unknown strength.

Don Carlos Buell had replaced Cump Sherman in Louisville. Like Sherman and Pope, Buell had preceded Grant on that famous May 17 promotion list of brigadiers. Buell, the cadet with the brilliant mind and all of the demerits at the Academy, the officer who had beaten a court-martial for taking his saber to an enlisted man back at Jefferson Barracks and then made three brevets to major in Mexico, was apparently proving just as cautious as Sherman had been. But he was a good friend of McClellan.

Grant had written to Sherman again, telling him, "Belmont has convinced me that our Volunteers, when properly led, can defeat the rebels in nearly any equal-strength confrontation—if only a commander will close and be tenacious, fighting for nothing less than victory." Sherman had replied that he now knew he should have been more aggressive, that he had regained his confidence, and that he was looking forward to a new command to redeem himself. Halleck appeared to be the answer.

Halleck was as aloofly starchy as Frémont had been grandiose. Grant had gotten off to a bad start with the new department commander over the telegraph thing. A spy had sent a fictitious telegram, and Grant had sturdily told Old Brains that he thought the problem was in Halleck's own headquarters. Even though it proved to be the truth, Halleck didn't back down gracefully and lightly reprimanded Grant.

Ever since his arrival in Cairo, Grant had been waging a secondary war—on the contractors and speculators who had obtained a monopoly on army business there. An example was forage that was selling for thirty percent above market value. Audacious collusion in bidding was common practice. Grant refused to sign vouchers for anything that was overpriced.

This brought him into conflict with a powerful Chicago lawyer named Leonard Swett, who got pushy with him and threatened to go to his friend the president. "Go right ahead," Grant replied. "And if I have to, I'll seize the Illinois Central to move my supplies." Swett owned part of the railroad.

"Furthermore, I order you out of this command," Grant added. "And if you don't leave, I'll either lock you up or shoot you."

Word came down from Washburne that Lincoln had made a humorous anecdote about the lawyer's report of this threat. "So I told Swett, if this man Grant threatened to shoot you, he's as likely to do it as not."

Grant also heard that the rumors about his returning to the bottle were emanating from these merchants of greed, but he paid no attention.

One positive result from the reports of misconduct and collusion was the board of officers that Halleck had sent to Cairo to investigate the way Grant was operating. Their report was favorable, and following it the command was redesignated the District of Cairo, with Paducah placed under it. Thus the very able Brigadier General C. F. Smith came into the fold. Grant couldn't have been more pleased; he still had trouble believing the magnificent officer whom he'd so admired as a cadet was his subordinate.

And Flag Officer Andrew Foote was a blessing as well. Since the navy had no current admirals, the fifty-six-year-old Foote was a commodore, equal in rank to a brigadier. There was absolutely no interservice rivalry between the naval officer and Grant. Foote was there to support the army commander, and was fully in concert with Grant's concept of offensive warfare. The crusty Foote was also a devoted temperance man, at least equaling Rawlins in his struggle against the demon rum. Rumor had it that he'd convinced his entire squadron, off the China coast, to take the pledge—in a day when grog was issued! To add to his religious makeup, he was an arch abolitionist. But none of these beliefs got in his way as a tenacious commander. He and Grant would make quite a team if the confounded new gunboats were ever finished.

According to Foote, the squat, well-armed, lightly armored, and somewhat underpowered "turtles" would be difficult to handle against the current, but would be far superior to anything the rebels could muster on the rivers. Drawing less than six feet of water, these menacing little monsters were designed to get close to a target, or be able to stand off at a distance and use their excellent firepower. Foote's eyes lit up when he spoke of what he'd be able to accomplish with them, as did those of his second-in-command, Commander Henry Walke.

Such was the situation as the Christmas season approached. Grant took stock. Just a year earlier, he'd been struggling in Galena, still the debt-ridden failure trying to be content in the family business. And now he was, in effect, running a ponderous company. That previous Christmas had not yet seen the sad rift in his beloved Union, and now a war of deadly proportions shook the land. What would Christmas a year hence hold?

Meanwhile, several hundred miles to the east, a troubled president sat in a window seat in the White House. His long face was mournful as he watched the lightly falling snow creating a velvet blanket of white on the ground below. With his long legs pulled up under his chin as he was sometimes prone to sit when he was alone and pondering his enormous troubles, he too wondered at the happenings of the passing year and at what lay ahead. Why, old man Lincoln, he said to himself—if you were going to beget a son who had to command the most massive army the North American continent had ever seen, why couldn't you have given him the insight to handle it better?

Or maybe some other farsighted fathers could have begotten some sons a president could count on—so he wouldn't have such confounded problems in the battle areas. McClellan was ill, but his effectiveness as commander of the Army of the Potomac was little bothered by his inactivity. Except for constantly building that vast army, Little Mac had been a master of sitting pat and not engaging the enemy. As general in chief, his effectiveness was also becoming suspect. Oh, he brought copies of correspondence he'd sent to Halleck and his friend Buell that were supposed to prove he wanted action. But what did those commanders do? Make excuses—particularly Buell.

Lincoln gazed out across the front lawn at the lamps on hacks as they moved like dark ants along Pennsylvania Avenue. Still, they were moving faster than any of his armies.

His own plan, the one he'd modified from Scott's Anaconda plan, was certainly that of an amateur general, but its concept seemed to be working out. It had started hazily and developed into what he thought had to be done to take the war to the Confederacy. How many nights had he stared at maps and tried to define and absorb the haphazard intelligence he received from political and questionable military sources? Then what had to be done had come together in his legal mind. He had arrived at the need, if not the means.

Now, the naval blockade of the Confederacy had already been put into effect. His plan had called for an amphibious force to proceed down the Atlantic coast and take Port Royal, South Carolina, providing a base for the blockading fleet and possible incursions into the enemy interior. This had been done successfully.

The failure had come with the other part of his plan. Simultaneously, a force was to have moved on the Cumberland Gap to seize and hold a portion of the railroad connection between Virginia and Tennessee. With the severing of this vital supply line, enemy forces in Virginia would suffer.

This plan coincided with information espoused by Senator Andrew Johnson that there were an extensive number of loyal Unionists in eastern Tennessee, his home territory. Johnson had promised an uprising and destruction of rails in this area, should Federal troops head that way. It was through this area that the heart of the Confederacy could be pierced; therefore, the movement through the Cumberland Gap should have begun at once.

And McClellan had agreed, had immediately so directed Sherman, who was then commanding the Army of the Ohio in Kentucky. But Sherman saw shadows behind every rock and had lost his confidence. Poor man. So nothing had happened through October and early November. Sherman was removed and McClellan sent Buell. Still nothing. Frémont out in Missouri overplayed his role as emperor and was replaced by Halleck. Halleck, whom Scott had recommended as his own replacement, fell in love with McClellan.

Expecting Federal troops, East Tennesseans rose and burned bridges. But no blue uniforms arrived, and the loyalists were hung, shot, or imprisoned. How do I answer Andy Johnson on that score? All he knows is that his president must have lied to him. Cumberland Gap is still held by the enemy. And all I hear from my generals is "cold winter, impassable roads, and not enough strength." Yet the army is growing at the rate of forty thousand men per month. How many myths can they concoct?

Ah, McClellan, speaking of emperors, how did you place yourself upon the throne? Because of an inexperienced president who didn't know how to read generals, that was how. Well, that president is learning that he'd better start taking over some of the command—if he ever expects to get anything done. But surely he needs help from some source. Are there no generals out there who will close with the enemy and destroy him—or at least follow orders?

Lincoln closed his eyes.

Did I lose *all* the good ones to Davis?

CHAPTER 24

Ulysses S. Grant, from his Cairo headquarters
Wanted to take two forts on the Kentucky/Tennessee borders.
These forts were the center of the Confederate line.
Said Grant, "I'll capture these forts and make them mine."
To Fort Henry they'd first go, then twelve miles to the east,
Where Fort Donelson would be captured, to say the least.
From "Brave Boys in Blue" by Katee Seal, age thirteen

HEADQUARTERS, DEPARTMENT OF THE WEST
ST. LOUIS, MISSOURI
JANUARY 6, 1862

General Halleck *did* look like an owl. His large, round, rather close-set eyes didn't even blink as he stared, and he usually stared. Except for the heavy hair at his jowls, his round face was clean-shaven, with a huge forehead accentuated by frontal balding. Not a touch of warmth invaded his expression as he returned Grant's salute. "Sit down, General. What brings you up to Cairo?"

Grant felt uncomfortable. He couldn't use the maps if he sat several feet away. "I felt I should meet you, sir, and present a plan I have in mind."

Halleck continued to stare from behind his busy desk. "Well, we've met. As you can see, I'm quite well occupied, so proceed."

He hadn't expected it to be *that* abrupt. "Well, sir, I'm fully convinced that we can sever the Confederacy by controlling the major rivers. At the present, Columbus negates our access to the Mississippi, but the Tennessee and the Cumberland are inviting. I'm confident—in fact, General Smith has recommended it—that we can take Fort Henry on the Tennessee without too much trouble, freeing our navy people to roam the river and bombard at will. This might also force the enemy to withdraw from Bowling Green, and permit us to encircle Columbus. As you are aware, Columbus is so heavily fortified that it would take an extensive siege to defeat the rebs there."

Grant started to unroll his maps. "Now, I've—"

"I'm perfectly aware of these points, General."

"Uh, yes, sir. I was thinking of perhaps taking Dover on the Cumberland. I don't know much about Fort Donelson there, but I think the rebs have quite a few troops. With that place in our hands, the door to Nashville would be open. And—"

Halleck's interruption was icy. "I also know where Nashville is. General Grant, I hope you didn't come all the way up here to tell me how to conduct my campaigns. Any student of warfare can readily see what you're recommending."

Grant couldn't tell if the baleful eyes were angry or just impatient. "Yes, sir. I just thought we ought to move while the timing is in our favor. The gunboats are near ready, and Buell seems to be in no hurry. I—"

"I really don't think the decisions of department commanders are your concern, General. There are larger issues at stake, which don't presently concern you. When the time comes, you'll have ample opportunity to play your part. Now I suggest you go back to Cairo and do your own housekeeping."

Grant had difficulty controlling his rising anger as he rerolled the maps. He tucked them under his arm and saluted. "Yes, sir." Turning, he walked silently from the general's office, avoiding the stare of Halleck's aide.

The telegram to General Halleck had been short and simple: "With permission, I will take Fort Henry on the Tennessee, and establish and hold a large camp there. Grant, B.G." Foote's request, strongly supportive, promised the assistance of four ironclad gunboats in such an operation. Now on the 30th of January, two days later, he had just settled into his quartermaster's frustrated report of equipment shortages when Rawlins burst through the door to his office. *"General, read this!"*

Grant looked up, startled, as the adjutant waved a message at him.

"The old son of a bitch is going to let us go!" Rawlins danced a little jig in front of the desk.

"Would you mind letting me read it?"

Halleck was no more verbose in his telegram: "Make your preparations to take and hold Fort Henry. I will send you written instructions by mail."

Grant reread, making sure. It was real. *He was going into major battle.* No guesswork on his part, no Belmonts, no demonstrations. He was going to take an army into the field to attack the enemy in his lair! He handed the message to Webster. Staff officers began crowding around the door. Rawlins was still grinning and cavorting around. Grant had to shake his head and smile.

But only for a moment; there was a lot to be done.

Halleck's instructions arrived the next morning, stating almost to the letter what Grant had expected. Move by water; take and hold Fort Henry; cut the roads that led to nearby Fort Donelson to cut off retreat; utilize cavalry to break the railroad; render the railroad bridges crossing both rivers impassable, but not destroyed; anticipate possible attack from Columbus. Additional regiments would be sent, including three batteries of artillery. His chief engineer officer was to be the highly regarded Lieutenant Colonel James B. McPherson, another Ohioan.

The instructions also informed Grant that Beauregard had left Manassas four days earlier with a possible fifteen regiments to reinforce the line from Bowling Green to Columbus. He was to move with the least delay, to organize his command as he saw fit, without regard to any political implications about regiments and brigades.

The speed element pleased Grant.

The Cairo machine jumped into gear.

Before dropping into bed for a few precious hours of sleep early on the 3rd, Grant penned a quick note to Covington, where Julia was visiting his family. "My dearest Julia, I'm about to embark on a major attack that you will undoubtedly read about by the time you get this note. My hand is relatively free, so we'll see if I've learned enough about being a general yet. I hope to give the Union the victory she so sorely needs. Pray for the brave lads who will fall in this effort, just as I pray for you and the children. Your loving Ulys."

Tired as he was, he lay awake, wondering what he could have forgotten. The telegram to Halleck had been sent: "Will be off up the Tennessee at six o'clock. Command 23 regiments in all." Twenty-three regiments, and just a few months earlier he'd been frantically seeking command of just *one!* Now, here he was, lying in a bunk aboard Foote's flagship, the *Cincinnati,* wondering if he would get as many as ten additional regiments in the coming engagement.

There were many questions to be answered in the next few days. Could the assorted regiments, with their individualities and lack of training, come together effectively? Smith was a rock, but could McClernand control his brigades? Of what caliber was thirty-four-year-old Lew Wallace, his latest and third-ranking brigadier? What effect would the cold, rainy weather and muddy roads have? How valuable would the gunboats' fire be on the rough and swollen river?

And finally, would he himself measure up?

Allowing two days for landing, assembly and preparation, the attack would begin on the 6th. He'd get his answers then—or in the following days, because he had absolutely no intention of stopping at Fort Henry.

Shortly after the first transports arrived at the rain-swept landing point, some nine miles below the Confederate site, the officer commanding Fort Henry, Brigadier General Lloyd Tilghman, was alerted that a major Federal force was heading his way. Tilghman, an 1836 graduate of West Point, had an extensive background as a railroad engineer, and had served as General Twiggs's aide during the Mexican War. With a neatly trimmed beard, the dark-complexioned and slender commander carried himself as if he'd never been out of uniform. But this was no railroad company boardroom. The next three hours were agonizing to the Confederate general, as he listened to reports of growing enemy strength. At 5:30 he called his commanders and staff together.

"Gentlemen," he said gravely, "I've made a difficult decision. It appears the enemy will attack within the next forty-eight hours. And reports indicate that we will be heavily outnumbered. Most importantly, he has the new gunboats, which our intelligence informs us are heavily armed. And I don't have to tell you about the water problem in this abortion called a fort. If I had the idiot son of a bitch who designed this farce, I'd shoot him myself. Six of our seventeen guns are underwater, and the magazine is threatened.

"Therefore, I want the brigade, with its five regiments, plus all the field guns, to depart under cover of darkness tonight for Fort Donelson. I'll remain with part of my staff, all fixed gun crews and ammunition handlers, one company of infantry, and the sick in quarters. The road is bad, but getting to Donelson is far better than getting caught or decimated here."

"But Lloyd," the brigade commander asked, "how long do you think you can hold out here?"

"I don't know, maybe twenty-four hours. Depends on the rain."

"Why don't we all pull out and rechristen this mistake for the damned engineer who designed it?"

"I can't. They might even attack tonight, and your columns would be vulnerable. Besides, there's the slim chance that this whole thing is a feint. No, I have to remain. Gentlemen, you have your orders."

The firing from Foote's little armada had begun a scant thirty-five minutes earlier, but to Grant it seemed an eternity as he listened to the muffled sounds of the gunnery duel. His two divisions were both bogged down by the muddy roads, Smith's on the west side of the river trying to reach Fort Heiman—an incomplete structure that looked down on Fort Henry—and McClernand's on the east side. The miserable rain had ceased just about the time Foote's first rounds were fired, and now the sun was peeking like a curious cat through the bright holes in the overcast.

Grant fretted. All of this effort, the waiting and the planning, and the commodore's prediction would probably prove true; Foote had said that he'd beat Fort Henry into submission before Grant's troops could get unstuck and get to the objective. He should have gone along with the admiral instead of setting up his command post on the river bank.

Suddenly the sound of firing ceased.

Stillness settled over the misty river, and Grant felt his nerves jump. *What was going on?* He'd better get up to the signal point. Jamming his pipe into his pocket, he waved to his adjutant. "Come on, Rawlins, let's see what's happening."

They were up the steep hill in a few minutes, arriving at the side of the naval ensign Foote had left behind as a communicator. The young officer had his glass trained on the *Tyler,* stationed three quarters of a mile away. "What's going on, Mister?" Grant asked.

The ensign held up one hand as he continued to stare through the small telescope. "The *Tyler* is running up a signal now, sir . . . just a minute and I'll—*yippee! They've struck their colors! The navy did it!*"

Grant was dumbstruck. McClernand and Smith weren't even close to their objectives. He felt a quick twinge of jealousy. Cheated. No, such a selfish emotion was ridiculous. But it *had* been too easy. Had the rebs taken off, except for a token force? If so, where had they gone? Donelson? Well, he'd soon find out. The ensign's words came back—*"The navy did it!"* He felt another pang of regret, but brushed it aside. The gunboats were still under army command, part of his team. What did it matter which part brought about the victory? Still—what was it, some old pride, some tradition that dated back to West Point, that caused him to—*no, that was ridiculous!* Look at how many soldiers had escaped death and maiming. "All right, Rawlins," he said quietly, "let's head upstream and congratulate our victorious naval arm."

Grant and Foote received General Tilghman in the ward room of Commander Walke's *Carondelet,* which was anchored beside the shattered and nearly submerged fort. A total of seventy-eight officers and men and sixteen hospital cases comprised the enemy force. Foote's gunboats had taken fifty-nine hits in the short but vicious gunnery duel, but only one—a hit on the boiler room of the *Essex*—caused any severe damage and casualties. Foote would head back to Cairo with the *St. Louis,* the *Cincinnati,* and the crippled *Essex* for required repairs, while the *Carondelet* would remain on station with the three older boats.

Following the quick surrender ceremony, in which the Confederate general was given permission to send a report back through rebel lines, Grant eyed the quiet, emotionless Tilghman. "From the size of your complement, General, I'd say you did quite a job."

"The water defeated us more than your gunboats, General. That and losing our six-inch rifle. If that gun had stayed in commission, you might not have any gunboats left. But," he shrugged, "that's conjecture. Your army would surely have invested us in a few hours anyway."

Grant lit his pipe. "Where's the rest of your command?"

A slight smile touched Tilghman's lips. "Come now, General. You've seen my command."

"Did you send them over to Donelson, or are they lying out there in the woods somewhere?"

"I'm afraid that's something you'll have to work out by yourself, General."

Grant nodded. "Yes, I suppose so. Well, commend your brave soldiers for me, and I hope your stay in one of our prisons will be soon terminated by a Union victory in the war."

After they shook hands, Grant turned to Rawlins. "Send this message to General Halleck: 'Fort Henry is ours. The gunboats silenced the batteries before the investment was completed. I think the garrison began the retreat last night. Our cavalry followed, finding two guns abandoned in the mud.' "

"Is that all, General?"

"No. Add, 'I shall take and destroy Fort Donelson on the 8th and return to Fort Henry.' "

CHAPTER 25

Lieutenant Colonel James Birdseye McPherson was a handsome graduate of the West Point Class of '53. In fact, he'd stood number one in his class. When the war began, he was a highly regarded first lieutenant of engineers, and it was when he became Halleck's aide the previous November that he was jumped from captain to his present grade. The Ohioan was from Sandusky County, near Lake Erie, and was now thirty-three, not having become a cadet until his twentieth year. Grant had liked him from their first meeting, and had marked him for a promising future. Now, reporting back to the command post, damp, from an extended reconnaissance in the rain, McPherson stood in front of a crackling fire and summed up his opinions about Fort Donelson. "Sir, captured pickets report that between twenty and twenty-five thousand rebel soldiers are in the Dover area. But I believe the strength to be closer to twenty. Whatever it is, it's considerable for a well-entrenched enemy. And they *are* dug in, General.

"As you know, the Cumberland comes down from the north and bends east just before it reaches Dover. The fort itself is not large and is located a little over a mile west-northwest of the town. It's situated on a hill, facing north so its guns can bear on anything coming south, like our boats. What makes it difficult for a ground attack is that the rebs have dug rifle pits in an arc that extends from the flooded area south and east of Dover around to the swampy, impassable land to the north of the fort. Added to these entrenchments are felled trees positioned outward with sharpened limbs. These make a particularly effective abatis."

"What about that road out, south of Dover?"

"It's under three feet of water, if you're thinking about an escape route for them. I know you don't want another Fort Henry situation."

Grant sucked on his pipe as he digested the engineer's information. It confirmed and added considerably to what he knew about the enemy site and intelligence he'd assembled from other sources. "Thanks, Colonel. The old European philosophy of having at least three-to-one odds when attacking a fortified position certainly doesn't apply here, does it?"

"No, sir."

"Fortunately we'll have the gunboats."

"I must warn you, though, that the rebel guns will be bearing down from above this time."

"I trust Foote to win out from that side. Now, if Beauregard doesn't show up with his purported fifty regiments from Bowling Green, we might do all right. A place like Donelson can also be a trap, you know."

"Then you are proceeding with an assault, General?"

"Yes, but it will probably be on the twelfth or thirteenth now, when we get all the boats upriver." Grant thanked McPherson and frowned as he further digested the new information. Donelson was going to be more difficult than he had thought.

The next day Grant handed a message to his adjutant. "Rawlins, I want you to get this telegram off to Washburne right away. As you know, the Senate failed to confirm General Smith's promotion to brigadier for some stupid reason, I guess because of his failure to play politics. I've asked the congressman to do everything in his power to right the most grievous wrong in the history of promotions."

Rawlins took the message. "And I'll stick in my two cents in another one, if you don't mind. With all the conniving and so-called cooperation between Halleck, Buell, and Little Mac, we sure don't need these damned civilians in Congress messing things up."

Grant's smile was gentle. "How quickly change occurs."

"Sir?"

"Oh, I was just thinking about how a certain civilian became a dyed-in-the-wool adjutant so rapidly."

Rawlins spun on his heel. "Well, I'm a soldier for the time being!"

The Galena lawyer was closer to the truth than he knew. In St. Louis, General Halleck was pulling strings like a master puppeteer. A constant flow of telegrams between himself, Buell, and McClellan had continued since before the first of the year. Halleck wanted supreme command of everything west of Virginia, and Buell was jockeying for the same thing. But on the surface, *concert* was the most overused word in their vocabularies. Halleck was in concert with Buell, and Buell with Halleck. And McClellan, at the urging of an impatient president, was the incompetent conductor whose arrogance kept him from understanding the music, and his concert-master, Buell, was afraid to touch his instrument.

Old Brains looked on Grant with contempt. Seedy in appearance, the man slouched and walked pitched forward on his toes. One of his eyes even seemed to be a bit lower than the other. And he'd heard the old army stories about Grant and his drinking. Couldn't ever trust a drunk all the way, no matter what. Oh, the man was a fighter, but what about his judgment? The jury would be out forever on Belmont. But he'd keep him on a short rein and use him for the time being. Couldn't let him get too much glory.

Fortunately, he could heap credit on Foote's head, as he'd done when Fort Henry fell. This thrust into Tennessee was the golden opportunity. If Foote could take Donelson the same way, Buell would be totally out in the cold. The message he'd just sent the commodore read: "Push ahead boldly and quickly. Time is now everything for us. You have gained great distinction by your capture of Fort Henry. Everyone recognizes your services. Make your name famous in history by the capture of Fort Donelson and Clarksville."

He smiled to himself. Once Foote wins out, Grant can be pushed back into obscurity, where he belongs.

He looked up as his aide stuck his head through the doorway. "General Sherman reporting, sir."

Ah, Halleck thought, the other nail. Sherman is my key to Washington. With his powerful father-in-law and senator brother, he'll be my access to Congress. Now if only he isn't too damned fidgety. . .

Meanwhile, on the same day, a man named Cyril Albertson reported into the army telegraph office at Cairo. In his middle forties, Albertson was small, waspish, and bald-headed. Born in Kentucky, he had spent time in South Carolina a decade earlier. He'd been with the Telegraph Service for five years when the war broke out, and was now transferring from Cincinnati. Although thought had been given to placing the Telegraph Service—or at least the part servicing the military—within the army itself, McClellan had decided it should remain separate.

Albertson was a perfect example of the mistake.

The telegrapher had developed a deep, sentimental attachment to the Confederate cause, and he was serving that cause more importantly than he knew. Before Cincinnati, he had been assigned to St. Louis, where he had disrupted the flow of messages between Halleck and his subordinate commanders, creating the initial trouble between Old Brains and Grant. In Cincinnati, he had lain low, but now he had another golden opportunity for disruption. All he had to do once he was settled in was conveniently destroy certain messages as they came in. With all the existing confusion, the chance of his subversion being detected was minimal.

Halleck and Grant would again be perfect foils.

"Colonel John Hellstein, sir. Commanding the Twenty-ninth Indiana."

Grant looked up from the order he was writing in the Crisp house, his headquarters outside of Donelson, and casually returned the officer's salute. "What may I do for you, Colonel?"

The regimental commander handed over an envelope. "I've just arrived with my regiment from Paducah, where General William Tecumseh Sherman has just taken over command. He asked that I personally deliver this to you."

Grant thanked him, asked about his regiment, another of the new ones, and opened the envelope. The short note read:

> *Sam:*
> *I'm the new boss in Paducah, charged with supporting your exciting campaign. I'll get every regiment, every ounce of food, every bullet I can find to you as soon as possible. I know I rank you, but if you can use me in any way, in person, I'll waive rank to serve you. Good luck, my friend.*
> *—Cump Sherman*

Grant puffed on his pipe and handed the note to Rawlins. "Seems we have a friend," he said quietly, stifling the emotion that welled up in his throat.

The only gunboat on station, the *Carondelet,* had engaged the fort, and had taken a large-caliber solid shot through her side just before noon. Then she had retired out of range to transfer her wounded and wait for help. Colonel McPherson's prediction had proved correct. The Donelson gunners wouldn't be easy to defeat. Additionally, McClernand had gotten part of his division into a fight early in the day, and had gotten his nose bloodied. His division was in position on the right of the fan that surrounded Donelson; Smith's division was on the left, and the new brigadier, Lew Wallace, had a makeshift command in between. When Foote made it with the other gunboats, Donelson would be pretty well bottled up.

Grant was impatient, but had to wait for the commodore.

And now this doggone change in the weather bothered him. The temperature had taken a nosedive, beginning at dusk, and a cruel north wind had rushed menacing clouds and driving rain into the battle area. Sleet had soon turned to snow, announcing a howling blizzard. By nine P.M., there was five inches of snow outside the command post at the Crisp house.

All at once, Grant tired of the report he was writing and threw the pen down. Rising from the table, he began to pace the room. Rawlins watched, knowing his commander's agonies. "How about a cup of hot coffee, sir?" he asked. "I think the cook just made a fresh pot."

Grant moved to the window, staring out. "The men out there don't have hot coffee. No, they don't have hot anything. No tents and no fires. And I'll bet three quarters of them threw away their overcoats and blankets two days ago on the march over."

"They'll make it, sir. Many are western farm boys."

Suddenly Grant turned, moving swiftly to where his overcoat hung. "C'mon, Rawlins, we're going on a little inspection trip."

"But, sir, what sense will it make for the commanding general to catch pneumonia?"

"Just as much as sitting on his fat tail by the fire here."

Grant led his small entourage of Rawlins, his aide, and his orderly through the knifing cold to different groups of huddling soldiers in Smith's division. Lieutenant Laglow supplied the countersign when challenged, which was seldom. Grant listened patiently while his aide berated one shivering collection of Illinoisans for not challenging them. Riding on, Grant said, "You were right, but those boys are smart enough to know that no rebel soldiers are going to be traipsing around in this weather."

At each snowy stop, his empathy increased. Poor devils. How would they be able to fight in the morning? Well, at least some of them would know their commanding general had cold feet too. If this weather held, he'd have to get tentage to them somehow, and more blankets. Have to send word off to Sherman as soon as possible. Why was it an age-old custom for soldiers to discard anything heavy that wasn't of immediate need? Army supply was bad enough without help!

Shortly after ten, Grant stopped at the field hospital between the two main divisions. A weary Dr. Brinton met him at the opening of one of the few large hospital tents. "Well now, General," the surgeon asked, "are you out for your evening constitutional, or just trying to get sick from exposure?"

At least the tent was warmed by a small stove. "Just looking around, Doc. Are your patients making out all right?"

"No one is dying from heat prostration."

Grant walked up to two patients playing cards by candlelight. "Evening, men. Who's winning?"

"I am, General," replied the one with a bandage over one eye. "Straley here has trouble cheating with only one hand."

"Where are you boys from?"

"Outside Chicago. Earlier today, when we was wiping out them rebs, we was from outside Dover." Both soldiers chuckled.

McClernand's men. "Tell me about it."

"Well, you see, General," the one with the bandaged arm said, "I had trouble loading my musket after that reb shell hit me, but Turner here, he kept loading for me, 'cause I'm the best shot. And I kept shooting at this here reb field gun until it plumb went out of action. Musta killed all of them!"

Grant spoke sharply. "I don't like liars. You didn't hurt *anyone,* did you?"

The soldier's mouth dropped open. "Well, I, uh . . ." He saw the slight smile touch Grant's lips. "I dunno, General—I reckon I just scared hell out of them and they fainted."

Grant nodded. "Good boy. Now, as soon as that arm's better, you can scare a few more of them."

"Yes, *sir!*"

They'd do all right. Western soldiers usually had a lot of spunk.

Returning to the Crisp house shortly before midnight, Grant found that Foote had finally arrived on the river. And behind his squat turtles were two of the old wooden gunboats, as well as more puffing transports and supply ships. The final scene was being set.

But it wasn't the final scene. Foote and his gunboats were soundly thrashed by the Confederate guns the next afternoon. In fact, there had been some doubt as to whether the commodore's flagship, the *St. Louis,* would survive after a hit that nearly wiped away her pilothouse. The flag officer himself received a bad foot wound, but decided to remain on station, downriver, for the time being. Other gunboats had taken hits that had nearly knocked them out of commission.

While the navy still had some firepower, the rebel garrison was far from bottled up. Disappointed, but still confident, Grant sent a message to Halleck, stating that Donelson might now require a siege. He hated the idea, because it could give the rebels time to bring in reinforcements. And inactivity, particularly in this cold, could hurt his army as much as enemy fire. But a general attack on those fortifications, now covered by icy lacework, could also be deadly.

There was no simple answer.

Grant had no idea that his decision was being made for him. In the commander's office at Fort Donelson, four brigadiers were discussing rebel plans. The senior was John Floyd, fifty-five, who had been secretary of war under President Buchanan. He was under indictment in the North for concentrating guns in the Southern arsenals, anticipating their capture by Confederate forces. He had been appointed a brigadier general in the Confederate Army in May 1861, and had little experience as a military leader.

Second in rank was Gideon Pillow, fifty-four, remembered by Grant and many others as the fire-breather whose conduct in Mexico had been questionable. He was sanguine, often eager to undertake a dangerous venture—at least on the surface—and flighty. Now, perhaps thinking that a victory by his division would forever wipe away the Mexican stain, he wanted to fight.

Third in line was handsome Simon Bolivar Buckner, thirty-eight, who had been active in Chicago real estate after resigning from the army in 1855.

In 1858, he had moved back to Kentucky and prior to the war had organized the state's militia. Trying in vain to keep the state neutral, he had turned down offers of stars from both sides. But when the Kentucky legislature opted to join the Confederacy, he accepted a commission as a brigadier general in that army. Now he commanded a division and tried to quiet his qualms about the situation at Donelson. With good reason, he had little use for either of his seniors.

The fourth general was Bushrod Rust Johnson, Class of '40, who had been wearing stars for only a fortnight. He had served in the Mexican War, but had resigned in 1847 to go into the academic world. He was deferential, had been treated indifferently by his peers, and might as well have been a ghost at the meeting.

Finally Floyd said, "All right, the decision is that we must break out. By attacking Grant's right, we'll open the way south. Pillow's division, reinforced by part of Buckner's command, will strike at sunup tomorrow morning. The remainder of Buckner's force will hold the Union left. And the fort's gunners will maintain a watch over the river, although I'm sure those navy boys have tucked their tails between their legs and taken their wrecked gunboats home."

Pillow grinned. "I'll smash them into the snow."

The cautious Buckner raised an eyebrow. "I hope so."

It had snowed again the night before. Half-frozen soldiers on both sides of the lines shook themselves and tried to beat the frost out of their bones. The rebels, however, were enthusiastic about the ordered attack, while the unsuspecting Yankees were simply eager to get some warm food and coffee into their hungry stomachs. Grant, drinking coffee at the Crisp house, didn't hear the first snow-muffled sounds of a battle from McClernand's lines two miles away. And he had no idea that Pillow's men were rising like gray and white phantoms from their positions and crashing into his right.

Because it would make no sense.

The seaman was ushered into the kitchen with Foote's message. It read, "Unable to travel due to my wound. Please come to the *St. Louis* for a conference. Immediate decisions imperative." Grant scribbled on the note, "Will be along later."

Shortly, as he was leaving with Laglow, he told Rawlins, "Get messages to Smith, McClernand, and Wallace that I want no adventures until I return from seeing Foote. After I talk to the commodore, we'll see what the situation looks like and act accordingly."

CHAPTER 26

We be of one blood, you and I!
—RUDYARD KIPLING

Grant had been pleased with Foote's agreement to keep his boats on station to render whatever support he might be able to muster. Now it was a pleasure to see the well-functioning operation at the landing site. The major in charge of the unloading and distribution of supplies seemed to have things moving smoothly. Some of the regimental quartermasters were on hand, reminding him of his years as a drudge. Now he could appreciate how vital it was to those commanders to have capable officers in such jobs. For it was even more important to himself. Walking down the gangplank of one huge side-wheeler, he was startled to hear a shout from his adjutant. *"General, General Grant!"*

Grant looked up in surprise—what could bring Rawlins all the way down here on a hard-ridden horse?

Rawlins jumped down. "Sir, you've got to get back right away! The enemy smashed into McClernand shortly after you left, and things look pretty bad. His division's been thrown back with heavy casualties and it looks like the goddamn rebs are going to run him over!"

Grant turned quickly to his aide. "Get the horses, Laglow!" Impossible! Why would they hit the right—just where he had no reserves? Why would an entrenched force come out of its cover to *attack?* It simply made no sense. "Is anyone helping McClernand?"

Rawlins was already remounting. "You told the commanders to sit tight, so no one could reinforce him. General Wallace finally sent him Thayer's brigade, but I think they got lost. Things were pretty bad when I left."

Grant climbed into the saddle. "Why wasn't I notified sooner?"

"By the time McClernand found out how heavy the attack was, we thought you were on your way back. And we didn't know exactly where you were. As soon as we saw it was getting out of hand, I came looking for you."

Grant grimly urged his mount forward. Down here talking to sailors and supply people when his army was disintegrating! Doggone it! Seven miles back. A lot could happen during a seven-mile ride through rough, snow-bedeviled country. No, fourteen, counting Rawlins's ride. Keep it together, McClernand, just keep it together!

*   *   *

It was eerily quiet, except for the report of a sporadic musket.

A lull?

Why?

The acrid smell of gunpowder and its accompanying clouds of dense smoke hanging over the sullen black trees could only be a product of the folly of battle. Or the exhilaration of battle, which Grant began to sense. Was he in time? Certainly. Federal troops were milling, quiet, waiting for direction.

Riding up a slope to a small bluff, he saw both McClernand and Wallace standing next to the charred skeleton of a shattered oak. Map in hand, Grant swung down from his weary horse. Strange how the strength seemed to pour into his body, and equally strange how calm he felt. He ignored the stares, the slight stirring and the few halfhearted salutes. Gazing up into the weary black eyes of John McClernand, he said, "I understand you've had a difficult morning, General."

The former congressman's deep voice worked slowly and with an edge. "Well, I haven't been picking daisies."

"What's the situation?"

McClernand glared back. "This army needs a head."

"Seems so. Also seems it's got one. Tell me about it."

McClernand shrugged, apparently relieved to unload the pressure. "As you probably know, the rebs hit me in force about breakfast time. And I mean in force—must have been six or seven brigades. My God, how they kept coming. We held as fast as we could, giving up every yard with blood, but we were too thin, too damned thin . . ." His voice trailed off. "How heroically the boys fought. I've lost over fifteen hundred men. And God only knows how many the extra brigades have lost.

"I sent for help and sent for help, but you weren't available and your goddamn staff wouldn't make a decision. Lew, here, finally sent help, or we wouldn't even be here. Thank God I had commanders like Logan and Oglesby and . . ." His voice trailed off again. "I'm afraid they've licked us. The whole right side is open."

Grant spoke firmly, "Then it must be retaken."

"How, for God's sake?"

"Reform and refill your ammo pouches. I see box after box of ammunition lying all around us. General Wallace, get another brigade over here as soon as possible." He paused, struck by the continuing lull in firing. The enemy could be disengaging. And why not? Five hours of intensive fighting could wear out the rebs too. And hadn't someone mentioned that the wounded rebs had full haversacks—as if they might be going somewhere? Belmont had taught him one thing: *When both sides are fought out, victory is in the grasp of the man who makes the final effort.* Well, by lightning, he was going to make that effort! "Gentlemen," he added, "I think the starch has gone out of our enemy."

He sat on a rock and scribbled a note to Foote. "Get the remaining gunboats upriver for a demonstration, if nothing else, at all costs. At least fire some shells from long range, let the rebs know you're there . . ." The wording came easily. He turned to Laglow. "Get a courier on the fastest horse around and get this to the naval commander at once."

Lazily cocking one leg, he looked up at his division commanders and spoke casually. "Whoever attacks first will be victorious, and the enemy will have to be in a hurry if he gets ahead of me. Organize the counterattack. I'm going down to get Smith into their right, which should be pretty thin by now."

General C. F. Smith eased to his feet as Grant reined in. Without dismounting, Grant said, "General, we've nearly lost the right in an all-out rebel effort. I think they've massed their forces there, so your front should be lightly held. You, sir, hold this army's fate. You must take Fort Donelson."

Smith's hand unconsciously stroked the hilt of his saber. His deep voice was emotionless. "Then I'll do it." He turned to an aide. "Get the division in line with a column of regiments to attack at once." Turning back to Grant he asked, "How bad is it?"

"Nearly a rout, but they've faltered. McClernand and Wallace should be counterattacking with everything shortly. And I've asked for supporting fire from the gunboats, so if your assault is successful, get word to the navy to cease fire."

The old ramrod body seemed to grow even taller as the recipient of three brevets for bravery in Mexico looked coolly at his former cadet. "General, I told you I'd do it. Go on back to your amateur generals and don't worry about this end."

While Grant rode back to supervise the battle on his right, he missed a show that would have stirred the heart of any soldier. Smith rode his spirited mount up a small rise and drew his saber as his lead brigade quickly formed. His voice carried clearly. "Second Iowa, you must take the fort. Remove the caps from your guns, fix your bayonets, and I will support you!"

And with that, the tall, white-haired general raised his saber and spun up the slope toward the forbidding entanglements of felled trees and Confederate trenches. Immediately the Second Iowa surged forward, knowing that their cold steel would somehow overcome enemy bullets. There would be no faltering, no indecision. Old Smithy, in his flowing white mustaches would see to that!

And see to it, he did. Smith seemed to be everywhere—swinging that flashing sword, swearing, cajoling. Many heard him shout at one lagging element, "Damn you, gentlemen, I see skulkers! I'll have none here. Come on, you damned Volunteers, come on. You volunteered to be killed for love of country and now's your chance. *Move your asses and be heroes!*"

Grant had been right; Smith's front was lightly held. But even a small force such as Buckner had left there could be effective behind such fortifications—particularly with shotguns at bayonet range. The sheer drive of Smith's thrust, however, provided the deciding factor. The general was the first through the enemy trenches, almost asking to end his magnificent career in the utmost of glory. Yet, miraculously, he remained untouched as his inspired troops swept on to the edge of the fort, where enemy artillery fire finally stopped the assault. But he had rolled up the enemy right.

In a war punctuated by heroic leadership, Smith's Donelson attack would live in history as one of its most spectacular.

The general called his commanders together. "Well done, gentlemen. We've breached their lines and gotten their attention. A major attack is going on to our right, made possible by your valiant efforts. We'll dig in here and finish the job in the morning. Tend to your wounded and convey my heartfelt thanks."

Grant sat quietly on his horse, watching the sea of blue uniforms advance. Reports from his two division commanders confirmed that the enemy's will to fight was gone. Nearly all of the ground lost that day had been regained. Grant looked toward his thoughtful adjutant. "Well, Rawlins, you don't make money getting back what you started with, but I think we've won a great battle today. Demoralized men have found themselves and regained their dignity. A day or two more should do it, but the victory came today. Put out the order that campfires will be permitted tonight. Our warm men can flaunt their confidence right in front of the enemy. And we can all thank God for our deliverance."

John Rawlins nodded, looking into the quiet blue eyes. Before this day, he'd been an admirer; henceforth he'd be a disciple. For this man, this simple farmer from Ohio was certainly a savior—possibly the savior of the Union. He *knew* it. He softly said, "And thank God for a general like you."

That night, as Grant finished a letter to Julia, three Confederate brigadier generals—Bushrod Johnson wasn't even included—sat in a final council of war in the Rice house that served as Pillow's headquarters. They were tired officers, who had in one day fought a battle and won, only to fight another and lose. This terrible fact weighed on them most. Victory had been in their grasp, and then Pillow—who had been in command of the attack— had made the unfortunate decision to continue the fight, instead of sticking to the original plan of simply opening the road south for the breakout.

So, instead of escaping, the weary Confederate force had faltered and had been thrown back by a vicious Union counterattack and was now watching Federal campfires blazing away as if that damned Grant owned the place. Pillow swore it was his bad luck.

Floyd didn't know what had happened. Buckner knew, remembering Mexico; and he also knew what that old fanatic, Smith, had done to what had remained of his division on the Federal left. Sitting in a dimly lit corner, the brilliant, still-seething Nathan Bedford Forrest knew; his dismounted cavalry had spearheaded the original victory that morning. Colonel Forrest, a wealthy, powerful, six-foot-two Tennessean with a commanding presence, had had no formal military training or experience, but was already showing a winning feel for battle.

"So then it's agreed," General Floyd said, "We cannot sacrifice this number of men, not in any sense of clear conscience. Sidney Johnston has moved back to Nashville, so reinforcement from that quarter is hopeless. It's better for these lads to be in a Northern prison, where they might later be exchanged. But *I'm* not going to do it."

"You're the commander," Buckner said.

"Yes, but you know about that indictment," the former U.S. secretary of war said. "Out of pure spite, they might just shoot me. No, I'm going to take my brigade out, or at least as much of it as I can. We still have some transports close by."

Buckner contemptuously threw his cigar in the fireplace. "All right, give me command and I'll surrender the garrison. Grant will treat me with honor."

"Will you give me time to get out?"

Buckner's tone was bitter. "You'd better move fast. But let's get things straight. General Pillow ranks me."

Floyd turned to Pillow. "I turn over the command, sir."

Pillow shook his head. "No, I'm leaving too. The Confederacy needs my experience in other campaigns. I pass."

"All right, then it's settled," Buckner said gravely. "I assume command."

"Just a goddamned minute!" Forrest came out of the shadow. "I'm not turning my cavalry over to any damn Yankees. That flooded road's still open to the south. I'll lead them out, and anyone else who can mount a horse and wants to come along. I'm a long way from finished with this war!"

Buckner nodded. "As you wish, Bedford." He turned to an aide. "Get me pen, ink, and paper. And send for a bugler."

Shortly after three in the morning, General Smith kicked the snow off his boots in the kitchen of the Crisp house. Grant shook off the sleep as his division commander said, "I have something for you to read, General. Just got it from a rebel flag-of-truce officer."

Grant pulled on his pants, then held the letter up to the light of a kerosene lamp. It read, "Sir: In consideration of all the circumstances governing the present situation of affairs at this station, I propose to the Commanding Officer of the Federal forces the appointment of Commissioners to agree upon terms of capitulation of the forces and fort under my command, and in that view suggest an armistice until twelve o'clock today." It was signed "S. B. Buckner, Brigadier General, C.S.A."

Grant stared solemnly at the note for a moment, then smiled at Smith and his staff members who'd awakened. "Gentlemen," he said softly, "Donelson is ours."

When the cheers subsided, Grant handed the letter to Smith, asking, "What answer should I give him, General?"

"No terms whatsoever!" Smith barked in reply.

Grant sighed as he picked up a pen. He'd seen what commissioners had done to an honorable victory in Mexico. But this was his old friend, Buckner, asking to be treated gently. He certainly owed the man, but this was war and neither personal friendships nor debts could affect a commander's decisions. He began to write. As soon as he finished, he stood and read, "Sir: Yours of this date proposing Armistice and appointment of Commissioners to settle terms of Capitulation is just received. No terms except unconditional and immediate surrender can be accepted. I propose to move immediately upon your works. I am, sir, very respectfully, your obedient servant."

Smith smiled his approval as the rest again cheered. What was to become one of the most famous dispatches in American military history had just been penned.

Grant chose the Dover Inn as his new headquarters, meeting Buckner and several of the Confederate colonels there for a cornbread breakfast. His old friend was angry over the terms. "I really think you could have been more considerate, General," he said stiffly as a waiter brought coffee. "After all, we have known each other a long time."

Grant's voice was low, his eyes troubled. "I'm sorry, my friend, but I had no other choice. This isn't Mexico or some European battlefield. The Union has been threatened by insurrection, and it must be crushed. I well remember what you did for me in my time of need, but you have chosen the wrong path, and I can't give in to private wishes."

"I consider my path the honorable one, sir!" Buckner retorted.

Grant shrugged. "Your Confederate scrip won't be any good in a Federal prisoner of war camp. All I can do is offer you some money."

Buckner jerked up from the table. "You can take your money to hell!" He stormed away.

Grant watched sadly. After a moment, he turned to Rawlins. "Any news of Bushrod Johnson, the other general?"

The adjutant shook his head. "No, sir. He probably got away with the others."

"What's the tally?"

Rawlins raised an eyebrow. "Near's I can guess, nearly fifteen thousand prisoners, twenty stands of arms, forty-eight pieces of artillery, seventeen heavy guns, over three thousand horses, and a large quantity of commissary stores. Do you know, this is probably the most successful bag of prisoners an American army has ever taken?"

Grant smiled briefly.

He knew.

CHAPTER 27

M any others knew, as well.
      Grant's name burst across the Union sky like a brilliant new star. Starving for a resounding Federal victory and for a major hero, the people of the North rejoiced. A general who had come from obscurity had given both to them. The press jumped on "Unconditional Surrender Grant," shouting the great news from massive headlines, making it a household name overnight.

Every schoolmarm in the country wrote *Donelson* on her blackboard.

When the word reached St. Louis, General Halleck was elated. This was his chance! He'd invite Buell down to take over the Cumberland, Sherman would have the District of Cairo, while Grant—the temporary hero—would be given the new District of West Tennessee, an undefinable region that would allow him to keep the sloppy officer under whatever wraps he might choose. Grant was nothing more than an upstart, but he was so much in favor in Washington that he'd have to recommend him for promotion. But he'd stick in two other names. Carefully, he penned the message to McClellan—"Make Buell, Grant and Pope major generals of Volunteers and give me command in the West. I ask this for Forts Henry and Donelson."

To the request for extended command, McClellan turned a cold shoulder. But the young general in chief rushed to the White House with the recommendation for three promotions. This was Buell's chance. And Grant had given him his first major victory since his ascension to head of the army, so why not? What was another two-star in the vast sea of general officers?

Lincoln rubbed his chin whiskers as the imperious general added his verbal endorsement. His decision wouldn't be difficult. In a way it was political, but then, so was everything else. It was also a reward, and a heartfelt expression of gratitude from a personal standpoint. He'd finally, by damn, found a general who could fight! As soon as McClellan left, he wrote a short note to be delivered to the senior senator from Illinois. "I wish to appoint Ulysses S. Grant major general of Volunteers with a date of rank of February 16th. Since the Senate is equally proud of his achievements in Tennessee, please see if you can forgo the usual committee holdup and approve him immediately."

*   *   *

In the meantime, the telegraph line to Fort Henry from Dover had been completed. But amidst the bustle, the arrival among the telegraphers of skinny, quiet Cyril Albertson went unnoticed. As soon as he had heard that the line would be Grant's major relay point, he had guessed Fort Henry would be his truly golden opportunity to help the glorious South.

With the disposal of prisoners and matériel continuing at Donelson, Grant sized up the situation and decided that Johnston was falling back all along the line. Kentucky was out of the question for the rebs, and now the same could be true of western Tennessee. With Buell finally unsticking himself and moving south, a perfect chance had arisen to strike the enemy at Nashville. In a supporting or primary role, he could move his strong, well-equipped army and smash into the Confederates there. In addition to a recommendation for promotion for General Smith, he sent a telegram to Halleck: "I have sent General C. F. Smith and his division to Clarksville to stand ready for a new thrust at the enemy. Request permission to move on Nashville as soon as possible."

Grant was conferring with Colonel Webster in his office in the Dover Inn when Rawlins walked in carrying a box of cigars and wearing a big smile. "General," he said, "these cigars just arrived, along with dozens of other boxes. Seems a picture of you with a stogie in your hand has hit the papers all over the country. Looks like every Tom, Dick, and Harry will be sending them to you."

Grant picked one out of the box, smelling it. "Hmm, it looks like I can retire my pipe for a while, doesn't it?"

Rawlins was still grinning. "I think you'd better light it, sir. You have something to celebrate."

"Oh, what's that?"

Rawlins pulled a set of major general's shoulder boards from his pocket. "The word just came in that you are out of uniform."

When further word arrived of the change in command of the District of Cairo and the establishment of the new district, Grant wrote a congratulatory note to Sherman, ending it with, "I hope we can soon serve together, my friend. I can't imagine one of your capability being kept under wraps when battles are yet to be won."

An hour later, he sent a telegram to Halleck through the Fort Henry relay:

> *I have a report from two spies from the Eighth Missouri who have just returned from Memphis. The long-anticipated Gen. Beauregard has been sick in Decatur. He recently proceeded to Columbus where he will supervise the abandonment of that fortress. Apparently the enemy will retire downriver to a new line of defense. 12,000 rebel soldiers are reported at Mem-*

phis. General Buell has ordered General Smith to take his division to Nashville. Although Smith is under my command, I found no need to countermand the order, but I feel I should go to Nashville to see what is transpiring there. I shall go there should you not order me otherwise within twenty-four hours.

Arriving in Nashville early on the morning of the 27th, Grant found his estimate to be correct. As soon as the transports bearing Union troops had appeared on the Cumberland, the city had emptied of the remaining Confederate troops. Only a rearguard element was close. And they were merely looking for a chance to salvage something from the vast stores of military equipment and foodstuffs stockpiled in the city. But even this activity had ceased when the Union transports steamed in.

Since Buell had not arrived, Grant rode around the city, storing up information in the event he should have to fight there someday. He stopped at the home of former president James Polk to pay his respects to his redoubtable widow. Although she received him and his staff cordially enough, she coolly made it clear that she was a Southerner through and through. Understanding her dismay, Grant thanked her and ended the visit quickly.

At five o'clock, he penned a short note to Buell, telling the general that he could wait no longer. When he arrived at the wharf where his gunboat was tied up, he found that Brigadier General Don Carlos Buell had just gotten there. From the Class of '41, Buell was robust, had a hawklike appearance with piercing, close-set eyes, a beak of a nose, and a salt-and-pepper beard. He wasn't noted for pleasantries. Although Grant had known him at West Point, Buell's tone was particularly cool. "Well, General, I'm glad I caught up with you. There are several things we should discuss," he said curtly.

Grant shook his hand. The last time they'd seen each other had been in St. Louis. Buell had been a captain, and he had been hauling wood and wearing a faded army overcoat. The captain's tone had been a mix of sympathy and condescension. "Yes, General," he replied, "we do have a few things to talk about."

"May we do so alone?"

"Certainly. Do you want to go for a stroll?"

"Suits me."

As they moved away from their subordinates, Grant said, "General Smith should be in with over two thousand troops within the next two hours. I would like to have him back in a few days. I'll probably have use for him shortly."

"But you're remaining at Fort Henry, according to Halleck, and the situation here is tenuous, perhaps dangerous, with my limited strength."

Grant spoke quietly. "Nonsense. I've been riding leisurely about town all day. Even had a quick cup of tea with Mrs. Polk. Nashville is an open city."

Out of earshot from everyone, Buell's voice rose. "Don't tell me it's nonsense! Fighting is going on just a few miles away."

"Rearguard action by Forrest. The main body of Confederates are scooting for the state line as fast as they can move."

"But I tell you an enemy attack is imminent!"

Grant stopped, turning to his former senior. "General, Nashville is yours, not mine. If you wish to keep your troops over there across the Cumberland watching shadows, that's your business. But you're not keeping mine. I'll expect Smith back at Clarksville shortly."

Buell glared. "I don't think General McClellan will like your attitude."

"Possibly not. But then—" Grant smiled—"sometimes *I* don't like my attitude." He reached inside his coat. "Here, have a cigar."

In the meantime, Cyril Albertson was busy destroying more and more messages. Halleck, uninformed about Grant's or Smith's whereabouts, reported to McClellan that he would sit tight until further information about enemy dispositions could be obtained. Further, that he'd ordered Grant to move the bulk of his forces to the vicinity of Danville, some thirty-five miles down the river from Fort Henry, in readiness for an operation on the Tennessee River.

On March 1, when he heard that Smith was in Nashville, his courtroom polish blistered. Glaring at his aide, he exploded. "What the hell's going on down there? Can't those bastards follow orders? And now McClellan's demanding strength reports. Hell, I don't know what Grant's got! I haven't received a strength report from that prima donna in two weeks!"

Just then, a staff officer entered, handing the general a note from Buell that mentioned his meeting with Grant in Nashville. Halleck stared at the message, then rolled it into a ball and threw it against the wall. "Goddamn it, he's supposed to be at Fort Henry running his own command!"

Old Brains went back to his desk and began to scribble a message to McClellan. "I've had no communication with General Grant for more than a week. He left his command without authority and went to Nashville. It is hard to censure a successful general immediately after a victory, but I think he richly deserves it. I can get no returns, no reports, no information of any kind from him. I am worn out and tired with his neglect and inefficiency. C. F. Smith is almost the only officer equal to the emergency."

But Little Mac, in the midst of his own troubles, had scant time for squabbling generals in the West. He fired back a quick reply: "Generals must observe discipline as well as privates. Do not hesitate to arrest him at once if the good of the service requires it, and place C. F. Smith in command."

By the time Halleck received this answer, he'd cooled down a bit—deciding that the arrest of a popular general could be a sticky wicket. He'd better have something more on Grant, and decided to cut him down another way. He sent another message to the general in chief: "A rumor has reached me that since the taking of Fort Donelson, General Grant has resumed his former bad habits. If so, it will account for his neglect of my orders. I do not deem it advisable to arrest him at the present, but have placed General Smith in command of the expedition up the Tennessee."

And to Grant he telegraphed: "You will place General Smith in command of expedition and remain yourself at Fort Henry. Why do you not obey my orders to report strength and positions of your command?"

Of course, even the most treacherous telegrapher could not intercept all messages, so this one got through. When Grant received the testy message, it was his first inkling that something was amiss in St. Louis. What was wrong? No reports on strengths and positions? Such was reported daily! Surely they were going through Cairo by wire. Smith in command? Why, suddenly?

What was wrong?

He notified Smith and sent Halleck a message confirming the change, along with a statement that he had been forwarding the required reports continually.

On the 6th of March, Rawlins came into his office seething. His face was white, and he had trouble controlling his voice. He read the latest message from Halleck: "Your neglect in forwarding reports has seriously interfered with military plans. Your going to Nashville without authority, when your presence with your troops was of the utmost importance, was a matter of serious complaint in Washington, so much so that I was advised to arrest you on your return."

It was Grant's turn to flush as he read the message. *Arrest?* What was going on? He felt sudden hurt and anger.

"This nonsense about Washington has to be Halleck's doing," Rawlins ground out. "What else? And *arrest?* My God, you're the biggest hero in the country!"

Grant felt the heat on his face as he reread the unbelievable words. Something Sherman had written to him came back: "A political personality or the devil can live down slander, but not a military man."

"I'm going to notify Washburne right away," Rawlins said.

Grant moved to his desk, barely hearing. His defense was simple—the truth. The words tumbled from his pen as he again explained everything, ending with, "I have done my very best to obey orders and carry out the best interests of the service. If my course is not satisfactory, remove me at once."

Grant sat in his tent staring at the bottle of whiskey he'd had his orderly bring. He'd been without a drink for a very long time, in spite of all the accusations. But the tales didn't matter because they were untrue. He hadn't touched spirits since that winter night in the tavern back at Hardscrabble.

But this was different. His honor had been stained.

He couldn't remember when he'd felt so dejected. A drink or two wouldn't hurt, and maybe he'd feel a little better. He couldn't even write to Julia and tell her what Halleck was accusing him of. He opened the bottle and stared at it.

Arrest!

He tipped the bottle back and took a long drink, the whiskey burning as it went down his throat. He drew in a deep breath, held it a few moments, and blew it out. He could resign. Or maybe request a court of inquiry. But it would all be so sordid. He hated to think of the whole country reading a headline like GRANT GETS COURT OF INQUIRY FOR DISOBEDIENCE. It would all be so terrible on Julia and the kids.

His mother.

His father.

Julia.

He nodded his head. Yes, he could resign, maybe that was best—

A slightly familiar voice broke his thought. "You got a minute, General?"

He looked up to see a redheaded man outlined in the tent entrance. He was wearing the star of a brigadier on his shoulders and a broad smile on his face. "I got tired of being a goddamned paper shuffler and decided to come down and see you. Rawlins just told me about your little misunderstanding with Old Brains."

Ordinarily he'd be delighted to see Sherman after all these years, but right now he was ashamed to do so under these conditions. Rawlins didn't have any business telling the man—

"Aren't you going to invite me in?"

"Uh, yes, come in. There's a stool over there." He put the bottle down on his camp desk.

Sherman looked at it pointedly. "When did you start that?"

"Just now."

"Think it'll help?"

"Can't hurt."

"Yes, it can. When I was having all those troubles up in Louisville— you know, when I was fighting with the damned press and the rest of the world—well, I drank my share every night, and you know what? It didn't help a goddamned bit. In fact, I know it increased my problems."

"You want some?"

"No, but I'll take one of those cigars you're getting famous for."

Grant pulled out a cigar and held a match to it for his friend. Looking back at the whiskey bottle, he suddenly thought of Julia. Sherman was right—it really wouldn't help. He quietly replaced the cork and handed it to his visitor. "Here, call it a reunion gift."

"Thanks." The other Ohioan took the bottle and blew out a big cloud of blue smoke. "I'll save it for a special occasion."

"I'm thinking about resigning," Grant said directly.

Sherman snorted. "Why? You're the most popular hero in the whole damned Union. Don't let Halleck get you down. He's a vain man and probably a little jealous of you."

"Why? I gave him a big victory."

"You have to know how devious he can be. It'll blow over. You know, I came awful close to resigning myself back there during those dark days in Ohio. And this is nothing that serious. Everyone in the country doesn't think *you're* crazy!"

Grant watched him a few moments. Putting it that way, he was probably right.

Sherman leaned forward. "We've got a war to win, Sam. And it's going to take fighters like you and me to do it. Maybe we have to be tested in some bad way like this before we can get there—I don't know. Someone once told me some people have to go *through* to get where they're going; there's no way around."

Grant just shook his head.

Sherman's eyes never left him. "I'm just sure of one thing, you can't be spared."

Two developments caused Henry Halleck to back off. The first was a message from the adjutant general—which had been prompted by Lincoln—to be specific in his accusations and innuendos about Grant. The order had been directed by the secretary of war. Lawyer that he was, Old Brains knew that he had to put up or shut up, and he simply didn't have a case.

Secondly, Grant no longer was a threat—Halleck had just received word that he had what he wanted—complete control in the West! His command ran all the way to a north/south line that ran through Knoxville. He was elated. He sent a telegram immediately to Grant.

Grant, who had followed Sherman's advice and had cooled his heels, read it with a sense of relief: "You cannot be relieved from your command. There is no good reason for it. The power is in your hands; use it and you will be sustained by all above you. Instead of relieving you, I wish you, as soon as your new army is in the field, to assume command and lead it on to new victories."

Grant shook his head. He couldn't understand the whole thing.

Standing beside his desk, Colonel Webster said, "He's a strange man, General."

Rawlins strode in, waving a message. "Just got this from Washburne! Lincoln has fired McClellan! The little bastard will still command the Army of the Potomac, but he'll be out of our hair."

Grant looked up in disbelief. "Who's the new general in chief?"

"The president himself. And it's about time. He certainly can't do any worse."

Grant shook his head, imagining the problems. Lincoln had recently lost a son and it was rumored that his wife was mad. "He already has his hands full."

"They're supposed to be big hands. Oh, and one final bit of news. Halleck is now in command of the new Department of the Mississippi. What do you think of that?"

"Makes sense to me. I guess I'd better accept his peace offering for what it's worth."

But the wound still hurt.

CHAPTER 28

The peach trees near Shiloh meetinghouse
were in pink blossom,
the clear streams ran down the ravines
to the flooded river,
and between Snake Creek and Lick Creek
the high ground was waiting
to absorb the blood that would flow so soon.
— CAPTAIN C. L. SUMBARDO

How in the living hell a grown-up man like me could fall getting into a boat, I don't know." Major General C.F. Smith bristled as he told Grant about his accident. "Jumping into this stupid yawl, I raked my right leg, shin and calf both, on a damned seat. Now it's infected and I'm laid up just when I should be out there chasing rebs."

Grant and he were talking in a large bedroom of the fine old mansion Smith had taken over for his headquarters in the village of Savannah, near a bend in the Tennessee some thirty miles northeast of Corinth. The latter place was a hamlet at the intersection of two important railroads, where it was believed a large Confederate force was being assembled by Albert Sidney Johnston. Grant was eager to attack Corinth, as was Smith, but Halleck had them under tight rein.

"We should've gone right after them following Donelson," Smith growled. "Their entire forces were split. But no, we sat on our asses just like we are now. Halleck hasn't got any more balls than McClellan back East. We're just chafing like hounds on the leash."

Grant was chafing just as much as the gallant old soldier sitting up in the bed. "I was ordered to fortify and wait on orders," he said.

"Fortify!" Smith snorted. "If the damned enemy will just come out and attack us, we can whip them to hell. If we begin to spade, it will make our soldiers think we fear the enemy!"

"I agree," Grant replied. "Soldiers who dig holes lose their will to fight!"

Pittsburg Landing, on the west side of the Tennessee, was a shelf of land below a hundred-foot yellow mud cliff where cargoes had long been unloaded for Corinth. Above it was a plain gutted by shallow ravines and light timber. Dotted by cleared farmlands of grain and fruit orchards, it was flanked by the Snake and Lick creeks, and constituted a square roughly four miles to a side. Five of Grant's divisions were camped there. Cump Sherman, still a brigadier, commanded the largest, a four-brigade collection of green troops that he was feverishly trying to train. Brigadier General Prentiss and his two-brigade division were on line with Sherman, with McClernand—now a major general—just behind with his three brigades. Hurlbut and W. H. L. Wallace, with their three-brigade commands, were closer to the landing, while Lew Wallace, also a new two-star, had his division five miles north, across Snake Creek at Crump's Landing. Sherman was head-quartered on the right flank next to a Methodist log structure called Shiloh Church.

Grant's army was more than forty-two thousand strong.

And two roads led to Corinth.

The plain was a good staging area where the regiments could comfortably drill while everyone waited for Buell to bring down his army of an additional thirty thousand men. Then Halleck would cut loose his aggressive leaders. Waiting until vast numerical superiority was attained seemed to be a common command disease among the senior Union leaders at this point of the war, and Grant pondered its reason as he waited. He knew without being in on rebel councils that the seven weeks since Fort Donelson had given the enemy a chance to save the West, but he didn't believe they could—not in the long run.

Not unless something totally unaccountable happened.

He barely considered that those two roads also led *from* Corinth.

At eleven P.M. on Wednesday, April 2, General Albert Sidney Johnston sat gazing at the dying ashes in the fireplace of his bedroom in Corinth. Tall and handsome, the fifty-nine-year-old Texan wasn't happy about his long retreat from Bowling Green, but he wasn't one to dwell on failure. The Army of the Mississippi that he had assembled here was the largest force the Confederacy had yet pulled together, and if Van Dorn could arrive with his Elkhorn Tavern veterans, the command would swell by another fifteen thousand men. Right now, with over forty thousand troops, he thought his strength was equal to that of Grant up at Pittsburg Landing.

Grant had done well at Donelson for a green general, and he had Smith—who had served as his own executive officer in the Mormon campaign shortly before the war. God knows that man could fight, but a spy had reported that he was sick. The rest of Grant's division commanders, except for Sherman—who had seen no real battle in the Mexican War and was considered unstable—were civilians.

His Southern generals, on the other hand, were consummate professionals. As second in command, he had the brilliant P. G. T. Beauregard, hero of First Manassas. Then came his corps commanders: his First Corps was commanded by Leonidas Polk, the Bishop and his onetime roommate at West Point; for his Second Corps he had Braxton Bragg, the tempestuous North Carolinian who'd been such a hero in Mexico; and commanding his Third Corps was the Class of '38 graduate, Dragoon William Hardee, the tactics expert who had been commandant of cadets at West Point before the war. And lastly, he had John Breckinridge, former vice president of the

United States and the only nonprofessional. Commander of the Reserve, the Kentuckian was considered very capable.

And he had some fine brigadiers.

God, he had generals!

It was the lack of training of many of his soldiers that bothered him. Still—

The knock on the door was demanding.

Answering it, he found Colonel Thomas Jordan, Beauregard's adjutant and a onetime roommate of Sherman at West Point. "Sorry to bother you so late, sir," Jordan said, holding out a telegram."But I have some interesting information."

"Come in, Tom."

Johnston held the message up to the lamp. It was from a spy and described the movements of General Lew Wallace, up near Bethel. The spy thought Wallace was going to move on Memphis. The handwriting at the bottom was Beauregard's: "Now is the time to advance on Pittsburg Landing."

The Texan raised his eyebrows. "What do you think?"

"Sir, Wallace is well away from Grant at this time. That's a whole division."

Johnston stroked his mustache. It was tempting. Surprise and numerical advantage. Ought to get another opinion, though. In addition to commanding his corps, Major General Braxton Bragg was doubling as the army chief of staff. "C'mon, let's go across the street and see what Bragg has to say," the Texan replied.

The artilleryman was reading in his long underwear when his commander knocked. "C'mon in, General," he said, opening the door. "Want a drink?" He nodded toward Jordan. "What'd you do, steal an adjutant?"

"I'll pass on the drink," Johnston replied. "I want your opinion on whether we should attack on the basis of this." He handed Bragg the telegram.

Bragg scanned the message. Without hesitation, he said, "Hell, yes."

"The risks could be high."

"They always are. If we wait much longer, Buell will be here. Let's hit 'em while they're sitting on their ass!"

"But Wallace can get back in short order."

"If we surprise them, he'll be too late. First we smash Grant, then Buell will be easy."

Johnston went to Bragg's fireplace and stared into it.

Colonel Jordan said, "They haven't entrenched, according to a report we received today."

Bragg walked over to his chief. "Let's kick 'em in the ass, Sidney."

The Texan continued to stare, frowning. After a moment he turned to Jordan. "Did Beauregard have any ideas as to how?"

The colonel grinned. "Sir, I can have a plan ready in a hour. I just happen to know one that Napoleon used in a similar situation—the best concept for a three-corps attack. It can't miss!"

Johnston turned back to the fire for several moments, then started for the door. "Draft it, Tom—and, Braxton, get the commanders together for a conference over breakfast."

Three nights later and thirty miles to the north, Grant was soaking his badly wrenched ankle in a pail of hot water. He was restless, feeling an uneasiness he couldn't pin down. Maybe it was his silly accident. Imagine, a rider like him getting caught under his falling horse! Well, it had been raining awful hard and had been very dark. He'd just written to Julia and repeated what he'd sent to Halleck that day—that he didn't think the rebs were ready for any kind of an attack. But word had since arrived that Johnston was stronger than he had thought, which made him pay more attention to the reports of nearby rebs and minor enemy contact over the past thirty hours.

Could they possibly be coming up from Corinth for a full-scale attack?

Even if this were so, his divisions were in position and alert. He knew Sherman was vigilant, and even he had called the idea of a major rebel attack nonsense.

Johnston had to know about Buell coming—everyone did.

Unless the great old general had a hundred thousand men, he couldn't attack. No, it was out of the question.

Nelson's division from Buell's army had arrived and Grant had told the brigadier he could move his troops down to Pittsburg Landing by boat in a couple of days. He wondered if Buell would be troublesome about it. Buell himself should be in with his column before long.

Fortunately, he had the brilliant McPherson on hand as a trouble-shooter.

Still, he felt restless.

He lifted his foot out of the pail and reached for a crutch. Smith down with that infection, and doggone it, now this!

"You can march to a decisive victory over agrarian mercenaries, sent to subjugate and despoil you of your liberties, property, and honor . . . The eyes and hopes of eight millions of people rest upon you." These were some of the words of Sidney Johnston's message to the troops of his Army of the Mississippi before they marched off toward the enemy. They merely bolstered the widely held opinion of the average Southern soldier that he could "lick three Yankees without half trying." Now, as daybreak arrived on Sunday, April 6, the boys in soggy gray were poised to attack the Union host. Prepared to smash into Sherman and Prentiss was the Confederate juggernaut of three corps, with Hardee in the advance. But Johnston's prized element of total surprise was not to be achieved on this fateful day.

Although there had been confusion in the placement of his army, and Van Dorn had not arrived, plus the fact that Beauregard had decided that Buell was already in the vicinity, General Albert Sidney Johnston of Texas made his decision. "I would fight them if they were a million," he said firmly.

But strangely, it would not be the Confederates who would start the great battle that would forever be known as Shiloh. The commander of Prentiss's First Brigade awoke in a cold sweat at two-thirty on the morning of April 6. In a vivid dream, he had been surrounded by rebel soldiers, wounded, and finally killed by a bayonet lunge. He summoned his field officer of the day and ordered him to take three infantry companies on a reconnaissance down the Corinth Road.

The major left shortly with his large patrol. Just before sunrise he encountered Confederate pickets from the Third Mississippi Infantry Battalion and chased them back to their main body. Following a short pitched battle, the Union patrol pulled back to the lines of the Twenty-fifth Missouri, the regiment that would soon hold off an entire rebel brigade while Prentiss was being informed.

As the pink spring dawn spread over Sherman's green troops, their redheaded general listened to the wake-up call of a clear bugle echoing through the wet morning air. For some unknown reason he felt a sense of nervous urgency as he sipped from his steaming metal coffee mug. It was something like what he'd known at Manassas. Probably that dull "pop-popping" of nervous pickets over in Prentiss's sector, he thought. What the hell were they doing shooting so much this early?

Just then a courier rode into his headquarters camp. "Sir!" the wild-eyed young lieutenant shouted. "Prentiss is being attacked in force by a flood of graycoats!"

Sherman jumped to his feet. "Where?"

"All along his front!"

"My God!" Sherman replied, his mind racing. He had probed five miles down the muddy Corinth Road the night before and there had been nothing. Where in hell had they come from?

At that moment the first rebel artillery shell crashed into his nearby front. It was instantly followed by several more, and the close-in blast of shotguns and muskets told him the worst. "Get my horse!" he shouted to his orderly.

Grant hobbled into the dining room of the mansion in Savannah. Resting the hated crutches against the wall, he looked once more at his swollen ankle and growled, "Doggone it!" He took the proffered cup of coffee from the orderly and asked Rawlins, who was sorting mail, "Anything interesting?"

"Don't know, General, I haven't opened anything. Here's a letter from your wife."

"Oh, good. Are you ready to move the headquarters down to Pittsburg today?"

"Yes sir. Soon as you leave to meet General Buell."

Buell had arrived the night before.

Grant sipped the coffee as he opened the letter from Julia. She and the kids were still in Covington. "My dearest Ulys, I hope you are well and that General Smith is better too. I—"

"Did you hear that?" Grant asked, lowering the letter as he listened to the faint sounds of what could be cannon fire from the south. A sudden silence in the room made the sounds more distinct and confirmed his suspicions.

At that moment, Captain Hillyer, another member of Grant's staff, burst into the room from outside. "Sir!" he exclaimed. "It sounds like a hundred guns are being fired down by Pittsburg Landing!"

In spite of everything, Johnston must have made his move! Grant hauled himself to his feet, reaching for his crutches. "Gentlemen," he said, "the ball is in motion. Let's be off." He scribbled two hasty notes, one to General Nelson ordering him to proceed with his division down the left bank of the river to a point opposite the Landing. He explained this order in the second message, which was to Buell.

His command steamboat, the *Tigress,* was standing by with steam up. As soon as Grant and his staff, horses and all, were aboard, the craft was ploughing at full speed upriver, since the Tennessee flowed north. Crump's Landing on the west bank came into view directly. As the steamer slowed and swung into the wharf, Grant saw Lew Wallace, currently the youngest major general in the army, waiting on the jetty. Not wasting any time, Grant shouted from the rail, "General, get your troops under arms and have them ready to move at a moment's notice."

"I've already done so!" Wallace yelled back.

By now the sounds of cannon fire and musketry were coming in more clearly, and Grant wondered how bad it could be. As the *Tigress* headed back into the mainstream, a small steamer, the *Warner,* churned to a halt beside her. A captain stood at the rail with his hands cupped at his mouth. "Tell General Grant the rebs have attacked in full force from the southwest. But we don't know the full strength of the enemy because the battlefield is such a shambles. This message is from Colonel McPherson."

Grant nodded and Rawlins shouted, "We understand!"

Grant's mind raced on in the myriad thoughts of an army commander who has been gravely struck by a serious and capable opponent. Morale? Ammunition? Leadership? Cooperation? Why did Smith have to be laid up? What if he lost Sherman? Could he trust McClernand? Prentiss worried him too. He felt the tense pressure as he nibbled on an apple, possibly the last food he'd taste for some time.

As soon as the gangplank dropped at Pittsburg Landing, Grant urged his horse down to the muddy bank. His staff was right behind him. The landing certainly was a shambles! Steamers, jammed into the wharf area, were disgorging supplies that were piling up like random goods at a noisy rummage sale. Interrupting this activity were seemingly hundreds of blue-coated deserters who were teeming around in various stages of bewilderment.

Many were wild-eyed, but most wore the dull, vacant stare of men who had failed the first major test of their lives. How far had these men run in their panic—all the way from the front to the safety of the landing? His first instinct was anger, but he pushed it aside. He wondered if these stragglers should be reorganized and sent back. But he quickly decided it would be useless; they might fight well another day, but now they were useless.

They had "seen the elephant" and he had crushed them.

He pushed his horse up the sticky saffron bank. More young men in blue were straggling, weaponless, toward him. Others, loosely in ranks, appeared to be new. Confusion ruled. He rode up to a higher point and looked southwest through his glasses. The din of battle carried clearly, even though it was two miles away. Artillery fire was so steady it barely allowed the smaller arms their insistent, chattering voice. A great pall of gray-black smoke had worked its way up through the distant trees, only to level out, flat-topped like an anvil, where the innocent morning breeze had assumed command.

The center of Sherman's rear—if there was a rear—was a tangle of frenzied activity. Wounded, dazed soldiers were everywhere. Muddy blue uniforms were moving forward and back through the busy area in a maze of apparent confusion. Yet, somehow, there seemed to be a semblance of order. Grant thankfully sensed no panic.

The midmorning sun, fighting its way through the smoky haze and freshly budding trees, provided an eerie glow of unreality. It was as if the world had turned to a murky sepia, saturating everything into an overexposed photograph. The noise, however, was real. The thunder of Sherman's nearby guns, the sharp popping of musketry just a few hundred yards away, and the crash of incoming artillery dealt an urgent sense of awful truth.

The acrid smell of gunpowder filled the air; crimson blood stained the walking wounded. Cries of other men with torn and mutilated bodies harmonized with the shouts of just plain angry men, or orders and warning, of young soldiers simply making noise to bolster their confidence and shield their fearful truths. Rebel yells pierced the din; wounded horses screamed. It was all familiar to Grant as he quietly sat his horse.

Sherman rode up, casually saluting with a bandaged hand. His face was grimy and his bloodstained uniform was torn. "Thought you'd be here pretty soon," he said.

"What happened to your hand?" Grant asked.

"Just a scratch. Got it when they shot my first horse out from under me."

"How many times has that happened?"

"Three." Sherman's busy eyes swept his command post, then returned to Grant. "I've had a busy morning."

"So I've heard. Tell me about it."

Sherman's usually nervous hands were quiet as he said, "We got hit by about a corps at dawn. I lost two Ohio regiments right off. Their goddamned colonels took off like scared rabbits after a few volleys. Naturally, their men, except for a couple of companies with gumption, ran right behind them. And the colonel of another regiment was drunk, so its efforts were wasted initially. But we filled the holes as best we could. McClernand moved down to support my left. Have you seen him?"

"Not yet. I'm going over there next. Buell's divisions are on their way, and Wallace should be here within two hours. What do you need besides about ten crack regiments?"

Sherman's horse jerked up as an artillery round burst nearby. "Send me a good aide," he replied. "Mine got killed within three feet of me. No, Sam, all I need is enough ammunition to keep fighting."

"I'll keep it coming." Grant looked into the steady gaze of his friend's brown eyes and felt a wave of trust he'd never forget. "This army's lucky you're here, General."

Sherman touched the brim of his hat in salute, smiled fleetingly, and turned back to his war.

Grant found Prentiss just before eleven. The brigadier's command post was in a clump of trees some five hundred yards south and to the front of the general Union line. It was also close to a washed-out road where Prentiss had set up his latest defense line in defilade. The same sepia air, shattered by the intense cacophony of battle, clung to this area. The combat was raging so close that the whole thing was hypnotic to Grant. For some reason the memory of a bright day outside the City of Mexico flashed over him. Ditches, cornfields, a belfry with a little howitzer—all so clean and simple, compared to this fumy, murky bedlam.

Prentiss jumped off his horse, his uniform torn in several places, his face streaked with grime. "General," he said, "I don't think this is a very safe place for an army commander."

Grand handed him a cigar. "No, I don't suppose so. What's going on?"

"We've had the shit kicked out of us since before daybreak. I've lost several hundred yards and a hell of a lot of men, but this division is still fighting."

"How many effectives do you have left?"

"Don't know—a little under three thousand with the reinforcements."

"What do you think you're facing?"

"Can't tell. Possibly two or three divisions, maybe more."

Grant relit his cigar. "You think you can hold here for a while?"

Prentiss sighed. "Suppose so. The sunken road is a pretty good position, and that bramble field in front of it affords some protection, but the boys are about tuckered out."

Grant searched the general's eyes for what he needed to know. He was pleasantly surprised by this unproven Volunteer commander's tenacity—at this point, no regular officer could be doing more. He hated to leave this courageous command so exposed, but he couldn't afford to lose his salient. He said, "I've got at least three divisions coming in, but we need time. General, I need for you to stay here—at all costs."

Prentiss uncapped his canteen, staring at Grant while he drank. "I'll do what I can. By the way, do you know what the rebs have already named this place?"

"What's that?"

"The Hornets' Nest."

Where was that doggone Lew Wallace?

By lightning, he should have had his division here well before this!

Or Nelson, for that matter. There should be some word from him. He'd left Savannah in plenty of time to be adjacent to the Landing by now.

Often a battle could depend on the most trivial of happenstances, but these were *divisions* he'd counted on!

Grant sat on a tree stump, easing the pain in his throbbing ankle. He pulled out his watch. It had eight minutes after twelve. Over six hours of fighting. Were the rebel soldiers tired too, maybe ready to quit? He— There was something vaguely familiar about the sergeant of dragoons who stood before him saluting. Grant touched the brim of his slouch hat. "Yes?"

The sergeant removed his hat, looking at it, turning it around in his fingers. "Sir, I, uh, you don't remember me, but I'm, well, I'm pleased to see you again. And mighty proud that you're a general and all. I knowed you was going someplace, someday. Never had no doubts back at Monterrey."

Grant peered more closely. "What's your name, Sergeant?"

"Bolding, sir. From your quartermaster section in the Fourth Infantry. Remember those little skirmishes we went on without orders?"

Certainly, the boy, no—the corporal. Bolding. He stuck out his hand. "Of course. How are you? What's an old quartermaster roustabout like you doing in the dragoons?"

Bolding put his hat back where it belonged. His sun-creased face held a wide grin. "I transferred after the war, General. As to what I'm doing, I'm part of this detachment of cavalry that's holding this here bridge. But ever since you rode up, I been keeping a close eye over you."

Grant nodded as more memories of sunlit cane fields flitted back.

"You never was one to stay out of the shooting, but you ain't no lieutenant anymore, General."

A smile touched Grant's lips. "Bolding, how would you like to keep a real close eye on me? You must know horses, and you're a good shot. How would you like to become my new orderly?"

The grin widened as Bolding patted his carbine. "General, sir, you done got yourself a dog-robber."

Much to the consternation of his staff, Grant stayed in the thick of the fighting as he went from one command to another. As Rawlins would later record, the commanding general never stopped believing that his army would win the battle. His presence and unflagging, even obstinate, trust in that victory provided immeasurable encouragement to the many soldiers who saw him. In several cases, he personally moved commands around, placing them where they would do the most good. Twice the 11th Iowa broke and was ready to run when Grant turned it around and back into the fight.

The first general he lost was W. H. L. Wallace, who was mortally wounded. The middle of a battle this fierce was no time to be changing commanders—particularly with a division so close to breaking, but he had no choice.

At two o'clock, there was still no sign of Lew Wallace.

The situation was grave.

Grant had finally met with Buell at the Landing. Buell had stated that Nelson had been badly slowed by boggy ground. And the troublesome general hadn't yet given his division commanders orders to join the battle. Union soldiers were dying right and left, and the outcome of the fight looked grim, but Buell still held off. Somehow Grant had held his temper. Now, he looked again at his watch and faced McPherson and Rawlins. His voice was flat. "I want both of you to ride north and find General Wallace. When you do so, tell him to somehow get down here at once."

Both officers nodded and swung into the saddle.

General Albert Sidney Johnston, for some reason known only to him, was using a tin cup to point directions, instead of his saber. Now, at a little after two o'clock, he touched the tips of several bayonets with it as he leaned down from the saddle to speak to a group of dazed soldiers who had just been repulsed in an attack. "Men, they're stubborn. We must use the bayonet. These must do the work."

The Southern soldiers had just tried to take a strongly held peach orchard on the flank of the still-stubborn Hornet's Nest. Like Grant, the Texan had been personally involved in the battle all day long. Now, as one who knew anything about the great officer would expect, Johnston rode in front of the line of battle, stood tall in the stirrups, waved his hat, and shouted, *"I will lead you!"*

His uniform was torn in several places and the sole of one of his boots flapped loosely where a Federal Minié ball had struck it. His teeth flashed in a grin beneath his sweeping dark mustache. This was the epitome of leadership to him. The Confederates cheered, let out their yells, raised their flags, and stormed through heavy fire to the objective. Before long, he watched proudly and quietly as the men he'd just led exulted in having taken the withered peach orchard.

Suddenly, his aide saw him sway in the saddle. "General—are you all right?" he cried out.

Johnston clutched his right thigh and leaned low over the pommel. The aide guided his horse close and held the general. "What is it, sir? Where are you hit?"

Johnston's eyes fluttered as he lost consciousness. "Sir!" the aide cried. "General, don't—" He leaped down from his horse and eased his commander to the ground. Frantically feeling around for a wound, he suddenly noticed a wide stain of blood spreading above the general's right boot. Moments later, he found the wound—a bullet hole above the knee that had severed the femoral artery. Blood was gushing out with each pump of the heart, and the aide didn't know how to stop it. "Help!" he screamed, but the gathering soldiers just stared. Not a one knew how to apply a tourniquet. The gallant Texan's life was spilling out on the ground in a pool of crimson, and his staff doctor was a thousand yards away, attending to some wounded Yankee prisoners. Just thirty minutes earlier, Johnston had ordered him to stay with them and do so.

It didn't take long.

A colonel from his staff arrived and knelt over the general. "Oh, my God, General, don't . . . Oh, hang on, hang on!" He wiped a tear from his eye. "We need you too much, sir. Don't leave us."

But Albert Sidney Johnston couldn't hear him.

He was dead.

"Sir," Webster said, "there's some good high ground running westward from the Landing. And in front of it is a good backwater to protect it. If I can round up our reserve and other available artillery, we can mass the guns along that ridge and give 'em hell. No one will get near the Landing."

Grant looked at the map his chief of staff handed him. Joe Webster had come to him from the First Illinois Light Artillery, and was still that regiment's nominal commander. In fact, it had been through Webster's insistence that he'd pressed Halleck to send the remainder of the First's guns down. "How many pieces do you think we can get into action?" he asked.

"I'll use everything I can find. Probably around fifty."

Grant nodded his head. With no shortage of artillery ammunition, such a formidable battery could be just what he needed to stave off any breakthrough by the rebs. "Go to it. And pour some fire around the hornets' nest as soon as you can."

Grant turned to Captain Hillyer. "Get word to the *Tyler* and *Lexington* to step up their shooting while Colonel Webster gets organized. But I don't want any short rounds from those eight-inchers."

"Yes, sir!" The aide hurried off.

"All right, Clark," the general said to Laglow as he put his bad foot into the stirrup, "let's go find out how McClernand's doing."

Rawlings and McPherson cantered southwest along a dirt trail known as the Shunpike Road. They had already covered the River Road north almost to Crump's Landing, then had turned west on the road to Adamsville for two miles. And they had seen nothing remotely resembling a missing Federal division. McPherson was anxious, Rawlins was furious. At three-ten they crossed another dirt road, rounded a bend, and saw the bright flash of sunlight on metal and a large number of blue uniforms ahead. They burst into a gallop, quickly reaching the first elements. Union soldiers were everywhere, mostly lying and sitting down around the road.

As the two staff officers pulled their horses up, Rawlins shouted at a lieutenant, "Where's General Wallace?"

The officer jerked a thumb down the column. "Down there somewhere."

Two minutes later they found the division commander talking to some of his officers under a tall oak tree. He touched his brim, returning McPherson's salute. Rawlins was livid. "What the hell are you doing, General?"

Wallace scowled. "Taking a break. What's it look like?"

McPherson caught Rawlins's sleeve, speaking quietly, "Take it easy, John. We've got to get them moving, not get you shot."

Rawlins's eyes flashed as he turned back to the general. "General Grant has been expecting you in the battle lines for over four hours. Thousands of our brave boys have died because your division is sitting here on a Sunday picnic, and you ask me what it looks like. I—"

"General Wallace," McPherson interrupted pleasantly, "I assume you took the wrong route, but apparently you are aware of that. If you'll be so kind, please get your division moving back up this road. If you'll give us a handful of cavalry, we'll scout out a cross-country route. Shouldn't be more than five miles to our front."

Wallace switched his glaring gaze from Rawlins to the engineer. "All right, Mac. But we haven't been just sitting on our asses. This division has already marched twelve miles today along these damned roads. And I just countermarched them an hour ago, when I realized we were not headed for the Landing."

"Countermarched?" Rawlins bit out. "Why didn't you reverse march?"

Wallace had had enough. He snapped, "I don't think any captain, even Grant's pet, has any damned business criticizing a general officer, Rawlins!"

McPherson jumped off his horse, unrolling a map. "Here's where I propose to move cross-country, sir."

Wallace turned angry eyes to the map.

Softly, McPherson said, "General Grant needs you immediately, sir. The battle hangs in the balance."

The drizzle had begun a half-hour earlier, making the Sixth Division's heroic stand in the hornets' nest even more dismal. Sitting bareheaded on a log in a narrow gully, Brigadier General Benjamin Prentiss wiped his face and tried to think of an answer for his chief of staff. He looked at the colonel's pained expression. The man was right—to continue would be sure suicide. The crash of incoming artillery was deafening. The air around them was a stinking fog of smoke. The screams of wounded and dying soldiers filled the air. There had to be at least three rebel divisions coming at them through the splintered remains of trees, coming in their hated gray or butternut uniforms, shouting their hideous rebel yell, bringing their undiscriminating death.

Still packed along the sunken road, his men were hanging on. That's what Grant had asked him to do—hang on. And his brave boys had done so. But it couldn't last much longer. The rebs were all around them now. His survivors were a stubborn island of muddy blue and blood-crimson. How many effectives left—maybe twelve hundred? Every minute wasted would mean more deaths.

What a terrible disgrace, surrender. Was that what a proud man from Illinois did? But pride had nothing to do with fact. There was a time when a commander had to put aside patriotism and courage for the truth, when his responsibility to his men overshadowed everything else.

That time had come.

He sadly nodded his head in acknowledgment.

Wiping a grimy, blood-caked sleeve over his brow, Prentiss sighed and said, "I hope someone will understand." He rose, sticking his battered slouch hat back on his head. "I guess it's time to send them the white flag."

Colonel McPherson jumped down from his tired horse, shaking off the water. "Sir, General Lew Wallace is finally in place on Sherman's right. That should secure our whole right flank. With this rain and Sherman's having to fall back so far, I thought it best to leave him there until I reported to you."

Grant had received word about Prentiss's surrender just a couple of minutes earlier. Now he broke away from those sad thoughts. "Good work. Where's he been all day?"

"Took the wrong roads."

Grant unrolled his map. "Show me where they are."

McPherson traced the positions of both divisions with his finger, saying, "The fighting has fallen off considerably."

"Good. I think the rebs have run out of steam." He told the engineer about Prentiss. "Sometimes it takes a lot of soldiers to take care of capitulating troops, particularly when there are many wounded. Then there's the rain. The way Webster's pouring artillery into them, they'll have to dig in for the night. We're secure, Mac. Our army took a lot today, but Sherman, and Prentiss in particular, saved us."

"Then you're not thinking of retreating tonight?"

Grant looked at his engineer in surprise. "Why should we retreat when we're winning? We've got a fresh division of our own, part of one of Buell's, and a friendly army sitting just across the river to help us tomorrow. We'll maintain contact tonight and hit 'em at first light."

McPherson grinned. "Yes, *sir!*"

*　　*　　*

Shortly after midnight, one of the navy's intermittent harassing rounds crashed behind the Confederate lines and broke the wet stillness. Sitting huddled under a blanket on the bluff above the Landing, Grant shifted position and flexed his arms. The tree under which his little command party was seeking shelter allowed a steady dripping of cold raindrops to filter down, making sleep difficult. Captain Hillyer had insisted on joining him and was curled up in a nearby slicker. And Sergeant Bolding, who hadn't been more than twenty feet away since their original conversation, sat off to the side, eyes lidded and carbine at the ready.

Grant pulled the blanket back over his shoulders. What was a little more rain to a man with a badly swollen ankle and innumerable thoughts that prevented sleep? His battle-weary troops were lying exhausted in the same water, many of them wounded, others in low spirits. At least they'd been fed. He'd done his best to jack up their morale, but cold, wet, tired soldiers are often hard to convince.

Particularly if one had just lost a close friend.

He'd tried to find a corner in the nearby farmhouse where he might doze off, but the cries of pain had torn into him. A makeshift hospital was no place for a commander to relax. Those poor, marvelous soldiers—would they ever understand? He didn't know the number of casualties, but he guessed it would be in the thousands. Terrible, probably the worst ever on the North American continent.

But the Union had to be preserved.

How would their mothers ever understand?

It would be over on the morrow. Had to be. The rebs simply wouldn't be able to sustain any further momentum. If they couldn't blow his army into the river today, they wouldn't be able to do it in the face of his reinforcements. But how easily would they quit? Prisoners reported that Beauregard was in command following Johnston's death. He was a fighter. And Bragg would be pushing him. Still, the little Frenchman was too smart to sacrifice what was left of his army. . .

Bolding swung his carbine up as the dark forms approached. Rawlins shook off the water and stood before him, scowling in the harsh light of the lantern. "Goddamn it, General," the adjutant complained, "why are you out here in this miserable weather? A commander needs rest to make sound decisions. And this rain isn't doing that ankle of yours one damned bit of good."

Grant relit the stub of a cigar. "Now, Rawlins, quit playing mother hen. If the troops can stay out in this, so can I. Who've you got with you?"

Sherman stepped into the light, his eyes dark in the shadow of his dripping slouch hat. "Hello, Sam. I thought I'd see how you are and—well, I was going to ask you to move my beat-up boys back out of tomorrow's fight. But somehow when I see you, I think it's a stupid idea." He paused, then added, "We've had the devil's own day, haven't we?"

Grant nodded. "Yes, we have. We'll lick 'em tomorrow, though. Here, have a cigar."

CHAPTER 29

On Shiloh's dark and bloody ground,
The dead and wounded lay.
Amongst them was a drummer boy,
Who beat the drums that day.
A wounded soldier held him up—
His drum was by his side.
He clasp'd his hands, then raised his eyes,
And prayed before he died.
> —WILL S. HAYS, "THE DRUMMER BOY
> OF SHILOH"

John Rawlins leaned close to the kerosene lamp. The general had long before given him carte blanche to write to Congressman Washburne about any aspect of the command or the war. And at times—such as now—the general needed someone to step in and tell the damned truth. Those who weren't close to him simply didn't know the quiet man's strength and honesty. They didn't know that he'd never blow his own horn. And mostly, he wouldn't even defend himself against the false accusations and insinuations that seemed to land on his head like snowflakes in a blizzard.

Like this deluge of criticism about the battle.

Half aloud, Rawlins repeated the old adage, "Falsehood will travel from Maine to Georgia while Truth is putting on its boots."

He held the letter up to the light to see if he'd make any mistakes.

Pittsburg Landing, Tennessee
April 21, 1862

Dear Washburne,

    I'm sure you've read the varying newspaper reports of the Battle of Pittsburg Landing, or Shiloh, as some are calling it. I now feel I must give you a personal acount. The enemy hit us with great force the morning of the 6th inst. and drove us back throughout most of the day. By sunset that evening, their major thrust had been spent and General Grant knew victory had eluded them.

    Sure enough, the following day proved him correct. Our Federal forces attacked at dawn and fought heroically throughout the morning, sending the enemy running back toward Corinth in the afternoon. The final action of the battle was an attack by two regiments led by General Grant himself. Elements of our proud Army of the Tennessee maintained contact with the retreating enemy, but we were just too spent to capitalize.

Buell, who arrived quite tardily on the 6th and contributed little, was important in assuring victory on the 7th, but didn't follow up on the retreating rebels as he should have, and as General Grant urged him. He is a prima donna, jealous of his prerogatives. I must add that General Lew Wallace, who lost his way on the 6th, was also a major factor in the fighting on the 7th.

There are newspaper accusations joining those of politicians from states like Ohio—from which two regiments fled the battle in sheer terror—and from stragglers trying to cover their cowardice, that our army was caught by surprise, and that we were poorly generaled. These are barefaced lies. Both Sherman and Prentiss, who, by the way, led heroically the first day, were deployed for battle prior to the first shot (fired by a Union soldier on patrol) on the morning of the 6th.

This leads us to the man who really won this great victory for us. In his calm, competent manner—rising to the occasion of possible defeat, as he always seems to do—from the moment of his arrival on the battlefield on the 6th, General Grant instinctively made decisions that welded our forces together. On the 7th, he blended Buell's troops into the common objective and our proud victory—over a powerful and well-generaled enemy army.

For those who say we suffered a defeat, I ask: Who retained the field, and who retreated?

I must say the Confederate army fought with the utmost gallantry, and we were able to defeat them only because our cause is just, and because we had U. S. Grant as our commander. As you know, I'm somewhat prejudiced about the man, but these are facts.

I remain your friend.

John A. Rawlins

Three days later, hearing that General Smith's condition had worsened, Grant went to the old mansion in Savannah, arriving in midafternoon. Smith was sitting up in bed, lucid and as abrupt as ever. He waved the medical orderly out as Grant sat by his bedside. "Got one of those famous cigars of yours, Grant?" he asked.

Grant smiled, handing him one and holding a match to it. "Are you supposed to smoke?"

"What's the difference?"

Grant nodded, lighting his own. As blue smoke filled the air, he asked, "Giving you much pain?"

"What's pain?"

"When are you coming back to duty, General?"

"Don't think I am. Matter of fact, I don't think I'm leaving this bedroom alive."

"That's not what I—"

"Don't give me any of that phony shit. I ought to know."

The two pragmatic men smoked in silence for over a minute. Finally Smith said, "I heard about all that crap they're accusing you of. Damned shame. Don't know which is more treacherous—politicians, cowards, or the press. But don't worry about it. You'll ride it out because you've got the stuff. I guess I can tell you now that I wasn't too pleased about serving under someone so far behind me in years, rank, and all. But when I found out you had the stuff, I figured I was the lucky one.

"Don't interrupt me. I'm only sorry I can't go all the way with you. I think we'd've made a fine team, probably cleaned up Virginia for them, and everywhere else. But you're going to have to make it alone. Oh, you've got Sherman and these other young hotshots, but don't count on them, Grant. Stick to your own way. That's all that counts."

Grant choked up momentarily, finally finding his tongue. "Thank you, sir. Coming from you that's mighty high praise. I'd be your lieutenant any day."

"Nonsense. You're the right man. I—" Smith started to cough, then his eyes fluttered and he lost consciousness. Grant grabbed the cigar and shouted for the orderly.

It was the last time he saw Charles Ferguson Smith alive.

Grant stood at the funeral service, grieving more deeply than he could imagine. Memories returned of the tall, erect, mustached Smith, standing on the reviewing stand at West Point. Wearing his full dress uniform, beside the imposing Scott. Capturing the fancy of a young plebe from Ohio, the epitome of a soldier, of a great officer—perhaps one of the greatest in any army, anywhere. He saw Smith in battle in Mexico—magnificent, as always. And now, snuffed out when his fame as a general was just beginning, by a freak accident. The man who'd stormed God only knew how many entrenchments, the man who'd been such an influence on so many hundreds of cadets, officers, and men.

The red, white, and blue flag was so vivid.

It personified this soldier.

Or did this dead soldier personify the flag?

He remembered the plaintive bugle call for General Hamer, so long ago at Monterrey, and how he'd felt such a grievous loss. But that memory had dulled; this pain was all too fresh. Smith's remains should go to West Point, to be buried on the Plain where perhaps his sublimity could be felt by all those generations of cadets to come.

He would write to Mrs. Smith tonight, hoping God would give him the words to at least partially express what he felt.

Suddenly he thought of Albert Sidney Johnston and wondered if perhaps a Confederate general had stood at his funeral in the same sorrowful awe. Perhaps an old comrade or aide. Probably *all* of those strong generals who'd been at the battle had done so. Many had thought Johnston the greatest soldier in the army. Smith had been the Texan's deputy in Utah before the war; what a team they must have made! And now they were dead in the same month.

Smith had been so clear for those precious minutes in the bedroom. Had said some nice things. Could a boy from Georgetown, Ohio, be the man Smith thought him to be? "Stick to your own way," the old soldier had said.

It might be difficult.

Might be impossible.

But he'd try.

The clear notes of Tattoo were so haunting, so moving, as they echoed over the gravesite.

Once more Halleck had neutered him. This time, with Old Brains in the field, Grant had been relegated to deputy commander—about as important a job as vice president, he'd complained to himself. But it was just as well, for Halleck would have driven a snail crazy, so slowly did he entrench his way to Corinth to attack Beauregard. And once more the Little Frenchman had been given time to pull his outnumbered army away to fight another day.

Grant chafed at the inactivity, thought seriously about trying to get another command. But Sherman, who had been promoted to major general of Volunteers on May 1, shored him up once more, telling him he would get another chance to command in the West. His words, "Sam, these boys in the Army of the Tennessee are fighters, and they need a fighter like you to lead them," rang in his ears and stilled his impatience enough for him to hold on.

His forbearance was rewarded when he was given direct command of his army again. He moved his headquarters to Memphis, but his stay there was cut short when he received a cryptic telegram from Halleck stating, "You will repair immediately to this place and report to me."

Arriving back in Corinth on July 15, Grant was quickly ushered into Halleck's office. Old Brains immediately solved the riddle: "I have been summoned to Washington to become general in chief of the army. I'll depart in two days. For the time being, no successor to my command will be named. As second in rank, you will be given command of an enlarged district and assume many of the duties I now hold."

Halleck's owlish look was almost pleasant as he went on. "As you know, General Pope assumed command of the new Army of Virginia three weeks ago. His old Army of the Mississippi, now under the command of General Rosecrans, will also be under you—as well as your own Army of Tennessee. General Buell's Army of the Cumberland will operate independently in eastern Tennessee. He, like you, will be under my direct orders from Washington."

Grant wanted to throw his fist in the air and cheer. Halleck was leaving! And he was to be in command of two armies and a district that embraced everything between the Tennessee and the Mississippi!

Halleck's words broke through. "We've had some problems, General. Frankly, I attribute most of them to lack of communication. Others to your inexperience. I hope any unpleasantness can be forgotten. I wish you good luck."

Grant shook the proffered hand, concealing his excitement. "Thank you, sir. Is there anything specific in the way of orders?"

"Only that you'd best become one hell of a railroad man. You're going to have almost four hundred miles of it to maintain and protect."

Grant saluted and walked out, wondering if he'd ever be able to communicate with the man. Railroad track! There was a huge enemy out there, and a place named Vicksburg that he'd been thinking about. Webster and the newly promoted Major Rawlins—who had accompanied him to Corinth—waited quietly as he returned from Halleck's office. He smiled slightly as he said, "Start figuring out how you want to set this place up, gentlemen. We're taking over command here."

CHAPTER 30

Corinth, Mississippi, in July was hot and oppressively wet. When it wasn't raining, the air was still heavy enough with moisture to make the place feel like a huge Turkish bath. Grant, having settled into his massive administrative duties, was trying to put a semblance of order into the problems he faced. Not only did he have to spread his infantry divisions out to a point where his command lost its cohesion, but he had to use the troops to maintain the railroads. And he didn't have enough cavalry to police the many stretches of those tracks. Shortly after pinning a star on the brilliant McPherson's shoulder, he had assigned the engineer as superintendent of railroads—a waste for a man with his command brilliance.

Grant put his pen down and moved to the large window, where he looked out at the busy street. Wiping the sweat from his moist forehead, he lit his meerschaum and blew out a cloud of grayish smoke.

Back in Cairo, he'd had to fight with the swindlers and thieves, but at least it had been in friendly territory. Here, among enemy citizens, every Tom, Dick, and Harry could turn into a marauding night rider when the sun went down. The guerrillas destroyed track, killed pickets, shot couriers, and burned supplies. And spied. Seemed that everyone who could see was a doggone spy. How could he ever move troops around when the enemy knew about it at first light?

Halleck had said, "Use a lot of hemp." And his own order had read, "Persons acting as guerrillas without organization and without uniform are not entitled to treatment as prisoners of war when caught."

But he hadn't hung anyone yet.

Bolding stuck his head through the door. "Sir, your son wants to see you."

Young Fred came in, acting as adult as possible in his brown suit and tie. Only the cap gave away his twelve years, and his mother wouldn't give in on letting him wear a man's hat. Ever since the previous summer when

Grant had let him tag along on a march with the Twenty-first Illinois, the boy had been eager to enlist in the army. Fred smiled as he clicked his heels and jerked a bow to his father. "Are we going for that ride, Papa?"

"Yes, son. I have to sign a couple of papers and then we can go."

Fred looked relieved. "I was afraid you'd be too busy again."

"No, I told everyone I'd shoot the first person who stopped us. In fact, Sergeant Bolding has the horses saddled and waiting."

Fred pointed to the corner of the big room. "I could have a desk right over there, Papa."

Grant was puzzled for a moment. "What—oh, your being my aide. Well, your mother and I talked about it just a couple of nights ago, and she just won't give in. You're still too young, you know."

"But some of those drummer boys are my age. And the navy has midshipmen even younger than me."

Grant's response was gentle. "Wait awhile and we'll see." The family had been with him here at Corinth for a fortnight now. His son Buck—so nicknamed because he'd been born in Ohio, the Buckeye state—had enlivened the visit by getting kicked by a horse. But the accident hadn't been serious. At ten, he also wanted to get into the army. Little Nellie, now seven, was a joy, always able to find her father's welcome knee, and able to twist him almost any way she desired. And bustling little Jesse was everything a boy working on five should be. Julia and the boys were leaving the next day to go back to White Haven, so he couldn't let anything interfere with this chance to ride with his oldest son.

"But that's what you always say," young Fred said with a frown.

Grant put his arm around the boy's shoulder. "That's because we have to wait awhile and see," he replied with a smile.

Rawlins came into the office and greeted Fred. "General," he said to Grant, "that new cavalry brigadier, Sheridan, wants a minute with you. I told him you were busy, but he said he'd wait."

Grant glanced at the wall clock. "It's okay, send him in."

Philip Henry Sheridan was short, swarthy, bandy-legged—a thirty-one-year-old Irishman from Ohio. Combative, with dark brown eyes and wavy dark hair, he had taken five years to complete West Point owing to a fight with a cadet sergeant. He was clean-shaven except for a clipped mustache, and his gestures were nervous and jerky. From the Class of '53, he had served nearly eight years as a second lieutenant. Halleck had made Captain Sheridan his quartermaster until the governor of Michigan had offered him a commission as a colonel to command a cavalry regiment. Less than a week later, he had been in command of a cavalry brigade, and thirty-five days after that, following his brilliance at the battle of Booneville, he had been promoted to brigadier.

"What can I do for you, General?" Grant said, returning Sheridan's salute.

Sheridan gave him a cocky grin and said, "I'll be going to Buell's army, General, but I want you to know that I'd rather stay with you."

Grant donned his slouch hat. "And why is that?"

Sheridan continued to grin. "Because we're both fighters, and someday you're going to have a lot of cavalry to command."

"What makes you think so?"

"Because it's going to be a cavalry war before it's over."

"You sound pretty sure of that," Grant said. For some time he'd been thinking that the enemy armies would have to be defeated in the field, that the taking of cities without vanquishing opposing armies normally would not win the war. There would be exceptions. And cavalry had little to do with taking cities, but would be a vital necessity in other kinds of warfare. Right now, the South's two top cavalry commanders in the West—Forrest and Morgan—were giving him fits along his rail lines. And Jeb Stuart was practically a legend back in Virginia.

"I know so, General. But we're gonna have to learn how to use it."

"How do you propose we can do that?"

The little Irishman grinned again. "By fighting, General."

As Grant motioned for Fred to follow him and headed for the door, it was his turn to smile. "Glad you came by, Sheridan. We'll talk about this more one of these days."

It was in the middle of August that Major General John McClernand took a leave of absence and journeyed to the nation's capital to begin a campaign that he hoped would make him the most important general in the war. A day after his arrival there, he removed his hat and was shown into the president's office. The tall form of Abraham Lincoln was standing in front of a window, outlined in the bright morning sunlight. After greeting the seated secretary of war, Edwin Stanton, the former Illinois congressman addressed the president. "Good morning, your excellency. I'm pleased that you could find time to see me."

Lincoln smiled engagingly. "Nonsense, John, I always have time for an old friend from back home. There's whiskey at the sideboard, if you wish."

"Never at this time of day, sir."

"Good. Now, what is this plan you have in mind?"

McClernand took the proffered chair. "Well, Mr. President, we've been on opposite sides of the political fence for a long time. But now we're united in a common cause, fighting a dangerous enemy who wishes to tear down our beloved Union." McClernand's voice took on its noted poise as he moved smoothly on. "I'm sure you share my awareness that a grave political problem is approaching in the western states—that of continued support of the war. The problem is simply financial.

"We're talking about the greatest area of farmland in the world, and states that produce vast quantities of grain and meat—products that have for years found markets via the mighty Mississippi, a waterway now closed to them by the enemy at Vicksburg. These products must now move via the east-west rail lines and by vessels plying the Great Lakes.

"And who owns these modes of transportation? The monopolistic cartel of greedy eastern railroad barons and their partners, the kings of Yankee industry. In the midst of their making the war a huge profit-making scheme, these hoggish opportunists have raised the freight rates so high that the producers can't make a profit. Our proud farmers will soon see no way out but to accede to the wishes of the Confederacy, declare peace, and reopen their waterways."

McClernand paused, then resumed with dark eyes flashing. "To accomplish this return to the old ways, they are beginning to elect antiwar men to political office. They may even gather enough strength to form a powerful new party, even decide to secede from the Union."

Secretary of War Edwin Stanton interrupted, "Isn't that carrying it a bit far, General?"

"Perhaps, but the concept has backing out there. Unless the government does something to open the river, it could become a reality."

Lincoln nodded, returning to his desk and folding his cranelike body into a chair. "He's right, Ed. You know there's been talk. We've heard John's assessment, now let's hear how he proposes to fix it."

The smile softened McClernand's hawk features. "Thank you, Mr. President, I have a surefire answer. We've entrusted the operation of this war to the professionals too long. West Point strategy hasn't produced a damned thing, and I ought to know—I was at Shiloh and Corinth."

The president spoke softly. "It's our impression that Grant won at Shiloh."

McClernand shrugged slightly. "Let's say that thanks to some of us in command, he didn't lose. Anyway, it's time for a vigorous volunteer to step forward and give the Union a signal victory, one that will open the Mississippi forever. I believe I'm that man. My battle record speaks for itself. Furthermore, I'm a Democrat, well-known in Democratic country. I propose to go back to our great farm belt and build fervor for winning this damned war. I believe I can find new recruits by the thousands. I'll weld together a mighty army to conquer Vicksburg and clear the river all the way to the gulf!"

Stanton appeared interested. "We could certainly use the troops. You wish to command this force. Is that correct?"

"Precisely," the general replied. "If all these lads answer my call to the colors, they'll certainly want to follow me into battle. And, gentlemen, I know how to lead without a West Point textbook. We'll clear the Yazoo, surround Vicksburg, and smash it into capitulation!"

Both Lincoln and Stanton nodded their heads. Finally the president got up to shake McClernand's hand. "Your plan sounds interesting, John. I want to present it to some other Cabinet officers, and of course to General Halleck. I'll let you know."

"Well," Halleck said after the president consulted him, "I don't particularly like the idea of giving McClernand a private command. He is proven in battle, but he's somewhat insubordinate, or he would have gone to Grant and myself before coming to you. And while I was in Corinth, I heard rumors that discipline was suffering in his division because of his penchant for making political promotions."

The general in chief widened his owl eyes. "I believe, Mr. President, that he's primarily interested in building a political base for higher office later on. If this is the case, you should be wary of how he goes about it. Is he fit to command such an expedition, and if not, what deleterious effects will such an appointment have on our present command structure in the West? I've recently received feelers from Grant in regard to Vicksburg, and I've given him a free hand to look toward that objective."

"What about the troops McClernand might raise?" Lincoln asked.

"By all means, he should be given a free hand. If he raises an army, we'll work out the details of his command position later."

The president frowned. "I don't think he'll buy that."

"It's your decision, sir. Right now, we need the men."

Back at Grant's headquarters, John Rawlins had interesting information. "General," he said, "I have an odd report here. It seems that one of our telegraphers from Fort Henry got drunk recently and rattled off a wild tale about tampering with messages between you and General Halleck early in the year. Seems he's a rebel sympathizer."

Grant looked up from his desk. *Of course!* "I knew there had to be some plausible answer. What has been done with this fellow?"

"Nothing, sir. He disappeared. But one of his fellow telegraphers thought he had hightailed it to Richmond or someplace else in the South."

"Hmm. Just as well. Probably would've been hard to convict him anyway."

"I have something else that ties in with it," Rawlins said, holding up another letter. "The War Department is assuming direct control over the military telegraph system. Most of the operators will still be civilians, and they will be assigned to major commands. Not only that, but to ensure secrecy, ciphers will be put into use."

Grant's mind flew. A private cipher and telegraph operator! That should certainly ensure security of communication.

The telegrapher's name was Samuel Beckwith; as a sergeant he had served as private secretary to General W. H. L. Wallace, the brigadier who had been killed at Shiloh. Now he was a civilian, the newest member of Grant's personal staff.

Grant felt an immediate sense of trust the day he met Beckwith.

The weeks seemed to fly by. Bragg led his army against Don Carlos Buell, trying to burst through Kentucky from eastern Tennessee and drive into southern Ohio. It was an audacious plan to win the war that nearly succeeded.

In the meantime, with Corinth threatened by the combined armies of "Pap" Prince and Earl Van Dorn, Grant had moved his headquarters to Jackson. The pitched battle of Corinth followed, and proved to be yet another instance of failure to capture a losing enemy army. This time it was an arrogant Rosey Rosecrans—the cadet corporal who had first drilled Grant at West Point—who failed. Refusing to follow orders, he neglected to follow up and close the trap that Grant had set.

A month later, after first outmarching and passing Buell, Bragg collided with his Army of the Cumberland at Perryville, southeast of Louisville. The two commanders would reach a zenith following a bloody battle in which Sheridan distinguished himself and a smaller Confederate force won a draw. Somehow Braxton Bragg, the cantankerous and aggressive hero of the Mexican War, unbelievably ran out of resolve and withdrew. When Buell failed to go after Bragg and destroy him, Washington finally gave up and fired him. He would later get a court of inquiry.

Grant had no idea what his missing general, McClernand, was up to during the latter's extended leave of absence. In fact, the former congressman was being highly successful in recruiting his private army to take Vicksburg. Changes in Grant's command included chief of staff Joe Webster's promotion to brigadier and his being placed in charge of the railroads—thereby freeing McPherson, who was promoted to major general of Volunteers, to command the Second Division. Also promoted to major general was John Logan, the other congressman who had given Grant's Twenty-first Illinois reenlistment speech.

In another of those strange twists that continued to mark this remarkable war, this conflict that was said to put brother against brother, General Pap Price was deeply hurt when his son, Brigadier General Edwin Price, denounced the Confederacy after being exchanged for General Ben Prentiss—the hero of the Hornets' Nest.

An officer who would be a valuable addition to Grant's staff was Lieutenant Colonel James Harrison Wilson. A graduate of the Class of '60, he was twenty-five when he reported in to Lieutenant Colonel Rawlins—who had recently received his second promotion. Slight of build, Wilson had a light complexion and a sweeping brown mustache over chin whiskers. Like Grant, he had been a superb horseman at the Academy. And no one had ever accused him of being bashful, as evidenced by a couple of incidents . . .

While Wilson was in Washington getting his new assignment, the Antietam campaign had been in progress and he had volunteered to serve temporarily as an engineer on McClellan's staff. He reported in to Little Mac in the company of another young officer who would have an impact on the war—George Armstrong Custer. While serving as an aide, Wilson took it upon himself to send General Joe Hooker a message. Hooker, the satyr who had been Hamer's brilliant chief of staff in Mexico, had just received a foot wound and was retiring from the field of battle. The message from the young engineer urged Hooker to return to the field, even if he had to be carried by stretcher, with "his bugles blowing and his corps flag flying over him."

It was not known how the imperious Hooker replied.

Before leaving McClellan, Wilson had offered more counsel. Upon learning that he was to be relieved of command of the Army of the Potomac, Little Mac had stated that he didn't want another command. To this the brazen Wilson had replied, "If you're not offered an independent command, you should take a corps or division. If neither of these can be had, you should take a brigade, and if not that, a regiment. If this fails, you should shoulder a musket and serve as a private soldier!"

It was also not known what the lordly McClellan replied.

"General Grant is away from the headquarters," Rawlins told him when he reported in. "But you will be assigned as acting inspector general."

"But I'm an engineer!"

"The general knows. McPherson has already told him you are a bright young man, and right now we need to know what condition this command is in. He's handing you a high position of trust on face value, Wilson."

The new arrival slowly nodded his head, then broke into a smile. "Then I guess I'd better be a good I.G., hadn't I?"

"That would be a wise idea."

"What's the general like?"

Rawlins pulled out a newspaper clipping. "We now have a newspaper correspondent with us whom we feel we can trust—a distinct rarity. His name is Sylvanus Cadwallader from the Chicago *Tribune*. This article will tell you about General Grant. Here's an excerpt: 'General Grant is invested with large discretionary powers and we are sure he will use them wisely. His forward movement is an indication that he means work, and with him work is not bloodless strategy but strategy that leads to hard fighting and decisive results. He is looking for the enemy and when he finds him there will be bloodshed.' "

Wilson took the clipping and quickly read it. "I guess I'd better be a very good I.G., hadn't I?"

Rawlins nodded. "Yes. And General McPherson also told me that you're a teetotaler. Is that correct?"

"Yes, I abstain from all alcoholic drink."

"Good. I've just gotten rid of a drinking colonel by the name of Laglow, and others will be sent packing before long. Before I'm done, this headquarters will be totally sober."

Wilson raised an eyebrow. "Including Grant?"

Rawlins's black eyebrows came together in an instant scowl. His voice lowered as he snapped, "Don't you ever intimate that the commanding general imbibes. That is an old army story, and he is as abstemious as I am now. And, Colonel, I not only break bottles of whiskey, I break the arms of those who bring them here!"

Wilson nodded his head. "Very well, I'll help you break them, Colonel."

It was just before midnight on Thanksgiving Day that Grant went back to his office. He turned up the kerosene lamp burning on a low credenza beneath the large map that included parts of western Tennessee, eastern Arkansas, western Mississippi, and eastern Louisiana. Standing quietly before it, his eyes traced the path of the broad, curving Mississippi River as it cut through the center like a giant serpent with a thousand coils. His eyes locked on a point in the center, where the river hooked east. There, waiting like a menacing octopus with long, stinging tenacles, was Vicksburg, guardian of the central Mississippi.

Grant's eyes narrowed as he fixed on the Confederate strongpoint. It was the most important objective in the country, in his opinion. Open the Mississippi and the Confederacy's death knell would be sounded. It was an exception to his theory about cities not being vital. Vicksburg. Well fortified, but not invincible. The composite derived from drawings by prisoners of war and riverboat personnel's descriptions indicated that it was a typical river town situated on a bluff some two hundred feet above the east bank with a sweeping view to the west; below it the river, in places a mile or more wide, made a hairpin turn as the riverbed pushed northeast, then quickly southwest; the land within the hairpin was barely above water level, easily flooded, and commanded by the bluff; it occupied an impregnable position from the west.

If the prisoner reports could be believed, the rebs had many heavy-caliber guns inside their works, guns that would command the river and western approach for several miles. The town was heavily entrenched, its population entirely Yankee-haters.

And to the north, outside the long range of the guns, the Yazoo River was in command. Nearly as wide and yellow as the big river, the Yazoo produced a vast network of swamps and shallow creeks, providing a huge wilderness of mud and fallen trees. It was almost impregnable if the rebs fortified its few passage points.

To avoid the Yazoo network, it would be necessary to move an army all the way around through the Jackson area, some forty miles to the east. And Joe Johnston was reported to have a strong army in that direction. The other option was to come in from the south. But how would one get to the south and get a huge army across the river without ferryboats?

"Excuse me, sir."

It was Lieutenant Colonel Wilson, the field officer of the day. "Yes?" Grant replied.

"I was wondering if I might speak with you, sir?"

"Certainly."

"I've been thinking about Vicksburg, and I have a thought you might keep in mind."

"Which is?"

"If you ever need to, you might make a run under those guns at night—gunboats, ferryboats, and all."

Grant turned back to the map. It would be a daring effort, probably far too dangerous. "Thanks, Wilson, I'll keep it in mind." Pemberton might have to be beaten outside his castle. Pemberton. He thought back to a bright, smoky day at Cosme Garita on the edge of Mexico City. A belfry and a little mountain howitzer raining shells down on the enemy. A general's aide: John C. Pemberton. Now a Confederate lieutenant general, even though he was a Pennsylvanian. Commanding the army at Vicksburg.

How good was Pemberton?

He'd find out.

CHAPTER 31

OXFORD, MISSISSIPPI

Occupying portions of some nine thousand square miles of northwestern Mississippi brought on the intricate problem of freed slaves, or "contrabands" as they were labeled. Having heard that the invading Yankees were bringing their freedom, these people had simply walked away from their masters or their deserted plantations. Now they turned to their liberators for succor. They swarmed helplessly around every army camp, clogging the muddy roads, looking for the promised manna. There was no plan to the exodus, no Moses to lead it. Blind hope conquered terror and led them from their familiar haunts. There were men, women, and children in every stage of disease or decrepitude, often nearly naked, always hungry.

Grant was deeply concerned with the contraband problem. Aside from the immense numbers involved in the human flood, he simply could not disregard the tragedy involved. One night, with Bolding only a few feet away in the dusk, Grant stood under a tree and watched a nearby group of the former slaves huddled around a small orange fire. An old white-haired woman, whose skinny body was encased in a dirty and tattered blue army blanket, stood on the outside of the gathering. She held out a tin army cup for her meager share of the soup that was being rationed out from the black kettle over the fire. An equally scrawny dog, a hound of some kind with its ribs showing through its mangy brown coat, sat beside her feet. As soon as the tall woman doing the serving poured her portion into the cup, the old woman hungrily drank from it. After a few moments, she poured the remainder into her hand and let the dog lick it.

Grant felt a fierce tug. That woman could be his own mother. And she had to be terribly hungry. But still she had kept a taste for her starving dog, probably her only possession. He closed his eyes momentarily and prayed silently. "Oh, Lord, give me the wisdom to solve the problem of these poor people." Turning to Bolding, he said, "When we get back, I want you to get a case of hardtack and bring it to that woman with the white hair."

Bolding looked quizzical.

"Just give it to her. She'll know what to do with it."

He looked back at the woman, and just then she glanced up into his gaze. Her eyes seemed to glow in the fading light. He touched the brim of his hat in greeting, and a smile touched her lips.

As he turned away, he again thought of Hannah Simpson Grant. He hoped she would never have to share the dregs of her only meal with a dog.

The next day Rawlins came to him with a file folder and a recommendation. "I think I've found the man to handle the contraband situation," he said brightly.

Grant looked up from the stack of papers on his desk. "Good. Tell me about him."

Rawlins handed him the folder. "He's Chaplain Eaton of the Twenty-seventh Ohio. I have here some letters from officers who know him. His qualifications are excellent."

"A chaplain? I know your missionary zeal, Rawlins, but I don't think a preacher's prayers are the answer."

The adjutant smiled. "I knew you were going to say that. But this chaplain is more than a country preacher. Coming from a New Hampshire farm, he worked his way through Dartmouth and became superintendent of schools in Toledo when he was only twenty-seven. In 'fifty-six he studied for the ministry, getting ordained just before the war.

"Heroically sticking by his sick colonel's side in a battle outside of Springfield in 'sixty-one, he was captured, and so impressed the rebel commander that he was allowed to preach while in prison. After being exchanged, he has been with his regiment in its last five battles. He's a soldier, General. Oh, and there's a rumor that he even clashed with Halleck at one time." Rawlins smiled again. "Which shows good judgment."

"Sounds like quite a package. Get him in to see me as soon as possible."

John Eaton was surprised to receive an order to report to the commanding general about whom so many unsavory rumors had circulated. Entering the small frame house where Grant was headquartered, he found several generals and colonels gathered around the small man at his desk. He started to excuse himself and back out, but Colonel Rawlins told him to be seated, that the conference would soon be over. Not wanting to be conspicuous,

Eaton found a chair in a corner and tried to read the book he'd brought along.

Ten minutes later the officers filed out and Eaton looked up into the steady gaze of the commanding general. "I guess you're the chaplain who's going to solve one of my biggest problems," the general said. "Come, sit by my desk and we'll talk."

Eaton was surprised at the quiet, earnest tone. Was this the great dissipator?

Grant searched the chaplain's eyes and found them steady, a good beginning. He spoke simply and directly. "As you know, Chaplain, the president issued his Emancipation Proclamation in September and it's to take effect New Year's Day."

Eaton nodded his head as Grant explained the contraband problem and its possible solutions. At length the chaplain said, "I know this is a terrible situation, but where do I fit in?"

"You're the man with all these darkies on his shoulders. I want you to take charge of this program."

"But, sir, there must be some mistake. I'm a chaplain now, not an administrator. Besides, I have my responsibilities to my regiment."

"I appreciate that, but I'm giving you much greater responsibilities. We're talking about thousands of lost souls who have been broken out of their way of life and forms of paternalism. The Southerners refer to them as children. Now they are *lost* children. Frankly, Mr. Eaton, I don't see how you could receive a higher calling."

Eaton sat quietly for a moment, struggling, then said, "But I have no rank, and frankly, I don't think I can measure up. I wouldn't know where to begin."

Grant handed him several pages of handwritten notes. "This will help. We'll set up special camps adjacent to army camps. We'll provide medical facilities and food, some clothes. We'll keep their idle hands busy by having them perform many of the fatigue duties of the soldiers. They can help in all nonbattle work.

"And all around us, Mr. Eaton, are fields of cotton, just waiting to be picked and baled for shipment to the North. We'll work out a means of paying for this labor because few of them will know what money is. The same will apply when we hire them out to the Secesh who didn't leave. We can use the women in various capacities, such as kitchen help and in hospitals. And," Grant smiled, "maybe you can keep those hordes of little ones busy in Bible schools."

John Eaton shook his head. "You make it sound simple, General, but I can see opposition brewing from senior officers who might have their own plans."

Grant's blue eyes bore into his gaze. "You'll notice I've used the term *we* throughout. That means you and me, Mr. Eaton, all the way. I'll give you special authority and no one will challenge it more than once. If I'm not available, Colonel Rawlins wears these stars.

"My wife's family had slaves, and I didn't think too much about it because they were well cared for. In fact, *I* was a slaveowner at one time. But that was more or less complacence. Now, I'm troubled over a long-range solution for these people. They are presently in a void—half-free, half-slave. And they need careful guidance in how to live on their own . . . " Grant paused a moment. "I see them adjusting, becoming slowly educated. I see them in uniform, helping to win this war . . . maybe someday becoming valuable citizens of one Union, voting and holding office. But right now they need to survive."

Eaton stood, walking to the window, staring out. Finally turning, he came to Grant and stuck out his hand. "General, if God can provide you to get this started, I guess He can give me the strength to help. When do I begin?"

"You just did."

Grant watched the square shoulders of the soldier-clergyman depart. He had the right man, he knew it. Now, if Halleck and the powers that be would only provide the funds . . .

He smiled to himself. It would take several lifetimes to deduct that kind of money from the pay of a Volunteer major general, so why worry?

After setting up a camp at Grand Junction, Tennessee, John Eaton began running into mounting problems with his Negroes. Getting assistants was difficult, since the soldiers resented having to do anything that smacked of serving the contrabands. He quickly learned that it was one thing for these boys to fight against the principle of slavery, but quite another to bring the victims to their breast. Thus, his assistants were reluctant enlisted men who were detailed to the job. Just getting one assistant for every one thousand contrabands was a major accomplishment.

And when the chaplain was getting this settled, Grant's supply depot at Holly Springs fell to General Von Dorn, and the contraband camp had to be moved to Memphis. A few days after this, Grant received a letter from Eaton.

> *Dear General Grant,*
>
> *You can't imagine what a difficult trip it was to Memphis. Just imagine moving several thousand frightened and bewildered, mostly helpless Negroes by rail. They so jammed the trains that they had to cling to the roofs and platforms of passenger and freight cars—right in the middle of smoke and cinders. When they arrived here, there were insufficient places for them to stay, so they huddled around little bonfires in the falling snow. But now, we at least have roofs over their heads. As you know, the contraband is an alien, unwanted by anyone, particularly the townspeople. But, in an attempt to give him more identity, I'm striving to keep the families together. Many of them want a formal marriage. One day, Chaplain Gale Williamson, my assistant, performed over two hundred marriages.*

I know, sir, that you have no guidelines from Washington on how to treat these people, but I find your solutions always logical. The day will arrive when someone will look back and see that our handling of the contrabands was a basis for future policy.

I thank you, sir, for trusting me with this problem—and also for your continued support, regardless of other military necessity.

Yr. Obedient Svt.,
John Eaton

CHAPTER 32

December was not a good month for Grant or the Union. In the East, Major General Ambrose Burnside led the Army of the Potomac to disastrous defeat by Lee at Fredericksburg. In Mississippi, when the depot commander at Holly Springs failed to act on information that the enemy was headed his way, disaster struck in the form of General Earl Van Dorn. The Army of the Tennessee's major supply center, filled with over a million dollars worth of equipment and other requirements, fell to the enemy and crippled Grant's plans to clear the Mississippi. Rawlins wanted to have the depot commander shot, but Grant shrugged, knowing it wouldn't solve the problem.

Only one thing mattered at this point—that Vicksburg was no longer a hazy idea; the river fortress had to be taken!

Then an ominous message arrived from Halleck: "The president may insist upon designating a separate commander for Vicksburg." Grant stared at the words. Now there was no doubt as to what McClernand had been up to. As his XIII Corps commander, he was senior to every other general in the field. The rumor must be true: they were going to give the political general command of the Vicksburg campaign.

Rawlins's stream of obscenities filled the air.

Grant stifled his displeasure. Now he knew what had troubled him so long about the Illinois congressman. He was a self-seeker, and would probably go to great lengths to promote his designs. "What do you think he wants in the end?" he asked his adjutant.

"The son of a bitch wants to be president," Rawlins growled.

"Is that such a bad desire?"

"It is if the man tramples others to get there. In this case, he has been deceitful with you by going over your head without informing you. And we both know he's incompetent of high command. What are you going to do?"

Grant shrugged. "Handle the problem when it's a fact."

*   *   *

The next December problem was the complete loss of communication.

On the 19th, Brigadier General Nathan Bedford Forrest sat on a tired mount atop the crest of a hill on the east bank of the Tennessee. The light rain had stopped, permitting a brief glimpse of sunlight to warm his wet, fatigued body. He'd had only snatches of rest in four days, but now he could sleep for a whole day before resuming operations. With rich satisfaction, he watched the last of his hard-riding cavalrymen complete the crossing of the river. What marvelous men!

He'd done it just like he knew he could. Against great odds and heavy numerical superiority, he'd outwitted those stupid Yankee sons of bitches and torn a big hole in Grant's rear. There were so many rips in sixty miles of track that no supply trains would get through for weeks. He chuckled to himself. Old Ulysses would sure have fun trying to talk to anyone by wire—there was enough chopped telegraph line to start a fence company! Yup, the skinny Tennessee country boy had shown them; he'd outmaneuvered, outguessed, outfought, and outrun them at every turn. They'd never learn this kind of warfare at West Point, that was for damned sure. And now they know that western Tennessee will never be secure, not ever!

He turned his horse to head for the warm farmhouse that would be his headquarters. Having made a lot of money before the war, he'd had a fine string of horses. But so far, eleven had been shot out from under him.

He smiled grimly.

This was his country.

The disconcerting 19th of December also held personal concern for Grant. His father had arrived a few days earlier, intent on arranging a cotton supply source within the territory occupied by Grant's army. Old Jesse had gone into this new business venture with three brothers in Cincinnati, apparently promising his son's cooperation in the matter.

Grant had welcomed his father warmly, but had cooled quickly as the gist of the visit began to surface. Already Grant had been alarmed by the swarm of opportunists and adventurers flooding through his command, trying to get rich quickly off the spoils of war. It was Cairo all over again, only the faces and the schemes were new. And it wasn't the first time Jesse had tried to use him to make money.

And now on this day when the rear of his command was falling apart and staff officers were filling his office, his father stood before him, demanding time to talk. He grabbed his slouch hat, jammed it on his head and led the way out the door."Let's walk, Papa. It's the only way we can be alone."

Jesse Grant nodded, following him. The man had changed little in his advancing years. His body was heavier, his hair had departed from the front of his head, his whiskers were gray, and his small eyeglasses thicker. If anything, his manner had become more obstreperous and narrow-minded.

Grant smoked a fresh cigar as they strolled down the main street of Oxford. They spoke of home, of his mother and siblings, of the tanning and retail business. Grant's practiced eye took in the uniforms of his soldiers as he returned salutes and greeted them. At length he stopped, saying, "Papa, I have to be getting back. Some bad developments are taking place up north and I want to be available."

Jesse's look was determined. "Just a minute, son. We've still got to talk about the cotton."

Grant began to walk. "We've been over that."

"But you're not thinking, Ulys. Someone's going to make this money and it might as well be me. Our whole family will benefit in the end."

Grant stopped, his blue eyes cold. "Papa, I've tried to be respectful to you all my life. And I'm appreciative for all you've done for me. Now you come to me because I'm the commanding general and a means of you turning profits. You embarrass me. The answer is positively no."

"But—"

"I won't stand for one more doggone word about your money schemes. Is that clear, Papa?"

Jesse stared at his son for several moments, then dropped his eyes. "I never thought I'd live to see the day when my own son would talk to me like that." His voice showed hurt.

"Those words were not from a son to a father."

"I'll leave tomorrow."

Grant touched his father's arm, finding a smile. "We'll have dinner tonight."

The Battle of Stones River took place on the last day of the year. Although Rosecrans left much to be desired in its conduct, his subordinate leaders, such as Philip Sheridan, proved brilliant and determined. His opponent, Braxton Bragg, seemed to have his old determination back, but had to pull his army out of the battle. Once more a rebel army escaped. The North proclaimed Stones River a victory, setting the stage for Lincoln's masterful announcement of emancipation:

> *Whereas on the twenty-second day of September, in the year of our Lord one thousand eight hundred sixty-two, all persons held as slaves within any state, or designated part of a state, the people whereof shall be in re-bellion against the United States, shall be then, thenceforward, and forever free; and the executive government of the United States, including the mil-itary and naval authority thereof, will recognize and maintain the free-dom of such persons and will do no act or acts to repress such persons, or any of them, in any efforts they may make for their actual freedom . . .*

The president had labored long with the proclamation, not only in its word-ing, but in its far-reaching impact. By announcing the preliminary edict in the early fall, he had given the country advance notice of what he referred to as "100 days." Though slavery was not necessarily the major issue of the war, he felt its abolishment would tend to weld the North back together.

But the Emancipation Proclamation had even further implications. After its issue, sympathy with the Confederacy would be identified as support of slavery. Both Great Britain and France were friendly to the South and were a strong interventionist threat. In fact, they were the Confederacy's strongest hope for victory. In England, British textile millworkers were out of work because of a shortage of cotton, and the French were eager to have their supply replenished. But, since antislavery sentiment ran so high in both countries, the proclamation should stem any possible involvement in the war.

> . . . And I further declare and make known that such persons of suitable condition will be received into the armed service of the United States to garrison forts, positions, and to man vessels of all sorts in said service. And upon this act, sincerely believed to be an act of justice, warranted by the Constitution upon military necessity, I invoke the considerate judgment of mankind and the gracious favor of Almighty God . . .

On January 2, Major General John A. McClernand took his chartered steamer, *Tigress*, down the big river to take command of what he called the "Army of the Mississippi." His primary subordinate was Cump Sherman, commanding a two-division corps. Sherman had made an ill-starred expedition up the Yazoo—an Indian word for death—at the end of December, and had been strongly repulsed in that impossible morass. Grant had faced McClernand's superseding him in the Vicksburg area with no outward emotion, although he felt nothing but contempt for the man.

No sooner had the Illinoisan assumed command than he organized an attack on nearby Arkansas Post with Sherman's troops. This caught Grant by surprise when he arrived in Memphis a day later. He sent a sharp note to McClernand and a questioning message to Halleck.

Halleck's reply read, "You are hereby authorized to relieve General McClernand from command of the expedition against Vicksburg, giving it to the next in rank or taking it yourself."

"There it is," Rawlins beamed as Grant looked up after reading the message. "They've discovered that McClernand isn't the man. Kinda nice to know they aren't always stupid in Washington, isn't it? Do you want me to write the order?"

"What order?"

"The one relieving McClernand and you assuming command."

"No. I can assume command by virtue of rank anytime I go downriver. In the meantime, I imagine the man will be successful on the Arkansas, and even a small, one-sided victory won't hurt us. Besides, if he'll behave, he might be quite useful in this campaign."

Rawlins shook his head. "General, you're a dreamer."

Grant's headquarters steamer, the *Magnolia*, took up residence at Young's Point, located at the bottom of a river crescent called Milliken's Bend, thirteen miles above Vicksburg. Shortly after arrival, Sherman gave him a bleak appraisal of the situation. Other than somehow getting a large force behind the bluffs to the east, Vicksburg was practically impregnable. Grant listened grimly. At length he said, "We'll get to work on it. But first I have to deal with McClernand."

"Do it fast, Sam. He might do something impetuous or plain stupid."

Grant showed him a letter he'd just received from the ambitious general. In it, McClernand complained about orders being issued directly, rather than going through him. He ended it with, "One thing is certain, two generals cannot command this army . . ."

Sherman smiled wryly. "He's absolutely right."

Rawlins held up an envelope as he joined Grant at the wardroom dinner table on the *Magnolia*. "This just came in from Washburne. It includes a copy of a letter he received from Joseph Medill. You know, the great patriot who's editor of the Chicago *Tribune*. It's kinda chilling to hear how his confidence is shaken, particularly when his respected words reach so much of the public."

Grant swallowed a piece of nearly charcoaled steak. "What does he have to say?"

"He's about ready to give up on the war. He mentions reaching an agreement with the South sometime this year, and thinks we should consider our bargaining position on a boundary line. He thinks that if we don't take Vicksburg, the Secesh will have a ring in our nose and the string in their hands—a straight quote. He wants the War Department to pull some sixty thousand troops out of the Washington area and send them to General Banks in New Orleans. He thinks Banks can then fight his way upriver, and our two commands can squeeze Vicksburg."

Rawlins motioned to an orderly to bring his food. "He doesn't think you are Napoleon, but he believes you can plan and fight, where other generals can't or won't. He lambastes Halleck, but his attack on the president is scary. Let me read his exact words: 'Lincoln is only half awake, and will never better what he has done. He will do the right thing always too late and just when it does no good.' "

Grant frowned. "That's pretty bad. What does Washburne think?"

"He believes Medill is overly upset because he's too close to the move to end the war, but he's also concerned about our ability to take Vicksburg. He believes that if it can be done, you're the man to do it."

Grant shrugged. "I hope he's right."

Grant looked up to see McClernand's angular frame fill most of the doorway. "Come in, General," he said quietly.

The former congressman touched his brim in a casual salute, but his eyes were an angry black, his voice cold. "You wanted to see me, General?"

"That's right. Have a seat."

Rawlins closed the door and they were alone. McClernand began removing his gauntlets, making no move toward the proffered chair. Grant shoved a letter to the front of his desk and cut right to the heart of the matter. "Here's a copy of a special order published this morning. You will note that I am assuming command of this campaign and that department headquarters will be here, or wherever I choose to move it. You will further note, General, that army corps commanders—of which you are one—will resume command of their assigned corps, and will get orders from and report directly to me.

"You will also note that your Thirteenth Corps is responsible for garrisoning Helena and maintaining other positions on the west bank of the river south of Helena. I believe this order clearly states your position, General. As you so ably said in your letter, this expedition doesn't need two commanders. Do you have any questions?"

McClernand's eyes strayed down to the special order, then broke away to Grant's steady gaze. "But, General, I—" His years as a lawyer came quickly to the fore as he found his composure. "There seems to be some mistake. I know you are fully aware of my position here. I am the architect of this expedition, with full approval of both the president and the secretary of war. I have orders authorizing my command. To relegate me to a corps commander's position usurps the authority of the entire governmental structure. I've made plans, General. Right now, I'm ready to rechannel the river. And Vicksburg will be taken in a few weeks."

"Overall plans are no longer your prerogative," Grant replied.

McClernand stiffened. "Then I will temporarily accept the order for the purpose of avoiding conflict in the face of the enemy. But I strongly challenge your right. The matter should be referred through channels to the president."

Grant nodded. "Put it in writing and I'll endorse it and forward it immediately. If there is a reversal, I will cheerfully submit. In the meantime, General, I expect full and cheerful cooperation from you as an army corps commander."

McClernand raised a hand in angry salute. "Yes, sir!"

CHAPTER 33

And now, where circling hills looked down,
With cannon grimly planted,
O'er listless camp and silent town
The golden sunset slanted.
—JOHN REUBEN THOMPSON

Tom Knox, a correspondent of the New York *Herald,* was ushered into Grant's cabin office on the *Magnolia* by Rawlins. The newspaperman handed over orders from the White House authorizing him to return to the Vicksburg area. Grant glanced at the orders and quietly regarded the correspondent. Knox had run afoul of Sherman when he wrote critical articles about the general's misadventure on the Yazoo. He had even gone so far as to bring up the old charges of Sherman's insanity.

And that had brought the furious redhead down on his neck. Charging that the articles had given the rebels Union troop strength and tactical information, Sherman called Knox a spy and had him court-martialed. Knox had been acquitted of espionage, but had been ordered out of the war area under threat of imprisonment. Going to Washington, Knox had enrolled support that reached Lincoln and the president had rescinded the order.

"What do you want from me?" Grant asked.

"These orders say I can stay here if you give your express consent."

Grant glanced at the orders again. "I won't overrule General Sherman, Mr. Knox. Make your peace with him, and you have my permission."

Two weeks later, Tom Knox was back in Grant's office, showing him the letter he'd written to Sherman. The tone of the communication was cool and in no way apologized for the *Herald* reporter's earlier conduct. Knox's face was white as he handed over Sherman's response.

Grant read, "Sir: Come with a sword or musket in your hand, prepared to share with us our fate in sunshine or storm, in prosperity and adversity, in plenty and scarcity, and I will welcome you as a brother and associate. But as a representative of the press which you yourself say makes so slight a difference between truth and falsehood, and my answer is Never!"

Grant handed Sherman's letter back, saying, "Apparently you didn't listen to my advice, Mr. Knox. I will not override General Sherman's decision."

The *Herald* and the president should have known better.

But then, Mr. Lincoln had probably guessed that Grant would support Sherman. He had merely appeased the press. It was Knox who should have known better, Wilson noted in his journal the next day after the newspaperman's departure.

Rawlins stood on the dock, watching the steamer pull in. The visitor he was expecting was Charles A. Dana, the Harvard-educated intellectual, world traveler, poet, coeditor of the *New American Encyclopaedia,* and longtime editor of Horace Greeley's *New York Tribune.* Dana was coming to spend some time at Grant's headquarters on a special mission from the War Department. Ostensibly, the special commissioner was on a tour to report on pay conditions in the armies west of the Alleghenies.

Rawlins had heard that the former editor had left the *Tribune* recently, no longer being able to stomach Greeley's eccentricities—which, to him, bespoke integrity, independence, and perhaps sound, objective judgment on Dana's part. Such a man might see the truth about Grant and become the spokesman the general so badly needed. If not, nothing would be lost.

He extended his hand to the forty-four-year-old commissioner. "I'm

John Rawlins, sir, General Grant's chief of staff. Welcome to Young's Point, Louisiana."

Dana looked surprised. "I didn't think my visit would bring out such an important person, Colonel."

Rawlins smiled. "Just a country lawyer welcoming an important visitor, sir."

"That isn't quite the way I hear it. Washburne told me about you, and I've heard some other tales about the influence you exert over this command."

Rawlins shrugged as they began to walk. "Just a front, Mr. Dana, to keep the parasites away from the general."

"And how is General Grant?"

"Except for not having Vicksburg in his pocket yet, he's fine. And his pocket will soon be full."

Dana raised an eyebrow. "Is that so?"

"Yes, and you might use that term in your first report."

"Report?"

Rawlins stopped, looking directly into the commissioner's eyes. "Yes, sir. The first of the ones you'll be sending Mr. Stanton about the general. You see, our friends have already notified us that a well-regarded spy would descend upon us."

Dana's smile was warm. "Well, I'll be damned. I guess that puts it all up front, doesn't it. Colonel? Will this affect my welcome at the officers' mess?"

"Hardly, sir. The general wants you to be privy to everything."

"Everything?"

"You have the run of the place."

Grant stood at the stern of the *Magnolia* watching the large white moon flit in and out of the few thin clouds. Above and to the right of it, he could make out most of Orion. Even the red planet, Mars, blinked back at him brightly. Like the galaxies above, spring was upon him, meaning that most of the winter had been wasted. A whole season had gone by, a season in which the Union had floundered around, wondering if it should continue to fight, and if so, whether victory could be had.

In his case, little was different. Vicksburg was still firmly in rebel hands, and nearly four miles of the Old Man—the Mississippi—was still denied to Union traffic. To some, it appeared that he had floundered. He'd tried one plan after another and each had failed, seven of them. Someone brought up the old saying, "Seven times against the city." Yes, he'd failed. But he hadn't quit and wasn't about to.

He couldn't just get behind the town and assault it; Joe Johnston could hit him from the rear and his army would be like a piece of cheese in a sandwich if Pemberton attacked at the same time. No, he had to get his troops south of Vicksburg. The idea that young Wilson had planted in his head months earlier now made more sense. Run the enemy batteries. March his soldiers down the Louisiana side of the river, over the improvements that had been built, or around the other bayous, then run the batteries with transports that could ferry them safely across the river. Then he could deal with Johnson alone, or Pemberton alone—if the latter chose to come out of his entrenchments and fight. It would be a dangerous plan, since essentially his army would have to live off the land, something no general in his right mind would do. But sitting on his tail wouldn't accomplish anything!

He'd, by lightning, do it . . .

When Flag Officer Andrew Foote was promoted and transferred, David Porter, an acting rear admiral, assumed command on the Father of Waters. Son of the famous Commodore Porter, the gruff, salty admiral was stocky and bearded, and even more aggressive than his predecessor. He had pushed his doughty little fleet into the bogs of the Yazoo to support Sherman's ill-fated December adventure—and had nearly lost it. He now greeted Grant pleasantly and listened while the general laid out his plan to run the Vicksburg batteries.

Admiral Porter had his own free rein, so he could easily turn Grant down. But as the army commander waited, a now-cold cigar clenched between his teeth, the naval officer nodded his head energetically and said, "By all means, let's do it! But I must warn you that once these craft get downriver, there's no coming back. The four-knot current will slow my gunboats too much to make it past those damned guns."

Grant nodded. "We'll need them down there to link up with General Banks later on." Banks had assumed Federal command in New Orleans after General Butler's departure.

"When, General?"

"As soon as I can get the troops downstream and this moon becomes a sliver."

Julia Grant touched her waterfall of curls as she waited for the show to begin. It seemed only fitting that she should do something special with her hair for the festive occasion. The good Lord knew she had so few occasions to even pretend like this. *Theater on the water* was the phrase she'd coined while talking Ulys into letting her come along on the steamer. He'd been adamantly against it until she sold him on the idea that his having family right there on the river would set an example, would show that less danger existed in running the batteries. He'd wanted to put them ashore until after the big gamble was over. But, although out of range, she was still *here* for what would be one of the most exciting adventures of the war!

The *Magnolia* swayed gently in the dark, mild current, anchored where Grant could watch the hazardous operation without danger. She knew he must have argued with his staff over their location on the river, wishing he could be down in the thick of it. But Rawlins had put his foot down again.

Glancing at Ulys, she could tell by the way he clenched the wooden rail of the steamer that he was knotted up inside. It wouldn't be long now—history would be made right in front of her. He'd promised that their separations would occur only when he was in the field, and she was certain he was planning an extensive campaign now. Otherwise he wouldn't have let them come down to Young's Point to stay with him on the riverboat.

It seemed unearthly silent on the steamer; even the kids were keeping quiet. She glanced at young Fred, standing beside Ulys. The decision to take the boy out of school and let him stay with his father had been difficult, but Ulys felt it was all right. She'd heard that "older than most midshipmen" line until she hated it. He had his father's sword and yellow sash on now, as well as a serious look on his face as he stood by the rail.

My, a son practically in the army—what was she coming to? She'd put on a little weight at the age of thirty-seven, and didn't move quite as quickly on the dance floor—if she ever got a chance these days—but she felt healthy and vigorous, almost like a bride when her lusty Ulys finally came to bed at night. She felt just as youthful when he held her hand while they were alone now and then on the stern late at night. She had stopped asking about the awful things he had to do in battle. He wouldn't tell her anything anyway, not anything that he considered too harsh.

He spoke sometimes of everyday happenings, but she knew he shielded her from the terrible burdens he bore. Now and then, she heard him mumble in his sleep, felt him toss and turn fitfully, bedeviled by the busy mind that couldn't relax.

She touched his sleeve as he intently watched the bend of the river through his glass. "It won't be long now," he said around the cold cigar.

She glanced back to the chair where Mr. Dana smiled so reassuringly. Her sleepy little Jesse was asleep on his lap. The handsome young Colonel Wilson also smiled at her—*Lieutenant* Colonel Wilson. You'd think after all these years, she could keep the ranks straight. Mr. Dana was so pleasant and gentlemanly. Ulys was quite pleased that Washington had sent him out.

"There!" Ulys pointed as the first dark, shadowy shapes of the gunboats began to move past the *Magnolia*. "We'll soon know." He'd told her only that he was undertaking a great gamble, one that could put him behind a desk in Cincinnati or somewhere, if it didn't work out.

Larger shapes were approaching, the transports and supply steamers, dark behemoths moving quietly on the softly lapping, quicksilver water.

How suspenseful!

She waited, hearing her own breathing, saying a silent prayer for the crews.

The first tiny flash of an enemy gun preceded the muffled explosion by several seconds. It was followed by another, and quickly many more, as the high, dark mass that was Vicksburg began to sparkle. It seemed as if a swarm of tiny fireflies had come out, as if dozens of tiny champagne corks were popping in accompaniment. Suddenly a small blaze broke out at a lower level. It grew quickly, like an accusing floodlight, yellow-orange and brightening, giving form to the dark shapes plodding past the town. "They must have saved some old evacuated houses for this," Rawlins said at Ulys's elbow.

Her husband nodded, his eyes glued to the scene.

Small white splashes, the size of raindrops, marked where enemy shells landed around the shadowy figures of the flotilla. Periodic hits could be detected, but still the Union craft lumbered on. Suddenly a transport burst into flames and Ulys's grip tightened on the rail again. He nodded, speaking to no one in particular, "That's why we can't move the troops this way."

The bright red trail of a rocket across the inky black sky caused Julia to think of Francis Scott Key's immortal words:

The rocket's red glare.
The bombs bursting in air,
Gave proof through the night
That our flag was still there.

Instinctively, she looked up at the mast. Yes, the stars and stripes were still there. As was the scarlet, two-starred major general's flag that announced the presence of her husband on board.

Minutes passed. Finally an exultant Wilson lowered his glasses and turned from the rail. "By God, they're making it, sir! We may have lost some barges, but they're getting through!"

Julia felt a flash of happiness as she saw Ulys's grim expression relax. He heaved a sigh and nodded. "Yes, I believe thay have. Now we can get down to business."

She knew her stay on the river was over.

The next morning, the 17th of April, Grant hurried by horseback down to New Carthage, some twenty miles below Vicksburg. The sunken transport that had burst into flames in front of Vicksburg had been his old headquarters steamer, the *Tigress*. One of the turtles had been damaged and a few coal barges had been sunk, but Porter was enthusiastic. "No troops or explosives, but by God, we can get everything else down here. We just can't get back."

Grant nodded in agreement. "I know. The ammunition will just have to come down the west side. As long as we can get forage and primary rations down here, we'll be all right."

"What does Halleck say about all of this? Does he know you're going to go without a supply line?"

"He'll find out."

"Do you know how far your neck is out?"

"Yup."

CHAPTER 34

After Joseph Johnston pulled out of Jackson, the capital of Mississippi, Grant occupied it for a short stay, enjoying the thought that it was Jefferson Davis's home town. That brought the defenders of Vicksburg our of their nest. The hard-fought battle of Champion's Hill followed, ending in a resounding Federal victory. When it was over, Pemberton pulled his demoralized command back inside the defenses of the river fortress and licked his wounds. In addition to losing many men and guns he couldn't replace, one of his top brigadiers—Lloyd Tilghman, the brave commander who had surrendered Fort Henry to Grant and been exchanged in the fall of 1862—was killed in the battle.

Grant was now filled with mixed emotions. His army had fought well and he had bottled Pemberton's command up in Vicksburg, but the thought of a prolonged siege was completely distasteful. He decided to storm the emplaced enemy. On May 19, he was repulsed. Regrouped on May 22, he ordered all three of his corps, Sherman's, McClernand's, and McPherson's, to attack along a line. Although several Federal regiments got inside the rebel works, they couldn't hold. The assault failed and was made more painful because false information from McClernand caused unnecessary casualties. But outlying forts and batteries were in Federal hands, permitting full resupply.

Now it was obvious—nothing other than a siege would bring Vicksburg to its knees.

And Grant finally fired McClernand, banishing him to "somewhere in Illinois, where he could await further orders." Major General Edward Otho Cresap Ord was given command of his XIII Corps.

Admiral Porter brought his river fleet to bombard the town's fortifications and Grant's artillery pounded away daily. What the Federal artillery most needed was coehorn mortars so shot could be lobbed into Vicksburg with a high arc and little chance of overshooting. They weren't available, so makeshift mortars were made from hollowed-out logs. Grant's army grew, strengthened by the first of the Negro regiments he would use for the rest of the war.

Pemberton knew he was doomed, but hung on tenaciously. Once he got word through to the lurking Johnston, asking the general to approach Grant with the idea of giving up Vicksburg if the Union commander would let him march out with his army and guns. Johnston, whose command was too weak to attack Grant, scoffed at the idea. Pemberton, of course, had no idea that Grant wanted his army as much as he wanted to clear the river.

And food supplies continued to dwindle in the beleaguered town.

*   *   *

Grant didn't know what made him do it. Perhaps it was the protraction of the siege, or just a simple weakness on his part. But one night he just *had* to have a drink. It wasn't a matter of violating any pledges, it had nothing to do with Julia or Rawlins, not anything. He just *had* to have a doggone drink!

He knew that Surgeon Daly, who had been at the headquarters for only a short time, might have some spirits. Rawlins had mentioned that he suspected the doctor of imbibing. He made his way to Daly's tent feeling an overpowering urge for that drink. Once he got it into his head that he might have a drink, it was unexplainable, a driving desire that blotted out everything. He didn't even think about resolve, promises, or anything except the thought of that drink going down his throat and spreading its warmth in his body. He didn't care what it was, just as long as it had alcohol in it.

It was quite dark at nine-twenty, but a shaft of light marked the entrance to the surgeon's tent. As he reached for the flap, he heard voices and stood still for a moment. Daly had a visitor, but it didn't matter. All he wanted was that drink. As he pulled the flap back, he heard a voice say with alarm, "It's Rawlins!"

Entering, he saw a bottle of rye and a tin cup sitting on a makeshift desk. He nodded to the two officers inside and pointed to the cup. "May I have some of that, gentlemen?"

Both Daly and the other officer, a visitor, stumbled to their feet. "Uh, yes, I mean yessir!" the surgeon replied.

Grant poured a healthy portion of the whiskey into the cup and held it up. "To the president," he said quietly, then drained the contents. Putting the cup down, he thanked them, touched the brim of his hat in salute, and departed.

Heading back to his tent, the taste of the rye stayed with him for a few moments. It was neither good nor bad. It was whiskey. The warmth was leaving his gullet and it was too soon to feel any effect. But he liked it. He glanced up at the sky as the half-moon darted out from behind a cloud. The drink was like a beam of moonlight.

It meant nothing.

Just a drink.

Grant laughed at the joke Dr. Daly had just finished and sipped from his glass. He had invited the surgeon and his guest, Dr. McMillan from Sherman's command, to his tent for some wine. It was a sort of repayment for the drink of whiskey he had "stolen" the night before. Sergeant Bolding had brought him the case of wine at noon, and he had intended to save it for the day when Vicksburg fell. But, like a kid with a sweet tooth who finds a bag of candy, he'd opened a bottle right after Bolding had left. It was after supper that he'd gotten the idea about returning the doctor's favor.

Now he felt pretty good. The pressures that had been on him for some time had crawled under a rock somewhere and he felt very relaxed.

"I'm not much of a storyteller," he said, "but let me tell you about what General McClernand did. One day I sent Colonel Wilson to tell the general to strengthen his troops at a certain point on the line. Well, McClernand didn't like it and he shouted, 'I'm tired of being dictated to! I won't stand it any longer and you can go back and tell Grant so.' He followed this with a stream of swearwords. Wilson then reined his horse in close and said, 'General, in addition to your highly insubordinate language, it seems you are cursing me as much as General Grant. If this is so, even though you are a major general and I'm only a lieutenant colonel, I'll pull you off that horse and beat the boots off you.' McClernand quickly apologized and said, 'I was only expressing my intense feelings on the subject matter.' " Grant chuckled. "A couple of days later, after Colonel Rawlins got angry and loosed a stream of oaths in my presence, he came back to me and apologized. I told him I understood—that he was merely expressing his intense feelings on the subject matter."

Grant chuckled while the other two officers laughed uproariously.

It was *really* good to relax.

And a little drinking wasn't hurting him a single bit.

The following noon as he was finishing lunch Grant said, "Mr. Dana, I'm going to Sartartia today. Would you like to go along?"

The commissioner smiled. "Why, yes, General, I would."

Sartartia was a hamlet a little over halfway between Vicksburg and Yazoo City on the Yazoo River. There was a Federal outpost there. Taking a cavalry escort, Grant and his small party rode horseback up to Haynes' Bluff, where they boarded a steamer named the *Diligent*. The captain quickly showed Grant to a rather elegant stateroom. "Just make yourself comfortable, sir," he said, pointing to a sideboard that securely held several nearly full whiskey bottles. "It'll be almost nighfall by the time we get to Sartartia."

Grant thanked him, told his aide he could go forward and enjoy the trip, then turned to Charles Dana. "I don't feel too well," he said, "will you excuse me for a while?"

"Yes, sir," the commissioner replied. "I'll go find my own stateroom. I have some letters to write."

As soon as the door was closed, Grant stared at the sideboard. He had a prickly feeling, and drew in a couple of deep breaths. The headache was probably caused by the wine he'd consumed the night before. It could do that if one wasn't used to it. He went to the sideboard and pulled a half-full whiskey bottle from the shallow well that kept it from rolling around. It was scotch whiskey—Crawford's. He hadn't heard of it before. Had to be imported from the British Isles. He'd drunk a small amount of scotch whiskey back in the old days, and had liked it. But it had been too expensive. How could a bottle of this Crawford's be here on a second-rate river steamer?

He pulled out the cork and smelled it.

The pungent odor was appealing.

He tipped it, putting his forefinger over the opening, and tasting it.

The memory was there. It tasted good, exciting.

He reached for a glass and poured in about an inch of the golden liquid. He took a sip and then a couple of large swallows. It stung, but it was good. Warming. He drained the glass and poured again, this time the old four-fingers amount.

"General." It was Dana, tapping on the stateroom door. "General, wake up! General Grant, do you hear me?"

Grant rolled over in the bunk and forced his eyes open.

"General, I have to talk to you!"

Grant shook his head, but nothing made sense. He looked at the whiskey bottle, lying on the bunk beside him. It was almost empty, but the cork was in it. He glanced around the stateroom, barely remembering. A steamer—

"General, are you all right?"

"Yes," he managed.

"A gunboat captain was pulled alongside. He says that our command at Sartartia has removed itself, and that the place might be occupied by the rebels. What do you want to do?"

He didn't quite understand. After a few befuddled moments, he heard Dana say, "Do you want to go ahead or stay here overnight?"

He shook his head again, but it still didn't make sense. "You make the decision," he managed.

After a moment's silence, Dana replied. "Very well."

Grant pulled the cork from the bottle and drained the last of the whiskey. Rebs where? Didn't make sense.

Grant awakened at 5:50. His mouth tasted bad, but yesterday's headache was almost gone. And there was little doubt that he'd consumed a fair amount of whiskey the previous day. He turned up the wick in the kerosene lamp, saw the empty Crawford's bottle, and remembered. Looking back at the sideboard, he thought—a little drink wouldn't hurt anything this morning.

Always made things better.

But a scene from California flashed through his mind. No, that was for someone who *had* to drink. And he could take this stuff or leave it. Hadn't he proved that in all these years? He poured cold water in the white china washbowl and dunked a towel in it. Wrapping it around his head, he sat down in his summer underwear and thought about other California scenes. None of them were pleasant, so he pushed them out of his mind.

He pulled the towel away. He'd played the old backsliding game, but whom had he hurt? When he got right down to it, whom had he actually hurt by drinking yesterday? Had he lost a battle? Had he lost any men? Made *any* kind of a mistake? Had he hurt Julia and the children?

He'd broken his pledge, but that was all. He'd get back to Vicksburg and pour himself back into the siege and the management of his big army. His imbibing in the last couple of days would have absolutely no deleterious effect whatsoever.

Suddenly he thought of Rawlins.

Someone would leak the story of how Grant had disappeared into a stateroom full of whiskey for so many hours. And hadn't there been something about the rebels, someone asking him for a decision?

All at once he felt terribly guilty.

He returned to the washbowl and picked up a bar of soap, not at all proud of the image in the small mirror on the wall.

Fifteen minutes later, wearing a fresh shirt and feeling a little better, he went out on deck and lit his first cigar of the day. The steamer was sitting quietly by a wharf, the dirty water of the Yazoo lapping gently at its sides. The soft orange light of dawn softened everything as it spilled over the other boats in the anchorage and on the nearby buildings. He took a big drag on the cigar and blew it out. He was all right.

Yes, all right, but no matter how he shaded it, he'd been drunk twice lately . . .

Just then Dana walked up. "Good morning, General. Feeling better?"

"Yes, very much so. How's everything here at Sartartia?"

Dana answered quietly, "We are at Haynes' Bluff, General." He went on to describe the previous afternoon's happenings.

When he finished, Grant nodded his head and said, "You made a wise decision, Mr. Dana. Shall we find some breakfast?"

Returning to his headquarters behind Sherman's corps on the north side of Vicksburg at shortly after ten o'clock, Grant ran into a white-faced John Rawlins. As usual, the chief of staff went abruptly to what was on his mind. "General, I have broken every bottle of spirits I could find in this god-damned headquarters this morning—including those damnable quarts of wine in your tent. And I've written you this letter. I finished it this morning at two o'clock." He handed Grant an envelope. "Now before I completely lose my temper, I'm going to get away from you!"

"What is it, Rawlins?"

The chief of staff's eyes were black ice. "Read the letter, General!" With that, he stomped out of the room.

Grant sat at his desk and opened the letter, which read:

> *The great solicitude I feel for the safety of this army leads me to mention what I had hoped never again to do, the subject of your drinking. I hope I am doing you an injustice by unfounded suspicion, but if in error, it had better be on the side of the country's safety than in fear of offending a friend.*

I've heard that you have imbibed, and this gives me sorrow. You have full control over your appetite, and can let drinking alone. Had you not pledged me the sincerity of your honor that you would drink no more during the war, and kept that pledge during your recent campaign, you would not today have stood first in the world's history as a successful military leader. Your only salvation depends upon your strict adherence to that pledge. You cannot succeed in any other way.

The lives of the brave officers and men in this command depend on it, and you owe it to their mothers, wives, and children.

If my suspicions are unfounded, let my friendship for you and my zeal for my country be my excuse for this letter; and if they are correctly founded, and you determine not to heed the admonitions and prayers of this hasty note, by immediately ceasing to touch a single drop of any kind of liquor, no matter by whom asked or under what circumstances, let my immediate relief from duty in this department be the result.

John Rawlins

Grant slowly replaced the letter in its envelope and bowed his head. It was then that he finally felt the deepest remorse.

An hour later, buried back in the paperwork on his desk, Grant turned down a request from Major General Nathaniel Banks for assistance in taking Port Hudson, a smaller downriver stronghold a little over a hundred direct miles northwest of New Orleans. Banks, a former governor of Massachusetts and also a former speaker of the House of Representatives, was another political general. But he was considered to be capable, having taken over the New Orleans command from Major General Ben Butler, whose conduct there was now under scrutiny.

Port Hudson would fall easily, once Vicksburg was in hand.

This done, he glanced once more at Rawlins's accusatory letter and felt bad. When the chief of staff returned that evening, they would have to have a talk. And he dreaded it. He'd never cared very much about what people thought, but Rawlins was his best friend . . .

Two hours later, he inspected the entrenching going on in Ord's corps. The rebel musketry was heavy, he noted, but the enemy artillery fire was quite sporadic—as if the Confederates were saving their shells for a final effort. Or were running short of them. He'd bank on the first opinion. *"Hey, you, get down!"* a rough voice with a Chicago accent shouted at him. Just then a sniper's bullet tore through his sleeve. The voice sounded again. "I don't care if you are a goddamned officer. You needn't draw fire on us!"

Another voice quickly said, "Hush, Jones. Don't you know that little fella is Grant?"

"I don't care if he's Jesus Christ. He's got to get down!"

Grant smiled as he rode back toward the rear. His soldiers were doing just fine, in spite of the less than rewarding work with a spade. He now had seventy thousand mostly entrenched troops in the Vicksburg vise. The June heat was around 95 degrees and he hated to wait, but he knew Pemberton couldn't last much longer.

CHAPTER 35

The 1st of July arrived, and with it a mounting tension in Grant. He sensed the approaching climax and, like an old hunting dog, he had his hackles up. He had sent Sherman out a week earlier with a large screening force to make doubly sure that Johnston had no adventuresome ideas. But the wily rebel general was too smart to risk losing his small army to save a doomed town. Sherman had made no contact.

Prisoner reports indicated that Vicksburg was on its last legs. Rebel morale was low, illness prevalent, the water supply so short it had to be guarded, and already the troops and town's civilians were reduced to eating mules and rats. His "groundhogs," as he called the tunneling Union soldiers, had burrowed their way to the gates, sometimes in passages wide enough to permit four men abreast. Above, they were backed by 220 guns, not counting Porter's gunboats and waterborne mortars. Prior to the assault, a rain of exploding hell would burst devastatingly on the enemy, which would be smashed. His boys would experience no bloodbath this time; they would burst out of the ground into a sick and withered enemy, and overwhelm it.

Everything was being readied for the 6th. By nightfall that night, the Mississippi and Pemberton's army would belong to the Union. It was as sure as a royal flush. Grant sighed as he put his pen down after finishing the order. All these months, all these disappointments and massive problems, all this frustration would culminate in a final engulfing victory.

On the 6th . . .

Lieutenant General John Pemberton stared at his whiskey glass the night of the 2nd. Seated beside him in his large, high-ceilinged bedroom was Major General John Bowen, the subordinate commander on whom he most relied. It was a stifling evening, the still air barely stirred by the gray-haired house servant waving a large palm leaf from the corner of the room. Both generals drank quietly, Pemberton alternating between depression and last-ditch hopes. He was the interloper, the Pennsylvanian who would be blamed for Vicksburg. The obvious scapegoat. What did it matter that he had married a Virginian and lived in that fine state?

He'd done all he could possibly do.

And now it was time. Almost out of rations and water.

He commanded a broken army that wished only to quit and go home, an army well aware that many thought it would never survive if Grant delivered the coup de grâce.

He had few options. "What do you think, John?" he asked quietly. "You knew Grant back in Missouri when he was farming. Will he be a gentleman about this?"

Bowen shrugged. "One never knows what that quiet man will do. Remember Donelson?"

"You mean about unconditional surrender? Well, I won't have it!"

Bowen poured himself some more whiskey. "I don't think you're holding any aces."

"There's still the breakout possibility."

"With what? The men not only won't do it, they wouldn't be worth a plugged nickel if we did manage to squeeze out. Grant's legions would annihilate us."

Pemberton's voice wavered. "But I can't let Davis down."

"It's beyond that, General. We're talking about the survival of thousands of brave young men."

Pemberton stood and angrily threw his glass against the wall. *"I know that!"*

The 3rd of July broke cloudy and muggy, promising some much-needed rain. After an early morning sortie among the troops, Grant busied himself with a long letter to Eaton. The man was doing so well with the contrabands—he doubted if he'd ever make a better find. Then he penned a note to Sherman to plan an immediate campaign against Johnston the moment Vicksburg fell.

He was sipping coffee when an excited Rawlins burst into his tent. *"General, they want to negotiate!* They ran up some white flags a few minutes ago in McPherson's sector, and General Bowen rode out to meet with him. Bowen has a letter from Pemberton to you and wants to meet with you."

Grant lowered the cup as he slowly nodded his head. By lightning, the reb has come to his senses! Maybe the final, bloody finish of this thing could be avoided. But there was still some poker to be played. He said, "I don't think I should see Bowen now. Just bring the letter and we'll see what price Pemberton's demanding."

At three P.M. sharp, under glowering gray cloud formations, Grant watched three mounted men under a white flag ride out of the Confederate works. He lowered his glasses. "It's Pemberton," he said. "C'mon, Rawlins, let's see what he wants this time." The rebel leader, like Buckner at Donelson, had asked for commissioners to arrange the terms of capitulation, but, as at Donelson, Grant had demanded unconditional surrender.

Shortly, Grant and his officers pulled up before Pemberton. Salutes were rendered and everyone dismounted. The center of the battlefield that had echoed the voices of war for seven weeks now lay completely still. Grant spoke evenly, "Shall we go for a walk, General?"

Pemberton looked stiff and sullen. "I suppose that's best."

Just out of earshot, they stopped by a large, shredded tree stump. A few raindrops from the threatening clouds spattered on them. "General Grant," Pemberton began, "now that we're alone together as two professional soldiers and gentlemen, we can work out something satisfactory to both sides. You have a penchant for unconditional surrender, but we can be more civilized and reasonable, I think. You don't wish to lose thousands of men any more than I do. Now, what are your actual terms?"

Grant removed the cigar from his mouth. His face was expressionless. "I believe my letter was clear enough, General. Nothing has changed."

Pemberton's anger reached the surface. "Good God, man, can't you be reasonable? This isn't some kind of a chess game!"

"I know, but then war isn't reasonable, is it?"

Pemberton turned to go. "There's nothing more to discuss."

General Bowen met them a few paces away. "General Grant, may I please have a word with you?"

As Pemberton stalked off, Grant shrugged. "Go ahead, John."

"Well, the general's got a great deal of pride at stake here, him being a Yankee and an old friend of President Davis and all. He's between a rock and a hard place."

"That's his choosing, not mine."

"But, General, I'm not just thinking of him in this. My interest lies in the men—an awful lot of whom are going to die or get maimed if we don't reach some kind of an agreement. I was thinking that a parole might be acceptable to him. It would be an expensive headache to ship us all up North. And you know as well as I that paroled prisoners are nothing but trouble if we cheat and try to use them again. They think they're out of it and never are worth a damn again. These hungry boys just want to drift off and go home."

Grant peered at the man he'd known from Hardscrabble days. "Thirty thousand men is a pretty big gamble, what with the Confederacy needing troops so badly."

A quick flush showed in Bowen's cheeks. "Sir, we still have honorable leaders."

"I know."

"Just consider it. Anything is better than more bloodshed."

Grant nodded his head. "I'll think about it."

That night, word flashed over the wire that Major General George Meade, the recently appointed commander of the Army of the Potomac, had defeated General Robert E. Lee's Army of Northern Virginia outside an obscure Pennsylvania town called Gettysburg. The logical part of Grant that was also noble was greatly pleased; the small part of him that was all too human thought, Bad timing.

Rawlins said it for him, "That battle sure stole our thunder. While they're shooting off rockets up North, they'll barely know what's happening here."

"Our boys will know, and so will Davis," Grant replied. He looked into the light of the kerosene lamp near his elbow. "I wonder what happened up there?"

"No details. Just that Lee is leading his shattered brigades back into Virginia in driving rain."

Grant shook his head. "And another one gets away."

"What does that do to your decision, General?"

"Nothing. I'm going to offer the parole."

"Can you really trust them?"

"I hope so."

At a few minutes past ten on the morning of the Union's eighty-seventh birthday, white flags suddenly appeared in the sunshine above the Confederate lines. Southern soldiers in ragged gray and butternut had heard that they were out of the war, and most rejoiced, at least inwardly. Soldiers in blue handed out hardtack and water, and the only cheer that went up was raised from a Northern regiment for the gallant defenders. In a house on the Jackson Road, where Grant and his staff met with Pemberton and his officers, all was not as warm. The Southern commander and most of his staff were disagreeable to the point of rudeness, and when Grant asked for a drink of water, he was told he could get it himself.

Grant shrugged off the rebel boorishness. The conquest of Vicksburg was complete. The Union had a great, bona fide victory to celebrate, the Mississippi was about to be reopened, the will to preserve the Union had been salvaged, and the Confederacy had just been shrunk considerably. He'd send some troops down to help Banks with Port Hudson, but that final rebel point on the river would fall easily.

It was simply a *great* day.

CHAPTER 36

It was a time for plaudits and they flooded in from a grateful nation, from Grant's friends, and from his superiors. A telegram from Halleck announced: "It gives me great pleasure to inform you that you have been appointed a major general in the Regular Army, to rank from July 4, the date of your capture of Vicksburg." Grant accepted all of the acclaim with his customary shrug, except for the one letter that moved him. It was from the greatest man of the time, and he would keep it the rest of his life.

My Dear General:

I do not remember that you and I ever met personally. I write this now as a grateful acknowledgement for the most inestimable service you have done the country. I wish to say a further word. When you first reached Vicksburg, I thought you should do what you did, but later I doubted your plans. Now, I wish to make the personal acknowledgement that you were right and I was wrong.

Yours very truly,
A. Lincoln

Grant read the preliminary report of the battle of Gettysburg with interest. George Pickett, the second lieutenant who had torn down the enemy colors at Chapultepec, had led his division in a fatal but heroic charge on the third day. Dick Ewell, "the eagle with a lisp," had commanded one of Lee's corps—on one leg. How well he remembered coming back from leave at Jefferson Barracks after the Fourth Infantry had departed, and getting those extra days of leave from Dick Ewell. And what was that old joke Ewell used to tell—"When an Indian was asked whether a child was white, he'd answer, 'Part Indian, part missionary.'" Longstreet was mentioned often, also as a corps commander. Pete Longstreet, the great friend tied to a thousand memories. Would they ever meet in battle?

Miss Mary Emma Hurlbut sort of came with the new headquarters establishment. Immediately after the surrender, Grant moved into part of the twenty-six-room mansion owned by William Lum. The Lum estate was located on lovely grounds, high on a prominent hill that afforded a sweeping view of the river. Lum was a wealthy aristocrat, cut from the grand old Southern bolt, who had accepted the fortunes of war and decided to make the best of it. He and his family made do in the mansion, along with Grant and his staff.

Emma Hurlbut—no relation to the Shiloh general—was a charming, fair-haired young woman from Danbury, Connecticut, who had come to visit the Lums just before the war. Her stay had been extended through the hostilities. To keep busy, Miss Hurlbut had assumed a semi-governess role with the Lum children. Partly at Grant's suggestion, and partly because of his own morality, Rawlins had assumed the role of protector of the Lum women and their friends who came to the house. And none of the hotbloods on the staff wanted to tangle with him.

But it was more than that with Rawlins; from the first day when he set up the headquarters he had been taken with the attractive, witty Emma. Three days later, he asked her to go for an evening stroll and was delighted by her strong Union sentiments.

"But how could you stay here," he asked, "feeling as you do about the wrongs of this war?"

Her smile was bright. "I didn't feel like taking a long swim or walk."

"What about the Lums? How do they feel about your views?"

"Out of respect to them, I keep my opinions mostly to myself. But Mr. Lum was against secession from the beginning."

They found a pleasant bench under a huge oak near the edge of the grounds. Rawlins spoke earnestly. "Miss Hurlbut, you don't know how delighted I am to find you here. My wife has been dead for two years now, and I've been so wrapped up in the war and General Grant that, well, I hardly know how to talk to a fine young woman like yourself. I'll be damned if I do—excuse me for swearing."

Little crinkles marked the corners of her deep blue eyes when she smiled. "Why don't you just be yourself, Colonel? My father cursed now and then, and didn't mean anything by it. As a starter, why don't you tell me about your wife? Surely there must be something you've never been able to talk about."

She was so right, he thought. He had never really been able to share his loss with anyone. He'd unloaded some of it on Grant, but hadn't wanted to burden him with it. "Well, if you don't mind, I'd kind of like that. Her name was Elly and she was sweet and gentle, and . . ." The pain was still there. "And we were good friends, Miss Hurlbut, good companions. She bore me three fine children and God found a reason to take her from me before I ever had a chance to make things easy for her. I loved her very much."

They began to walk again and without realizing it, John Rawlins talked on for nearly thirty minutes, interrupted and encouraged only by Emma's gentle questions. And in the end, he felt cleansed, comforted. As they reached the house he spoke softly, touching her hand. "Thank you so much for listening."

She paused, looking deeply into his dark, earnest eyes. "Thank you for trusting me enough to tell me."

"May we do this again tomorrow night, if I promise to be more fun?"

Her smile washed over him. "I laugh easily."

Their evening walks became ritual, a part of the day Rawlins anticipated more and more. He knew he was falling totally in love with her. Sundays, he rented a rig for drives in the country. On the second of these, he drove down to the base of Haynes' Bluff and described the disappointing early days of the campaign. Her eyes reflected her interest. "Just think, John, I was probably the only person in the whole town who wanted you to get up there."

Rawlins stared out at the Old Man's broad expanse of slowly moving, muddy brown water. After a few moments he said, "Emma, there's something I have to tell you, something that may change our relationship."

"Yes?" She looked at him calmly.

There was pain in his eyes as he turned. "No one knows about this. I've just never told anyone before. I have some fears that have been growing stronger lately—at least until you entered my life. Both of them involve death. One has haunted me since childhood and the other is more recent.

"The latter is consumption. I haven't coughed much here in Vicksburg, I guess because of the warm weather. But I did last winter, every now and then. Anyway, you know how Elly died, and I may have the early symptoms."

She took his hand and held it firmly. "Nonsense. Anyone can cough when he's traipsing around with an army, sleeping in tents and all. You just had a cold that hung on, that's all. Such a meaningless thing couldn't change the beauty we've found."

"I hope you're right. I just had to tell you."

Her smile was tender. "Now what's the other terror?"

"I've told you about my father and his drinking. Ever since I can remember, I've had this fear that I would die a damned drunkard—that I had inherited this blighting weakness for drink from him. I show it only in my unbending stance against intemperance, but deep down it gnaws at me constantly. I'm afraid that something will let go within me, let the floodgates down, and I'll jump into a whiskey barrel with both feet, and never be able to get out."

Emma leaned up and brushed his cheek with her lips. "You're never going to be a drunk, darling. Not you, not the strong-willed John Rawlins I know so well and have heard so much about. Why, I've heard that you are the scourge of the command, the straight-laced old dictator who rides herd over all the ne'er-do-wells on the staff. And on the general, himself. Rumor is that you taste his water, just to make sure he isn't nipping."

Rawlins chuckled. "Hell, I'm not that bad."

"Neither are your chances of becoming a drunk. You've only nourished a sense of guilt for your father. You saw what it did to your family and feel a dirtiness you can't wash off. You, my handsome John, have as much chance of being a sot as I have of becoming president of the Confederacy."

For several moments they looked deeply into each other's eyes. The pain disappeared as he drew her into his arms. He kissed her gently, then responded to her darting tongue. Smiling down into her eyes, he said, "All right, if you can quell those fears of mine and heat up everything else in this body, then, by God, you ought to marry me."

She sighed and snuggled tightly. "That would make me a very lucky Yankee lady, darling."

"We'll talk about it when I get back from Washington."

She looked up in surprise. "What?"

"I've decided I should go in and represent the general briefly at court."
"How?"

"I'm going to see the bigwigs—Stanton, Washburne, and the president."

Her eyes widened. "You're going to see Abraham Lincoln?"

He grinned. "He needs to know why Grant is the best general in the army, and I'm going to tell him."

Rawlins was warmly accepted by everyone in Washington, including the president. His knowledge, fervency, and the manner in which he presented matters in the West impressed Stanton, even Halleck, and particularly Lincoln. He even waylaid a plan to make his boss the new commander of the Army of the Potomac, an assignment that would have thrown the Westerner into a cauldron of petty jealousies. When he returned to Vicksburg, he was secure in the knowledge that Grant was both understood and respected.

Shortly after his return, Grant surprised him after dinner one evening by leading him into the large parlor of the mansion. Waiting there were the staff, Mr. and Mrs. Lum, Emma Hurlbut, James Wilson, Chaplain Eaton, Cump Sherman, and James Birdseye McPherson. Rawlins looked every bit like a displeased chief of staff who should know about such things. But before he could ask what was going on, everyone formed a circle around him and General Grant said with a frown, "It's pretty bad when the chief of staff of a command at this level can't keep his rank straight."

Grant pulled a pair of brigadier general's shoulder boards from his pocket as James Wilson quickly read the special order from Washington that promoted John Rawlins to that rank. Asking Miss Hurlbut to help him snap them on, Grant grinned. "You've come quite a way, my friend."

The profane country lawyer who hadn't known how to stand at attention two years earlier *had* come quite a way.

The horse's name was Blazer because he liked to gallop. He was a big bay, imperfectly broken for some reason, a gift from Banks. Grant had liked the fire in the charger's eye the moment Banks's orderly had led him out of the stable. And how they had flown on an early morning ride. With a little getting to know each other, he and the horse should form a fine friendship.

How fast the animal was!

He'd liked to have had him back in Detroit, where he could have won some money on him. Now, as they raced along the railroad track on the way back into town, he'd outdistanced the other horsemen by at least a hundred yards, and was gaining even more . . .

The animal was just one of the several nice things that had happened to him since arriving in New Orleans on September 2. He had been honored, serenaded, and cheered in these three days. The corps he had loaned to Banks after the fall of Vicksburg was Ord's, the old XIIIth. It had been drawn up at parade to salute him that morning. And though he didn't normally care for such formalities, he had caught himself waxing sentimental as his former troops passed in review.

Next he had attended a most pleasant luncheon with Banks and Adjutant General Lorenzo Thomas, who was visiting from Washington. One of their points of discussion had been the use of Negro troops in combat, a development he favored. He'd heard that the rebels had been employing a handful of colored sharpshooters all along. He figured that sometime soon the South would be down to such manpower bare bones that Davis would have to use his black pool of bodies as replacements. Interesting concept—enslaved coloreds fighting to preserve their bondage!

Yes, the luncheon had been enjoyable, a lot of backslapping over Vicksburg. He'd sipped from a single glass of wine during the toasts, but hadn't felt any effect from the alcohol. It was okay, Rawlins, no breach of trust.

As he rode on, the fine horse sent him signals that he wanted to run. An animal could do that to a sensitive rider. "All right, Blazer, you want to go, we'll do it!" Urging the big animal into a gallop, he quickly lost himself in the pure joy of riding. His entourage streamed out behind him, so after a couple of minutes he pulled back on the reins to wait for them. After all, he was in town and—

It all happened so fast that nothing could be done. The locomotive rounded the bend in the track and simultaneously its whistle *blasted!* Blazer shied, rearing, and lost his footing. *No, he was falling!*

NO!

Grant lay sweltering in the bunk of the steamer. Tossing the book he'd been reading aside, he painfully reached for the water glass. Two weeks and the pain was still plaguing him. Most of the swelling in his leg and hip had gone down, but his ribs were still as touchy as boils. Childish trick he'd pulled down there in New Orleans, but he'd just felt like cutting loose with that big bay. They said the animal had landed right on him. If whoever had tried to break that willful horse had just taken the time to expose him more to street sounds, he wouldn't have been so doggone skittish at a train whistle. He'd never been knocked out and banged up so badly on a horse before— not even close, even though he'd ridden some pretty wild ones.

The stay in the hospital had been highly unpleasant, even with the special care afforded an army commander. But that was due to his extreme discomfort. He'd be a little more careful the next time he rode a restive horse in town.

He picked up the New Orleans newspaper and reread the story about Rosecrans. Apparently the arrogant Ohioan had finally gotten off his butt in East Tennessee and was outmaneuvering Bragg. Now he was pushing the North Carolinian out of Chattanooga, apparently headlong. Maybe Rosecrans would prove himself yet.

For some reason, he felt a strong pull toward East Tennessee. Did he have further destiny there? Would he be sent there to essentially end the war in the West, forcing the Confederacy to sue for peace? Could he do it if given the chance?

CHAPTER 37

October 17 was a pleasant, sunny day in Indianapolis. Grant had just returned from a short hobble around the train, when Rawlins handed him the message stating that they should await another train bearing Secretary Stanton. The message had arrived just in time, because the train carrying Grant, his family, and his entire headquarters had been scheduled to depart for Louisville in just fifteen minutes.

Grant edged up into his car with Bolding's help. His left leg was still stiff and somewhat painful during various movements; otherwise he was getting around quite well with the aid of a cane. He glanced at the message again. He was to meet "an officer from the War Department."

Such evasive wording was unnecessary—it was no secret that the "officer" was the difficult and abrasive Stanton himself. Although he'd never met the secretary, he had communicated with the man by telegraph on various occasions. What had brought him out of the capital to issue orders? And why Indianapolis? Well, he'd soon find out. In the meantime, he went back to Dana's letter. It had finally caught up with him at Cairo.

> *With the Army of the Cumberland*
> *Chattanooga, Tennessee*
> *Sept. 28th, 1863*
>
> *My Dear General,*
>
> *I hope you are mending well from your accident. We certainly need someone like you here to straighten things out. General Rosecrans appeared quite brilliant in the beginning of this campaign, outmaneuvering Bragg so well, but then he became overconfident. As you will have heard well before you get this, he met his Waterloo at Chickamauga Creek, about a dozen miles south of here.*
>
> *Rosecrans must have thought he was chasing panic-stricken recruits all the way to the gulf. But there wasn't any panic in Bragg. He pulled everything together and counterattacked with the help of Longstreet, who had just arrived with his famous corps from Virginia. The Army of the Cumberland was all but routed and might have been decimated except for an amazing holding action by General Thomas.*
>
> *Now we're locked into Chattanooga, with a terrible supply problem. The only route in is a horrible muddy and hilly route that requires an eight-day wagon trip. And if the rebels get smart, they'll close that. We've received word that General Hooker is bringing the Eleventh and Twelfth Corps over from Virginia, but that'll just add to our supply difficulty.*
>
> *I've also heard that you've been directed to move Sherman over here,*

but he'll have to repair track as he comes—meaning the game here may be up before he arrives. I don't trust Rosecrans. Something seems to have snapped since Chickamauga. He is totally lethargic and indecisive. I reported to Stanton that I wonder if he is of sound mind.

Therefore, General, I sincerely hope that Washington sees fit to bring you here. All this army needs is an iron hand to put it back together. The Gordian knot needs to be cut.

Your Respectful Servant,
Charles A. Dana

Grant put the letter away and looked up as Rawlins, standing near the front of the car, said, "Here they come, General."

The hard-headed Edwin McMasters Stanton had come out of Steubenville, Ohio, to become a skillful attorney on the Washington stage. By the mid-'50s he was appearing before the Supreme Court; in 1860 he was Buchanan's attorney general. Politically he had been a Jacksonian who deplored slavery but upheld the civil rights of slaveholders. He'd been Lincoln's secretary of war since '62. Grant waited in the middle of the car, next to his chief surgeon, Dr. E. D. Kittoe. Stanton removed his stovepipe hat, revealing his bald head, as he came into the car. The dark, rather close-set eyes were well-bagged; the downturned, thick lips rode like a skullcap over the long beard that was dominated by two nearly white columns of forward-pushing, lightly curling whiskers. The second most powerful man in the Union stepped forward, hand outstretched, saying, "General Grant, how good it is to finally meet you in person. I'd recognize you anywhere from your pictures." Grant suppressed a smile as Stanton lustily shook the hand of the bearded and startled Dr. Kittoe.

"But, sir," Kittoe managed. "*This* is General Grant."

Two dozen years of courtroom experience rescued the surprised secretary. "Oh," he said, turning, "excuse me. It's an honor, sir."

Grant smiled, shaking hands. "The honor is mine, Mr. Secretary."

Stanton had decided to come to Indianapolis so he could share the trip to Louisville with Grant. The train ride was shortened by the secretary's expansive description of the war around Washington, and finally the campaign at Chattanooga. He explained that Burnside—ex-commanders of the Army of the Potomac seemed to be everywhere, Grant thought—had recently moved his depleted Army of the Ohio down to eastern Tennessee to meet the president's longtime wish to support the loyalists there. Finally, an hour from their destination, Stanton produced two orders—each designating Grant the commanding general of the Division of the Mississippi, a new command that encompassed the old Department of the Ohio, the Department of the Cumberland, and the Department of the Tennessee. Except for Louisiana, where Banks was senior to Grant, everything west of the Alleghenies was his.

The only variance in the two orders was in the name of the subordinate general officer to command the Army of the Cumberland. One kept Rosecrans, the other named General George Thomas to replace him. Grant read the two orders, then glanced out the window. As the browning countryside rolled by, his mind drifted back through the years to West Point. It was evening, and a cadet corporal was escorting three seniors into his lowly room. He jumped to attention as they spoke to him. One was Ewell, one was Sherman, and one was Thomas; the cadet corporal was Rosecrans.

"Do you want some time to think it over?" Stanton asked.

Grant turned back to the present. "No, I want Thomas."

After seeing Julia and the children comfortably situated with Louisville relatives, Grant headed his train on down to Stevenson, Alabama. Arriving there, he was briefed by the one-armed Major General Oliver Otis Howard, commander of the XI Corps. Rosecrans, on his way north to oblivion, spent a cool half-hour with Grant, explaining the "great" plan that he claimed no one would let him execute. Then came the arduous two-day horseback journey to Chattanooga via the muddy, mountainous wagon road. The trip was difficult enough for the injured Grant until his horse slipped and came falling down on his bad leg. The pain was terrible after the spill, requiring many tightly clenched cigars as he continued the journey.

He rode into the little town of Chattanooga just as dark was falling on Friday, October 23. The storm he and his party had ridden through had been raging for two days, and a chilling rain was still falling. His topboots were spattered with mud and his uniform soaked, as he was helped into the living room of the plain, one-story building that housed Thomas's headquarters. Dropping into an armchair in front of a cheerfully burning fire, he accepted a cup of hot coffee. He was chilled and bone tired. He hadn't eaten in several hours and his leg hurt dreadfully. Leaning back, he closed his eyes.

Major General George Henry Thomas, recently nicknamed the "Rock of Chickamauga," was the opposite of Pemberton—a Virginian who stayed in Union blue. An artilleryman, he had won two brevets in the Mexican War. He had been on active duty as a major under Lee and Albert Sidney Johnston in the Second Cavalry in Texas just prior to secession. Shortly after the war began, he had been promoted twice to command that regiment, and had gone on to glory as a general officer.

Thomas was a huge man, imperious-looking, ever in control of himself, and reserved to the point of coolness except to his closest intimates. His deep-set, widely spaced eyes were guarded by bushy brows that added to his apparent aloofness. A strong chin, enhanced by a short, graying beard, touched off his fierce look. He was six years older than Grant.

Grant sipped his coffee and asked, "Do you have a plan to break the siege?"

Thomas's voice was flat. "Yes. When you're ready to ride, I'll show you the terrain and explain it to you."

"That'll be tomorrow morning."

"I heard your horse fell."

"I'll live. Now tell me what you have in mind."

"Do you know Baldy Smith—William F. Smith?"

"Engineer, isn't he?"

"Yes, Class of 'forty-five. He commanded a corps at Fredericksburg, but got crosswise with Burnside and wound up losing his second star. Baldy's got a good plan that I've already approved."

Grant stared into the fire. Here was a general, after one week in command of a major army under siege, with what he called a good plan that he hadn't acted upon. "Let's hear it," he replied.

Thomas told an aide to bring a map and an additional kerosene lamp. Using his finger as a pointer, the big man showed him the town, the river, the location of Federal troops, and the positions of Bragg's troops atop Missionary Ridge to the south and Lookout Mountain to the southwest. He then pointed to a place where Baldy Smith planned to set up a night river crossing to open a supply line from Bridgeport, Alabama, thirty miles southwest. This was followed by more specific details. When he finished, Grant asked some incisive questions and finally nodded his head. "Risky, but I like the concept. Besides, we haven't got many other choices. We've got an army without enough shoes, on half rations, with hardly any ammunition. Can't fight that way. I'll be ready to ride in the morning."

Shortly before noon the next day, Grant sat astride his horse on a little hill just south of the city. He was fascinated by the view. Before him lay Missionary Ridge, a long crust of a hill that rose northeast of the town and ran nearly seven miles to the southwest. It was some four hundred feet high, more in places. Through his glasses, he could easily discern the movement of rebel troops on it. Thomas was even able to point out where Bragg's command post was located. Grant thought it highly intriguing, as if it were some European scene where the generals were surveying a battlefield like the marshals of God.

"They're heavily dug in," Thomas added.

Off to the southwest, beyond a turn in the river called Moccasin Bend, rose majestic Lookout Mountain, a sharp-pointed reef over a thousand feet high. It appeared to have thrust itself northward from Alabama to explode in covetous control of the valley below. Abruptly from the river, the cultivated and tree-held slope surged upward to three hundred feet of solid rock cliff that capped off its top. Grant had been fascinated by this amazing natural fortress since part of the clouds had lifted and revealed it during his earlier ride that morning.

They rode back to the house that Rawlins had selected to be Grant's headquarters. The reconnaissance had been well worth the discomfort. After giving official approval to Baldy Smith's river escapade for the 27th, Grant turned to other pressing matters. A telegram from Halleck asked if he could help Burnside to the east in Knoxville. He sent a quick no, explaining that he still didn't have supplies, nor enough men for his own mission. He also sent orders to Sherman to get out of the railroad business and speed his command to Chattanooga without delay.

Since the bad blood between Hooker and his XII Corps commander, Major General Henry Slocum, was well-known, Grant ordered the latter to remain in the rear with one division to guard the Nashville railroad. Hooker with his remaining three divisions was ordered out of the Stevenson-Bridgeport area to come east in coordination with the river gamble.

Well before dawn on the 27th, Baldy Smith's plan to open what would be called the "cracker line" was put into motion. A brigade was floated on flatboats with muffled oars downstream on the Tennessee, around Moccasin Bend, to its destination at Brown's Ferry. A welcome morning fog concealed the movement from prying rebel eyes on Lookout and along the west bank of the river as Baldy's navy stealthily landed, seized the area, and allowed the engineers to fasten together the pontoon bridge.

The whole thing might work.

In the two-story house on the bluff that housed Grant's staff, several pots of weak coffee had been consumed since Thomas and a number of his officers had joined Grant at daybreak. Now, at shortly before nine, a courier burst through the door, breathlessly handing a dispatch to James Wilson. Seconds later, he read aloud, "River mission a total success. Only thirty-eight casualties. Ferry and opposite valley in firm Union hands. Bridge soon ready for supply elements. Signed, W. F. Smith, Brigadier General, Commanding."

One of Thomas's aides let out a whoop. A resounding cheer followed, as staff officers lost their dignity, some pummeling each other, the quietest ones grinning from ear to ear. Baldy's plan had meshed like clockwork!

Grant pulled himself stiffly out of his chair and walked around the table, hand outstretched to Thomas. "Congratulations, General, you pulled it off in great style."

Thomas couldn't conceal his smile. "It was Baldy's show all the way."

Grant nodded his head. "Maybe we can get his second star back."

"I'll write the recommendation."

Grant reached for a cigar. "Now we can get down to the real business of beating Bragg."

CHAPTER 38

Even Thomas's chief of staff, Major General Joe Reynolds, had once admitted that his boss *was* slow. But it was a common disease of many of the leaders on both sides of the war. Another common failing of many officers was the inability to carry their brilliance at lower levels over to top command. Outstanding commanders at regiment, brigade, and division, they failed at corps and army level. Some had this failing in addition to being slow. Two such Confederate generals were about to meet at Braxton Bragg's headquarters above Chattanooga. One had failed at Gettysburg, the other was faltering now.

Tall and gangling, with a sparse, gray-shot beard, the forty-six-year-old Bragg had been well known throughout the regular army for his short temper and testiness. Appearing ten years older because of a chronic stomach disorder that was probably aided and abetted by his choleric disposition, he looked even more difficult because of his black beetle brows. The heroic artilleryman who had received three brevets in Mexico had been a full general in the Confederate Army since shortly after Shiloh.

Now, as he awaited the arrival of General Longstreet, Bragg stood on an outcrop of rock staring down at Chattanooga and thought about his plan. During Jefferson Davis's visit three weeks earlier, the president had been in favor of sending Longstreet to kick Burnside out of Knoxville. Now, he was going to do just that. Old Pete, as he was familiarly known, had been part of the recent "palace revolt" that had brought the president to Chattanooga. The corps commanders in the Confederate Army of Tennessee had somehow had the audacity to petition Davis to get rid of him—remove Braxton Bragg, one of the most brilliant officers in the army, from command! Davis, of course, had retained him, although it had been rumored that Polk, Hardee, Buckner, and Longstreet had all turned down the top command. Nonsense—they couldn't *handle* it!

Crybabies. They had wanted to charge right into Tennessee and take a big chance of losing their army after his great victory at Chickamauga. The Confederacy had dearly needed that victory, and he hadn't been about to let a follow-up defeat mar its significance.

He had insisted that Missionary Ridge was a natural fortress, the best place to hold off the Army of the Cumberland from any major operations in the Deep South. Now he had it practically imprisoned down there.

So, by God, he was still in command and intended to stay there!

Longstreet certainly didn't have any complaints coming. Word had gotten around that Lee wouldn't have lost at Gettysburg if Old Pete hadn't dragged his feet like a petulant schoolboy when he didn't get his own way. So, if the goddamned troublemaker wanted to face the facts, he had already kept the South from winning the war . . .

Lieutenant General James Longstreet was, at forty-two, a big man. He wasn't quite six feet tall, but he was bulky and gave the impression of being powerful. He had a receding hairline, but was blessed with a handsome nose, high cheekbones, and a luxuriant, slightly graying beard. Nicknamed "Lee's Warhorse," the South Carolinian turned Georgian didn't like the idea of having his proud First Corps out here in Tennessee under Bragg, not when Lee needed him in Virginia.

He pulled on the cigar as he strode toward Bragg's headquarters through the light drizzle. Now he'd finally be fighting Sam Grant. He'd hoped it wouldn't come down to that, but wars didn't always choose bedfellows or opponents with very much sensitivity.

Sam Grant.

He'd never for the life of him figured out what had gotten into Sam in the years since they'd last met. The man had been a downright poverty case then. Who would ever have guessed that damned Ohio farm boy could learn the trade of generaling so quickly? But old Sam had always been a quiet force. Strong and steady, except when he was supposed to have gone off his rocker a little bit in California. And he could make his men fight, all right. What was it that Yankee prisoner had said? "When the boys heard General Grant had come in, they all seemed to stiffen somewhat. Everything seemed brighter, more organized, something they could just *feel*. They'd done got a general who knew how to *win!*"

Well, Sam, we'll see about that.

Now he had to see that goddamned Braxton Bragg. Why had it been his plight to be hooked up with this egotistical, contentious North Carolinian anyway? The bastard had been fighting with *somebody* his whole career. What was the story that followed him in the old army . . . when he was stationed at a post where he was a temporary battery commander *and* the post quartermaster, he had requisitioned something for his battery, only to turn down the request as the quartermaster, proving that "not only could he not get along with anyone else in the army, he couldn't get along with *himself!*"

Longstreet entered the headquarters tent ready to do battle.

It was chilly in the big tent, but Bragg sat in shirtsleeves at a field desk in the private cubicle that served as his office. He pointed to a stool and quickly dispensed with the formalities. Launching directly into the purpose of his summons, he said, "General Longstreet, you will be moving your corps east to attack the Yankees at Knoxville, taking two divisions of infantry with supporting artillery and cavalry. You'll move up the railroad to Loudon, where you'll organize for the assault on Burnside—whom you'll destroy, capture, or drive out of East Tennessee. You'll accomplish this mission as quickly as possible and return here. As you know, Sherman is on his way and I'll need you to balance the odds."

Longstreet stroked his beard, speaking quietly, "Then why send me in the first place?"

"Because those are your orders, sir!"

"Well, they don't make much sense to me. Would you afford me the courtesy of your reasoning? Seems to me we should attack and defeat Grant right now, before Sherman gets here."

Bragg was losing his famous temper. "Dammit, General!" He paused, drew in a deep breath and blew it out, then went on. "All right, Burnside is spread all over East Tennessee. He's weak and undersupplied in Knoxville, a sitting duck. Secondly, when Grant finds you gone, he may send someone after you, weakening his force here. If he does, you'll outmaneuver that force, and we'll crush Grant's remaining army once and for all."

Old Pete locked into Bragg's dark glare. "It still doesn't make much sense to me."

"Goddammit, Longstreet, those are your orders. *Now, carry them out!*"

The First Corps commander nodded, tossed off a casual salute, and turned to leave. At the tent flap, he stopped and turned around. "I'm on my way, General, but between us, it seems this army's sad fate is to wait until all the good opportunities have passed, and then in desperation seize upon the least favorable."

Grant received the news of Longstreet's departure with mixed emotions. To Rawlins he said, "I don't know what Bragg is thinking of, unless he assumes we'll just sit here. That's a mighty big corps to send away."

Rawlins shrugged. "Can there be any other reasons to split his force?"

Grant shook his head. "I don't know, unless it was Davis's idea. The only thing I'm certain of is that Burnside had doggone well better have some starch in him. His messages have been pretty resolute, so I think he does. Still, I have to come up with a way to help him."

"Yes, because Halleck will keep burning up the telegraph until you do."

"I sure wish Sherman would get here. If I had him now, I'd attack Bragg immediately. This sitting still, letting him call the shots, isn't the way to fight a doggone war."

"Maybe he still thinks they beat us at Shiloh."

Grant frowned, going to the map. "I sure hope so."

Grant sent word to Halleck that he couldn't help Burnside. The general in chief shot back a request that Grant do his utmost to encourage the East Tennessee commander. Grant knew only one way to do it. When Burnside reported that Longstreet's new dispositions lacked effectiveness, that he seemed torpid, Grant's subtle message to him read, "I see no reason to retreat from East Tennessee. If I did so at all, it would be after losing most of my army. Apparently that will not be necessary for you."

On November 13, word came that Sherman was in Bridgeport and would be in Chattanooga the following night. Grant invited Thomas, Hooker, and Dana to join him for dinner that evening, so planning could commence immediately. When the independent Hooker sent word that the likable one-armed Howard would come instead, Rawlins groused, "Just like the son of a bitch. He can't get over having commanded the great Army of the Potomac, and doesn't want to defer to you one iota." But Grant didn't answer; the invitation had only been a formality. He looked forward to getting his army moving—and seeing the redhead.

Sherman had never been accused of flamboyance, but he could enter a room with such spontaneity, with such brisk movement, that those present often felt a current of decisive strength. Even to his detractors and competitors, Sherman was a presence. And so it was when he finally arrived at the house on the bluff at nine-thirty the night of the 14th. He looked around as he shook the rainwater from his slicker and slouch hat. His ungloved hand tossed off a salute and quickly found Grant's warm grip. He nodded or spoke to everyone, then looked back into the warm blue eyes he knew so well. "Any brandy around here, or do I have to settle for a cigar?"

Grant chuckled. "In a headquarters managed by Rawlins?"

Sherman handed his slicker to an aide and dropped into a chair. "Well, when does the war start? I'm tired of playing railroad and marching around this damned country. I've brought seventeen thousand lean fighting men who are itching to send Bragg packing, and if you don't have too many newspaper reporters around, they'll get at it as soon as I bring them up."

Charles Dana smiled. "Does that include me?"

"No, you're an *ex*-newspaperman who has become one of us."

The levity was soon replaced by the serious problem confronting the generals, and they tackled it as a team. Sherman, fresh to the scene, was full of exuberant ideas; Thomas, the plodder, called upon his shrewd powers of observation and memory to erase the unrealistic. Grant mostly listened, posing a question now and then. Howard would later describe the informal meeting as a courtroom session—with Sherman the illustrious advocate, Thomas the astute judge, and Grant the qualified jury who would sift through the evidence for a plausible verdict.

The plan was firmed up the following morning: Sherman would march his army around the north side of the hill mass above the town, and out of sight of prying rebel eyes on Missionary Ridge, to a position three miles to the east. There he would cross the river by the pontoon boats Baldy Smith was ingeniously building at a sawmill he'd "requisitioned," and ready his command to strike at the thinly held east end of the Ridge. Meanwhile, Hooker would have attacked and cleared Lookout Mountain. Howard, with two divisions, would follow Sherman and support him. Hooker then would be free to hit the Ridge from the west.

Explaining it to Rawlins, Grant said, "Sherman calls this a *Cannae,* or something like that. It's a term the Germans use for a tactic that Hannibal once used to defeat the Romans in a town by that name in Italy. To me, it's a double-envelopment, or simply 'hit 'em from both ends.' Anyway, I think Bragg will have to shift most of his strength to meet Sherman's thrust. That's when Thomas will strike the center with the Army of the Cumberland. If everything works right, we'll knock Bragg right back into Georgia."

Rawlins chuckled. "*Can-eye?* General, you surprise me."

"Oh, Sherman reads a lot."

Rawlins turned quickly serious. "There's a rumor among Thomas's men that you favor Sherman's troops, and that they'll be given the glory."

Grant frowned. Was he too involved with Sherman? After all, the man had never let him down, had always followed orders directly and aggressively. What commander wouldn't rely on a proven leader with proven troops? Thomas would get his chance. "Well, Rawlins, you just let the word filter down that there'll be plenty of glory to go around."

Tall, dapper, clean-shaven Joe Hooker watched General Geary's maneuver through his expensive Belgian glasses. Good! The division right was well up the slope, continuing to climb sodden Lookout. And now the extended arm of blue infantry began to pivot like a long minute hand reaching backward for twelve, edging upward and upward, just like it was supposed to do. He hadn't known whether to trust Geary—one of Slocum's generals— but the man probably couldn't help that and seemed cooperative enough. Now his execution was almost as good as Von Clausewitz might have wanted it. But did Clausewitz ever execute this pivot on the slope of a mountain?

Maybe someday they'd quote *Hooker* instead of the German.

Now the damned cloud base dropped down again, obscuring the right wing . . . then the left, as the steadily climbing troops evaporated into the gray-white mist. My God, how would they see to shoot, moving like ghosts? But it would be almost as difficult for the rebs.

As the final elements of Geary's division were enveloped in cloud, Hooker swung the glasses down to the left where the other two divisions were moving up from Lookout Creek. The men were pushing, pressing the graycoats up the steep, boulder-strewn slope—until finally they too began to fade into the vapor, and only the crash of artillery blasts reverberating off the granite cliffs told him the battle was progressing.

He was pleased.

Would these unknown troops do him justice in their obscuration? Would this imposing mountain be his resurrection, his answer to the infamy of Chancellorsville, his relief from command of the Army of the Potomac? Or would some unknown fate impede him, cheat him of his due again?

He couldn't stay in this position—it was time to move up to where he could at least get quick dispatches.

From one vantage point to another, from one group of viewers to the next, from above and below, the battle of Chattanooga was theater at its grandest. In a normal battle, a soldier, even a lower-grade officer, was seldom involved in, or could see, more than a hundred yards of the conflict—and much less in dense smoke. But in this encounter on hills affording such superb views, the incredible drama between blue and butternut/gray was observed by the many who were not engaged. The entire locale was a vast, spectacular stage, centered by the Ridge and extended by suspenseful theatrics on lesser wings. Grant set up his headquarters on Orchard Knob, a small hill east of the town, below the high spine, as his regal box.

But frivolous cloud, often a wispy curtain, had shut down the scene.

The Army of the Cumberland watched the northern slope of Lookout in vain, wondering what was taking place on the unseen western slopes and in the gray mist. The muffled reports of Hooker's guns reached them over the four- to five-mile separation, but they couldn't see the action. They knew Sherman's boys were the fair-haired ones, and now Hooker's lads were up there looking for their own glory. Were the Cumberlanders to be the bridesmaids? Was the stain of old Rosecrans to keep them from their just due? Chickamauga wasn't *their* fault. Besides, many of them had fought for old Pap Thomas and had earned their own right to respect.

Then, just after Grant returned from visiting Sherman, as if on signal, the clouds at the peak of Lookout lifted. A full, clear view of the northern slope was exposed in bright sunshine, revealing the blue crawling ants as they worked their way around the narrow front of the mountain. Reflections of sunlight on metal, along with tiny swatches of color from flags, flickered in the distance. Shouts went up from Thomas's troops, regimental bands began to blare, and soldiers grabbed hands to dance the jig. *Hooker was winning!* Then suddenly the clouds closed again, as if the joy of victory was rationed.

Grant turned to Rawlins. "Have Thomas send a reinforcing brigade. Have the commanding officer tell Hooker we'll give him more help if he needs it. And also tell him I think the rebs will be gone from Lookout by morning. I have an idea that Hooker's resistance up there has been lighter than he will have us believe."

Grant was right on all counts. The famous "battle above the clouds," as Fighting Joe Hooker would term the engagement, was over and an unfounded legend was born.

Sherman had done well in executing his movement over the river and the occupation of Tunnel Hill, the first eastern peak of Missionary Ridge. In fact, it had been so easy that he wondered if Bragg had withdrawn. But when Grant assured him the enemy was still there in force, he was puzzled. On the morning of the 24th, he was ready to smash on over the remainder of the Ridge.

Only he couldn't.

Grant opened the message a little after eight. "I regret to inform you that I am not on Tunnel Hill, but a detached hill separated from Missionary Ridge. A sharply cut valley stands between me and the objective I supposedly held last night. You'd best hold off Thomas's attack until we can fight our way over this gorge and start getting up the real Tunnel Hill. That action is in progress, but strong enemy fire is coming right down our throats. A prisoner reports that he belongs to Cleburne's division, which is firmly dug in. This isn't good news, since Cleburne is supposed to be Bragg's best. I hope to be atop Tunnel Hill by noon. Sherman."

Grant handed the message to Baldy Smith as he spread out the map. "It's impossible," the engineer said. "Not only do the maps not show a separate hill, but all of us examined the area with our glasses from across the river."

Grant shrugged. "Sherman ought to know."

"Well, I still don't believe it."

Rawlins asked, "What can be done?"

"Have Thomas send a division over to help, while we wait and see," Grant replied. "I know Sherman will get on the Ridge sooner or later. In the meantime, we'll get an order over to Hooker to move down to the southern tip of Missionary and attack as planned. He should be able to do so well before noon."

Hooker, Grant thought, an enigma. So bright in Mexico. Chief of staff to the tragic Hamer, but totally incompetent leading the Army of the Potomac. Contentious, vain; they called the women who were always in his trains "Hooker's girls," and sometimes just "hookers." But maybe the satyr could still be of value.

He thought again of Hamer, who might have been president. The man was still a sad memory . . .

At that moment, the dramatic Hooker unfurled his largest flag on the high northern tip of Lookout. His redemption was partially complete. But fickle fortune also ducked behind the clouds—for he later ran into a major obstacle on his march down the Chattanooga River Valley. The creek turned out to be a major torrent, offering no fording positions. The only bridge had been destroyed by the rebs the night before, and the process of building a new one would take him most of the day, keeping him away from Missionary and the glory he so wanted.

By two o'clock in the afternoon, Grant was wondering if his plan was finished. Sherman was still getting nowhere in his attack, and at best wouldn't take Tunnel Hill for another two or three hours. The redhead had even sent Thomas's division back, stating that he had plenty of men for the confined approach. It was the withering fire from above, not a shortage of troops, that made the assault so difficult. And with Hooker stalled, his double-envelopment was a mockery.

As Grant sat on a stump, grimly chewing a cold cigar butt, Rawlins came up. "What are you going to do, General?"

Grant snapped a stick he'd been absently whittling. "I'm not going to sit here much longer. I suppose we ought to see what Thomas can do. Bragg must have weakened his center to hold off Sherman. If he shifts back to meet Thomas, it may spring Sherman loose."

Thomas was standing several yards away, watching the Ridge through his glasses. Grant walked over to him and said, "Doesn't look like Sherman's going anywhere. Don't you think it's time to order your troops to advance against the enemy's first line of rifle pits?"

Thomas nodded. "I suppose so."

Tired of inactivity, Grant decided to go down the hill for something to eat while the attack was being formed. He returned to Orchard Knob forty minutes later, surprised to find that Thomas was still in the same place. "What's going on?" he asked Rawlins.

"Not a goddamned thing!" Rawlins fumed. "I suggest you give the general a direct order if you expect him to do anything."

Grant hated to be peremptory with the respected Thomas, but, inexplicably, the general had done nothing about the attack. His temper tugged at its bonds as he strode over to Thomas and said evenly, "General, order your troops to advance and take the enemy's first line of rifle pits at the base of the ridge—*now!*"

Thomas scowled. "What do you propose for a reserve?"

Grant's eyes were hard. "Bragg isn't coming off that hill today, at least not in our direction. Our reserve is going to *attack!*"

Thomas shrugged and gave the orders.

Thomas's four divisions, including Phil Sheridan's, were soon formed abreast—a solid sea of blue, stretching out three lines deep for nearly a mile. Regimental colors flickered in the light breeze, and the glint of bayonets could be easily seen from Orchard Knob. Periodic cheers drifted up. The Army of the Cumberland was ready to strike; its chance for glory had arrived. As the roar of its artillery signaled the advance, the maze of blue began to edge toward Bragg's first line of defense at the base of the Ridge.

The curtain was going up.

Grant watched quietly, stirred by his first full view of twenty thousand troops attacking as one. Dana and Rawlins, standing at his elbow, were fascinated. As the tide moved on, Grant anxiously watched the enemy artillery on the Ridge. When the attackers were less than a quarter of a mile from the rifle pits, puffs of smoke belched from the enemy guns. Shell after shell poured into the blue ranks, but the mass of Federals continued to sweep forward.

The crackle of enemy musket fire joined the tumult just as the forward edge of Thomas's blue wave turned ragged. Were they faltering? No! Just some elements edging out more quickly than others. Grant couldn't believe his glasses—gone was the rigid execution of a well-drilled battle formation; the first lines had broken into a running, scrambling, biting saw! The first teeth of the saw poured over the enemy fortifications and swarmed into the pits. In what seemed only moments, the entire first line of enemy defenses was engulfed by blue.

Almost immediately the moving forms were mostly in butternut, as rebel soldiers appeared to be running up the slope in full retreat. Enemy artillery fire stopped abruptly, apparently waiting to zero in on the pits area as soon as the defenders were clear. Rawlins and Dana joined in the cheers that shook the Knob. Grant was about to walk over to Thomas and offer him a cigar when Dana grabbed his sleeve. "Look, they're moving up the slope!"

Grant quickly raised his glasses. What was going on? The uneven blue clusters were breaking out of the smoke of the rifle pits in motley, jagged groups, pressing upward, overtaking and mingling with the receding enemy gray. Grant held his breath in wonder as Rawlins said, "Jesus Christ, they're going all the way up!"

Now and then Grant detected the glint of officers' sabers; once he was positive he saw Sheridan's big roan next to an advancing flag. What kind of an army was he watching—had they gone berserk? No one person could have ordered such a crazy, disorganized movement. Without lowering his glasses, he muttered, "This has to be the most miraculous charge in the history of warfare. By lightning, look at them go!"

Up on the slope of Missionary Ridge, Little Phil Sheridan was in his glory. Although his orders had directed him only to the rifle pits, he wasn't about to stop there. One of his regiments had already followed the surge of other Federal attackers out of the pits. The momentum, the running, shouting rout at the pits couldn't be suddenly halted. Junior officers were ordering their men forward with flashing sabers. There was a wild-eyed fervor upon the men, an exhilarating frenzy of *winning*—and who wanted to stop it? Surely, he didn't.

He felt it himself!

Moments earlier he'd realized *the damned Ridge could be taken!* They could keep going all the way! These glorious, incredible boys would take hell today, give them a damned chance! With a wild sense of abandonment, he pushed his horse forward, waving his hat and swinging his saber. *"C'mon, boys,"* he shouted. *"Give 'em hell! We'll carry the line!"*

All along the slant of the Ridge, Confederate soldiers were dropping their arms and fleeing in panic. Bragg's gunners on top couldn't bring their guns to bear for fear of hitting their own men. Time flashed by and soon the panic spilled over the crest, as fear-crazed butternut soldiers ran into the gun emplacements. And right behind them came the Yankees, unstoppable, blood in their eyes. They poured onto the top of the Ridge like a swarm of vengeance, overrunning and scattering all resistance. Bragg himself was nearly captured as the rout forced even his most resolute defenders down the backslope. There was nothing for him to do but sound the retreat and hope to reorganize at some other point.

The bugle blew the Confederate knell.

Chattanooga was lost.

Back on Orchard Knob, Grant was still transfixed by what he saw at the top of the Ridge. There, the wildly exuberant troops of Thomas's Army of the Cumberland were cavorting like tiny children on Christmas morning. At last he lowered his glasses. Turning to the grinning Rawlins, he shook his head and said, "I still don't believe it."

CHAPTER 39

The recently proud Confederate Army of Tennessee fled in total rout, shedding its equipment and guns at every step. Only Confederate General Pat Cleburne's stout rear action kept the defeat from being worse. As it was, the vast rebel stockpile of supplies at Chickamauga Station was handed to Grant's troops, and only the rescue of Burnside kept him from going farther.

While Bragg's bruised and demoralized army was trying to put itself back together in Dalton, Georgia, attention focused on East Tennessee. But within days, Longstreet and Buckner had moved east and the steady Burnside, whose massively haired jowls would give the nation a descriptive word, had regained some of the pride he'd lost commanding the Army of the Potomac.

Grant was dissatisfied with the follow-up, and wondered if he'd ever completely destroy an enemy army in the open. He was emphatic about the factor of luck in the victory, stating that the battle had been won in spite of his generalship. But no one listened.

Then came the rumor that Bragg's resignation had been accepted.

Chattanooga was called the new turning point of the war and an exultant nation again toasted the hero of Vicksburg. Grant had now provided avenues into the enemy heartland by two decisive victories within five months. Even the Lincoln-hating New York *World* stated: "General Grant is one of the great soldiers of our age, perhaps of any age. Certainly, he is without equal in the list of generals now alive. If the incompetents in Washington had any sense, they would turn the war over to him."

And more cigars poured into his new Nashville headquarters.

Through early December, Rawlins suffered from various problems. He'd developed a severe cold at Chattanooga and couldn't shake the cough that worried him so much. Dr. Kittoe was puzzled and told Grant it was just a holdover and that most of Rawlins's problems were in his head. Yet the brigadier continued to lose weight and dark circles developed under his fierce black eyes. His thin patience became almost nonexistent as he continued to work long hours and fret over what problems Grant's success might bring.

He began to carry a handkerchief into which he could cough. And now and then, he detected a trace of blood on it.

Ten days before Christmas, Grant closed his office door and told Rawlins to sit down. "My friend," he began, "I think it's about time you got out of here. You've had only one short leave in two and a half years. You're getting married up in Connecticut at Christmastime, but I want you to leave now."

"But there's so much to—"

"You need rest. You need for your lovely Emma to relax you and nurse you back to health. You need to enjoy your children, who can be there when you arrive. You know what a lift mine give me when they visit. I want you to get out of here tomorrow morning and stay until you're on your feet, even if it takes two months."

"But General, we've got to finish the Chattanooga report, plus a dozen other things that need my attention. No, I can leave in a week and still get up there in time for the wedding. I'll—"

"You'll leave in the morning, General. That's an *order!*"

Grant sat back in the big overstuffed chair, watching the flickering reflections from the nearby fire wander around his water glass. On other New Year's Eves there had been different liquids in such a glass. But he was holding fast on his renewed promise to Rawlins, and he didn't want to get back into that terrible guilt he'd experienced over the Yazoo drunk. He'd been tempted to have some harmless Madeira tonight, but he couldn't chance what it might do to him.

Even now, he was still tempted. A glass or two wouldn't hurt.

He'd earned it.

But wasn't that what every drunk said, in one way or another?

What was he going to do, sneak the drink because his mother hen was away in Connecticut?

No, of course not.

If Julia were here, he wouldn't even think about it.

He wondered where Pete Longstreet was on this cold night. Are you still out there on the eastern end of Tennessee? Probably downing a couple of bottles with some of your generals and trying to convince each other that you can still win this war. Well, you are, you know. But you don't know why. You don't know that you are benefiting your beloved South by *losing.*

The North has the people, the institutions, and the territory to make a great and prosperous nation . . . while your South is burdened with an institution abhorrent to all civilized people not brought up under it . . . one that degrades labor, keeps it in ignorance, and enfeebles the governing class. With the outside world at war with this institution of slavery, you can never extend your territory.

The labor of your South is not skilled, nor allowed to become so. The whites cannot toil without becoming degraded and being called "poor white trash." Your system of labor will soon exhaust the soil and leave the masses poor. Assuming you could continue as a separate country, the nonslaveholders would soon leave, and the small slaveholders would have to sell out to their more prosperous neighbors. Soon the slaves would outnumber their masters, and would rise in their might and destroy them. And without education, they would make a wasteland of your beloved country before order could one day be restored. Yes, Pete, this war is costing a great deal in blood and treasure, but it just might be worth every bit of it.

228

He sighed, lighting another cigar.

He'd gotten a star for the bright young Wilson, but he'd soon be losing him to take over the Cavalry Bureau . . . Sherman was building up his army to go on the offensive into Georgia in the spring. There he would face the wily Joe Johnston, who had turned over the Confederate Army of the Mississippi to Bishop Polk and had assumed command of Bragg's shattered army—which was now mending quite well around Dalton.

He shook his head. What a year. It had begun with the frustration of Vicksburg, gone to the elation of finally taking that fortress, his injury, the victory of Chattanooga, and finally the nonsense of some people talking about him being president. It was a long way from peddling firewood in St. Louis . . .

Grant went to a window and looked out at the light Tennessee snow falling in large, soft flakes to the white blanket below. He remembered a snowy Christmas outside of St. Louis. Little boys and a baby girl, all bundled up and having fun on a sled he'd made for them. Julia throwing a snowball at him. Hardly any money for presents. A man with little future, except for the belief of his beloved wife. And here he was, with no sled or outstanding debts, surrounded by a war, and the recipient of near-adulation by many citizens in his beloved country. But none of that mattered on this particular night. He was simply too sad and lonesome.

The days rushed by, and in early February Abraham Lincoln reached into his political bag to solve a possible dilemma. Sitting in his White House office, the president pulled out his watch and glanced at it. It was time for that man from Chicago to arrive, the United States marshal who had known Grant in Galena. Washburne had recommended he summon this Russell Jones if he really wanted proof that U. S. Grant had no political designs. And he had done so. There was so very much at stake. Now that he'd finally found a general who could fight and win, he certainly didn't want to contend with him at the polls. McClellan, who was aspiring to the Democratic nomination, would be enough trouble. This country simply couldn't stand a change in regime.

He rose to meet the visitor. "Mr. Jones, I want to thank you for coming to see me."

After a few minutes of back-home Illinois talk, Lincoln went to the heart of the matter. "Congressman Washburne tells me you stay in touch with General Grant and have his confidence."

Jones was slender, with a short red beard. "Yes, sir, I think so. I'm handling some investments for him. Nothing very big, but steady little things that should give him a bit of a nest egg when the war's over."

"That's fine, Mr. Jones, but I didn't send for you to talk about money. I need to know where the general stands on this idea of making him president."

J. Russell Jones nodded, reaching into his inside coat pocket. "I have a letter from General Grant that I received the morning I left Chicago. I think it will answer your questions, Mr. President. It's in reply to a letter I sent him based on editorials in the New York *Herald* in December, which I'm sure you've seen."

Lincoln took Grant's flat, sloping scrawl to a lamp, quickly finding the passage he was looking for: "I am receiving a great deal of that kind of literature, but it soon finds its way into the wastebasket. I already have a pretty big job on my hands, and my only ambition is to see this rebellion suppressed. Nothing could induce me to think of being a presidential candidate, particularly so long as there is a possibility of having Mr. Lincoln reelected."

The president smiled. "Yes, I believe that settles my curiosity. And I can't tell you how gratifying such words are to me. No man knows when the presidential grub gets to gnawing at him, or just how deep it will get before he's tried it. I wouldn't think Grant would be immune to it."

Following Jones's departure, Lincoln returned to his desk and picked up the latest prod from Washburne on the Lieutenant General Bill. It had been the talk of Washington since mid-December. If he could trust Grant completely on the political thing, it certainly was the answer—what with so many members of Congress being down on Halleck. He couldn't understand what had happened to Halleck. Seemed like the man was a worse damned procrastinator at times than McClellan. Appeared plenty strong when he was brought into the job. Certainly bright enough. What had he told Stanton? "I'm Halleck's friend because nobody else is."

Washburne's note was bold: "This war cannot end until Grant is given the supreme command. He is the only general strong enough to bring it to a successful conclusion. It can't wait!"

On March 3rd, John Rawlins opened the telegram from Halleck. It read, "To Major General Ulysses S. Grant. The Secretary of War directs that you report in person to the War Department as early as practicable. If necessary you will keep up telegraphic communication with your command while in Washington. The Secretary of War also directs me to inform you that your commission as a lieutenant general is signed and will be delivered to you on your arrival at the War Department. I sincerely congratulate you on this recognition of your distinguished and meritorious service."

Rawlins stared at the words, shaking his head ever so slightly. It had finally come, what he had so wanted and now so dreaded. By special order of Congress, the rank was a great tribute, for the highest commission in the military was two-star. Winfield Scott had been breveted lieutenant general in 1855, but he had been the only one to hold Federal rank above major general in the entire century. Rawlins also knew what had to follow. No major general could give Grant orders, so Ulys would have to go to Washington and be the boss. There was no way around it.

And that was what worried him.

Rawlins coughed and reached for his handy handkerchief. Spitting sputum into it, he looked for that worrisome trace of red blood that was usually there. He had often told himself to quit looking, because it always made him worry, but he couldn't stop.

Quietly he went into Grant's office, held out the message, and said, "Soon you will be the one out of uniform with those shoulder boards, General." As Grant glanced up quizzically, he added, "Well, at least we can get even with that bastard Halleck now."

Grant read the communiqué and got to his feet. Turning away, he said softly, "I don't know if I'm qualified for this."

The emotion finally caught up with Rawlins. He felt his eyes brim, and remembered the day when a stocky leather goods store clerk who had been a captain in the Mexican War moved into the house next door . . .

CHAPTER 40

I want it said of me by those who knew me best,
that I always plucked a thistle and planted a flower
where I thought a flower would grow.
—ABRAHAM LINCOLN

Grant arrived in Washington late on the afternoon of March 8. With him were Rawlins and Colonel Comstock, his new engineer, along with young Fred. As soon as the train hissed to a stop, the two staff officers headed for the War Department to confer with Halleck. Privately pleased that someone had mixed up his arrival time, thereby killing the chance of any big fuss, Grant and his son made their way to Willard's Hotel.

It was a raw day, cloudy, with a nasty wind blowing in from Chesapeake Bay, and it was chilly in the open hackney. As they passed the White House, Fred stared at the structure in awe. "Are we really going there tonight, Papa?"

"Yes, son."

"And we're really going to see the president of the United States?"

"Sure are."

That kept the wide-eyed boy quiet until they reached Willard's, two blocks down Pennsylvania Avenue. It was in this famous hostelry that Lincoln had stayed in the days prior to his inauguration, and where a few years earlier Julia Ward Howe had written her stirring "Battle Hymn of the Republic."

Wearing a wrinkled duster that covered his travel-weary uniform, Grant led Fred through the hotel's busy lobby. Glancing around, he noted all kinds of uniforms and rank in the noisy place. It seemed as busy as his headquarters in Nashville on a Monday morning when all the contractors were rushing in to peddle their wares. He edged up to the reception desk, trying to catch a clerk's eye. Finally, a tall young man with a starched collar and a superior tone raised an eyebrow. "Yes?" he said with a touch of disdain.

"I'd like a room for me and my son," Grant replied in his usual quiet tone.

The clerk looked up and down a chart, finally saying in a bored voice, "We might be able to put you up in a small room on the top floor, but it'll cost you seven dollars a night."

"That'll be all right."

As Ulys signed the register, the clerk sniffed, "It'll have to be. We're expecting General Grant in tonight, and the hotel is full."

Grant chuckled inwardly, recalling the time he reported into Cairo without a uniform. The clerk reached for a room key, then glanced at the scrawl on the register which stated, "U. S. Grant and son, Galena, Ill." He looked up, staring, and dropped the key. "But, uh, sir . . . General, sir, I'm sorry. I, that is, we have the presidential suite, that's parlor six, reserved for you, sir. We thought, I mean, we expected your aide. Uh, will you follow me, please, sir?"

Grant nodded, winking at a smiling Fred.

Dinner in the hotel dining room was continuously interrupted by well-wishers, but Grant and his party finally got away and went to the White House, where a presidential reception was in progress. As they entered the mansion, Rawlins said, "You know, Lincoln may have begun by splitting rails, but he lives pretty well. And he certainly recognizes a political opportunity with the best of them."

Grant nodded as he looked around the lovely edifice in awe. He was filled with mixed emotions. At long last, he was to meet his commander in chief, the president with whom he'd corresponded, the man who carried the fate of the Union on his thin, stooped shoulders. Within moments, he would shake the hand of greatness. But unfortunately he had to move through the buzzing, leering crowd to do so. His name seemed to be echoing off every tongue as he forced his feet forward to the smiling, waiting Lincoln. It was a bedlam worse than Shiloh.

The president's handshake was firm as his words came down from so many inches above. "I've waited a long time for this pleasure, General Grant. Welcome to Washington."

Grant struggled to speak. "The pleasure is mine, Mr. President." He wondered if he should have addressed him as "excellency."

Lincoln chuckled. "Well, now that we know each other's pleasures, we can make plans. After the guests have had their share of you, I'd like to speak privately with you in my study. In the meantime, I believe Secretary Seward will be your host in the East Room."

Forty minutes later, the dazed Grant was led away from what was described in one of the newspapers as "a wild mob of hero-hungry admirers that forced the tiny general to stand on a crushed velvet sofa to keep from getting trampled to death." As the door to the presidential study closed, Grant heaved a sigh of relief and collected himself. A beaming Lincoln stood beside Stanton near a big desk. "Are you still in one piece?" the president asked.

"Yes, sir. Barely."

"Good. I know you must be tired, so let's get this over with quickly. As you know, a special ceremony has been planned for tomorrow at one o'clock, for the presentation of your new commission as lieutenant general. Having heard of your aversion for long speeches, I plan on making a short one—only four sentences. My secretary will provide you with a copy of what I'm going to say.

"There are two points I'd like to have you make in your answer. First, something that shall prevent or obviate any jealousy of you from any of the other generals in the service. And second, something that shall put you on as good terms as possible with the Army of the Potomac. Now consider whether this may not be said to make it of some advantage, and if you see any objection whatever to doing it, be under no restraint whatever in expressing it. The decision is yours, General. There are several objects to be gained here."

Grant gazed intently into the friendly gray eyes, not noticing how close-set they were, not seeing the elephant ears or warts. A feeling of trust and comfort quickly overcame the uneasiness he had felt since entering the mansion. This man appeared to be everything he'd envisioned, the leader with whom he could work. "Yes, sir," he replied.

"We'll have an opportunity to talk after the ceremony, at which time we'll start getting to know one another. You can give me your views on the conduct of the war and your working arrangements as general in chief."

There, it was official—he was the new general in chief. "Yes, Mr. President."

Lincoln again smiled and shook his hand warmly. "I look forward to tomorrow as a great turning point for the country, General."

"What are you going to say?" Rawlins asked.

"I don't know," Grant replied from his easy chair in the Willard's suite where he was trying to put words together. "I've mulled it over and I just can't bring myself to say anything the president wants. The other generals will just have to take me for what I am, and so will the Army of the Potomac."

Rawlins stepped close, looking down into Grant's frown. "General, there's something I have to say. Ever since Galena, I've admired you for what you are, for your forthrightness and honesty. Perhaps I've admired your lack of pretense most of all, your ability to continually be yourself. And perhaps I've assumed too great an imagined role in what I call your destiny. Although I've never doubted your ability to arrive at this level of influence, I now feel somewhat uncomfortable that the time has arrived. It'll be increasingly difficult for you to remain the same Ulys Grant I knew in Galena—for you really aren't that same man.

"You've learned how to handle power and men of power. In fact, I honestly feel at times that you are outgrowing me. But that's not the point. You are in the national view like perhaps no other American in history. And Washington, General, is not Cairo, Vicksburg, Chattanooga or Nashville. It's a den of wolves. And right now you have to begin playing the politician. The president wants you to make an overture and assuage this overrated eastern establishment. And it's only the beginning."

Grant toyed with the pencil for a few moments, finally saying, "I'm the way I am, my friend, and there's no rank or command in the world that's going to change that."

The city of Washington was warm and fresh on this early March morning. It had showered just before dawn and was bragging about it from mirrored puddles of rainwater in its streets. The *Evening Star* had predicted a high temperature of 82 degrees and recommended that no one go out after noon without an umbrella. The newspaper also noted that this early warmth would soon have cherry blossoms erupting all along the Potomac. But weather never fazed Washington residents; it rained or it snowed, or it didn't. Parades and outside parties had to make do as their luck prescribed.

The social whirl in wartime Washington was unceasing, with strong and beautiful women spending fortunes on appearance and status. In vogue were jaunty plumed hats with short coquettish veils and three-cornered, gaily flowing summer bonnets from William's exclusive shop up Pennsylvania Avenue. The discreet showing of a bit of leg, with dainty gaiter boots and white hose, was popular among the younger set. Other marks of status were superbly liveried coaches, surreys, gigs, and other types of carriages. But most prevalent in salon, tavern, theater, or on the street was the dizzying maze of uniforms. A popular saying was, "Washington is so overloaded with soldiers that a man threw a stone at a dog on Pennsylvania Avenue and hit three commissioned officers!"

On this early morning, Grant and Rawlins took advantage of the nearly empty sidewalks to go for a stroll. After some fifty yards, Rawlins asked, "What are you going to do about that goddamned Halleck?"

"Leave him right where he is as chief of staff to the general in chief. He'll be my right arm here in Washington, permitting me to stay in the field."

"Can you trust him?"

"I think so. He's an intelligent man, and has accepted my promotion as well as possible, considering that he's been my boss for over two years. And he gets on all right with the president and Stanton."

"Where does that leave me?"

Grant stopped to relight his cigar. "Well now, who do you think is going to run my headquarters in the field? Nothing changes. Halleck has the desk job and you get to put up my tents."

Rawlins chuckled. "You don't have to make me sound like an orderly."

"We'll be together all the way."

Rawlins nodded as they continued to move along. "What about the other commands? Everyone is jockeying for position. I heard Hooker even threw his hat back in the ring for the Army of the Potomac, while complaining that he didn't get enough credit for Lookout. And young Wilson's pushing Baldy Smith."

"Hooker had his chance. And General Wilson had better stick to his horses and stay out of it. The bullion on his stars isn't even beginning to tarnish yet. Besides, I'm going to pull him out of that Cavalry Bureau job and give him a command."

"Who's going to run the mighty Army of the Potomac?"

"I'm going out to see General Meade after the ceremony today. It all depends on what he has to say and how he strikes me. At this point, I don't see much need for change. He did quite a job at Gettysburg, I'm told."

"Yes, but Lincoln wasn't very happy with his failure to follow up."

"That happens to all of us. Look at Chattanooga."

Rawlins frowned. "That wasn't your fault."

"It never is."

"And in the West?"

"Sherman will assume my last job, with McPherson moving up to command the Army of the Tennessee. Logan will take over his corps."

"And the other commands here in the East?"

"We'll see."

The president had his entire cabinet assembled for the presentation. Joining those astute gentlemen in the East Room were Halleck, Washburne, Dana, and favored photographers and reporters. Since Julia was still in Nashville, Grant was accompanied only by Rawlins, Comstock, and young Fred. At eight minutes after one, Grant faced his commander in chief and looked up into the same pleasant smile he'd encountered the night before.

When stillness fell over the room, the president read, "General Grant, the nation's appreciation of what you have done, and its reliance upon you for what remains to do in the existing great struggle, are now presented with this commission, constituting you Lieutenant General in the Army of the United States. With this high power devolves upon you also a corresponding responsibility. As the country herein trusts you, so, under God, it will sustain you. I scarcely need add that with what I here speak for the nation goes my own hearty personal concurrence."

Lincoln handed Grant his scroll of commission and shook his hand warmly. Tucking the scroll under his arm, Grant glanced at Fred, then squinted at the words on which he'd finally settled. His voice was a bit raspy as he read them: "Mr. President, I accept this commission with gratitude for the high honor conferred. With the aid of the noble armies that have fought on so many fields for our common country, it will be my earnest endeavor not to disappoint your expectations. I feel the full weight of the responsibilities now devolving on me and know that if they are met it will be due to those armies, and above all to the favor of that Providence that leads both nations and men."

The beaming president showed no notice that Grant had totally ignored his request in regard to the two points. He shook Grant's hand again, and let the press take over. A short while later, the two men had a quick private meeting in which Grant told the president he wanted to get the feel of things before discussing plans. Lincoln readily agreed. The remainder of the afternoon was spent in the inspection of Washington's defenses with Halleck.

As the inspection party finally stopped in front of Willard's, Grant said, "Well, General, all I can say is the capital looks like it could withstand Attila and his hordes. I think we should shift some of these boys down to the Army of the Potomac shortly, where they can be better utilized."

Halleck nodded. "Whatever you say, General. Will you be planning an offensive shortly?"

Grant nodded. "After I get my feet on the ground."

"May I make a recommendation?"

Grant looked into the owlish eyes that had once treated him so haughtily. "Certainly. That's what you're getting paid for."

Halleck spoke softly, "Don't tell the president any details of your plans. He means well, but he has a habit of being too accessible and honest. He holds very little back from those he thinks he can trust."

Grant nodded. "Thanks. I'll keep that in mind."

Following an uncomfortable dinner at Secretary Seward's home that evening, Grant hurried back to Willard's for a late visit he'd long anticipated. Brigadier General Rufus Ingalls, the Army of the Potomac's quartermaster, was waiting when he arrived. Ingalls, wearing a dress uniform complete with ceremonial sword—literally dressed to the hilt—turned from the window and raised his glass. "Hail, Caesar! Little Fred let me in and I spent ten minutes looking for a drink." He raised a bottle. "Finally ordered a jug myself."

Grant shook his ex-roommate's hand warmly, and they spun quickly into catch-up talk. A lot of sand had run through the glass since Vancouver. Grant was tempted to accept Rufe's reasons for them to sit down and joyously consume the contents of the bottle: old times, their reunion, his promotion. But he simply couldn't. He poured himself a glass of water.

Grant picked his friend's brains about the overall personality parade and staff situation in Washington, getting direct and often critical views. Ingalls had never been accused of being bashful. Finally, the one-time scourge of Benny Haven's asked, "What are you going to do about Butler?"

"Butler—oh, the commander of the Department of Virginia and North Carolina. He's down at Fortress Monroe, isn't he?"

"Uh-huh, another one of your worthless commanding generals."

"Why do you say that?"

Ingalls poured himself another two inches of whiskey. " 'Cause he is.

He's one of the slimiest politicians we've got wearing stars. He's a lawyer in his late forties, who came in from the Massachusetts state militia. Before that he was known for shedding his skin like a wiggly snake. He actually supported old Jeff Davis for *our* presidency in 'sixty. Although he was one of our first Copperheads, you should've seen him turn into a powerful war Democrat when things started to pop.

"He wasn't any good in New Orleans and he won't do you any good here. But he has a lot of people jumping to his tune and will be tough to get rid of. The word is that Lincoln needs support from the war Democrats and the Republican radicals who are on Butler's bandwagon. This is going to be a tough election, and he can't take any chances."

"Will he fight?"

"Don't know. He's never had a chance to prove it."

"That's all I care about, but I'm glad you warned me. He's the least of my worries right now."

"You bringing Cump Sherman in for the Army of the Potomac?"

"No, he's needed in the West."

"You're going to have a hell of a time with this prima donna army. They're gonna resent you. They don't know how to get off their fat asses and win anything, and they're going to take umbrage with an upstart stranger who might have different ideas."

"They'll come around."

Ingalls grinned. "Under Meade?"

"Maybe."

"You'd best step lightly there, too." Ingalls threw up his hands in mock defense. "I know, I know. You don't give a damn about politics, but I'm giving you the Washington inside. This place seethes with it, and Meade's part of it. Pennsylvania carries a lot of popular and electoral votes, and he's a native son. He also saved the state from invasion at Gettysburg. To remove him from command now might mortally offend the proud Pennsylvanians enough to vote for their other native son, that little asshole, McClellan. So you have to be aware of Meade's importance."

Grant walked to the window and looked out over quiet Washington. He still couldn't believe an arrogant young general who never did much except inhibit the war effort in the East could actually be running for president. He still remembered his unpleasant encounter with the young Captain McClellan on the West Coast. Now these doggone politics in the army. Finally he turned. "I appreciate what you're saying, Rufe, but this war has to be won. If Meade were *Lincoln,* and the wrong man, I'd relieve him."

Major General George Gordon Meade, although raised in the Keystone State, was born in Spain. He graduated from West Point in 1835, but resigned from the army a year later to go into civil engineering. Grant remembered meeting him in the Mexican War, when he was back on active duty. He stayed in the army as an engineer until being appointed a brigadier general of Volunteers in 1861. He went on to command both the First and Fifth Corps of the Army of the Potomac, reaching that army's command following Hooker. He was bright and dedicated, his well-known temper being his major shortcoming. Balding, with a heavy mustache commanding short chinwhiskers, Meade's stern visage was created by a strong, hooked nose that separated his moody, heavily bagged eyes—which Grant now studied, as he listened to the forty-nine-year-old Pennsylvanian in his command tent.

"General Grant, I find it only natural that a successful commander would hold his recent subordinates in high esteem. They've proven themselves. Therefore, should you wish to bring in someone like Sherman to assume command of this army, I would fully understand and willingly perform such other duties as you might require."

Grant liked that. And he liked what he'd seen around Meade's headquarters; in fact, he had taken an immediate liking to the man himself. "No," he replied, "Sherman has other requirements. And it appears that this mishandled army finally has a commander it can count on. I don't know if a stranger could hold it together for the difficult job it faces. Now, let me ask you a question. Do you think you can work with me in the field— I mean in close proximity? It may appear at times that I'm usurping your prerogatives by being close by, particularly when it comes to the press, but I'll try to issue all orders direct to you, without interfering—unless a situation arises where this isn't feasible. Think you can handle that?"

"Yes, sir, I believe so."

"Good. Then I see no reason for change. Now tell me about General Humphreys, your chief of staff. I had the feeling he considered me an enemy agent on the way over from the station."

Meade smiled. "Andy's a bit possessive. In fact, he's one of the most loyal officers I've ever known. He's a West Point engineer who's doing a whale of a job for me, when he could probably be in corps command somewhere. He's so fearless in battle that someone once said, 'I like to see a brave man in battle, but Humphreys seems to *enjoy* getting shot at.' He's a pains-taker and expresses himself, shall we say, in a colorful manner."

Grant smiled. "I have one of those, too. What about your corps commanders?"

"I have three of the best major generals in the army. Winfield Scott Hancock has the Second Corps. He's a forty-year-old Pennsylvanian. Graduated from the Academy in 'forty-four. Got a star in the fall of 'sixty-one. Distinguished himself at Antietam, Fredericksburg, and Chancellorsville as a division commander. For whatever it's worth, McClellan called him 'Hancock the Superb.' He did an outstanding job for me at Gettysburg, where he was wounded. He's on leave and will be back next week.

"Gouverneur Warren has the Fifth Corps. He's the kid of the lot, coming from the class of 'fifty. He's a New Yorker and another engineer. Also taught mathematics at West Point. He—"

Grant broke in. "That's what I wanted to do early on. It once seemed to me the ultimate vocation."

Meade nodded. "An admirable goal. What stopped you?"

Grant puffed on his cigar. Several unhappy scenes flashed by: the death of Hamer in Mexico, card games in Detroit, drunkenness in Sackets Harbor and Vancouver, a captain named Buchanan . . . waste. He came back to the waiting Meade. "Lots of things, General. Maybe I just wasn't smart enough."

Meade chuckled. "I doubt you'll convince anyone of that. Anyway, Warren has a brilliant record. He's a good one. Then we get to John Sedgwick. He's a couple of years older than me, but graduated from the Academy two years behind me. You may remember hearing about his exploits in Mexico. When the war started here, he was a colonel of cavalry. His division took a pretty good mauling at Antietam, where he was twice wounded. His troops love him and call him 'Uncle John.' I consider him my rock, and recommend that he take over this army should anything happen to me, or if you change your mind about keeping me."

Grant stroked his beard, pleased. "They sound pretty good. But they're going to have to be. This army is in for a big fight to the finish, and there won't be any backing up. Unfortunately, until you took command, it didn't know how to win. I've been warned that caution is part of its breeding. Well, you and I are going to introduce a new strain." Grant shook his head. "But I shouldn't have said 'I' because that sounds like I'm already sticking my nose in your business."

Meade shrugged. "What's mine is yours. Have you formulated any plans yet?"

"No, not yet. I hope to go on the offensive by early May, though. So you can plan accordingly. I've already told Halleck to start cleaning house of garrison troops, so you could be receiving reinforcements shortly."

"Good. Some of those parade soldiers in Washington have been there for the whole war."

"Maybe they'll be able to show off their parade skills in Richmond some of these days—after they've fought to get there. Now, there are a couple more things. First, I'm thinking about bringing Burnside in to command the Ninth Corps. I know he ranks you, and was once the army commander, so for the present I'll keep him directly under me. He'll have some Negro troops, so I don't know how effective he'll be initially. Do you think you can work with him under these conditions?"

"I don't see why not."

"Okay. The other idea is bringing in a cavalry corps. We haven't used cavalry as well as we should. The rebs have made capital use of Forrest and Morgan, and particularly Jeb Stuart. I think he's one of Lee's strongest suits. I believe young Wilson over at the Cavalry Bureau will make an excellent division commander. And I have in mind an aggressive young general out West to command the corps."

"Is that part of the new strain you want to infuse?"

"No, I'm speaking of new tactics. Changing of attitude will have to come from within."

"Whatever you say, General."

CHAPTER 41

Julia's old nearsightedness had increased in the years since she worked on a quilt while her handsome young lieutenant was off fighting in Mexico. Now she had a minor eye infection that produced weakness and nausea. But Ulys's return to Nashville on the 12th quickly took her mind off the ailment. She could hardly contain herself as he recounted his adventures in Washington. "Do you mean you actually *refused* a presidential dinner invitation?" she asked with wide eyes. "Why, if I'd been there, I'd have gone without you, darling. Imagine!"

"I had to get on back here to wrap things up. I just told him I'd had enough of being in show business. But don't worry, there'll be other opportunities after we get back."

"You said you met Mrs. Lincoln. What was she like?"

"I don't know, dear. Charming, I guess. It was all such a mad rush that night."

"Did Fred meet her too?"

"Yes, he was with me all evening, except for the few minutes when I spoke with the president."

"And you don't even remember what she was wearing?"

"No, dear. The only thing I remember about clothes is that Mr. Lincoln's collar was too big." He chuckled. "And that's probably because it was about as high as I could see."

Julia rubbed her hands together excitedly. "Oh, I wish I could have been there! And you stopped briefly in Covington. How are your parents?"

"Same as ever. Although Mama seems to have quit talking altogether. Papa is still conniving and more than makes up for her. I missed the carriage he sent down to the landing. Seems like the driver never found me."

"Well, if you didn't look like a threadbare traveling salesman, it wouldn't happen. You probably rubbed dirt into your new shoulder boards so nobody would notice them. I've ordered two new uniforms for you, so you won't be so shabby when we get to Washington."

"I won't be in Washington much, dear, at least not any more than I can help. My staff is arranging some boarding rooms for you and Jesse. When I have to be in the city, they'll do just fine for the three of us. And when it's possible, I'll have you down to our field headquarters. In the meantime, I guess the Boggses will keep the other three kids in St. Louis, right?"

"Yes, they're so proud of you, they'll do anything."

Grant chuckled. "I was the worst real estate partner Harry ever had."

She took his hand. "Those were just hard times, darling. Now when are you going out with your generals?"

"Tomorrow night. It may be the last time we'll be together for a time."

"Will Rawlins actually let you have some fun, or aren't you taking him along?"

"Oh, no, he'll be there, watching the cork on the bottle."

"How is he, Ulys?"

"He still has his cough, but he seems strong enough. I only wish he'd quit worrying so much."

"He can't help it. He loves you like a brother."

"I just want him to take care of himself."

Julia came into his arms, brushing his lips with hers. "And I just want you to take care of me."

Grant worked over the last bites of the leathery meat, wondering whose idea it was to come to this restaurant. Oh well, the soup had been good. And his army hadn't exactly left vast herds of beef cattle on the hoof. Julia liked to say that he had no imagination beyond overcooked steak, but he didn't see anything wrong with that. Otherwise, he couldn't remember a more enjoyable evening. They were all here—six of the finest generals ever to cast a shadow—Sherman, McPherson, Logan, Sheridan, Granville Dodge, and Rawlins. Except for the quieter McPherson, they were some package of power-packed personalities. He couldn't even keep track of the conversation, what with so many of them trying to talk at once.

The visit to Governor Andrew Johnson had been pleasant, bringing on sly smiles when he told the governor that they hadn't had time to put on their dress uniforms—which hardly any of them owned. By lightning, his generals were soldiers. If their uniforms were a bit stained and worn in places, it was because they wore them in battle!

After dinner, the group hurried on to the theater to see *Hamlet,* a production that was so bad Sherman had to be shushed by Logan. Cump was quite knowledgeable about the play and knew how it was supposed to be produced, even knew many of the lines. Grant was enjoying himself immensely. He, too, liked the theater, but would never have time to learn anything about it.

The curtain had just come down when a loud voice interrupted them. "You soldiers are going to have to leave!" Grant looked up to see the stern, perhaps once voluptuous but now well-expanded proprietress glowering at them. "Your damned General Grant's curfew makes us all go to bed like children and close so early we can't make a living. So y'all have to get out!"

Sherman grinned. "But, madam—"

"What's good for us is good for you. I didn't see anything in that stupid order saying you soldiers had any special privileges."

Grant winked at Sherman, as they all laughed. Quietly, Sherman said, "Yes, ma'am, bring us the bill."

Sherman came to Grant's office at nine the next morning. After the redhead heartily agreed with Grant's decision to stay out of the capital, Grant moved to a large-scale wall map of the Confederacy. "You've asked me what my plan is, Cump. From the big picture, I see the enemy bottled up here, along the southeastern coast between Washington and Savannah. The capability to wage major war lies up this corridor between the mountains and the Atlantic Ocean—Georgia, South and North Carolina, and part of Virginia. If this territory falls, the rest of the Confederacy consists of dying limbs. Scattered armies in Missouri, Arkansas, or wherever, will have no further means of fighting, nor any reason to do so.

"And what have we at the ends of this great corridor, sealing it off? Two fortified cities—bastions where two major rebel armies can operate from sanctuary. At the northern end is Richmond, from which Lee has been able to roam as far as Pennsylvania. At the other end we find Atlanta, the base for Joe Johnston. Each city serves as a hub of communication, factories, barracks, depots, and hospitals. Each has well-built forts, behind which these roving armies can retreat and continue the stalemate."

Grant paused, sipping from his coffee cup. "The way I see it is this. As long as the rebs can keep both cities, they have a chance of the British intervening, or worse, a change of will in the North. It's quite possible for Lincoln to lose the upcoming election, and the Union pacifists to end the war.

"Therefore, we must destroy one of these major armies at the site of its fort, opening the corridor for a two-sided defeat of the other army and fort. We have the superior numbers and resources. We must bring them relentlessly to bear.

"We're going to chase both of these armies back into their sanctuaries at the same time. Which brings us to your mission, Sherman. As I told you, I must fight Lee in Virginia. The fort of Richmond is my problem. Atlanta is yours. By early May, I want you to head south into Georgia, chasing Johnston back into Atlanta, where you will defeat him."

Sherman's frown disappeared. "You make it all sound so simple, Sam."

Grant relit his cigar. "It's always easy to outline goals. Accomplishing them is another matter. Just remember one thing—we can't do this backing up, and nothing, absolutely *nothing* should dissuade us."

CHAPTER 42

I f one were to find the closest resemblance to a great white knight visiting 1864 from the days of King Arthur, it would be Robert E. Lee. His short beard was nearly white, as was his major vanity—his combed-over hair. His well-tailored uniforms were also a light gray, trimmed in gold bullion with his special insignia of rank as a Confederate general. Even his favorite horse, Traveller, was gray. But there was nothing gray about his beliefs. His erect, knightly appearance fitted his concepts of confidence and of *noblesse oblige*—the obligation of the highborn to display honorable or charitable conduct that included a sense of responsibility, and incumbent with this obligation, an unbending sense of fairness.

Five nights a week, his mess table provided boiled cabbage, corn bread, and some kind of potatoes—an austerity not particularly popular with his staff, but closer to what his enlisted men were eating. He slept unnecessarily on the ground so often that his adjutant, young Colonel Taylor, once said, "General Lee was never so uncomfortable as when he was comfortable."

While he was fondly regarded as "Marse Robert" by his lower ranks, and enshrined in a special shaft of sunshine from above, Lee was a hard-nosed, toe-to-toe slugger who was born to be a soldier. He was a superb war leader, a mid-Victorian Alexander who was at his highest pinnacle in battle. He was a tenacious competitor who would have humbled Napoleon, just as he had embarrassed Lincoln's marshals. He could turn even the most obvious defensive situations into a devastating offensive. As he once said, he had to be careful lest he "learn to love war too much."

He truly loved his veterans of the Army of Northern Virginia. He suffered as deeply from their continued losses as any compassionate captain in history, but he knew their role. His own was clear: uncluttered by intellectual or political distractions, he firmly and confidently strode his own path, followed his own immediate star. He vowed never to succeed Davis as president, even failed to exert his exceptional influence in dissuading his commander in chief from various blunders in strategy because of his ironclad adherence to civil authority.

Lee believed that every life had a purpose, and was called a praying soldier. He devoutly believed in God's management, trusting in Him and often calling for His help. While following his ordained course of arms, this scion of Virginia gentility managed to effect a total reconciliation of Christianity and war just as easily as his forebears had in the Crusades.

As he had been the perfect cadet, Lee was now close to being the perfect general. He was a superb tactician, with excellent generals of his own choosing to move about the totally familiar chessboard of Virginia. But seldom did his generals see an inner charm in him; he was either lacking in it in his rigidity or he was as taciturn as Grant. He could never have enjoyed himself in comradeship as Grant did with his generals in Nashville. Having fun did not fit his spartan role.

This was the titan Grant was finally about to meet in battle.

Now, on this third day of May, Lee stood on the peak of his observation post on Clark's Mountain, peering down through his glasses at the broad expanse of Union tentage at Culpeper, across the Rapidan.

Could those people have ninety thousand troops there, as his spies had stated? Well, he was certainly no stranger to the Army of the Potomac; it had come over that river before. McClellan had been the first, riding a crest of popularity and shouting, "On to Richmond." The boy wonder had wound up stymied in the Chickahominy swamps, purportedly blaming Lincoln for what was really Southern fighting skill.

Next came the bragging Pope, trying to build a reputation from his "headquarters in the saddle," saying he was going to track down and smash the rebel, Stonewall Jackson. Actually Pope commanded what was called the Army of Virginia, but this short-lived force had contained portions of the Army of the Potomac at what those people called Second Bull Run.

God bless your soul, Tom Jackson. He didn't know he was going up against the best general I ever had, did he? He didn't know you'd move so quickly between him and Washington on one of your famous quick marches, decisively trounce him at what *we* called Second Manassas, and send him off into oblivion.

McClellan tried again, this time in Maryland, just as I was about to descend on Baltimore and Washington. But he was better at Antietam and pushed me out of Maryland. Lucky for us that he stopped to shout about victory when he should have followed up.

Then it was Burnside's turn. The newspapers said he wept like a child, claiming he wasn't qualified for the job. And he proved he wasn't when he tried to charge a stone wall at Fredericksburg. He lost nearly thirteen thousand of his boys, and the Northern populace demanded his scalp.

And next came Hooker, the immoral one, across the Rapidan to Chancellorsville and into the Wilderness, where he lost sixteen thousand brave men and was almost routed. That's where your ghost walks, Tom, around the smoky Wilderness where you so roundly helped me trounce Hooker . . . and your men accidentally shot you. It broke my heart, Tom. We were so much together in our thinking, you so brilliant and audacious. I wish you could be with me in this coming campaign.

And then I decided to carry the war to Pennsylvania. But I didn't have you, Tom. And by this time, George Meade had the Army of the Potomac. He stopped me at Gettysburg. I was sick and Longstreet was slow, but I can't make excuses. If I'd listened to my own judgment, we might've defeated Meade. As it is, we were lucky he didn't follow up as we retreated back into Virginia.

Then Meade came over the river last November, only to turn tail without a major battle. And now you're down there, Meade, getting ready to come after me again. But it's not you who gives me pause for thought. No, it's your commander.

U. S. Grant. How much is truth and how much is fiction? Surely your record is impressive. They say your first foe ran away; then, when your star was barely out of the package, you took Paducah; then Belmont. Next came Forts Henry and Donelson, where you turned defeat into victory; and in spite of claims to the contrary, you won out at Shiloh, Corinth, and then that masterful job at Vicksburg. And finally you relieved that siege at Chattanooga and turned it into a smashing victory that may have opened the door to Atlanta.

And now, at last, you are here.

They say you are a sloppy, common drunk. But are you? No man befuddled by drink could have achieved those victories. If you are so common, how can you accomplish so much? Are you a Marshal Ney, who can come out of nowhere to become a brilliant commander? It is said that your tenaciousness is your formula. Well, my young general, it will take more than that to defeat the Army of Northern Virginia. Longstreet is back and my army is rested. We'll be playing in *my* backyard, sir, where my officers and men know the ground from tree to gully.

Maybe we should have just given you people Richmond, and consolidated one huge army around Atlanta. We could have had success attacking up into Tennessee and Kentucky, perhaps have retaken Vicksburg. But the president insisted that the soul of the Confederacy is here in Virginia, and here we remain.

How fitting that your name is Ulysses, for it may take you a long time to work your will. I will let you cross the Rapidan unmolested, and unless I miss my guess, I'll meet you in the Wilderness. There, your numerical advantage will be nullified. There, I will rise out of the ground like an avenging specter, slash your flanks and turn your columns. And when you are defeated, you, too, will pull your army back across the river to get ready for another try.

It's God's will.

After the Nashville reunion with Grant, Sherman dove into his task of organizing the western armies with firm resolve and his usual mode of rapid-fire flamboyancy. He'd gone north on the train with Grant to Cincinnati so the two could discuss at length their long-range ideas on the coming campaigns. His wife, Ellen, had joined the exuberant Julia in a shopping spree in the Ohio city. Then it was back to Nashville to his new command. He had a concept about discipline that he wanted to instill from top to bottom. The rigidity of the regular army would be relaxed with his free-thinking Westerners; he called it "the principle of harmonious action." It would have to be a selfless army if it were to succeed.

With his red hair seldom under control and his bright brown eyes often dancing, he was "Uncle Billy" to the troops, and constantly in their midst—even forgoing his private box at the New Nashville Theater to sit among his boys and lustily applaud the "points" with as much gusto as any of them.

Although his command was too new to have the rivalries of the Army of the Potomac, he was still dealing with a complex mixture of personalities. When the fiery, profane Logan, while in temporary command of the Army of the Tennessee, clashed with Thomas over railroad right of way, Sherman quickly called McPherson away from his wedding plans to smooth things out.

Thomas remained cool to him, particularly on the point of relaxing drill and discipline. The press tried to make something out of his being selected for the command over Thomas, but he laughed the situation away by snorting, "Not a bit of it. It doesn't make any difference which of us commands the army. I would obey Tom's order tomorrow as readily and cheerfully as he does mine today. But I think I can give this army a little more impetus than Tom can. These damned newspaper mongrels seem determined to sow dissension wherever their influence is felt."

From his first day in command, he fought the railroad problem. He decided that his single rail line between Nashville and Chattanooga simply would not be used for civilian interests. When the East Tennesseans complained to Lincoln, he answered the president by saying, "Either the East Tennesseans must quit or the army must quit, and the army doesn't intend to unless Joe Johnston makes us." When Christian commissioners demanded that Bibles and religious tracts be sent over the line, he growled, "Rations and ammunition are much better."

Acting as his own quartermaster, Sherman wrote, "Commissaries are too apt to think their work is done when the vouchers of purchase are in due form, and the price in Chicago or on the moon is cheap." To a civilian quartermaster he shouted, "I'm going to move on Joe Johnston the day Grant telegraphs me he's going to hit Bobby Lee; and if you don't have my army supplied, and *keep* it supplied, we'll eat your mules up, sir—*eat your mules up!*"

Now, on May 3, while Lee was contemplating what Grant might do, Sherman was pondering his own situation. A prolific letter writer, he'd just finished one to his wife and one to his brother, John, the U.S. senator. He poured a small glass of brandy and lit one of Grant's cigars before going to the window that faced south where the enemy waited . . .

"So we're about ready, Joseph Eggleston Johnston. I have nearly a hundred thousand fighting men to throw at you—some of the best-equipped veterans in the world, commanded by some topnotch generals. I'm satisfied, if ever a commander can be satisfied, that you can't hold out against us. I know you have some pretty good veterans yourself. And some pretty damned good generals too. You've also got some excellent terrain in your favor.

"But, you old defensive wizard, I'm not just going to assault you head-on. We're going to play the flanking game. I've got pudgy young John Schofield to worry you on one side, and the brilliant McPherson to hit you on the other. And while you're meeting their threats, steady old Tom will keep bearing in from the center. Three armies against your one, Joe, and two of them almost as strong as yours.

"It may take a while, Joe, but your days are numbered. Just like the days of the Confederacy. That goddamned Forrest sealed your fate last month, slaughtering all those helpless coloreds at Fort Pillow. Victory is one thing, but downright murder of surrendering troops—black or white—is barbaric. Every time a goddamned Copperhead voice is raised about us ending the war—which is your only hope—twenty others will remind us of Fort Pillow. I've always admired that great fighter, but now I question his sanity. The gloves are off now, Joe. Anything goes."

* * *

And on the same night, Grant lay on his bed in a house at Culpeper, reviewing his actions of the last few weeks and weighing the future. He bunched up his pillow and stared at the high, shadowy ceiling. Where did he stand? What could he have done that hadn't been done? There were always a thousand things.

Never could he have dreamed that his rapport with the president could have been so comfortable. The man was so gentle, yet strong; so sincere, yet so humorous; so exuberant, yet so weighed down by his huge burdens. So honest. Even he had fortified Halleck's advice about sharing plans. "General Grant, I have to tell you. People are always asking me what is going to happen next, and there's always the temptation to leak what I know. I guess I'm something like the child who sneaks a look on Christmas Eve, then rushes back upstairs to tell the other kids what's under the tree. So don't tell me what you plan, unless you really feel I should know. All I've ever wanted is a general to take responsibility and act, calling on me for assistance when he needs it. Armies sitting on their tails cost a lot of money, and there is a limit to resources. But you, General, seem to know the value of minutes."

Of course there had been, and would always be, problems.

Fortunately, Halleck had proven to be an excellent chief of staff in Washington. And there'd only been one difficulty with Stanton; he was used to running everything. But Lincoln had quickly settled this problem by telling the secretary that the general in chief, alone, was running the army.

Excluding those under the firm hand of Sherman, there were armies he didn't yet trust. Major General Franz Sigel was somewhat troublesome in the Shenandoah, and Banks was chasing an unimportant enemy out west on the Red River, when he could be adding forty thousand men in support of Sherman. Both were political generals with pull that reached to the coming election.

He'd been warned about Butler by Rufe Ingalls, but that political general had been more than cooperative about how his Army of the James could be used. Counting the ten thousand men from the South Carolina command, Butler had thirty thousand effectives. His mission was to move up the James River to City Point, where, if he could not proceed on Richmond, he was to entrench. And he'd given Butler the redoubtable Baldy Smith as field commander. So nothing should go wrong in that quarter.

Burnside was here to protect Meade's rear and rail lines; also to dash back to protect Washington if needed. His combination of many raw recruits, plus two brigades of untried Negroes, made his Ninth Corps an uncertainty. But he still had a number of veterans from the Knoxville campaign to lend some stability.

Meade. His respect for George Meade had grown each week. The press had been difficult on the Pennsylvanian, chiding him because the general in chief's headquarters at Culpeper was six miles closer to the enemy, and that he was only a token commander because of the lieutenant general being in the field. And it hadn't helped when the *Army and Navy Journal* had been so adamant that the "miracle worker from the West would straighten out this terrible Army of the Potomac."

No wonder he'd gotten the fisheye from some of its generals. But that didn't matter because when he'd inspected troops at the various reviews, he'd seen the steady, curious look of men who'd fight. And that was all he cared about.

Meade had readily accepted Little Phil Sheridan to command his new cavalry corps. The banty rooster was the only western general he'd brought east. If the little tempest could measure up to his previous exploits, he might just be the flame that was needed here. And he'd given Sheridan young Wilson as a division commander.

He knew his basic order to Meade had been far simpler than the means of executing it: "Seek out Lee and defeat him in the field." No one had done it yet, but he had told Meade just what he had told Sherman—there'd be no backing up. "Wherever Lee goes, you go."

In the morning they'd strike this tent city at Culpeper. The Army of the Potomac, ninety-seven thousand strong—but with only sixty thousand fighting men—would cross the Rapidan to meet a rebel army for the last time. For it would not turn back.

Lee.

Grant sat up in bed.

Yes, General Lee, the time has come. I've heard the whispers—"Grant hasn't met Bobby Lee yet." Well, with all due respect, sir, I'm not too concerned about that. I stood at the grave of a grand old general just after Shiloh, and I doubt that you could be any better than he. I'm also tired of people asking me what I think you're going to do. I figure that's how you've had so many of them buffaloed—always trying to outguess you. Well, sir, I'm too concerned about what *I'm* going to do to worry about that.

I've heard the stories that you're the silver-haired grandfather type, who pats children's heads and prays for your enemies. Well, that may be, but I give you credit for being a Herculean warrior who thinks right is on your side. But it just so happens that right isn't on your side, except in your own justification. You are the one who chose to break your oath and fight against your Union. Surely, you worship the same God as I do. And deep down, you must detest this horrible war as much as I.

I hope ever so much that we can end this quickly. Hundreds of thousands of lads can yet be saved from death and maiming. An untold number of civilians will also suffer and die. How many children in your beloved South will never see their first birthday? How many of our lads will never marry their sweethearts, or even meet them? How many will never beget their immortality? Do you want your sacred Richmond starved out, perhaps reduced to rubble?

If you'll come out of your defensive positions and join in one grand battle, we can avoid much of this. But I somehow feel that you will fight until there is no hope.

And that makes me terribly sad.

And makes me wonder if I'm up to it.

CHAPTER 43

There was an air of excitement in the night air as the Army of the Potomac began to break camp shortly after midnight. Hancock's II Corps led the way to the Rapidan. Escorted by Gregg's cavalry division, Hancock would cross Ely's Ford and quietly head for the ghosts of Chancellorsville. Another column headed for Germanna Ford—Warren's V Corps to go to Wilderness Tavern, with Sedgwick's VI Corps directly behind. Burnside would await orders at Brandy Station while the reserve artillery and the trains would follow Hancock over Ely's Ford. Cavalry-protected engineers with pontoon bridging were in the vanguard, ready to open the door to the last southerly crossing of the river to which blood was no stranger.

Was it really the Rapidan, Rawlins had asked, or Charon's Styx?

Meade's army moved smartly through the barely lit chill, wondering how soon it would be coming back, wondering how long it would take Lee this time, wondering also if this strange, quiet little general they'd inherited just might have some of his western magic to use.

Gradually the night noises began to diminish and the first streaks of dawn's early light played on lightly oiled muskets and flashing bayonets. The soldiers were greeted by the promise of a warm spring day, with its green shoots and curious new wildflowers. Before long, last winter's new overcoats would be shucked, an unnecessary as the jokers in their decks of cards. They knew why old Grant loaded them to the hilt—just so he would have to use fewer of them damn wagons. What the hell good were wagons if they couldn't be brought along to carry things like ammunition and rations? Damn generals!

Grant spent much of the morning watching from his big bay, Cincinnati, and wondering why Lee was letting his huge army splash across the river unmolested. He didn't like having to send the majority of his army down the Germanna Ford Road through the Wilderness, but the Rapidan had to be crossed where possible.

He could practically *feel* enemy eyes observing him.

As certain as the sunshine, Lee's legions would strike somewhere soon.

The Wilderness was aptly named, consisting of a wild tangle of second-growth timber and underbrush. It ran approximately thirteen miles from east to west and ten miles north to south. The Germanna Road ran southeast to an intersection with the main east-west highway, the Orange Turnpike, where the broken-down Wilderness Tavern was located. At this point the Germanna Road turned into the Brock Road, which crossed the other east-west route, the Orange Plank Road, on its way to Spotsylvania Courthouse.

So tangled was the Wilderness that these roadways were tightly edged by trees and brush, limiting their use to their actual width—anything but a tactical advantage for a huge invading army. Chancellorsville was located on the eastern edge of the Wilderness, while Lee's headquarters was at Orange Courthouse, a few miles west of the Wilderness. Hancock went into bivouac at Chancellorsville about noon, waiting for the cumbersome wagon train to catch up. Warren's corps reached Wilderness Tavern by midafternoon; Sedgwick camped between him and the Rapidan a short time later.

Tactically, Grant would have preferred moving more quickly through this huge entanglement, but that would have been a ripe invitation for Lee to initiate one of his famous slashes and cut the army off from its trains— which couldn't possibly complete the river crossing before the following afternoon. The die was cast. Grant was certain Lee was going to hit the flanks of his south-moving columns, not only because he'd be crazy not to, but because a rebel message from Clark's Mountain had been deciphered, indicating that Dick Ewell was moving his corps eastward.

Grant decided that Burnside could be more vital in a close supporting role, so he ordered him to leave Brandy Station, cross the river, and catch up by an all-night march.

Before dark that evening, Meade arrived at Grant's headquarters. After going over the map for half an hour and discussing contingencies, the next morning's plan was resolved. "So," Grant summarized, "Hancock will move south and east, commencing at five A.M. Warren will move southeast four miles to Parker's Store, and Sedgwick will go on into Chancellorsville, securing Orange Turnpike to the west of the town. I'm sure we'll make contact with at least part of Lee's army sometime during the morning, so your boys had best get to sleep early.

"Oh, and I almost forgot, I received word from Sherman, Butler, and Sigel that they've begun their advances. I don't expect too much from Sigel, but he can keep Lee concerned. To steal a phrase from Mr. Lincoln, 'If he can't skin himself, he can hold a leg whilst someone else does.' "

A smile touched Meade's lips. "You people from Illinois do have a way with words, General."

At eight o'clock on the 5th of May, as he waited for Burnside at Germanna Ford, Grant had his answer. Meade's message read, "The enemy have appeared in force on the Orange Pike and are now reported forming a line of battle in front of Griffin's division. I have directed Warren, whose corps is stretched out almost three miles, to attack them at once."

Grant turned to Colonel Comstock. "Warren's about to get hit on the flank near the turnpike. Could be Ewell or Hill."

The engineer scowled. "He should have been *past* the turnpike by now!"

Grant shrugged. "He's late. And Hancock's probably so far south that he's out of touch. C'mon, let's head for Chancellorsville. We'll set up our headquarters near Meade's." He scribbled out a message and handed it to Meade's courier. It ended with, "If any opportunity presents itself for pitching into any of Lee's army, do so without giving time for disposition."

Time, however, would soon be dispensed by generals in the Army of the Potomac as if it were the cheapest commodity on the planet. Meade's order to attack was relayed by Warren to Griffin, who in turn sent it to his advance brigade commander. That general decided the enemy was too well-situated for an attack, and sent word back to Griffin. Griffin went forward to see for himself, then ordered a staff officer back to tell Warren he agreed with his brigade commander. Time flew. Warren went to inform Meade of the delay, as Grant listened. Meade's temper remained barely leashed as Grant asked, "Is this whole army reluctant to fight?"

Meade turned to Warren, his face white. "Is a goddamned brigade commander running your corps, General?"

It took time to get the word back to Griffin, time which the Confederates spent well. It was Ewell on the turnpike, and although skirmishing had been going on for some time, he was now under orders to pace himself with A. P. Hill's corps, which was moving east along Plank Road. Lee's caution was based on the absence of Longstreet, who was still several miles away. Lee himself was riding with Hill, taking few chances on the loss of communication. When the ire from above reached Griffin, the hard-bitten regular threw his proud division into full attack, routing the lead rebel brigade and killing its commander. But, after proceeding nearly three-quarters of a mile, Griffin found that he was alone—an unprotected salient with reorganizing enemy troops on three sides. Bitterly, he gave the order to fall back through the murky, false twilight created by a combination of powder smoke and burning leaves.

This was only the beginning of V Corps incompetency. Warren was six hours late in his attack and his coordination of division movement was terrible. But his subordinate commanders were simply incapable of efficient movement in the maze of confusing forest. Brigades that were supposed to be facing west wound up looking north, exposing their flanks to crippling rebel fire; regiments were broken and a mounting casualty list began to reach fearful proportions.

Meanwhile, to the south, the Federal gap between Warren and the oncoming Hancock was filled by the VI Corps division of tough George Getty, a classmate of Sherman and Thomas. Just as Getty was preparing to meet the onslaught of Hill's two rebel divisions on the Plank Road, Hancock arrived at the head of his II Corps column. Hancock tried to talk Getty into waiting until more of his troops could arrive, but Getty was determined to follow Meade's insistent orders to attack. At 3:40, the battle exploded with full intensity.

The narrow confines of Plank Road quickly proved to be nothing more than a trap for immobilized, useless artillery pieces. Every element of textbook warfare was worthless, as kneeling troops on both sides sought whatever meager cover they could find and fired as rapidly as possible in the opposite direction. Heavy powder smoke quickly enveloped the front lines, joining in the already prohibitive labyrinth of saplings and undergrowth to limit visibility to almost nothing. Musket fire was incessant as the lines locked together. Officers, standing and trying to lead the advance, fell like flies. Hancock was able to bring his two available divisions in to support Getty, but progress was slow as the boys in butternut fought courageously. Yet somehow the Federals managed to push Hill back, while Warren's corps continued in its killing stalemate. Lee and Hill stubbornly hung on until dark, barely avoiding the total disaster that would have come with one more hour of daylight.

Grant was that close to winning.

With the eerie umber air fading to dark chestnut, nighttime brought a welcome battle lull. Weary, begrimed soldiers on both sides turned to the tiring but vital chores of the axe and shovel. The same frustrating trees that had been their nemesis now became their only means of safety for the forthcoming hours of respite. Intermittent musket fire continued, but casualties diminished—only to be replaced by a new horror. Sporadic fires of dead leaves refused to die, creating a choking fog of smoke that would kill some as surely as a Minié ball.

The first day of the battle of the Wilderness was over.

But only the fighting.

Shortly after nine, Grant acquiesced about the four-thirty jump-off for the next morning. "All right," he told Meade, "make it five, but no later. If the prisoner reports are correct, Longstreet will be up early, and Hill will have his other division. With our losses today, our numerical advantage will be trimmed considerably. But we must hit Lee's right while there's still a possibility that it's his weak point."

Meade tossed off a salute. "Very well, sir."

Grant watched the army commander's form disappear in the darkness. Turning grimly to the distant glow of flickering flames in the Wilderness, he thought the sporadic reports of musket fire sounded like miniature firecrackers as they carried to his hilltop. He turned to Rawlins. "According to Comstock, it was a terrible mess in there this afternoon."

Rawlins spoke quietly. "I know, I talked to him. It was a nightmare. I heard that General Getty lost nine hundred in his Vermont brigade alone. It's all that damned Warren's fault. But I'm sure Lee's losses were heavy too."

"Uh-huh, a lot of brave lads died on both sides."

"I only worry about our own. If you don't have anything else for me, I have to get back to my casualty reports."

Grant nodded. "And get some sleep."

"I won't need it as much as you."

Grant walked to his tent. His spartan quarters contained a cot, a washbasin on a tripod, a simple desk, two chairs, a kerosene lamp, and his clothing trunk. But he wasn't aware of furnishings, hardly of the tent. He sat down and stared at his boots, deeply troubled.

If he only had some whiskey . . .

The weight was so staggering. So many lives, so many limbs. The weary, blood-covered surgeons in their red-splattered aprons were probably throwing arms and legs away like chicken entrails. How many eyes would never see again? How many bodies were burning to a crisp in that godforsaken stretch of death-dealing wasteland? How many would not be recovered until the skulls were long a yellowed white—devoid of expression, except for the leer of bared jaws?

And he was the architect. On his head rested the blame. How many graveyards would he fill before this terrible campaign was over? How many mothers would mourn the rest of their lives over the carnage he now directed? How could they ever understand?

He recalled the end of a Gettysburg poem that had caught his eye:

Fold up the banners! Smelt the guns!
Love rules. Her gentler purpose runs.
A mighty mother turns in tears
The pages of her battle years,
Lamenting all her fallen sons!

Smelt the guns.

Sure.

Would all the guns of the world ever be smelted? Would there ever be a day when a tanner's son or his like would not have to wave the banner, not have to send such brave and innocent boys into a grotesque waste like the Wilderness?

He slumped in the chair. It seemed so long. Bloodstained corpses paraded before him, some in old-style uniforms, some in Mexican uniforms. Some in butternut, and many in blue. Most in blue. Limping and often hanging on to one another. Looking at him with lifeless eyes.

And this was only the beginning.

His eyes blurred.

Early on the morning of the 6th, Robert E. Lee knew as well as Grant that his weakness lay on his right, because Longstreet was still not up in battle position. He expected Grant to throw Hancock's powerful II Corps into Hill with everything he had. The only solution was to have Ewell get the jump by hitting Warren first, hoping the Union effort would be diverted in that direction. Just as Hancock's pickets began to probe, Ewell smashed into the V Corps. But Warren had stiffened his command and held firmly. By five-thirty, the entire line was locked in furious fire.

The II Corps would not be denied. It swept up Lee's right and pushed Hill almost back to the Confederate trains. Knowing disaster was imminent, Lee energetically directed the formation of a new defensive line in person. Had the visibility been better, one of many Federal sharpshooters could have ended his brilliant career then and there. But just as Union victory flirted, the mass confusion of too many troops in a confined area overwhelmed Hancock. His advance ground to a tangled halt, giving Lee just the amount of time he needed.

By the time II Corps commanders were able to sort things out, the lead elements of Longstreet's hastening corps came charging in. Hancock's luck ran out. It was Lee's warhorse's moment of glory. But suddenly the bad luck proved it had no favorites.

Having heard some firing that seemed out of place, Pete Longstreet spurred his horse forward to check on it. With several staff members in his wake, he rode toward a position where two of his brigades were abreast of each other. *My God,* he thought, *our men are shooting at each other!* Just as he raised his arm, a sledgehammer blow struck him at the base of his neck. The impact nearly knocked him out of the saddle. As blood spurted, he heard the staff officer behind him shouting, *"Don't—we are friends!"* His right shoulder was a mass of pain, his arm useless and dangling. *"Longstreet's hit! The general is hit!"* strange voices shouted in the murk. Somehow he stayed in the saddle until helping hands reached him and lowered him to the ground. The maze was turning scarlet as he faded away.

With Longstreet wounded much the same as Stonewall Jackson had been, confusion hit the overcrowded Confederate entanglements. During the ensuing lull, Hancock disengaged and withdrew to the entrenchments his men had constructed the night before. His brilliant victory had been wrenched away, but his position was now stable.

When Comstock returned from his visit to II Corps in midafternoon, Grant listened closely to his report, then turned to Meade. "Burnside's two divisions are now in position, so give the order to Hancock to resume the offensive at six."

Grant turned back to the stick he'd been whittling. Would they ever get out of this hell? They'd been so close the day before, and again today. It seemed like his feet were stuck in a quagmire, and just as he'd pull one out to step forward, the other would get stuck.

Could the handsome Hancock unstick the other foot and push the enemy far back into the forbidding thicket—start the beginning of the end of this horrendous combat? He was supposed to be "Hancock the Superb"— now was his chance to prove it.

Grant had his answer well before six.

Hancock never had a chance.

Lee threw Hill and Longstreet's corps into the II Corps entrenchments at four-twenty, nearly overwhelming the Federal line. But Hancock's reserves joined the desperately fighting main body just in time to make a stalemate of the furious battle. As darkness edged forward, the rebels again moved back to defensive positions, leaving a few hundred yards of smoking wasteland filled with a carpet of silent bodies.

Shortly after seven, Grant and Meade sat down for supper, assuming the entire front was stabilized for the night. But Grant had no sooner picked up his fork when a panting VI Corps staff officer was ushered into the tent by Rawlins. "General," Rawlins snapped. "They've just kicked the shit out of Sedgwick's right flank! Most of a brigade has been captured and part of a division is running all over the place. I guess the whole flank has cracked."

Meade threw his knife down. "Goddammit, I don't believe John could let that happen!" He glared at the staff officer. "What happened, Major?"

"We're not sure, sir. About six o'clock, all hell broke loose to our right. I guess the rebs were adventuring up near the river and found a hole. Before we knew what was happening, they'd smashed into Rickett's division and caught us with our pants down. Our boys started running, and, well, you know how that goes. When General Sedgwick found out what was going on, he was all over the place trying to stop them. I was right beside him when a rebel officer on a big black rode right up and pointed a revolver at the general. He shouted something like, 'Surrender, you Yankee son of a bitch!' But I shot him and Uncle John kept on going. Then he sent me to your headquarters, and General Humphreys ordered me here to report directly."

"Do you know what Humphreys is doing?" the irate Meade asked.

"Yes, sir. He told me to tell you he was throwing in some reserves and would take care of everything until you got there. But it may be too late. Lee is going to throw everything he's got between us and the river. We'll be cut off completely!"

Grant had been listening quietly. Now arising from the table, his tone was as angry as Rawlins had ever heard it. "He hasn't had time to mass his forces for that. And I'm heartily tired of hearing about what Lee is going to do. Some of you always seem to think he's suddenly going to turn a double somersault and land in our rear and on both of our flanks at the same time. Go back to Sedgwick and think about what we are going to do *ourselves!*"

The startled major mumbled, "Yes, sir," as Grant's stern expression relaxed and he sat back down at the table.

Colonel Comstock returned from Meade's headquarters at six-forty the following morning. He reported that Sedgwick had managed to shore up the north flank, and that the rebel attack in that sector had been of no more than division strength. Grant nodded. "I was sure that was the case." He handed the engineer the orders he'd just written for Meade. "Here's the plan."

Comstock read quickly. In that Lee had pulled back to fortified positions, the Federal forces would move some twelve miles south to Spotsylvania Courthouse on a march that night. When darkness arrived, Warren was to pull his corps out and move down the Brock Road to the rear of Hancock. As soon as V Corps passed, Hancock was to follow. In the meantime, Sedgwick and Burnside were to ready their commands to head for the same area. And the pontoon bridges at Germanna Ford were to be *dismantled!*

There would be no way back.

Comstock looked up, shaking his head. "My God, General, do you know what this means?"

"Of course. We came to fight."

Comstock looked into the steady gaze for a couple of moments, then replied in a low voice, "General, this may be the most momentous decision of your life."

Grant looked to his left. "Richmond is in that direction."

CHAPTER 44

If you want to smell hell—
If you want to have fun—
If you want to catch the devil—
Jine the cavalry!

Lee turned to his adjutant general, Lieutenant Colonel Walter Taylor. "All that dust means they are moving their trains, and that tells us Grant is going somewhere."

The twenty-five-year-old Taylor, darkly handsome and sensitive, had been with Lee since the beginning of the war. He replied, "Well, General, we know he's not going back across the Rapidan, unless he's going to swim."

"No, but he could be going to Fredericksburg, where he can cross the Rappahannock, or turn south. Or he could just be going south now, to Spotsylvania."

"Then you don't think he's going to quit?"

Lee's dark eyes narrowed. "No, sir, I do not. I think we'd best look to Spotsylvania. We'll rest today, then shift most of the army south on a night march, with General Anderson taking Longstreet's corps in the advance. If Grant *is* going there, we'll be waiting."

To himself he added, "My knights will await your queen, General." He felt the old thrill of being on the chessboard of war with a worthy opponent. The Wilderness had been a closer call than he had wished, but he still had the terrain and the advantage of starting a battle from a defensive posture . . . even though the attack was his strongest suit. The odds were still in his favor; if he could stop this young general one or two more times, Lincoln would never get reelected in the fall.

And it would all be over.

Shortly after eight P.M. Grant and Meade, together with their respective staffs, moved south to ride with Warren's advance down the Brock Road. It was a warm, dusty night, with the acrid smell of Wilderness smoke still hanging in the air. An early half-moon provided enough light to assist the guides. As they reached Hancock's sector, the column moved off to the side of the road to avoid trampling the dirty blue uniforms of II Corps soldiers, who were trying to sleep.

No announcement of victory or defeat had been made to the troops, so they were hanging on in limbo, waiting for the inevitable order to march back over the river. This was the Army of the Potomac, wasn't it? Get what sleep you could, and get ready for another long march. Don't pay any attention to the stench of burned bodies wafting in on a light westerly breeze, don't think of missing friends or the horror of the past two days. Just be grateful to be in one piece and think about the nearing end of your enlistment. Damn those generals!

But suddenly the word was passed that some heavy gold braid was going around them with a strong cavalry escort. It was Grant and Meade! *And the little bastard was riding south!*

Immediately the news spread, as soldier after soldier nudged his buddy to wakefulness. They must have won, certainly they had, because Grant was riding south. That little son of a bitch of a bulldog from the West had done it! No more running back with their tails between their legs. They were, by God, going on to Richmond!

Grant heard the first tiny cheer from somewhere to his rear. Quickly it was joined by another and another. Soon the whole Second Corps was on its feet on the west side of the road, cheering lustily. He turned to Rawlins, riding at his side. "Spread the word that the cheers are appreciated, but I don't want the enemy to figure out what we're doing, so they'd best quiet down."

Rawlins grinned. "From what I've heard, General, this army hasn't cheered a general in a long time. Let them have their fun. Besides, if Lee's boys haven't heard it by now, they're all deaf."

Grant pulled his hat brim lower and smiled briefly around his cold cigar. If these men could go through the horror of these last two days and still find a reason to cheer, they'd be doggone tough to beat.

Sheridan had taken two of his cavalry divisions down to Todd's Tavern on the Brock Road that afternoon to chase Jeb Stuart's cavalry away from the route of march. And he had done so, following sharp fighting. Assuming the rebel cavalry would hole up at Spotsylvania, he planned to move these divisions across the Po River at daybreak on the 8th, as Wilson struck down from the direction of Chancellorsville with his division. After Wilson drove Stuart's horsemen across the river, the three Union cavalry divisions would be in position to hold off any large body Lee might throw against Spotsylvania until a major portion of Meade's army arrived. But for some reason, Sheridan had neither issued orders to his two division commanders at Todd's Tavern, nor informed Meade of his dispositions and plans.

And for that he would suffer.

When Meade arrived at Brock's Tavern shortly after midnight, he found the route of his advancing army clogged by the *sleeping* cavalry! He'd listened to Sheridan's damned complaints about his use of cavalry too long for this dereliction! Angrily, he summoned the two division commanders—Gregg and Merritt, who was filling in for the sick Torbert. "Just what the hell is this?" he demanded. "A whole army is coming down this road shortly, and it looks like one huge outdoor bedroom!"

The two brigadiers shifted uneasily. Gregg decided to speak up. "Sir, we fought a hard battle today, and will probably be moving south before daybreak. So we thought it best to give the boys a little rest."

"If you'd been back guarding the trains like you're supposed to, you wouldn't be so damned tired. Where the hell is Sheridan?"

"Don't know, sir. I think he's back with Wilson. He should be along shortly."

Meade simmered down a bit. These officers weren't to blame. "Well, I want you to get these divisions up and ready to move. Gregg, bring your division southwest along the Catharpin Road and secure the ground east of Corbin's Bridge. Merritt, move yours on down the Brock Road toward Spotsylvania. Clean out whatever elements of Stuart's cavalry you run into, then send as much of your command as you can spare back to guard the trains. Do you understand?"

The "Yes, sirs" came in unison.

But it would be two hours before Sheridan's divisions could get moving, two fateful hours in which Lady Luck continued to bless the Confederates. Unknown to Meade, Grant, or even Lee, a forest fire would determine who won the race to Spotsylvania Courthouse. R. H. Anderson, in temporary command of Longstreet's corps, had left the lines at eleven P.M. Knowing the men would need some sleep, Lee had directed that he stop at three A.M. to let them grab a couple of hours of rest. But fate stepped in. The surrounding woods were burning out of control, and there was no place to get off the road. Anderson told his division commanders they had to keep moving. Without planning it, Anderson was slipping through toward Spotsylvania while confusion reigned in the federal advance.

The angry major general of Volunteers who sprang down from his horse in front of Meade's new headquarters was used to fighting. Townspeople in his hometown of Somerset, Ohio, had reported that he'd licked every boy in town before he descended on West Point. The bandy-legged little Irishman didn't quit swinging his fists as a cadet, and was finally on the coals in his third year when he attacked a haranguing cadet sergeant. Because he had impressed his tactical instructors with his grasp of maneuver and battle—and perhaps because Superintendent Robert E. Lee had seen something worth salvaging—the fiery cadet was suspended for a year, rather than dismissed.

Following his commission as an infantry officer when he graduated in the Class of '53, the social misfit was assigned to the First Infantry in Texas. There, a peer described him as "suggesting a low-comedy man who walked offstage all made up of funny parts, but upon a closer look, the stern, composed lines of his face were enough to make one forget his grotesque figure and careless dress." It was only natural that this eccentric should remain a second lieutenant, in spite of repeated bravery in Indian campaigns, until the rumble of battle reverberated from Fort Sumter.

Philip Henry Sheridan saluted abruptly. His black eyes narrowed as he bit out, "You wanted to see me, General?"

Meade was still angry. "Yes. I want to know why in the hell you think you can do what you want with my cavalry. First of all, you didn't follow my orders yesterday. Instead of guarding the trains, you went on your own offensive against Stuart. Then you left two divisions without orders, directly in the line of march of this whole army. What the hell do you think you're doing, General?"

Sheridan stiffened, every ounce of his Celtic blood in revolt. "It just so happens, General, that my massing of cavalry saved not only Hancock's ass, but yours as well! Just once, the cavalry of this army had the guts and opportunity to quit groveling under the spurs of that goddamned Stuart. Well, we showed him yesterday. When he thought he had us on the run, Custer whirled and damn near bit his balls off. Wilson and Greer wheeled right behind and we chased him damn near to Spotsylvania. *That's* why those two divisions were resting on your sacred road last night!"

The scion of Philadelphia gentility stared coldly into his subordinate's black eyes. "Why in the hell didn't you know the route of march?"

"Because I wasn't informed!"

"Why didn't your division commanders have orders?"

"For the same damned reason. But I had planned to get them moving right after you got in the act."

"What do you mean by *that* impertinence?"

"You gave orders to my goddamned command without going through me, *that's* what I mean. Look, General, I'm not one of your sit-on-his-ass Potomac generals. I don't need you to tell my generals what to do. You just tell me and I'll handle it from there."

"Like following my order to guard the trains?"

"I sent Wilson back."

"But only for a few hours. Do you call attacking Stuart guarding the trains?"

"Who in the hell else got into Spotsylvania today? If you hadn't interfered, my whole corps would have blocked the rebs. As a matter of fact, if you'd just leave me alone, I'd take my corps out and whip the hell out of that almighty Jeb Stuart, and then what would Lee do?"

Meade's cold wrath was barely contained. "So you don't think I have the right to give orders to *your* corps, huh?"

Sheridan leaned forward. "You have every right in the world, General. As a matter of fact, you can give *all* the orders, because I'm not going to give them *another goddamned one!*"

Meade pulled in a deep breath and blew it out. "Sir," he said in a low voice, "you are the most insubordinate son of a bitch I've ever met. You are dismissed, pending possible arrest."

Twenty minutes later, Grant listened as a still-fuming Meade recounted the incident. It sounded like his hard-fighting cavalryman was feeling his oats a little too much. He and Little Phil had held some long discussions about the effective use of cavalry, and Sheridan's theory of separate mass employment was indeed provocative. But the little Irishman *had* been wrong. Finally, Meade ended with, "If he weren't your own appointee, I'd see that he was a colonel tomorrow."

Grant sighed. "Well, General, I certainly agree that he went too far, and I'm sure you've tempered his remarks, but a couple of his points were pertinent. Stuart *has* had his own way for a long time. And some of your generals haven't been overly aggressive. I do think we ought to try some of Sheridan's ideas."

Meade frowned. "Oh, I forgot to tell you—he also had the gall to say that if I'd give him his own head, he'd go out and whip the hell out of Stuart."

Now it was Grant's turn to frown, but only to cover his own pleasure. "Did Sheridan say that? Well, he generally knows what he's talking about. Let him go ahead and do it."

Meade shrugged. "You're the boss."

"And General, I don't want you to feel that I'm not supporting you in this."

As soon as Meade left, Rawlins let out a low whistle. "You're letting that insubordinate little bastard get away with it. Do you know what this means to Meade's authority?"

Grant nodded. "Yes, but he'll be all right. I'm more interested in keeping a fighter in the command." The smile slipped out. "Besides, now Little Phil will have to put up or shut up."

As the afternoon of the 8th wore on, the question of what Lee was going to do about Spotsylvania was becoming quite clear: he was going to fight with everything he had!

The Wilderness was only the beginning.

Grant knew it, and his cavalry corps commander knew it.

Sheridan opened his orders from General Humphreys, Meade's chief of staff. "The major general commanding directs you to immediately concentrate your available force, and with your ammunition trains, proceed against the enemy's cavalry, and when your supplies are exhausted, proceed to Haxall's Landing on the James River, there communicating with General Butler, procuring supplies, and continuing against the enemy as the situation dictates."

Sheridan watched from a small hilltop as his cavalrymen began to move out of the tiny hamlet of Aldrich's Station at six o'clock on the morning of the 9th. Walking their horses four abreast, his troopers would eventually stretch out for some thirteen miles on the Telegraph Road that connected Fredericksburg with Richmond. Before the column was complete, nearly a hundred proud guidons would dance in the light breeze; one hundred troops and companies of fighting horsemen who could fire from the saddle or dismount and shoot like deadly infantrymen would have passed.

The familiar sounds drifted up to him—the subdued murmur of troopers' voices, the now-and-then laughter, the creaking of well-oiled and well-worn leather, the squeaking complaint of caisson wheels, the braying of unhappy mules, and the muffled beat of thousands of well-shod hoofs. Stretching out before him were nine thousand of the world's finest fighting men, eager to lock horns with Stuart again. The horseflesh was sound, after the well-deserved rest of the previous weeks. He never had agreed with his predecessors—pounding around the country at full tilt, horses and men too damned tired to do anything when the battles were joined. No, whenever possible, Sheridan's mounts would walk to their fights.

As the clank of loose metal and an occasional whinny reached him, he thought about his young generals. David Gregg, thirty-one, Class of '55, had been in nearly every cavalry action in the East; likable, dependable. Wesley Merritt, twenty-nine, Class of '60; bright and energetic. James Wilson, Grant's protégé, had so far performed admirably; maybe too big for his britches. But he was practically a wallflower compared to that reckless, luxuriant George Armstrong Custer.

My God, only twenty-three years old and a brigadier! Dashing, handsome in his long blond curls, the flamboyant Custer was unswerving in his rush to glory. Resplendent in gold-embossed uniforms, he always rode an expensive charger. A small voice warned against a lack of depth in the young swashbuckler, but he was a fighter, wasn't he? Absolutely fearless, and his four regiments of Wolverines would follow their Ohio-born leader right through the gates of hell.

Toss in the twenty-seven-year-old Henry Davies, and it looked like he was running a grammar school for generals. But weren't most of his troopers nothing but kids? And wasn't he himself commanding the Union's only cavalry corps at the age of thirty-three? Or at least he was commanding now—if Meade had anything to say about it, he'd be an old private on a lop-eared mule to nowhere!

So, Jeb Stuart, you so-called Knight of the Golden Spur, here we come. You can't ignore this march of mine because you know I might at any time wheel and slash into your boss's flank. Christ, I could raise hell there! Even though you can't afford a major loss to me, you have to pick up my gauntlet and come out to meet me.

That should appeal to your goddamned chivalrous opinion of yourself. I remember you, a year behind me at the Academy, two before I sat out. You were part of that clique of young Southern gentlemen, the cream of noble gentility and all that shit I resented so much. But then, maybe you don't have such a highfaluting opinion of yourself after all these years of war. Maybe this dashing hero, knighthood crap is just what the Confederate press has made out of you. I do have to tip my hat to you, Jeb, you're the best damned cavalry general this country has ever seen. You've been Lee's eyes and right arm for a long time. I salute you, sir, but when you come out, I'm going to sure as hell cut some fingers off that arm.

Major General James Ewell Brown Stuart received the news of Sheridan's departure shortly after seven o'clock. He stroked his luxurious chestnut beard and turned to his close friend, Lieutenant Colonel John Mosby, who was visiting the command post. "What do you think, Mosby? What's this little Irishman up to this time?"

The slender, blond Mosby shrugged. "Don't know, Jeb. And there probably isn't time for my boys to mix in with his column and find out, but I can try." He jammed his hat on his head and grinned. "I'll let you know if I learn anything."

Stuart went to the tent flap and watched the famous ranger commander mount and trot away. What was that pesky Sheridan about? He accepted a fresh cup of coffee from a mess attendant and sat back down at his table to ponder his next move.

Jeb Stuart, thirty-one, had graduated in the Class of '54. Commissioned in the mounted rifles, he saw duty in Indian country, where he married the daughter of his commander—Philip St. George Cooke, a Virginian who later stayed in the Union Army when the War between the States began. Stuart served as aide to Colonel Robert E. Lee during John Brown's short-lived insurrection at Harper's Ferry in 1859. When the war broke out, he joined the Confederate Army, and by midsummer was a brigadier commanding cavalry. Twice he led his command in rides around McClellan, enhancing his romantic reputation and making the little Napoleon look foolish. His well-trained troopers, employing his brilliant cavalry tactics, were the early scourge of Union commanders. Fun- and music-loving, he possessed great good humor and panache, yet was nevertheless quite religious. Lee came to trust him so much that he called him his eyes and ears when they were in the field. Only five feet nine, his flowing beard and massive shoulders made him look much larger under his black-plumed hat as he rode spirited horses into the thick of every battle.

The coffee was strong, the way he liked it.

For some reason he thought back to John Pelham, or as General Lee called him, "the gallant Pelham." How he had liked that brave, audacious young officer, his chief of artillery. Killed in the prime of his youth at twenty-four, a little over a year earlier. He could see his infectious grin now. And the grins of many others. Brandy Station, the first major cavalry battle, flashed before him. They called it a "draw" but he had the field when it started and still held it when the last trooper put away his carbine. It was just before the ill-fated Gettysburg campaign. Many of his fine young cavalrymen had gone to "Fiddler's Green" that day.

Fiddler's Green. According to a sixteenth-century legend, soldiers and sailors and all other "masterless" men went straight to hell upon dying. But cavalrymen were an exception; their long ride to the River Styx was interrupted about halfway along the road by a broad meadow, dotted with green trees and crossed by clear streams—a place of peace known as Fiddler's Green. Close by are the camps of all the dead cavalrymen, with their tents, picket lines, and campfires. Here cavalrymen are authorized to dismount, unsaddle, and stay forever, their canteens always full, to enjoy the companionship and reminiscences of old comrades.

Stuart smiled. It was always pleasant to think about that place.

But why was he thinking of ghosts now? Sheridan was his enigma.

What should he do? That Irish alley cat had better-equipped troopers, with sleek, rested horseflesh, good carbines, even decent boots. Could Sheridan be headed for Richmond? Was he after the Confederate supply lines? Ready to tear into the right flank? Well, whatever his plan, he couldn't be ignored.

No, General, I'll have to call my tired lads in from all over and go after you. With you out of the way, it won't be long before Grant will tuck his tail between his legs and go the way of all Yankee commanders in Virginia—*north!*

In midafternoon, Gordon's brigade of Confederate cavalry pounded down on Sheridan's rear guard, only to run into a confident and fully prepared Henry Davies. The Southern brigade was quickly repulsed and the Federal march continued leisurely to the North Anna. Sheridan ordered Merritt to cross the river to a place called Beaver Dam Station, while Gregg and Wilson were to camp on its north side.

Sheridan watched the crossing from the north bank, quite pleased with the day's accomplishments. The corps had moved some twenty-five miles in good order and had readily beat off a rebel assault. Now the Virginia Central Railroad lay at his mercy. Merritt's orders were simply to raise hell with it. The sound of gunfire brought his glasses up. Beaver Dam Station wasn't much, but at least three big fat trains were sitting there, plus some other waiting cars on sidings. His troopers were circling the station and trains, little puffs of smoke punctuating the firing of their repeating carbines. He spurred his mount toward the river bank, shouting for his aide to follow.

Just as he reached Merritt, the grinning Custer reined in, shouting, "We hit the mother lode, General! Must be enough rations here to last Lee for weeks, plus a big batch of medical supplies. And to top it off, one of these trains is loaded to the roof with prisoners. Must be four hundred of our boys from the Wilderness!"

Sheridan smiled. "Sounds like an ample day's pay."

Merritt asked, "What about the depot?"

"Burn it," Sheridan replied, "right along with the trains. I want Stuart's scouts to see the biggest damn bonfire in Virginia."

Sheridan's command spent the next morning in an easy move below the South Anna, where they tore up some ten miles of track. Rebel cavalry stayed close. Since there had been no major contact since the rebel attack on his rear guard, Little Phil was certain that Stuart was coming in force. Spies in Richmond had confirmed that Bragg, who had surfaced there in February as Davis's chief military adviser, had upward of five thousand troops to defend the Confederate capital. Although this was supposed to be a motley collection of wounded soldiers, government clerks, old men, and young boys, Sheridan knew they would be fighting from behind formidable fortifications and be ably led.

He figured that Stuart would concentrate his cavalry in the vicinity of Yellow Tavern, a crossroads hamlet located some six miles north of Richmond. From that point, he could permit the Federal force to move on into the outskirts of the city, then smash into it from the rear and trap it. Well, Richmond would have to wait—he wanted Stuart!

Dawn of the 11th arrived under cool, overcast skies. Shortly afterward, Sheridan received word from his advance guard that Stuart's cavalry had begun to position itself in the vicinity of the crossroads. Little Phil nodded his head, a touch of a smile on his lips. "That's just what I want!" he exclaimed to the courier. "Stuart's not going to let us get near Richmond. He wants to fight at Yellow Tavern, and my God, I'll oblige him!"

His column was seven miles away. The priority now was speed over rested horses. Sheridan moved out at a brisk canter, with screening forces on each side of the pike to warn of a rebel flank attack.

Stuart's troopers hadn't had time to dig in substantially when the first Federal troopers arrived. Two of Merritt's brigades smashed into the Confederate right, pushing it several hundred yards to the east. Immediately, Sheridan brought Wilson's division in. Except for a concealed rebel artillery battery that created some havoc, the rebel cavalry was no match for Sheridan's shouting, surging dismounted troopers.

As the blue wave swept forward, Stuart threw a powerful counterattack into Merritt's left flank—only to be met head-on by the saber-flashing Custer, leading his charging, mounted Michigan brigade over the Confederate left flank. The shouting Wolverines quickly smashed through, grabbing three artillery pieces and routing the rebel troopers. Immediately, the Federal attack was pressed all along the line. Mounted and dismounted troopers blasted their way right into the middle of Stuart's crumbling force. In moments, it was impossible to distinguish between blue and gray, as the battle melted into a hundred small fights. The Confederates bravely tried to hold their ground, but it was an impossibility. They were outnumbered and outfought, in spite of their commander's valiant efforts in their midst.

Jeb Stuart had once said, "I'd rather die than be whipped." Now, at shortly after four P.M. he was at his heroic best. Hurrying from position to position, personally encouraging his troopers, firing his pistol, waving his saber, he weaved his big gray horse in and out of the surging combat. Now he was with a handful of privates from Company K of the Maryland Riders as they battled with Company E of Custer's Fifth Michigan.

"Bully for old K!" he shouted. *"Give it to 'em, boys!"* He emptied his huge, silver-chased pistol at the bluecoats. His horse shied and started to rear, but he held him in tow. "Steady, men, steady!" he called out. He didn't even notice the forty-five-year-old private who had raised his long-barreled revolver. The Michigan trooper was only twelve yards away when he fired.

The .44 slug tore into his right side, nearly unseating him.

No!

He looked down at his yellow sash and saw the blood start.

He couldn't fall out of the saddle in front of his men!

He saw a captain, tried to grab his hand. "I'm shot. Save your men! See to your men!"

As they lifted him to the ground, he blacked out.

Minutes later, but too late, James Gordon's Confederate brigade attacked from the rear only to be met by the remaining two brigades of Gregg's entrenched troopers. Gordon quickly caught the worst of it and had to withdraw. It wasn't long before Stuart's famed cavalry corps was defeated, its surviving elements breaking off to return to Lee.

A victorious Phil Sheridan led his proud troopers into the outskirts of Richmond, lured by the fame of taking the capital. But he knew Bragg's makeshift army would be far from the soft touch it presented. He paused in the outer works of the city just long enough to let the populace know he was there, then confidently moved east to cross the James and join Butler. But instead of that general and his army being four miles away, as planned, it was busy adding to its fortifications some eighteen miles down-river at Bermuda Hundred!

Butler's telegram to Grant on the 6th reported that he had successfully moved his army up the James to a place called Bermuda Hundred, southeast of Richmond. The message had ended with the confusing statement: "We are landing troops at night—a hazardous service in the face of the enemy."

That was five days earlier!

Why in hell was an army of thirty thousand men that was supposed to be on the offensive sitting on its ass, dug in, at its debarkation point? Why, in nearly a week, had Butler not swarmed over the poorly held defenses of either Petersburg—the rail center—or Richmond? Or *both* of them? There were rumors of Butler's incompetence at New Orleans, even reports of scandal, but why hadn't his generals pushed him? Baldy Smith was with him.

Sheridan pondered these improbabilities the night of the 11th, just before a Federal spy came to his tent to tell him that the Confederates had sent out only a token force of skirmishers to meet Butler's legions—but they had been enough to chase the Yankees back into their entrenchments.

As soon as the spy left, Sheridan kicked his camp stool and glared at his chief of staff. "That bastard, Butler! He might have won the war, if he'd known what he was doing. Or, if he'd even been up here, we could have taken Richmond together! No sense staying around this place now. Let's get some supplies from that coward's quartermaster and get on to tearing up track and raising cavalry hell."

CHAPTER 45

*Their backbones cracked as they tugged at one an-
other with their mighty arms—and sweat rained
from them in torrents.*

—HOMER, THE *ILIAD*

It was after the prolonged battle of Spotsylvania ended on May 19 that both armies sat back on their haunches, took a deep breath, and licked their wounds. But four days later, they collided again at the North Anna. There had been no clear-cut winner or loser in these major engagements since Grant had crossed the Rapidan, although the Federal losses had exceeded those of Lee considerably. On the rainy night of the 27th, Grant was surprised to find his statement to Lincoln in the Washington *Star:* ". . . I shall fight along this line if it takes all summer." He again reminded himself to be careful of what he might put in writing to the president. On the other hand, he could see no harm in his comment being printed if it would give the public confidence in the administration and the conduct of the war. It was difficult enough, what with the newspapers constantly harping on losses.

He turned to a copy of the Richmond *Examiner* that a prisoner had been carrying. It was dated May 13th and its headline stated, JEB STUART DIES. The article described Stuart's shooting at Yellow Tavern on May 11 and how he had been taken by ambulance to the home of his sister-in-law in Richmond. Although four leading physicians had fought to save his life, he had succumbed there the evening of the 12th at seven o'clock. The grateful and saddened people of Richmond would pay homage to their beloved and courageous cavalry hero at his funeral that day at St. James Church and during internment in Hollywood Cemetery. The article then went on to extol Stuart's many exploits and to summarize his life.

Grant closed his eyes. He had learned from spies several days earlier that Stuart had died of his wound, but it seemed much more personal to read it in an enemy paper. He knew that Lee must have grieved, and for a moment put himself in Richmond the day this newspaper had come out. What if he had been a Confederate general and had known this brilliant and courageous young officer? He felt a sadness and closed his eyes.

But then the other voice, the one that had given him grim satisfaction at the time he had heard of the rebel cavalry leader's death, spoke up. The war was a crime, Stuart had broken his vow, and his death would certainly mean fewer Union casualties in the days ahead. Because, like Stonewall Jackson, Stuart simply could not be replaced. Lee had lost another vital member of his fighting anatomy.

His eyes went back to the *Examiner*'s front page. A smaller item noted that Lieutenant General James Longstreet was recovering from the serious neck wound he had incurred in the battle of the Wilderness on May 6. It stated that he was doing as well as could be expected, and that he was most probably out of serious danger.

Grant closed his eyes again and murmured a quiet thanks to the Lord. Old Pete had also chosen the wrong path, but they had been friends for so long that he couldn't help but feel relieved. He thought back to a night in St. Louis when Julia was descending the staircase of a small house in her lovely wedding gown. A harpsichord was playing in the background, and standing beside him at the bottom of the steps was a grinning Pete . . . the holder of the gold band he would put on her lovely finger.

He had heard of Longstreet being wounded the night after it happened from a prisoner report, but had learned nothing concrete since. He reminisced more, going back to the Academy and down to Mexico . . .

Then he picked up his best quill and opened the ink bottle. It was time to write to his commander in the West.

My Dear Sherman,

I am sure you are aware of our recent battles, so I will only state that Lee and the whole Confederacy know we mean business. No longer is Lee making us dance to his fiddler. Yet, I deplore our losses as only you can understand. I think you knew General Sedgwick. His boys called him "Uncle John." He tried to get them to ignore a rebel sharpshooter, telling them the marksman couldn't "hit an elephant at that distance." Moments later, the sharpshooter hit him in the face and killed him. He'll be sorely missed. I've given his command to Gen. Horatio Wright, an engineer and member of the Class of '41.

Gen. Sigel has failed in the Shenandoah, and Butler has been useless on the James. He's fortunate to still have an army. He gave Beauregard time to assemble 20,000 troops and barely got back into his works. I may have to do something about him if I ever get this army down to the James.

I can relieve Sigel. I think I'll give old David Hunter the Valley command.

This brings me to your campaign against Johnston. I know you're doing your best and I congratulate you on your patience with that old fox. But, Sherman, I must urge you to move as quickly as possible against At-

lanta. I don't see any kind of early victory here in Virginia, so the burden of providing a major success rests on your capable shoulders.

There is the coming election to think about, you know. Everyone is sure McClellan will get the Democratic nomination, and there is a rumor that he will have an "end the war" plank in his platform. Above all, we need to keep Mr. Lincoln in the presidency, and your actions are the best insurance.

Please give Mac, Logan, and Thomas my best regards. I wish I could come out to see you, but I'm probably stuck in Virginia until this terrible thing is over.

> *Your friend,*
> *U. S. Grant*

Little Phil arrived on the North Anna the next day and reported directly to Grant. The pleased general in chief smiled as he gave Rawlins a sidelong glance. "I guess Sheridan thinks he has been clear down to the James River, breaking up railroads, and getting a peep at Richmond. Probably this is all in his imagination, or he's been reading these stories in the newspapers. I don't suppose he seriously thinks he made such a march as that in two weeks, does he?"

Rawlins shrugged. "You know how these cavalrymen exaggerate."

Sheridan grinned. "Well, General, from what you just said, I feel doubtful as to whether I've been absent at all."

Grant warmly shook his hand. "You did quite a job, just as you said you would. It's too bad Butler wasn't able to join with you to take Richmond."

"Oh, he was *able*, General. He just doesn't know how to fight."

"So I've seen. Well, let's get back to here. First, I want you to go over to see Meade and make peace. I don't want any prima donnas—no matter how well they fulfill their boasts—fighting with an army commander. You proved your point, Sheridan. Now let's see you prove your diplomacy."

Sheridan frowned. "But he was wrong, and—"

"And so were you. You should've been relieved. Do as I say and we'll get on with things. From now on, you'll be attached directly to this headquarters and receive your orders from me. Now, come over here to the map and I'll show you what I want done. Once more, Meade is going to move south toward Richmond. And I want your divisions to do exactly as ordered—no independent action."

Sheridan raised an eyebrow in good humor. "Yes, sir."

"This is where I want you to go."

Sheridan squinted at the small print naming a crossroads—Cold Harbor.

That night, Rawlins stuck his head inside Grant's tent and said, "General, we've got a talkative prisoner for you to interview."

Grant got up from his desk. "Good. I need to get away from these reports. Does he know very much?"

"You'll see."

Several members of the staff were gathered around a figure in butternut in the headquarters tent. An armed provost-marshal captain stood by his side. The prisoner was slender, a comical-looking creature with a shock of blond hair that stood up and looked as if it hadn't seen a brush in months. He had a scraggly reddish beard and though his long face wore a solemn expression, the twinkle in his eye bespoke a humorous wit. His clothes included a Confederate Army blouse that hung to his knees with a shadow where sergeant's stripes had once been sewn. His big toe could be seen peeking out of one worn hightop shoe.

When Grant walked in, the soldier said, "My name's Lee Lane, suh," with a heavy accent. He stuck out his hand, which Grant shook.

"What command do you belong to?" the general asked.

"I'm in Early's corps, but I belong to a No'th Ca'lina regiment, suh."

"Oh, you're from North Carolina?"

"Uh-huh, and a good deal fathah from it jes' now than I'd like to be, God knows."

"Where were you taken and how did you get here, young man?"

A grin creased Lane's face. "How did I get h'yah? Well, when a man has half a dozen a them thah reckless and desprit dragoons a yourn lammin' him 'long the road on a tight run and wallopin' him with the flats a thah sabahs, he don't have no trouble gittin' heah."

Grant suppressed a smile. "Is your whole corps in front of us, and when did it arrive?"

Lane screwed up his face and shook his head. "Well now, 'fore I tell you 'bout that, I want you all to know that I'm fast losin' interest in this heah fight. I was a peaceful man, and I didn't want to hurt nobody, when this heah conscript officer down thah in the ole Tar State come 'round and told me I'd have to git in the ranks, and go to fightin' fo' my rahts. I tried to have him pint them out fo' me, and told him I'd as lief have 'em all, but I wasn't strenous 'bout it. Then he began puttin' on more airs than a buckin' hoss at a county fair, and told me to come raht along, that the country needed me. Well, I had noticed that you fellers was winnin' too many battles and I thought I might jes' kinda even things up, so I went along."

He sighed. "But they ain't treatin' us too well—you know, feedin' us half the time on crumbs so that one boy in my company, he's got so thin you have to throw a tent rope over him to get up a decent shadow. Anyways, I been gettin' peacefuller and peacefuller, and them South Carolina folks'll have to find someone else from the old Tar State to win their war for 'em."

Now Grant sighed. "Are there any men from South Carolina in your brigade?"

A big half-serious, half-humorous expression came over the prisoner's face as he replied, "Yes, suh, a few . . . in the band."

Grant couldn't hold back the laugh any longer. Shaking his head at the roaring Rawlins, he said, "I'll be in my tent if you get anything important from this man."

Again, it seemed that Lee looked at his giant chessboard and anticipated Grant's moves as if he had a crystal ball or a spy inside his opponent's staff. This time his knights distributed pawns all along the Federal approach to Richmond, permitting river crossings, but concentrating toward the same destination that Grant had pointed out to Sheridan. This small but vital war zone in Virginia was essentially flat farm country, with low areas that became swampy during rainy periods broken by swirling but not too abrupt ravines and low-lying hills—innocent enough in appearance, but deadly when properly utilized for military defense. A skillful defensive engineer like Lee could give an attacking force fits in such terrain. And the newer rifles with their longer ranges could wreak havoc from a fortified position. As Grant reported to Halleck, gone were the days of wide maneuver and bold flashes of brilliance by intrepid commanders. A command had to slug it out and take losses to gain an objective.

Lee sensed with certainty that the critical crossroads at Cold Harbor was the place to end Grant's leapfrogging toward Richmond. He ordered his diminished cavalry—now under Wade Hampton—to intercept Sheridan. He also directed Beauregard, who was barely pressed by Butler, to rush a large force to that vicinity. The major portion of his Army of Northern Virginia continued to sidle along, keeping pace with Grant's main body.

Cold Harbor was an old wooden tavern set in a grove of tall trees at the intersection of five different roads. The name, of old English origin, meant "lodging with only cold food." Grant would find its greeting unbelievably cold.

After initial success at the crossroads, Sheridan discovered the arrival of rebel infantry in large numbers and decided to pull back. Baldy Smith, whose XVIII Corps had been ordered up from Bermuda Hundred by Grant, took the wrong route, going far out of his way and losing part of his command, ammunition, and supplies. With Lee's troops feverishly digging trenches at Cold Harbor, Grant's fervent enemy—timing—was beginning to work its insidious magic. The attack was scheduled for daybreak—four-thirty—on June 2. To pivot into position, Hancock had to move his Second Corps around to the left on a difficult night march. His guide took him down the wrong road. Also, Meade's other commanders were sluggish in their movements, reducing his timetable to a farce and his temper to the boiling point. The attack had to be held off for twenty-four hours, a full day and night of precious time in which Lee could add to his growing fortress.

That night Grant sat alone in his tent, pondering his terrible decision. A hard rain struck a steady beat on the overhead canvas as he thought of the men of his army trying to get some sleep in their wet holes and under whatever dripping cover they might have found. They were to attack at first light, and he had to make up his mind whether he should stick to the plan. He fingered a cigar and decided against lighting it. He'd been through about twenty that day, and his mouth tasted like a charcoal spit. He regarded the silver tinder box in the light of the lamp. The gift of an admirer, it contained a flint and steel to strike a spark, and a coil of fuse that ignited easily and wasn't affected by the wind. He wished he could find as practical a means of packaging Lee.

He had an inefficient batch of commanders, and an army that had surprisingly high morale—considering all it had been through. He also had a major dilemma. He couldn't sit here in a stalemate, he couldn't turn back north because he'd moved his supply base south to White House, he couldn't maneuver around Lee because of the Chickahominy River and its swamps, and Lee was waiting for him at a nondescript and probably deadly crossroads on the way to Richmond.

His heart was heavy as he wondered how many times he could keep ordering men to their death. Closing the tent flap, he knelt beside his cot and folded his hands. He heaved a big sigh and prayed silently, "Help me, Father, in this matter. I know what awaits the lads tomorrow, and it makes me want to go out there and tell my generals to call it all off and tell them I resign. I need your strength to do otherwise. I need your help, oh Lord, to bear up and keep my resolution." He put his hand to his forehead, closing his eyes and adding, "Help me, dear Lord, give me the strength."

After another minute of prayer, he got to his feet.

He knew he could change nothing.

At dawn the gentle slope of Cold Harbor glistened in innocent freshness, a silver dew signaling its tranquility. The night's rain had left a thick blanket of stillness that even the birds and the movements of early stirring soldiers didn't quite disrupt. Knowing the command to attack was imminent, soldiers pinned last-minute scraps of paper to their blouses—name tags that would enable their loved ones to find out if they had been killed. It was a wordless and deliberate procedure—what could be said that hadn't already been uttered?

It was the same on both sides.

Suddenly the deafening crash of Federal artillery announced that the moment of yet another terrible assault had arrived.

Just as the blue-clad troops surged forward, the freshly turned amber dirt above them erupted into a blazing nightmare. Bursting shells from rebel artillery and mortars blasted in the midst of the advancing Federal wave, throwing bodies and parts of bodies into the brightening sky. The wave melted, was replaced by another that dissolved just as readily under the steady rebel gunfire that now included an unending sheath of small-arms flame from the Confederate entrenchments.

Union officers waved sabers and fired revolvers, shouting, cajoling, and going down with their men. Soon the brightening sky was no longer brightening, but growing dark and stinking from the rising cloud of burnt powder. The wounded and still fighting crawled behind the bodies of their fallen comrades, wriggling for any cover, any respite from the deadly fire from above.

All along the ragged front, regiments, brigades, and even divisions were stopped in their tracks. Not one Federal effort, large or small, lasted more than fifteen minutes. In what seemed an eternity, but was actually less than an hour, the terrible attack at Cold Harbor was broken. Yet the battle staggered on, with mounting Federal losses. Finally, at 1:30 P.M., Meade ordered further frontal assaults suspended.

Grant's fateful decision had produced nearly seven thousand Union casualties.

CHAPTER 46

> *Despair. Vast Union losses. Congress*
> *Pursed its lips; ate three meals daily; voiced*
> *Distrust; demanded with disdain things*
> *Be reversed. Snide, back fence experts argued,*
> *Probed, discussed the general's ouster. Grant*
> *Was a disgrace. Advice stormed Lincoln's days,*
> *Sniped through his nights. Then—*
> *Lawyer-president resolved the case. Brief*
> *Words: "I can not lose this man. He fights."*
> —MAY LYNCH, *DECISION*

Julia Dent Grant had been the novelty of Washington society when she arrived in late March to reside at the fashionable Willard's Hotel. Washington matrons had been quick to note that the rather dumpy little nearsighted lady from St. Louis and other points presented little in the way of a threat. Although she seemed adequately gowned, she certainly didn't appear to be the type who would get her bonnets from William, where the remainder of a roll of ribbon was thrown away once a snip had been incorporated in one of the proprietor's creations.

One of these matrons, a senator's wife, had this to say to a reporter— off the record of course:

> *She appeared to be, in fact, quite dull—quiet, prosaic when engaged in conversation, hardly a person capable of any juicy tidbits of gossip. Although rumored to have grown up in St. Louis society, apparently Mrs. Grant was more a product of austere army life on the frontier. She was supposed to be only thirty-eight years old, but she certainly looked older— again, possibly because of hardship in the West. Yet there were enough ambiguities to make her a bit intriguing. She'd had her own slaves, even while building and living in a log cabin. Really, a colonel's daughter in a*

log cabin? That sort of poppycock was all right for a politician like the president, but really? The next thing, someone was going to say she split her own firewood. And they said this buxom little woman had once been the belle of the ball—why she was almost awkward! If Mrs. Lincoln felt secure about her, she had to be terribly common. The only problem was that she was Mrs. Grant, and her husband was the most famous man in the country.

And she was also rather standoffish—seldom accepted invitations, even to the theater to share private boxes. And her husband, the lieutenant general, was even worse when he was in the city. When the prize catch did attend a function, he never said anything—handsome enough, but so uninteresting. And speaking of his good looks, how did that plain little nobody ever get him—her father's money? Now with him down toward Richmond leading stalwart Union soldiers to slaughter, one would think she'd come down off her high horse and welcome invitations.

Of course, that grasping Kate Sprague had her under her thumb. That red-haired young harlot had jumped on the bandwagon the moment Mrs. Grant came to town. She and her uppity airs, Paris gowns, all her money, her political influence—the way she flaunted her so-called beauty, turning men's heads and controlling their attention at functions. It wasn't enough to be pushing her father for the presidency at every turn, handpicking a senator for a husband, now she was controlling the lieutenant general's wife!

Julia had just returned from leaving Jesse with his temporary tutor, and she had a few minutes to kill before Kate would arrive. She decided to water the pretty red roses the mother of some lieutenant had sent. She liked it here in Williard's, and loved the bustle and vigor of Washington. There was so much to see and do. But it could become a chore at times, particularly with Ulys down in Virginia, and so many people wanting to monopolize her time. Oh, most of them meant well, but so many just wanted to capitalize on her being Mrs. General Grant.

They thought they were playing with a provincial babe in the woods. Ha! Little did they know how well the social jungle of St. Louis had prepared her for the shallowness of wartime Washington. And to think of how much she'd once dreamed of being famous and sought-after. Silly girl dreams. The fantasies of every young girl's aspirations—fancy gowns, huge ballrooms lit by sparkling crystal chandeliers with a thousand candles; the beauty of the waltz played by a thirty-piece orchestra, gliding and swooping with a handsome man in evening dress, a dozen more clamoring for a place on her dance card; receiving engraved invitations to great dinners, leaving her *carte de visite* after teas in elegant gardens, an ornate box at the theater . . .

But she was no longer a girl, and the dreams were no longer that alluring. There were still the simplicities of life, such as the grocery shopping. She checked her purse to make sure the list was there. Actually, she sort of enjoyed shopping in Washington; the markets were more like country general stores than one would expect in a supposedly modern national capital.

But, ah, the terrible prices: coffee, 20 cents a pound; butter, 29 cents; eggs, 18 cents a dozen; roast beef, 26 cents a pound. *What outrageous profiteering!* No wonder Mrs. Lincoln, or "Madame President," as she liked to be called, was so hard on the merchants who delivered to the White House. What was the funny story they told—she reached such a point of browbeating with one grocer that he complained to the president, only to hear Mr. Lincoln sadly reply, "My good man, you ought to be able to stand, for fifteen minutes, what I have stood for fifteen years."

But perhaps Madame President *had* to shop shrewdly, since she was reported to be so extravagant everywhere else—expensive gowns, hundreds of pairs of gloves, and who knew what else? Kate reported that she said Mr. Lincoln had to get reelected to pay off the $25,000 she owed. Oh, how Mrs. Lincoln hated the lovely Kate or any other attractive woman who came in contact with the president! There were so many stories about her insane jealousy. Kate just loved to tell the story about her wedding: Mrs. Lincoln refused to attend out of spite, and waited until the president—who had to go—was almost ready to leave, then hid the pants to the suit he was going to wear!

Surely many of these stories about Mrs. Lincoln were exaggerated—this city being so full of sharp-fanged gossips—but some of them had to be true. Poor Mr. Lincoln, carrying the weight of a nation at war, probably working over eighteen hours a day, bearing the tragedies, and still having to put up with her problems. It was a wonder the man didn't just collapse . . .

The knock on the door announced Kate's arrival. Julia gave her bonnet a last minute peek in the mirror and headed out for what she knew would be an enjoyable midmorning breakfast.

Kate Chase Sprague at twenty-three, or was it twenty-four years of age, virtually had the world in her lovely hands. Not quite redheaded, as the sharp-tongued rival had said, her hair was more dark gold. With lively hazel eyes, a profile that would make an artist stop on the street, and a figure to match, she was bound to elicit the dislike of women in general, and the interest of any man still breathing. The fact that she had been acting as her thrice-widowed father's official hostess since her teens, when he had been governor of Ohio, gave her an easy sense of confidence and maturity beyond her years. She had continued in this role during Salmon P. Chase's tenure as secretary of the treasury under Lincoln. Married the previous winter to Senator William Sprague, the wealthy former colonel of Volunteers, she was the undisputed queen of the Washington social world. But this morning she was subdued.

Shortly after the maître d' seated them in the flower-bedecked dining room of the Herndon House, Julia asked if something was wrong. Kate looked up from her coffee. "Have you seen the paper this morning?" she asked.

"No, I seldom do until afternoon. There's always so much bad news, what with the casualty lists and all. Why?"

"There's been another terrible battle at a place called Cold Harbor."

Fear stabbed at Julia. "Oh?"

"We suffered severe losses in a very short period of time, and the papers are blazoning that your husband is a butcher. I'm afraid there'll be a vast hue and cry over it."

Julia's voice was barely more than a whisper, "How many this time?"

"One paper said as high as eighteen thousand."

"Oh, my God."

Kate Sprague smiled as she touched Julia's hand. "But you know how they exaggerate, dear. Could've been only half that many. No figures have been released by the War Department yet."

Julia stared into her coffee cup. Poor Ulys, now they'll really go after him.

"This will really give the antiwar dogs and the Copperheads something to chew on," Kate said. "What does that make it—around seventy thousand casualties in this campaign?"

"I don't know. I don't keep track."

"What do you think he'll do now?"

"Oh, he'll probably just keep going. That's his way."

Kate sighed. "I just don't know how much more of this the country will stand."

Julia felt dazed, in a bad dream. "Did they really call him a butcher?"

"Yes, dear, in big, black letters."

As in the case of the first day in the battle of the Wilderness, Grant had been stunned by the ghastly cost at Cold Harbor. But he shook it off and forced himself to plan ahead. In the early evening of the 4th he sat at the headquarters dining table with Rawlins, Comstock, and his newest aide, Lieutenant Colonel Horace Porter. Porter, an ordnance officer from the Class of '60, had joined him in Washington in April. Grant put down his coffee cup and announced, "We can't sit here, so I've decided to move south once more. The only way we can isolate Lee's army and Richmond from the rest of the Confederacy is to cut off their supply and communication lines. Petersburg, twenty miles south of Richmond, looks like the place we should take."

"But we're only ten miles from Richmond now," Colonel Comstock said.

"And Lee won't let us get there," Grant replied. "No, I've made up my mind. We'll withdraw to the east, go down the south side of the James, and try to take Petersburg."

"How will we swing this whole army around and pull back?" Porter asked.

"Meade can have his engineers dig a strong line of entrenchments behind our left," Grant replied. "We want Lee to think we're beginning another of our flanking movements and heading straight for Richmond. But we'll actually pull out at night and move east."

"Won't that be dangerous as hell, General?" Comstock asked. "What if Lee catches us in the flank?"

"We'll send Sheridan with a couple of divisions up to join Hunter in the Valley. He can tear up the Virginia Central on the way. Lee'll have to send his cavalry to chase him and guard against an attack from his rear."

Comstock shook his head. "It's still a hell of a gamble."

Rawlins spoke up. "How are we going to cross the river?"

"We're going to erect the longest pontoon bridge in history."

Rawlins shook his head. "You mean we're going to cover moving a hundred thousand men away from Lee, march them fifty-some miles, then get them over a mile-long bridge that doesn't yet exist—all on *time?* With an army that can't even march through the woods without getting lost? General, that's going to take some mighty fine planning."

Grant smiled. "That's why I have a mighty fine staff."

CHAPTER 47

The narrow-fronted, three-story red brick house with white shutters at 707 East Franklin had long been known as "the mess," since it had served for some time as sort of an elite bachelor officers' quarters. Colonel Custis Lee, the eldest son of the commanding general, had held court there with several other single officers during most of his long tenure as aide to President Davis. But the arrival of Mary Custis Lee and his sisters on the previous New Year's Day had abruptly changed the complexion of the zestful male retreat. As Custis liked to say, "It became the most aristocratic sock factory in Richmond."

Now, as his carriage approached the low iron picket fence that guarded the entrance, Robert E. Lee looked out with anticipation at the small portico, supported by its two white columns. It had been weeks since he'd seen his wife and family. He felt his pulse quicken as he turned the door handle.

Lieutenant Colonel Walter Taylor started to jump out to assist him, but Lee stayed his hand. "No, you go on to your delightful young lady and give her my fond regards. I won't have any need for you until tomorrow. But have the driver pick me up at six forty-five, so I can get to my appointment with the president."

Lee stepped down from the carriage and stopped to stretch, trying to ease some of the annoying little aches that lately seemed to come more frequently when he sat in one place too long. He was barely through the black iron gate when his youngest son, Robert, now a captain, bounded down the steps from the portico. "Father!" he exclaimed as he reached Lee's warm embrace.

Seconds later, Lee was smothered by kisses, hugs, and joyful greetings as his three daughters surrounded him. After each had received her due, he looked up to see Rooney standing at the top of the steps, grinning broadly. Rooney was home for a couple of days to recuperate from a stomach ailment he thought was an aftermath to his long stay as a prisoner in the Federal prison at Fortress Monroe. Lee embraced his second-eldest son.

Mary's wheelchair was just inside the door; from it his arthritic wife greeted him cheerily. He kissed her gently on the cheek, then brushed her lips with his. "And how is my beloved sock knitter?" he asked as he took her hands.

"I'm fine, darling," she replied warmly. "Certainly not turning as white as you. My," she said as she tugged his short beard, "even a few weeks makes a difference. Must be all those burdens and not enough proper food. You shouldn't be so silly about the way you eat. Oh, I know all about your spartan fare—Walter's told me."

"Walter talks too much, dear. Now, Robert, if you'll be kind enough to fetch in my bag, I'll move in for a couple of days."

Thirty minutes later, Lee sipped some tea in the pleasant backyard with Rooney. Major General William Henry Fitzhugh Lee—Rooney to the family—had gotten into the war early, and as a tall young cavalry officer had risen rapidly in command under Jeb Stuart. He'd been wounded a year earlier, and while recuperating, had been kidnapped by a daring Union raiding party. Some Federal leader had thought to use him as exchange bait for certain important Union prisoners. Tragically, during Rooney's imprisonment, his lovely wife, Charlotte, had died of illness. The twenty-seven-year-old Rooney had been exchanged in March.

Lee inspected some new buds on a rosebush, then sat on the steps. "Well, son, how do you feel?"

"Okay, Father, except for this blasted stomachache. My wound's healed."

"How's the other wound? Is it working itself out?"

Rooney's expression hardened as he looked toward the lowering sun. "I guess so. It just seems such a shame. We had so little time together, and she . . . she was just so darned young and beautiful. She—well, I guess it was the Lord's decision. I just wish they had let me come home for the funeral."

"Custis tried. They wouldn't accept his offer to exchange himself for you."

"I know. And I appreciate it."

Lee wanted to take the son he remembered as a bright, loving child in his arms; wanted to drain off some of the grief. But those years were past. He just sat there and shared the silence for several moments. "Were you still with your division when Hampton got the word to go after Sheridan?"

The war was the bridge back to the present.

"No, where has he gone?"

"Toward the Valley." Lee explained what he knew about the Yankee cavalry's latest effort.

* * *

Nearly a half-hour later, he had his talk with Custis. Colonel George Washington Custis Lee had graduated first in his Class of '54 at West Point. A promising career as an engineer officer seemed assured for him, but he had resigned from the Union Army shortly after his father's decision to fight with Virginia. However, Davis had sidetracked him by attaching him to his personal staff. He'd been promoted to colonel in the first few months of the war, but had gone no higher in rank since.

"Doggone it, Father, I know I can handle that command in western Virginia. And the president knows it too!"

Lee sighed. "Son, we've been over this before. I know how frustrating it is for you to be chained to a staff job and have a brother five years younger who's a major general. But you just haven't got any field experience. It simply wouldn't be right to give you a major command."

Some of the Lee temper was showing in Custis's eyes. "Well, just how, pray tell, am I supposed to *get* this precious experience?"

"I don't know, son. But getting a lieutenant general's job over so many battle-tested commanders just wouldn't be right. You're going to be a brigadier in the next few days. Settle for that, for the time being."

Custis nodded, his mouth set in a bitter line, his dark eyes glaring. "And all because I'm Robert E. Lee's son—right? The great general refuses to let his offspring accept anything that might smack of favoritism—*right?*"

Lee's tone was patient. "I've never believed in nepotism, but there's more to it than that. Custis, you're filling an important assignment. His excellency needs you, needs your experienced understanding of his ways, of his moods. And the days ahead will be even more trying. If I didn't sincerely believe that, I'd request that he release you for a brigade command at once."

Custis got to his feet, turned away, then wheeled. "But this war is winding down, and I haven't got much time. Do you want it said that Lee's West Pointer son sat the whole war out on the presidential staff? How does *that* sound for favoritism?"

Lee sighed. "You know how little attention I pay to criticism."

"Then why did you offer to resign after Gettysburg—when the newspapers got on you?"

Now it was Lee's ire that was being pushed. "It was something I felt I should do. And I don't think you have any right to question my decisions, young man. Now, I've heard enough on this matter, so let's go inside and get ready to eat." A smile touched his lips. ". . . General."

Jefferson Davis brought to the Confederate presidency a military background that included West Point, command of his Mississippi Rifles in the Mexican War, some time as Old Zach Taylor's son-in-law, a period as secretary of war for the United States, and a number of years as a U.S. senator. This experience, combined with his high opinion of himself, produced a commander in chief who considered himself a military expert. Davis was a paradox—highly strung and easily shaken by human suffering, he was nevertheless prepared to sacrifice any amount of Southern manhood to win the war. While he was usually frank and direct, he exemplified the rhetorical, and was often unforgiving and unyielding. Like most dedicated dreamers, he was blind to undesired reality. Added to these complexities, Davis required subordination, deference, and respect from everyone, including Lee.

Lee had a firm grip on his relationship with Davis. The general's keen sense of judgment in people provided the delicate insight necessary in dealing with the man who, often, would rather be wearing his stars. Lee knew that his personal popularity was a periodic barb to the president's fragility. He also knew that more flies could be gathered with honey. Not that he flattered Davis; he simply knew the little ways to assuage that fragility by couching his desires in a manner that didn't offend the president. He cared not that a few critics thought him deferential; he'd always believed that a soldier was subordinate to civil authority, and Davis was his president.

Now, in the president's study in the Confederate White House on Clay Street, and after an hour's discussion on the tactical plight of the Confederate Army, the subject had switched to replacements. Davis was becoming irritated. "I refuse to believe that we have that many desertions, General. All armies have a certain number, but I can't conceive that our proud Southern boys would quit in such numbers. They know their just cause, and will fight to the death for it."

Lee's tone remained reserved and emotionless. "Sir, I see the strength reports. It *is* a serious problem. And even the new conscription law, taking them from seventeen years of age to fifty, won't make up the difference."

Davis frowned. "My information indicates that the new law will provide over a hundred thousand men."

"Yes, sir, it can. But it won't. Just about all the fighters are in uniform now."

"Well, we'll wait and see."

Lee thought about their previous discussions on the use of Negroes. He said, "I have a detailed report on how the Union Army has utilized the coloreds. I think you should read it, your excellency."

Davis got up from his desk abruptly. The widely spaced blue-gray eyes narrowed. "The people will never accept it! You know putting Confederate uniforms on nigras violates everything we stand for. It tells the world we consider them *equal!* One of the tools we've used to keep everyone behind the war effort—ever since Lincoln issued that damn fool proclamation of his—was talking about the Yankees putting uniforms on them and sending them down here to rape, pillage, and become our rulers. We sure as hell can't do it *ourselves!* And you said yourself that once they did some fighting, they'd have to be freed. How are we ever going to rebuild the Confederacy if we do *that?*"

"Sir," Lee replied, "I'm your commanding general, not a politician. In the coming year I will need a certain number of soldiers to conduct the war, and we're scraping the barrel right now. If it comes down to the survival of the Confederacy, and we can make soldiers out of them, I don't care what color they are."

Davis scratched his hawklike nose. "There are times, General, when I think you forget your heritage."

Heritage, Lee thought—Davis had barely scratched his way into the aristocracy he so staunchly advocated. And what did heritage have to do with winning the war? But all he could say was, "Respectfully, sir, that isn't true. War is a matter of numbers, and men happen to be the most important of those numbers."

"Well, I don't want to discuss it anymore today. Let's get back to what Grant might do."

Mary Custis Lee glanced at the red coals of the dying fire, put aside her knitting, and looked at her dozing husband in the overstuffed chair five feet away. The book he'd been reading, something on tactics by a Prussian general, had slipped into his lap. Poor dear, she thought, all worn out even when he was home for a day. And he was getting so white! But then, no man in the Confederacy, except perhaps President Davis, carried so much responsibility. Her nasty arthritis caused almost unbearable pain at times, but she didn't have to suffer pain of the heart as he did.

She rolled the wheelchair close to him. Oh, how she often wished he were like other men, lesser men. If he just weren't the great gray knight, if he were just ordinary enough to come to her bed and let it all out once in a while. Bury his noble, handsome head in her shoulder and cry the cleansing tears that would wash away some of his great sadness. But, no, he would contain it, and tomorrow he would go back to his army to ride around on Traveller and inspire those brave lads he led.

Led to what? He would never tell her, but she knew. She read the newspapers. She also knew that he, deep inside, realized that the great struggle was hopeless. She knew that in some hidden recess, a tiny voice now and then raised its whisper, telling him he'd been used, used in the name of the state he so dearly loved. Yes, there had always been Lees in Virginia.

Why, he didn't even believe in slavery, having freed their own slaves in '62, right in the middle of the war. And he'd written a paper about slavery being wrong six years earlier. It had been during those beautiful two years of absence he took from his regiment in Texas after her father's death. Oh, how he'd worked during that period trying to whip the Custis estate back into shape. And for what? Arlington, proud Arlington, was now confiscated property—stolen by the Federal government for the price of a good horse in back taxes, taxes they said had to be paid in person by the owner, knowing full well our leading general could not do so!

Oh, how it had torn his heart. He loved her majestic ancestral home almost as much as she did. It had been the site of their courtship and marriage, the birthplace of their children, the scene of lovemaking and joy.

Mary dabbed with a soft linen handkerchief at the tear that slipped down her cheek. She'd known the young Robert throughout her childhood, but hadn't actually been attracted to him until that summer of his graduation leave from West Point in '29. My, what a handsome lieutenant he'd been! Those dark eyes and that erect, athletic figure had been enough to turn any girl's head. And he'd been so attentive to his mother during all those years when growing boys were more interested in their manly pursuits.

How she'd fallen for the son of Light-Horse Harry Lee, bless his tragic soul. Her own father hadn't been too thrilled with their desire to marry. Fine historic Virginia family, he admitted, but too fallen from prosperity for the lovely, wealthy, and charming descendant of Martha Washington—his only daughter. But she'd prevailed. Her wedding to the promising young engineer had taken place on a marvelous June day two years later.

She sighed as the white cat, Tom Four, rubbed against her leg, purring, arching his back for the attention he usually managed to get. How Robert had loved the first Tom, the beginning of a long line of pets in the family.

She leaned closer, hearing the light snore, wanting to right the sagging head without disturbing him. And there, around the eyes, were the newer lines—mixed right in with the deeper, older ones. Oh, if only he would take better care of himself; he was fifty-seven, not twenty!

Inadvertently, her hand stole to his cheek. Dear God, let him live through this terrible thing and give me some peaceful years with him. Oh, dear God, I pray to you."

The dark, unfocused eyes opened slowly, then became alert as he raised his head. They softened as he turned his lips to her fingertips. "Well, my love," he said, stretching his left arm around her, "It appears I slipped away from my lovely bride. Not a very gallant thing for a young soldier to do, is it?" He touched her moist cheek. "Are you all right, my dear?"

"Yes," she replied softly. "I'm just very happy to be with you."

CHAPTER 48

John Rawlins's doubts about pulling the Army of the Potomac out of its position near Cold Harbor proved unwarranted—staff planning was superb, the commanders executed their orders well, the pontoon bridge was not only erected on time, but served its purpose, and—thanks to Lee's cavalry being occupied with Sheridan, as Grant had expected—the enemy wasn't aware of the move in time to do anything about it.

It was the next phase of operations in Virginia that the chief of staff should have worried about.

* * *

Out in Georgia on the 14th, as the sun climbed golden out of the eastern haze, several officers had no idea how their day's activities would draw them so fatefully together.

Sherman tasted his hot coffee and was fully alert after just four hours of sleep—the usual allotment for the general, who was a night person and who would get his two or three catnaps under any available tree later in the day. He felt edgy this morning and there were plenty of reasons why. He had been after Johnston for five whole weeks now, and all he had to show for it was an overextended supply line. If Joe Johnston was the world's master of delaying defense, then Mama Sherman's little boy must sure as hell be the flankingest son-of-a-bitch in the Union Army. He simply could not bring the wily old bastard to battle.

And he was worried that the slow progress would take the offensive spirit out of this troops—and commanders. Damn Thomas. What had he written to Grant about old plodding Tom: "A fresh furrow in a ploughed field will stop the whole column, and all begin to entrench—I have tried again and again to impress on Thomas that we must assail, not defend."

And he knew, with all the troubles Grant was having with those eastern laggards, that this damned Atlanta thing had to be settled. Damned Johnston. Everyone thought Lee was Jesus Christ—well, Johnston must surely be the Holy Ghost!

General Joseph E. Johnston also faced myriad problems on this June morning, as he reread a critical letter he'd received from Jefferson Davis the day before. He simply couldn't get it through the president's thick head that it was impossible for him to meet Sherman's superior force head on. He had to keep preserving his forces in delaying actions. Damn it, Davis knew that the whole war depended on holding off until the Union election was over in early November. If he could sustain against Sherman, the North was bound to elect someone besides Lincoln, and a favorable armistice would be assured.

But Davis still thought himself the greatest strategist on the planet, and believed that any little band of Southern soldiers could take on a whole Yankee army. And his favored adviser, Bragg—what the hell had he ever accomplished, except making people mad? He did win at Chickamauga, but he gave it all back at Chattanooga.

He'd had his troubles with Davis for a long time now.

And now Hood was giving him problems. One would think that hot-blooded, impetuous fire-eater would have had enough glory after losing a leg and the use of one arm. In spite of his proven courage, the young man just wasn't capable of corps command. His grasp of strategy above division level was just too limited. And he knew Hood was criticizing him in correspondence outside of channels—probably with Davis.

Damn it, if they'd just leave him alone, he'd keep Sherman swimming until Christmas . . .

Lieutenant General Leonidas Polk finished his morning religious office and turned to his first cup of coffee. Several things were plaguing him, the least being how he could lose some weight. He'd been leaning too much toward the material side lately. Being a soldier-clergyman had been easy enough to justify in the beginning. After all, he was a West Point graduate, and the war *was* a holy one. But he'd been too intent on glory in the past few weeks—trying to make up for being relieved under a cloud after Chickamauga.

He forgot too often that he was, first of all, an Episcopal bishop.

However, he was pleased at the religious fervor that had taken hold in the army in the past few months. Perhaps some of that was due to him. The fact that Johnston and Hood had undergone baptism had helped the movement a great deal. How moving it had been when the tempestuous John Bell Hood, strapped to his saddle as a terrible cripple at the age of thirty-three, had asked him for salvation . . . how at midnight that same night, he'd gone to the convert's headquarters to conduct the baptism. Hood had struggled to his crutches, insisting on standing, his sad, bloodhound eyes soft and wide in the candlelight. Gone was the general's harsh intolerance as he opened his soul to God and His Holy Son.

But the war always brought conversions, and the Lord didn't care how His new lambs came to Him. Certainly, He believed in the necessity of war in His grand scheme, or there never could have been so many of them down through the centuries.

Still, it was time for this one to end. So much of his beloved South had been destroyed, so many brave souls had been killed or maimed, and so many at home were suffering. It was, specifically, time for the war to end for himself. Yes, take off these general's stars and the other accoutrements of the soldier. It was time to get back to running the still-struggling Church in Louisiana—another type of war—in that Catholic-infested land.

Perhaps he should resign now . . .

Captain Hubert Dilger hadn't intended for his leave of absence from the Prussian Army to extend for several years, any more than he'd expected to get so involved in this strange American war when he came to visit his uncle in 1861. But the *Amerikaners* had readily welcomed his artillery expertise. Now, after all that time with the Army of the Potomac and Hooker, he'd found a general who liked his artillery right up close. *Ach,* this Sherman, he was a warrior—in spite of his disregard for military discipline.

He could never have had so much fun back home. And, ah, the fame! His Battery I, of the First Ohio Light Artillery, was probably the most famous artillery unit in the whole Union Army, possibly on *both* sides. He loved to remember one general's comment: "Leatherbreeches gets so close, we ought to mount bayonets on his cannons." That nickname truly pleased him. As a free-lancer in the Army of the Cumberland, he was not only able to roam at will, but permitted to wear his own uniform—usually a white shirt and highly polished boots, which set off his spotless doeskin breeches.

Ach, how they marveled at his accuracy. But it was simply a matter of extensive precision training. His gunners responded precisely to his hand-clap commands, a system he'd devised to eliminate any possibility of a language problem when his English was much worse than it was now. And, of course, he usually did the sighting.

He was excited about today as he pulled on the polished boots his orderly had just handed him. He was sure the redheaded general would visit, maybe even inspect his proud battery of rifled Parrott guns. Or maybe he could incite these *verdammt* rebels into fighting for a change.

He handed his cup back to the orderly. These Yankee cooks never got the coffee strong enough!

Sherman came up to visit Howard shortly after noon. The pious one-armed corps commander usually gave the redhead a chance for some humorous relief. Oliver Otis Howard at thirty-three had been a general officer most of the war. Like Rawlins, he was a temperance fanatic, but unlike Rawlins, he found profanity a burr under his saddle. Therefore, it was a continuing game with Sherman and his senior officers to go out of their way to needle Howard by discussing their hangovers in a most descriptive and profane manner. Sherman didn't actually drink a great deal, but his war consisted of a jam-packed seven-day week—no Sundays off for religion and rest. Conversely, Howard considered observance of the holy day as a sacred duty.

But Sherman wasn't interested in jesting today; he had to find a way to get through between Pine and Kennesaw mountains. That was where Johnston was dug in again. *Damn him!*

As he moved his glasses slowly over the slope of Pine Mountain, he settled on a group of Confederates gathered on a parapet. And they were staring back through *their* glasses, probably watching *him!* They had to be officers. Well, this might be his only chance for battle today, and, by God, he'd give it to them. He turned to Howard. "Look at those impudent bastards. Throw a few rounds of artillery in there to teach them some respect."

As Sherman rode off, Howard sent word to the nearby Captain Dilger. Without wasting a moment, the Prussian sighted in on the gray figures from a range of about eight hundred yards. As the gun roared, Leatherbreeches raised his glasses. The first round was close, and part of the group scrambled away. Three figures remained. As Dilger clapped for the second round, two of the gray figures ducked out of sight, while a third moved more slowly. The last one looked larger than the others. The shell seemed to land right on him.

No one watching from the Federal lines knew it, but that round killed a Confederate lieutenant general—the Bishop. Leonidas Polk had issued his last order and had celebrated his last Eucharist.

Even Rawlins's worst fears about failure would not have encompassed the folly that Union forces outside of Petersburg experienced in the next three days. It was another of those opportunities that would have cut the war short by months, but the timidity of a corps commander—Baldy Smith—snatched a stalemate from the jaws of an easy victory. Lightly manned Confederate fortifications were taken by Smith, but he refused to follow up, even with the arrival of Hancock's Second Corps to support him. And Hancock the Superb was not so superb, being ill and bowing to Smith's decision. When it was all over, the golden opportunity to take Petersburg had flown, strong rebel forces manned the heavy defenses, and Grant had to settle down for a protracted siege of that city.

In the first part of July, Lee sent Major General Jubal Early with a strong force to move on Washington and Baltimore. He was nearly successful, first beating a nondescript force under Lew Wallace, the tardy general from Shiloh. But the arrival of Wright's VI Corps that Grant had rushed up to the capital from the James dissuaded him from entering the city. In problems of command—or lack of it—in Washington, Halleck again showed his true colors and waffled. He told Comstock, whom Grant had sent to Washington, "*I* am no longer general in chief. As a staff officer, it is not within my prerogative to originate tactical orders. Such is General Grant's sole responsibility, as is any calamity that may result from such orders."

When Rawlins heard this statement repeated, he was furious. But Grant ignored it. He had immediate command problems. He relieved Baldy Smith from the XVIII Corps, sent him on leave, and replaced him with the competent Major General E. O. C. Ord. Ord, a solid commander, had been with Grant in the Vicksburg campaign. Now, another western general was on hand. But that didn't solve the Butler problem.

Now, as the political general waited outside, Grant was considering his outright relief as well. But the outspoken Rawlins, of all people, recommended caution before showing Butler in.

After a few minutes of small talk, the former Massachusetts Democrat got right to the heart of the matter. "I've heard about a reorganization plan for my army that would take me away from the front. Frankly, General, I don't like it. I don't like General Smith's criticisms of me, and I'm here to tell you there's no way you can remove me against my wishes."

Grant looked at the odd-looking man, whose round body had given an aide cause to nickname him "Humpty Dumpty." He said, "Smith is being relieved, General."

"Well, it's about time. I had to relieve Gillmore right off the bat, and I was about to tell you to do likewise with that other West Point son of a bitch. I'm tired of being surrounded by incompetents."

Grant spoke softly, "General, have you ever considered that incompetent action also reflects on the commander?"

"What the hell is that supposed to mean?"

"Who was responsible for your army sitting at Bermuda Hundred for

the entire month of May—when you might well have taken either Petersburg or Richmond?"

Butler's jaw jutted. "That was your goddamned Smith and Gillmore!"

"It was your command."

"Stanton and Lincoln understand, and that's all that counts. But that
isn't why I'm here. As I said, I'm staying in direct command of my army!"

"The army doesn't work that way, General. If there is a good reason
for you to be assigned elsewhere, a change will be made."

Butler leaned forward in his chair, looking every bit the master fixer
he was. His tone softened, his eyes hooded. "Let me lay it out straight,
Grant. I carry a pretty big stick, as you well know. If you persist, I'll resign
and make such a stink in the coming election that Lincoln won't be able to
be dog catcher. It's as simple as that."

Grant's eyes hardened. "Are you threatening me, General?"

"That's *exactly* what I'm doing."

Grant stared into the bleak eyes. It was clear and simple. Ingalls and
Rawlins had warned him, but he couldn't believe the stark reality of it.
Here was a man who wasn't even worthy of sergeant's stripes, but he had
the *power*—truly naked power at its raw worst. It was everything he detested
in politics, thrust right in his lap. He should throw this charlatan out with
his own hands, but what would be gained? Simply put, the war could not
be won without Lincoln. No, much as he hated it, his hands were tied.

And it smarted.

He nodded. "General, you will remain in your command."

Jefferson Davis turned from his office window, where he'd been watching
a pair of robins cavort under an outside tree. "Well, Braxton," he said to
his senior military adviser, "if I relieve Johnston, what am I to do with
him?"

"Just send him home to Macon," Bragg replied.

"I don't like to do it this way."

"You don't have any choice, your excellency. Look at the facts. The
man has no intention of bringing Sherman into a major battle. He told me
personally, two weeks ago, that our only salvation is in holding Sherman
off until after the Federal election. Jesus Christ, does that sound like a
commander who should be leading one of our last remaining armies?

"McPherson has cut the rail line at Decatur. Sherman's army is within
five miles of Atlanta. The governor of Georgia and much of our Congress—
to say nothing of the press—are screaming that we are giving up Atlanta
without even a good fight. Hood reports that Johnston has passed up many
opportunities and has lost twenty thousand men in his retrograde march—
and he doesn't even give us satisfactory answers to our questions about his
plans."

Bragg held up a form. "What did his last message say—this one that
came in two hours ago—his plan of operations must depend upon that of
the enemy? Hell, you should have relieved him over a month ago!"

"Lee has a great deal of respect for him, and thinks he ought to remain."

"Let Lee worry about Grant."

"And Lee is quite guarded about our giving the command to Hood. He respects Hood as a fighter, but questions his carelessness otherwise. He prefers Hardee."

"Again, your excellency, we need aggressive action to save Atlanta, and the Confederacy. If Hood can beat Sherman, Grant will have to pull away from Petersburg. Then we'll win in Tennessee, Lincoln will be defeated, and the North will sue for peace. It's as simple as that."

Davis sat down at his desk, and struggled over the decision. After a minute, he reached for his pen and wrote out the fateful order.

Word of the change in command came to Sherman on the banks of the Peach Tree River the next day, July 19. He quickly called a council of war with his commanders. McPherson, Howard, and Schofield—who was in command of the Army of the Ohio—had all known Hood at West Point. Thomas had observed him in a regiment in Texas. All agreed on one thing— the brash Hood would attack, and waste little time in doing so. A colonel from Kentucky told Sherman he'd once watched Sam Hood in a poker game, and the fearless young officer had "bet twenty-five hundred dollars without a pair in his hand, or a blink in his eye." Sherman gave the order to expect a rebel attack at any point.

Just before noon the next day, Hood smashed into Thomas's Army of the Cumberland, sending Hooker reeling. But Hooker quickly reorganized for a counterattack and helped Thomas hurl the rebels back to within two miles of Atlanta. Like a bare-knuckled fighter shaking off a blow to the head, the undaunted Confederate general merely examined the possibilities for his next assault, and made ready to swing back at his opponent.

On the 21st, Hood decided that Sherman was spread too thin in trying to envelop the city on three sides. Knowing that McPherson was head-quartered some twelve miles out of Decatur, he confidently picked the proud Army of the Tennessee as his next target. He ordered four divisions to march at night and strike the next day when McPherson was to start moving toward Atlanta. The deadly ambush was planned for the fateful July 22nd.

At nine-thirty that morning, the handsome James Birdseye McPherson rode over to Sherman's headquarters house, behind the center of the lines. It took just a few minutes for the redhead to brief his army commander on what he wanted after the displacement. As McPherson started to leave, Sherman asked, "How's your lovely Mary, back in Baltimore? Is she still mad at me for delaying her wedding plans?"

The engineer broke into his big, warm grin. "No, sir," he replied. "She's still put out a bit with me, though."

Sherman put his hand on McPherson's shoulder. "Blame it on Grant. Then we're both off the hook. And tell her that just as soon as we finish Hood off here, I'll give you a nice, long leave so you can make an honest woman out of her."

A slight blush rushed to the engineer's cheek. "I'm afraid that's all she's ever been. Can I give her a target date?"

"Well, if Hood keeps coming out to mix it with us, you ought to be there by the first of September."

"That should keep her mollified. I—"

The muffled roar of artillery off to their left interrupted. McPherson's eyes widened as a look of alarm erased his smile. "Sounds like something's happening with my column. I'd better get back."

Sherman followed him out to the hitching rail, where an aide handed him the reins. As the engineer swung into the saddle, Sherman said, "Get a courier right back as soon as you know what's up, Mac!"

McPherson touched his hat brim in a quick salute as he wheeled his mount and galloped away.

Sherman hurried back in to his maps. If Hood was opening a major effort on the left, some part of Atlanta was surely available. He stared at the map. But which part? How could the madman dare? Had he hit the Army of the Tennessee in the flank? If so, with a corps? With more? No matter, the important thing was that Hood was *out* again! McPherson could take care of himself with those veterans. He'd send Thomas in—right into the goddamned center of the city!

He had just finished writing the orders when one of McPherson's aides burst through the door. *"General, something's happened to General Mc-Pherson!"*

With a start, Sherman moved quickly around the table. "What do you mean?"

The young captain stammered, trying to get the words out. "I, I don't know, sir. I, uh, his horse came running up without him. He was bleeding, and the, the saddle was empty."

A chill sliced through Sherman. He grabbed the captain's arm. "How? What happened, boy?"

"Well, the general, he sent messages off, then he, he took off with Burley, another aide, down this road . . . and we heard shots, and not more than a minute later, his horse came running back. I don't know anything else, 'cause I came right back here to report."

Sherman blew out a deep breath. Son of a bitch! Well, maybe it wasn't serious, maybe he was just wounded. Probably captured, though. Back to the battle. "Captain, I want you to pull yourself together and ride to General Logan. Tell him General McPherson is missing, and he's to assume temporary command. And tell him I have the utmost faith in the Army of the Tennessee holding out on its own. Then I want an immediate report on what's going on. Do you understand?"

The aide was still wide-eyed. "Yes, sir."

Sherman turned to his own white-faced aide. "And you go with him, Terry."

*   *   *

Thirty minutes later, two burly soldiers ripped the front door off its hinges and centered it over two chairs. Two other soldiers carried McPherson's body inside and placed it gently on the door. His chest was a mass of blood. Sherman reached out to touch him as the surgeon said, "The bullet hit so close to his heart that he couldn't have lived more than a few minutes. I'm sorry, General."

Sherman stared at the white face above the curly beard, and his anger flared. Mac had just looked so handsome in full uniform, boots outside, new gauntlets—a true general officer if there ever was one. And now some ignorant son-of-a-bitch who probably couldn't even read, some misbegotten white trash who didn't even know why he was fighting, had ended the life of the man who could have . . . replaced both himself and Grant, had there been a need.

Once more he reached out to touch the cold cheek, the tears beginning to trickle down through his red beard. His voice was barely audible. "What will I tell Grant?"

Rawlins cleared his throat. His voice seemed choked. "Excuse me, General. I, that is, I just received this message from Halleck."

Grant looked up, seeing pain. "Is something wrong?"

Rawlins handed him the message, which read, "Word just received from Sherman. Hood attacked the Army of the Tennessee at noon on the 22nd with Hardee's corps. The Confederates were repulsed, losing an estimated 8,000 men, and returned to the fortifications of Atlanta. Sherman expresses his great sorrow in reporting the death by gunshot of Major General James B. McPherson in battle."

The words swam as Grant reread the last sentence—*death by gunshot of Major General James B. McPherson.* He slumped as he dropped the message to his desk. Mac. Bright, dependable, cheerful Mac, who had come to him at Fort Henry. His right arm at Donelson and Shiloh. Brilliant in higher command. Mac. Like a younger brother who always did the right thing.

He felt as if he'd been kicked by a mule.

His eyes brimmed as he stared at the message.

When would it end?

Rawlins's gentle voice came through, "I'm sorry, sir."

The idea of the mine came from a chance remark by a private in the 48th Pennsylvania. It was overheard by its commander, Lieutenant Colonel Henry Pleasants, a mining engineer. The 48th, composed mostly of coal miners from the anthracite area of the Keystone State, was occupying a strong position just opposite an equally well-fortified portion of the Confederate line. Their position marked the farthest point Baldy Smith had reached in his ignominious attack on the Petersburg defenses. This was no friendly part of the war; there was no more "winking" combat between

Billy Yank and Johnny Reb, where one might shout to the other, "If you don't get down in the next minute, I'll have to shoot you."

Pleasants began to think seriously about the idea of a mine that would go five hundred feet to a point right under the main enemy fort. With enough powder, the entire top of the hill could be blown off. And with proper timing, a whole damned division, maybe a corps, could burst through and drive straight to Petersburg!

Pleasants went to his division commander, who went to Burnside, who took him to Meade. The chafing Meade thought it would be a good way to keep a number of soldiers busy in the hated siege. Naturally, the concept appealed to the impatient Grant, so permission was granted to begin digging late in June. Now, with Grant trying to come to grips with McPherson's death, it was time to see if the long shot would work. Pleasants laid four tons of black powder under the rebel fort and plans for the military portion were issued. Immediately following the explosion Burnside would send a division into the breach. As soon as engineers cleared the surrounding abatis, Burnside's other division would follow. The IX Corps would be followed by two additional corps—all supported by heavy artillery fire. It was an excellent plan.

But then things began to go awry.

Burnside wanted to send his well-rested colored division into the breach, but Meade objected, telling Grant, "This is political dynamite. Do you know what will happen if anything goes wrong? If those coloreds run into heavy fire and get decimated, the goddamned abolitionists and Copperheads will have a field day. The headlines will be a foot high, screaming that we deliberately sacrificed Negroes instead of white boys."

Grant agreed.

Burnside had tried, and that was his last rational act in what became known as the battle of the Mine. He met with his three other division commanders, two of whom had long dependable records. But the third, Brigadier James Ledlie, was a cipher who had come into the army as a volunteer major and had only recently been given a division. By some fluke, Burnside did not know that Ledlie had cravenly drunk himself into a stupor during an attack on rebel entrenchments just six weeks earlier. What Burnside *did* know was that Ledlie's division had recently picked up a reputation for being gun-shy. Nevertheless, the corps commander pulled the most unmilitary, irrational stunt of his career—he told the generals to draw straws to see who would lead the assault!

And Ledlie drew the short straw.

The sad afternoon scenario of July 30 was set. Grant and Meade arrived to watch the show, and due to the availability of a telegraph, the whole country would soon know the results. But the explosion was delayed.

At first it was thought that the whole thing had fizzled, but at quarter to five a slow rumble began to grow. Thousands of eyes stared in awe at the Confederate entrenchments that started to rise as if a giant mole were surfacing. In another second, the most violent manmade eruption ever heard split the crest of the hill, emitting a giant sheet of flame and hideous black smoke as it tossed everything in its path sky-high. In moments, giant pieces of clay, mixed with bits of guns and human bodies, began falling back to the ground like massive pieces of hail for hundreds of yards around.

A huge crater of freshly ripped soil gutted the ground.

The crash of Federal guns followed.

And so did a debacle even worse than when Baldy Smith had made his dull-witted attack weeks earlier. A criminally ineffective and drunk Ledlie would send his men into the huge smoking pit with no way to get out, hundreds more would follow, the way would not be cleared for other brigades to go around the enormous crater, command was a farce, and Confederate soldiers would line the edge of the smoking chasm of panicky, trampling, screaming Yankees to shoot them like fish in a barrel. It was pure slaughter.

The battle of the Mine, or of the Crater, earned its place in infamy. The taking of Petersburg had once more slipped through Grant's fingers in the most grotesque comedy of errors in the history of war. A great scar would mark the ground for centuries to come, while another type of scar would remain with Grant as long as he lived.

CHAPTER 49

Being in Stanton's large office did not intimidate Grant at all. He looked back and forth as first Halleck, then the secretary of war, presented their arguments against his wish to send Sheridan into the Shenandoah Valley. Finally, he looked directly at Halleck's wide owl eyes and said, "General, I don't want to hear any more. Jubal Early is roaming at will, holding towns for ransom, burning others, and generally terrorizing Maryland and some of Pennsylvania as he sees fit. I want someone to get after him without delay. Write the orders sending Sheridan up there, and do it today."

He rose and bid them good day.

That evening, he went to the White House, where Lincoln had invited him for a private talk. As they disappeared into the presidential study and got comfortable, Lincoln immediately waxed political. "It all boils down to the simplicity of 'war or no war.' The Democrats, who will undoubtedly nominate McClellan, are attempting to grab the reins by acceding to the wishes of the Confederacy. The so-called Radical Democracy party that nominated Frémont in May is merely a splinter of the radical Republicans, but can drain off enough votes to ensure my defeat in November."

It was one of those periods when Abraham Lincoln wore chin whiskers and now he rubbed them as he went on, "The radical Republicans don't see eye to eye with me because they want revenge, primarily in land confiscation and punishment. I see the restoration of the Union only in terms of putting it back together, minus some of the ills that tore it apart in the beginning. And this can't be accomplished with stern retribution.

"The human rights of the Negro are still the hub around which the issue revolves, General. But the spokes are interested only in lip service. Freedom is fine, but equality is something else. As I told an Ohio regiment, every human right is endangered if our enemies succeed. If the Confederacy is permitted peace based on its precepts, the rights of all our children, and their children for generations, are threatened."

Lincoln paused, glancing at the window reflectively, then continued. "If, by some slim chance I win in November, you and I will face a tremendous challenge. We must win the war, and in that capacity I have the utmost faith in you. But after it's over, General, *then* we'll be tested. I think I'll have to lean on you then just as heavily as I do now. I hope to move quickly through the necessary military government stage to bring the rebellious states back into Congress and to eventual harmony."

The president smiled. "I know, it sounds like I've been at the whiskey barrel, but I know it can be done—if we don't exact too high or embarrassing a price from them, and they're willing to meet us halfway. But unconditional surrender is the only means. Anything less will leave them holding the reins, and the hideous losses in this war will have been for naught."

Grant nodded his head in agreement. How could politicians so enamored of their game not see that this great man was the only answer? Why did party always have to come first? Was that democracy? Why couldn't right be done by the most qualified leader? And he had barely thought about what his role might be in the aftermath of the war—if its outcome was favorable. Yes, he could see where the army would have an important function. He thought briefly of Chaplain Eaton and his Freedmen.

Lincoln's voice broke in, "So, what do you plan for the Shenandoah?"

"I'm combining the departments and field army into one command with Sheridan as the boss. Since Hunter is far senior, he'll remain in command of the Department of West Virginia, but I'm going to put it in such a way that he'll probably ask for another job. Sheridan is to seek out and destroy all rebel forces in the Valley, then wipe out all means of rebel military supply."

"And you?"

"Back to my headquarters at City Point, sir."

"How soon do you think Sherman can defeat Hood?"

"Possibly within a month. As you know, he has repulsed Hood three times in nine days, costing the rebel army an estimated fifteen thousand men."

Lincoln nodded. "Are you aware that Admiral Farragut is moving his naval force on the forts of Mobile Bay tonight or tomorrow?"

"Yes, sir. Maybe he can still the wolves until Sherman and Sheridan win for us."

"I hope they're in time."

"They should be."

"How's the situation between you and Halleck?"

Grant shrugged. "Let's just say that he knows who he's working for."

A few days later, Sherman wrote an angry letter to his brother:

> *I can't believe that a patriotic senator like you could possibly ask that I send nine Indiana regiments home on furlough from a vital campaign to vote! I don't give a fiddler's damn if the Speaker of the House did request it. What about the other states? Is every general supposed to stop fighting to elect politicians who couldn't run a country grocery store, much less a country?*
>
> *The closest support I will ever give to a candidate is this campaign for Lincoln. And I mean this military campaign, John, not a bunch of speeches from a damned soapbox. And that's because I believe he's the only one of the lot who can save the war and the Union. The rest of you can go to hell!*
>
> *It's up to the leaders of this army and this country to face its major problem, not which politician will be elected. War is the remedy our enemies chose when they fired on our noble flag at Fort Sumter, and I say let's give them all they want; not a sign of let-up, no cave-in til we are whipped or they are. The only principle in this war is which side can whip. It's as simple as a schoolboy's fight and when one or the other party gives in, we will be better friends.*
>
> *You talk about the lack of will to continue the war. It pains me greatly to hear that civilians, far from shot and fury, think they have a right to dissent on something they haven't even earned the right to be party of. They never seem to realize that being born in the United States was only a matter of good fortune. This luck of the sperm draw merely gave them cradle rights; continued freedom and liberty have to be earned!*
>
> *When patriotism is overcome by the desire to protest our country's declared obligations, we are finished. Therefore, please do not ever ask such a favor in the name of Congress—particularly a Congress that cannot be worsted. And you can tell the Speaker that had I a vote, I would not give it to one of you . . .*

At shortly after nine on the evening of August 31, Grant's telegraph operator brought him the results of the Democratic convention in Chicago. It was official: George Brinton McClellan had been nominated for the presidency of the United States. God help us, Grant thought. The night before, over supper with Meade, General Humphries had made an astute summation: "The man is blessed. Falling into major command with probably fewer tools than most regular officers with more experience, the Little Napoleon was toasted to high heaven by a hungry and not-too-discriminating press. But when he began to believe the newspaper accounts more than the facts, he did himself in by not keeping his goddamned mouth shut. And now, barring some miracle, he will probably be the next president of the northern half of the *dis*-United States of America."

Grant shook his head. He didn't even want to imagine that possibility. But he had to be realistic. Washburne's latest letter was gloomy. Even Farragut's victory at Mobile Bay, accompanied by his ringing, "Damn the torpedoes, full speed ahead!" had been somewhat coolly received by the war-weary populace.

He *had* to give Lincoln something big.

Five hundred air miles away and twenty-six south of Atlanta, Cump Sherman was sipping from a brandy and chewing on a cigar. It was almost midnight, as he sat on a log and stared into the dying fire. His adventures in Georgia were on his mind, and they didn't please him. It had been nearly four months since his proud army had marched out of Chattanooga to conquer this stubborn rebel army of the West. He had chased, fought, flanked, and fussed his way to and around Atlanta—losing his caution at Kennesaw Mountain, and regaining it with sorrow over the needless losses.

He had to give Hood credit as a fighter—the man certainly moved troops around and took up the gauntlet when it was thrown in his face. But it was also his undoing. He couldn't afford losses in the numbers he'd been suffering them. The battle that had just ended at Jonesboro was another example. But time was running short. Time, his old nemesis. Why couldn't the good Lord provide enough time and more patience when He handed out general's stars?

He had almost tricked Hood at Jonesboro, making him think the siege had been lifted. The rebel general had even gloated to Richmond of his great victory. Ha! Now, with all the railroads to the south of Atlanta in Federal hands, the city was surely doomed—what was that rumble to the north? Thunder? The muffled echo of guns? Slocum had the only command left north of the city. Had that crazy Hood attacked *him?* The distant rumblings ceased as suddenly as they had begun. He continued to stare north. There seemed to be some kind of a glow. Fires? What the hell was going on up there?

He threw his cold cigar into the muggy Georgia night, and walked away.

Major General Henry Warner Slocum, the skinny commander of the XX Corps, awoke from a strange dream in which he was running through a massive thunderstorm. He swung his legs over the side of his cot just as an aide burst through the tent flap. "Sir," the captain said, "did you hear it?"

Slocum shook the sleep out of his head. "Hear what?"

"The explosions from the city. The rebs must be blowing up munitions or something!"

Slocum finished pulling on his pants and stepped out into the warm moonlight. A bright orange glow extended like a massive bowl over Atlanta and he could see what looked like tiny flames flickering from its dark form.

Strange—no attack was planned, so friendly artillery couldn't have caused it. Could Hood possibly be pulling out? He looked at his watch. Four hours until first light. Turning to the aide, he said, "Have some pickets probe into the edge of the city, if they can. In the meantime, let's assume the rebs are evacuating. If that's the case, I want a division drawn up to march into that place at eight o'clock in the morning with bands playing and all colors waving. This corps may have the chance to be part of one of the most momentous occasions of the war!"

Before nine the next night, Slocum—not having contact with Sherman down south—sent the great news to Stanton in Washington. "General Sherman has taken Atlanta." The news was soon in Lincoln's hands. It was 9:50 on Friday, September 2. The president ordered an immediate release of the news to the press and set Sunday aside as a day of thanks for the victories of Admiral Farragut in Mobile Bay and General Sherman in Atlanta.

Shortly before midnight, the news was relayed from Stanton to City Point. Grant, who had been writing a letter to Julia, looked up in surprise as a sleepy but grinning John Rawlins handed him the message from Halleck. He sighed as he read it once, then again. A smile touched his lips as he looked up at his friend. He said, "Well, by lightning, part of this thing is done. At least the fort part."

Rawlins's black eyes danced in the light of the kerosene lamp. "Just like you planned it, General. Congratulations!"

"Sherman's the one who deserves them. I want to recommend him for permanent promotion to major general. Will you see to it, please?"

"Yes, sir."

The grin could no longer be contained. It creased Grant's face as he said, "Doggone!" He got to his feet and clapped Rawlins on the shoulder. "And another thing," he said gleefully, "I want the darnedest salute fired to Sherman in the morning that this army has ever seen." He threw a fist into the air. "I'll be doggoned!"

Rawlins laughed out loud. In all of their time together, he'd never seen Ulys Grant come so far out of his composure. "I'll see to *that* as well, General!"

CHAPTER 50

Sitting in a rocking chair on the front porch of the comfortable red brick house he'd chosen for his headquarters, Sherman looked up from the newspaper he'd been reading and watched the traffic going by in the sunshine on Courthouse Square. A hound barked mournfully close by, and two boys, no more than ten, stood staring at him from across the street. He raised a hand to wave to them.

Hood's army had escaped to the southwest, much to his displeasure, but the political impact of taking the city was just as important at this juncture. Before deciding his next step, he had decided to rest his tired army while the tribute of a grateful nation was pouring in. The victory-hungry Northern populace was eagerly according him plaudits equal to those Grant had received following his major victories. Lincoln, in a major announcement, had voiced "the applause and thanks of a nation." Grant had used superlatives in his praise, and even the hostile Cincinnati *Commercial* and New York *Herald* had come out with hosannas.

All very nice for the Ohioan they had called crazy.

But the dilemma of Atlanta couldn't wait. Even before Hood fled, the problem had been uppermost in his mind. In the past, he'd seen too damned many men pulled out of a fighting army to garrison a captured city. The answer was easy—the citizens of Atlanta would have to get out, then he could take his soldiers and get on with the war. For those Atlantans wishing to go north and remain in Federal territory, free transportation would be provided. Those desiring to go south would be hauled halfway to Hood's lines at a place called Rough and Ready.

Having determined after much brain-searching to put a regular officer in command of the Army of the Tennessee, he had chosen Howard over Black Jack Logan—a move that had displeased Logan and Hooker. Joe Hooker had angrily protested Howard's promotion over himself, and had resigned. The fact that his archenemy, Slocum, was appointed as his replacement was added salt in his festering ego.

But changes in command didn't matter at the moment. The mayor of Atlanta was at the steps. As his senior aide started to intervene, Sherman said, "No, that's all right. Come on up and take that chair, sir."

The Honorable James M. Calhoun got right down to the purpose of his visit and waved a sheet of paper. "General, there must be some mistake in this order about civilian citizens of Atlanta having to evacuate the city."

Sherman held out a cigar. "Are you related to the great John Calhoun of South Carolina, Mr. Mayor?"

The mayor declined the cigar offer. "No, sir, I am not. And I did not come here to discuss family. I'm here about the outrage you are about to perpetrate on the good citizens of this city."

"Oh, you mean all of those innocent people who had nothing to do with the war?"

"Precisely."

"Well, sir, I just don't know how all these factories that support the war have been able to operate without some of those innocent citizens helping. Do you?"

"That has nothing to do with the actual conduct of the war, sir!"

Sherman brushed back a shock of red hair. "Well, I happen to think it does. Now, I don't have anything against the people of Atlanta—other than the fact that most are traitors in the rebellion against the United States—but there are rules relative to the conduct of war, Mr. Calhoun, that give me the prerogative of that order."

A flush began to show on the mayor's face. "But there are children too young to be considered in that category."

"Granted, but they are the responsibility of those who bore them. If I want to blow this place off the map, I can do so. That's the harsh truth of the matter, sir."

"But what purpose can you have in this evacuation? The populace can't possibly harm your troops."

"The point is simple. If your constituency remains in the city, we'll soon have to feed them. Or watch them starve before our eyes. Naturally, we won't let them starve, and I can't ship food all the way down here to feed them. So they have to go. This war should be over soon, and then they can come back."

"Sir, you will be regarded as barbarous from now to eternity!"

Sherman's eyes glinted. "That, sir, will have to be as it may. My only answer is that war is war and not popularity-seeking."

"Then you won't rescind the order?"

"I cannot, Mr. Calhoun, because it's not designed to meet individual needs, but to suit the overall good. I would suggest that you understand this, and use your influence in the orderly and prompt evacuation of your people. Good day, sir."

Julia had brought the children east in August to find a house in Philadelphia. She and Ulys had discussed the matter at length and had decided that Washington was just not the place for permanent schooling for the kids. After searching vainly for a couple of weeks, she had been enticed to a place by an old captain who had taught Ulys mathematics at West Point. It was Burlington, New Jersey, a shoe-manufacturing town some twenty miles up the Delaware from Camden. There she had found what she described as "a lovely two-story wooden house with fir trees, French windows, and an ivy-covered porch, where Ulys and I can hold hands after the war."

It was on Wood Street, a fitting name.

Her brother Fred, a lieutenant colonel on Ulys's staff since the previous March, was staying with her while recovering from a lingering illness. Young Fred and Buck were already in military school, Nellie was attending the highly regarded Miss Kingston's School, and little Jesse was proudly showing off to neighbor kids how well he could ride the pony he'd been given at Vicksburg.

Now that she didn't have any colored help, she often reminded herself that keeping a house wasn't easy. She preferred the visits down to City Point, because she could be with Ulys much longer. He was always in such a hurry to get back when he passed through Burlington. But school was school, and her brother had to recuperate somewhere. She stood in the dining room glancing around the table. The flowers were a gift from a neighboring Quaker woman. The silver, including the candelabra, had been Ellen's.

She wondered how her sweet mother was enjoying heaven. Ellen had always said that Ulys had greatness in him. Wouldn't she be thrilled to know that he was the lieutenant general of the whole army? Or maybe she did know, looking down on them all, as she surely did.

Her "Victor"—that's what she'd often call Ulys in private since Vicksburg—her Victor would be along any minute now. He was stopping on his way back from seeing General Sheridan down in the Valley. She hoped he wouldn't be too tired. His stay would be short, as always. Three nights for the two of them, and two days to romp with the children and push all of his army worries aside. If he could.

She sighed.

A short time, stolen from his war.

John Rawlins's cough had gotten worse, so Grant had once more sent him home to be with his lovely Emma. An officer who had joined him in August was now his secretary. He was Lieutenant Colonel Ely Samuel Parker, the son of a famous Seneca chief, and a sachem of his tribe. After reading law, he was refused admission to the New York bar because he was not a citizen—no American Indian was considered a citizen. He then decided to become an engineer and graduated from Rensselaer. While living in Galena, he became a friend of Grant's. He applied for a commission when the war broke out, but it was denied by Governor Seward, who said, "This war will be won by whites, without the aid of Indians." Tall and dark-skinned, Parker was now thirty-six.

Sheridan had lived up to his boss's expectations by pulling Early's fangs and driving him back through Winchester. The Confederacy's great granary in the Valley was in grave danger. But the siege of Petersburg continued with little change. Grant did throw a military adventure over the James, as much to season new troops as to harass Lee, but it accomplished little else.

The lines outside of Petersburg were static.

And it was back to the frustration of inactivity.

Jefferson Davis was far from inactive. Confederate newspapers had come down on him heavily after the fall of Atlanta, justifiably berating him for relieving Johnston. Now, with Early's defeat and the governor of Georgia screaming for assistance, the president took to the country in a last-ditch effort to raise troops.

Grant watched his announcements with interest, since they were reprinted in the easily available Richmond papers. From Augusta, Davis promised a death blow into the Union rear, stating that Hood was poised to strike all the way to Ohio. From Macon, he announced, "If only half the men now absent without leave will return to duty, we can defeat the enemy." But the statement that would return to haunt Davis the most was, "Sooner or later, Sherman must retreat. And when he does, the fate that befell the army of the French Empire in its retreat from Moscow will be reenacted.

Our cavalry and our people will harass and destroy his army as did the Cossacks that of Napoleon, and the Yankee general, like him, will escape with only a bodyguard."

Both Grant and Sherman weighed this statement with speculation. There was a certain amount of truth in the message. Sherman could not stay in Atlanta much longer. Letters between them toyed with his next move. It was then that the redhead proposed his idea of the march to the sea.

Why, he asked, should he continue to risk being cut off from his distant supply base, when he could march to a *new* base to be provided by a naval enterprise—such as at Savannah! "I can sweep the whole state of Georgia, dealing a fatal blow to Southern independence. They may stand the fall of Richmond, but not all of Georgia. If you can whip Lee and I can march to the Atlantic, I think Uncle Abe will give us twenty days' leave of absence to see the young folks."

But Grant had well-based doubts. Even if the navy could put a fleet together for Savannah, it could take months. Besides, if Davis's threats about a Northern expedition carried any water, Sherman would be needed to thwart them.

On October 9, Sherman said he wanted to tear up the railroad to his base in Chattanooga, cut loose with his ample stock of supplies, and live off the rich Georgia countryside. He would destroy as he marched. He quoted Sheridan, saying that a hungry enemy would exert unbelievable influence to fill its bellies. He ended with, "I can make this march and make Georgia howl!"

Grant sent Comstock to Atlanta to discuss the matter, and the staff officer came back in favor of Sherman's proposal.

And Rawlins came back to duty, rested and adamantly convinced that Sherman should give Tennessee his first priority.

"The reason I never have a council of war is because I think once an officer gets lined up too strenuously on one side of an argument, he sometimes loses sight of the reason and just wants to win his point."

Rawlins scowled back at Grant. "That isn't the case in this instance. Wilson told me Sherman is needed most in Tennessee and I believe him. The whole war could depend upon what he does."

"I know that, but I have to make up my own mind."

"Comstock was swayed by Sherman. Christ, you know how convincing that man can be."

"He's a talker all right."

"Then you should disregard what Comstock says."

"How can I do that? I sent him down there to evaluate the proposal."

At times, Rawlins far exceeded Grant's example; he would become so enamored of an idea that he became almost Messianic about it. The Sherman problem had reached that proportion with him. "That doesn't mean his evaluation is right. Goddamn it, General, you *have* to deny that stupid march to the sea!"

Grant nodded. "I'll think about it."

Two days later, while in Washington, John Rawlins stated his case on the Georgia problem to Congressman Elihu Washburne and now Assistant Secretary of War Charles Dana.

Both appreciated the chief of staff's zeal and deep concern on the matter, but when Washburne spoke to Lincoln about it, the president replied, "I trust Grant implicitly to make the right decision, but I will ask him about it."

It was the first time John Rawlins had ever gone behind Grant's back.

CHAPTER 51

T he crows will carry their own rations."

That saying was on Major General John Gordon's mind as he dismounted at Jubal Early's headquarters near Fishers Hill the afternoon of October 18. At thirty-two, the Georgia lawyer had been a hard-fighting general officer for nearly two years. Aside from being a top infantry division commander, he was one of the few Confederate officers whose wife traveled with him in all campaigns. In fact, it was said that Fanny Gordon was such a pain in the behind that old Jube had once wished to God the Yankees would capture her.

If Sheridan continued to rule the roost in the Valley and destroyed the Confederacy's breadbasket, Gordon thought, the crows *would* be carrying their own food. But he had a plan to change that.

Tall, arthritic, dour, and profane Lieutenant General Jubal Early—who had entered West Point when Philip Sheridan was two years old—listened quietly as Gordon described what he had found on his reconnaissance. "In short, General, if we smash into them in the morning, the route we've discovered at Cedar Creek will take us flush into the sleeping flank of Crook's corps on the south side of the Valley Pike. We can roll over Crook's two weak divisions and Emory's two divisions before they ever get out of their blankets."

Gordon grinned. "The Federal cavalry is too far away to be much help, so we should be hard into Wright's corps well before midmorning—except there may be so many skedaddling bluecoats by then that the battle will be over."

*   *   *

Early stared at the map, biting on the cold stem of his old corncob pipe. Sheridan had caused him a hell of a lot of embarrassment since coming to the Valley. Now maybe he could smash the upstart. His army wouldn't be able to stay in the barren Valley after the victory, but it could march proudly back to Richmond carrying Sheridan's flags. And guns. Goddammit, how he wanted those guns! So much had been made over his loss of guns in recent battles that some self-styled humorist at the factory in Richmond had chalked, "To Gen. Sheridan, care of Gen. Early" on the tubes of his new pieces. Well, they wouldn't laugh at him tomorrow, by God!

He looked up into Gordon's waiting eyes. The division commander asked, "What do you say, General? Do we hit 'em at daybreak?"

Early's strong jaw jutted forward. "You're damned right we do. And we'd better get an early start when darkness falls, if we're going to get there on time. Tell your boys they'll be drinking Yankee whiskey at this time tomorrow."

Sheridan was tired as he rode through the moonlit night with his cavalry escort. He'd gotten away late from Washington, where he'd been summoned for a needless conference with Halleck and Stanton. Damned cutthroats, trying to undermine Grant. They didn't trust anyone! He knew for a fact they didn't trust him, not the outspoken Irishman who was saving their asses in the Valley. Always intrigue and power playing. He hadn't even wanted to go, not with that probably spurious message Wright had intercepted from the rebel signal post. It was to Early and had stated, "Be ready to move as soon as my forces join you, and we will crush Sheridan." It had been signed *Longstreet!* Well, he knew Longstreet had returned to duty, but he doubted Lee would be sending his much-needed corps out of the defense of Petersburg and Richmond. No, it had to be a bogus message.

Had to be.

Still—

He *had* canceled a cavalry raid on Chancellorsville because of it.

And now, as he neared Winchester, he had an uneasy feeling. He knew his army was safely deployed along Cedar Creek, some fifteen miles below that oft fought-over town. It would require foolhardy audacity for a rebel attack.

Still—

The train from Washington had been able to take them only to Martinsburg, arriving at midnight and leaving them a thirty-mile horseback ride to Winchester. He flexed his shoulders, trying to shake off the fatigue. Spending the previous night with the young widow in Georgetown hadn't been too wise, not with her voracious appetites in bed. But he'd needed it. A man his age shouldn't be so wrapped up in war that he forgot about women. What a golden-haired beauty she was. He could feel her smooth legs around him now. He could also feel the scratches on his back. Next time, he'd put gloves on her . . .

The buildings of Winchester appeared, and shortly they reined in at the house that served as brigade headquarters. The windows were ablaze with light as the commander saluted from the front porch. Climbing stiffly down from his handsome black stallion, Rienzi, Sheridan asked, "Any dispatches from General Wright?"

"Yes, sir. Everything's quiet at Cedar Creek. Will you be spending what's left of the night, General?"

"Yes. Nothing I can do down there."

The full moon cast a silvery light on the sleeping countryside south and west of the Federal army as the hushed movements of Early's veteran troops brought them to Cedar Creek. They were in position at shortly after three A.M. when the moon dropped over the horizon and the night turned inky black. Lack of Federal pickets near Cedar Creek ford and on Crook's flank eliminated any chance discovery of the Confederate arrival. One Union officer of the day thought he heard noises outside the perimeter just before three, but rather than bother anyone, he strolled out alone to investigate. He was about to stumble into the middle of one of Gordon's infantry companies when a sergeant's hand clamped over his startled mouth. A whispered drawl announced, "Sorry, Yankee, you just done quit the war."

Sheridan opened his eyes and tried to awaken fully as his aide, Captain George Forsyth, tapped him on the shoulder. "Sir, it's seven o'clock. Here's coffee and hot water." Sheridan swung his bandy legs over the side of the bed and got to his feet, squinting into the early morning sunlight as it poured through the open window. Splashing water over his face, he asked, "Any news from General Wright?"

"No, sir. Status quo."

As Sheridan toweled his head briskly, he suddenly stopped. "Is that cannon fire I hear?" He cocked his ear. "There, hear it?"

"Yes, sir," Forsyth replied. "The duty officer first noticed it when he arose about six. It's been irregular and fitful ever since. We decided one of our brigades is probably out on an early morning reconnaissance in force. Or else General Wright is giving the rebs some artillery for breakfast."

"Possibly," Sheridan replied, reaching for a shaving cup. "And maybe Old Jubal is sending some back."

Forty minutes later, Sheridan finished breakfast with his aide and walked out on the front porch. Again he cocked his ear to the sound of distant thunder. Frowning, he said, "Whatever in the hell that is doesn't seem to quit. Did you try the field telegraph again?"

"Yes, sir," Forsyth replied. "Nothing. Mosby must have cut it again."

"That bastard. Okay, George, get me an escort of about twenty cavalrymen and let's saddle up. I've got a hunch we might be needed down south."

A short while later, after crossing Mill Creek, Sheridan and his party reached a rise that gave them a full view of the pike below. Sheridan's lips compressed as he saw a long line of disorganized blue uniforms moving north. They looked like *stragglers*! It could be only one thing—there'd been some kind of a battle and they'd been routed! Could it actually be Longstreet? He nudged Rienzi into a gallop.

In minutes he reached the first of hundreds of walking wounded, stragglers, and the rest of the flotsam that flees from battle. Fearful eyes and voices told him that the rebs had hit at dawn, overrunning the Eighth and Nineteenth Corps before they could get out of their tents. They spoke of their comrades being shot and bayoneted where they slept, and of a terrifying artillery barrage. Death, disaster, and rout! He spotted his quartermaster in a wagon. The colonel reported, "Things are bad down there, General. Your headquarters was overrun, and I don't know what happened to the rest of your staff. Crook's corps has been shattered, Emory's corps overrun, and Wright's Sixth Corps, backed by Custer's cavalry, was making a fruitless stand."

The column of wounded and skulkers looked unending.

Sheridan looked back at his colors being carried by the trooper behind him. Good thing they stayed with the commander. Well, should he round these people up and go on back to Winchester for a stand? He looked at them closely. The look in their eyes said they might still fight. Some had even given him a semblance of a cheer. No, he didn't even know for sure how bad it was, so how could he make a stand? "Colonel," he said to the quartermaster, "Stop right here and have the escort get busy rounding up these people. And get word back to Winchester to bring that brigade up to Mill Creek to block any troops from proceeding."

"What are you going to do?" Captain Forsyth asked.

"We'll fight back from where Wright is."

"But, General, it's nearly eleven miles from here!"

"I don't care if it's *fifty* miles, we're going to Cedar Creek!"

Sheridan's Ride was about to begin.

At ten minutes to nine, General Gordon reported to Early on the smoky, nearly quiet battlefield. "Is it true that we're stopping, General?"

A pleased smile crossed Early's face. "Yes, Gordon, I think this is enough glory for one day, don't you? We've taken almost two thousand prisoners, captured eighteen guns, and driven seven infantry divisions from the field. A remarkable victory!"

"But, General, we haven't sufficiently damaged Wright yet."

Early smiled patiently. "But there's no more fight in them. They'll go directly."

"But, sir, it's the veteran Sixth Corps. It won't go unless we drive it from the field. And if we stop, we'll lose momentum. Our boys are already looting and celebrating in the camps, and you know what that means."

Early shook his head. "The boys have it coming. Don't worry, Sheridan is whipped."

Sheridan galloped along the turnpike full of defeated Union soldiers, creating his unique brand of command magic. Little flat hat in hand, he shouted to one and all, "Follow me to the front, boys! We're turning around to smash 'em, boys! *Back to victory!*" Now and then, he reined in to speak a few words to different groups and cheer them back. One referred to him as Jack the Giant Killer. And slowly but surely, the blue column turned and followed its doughty commander. "If that little devil says we'll whup 'em, we will!"

Sheridan galloped on, continuing to wave his little hat and exhort his troops. "About-face, boys. We're going to put the goddamnedest twist on them you ever saw." "We're going back to recover our camps!" *"Come with me, and we'll lick 'em out of their boots!"*

Cheers followed him. "Here's Phil Sheridan, he said we'd lick them out of their damned boots!" "Little Phil's here to lead us back!" "We're going back with Sheridan to whip them!" And more cheers. By the time the general reached the battle lines on his foam-spattered Rienzi, thousands of his soldiers were heading back from dismal retreat to promised victory.

Little Phil had said it!

Now it was time for reorganization. Sheridan couldn't fathom the rebel lull, unless Early was waiting for Longstreet. He consolidated his forces on Wright's left, with the cavalry just behind. Sheridan ordered Custer to get some prisoners. At three, Gordon probed the XIX Corps front, only to be thrown back. Minutes later, Sheridan finished interrogating the prisoners. Longstreet was neither in the area nor expected. Commanders were notified that the counterattack would be readied. The proud Army of the Shenandoah had been glued back together!

As the warm autumn sun began to fall behind the Alleghenies, four o'clock arrived. Union guns crashed and Federal blue surged forward. At first, Early's troops held steady behind hasty breastworks, but the cheering, shouting Union wave would not be denied. When Emory opened a gap between two of Gordon's brigades, Custer and his shouting Wolverines smashed through, blazing away with their rapid-fire carbines. And Sheridan was everywhere, waving his hat and shouting encouragement.

Panic spread through the weary, disrupted Confederate ranks. Early, unable to believe that his brilliant victory was flaming into the bitter ashes of defeat, did all he could. But the retreating gray mass couldn't be shored up. In the fading light, he shrugged and gave the order to withdraw to New Market. But the pike had been ruptured by a lightning thrust of Federal cavalry that had demolished a vital bridge just west of Strasburg. Fleeing Confederate guns, caissons, ambulances, and wagons of every description were clogged on a three-mile stretch of road.

By the time darkness drew its curtain, General Early had delivered the new Richmond guns to their addressee.

An elated Grant ordered a one-hundred-gun salute from his guns outside of Petersburg. Not only was Early's Valley threat at an end, but Little Phil's ride had established him as the most colorful hero the Union could remember. Assistant Secretary of War Dana personally delivered his regular commission as a two-star, and told him that the president had said, "He always thought a cavalryman should be about six foot four, but now five foot four seems about right." The pleased Sheridan didn't bother telling Dana that he was being cheated out of an inch.

Rienzi, his black mount, would be renamed Winchester, and after his death would be stuffed to grace the halls of the ambitious red palace—the Smithsonian Museum. Further immortalization would be provided by poet Thomas Buchanan Read in his famous ode, "Sheridan's Ride."

> *The first that the general saw were the groups*
> *Of stragglers, and then the retreating troops;*
> *What was done? What to do? A glance told him both,*
> *Then, striking his spurs, with a terrible oath,*
> *He dashed down the line, 'mid a storm of huzzas,*
> *And the wave of retreat checked its course there, because*
> *The sight of the master compelled it to pause.*
> *With foam and with dust the black charger was gray;*
> *By the flash of his eyes, and the red nostril's play,*
> *He seemed to the whole great army to say:*
> *"I've brought you Sheridan all the way*
>   *From Winchester town to save the day!"*

When the celebration at City Point settled down, Grant went back to his other problems. Rawlins was still adamantly insisting that Sherman go after Hood and abandon his plans to sever the bowels of the Confederacy. On November 2, Grant settled the issue by giving the redhead permission to act as he saw fit, and let Rawlins work off his own steam. It was a clear reminder to all concerned: Grant would always follow his own counsel. Back in September, Sherman had sent Thomas's army north into Tennessee to counter any concerted effort Hood might make in that direction. And now, as Davis had warned, the crippled rebel general was threatening to exert his will there. Young Wilson was with Old Pap, reorganizing his cavalry. A message arrived at City Point from the former staff engineer who had recently been promoted: "Inasmuch as I now wear two stars, please forget my suggestion about Colonel Ely Parker."

This caused a loud laugh around headquarters because only a few weeks earlier, when he was angry about the incompetence of certain commanders, Wilson had said, "General Grant, I recommend you give Parker a scalping knife, fill him full of commissary whiskey, and send him out to bring in the scalps of as many major generals as he can find."

Grant continued to tighten his grip on Lee, who now referred to him as a bulldog, but the Weldon and the Southside railroads were still bringing in Confederate supplies—mostly from Wilmington, North Carolina. And Grant simply couldn't get to these rail lines.

But the war dimmed on November 8, Union election day. In spite of the great victories Lincoln's military leaders had handed him, everyone knew how capricious the electorate could be. McClellan and the Democrats might still sweep in. As Grant sat around a bonfire outside his tent late that night, his staff surrounded him. He felt both confident and mischievous, and got a bright idea. Each time Beckwith, the telegrapher, brought in an election report, Grant would look at it, shake his head grimly, then read the report aloud. The first time, he announced, "McClellan's leading by twenty-six hundred votes in Wisconsin." A groan from the staff followed. Next, his voice was barely audible as he said, "Looks like McClellan is carrying Massachusetts." Then, "McClellan's eighty-four hundred ahead in Indiana." "Little Mac is ahead of Lincoln by thirty-six hundred in Ohio."

Conversation around the campfire was stilted, the mood dark.

Finally at nearly one A.M., Grant got up from his chair, smiled, and said, "Rawlins, I think I'm going to bed. Would you have someone stay up to make sure Mr. Lincoln carries the rest of the states?"

The downcast Rawlins looked perplexed. "Sir?"

Grant laughed as he handed him the pile of reports. "The president is so far ahead, he ought to win by a landslide. Good night."

Lincoln's margin over McClellan was approximately a half million of the four million votes cast; in the electoral race it was 212 to 21. The president had a clear mandate to carry through to unconditional surrender. Grant and most of the Union Army were delighted.

There was no joy in the Confederacy. Its most favorable hope for a favorable solution to the war had sputtered out. Now it was a matter of foreign recognition and intervention, or the slim chance of victory.

But Davis wouldn't let anyone quit.

General Howard ate supper with Sherman on the 9th. Over coffee, the host confided, "I tell you, Oliver, you are about to make history. This goddamned army is going to march right off the map. Yessir, all the way to the Atlantic Ocean! That's right! You and Slocum are to be the wings, while that battle-crazy Kilpatrick leads the cavalry. We'll move eastward in four columns at fifteen miles per day, with only the minimum of wheeled vehicles and only ten days' rations. Kilpatrick will threaten Macon to the south, the left wing will feint at Augusta to the north, then we'll all swing in on Milledgeville a week later."

"No supply base at all?"

"None. The country is fat, and the orders will read, 'Forage liberally.'"

"What about communications?"

"I just told Grant I'm cutting the telegraph. He'll know where I am from the Richmond papers."

"What are you going to do about Atlanta?"

"Burn everything of military value."

"Won't the whole city burn?"

"Nope. Captain Poe and his engineers will contain the fires."

Howard shook his head. "You'll be the most hated man in the South, you know."

Sherman shrugged. "I'm not down here to run for Davis's job. Atlanta's the last major war-making center in the South, and I'm putting it out of business. Besides, burning part of a city isn't close to what Forrest did to those coloreds at Fort Pillow. It just depends on which foot the shoe is on."

"Well, I don't envy you."

Sherman laughed. "*I* envy me, Oliver. What man in the history of our great country ever had the opportunity to lead a legion of sixty-two thousand men on such a challenging campaign? Why, we'll rewrite the European military manuals!"

Chapter 52

Sherman had been correct in his assumption that the Richmond papers would be his couriers. Almost daily coverage was afforded his swath through Georgia. He was dubbed the "Judas Iscariot of Atlanta," although "Attila the Yankee" seemed more appropriate. He later told Grant that the indiscriminate burning and looting of private property in Atlanta was the work of local predators. And while Sherman's legions left little in their wake, Confederate newspapers requested that the citizens of Georgia residing ahead of his march destroy everything of provision value before he arrived.

The Georgians were two-way losers.

On the 30th of November, Hood slashed into a waiting John Schofield at Franklin, Tennessee, only to lose more than six thousand men in an unnecessary and reckless effort. Hood's losses included a dozen general officers, the most important of whom was Pat Cleburne, the Confederate hero of Missionary Ridge and one of the ablest leaders in the rebel army. Hood somehow reassembled his broken army and pursued the withdrawing Schofield to the hills south of Nashville, where he posed only a minor threat to Thomas. Old Pap's forte was defense, and he was putting his new army together inside the most stoutly fortified city west of the Blue Ridge. He was told to get after Hood and destroy him once and for all. But, as usual, he was taking his sweet time.

Grant's messages to Thomas became more urgent every day. Then the most severe ice storm in memory hit the Nashville area, and the Rock of Chickamauga reported that he would be uanble to move until a thaw occurred. A history of delays and excuses, plus the Thomas habit of methodical operation, plagued Grant. Ice? What next? He ordered Old Tom to attack or be relieved.

Black Jack Logan was on leave and visiting City Point when Grant sent for him on the 14th of December. After describing the situation, the general in chief said, "Logan, I've never heard anything but the best reports about you. I'm sure General Sherman wishes he'd kept you in command of the Army of Tennessee, but circumstances required otherwise. Nevertheless, he thinks you are the best civilian general he's ever met."

The handsome Logan smiled. "Well, thank you, General. I never thought I'd be hearing such words from a man for whom I gave a little recruiting speech all those years ago."

"Yes, and if you hadn't, I probably wouldn't be here today. Now here's what I've decided. I've written an order relieving Thomas. I want you to hand-carry it to Nashville. If, by chance, he has attacked Hood by the time you arrive, just keep the order and telegraph me. If he's still sitting on his tail, you are to assume command."

The former congressman frowned. "That could be a bit delicate, General. Thomas and I have never been the best of friends."

"That makes little difference at this point." Grant extended his hand. "I look forward to your report from Nashville."

Logan never got to Nashville. By the time he reached Louisville, word met him that the ice had melted and Thomas had routed Hood's already damaged army—chasing it below the Tennessee line and forever ending its effectiveness. The ferocious Hood's star had burned out in its bright flash across the firmament. After the first of the year, he would ask for relief from command of the shattered remnant of the Confederate Army of Tennessee, and his request would be accepted.

Sherman continued to strip his way toward Savannah, his "foragers" leaving little to be remembered by except hatred. In addition to Braxton Bragg, Davis sent Hardee and Beauregard to stop him. But even these highly experienced commanders couldn't be effective without numbers, and that was just what the Confederacy was running out of. All the stops were out. Sherman had said he'd disembowel the Confederacy, and he was doing just that. His juggernaut rolled almost unchallenged to what Sherman estimated was $100 million worth of damage.

On Christmas Eve, President Lincoln received the redhead's telegram, which he in turn shared with the nation the next morning. "I beg to present you as a Christmas gift, the city of Savannah, with one hundred and fifty guns and plenty of ammunition. Also about twenty-five thousand bales of cotton."

On Christmas Day, Butler finally found the weather perfect enough to put his troops ashore at Fort Fisher, outside of Wilmington, North Carolina—for a few hours. Determining that the fort was too strong to be taken, he withdrew and sailed back to Hampton Roads. Profane Admiral David Porter of Vicksburg fame, who was the naval commander in the amphibious operation, was furious and asked Grant to provide an aggressive general to lead another attack.

Three days later, Grant ordered Butler to report to him in person. "General," he began, "I cannot conceive that any commander could possibly attack a major objective and pull out with *fourteen* casualties. I consider your decision to abort the Fort Fisher assault a total disgrace."

Butler blinked, then trust his fleshy jaw forward. "You weren't there, so you don't know that the navy's bombardment was totally ineffective. My losses would have been catastrophic!"

"Comstock was there, and he disagrees. As does Admiral Porter."

"You're taking the word of a goddamned *colonel* over mine?"

Grant's eyes narrowed. "That's *exactly* what I'm doing."

"Well, we'll just see what Washington has to say about that."

"No, I'm not even going to waste the time, Butler. You're through."

"What do you mean?"

"Just what I said. Orders will be issued relieving you of command."

Butler pounded his fist on the desk. "You can't do that! I'll have you charged with incompetence and there'll be a court of inquiry."

Grant's voice was low and controlled. "If there's a court of inquiry, it'll be over the contraband goods that have been moving through your lines to Lee, and over your arrest of people who seem to know too much. While you were pretending to be a commander down in North Carolina, I ordered an inspector general to Bermuda Hundred."

Butler's expression lost its defiance. "I don't know what you're talking about."

"Incompetence, negligence, coercion, and criminal fraud, General."

"That's preposterous!"

"No, Butler, *you're* preposterous. If I had my way, you'd get a firing squad tonight. You tromped on me once, but the election is long over. Get out of my sight."

It was another New Year's Eve, but this time Grant was in the pleasant house in Burlington, New Jersey, where he was spending three days with his family. Sitting at a small desk in the master bedroom to escape the distractions of the children, he wrote to Sherman:

>   . . . *Wilmington will be in our hands within a fortnight, so Lee will get no more supplies from blockade runners using that port. Ord has taken*

over the Army of the James from Butler, and Wilson will rove through Alabama and Georgia with his cavalry corps, hoping to destroy Forrest. Sheridan will soon join me here.

I've decided against moving your army north by sea. Instead, I want you to march through South Carolina to Goldsboro, North Carolina. And come with haste, so you can combine with Meade in the final campaign against Lee.

I am pleased with your gentle actions to provide food and a respectful means of returning citizenship to the citizens of Savannah. While the whole South condemns you, I find it humorous that your magnanimous effort should bring this comment from the Richmond Examiner, *"What Sherman does is a dangerous bait to deaden the spirit of resistance in other places."*

So much for humor. Sometimes, I feel that I am never going to walk into Richmond. It seems that I am Sisyphus trying to push that huge stone up the hill, and watching it as it keeps on rolling back down. But there must be some of Sisyphus in all commanders, I suppose—at least those who are opposed by Lee.

In closing, I wish to add my personal solace over the death of your infant son. He never had a chance to know what his great father has done for his country.

Your good friend,
U.S. Grant

Grant put down the pen and got to his feet. Stretching, he went to the fireplace and stared down at the gray-crusted red embers. Another year of war, the worst yet when it came to the blood of soldiers he commanded. Faces and places flashed by—the eerie, deadly Wilderness; Spotsylvania; terrible, swift Cold Harbor; the debacle of the Mine; the other battles he hadn't witnessed, but whose conduct was on his head. Blue- and gray-clad corpses in different distorted body positions paraded before him, blank faces; the piles of blood-drenched arms and legs stacked outside a surgical hospital. Real faces, animated, smiling, speaking to him, passed over the fading coals—Hamer, now hazier, as if covered by the gauze of time; grand C. F. Smith, with his magnificent mustache; bright, cheerful Mac McPherson; others who had not been so close, such as Uncle John Sedgwick. The self-seekers and incompetents who had cost so many lives and had been sent on their way formed a different file: Hooker, McClernand, McClellan, Burnside, Butler, Rosecrans . . . others.

He saw the faces of those he didn't know, except from photographs or chance encounters in earlier years, and wondered if Robert E. Lee was staring into a fire tonight as a new year waited to be born, if he was seeing and mourning those who had been close to him, such as Tom Jackson and Jeb Stuart. He wondered if Lee was at home with his family.

They said his wife suffered, was an invalid.

At least a healthy Julia awaited him downstairs.

He closed his eyes, speaking softly, "Thank you, oh Lord, on this eve of a fresh year, for my family and other blessings. And let me pray for those fine soldiers who have passed on, as well as those who have survived this terrible carnage. And for their loved ones, Father. I pray that you will give the proper insight to our enemy leaders, and that this conflict will come to an early end in these still-dark months ahead . . ."

On the 2nd of February a grinning Rawlins walked into Grant's office. "I thought you might be interested in a couple of tidbits of intelligence, General."

Grant welcomed the break from his paperwork. "From the look on your face, I'd guess Jeff Davis fell and broke his neck."

"No, this is a financial matter. The big hair sale is off. The master plan to sell forty million dollars worth of Confederate ladies' hair to Europe has been canceled because without the port of Wilmington, they can't get it shipped."

Grant smiled. "If you'll pardon the pun, it was a hairbrained idea anyway. What else have you got?"

"The rebs are finally considering the use of colored troops."

"I wondered when they'd wake up. Do you know how far along they are?"

"It's still in the argument stage. A cornerstone of their society is built on the inferiority of the Negro, and to put guns in the hands of slaves to fight for the Confederacy would be an admission of equality."

"Yes," Grant said, "and after they fight, they'll have to be freed. I know Davis is desperate, but I don't think they'll ever do it. Keep me informed."

"There's also the matter of Captain Robert Todd Lincoln."

Grant sighed. "Keep him busy and safe. What is he, twenty-two and just out of Harvard? The president hated to use his influence and have him assigned to us, but Mrs. Lincoln has apparently been against his serving at all. It's due to her losing their other son, and I'm sure it's been difficult for the young man. Use your judgment, but keep him out of danger."

As Rawlins departed, Grant turned back to Stanton's messsage. Longstreet had recently met Ord under a flag of truce to discuss a means of peace. This was followed by a letter from Lee to himself, which he'd forwarded to Stanton immediately. This was the secretary's reply:

The president directs that he wishes you to have no conference with General Lee unless it be for capitulation of Gen. Lee's army, or on some minor, and purely military matter. He instructs me to say that you are not to decide, discuss, or confer upon any political question. Such questions the president holds in his own hands; and will submit them to no military conferences or conventions. Meanwhile you are to press to the utmost of your military advantage.

Grant put down the message. It was clear enough; Lincoln was making sure no general would take the shovel out of his hands. As it should be. Grant slowly wrote out his response to Lee.

Robert E. Lee poured another cup of the tepid coffee and sipped. For hours he'd paced, praying, and searching fruitlessly for answers. He'd finally called in Longstreet, who had arrived shortly after midnight. Now, at three A.M., with the black stillness broken by the golden light of a single kerosene lamp, the I Corps commander had assimilated the dozens of reports from every command in the army.

"Not a pretty picture, is it?"

Old Pete looked up from his chair at the long table. "My God, it's terrible, sir. I had no idea that desertion was so rampant and that so many commands were in such bad shape." His low voice was soft in the still room. "I don't see how we even have an army."

Lee sat down across the table. "Grant must have a hundred and fifty thousand men here, Sheridan is streaming down from the Valley with twenty thousand hardened cavalrymen, and Thomas is supposed to be coming east with thirty thousand. Schofield will join Sherman in Carolina, which will give him eighty thousand marching north. And Grant knows exactly what he's about. He's the hardest man to fight I've ever met."

"I've know him a long time, General. He doesn't understand backing up."

"I have fifty thousand men here, but no more than thirty-five thousand can fight. I finally convinced the president that Joe Johnston was the only man capable of slowing Sherman, but he's only got fourteen thousand men. And our supply situation is getting perilous."

Lee stared into his cup for a few moments, then looked up with the most naked expression Longstreet had ever seen in the great man's eyes. "I'm haunted by hungry, dejected soldiers, freezing in their remnants of uniforms, and looking to us generals for deliverance. We have a duty to them and to the rest of the people of our young country, and it frightens me. What do you think should be done?"

Longstreet shrugged his big bear shoulders, looking into the pained dark eyes for several moments before replying. "You know the answer, sir. If we can't make favorable peace terms, we can retreat—abandon Richmond and Petersburg, unite by rapid marches with General Johnston in North Carolina, and strike Sherman before Grant can join him . . . or we must fight here, without any further delay."

Lee nodded, dropping his gaze to the table. "The president is prickly about any kind of peace that will end the Confederacy. But I will approach him again tomorrow."

"I think you must, General."

"So be it. I don't think we can fight Grant here, so let's consider what must be done to join Johnston. Pick a point where we can hit Grant to make him open up his left flank. I think that's our only chance of breaking out."

"I already know, General. Fort Stedman, east of the city."

Lee nodded. "Let's try it."

Julia Grant stared out the tiny window of the army ambulance as it bumped along the corduroy road toward General Ord's review. Large puffs of broken clouds created fast-moving shadows as they scurried by on the wings of a brisk wind. They promised to behave at least until the big parade was over. Julia shrugged inwardly. The last few days had been nothing but a pins-and-needles ordeal, and today promised nothing less. Mary Lincoln was in another of her pouty moods, saying little and imagining God knows what. Well, she could just sit there, or talk to Colonel Porter if she wished.

When Ulys told her that the president was coming down to City Point for a prolonged escape from Washington, she'd been highly excited. As official hostess, this would be the most important social period of her life—what with entertaining Mrs. Lincoln and working out all types of social activities with the other generals' wives. What an exciting situation it had promised. But the last few days had been total disaster.

The day after the presidential party arrived on the *River Queen,* the Confederates launched a hopeless attack on a little fort named Stedman. Their commander apparently hadn't known that Ulys's troops were massed there for a huge review. Of course, Ulys was pleased over the rebels losing some four thousand men against minimal Union losses, but it had been a sickly sight to see all those dead bodies on the way.

Then Mrs. Lincoln had pulled another of her tantrums when she heard that General Griffin's lovely wife had a special pass from the president. And last night's dinner party—what a scene that was! Was the woman truly ill, as so many said? She was certainly impossible when she was in one of her moods.

What would she do at today's review? Mrs. Ord was not only one of the most beautiful of the generals' wives, but also an accomplished horse-woman. How would Mrs. Lincoln react when she saw her in the president's reviewing party?

As the ambulance bounced to a halt, Colonel Porter smiled. "It looks like we're here, ladies."

Mary Todd Lincoln pulled her hoops in and moved to the door. "Well, it's about time, Colonel." As she stepped down, she saw Mrs. Ord turn a fine chestnut mare away from the tall man in the stovepipe hat and head for the ambulance. Turning to Julia with a scowl, Mrs. Lincoln snapped, "What is *that* woman doing with the president?"

Julia shrugged. "She came earlier with her husband, I believe."

"She has no business being here ahead of *me!*"

Mrs. Ord reined her horse in, smiling. "Good afternoon, Mrs. Lincoln. I'm sorry you were held up."

"Don't you lie to me, you hussy," Mary Lincoln retorted. "I saw you over there with my husband!"

Mrs. Ord blinked in surprise. "But, I, well, the whole reviewing party is there. I was with my husband."

"Don't you lie to me. I saw you flouncing yourself in front of him like a cheap harlot!"

Mrs. Ord pulled back, moving a hand to her cheek as if she'd been slapped. Tears came to her eyes. "I, I don't know what you're talking about."

Julia moved quickly between the two women. "Excuse me, Mrs. Lincoln, but I'm sure you're making a mistake. The president probably hasn't even spoken to Mrs. Ord."

The angry eyes darted to Julia. "Ha! Little do you know, in your simpering *Mrs. Grant* facade! Little Miss Goody Goody from St. Louis. All of you generals' wives are the same. You think because your husbands are winning the war, that you can do anything you please—including turning the president's head. Well, I'm on to you, you know."

Julia forced a tight smile. "Why don't we move on over to the review?"

Mrs. Lincoln pushed her solicitous hand away. "Don't you touch me! I know what's in the back of your mind. The *White House,* that's what! You think you'll take *my* place some of these days, don't you?"

Julia replied softly, "Mrs. Lincoln, I never dreamed I'd be *here.*"

CHAPTER 53

Two hours after supper on the 30th of March, John Rawlins came to Grant's tent at his new headquarters location behind the Federal left at Gravelly Run. He stepped out of the mud, glad that at least the general's tent had a floor. He removed his wet hat, but couldn't do anything about his dripping slicker. "General," he said, shaking his head, "this is no weather for an army."

Grant nodded in agreement. "You want a transfer to the navy?"

"No, I'll settle for a new pair of boots."

"Have a seat and organize your puddles."

Rawlins eased into the canvas chair. "Sheridan rode up a little while ago, if you could call it that. His famous horse must have waded up to his knees. He's got everyone stirred up about the attack, but I think he's wrong—just as I think you are—to press it under these conditions."

Grant turned from the small field desk, laying aside the pen. "It's just as bad for them as us. I have five infantry corps on line, waiting to smash through when the opportunity presents itself. And Sheridan is loose on the left—or will be as soon as his horses can move. I figure Lee has only two avenues left. That costly feint at Stedman was a desperate effort to open our left flank, so he's thinking of moving south to join Johnston. His only other possibility lies in trying to get to Lynchburg and the mountains to the west.

"Once we take the Southside Railroad, he'll be completely cut off, so he has to do something. We've had a tough fight for almost eleven months, and if we just keep up the pressure, victory is in our grasp. I can almost smell it."

Rawlins shrugged and got to his feet. "I just thought dryer roads would save some lives. Do you want to see your enthusiastic cavalry leader?"

"Certainly. I can use all the enthusiasm there is."

Rawlins tugged his slouch hat over his brow and opened the flap. "I'll send him in."

Sheridan was covered with mud. Grant smiled as the dripping Irishman touched his hat brim in salute. "I hear you're a bit enthusiastic, General."

"Damn right, General. I can kick the hell out of Lee's cavalry out there at Dinwiddie Court House, if he comes out. Now, if I just had some infantry, I think I can turn his whole flank. And I can wrap up that railroad so he won't get another ounce of supplies, then smash him up from his right!"

"What about forage? You can't be supplied that far out—not in these conditions."

"I'll build my own goddamn roads, if it takes half my command to corduroy at night. Don't worry about that. I tell you I'm ready to strike out tomorrow and go to smashing things!"

Grant watched the fervent black eyes, believing this wild little man could do anything he said. "All right, Sheridan, I'll give you Warren's Fifth Corps. He ranks you, but you'll have overall command. Orders have already been issued for Wright, Parke, and Ord to attack in the morning. But we'll delay that assault until I hear from you. If this rain holds you up, they can move later."

"Thank you, General, but can I have Wright instead? We worked well together in the Valley."

"No, he's too far away. It has to be Warren."

Sheridan turned to go. "Very well."

"And Sheridan—thanks for dropping by."

The Irish face creased into a grin. "The pleasure was all mine."

The names Dinwiddie and Five Forks, two tiny locations that would never have been known outside the county, were about to become the center of world focus. While Sheridan urged Rienzi back through the deep mud to his headquarters in the Dinwiddie Tavern, Lee set the stage for his last desperate attempt to preserve the right of his command and the all-essential Southside Railroad. He sent George Pickett, the hero of Chapultepec and Gettysburg, with twelve thousand men to crush Sheridan's cavalry threat.

At noon on the 31st, Federal General Thomas Devin's division ran into

Pickett's force while probing the few miles north to Five Forks. Strongly outnumbered, Devin fought his way back to Dinwiddie, where the dismounted troopers of Crook's and Custer's divisions stopped Pickett right in front of the tavern headquarters.

Even at bay, Lee could still hurt his enemy.

Shortly after nightfall, a courier brought word to Sheridan that Warren's Corps had been caught in column by a strong Confederate force under A. P. Hill. But the hard-fighting Andrew Humphreys and his Second Corps had come to the rescue. Sheridan paced the tavern floor for over a minute before turning to his brother and aide. Pounding a fist on the table, he exclaimed, "Goddammit, we've got them!"

An hour and a half later Captain Sheridan rode into Grant's headquarters, where the lieutenant general had just finished a biting message to Meade regarding Warren's mishandled engagement. When Porter came to his tent, he clamped down on a cold cigar butt and said, "By all means, send him in. Maybe Little Phil has some *good* news."

He took the message from the aide and read quickly. Looking at the captain, he said, "So General Sheridan thinks Pickett is too far out and can be cut off, eh? Did he discuss this with you?"

The younger Sheridan lacked none of his brother's aggressiveness. "Yes, sir, he did. Pickett's got somewhere around eleven thousand infantry and cavalry, but we think he's under strict orders from Lee to hold the Southside Railroad, some three miles north of Five Forks. If an infantry corps can attack in concert with our artillery, we can defeat him."

Grant lit the cigar. "Well, I can't give him Wright, as he requests. It'll still have to be Warren. I'll get orders to him right away, so he should be near Dinwiddie shortly after midnight. As I told him before, Captain, he's to assume overall command. If there's any procrastination on this one, it'll be his fault."

"General, you know my brother."

Grant nodded. He also knew Warren. The Federal hero of Gettysburg had once said, "I'll be goddamned if I'll cooperate with anyone!" Grant turned to Porter. "Go on back with Captain Sheridan as liaison."

Phil Sheridan had been boiling for so many hours that he couldn't remember speaking in anything but a snarl. Awakening at dawn, he found *none* of Warren's corps in position. It was past noon before they were up, and almost four o'clock in the afternoon before the attack at Five Forks began in full force. Sheridan had insisted the battle be won during daylight, or their golden opportunity would be gone. He had no way of knowing that the ringleted and perfumed Pickett had retired to the rear with his cavalry commander for a *shad bake!* How could he even imagine that, with the war falling apart, those leaders would be at a frivolous fish feast?

Four hours later, Colonel Horace Porter galloped into headquarters, leaping from the saddle and gleefully shouting, *"He did it! Sheridan smashed Pickett!"*

As staff officers jumped up from the campfire to surround the exuberant Porter, Grant watched from his camp chair. In moments, Porter was standing before him. "I tell you, General, that little man is the goddamnedest fighter I've ever seen! They say he carries forked lightning in a battle. Well, he sure had it crackling today!"

Rawlins interrupted. "Tell us about the battle."

"First of all, Warren was late as hell and had a bunch of excuses. And God, was Sheridan mad. The Fifth Corps didn't get into it until after four o'clock, then—when the whole Federal front was supposed to wheel into Pickett—Warren's two right divisions went too wide. As the rebs started to pour heavy fire into Sheridan's cavalry and Griffin's division on the left, Sheridan grabbed his command flag and spurred that big black of his straight at them.

"He dashed from one point to another, waving his flag, shaking his fist, encouraging, threatening, swearing—the very incarnation of battle. He was so furious at Warren's lack of control that he snapped at some of those Fifth Corps brigadiers as if they were privates. When Generals Griffin and Crawford finally got in the right place to throw a hook around the rebel left, he managed to settle down a bit. But I tell you, the battle was all Sheridan."

"What about Warren?" Comstock asked.

"He relieved him just before sundown by field order, and Sheridan wouldn't listen when he tried to plead his case. Griffin now has command of the Fifth Corps. I'll bet Lee lost a third of his army, including six guns, thirteen battle flags, and at least a dozen general officers. And—"

Grant spoke for the first time. "How many prisoners?"

"Over five thousand, General!"

Grant nodded. "Then Lee is weak everywhere. I'll order an immediate assault all along the lines."

Shortly before daylight on April 2, the Union corps of Wright, Parke, and Ord crashed into the thinly manned Petersburg defenses. They were followed by Humphreys, Sheridan, and Griffin in the massive attack along the line. The gallant Confederate defense did its utmost, but the blue host would not be denied this time. Gone were the fumblers and procrastinators—the Burnsides, the Butlers, Baldy Smiths, and Warrens. Grant and Meade had welded the huge assault package together and Petersburg was doomed.

On the 3rd, standing in the center of Petersburg, Grant received Lincoln's warm handshake and congratulations. "I think, Mr. President," he replied, "That the Army of the Potomac deserves your kind words. The officers and men of that proud army have redeemed themselves from any past shadow."

"I thoroughly agree," the president said heartily as he turned and shook George Meade's hand.

Later in the day, word arrived that Federal troops were in Richmond, but they were too busy to be conquering heroes because they had to fight massive fires started by Lee's departing troops. Grant would later learn that the rebel army had ordered warehouses and munition magazines burned to keep them from Union hands. But the hungry flames, fueled by a brisk wind, had spread to much of downtown Richmond. No Nero was available to fiddle, however, since Jefferson Davis had fled and looters were busy in their usual pillage.

Richmond! Grant thought. Was it finally possible?

The Confederacy's northernmost fort had fallen.

Now it was time for the climax—destroy or capture the last major enemy army. Lee could be bent on only one course, a rapid move toward Lynchburg and the supplies that should meet him from that direction. One railroad remained, the Richmond and Danville, which connected with the Southside. "Rawlins," he said, "have a courier ready to depart at once for Sheridan's headquarters. I'm going to have him head Lee off, with the Fifth Corps following as fast as possible."

He reached for his pen.

The last race was on!

Lee, troubled by the death of fiery Ambrose Hill in the Petersburg attack, divided his fleeing army into two wings, the left moving along the south side of the Appomattox River under Longstreet, the right on the north side under the one-legged Ewell. Sheridan quickly guessed that Lee had to avoid any major battle as he took up the chase—he simply couldn't fight and survive.

Arriving at Amelia Court House after an all-night march, Lee gave his bone-weary troops a brief rest and an opportunity to gather some food and forage in the nearby area. Then it was off on another night march, which left hundreds of stragglers and tons of discarded equipment.

On the 6th, Sheridan saw a chance to strike a vital blow. Ewell's wing was ahead of Longstreet, at a point where the Appomattox crossed Sayler's Creek, eight miles east of Farmville and some fifty air miles west of Petersburg. With infantry in support, Sheridan threw his three cavalry divisions into action. The Confederate wing was broken in several places, requiring Richard Ewell to surrender or needlessly sacrifice thousands of lives. Sayler's Creek was as big a Union victory as Five Forks because once more Lee had lost nearly one-half of his remaining army, along with Ewell and several other generals—including his son, Custis.

*　　*　　*

That night, after supping with Sheridan, the "eagle with a lisp" sat by the campfire, hugging the knee of his remaining leg. He spoke softly, staring into the flames. "You know, I once gave Grant some extra leave when I was adjutant of the old Fourth Infantry. He was courting that gal he later married. He was a young second lieutenant. It was just before we headed off toward Mexico . . . a thousand years ago." He sighed. "General Sheridan, why don't you send an emissary over under a flag of truce to General Lee, and ask for his surrender to save further sacrifice? I think it's all over."

Sheridan watched the flickering yellow firelight play over Ewell's dejected features. He had been a struggling captain when this fighting man had been Stonewall's right arm. And here he was, a worthy general, brave beyond question, crippled, sitting here in an enemy camp brooding in final defeat—thinking only of how to save lives. Why had officers like him made those disastrous decisions so long ago? He finally spoke. "I'm afraid such action is out of my province, but I'll pass the suggestion along to General Grant."

CHAPTER 54

But Lee wasn't ready to give up, not as long as supplies awaited him at Appomattox Station, some twenty-five miles west of Farmville. Although Union troops were nipping at his heels, and Sheridan was on his flanks, he still had a chance. The race continued. Late in the afternoon of the 7th, Grant, who had caught up, decided to approach Lee. From Farmville, he wrote, "The results of the last week must convince you of the hopelessness of further resistance on the part of your army in this struggle. I feel that it is so, and regard it as my duty to shift from myself the responsibility of any further effusion of blood by asking of you the surrender of the Army of Northern Virginia."

Shortly after midnight, Lee's reply arrived by staff officer. He wanted to know what the terms were. Grant was ready to provide the widest latitude in terms, but decided to think about his wording. The next morning he wrote,

In reply I would say that, peace being my great desire, there is but one condition I would insist upon—namely, that the officers and men surrendered shall be disqualified for taking up arms against the government of the United States. I will meet you, or will designate officers to meet any officers you may name for the same purpose, at any point agreeable to you, for the purpose of arranging definitely the terms upon which the surrender of the Army of Northern Virginia will be received.

The door was open, but Lee was still looking for a long shot. The remaining wing of his broken army was using its last legs to reach Appomattox Station. His return note that night mentioned meeting with Grant to discuss terms for surrender of Confederate States forces, but not specifically the Army of Northern Virginia.

Grant sensed that he was hedging, but could in no way step into an arena of full peace negotiations. Lincoln had made that clear enough. Yet Lee was commander in chief of all rebel forces, and if he could surrender them . . .

Rawlins read the note and said, "You aren't swallowing this crap, are you, General? This is just a damned underhanded ploy to buy time. He's not being honest!"

Grant shook his head. War wasn't honest. "Maybe talking to him won't hurt. If I can have an hour with him, it'll all be over. I'm sure."

"Don't give him a plugged nickel. He's stalling and you hold all the aces. I haven't gotten around to telling you, but word just came in from Sheridan that Custer has driven the rebs out of Appomattox Station, captured four supply trains and a bunch of guns. Lee is finished." A grin spread over Rawlins's face. "It's true, General. You've cut him off. He's done."

Grant nodded, blinking. *That was it! Lee had no alternatives!* He nodded his head again. "Yes," he said, actually stunned that finally there was no place for Lee to go. "Yes, I think we can take him tomorrow," he said quietly. "Send my congratulations to Sheridan, but tell him to hold back."

Grant applied the mustard plasters the surgeon had given him to his wrists and the back of his neck, while soaking his feet in hot water and more mustard plaster. *Anything* was worth a try with these blessed migraine headaches. He got the doggone things every once in a while and they laid him low. But in the midst of this severe pain was a twinge of excitement. Was this really it? He was afraid to believe it, yet it had to be. The long road was finally running out . . .

Tomorrow was Palm Sunday, a fitting day for peace.

But would Lee realize it? Or would the grand gray knight fight to the bitter end? He was purported to be a man of God; surely he must see how further sacrifice was utterly needless.

Rawlins was right, his answer to Lee had to be firm. He must state that legal peace could not be established on the field of battle, but—well, the words would come to him in the morning when he felt better. Somehow he had to convince Lee, or he could not stay the sword of his generals. Sheridan wanted to smash them up and force the surrender in a final burst of glory. And Meade, well, Meade had a right to part of that glory. After all, the Army of the Potomac had finally won its spurs.

Grant arose shortly after sunrise, still suffering from the terrible headache. He said a short prayer honoring Palm Sunday, then sent the message he'd written in the middle of the sleepless night through the lines to Lee. He tried some breakfast, then rode painfully forward with his staff to be in easy proximity to the lines in case Lee came up with something.

Lee did. The last desperate Confederate attack of his army was made by John Gordon against Sheridan's troopers near Appomattox Courthouse. Gordon's corps, now reduced to an over-strength brigade, crashed into the Federal cavalry and was initially successful. But just when it seemed a breakthrough was possible, the opening revealed Ord's massed infantry, wave upon wave of blue uniforms accented by the sun's glint on thousands of bayonets, waiting motionless to surge forward. And then the cavalry began to re-form, richly colored guidons and battle flags snapping in the breeze on the crest of higher ground . . . *a whole corps!*

It was like a glimpse of one's death.

Gordon, in a forward position, watched in awe and felt the tightening of his diminished command. He sensed the sucking in, the apprehension and the futility. He looked at his battle flags, now clustered among such a small number of troops. It was just so hopeless. Was this, then, the end of it all? Speaking softly, he turned to an aide. "Get a white flag."

While Sheridan testily observed a temporary cease-fire with Gordon, Lee was in a quandary. His invitation to Grant for a peace parley had been extended to ten A.M. on the old stage road to Richmond. Had Gordon's breakout worked, the meeting would have been superfluous; now it was imperative. Lee had known since arising at four that this would be the day. It hung over him like a pall. He was so certain, in fact, that he had put on his elaborate new dress uniform, complete with silk sash and his ornate dress sword. Or maybe he'd dressed in that manner to tempt fate to give him one last chance. Now it didn't matter. Now he'd lost all bargaining power. Longstreet had insisted that Grant would be fair, but not receiving a reply from him was an ominous sign. Perhaps he shouldn't have stalled. Certainly he shouldn't have ordered that final assault—more death and maiming. Absolutely needless. Where would they have gotten supplies if they had broken out? No, it was just a stubborn old general's last-ditch vanity at work. Those final casualties belonged on his own head, just as Grant had stated. It made him feel even worse.

The Union commander had offered to let appointed officers handle the surrender—an obviously gracious gesture to spare him the humiliation of the flag of truce, carried by his color bearer. Never in thirty-nine years of military service had he ridden under such an abhorrent symbol. But then, he'd never had cause to surrender before.

Surrender!

The word lashed back at him, twisted his bowels.

Finally they were at the appointed place on the old stage road. But no Grant. After ten minutes he decided that Grant had simply decided not to meet with him. Then, just as he was about to start back to his own depleted lines, a blue-clad officer and escort rode out of the Union lines under a white flag. Grant? No, it wasn't a general.

Lieutenant Colonel Whittier, from General Humphreys's staff, saluted and presented Grant's letter. As Lee opened the message, he asked, "Do you have any verbal instructions, Colonel?"

"No, sir," Whittier replied.

Lee adjusted his spectacles and began to read.

> *Headquarters, Armies of the United States*
> *April 9, 1865*
>
> *General R. E. Lee*
> *Commanding C. S. Armies*
> *General: Your note of yesterday is received. As I have no authority to treat on the subject of peace, the meeting proposed for 10 A.M. today could lead to no good. I will state, however, General, that I am equally anxious for peace with yourself, and the whole North entertains the same feeling. The terms upon which peace can be had are well understood. By the South laying down their arms, they will hasten that most desirable event, save thousands of human lives and hundreds of millions of property not yet destroyed. Sincerely hoping that all our difficulties may be settled without the loss of another life, I subscribe myself,*
>
> *Very respectfully, your obedient servant,*
>
> *U. S. Grant*
> *Lieutenant General U.S. Army*

General Lee silently handed the letter to his adjutant, Colonel Taylor, and removed his glasses. He looked up at Whittier. "Is General Grant close by?"

"I believe he is, sir."

"Then I will dictate a reply." Lee turned to Taylor, who had produced paper and pencil. "Give me a few moments, please."

Rawlins looked up as Whittier galloped in and jumped from his horse. The colonel saluted with a grin, handing him Lee's sealed note. "General, I just got this personally from Lee!"

The staff quickly gathered as Rawlins tore the envelope open and began to read. He turned to Grant, who was quietly smoking a pipe on a nearby tree stump. *"Look at this, General!"*

Grant took the single sheet and read, "General: I received your note of this morning on the picket line, whither I had come to meet you and ascertain definitely what terms were embraced in your proposal of yesterday with reference to the surrender of this army. I now request an interview, in accordance with the offer contained in your letter of yesterday, for that purpose. Very respectfully, Your Obt. servt., R. E. Lee."

Grant drew in a deep breath.

322

There it was!

He quietly handed the note back to Rawlins. "You'd better read it aloud."

As soon as the Galenian finished, hearty cheers followed, rocking the air. And suddenly, Grant's headache was gone. He said, "Well, Rawlins, does the tone of that note suit you as well as it does me?"

Rawlins grinned through his heavy black beard. "Yes, sir, it suits me just fine!"

Grant pulled his order book out of a pocket and began to write. He acknowledged Lee's note and asked him to name the time and place.

CHAPTER 55

The red brick McLean house in the hamlet of Appomattox Courthouse was the site that was quickly selected for the surrender. By a strange twist, the owner of the house—Wilmer McLean—had owned the farm on Bull Run near Manassas Junction where the first major battle of the war had been fought. Wanting to get away from shot and shell, he had later moved his family to the rural hill country well west of the capital and apart from railroads and other features of military value. Now, inexplicably, the very war he was trying to escape was about to culminate in his living room.

Young Walter Taylor, Lee's adjutant, had been so overcome by the thought of forthcoming surrender that Lee had excused him from attending the ceremony. Lieutenant Colonel Charles Marshall, his secretary, and Lieutenant Colonel Orville Babcock, the aide Grant had sent ahead, accompanied the silver-headed Lee into the house to await the arrival of the Union commander.

Some thirty minutes later, Grant, accompanied by Rawlins and most of his staff, rode Cincinnati into the little village. Somehow, on the move from City Point, the trunk containing his fresh uniforms and ceremonial sword had been misplaced, so he wasn't dressed for the occasion. This would never have worried him, except that he didn't want to slight Lee. In any case, he wouldn't have worn the sword—and it was the occasion that mattered, not one's appearance. Mud had spattered his worn, plain uniform and had covered his boots. The braid on his epaulets was tarnished and barely proclaimed his rank. Even the slouch hat looked as if it had been thrown in too many corners.

Sheridan was waiting. He saluted.

Grant touched his hat brim. "How are you, Sheridan?"

"First-rate, thank you. How are you, General?"

"All right. Is Lee here?"

"Up in that brick house."

"Well then, let's go up."

It all seemed so casual, but Grant felt a rushing in his ears, a tightness in his stomach, as he swung down from the big horse. He had prayed for this moment, had always been sure it would arrive—perhaps not in this manner, but in some way. Now, as if in some surreal pantomime, he was moving toward perhaps his country's most historic moment. A horse neighed in the bright sunlight. Leather creaked. Out of the corner of his eye he saw his red flag with the three white stars suddenly flap, as if to urge him on. For a brief second he saw himself in an old army overcoat driving a wagon full of wood through the snow. For some odd reason, his next thought was of Chaplain Eaton.

Was it really Palm Sunday?

His staff and escort sat quietly on their horses.

He noticed Lee's gray horse, Traveller . . . that fine horse he'd read about in the Richmond papers. He had his bridle off and was eating grass. An orderly stood by his side.

The wind stopped and for a moment it was totally silent.

He looked up into the spring sky and squinted at the sun, remembering that Easter wasn't far away. But that had nothing to do with the present, with ending a bloody war.

The rushing was in his ears again.

Reaching the top step of the porch, he looked into Babcock's smile. The colonel said, "Come in, sir. General Lee is waiting."

Removing his hat as he entered, Grant followed his aide up the stairwell to the parlor on the west side of the house. He was greeted by a relatively small room that held chairs, a sofa, and two small marble tables—one round, the other rectangular. Standing in front of the fireplace was the erect, patrician figure of Robert E. Lee. How gray he was, so different from the hazy major he recalled from a glimpse of yesterday.

As Lee came forward, extending his hand, they exchanged greetings.

Babcock motioned toward the round table in the middle of the room as Lee returned to the other one. Leaning over as Grant seated himself, the aide quietly asked, "Don't you think it would be a good idea, sir, to invite the senior staff and generals in?"

Absently, Grant nodded. Moments later, Sheridan, Ord, Rawlins and others clanked in amid the noises that boots, spurs, and sabers always make. They quietly lined up along the wall behind Grant. Lee's only aide was Charles Marshall, who stood silently behind the waiting general.

Grant drew in a breath.

The air seemed charged. It was time.

He cleared his throat and spoke in his normal quiet tone. "I met you once before, General Lee, while we were serving in Mexico. I have always remembered your appearance, and I think I should have recognized you anywhere."

"Yes," Lee answered tonelessly, "I know I met you, and I've often thought of it and tried to recollect how you looked. But I've never been able to recall a single feature."

A slight smile softened Grant's expression. "Most people don't. Those were different days, General. You were a major and I was a second lieutenant. Funny, I can recall so many scenes as if it were yesterday, but the rest seems in another century."

Lee nodded, obviously anxious to get on with it. "I suppose, General Grant, that the object of our present meeting is fully understood. I asked you to ascertain upon what terms you would receive the surrender of my army."

Grant looked into the dark eyes for a moment before replying. "The terms I propose are those stated substantially in my letter of yesterday. That is, the officers and men surrendered are to be paroled and disqualified from taking up arms again. And all arms, ammunition, and supplies are to be delivered up as captured property."

Lee nodded without breaking the gaze. "Those are about the conditions I expected."

Grant glanced up and caught Colonel Ely Parker's eye off to the right. Then he spoke of peace, loss of life and property, and the hope that their actions of the day would be of mutual benefit. Then, on Lee's urging, Grant proceeded to write out the terms in his manifold order book. Pausing now and then for a word or phrase, he scratched away with a pencil. He labored over the ending, knowing he might be stepping on Lincoln's toes. But he wanted to make sure that brave soldiers who believed in a cause—no matter how wrong—would never be tried for treason. He wanted to include something that would forestall any government reprisal, that would have the effect of a general amnesty. Finally, he motioned to Rawlins, who came over and read the two pages. Rawlins nodded, then stepped back against the wall, where Sheridan uneasily shifted his weight from one foot to another.

Even the breathing in the room was hushed.

Grant arose and walked to Lee, handing him the order book. After pointing out a missing word, Lee reread the draft. He lingered over the final sentence, which read, "This done, each officer and man will be allowed to return to his home, not to be disturbed by the United States authority as long as they observe their paroles and the laws in force where they may reside." His expression softened somewhat. "This will have a very happy effect on my army."

"Then I'll have a copy of the letter made in ink and sign it."

Lee removed his spectacles and frowned. "There is one thing. The cavalrymen and artillerists own their own horses in our army. I'd like to understand whether these men will be permitted to retain their horses."

"The terms as written do not allow this, General. Only the officers are allowed to take their private property."

Lee replaced his glasses and read the second page of yellow foolscap again. Looking up with a touch of fleeting pain, he said, "No, I see the terms do not allow it. That is quite clear."

Grant felt Lee's discomfort. The great man would not beg, not even for his men. And Lincoln had said, "Get them back to their farms." Again he saw himself in that wagon, hauling wood from Hardscrabble. How would he have survived without horses? No, it would be bad enough for these men *with* the animals. He stroked his beard, replying, "Well, the subject is quite new to me. Of course, I didn't know that any private soldiers owned their animals, but I think this will be the last battle of the war—at least, I sincerely hope so—and the surrender of this army will soon be followed by others.

"And I take it that most of the men in the ranks are small farmers, so I will arrange it this way. I will not change the terms as written, but I will instruct the officers I shall appoint to receive the paroles to let all the men who claim to own a horse or mule to take the animals home with them to work their little farms."

Lee nodded, relaxing. "This will have the best possible effect on the men. I believe it will be very gratifying and will do much toward conciliating our people."

Grant turned to Rawlins to have the letter copied. While this was being accomplished, Grant presented a somewhat aloof Lee to his assembled officers. Lee moved back to the table when the introductions were complete. After a minute, he said, "General Grant, I have about a thousand of your men as prisoners. I shall be glad to send them into your lines as soon as it can be arranged, for I have no provisions for them. I have, indeed, nothing for my own men. They've been living for the past few days on parched corn, and are badly in need of both rations and forage."

"Yes, by all means," Grant replied. "I should like our men back as soon as possible. How many men are in your present force?"

"I can't say. I have no means of ascertaining our present strength."

"Suppose I send over twenty-five thousand rations. Will that be enough?"

Lee nodded. "Yes, I think that will be more than enough."

General Lee then turned to Colonel Marshall, and the two spent the next twenty minutes on the draft and then the ink copy of Lee's acceptance. This done, Lee signed the letter and handed it back to Marshall, who sealed the envelope and exchanged it for Grant's letter.

It was 3:40 on the 9th of April, 1865.

Lee's surrender was complete.

The gray-bearded general rose stiffly from his chair and moved to Grant, hand outstretched. Grant shook the hand, looking directly into Lee's unseeing eyes, feeling for this magnificent soldier, torn in the climax of victory by the sadness. Lee nodded his head to the other Federal officers, and, with shoulders back, walked out the door. Several officers sprang to their feet and saluted.

Moments later, Lee mounted Traveller and turned back for a final look at the McLean house—just as Grant stepped out on the porch. Grant removed his hat and stood at attention, as did the other officers present. Erect in the saddle, Lee raised his hat and barely nodded his head, then turned his horse to return to his vanquished army.

CHAPTER 56

BLOODGOOD'S HOTEL, PHILADELPHIA
GOOD FRIDAY, 1865

Grant looked up at the knock on the door. They hadn't even had time to settle down after the tiring train ride. He'd left word that they weren't to be disturbed, and was busy eating a piece of chicken from the small buffet that had been laid out for them. Who could be bothering them at midnight? He looked at Julia, who was unpinning her hat where she sat on the settee. Shrugging, he wiped his mouth and opened the door. A youth wearing a messenger's uniform greeted him.

The boy handed him a telegram and spoke hesitantly. "Sir, I'm sorry to bother you, but I've been waiting until you got to your room. This is an urgent message from the head telegrapher in Washington."

Grant took the wire, handed the boy a nickel, and opened it. He read its contents in shock. *No, it was impossible.* But the cold hard words blazed at him:

> *The president was assassinated at Ford's Theater at 10:30 tonight and cannot live. The wound is a pistol shot through the head. Secretary Seward and his son Frederick were also assassinated at their residence and are in a dangerous condition. The Secretary of War desires that you return to Washington immediately. Please answer on receipt of this.*
>
> *T. Eckert, Major, Chief Telegrapher*

No!

Julia stared at her silent, stricken husband. He looked calm, but she read sudden, naked pain in his eyes. "What is it, Ulys?" she asked in a fearful voice.

Without saying a word, he handed her the telegram.

As soon as she finished reading, the message fell to the floor. "Oh, my God," she said, then buried the onrushing tears in her hands. A sob racked her. "How could such a dreadful thing happen?"

Grant blew out a deep breath. "It had to be someone insane."

Two hours later, after dropping the distraught Julia off in Burlington, Grant sat staring out the window of the speeding train, seeing nothing, feeling a deep sadness. The passing countryside was a black maze of wet shadow. The color of death, of gloom. Of tragedy. How could it be? Surely it was some kind of a mistake. How could the man who had put the most meaning in his life be gone? And that's what Lincoln had done. He was more than a war president, he was an honest politician trying to reweld a Union.

In just five days—the short time in which the people of the North had rejoiced and lavished honor upon the president and himself—the country had turned from exultation to what could easily be anarchy. The "soft peace" president, that's what the hardliners had called him. And there were plenty of them. The president had tried to reach the public in midweek, bring them down from their jubilation to understand that it would be necessary and difficult to apply a gentle form of reconstruction to get the seceded states successfully back into the Union.

And now the great man had been blasted away by a murderous assassin's bullet, struck down before he could even see the complete peace that should be only a few days away. Sherman, at this very moment, was in contact with Joe Johnston regarding the defensive fox's surrender. Kirby Smith, in command of the only other sizable rebel army, would soon capitulate out West. Canby had entered Mobile, Wilson had ridden into Montgomery.

But Abraham Lincoln would never see it.

Some twelve hours earlier, the president had been so vibrant at the Cabinet meeting, relating how he'd had a strange dream the night before—the type of dream that always portended something important, similar to ones he'd had on the eve of great victories of the past.

And after the meeting, they'd had a few friendly minutes together. That was when Lincoln had invited Julia and him to join Mrs. Lincoln and himself at the theater. But Julia had not wanted to spend an evening with the difficult and unpredictable Mary Lincoln, so she had used as an excuse the need to visit their children in Burlington. The president had been gracious about it. But he was a gracious man.

"—and cannot live." The terrible words from the telegram flashed back.

If he'd only known.

If he'd only gone to the theater. If he'd been in the box with him—if that was where it had happened—he could probably have stopped the assailant. Or if he'd had an aide with him, the assassin might never have gotten near the president. *Oh, God, was it his fault?*

But Seward and his son? What was that all about? Was a master conspiracy afoot? Julia had mentioned a strange man staring at her earlier in the day at Willard's. Then there was the unknown horseman who had ridden up to their carriage on the way to the train station—peering in with a wild look. And the man who had tried to get into their car on the slow ride to Philadelphia—and had been thrown off the train. And lastly, Dana's telegram of warning, telling him to be wary on the return trip, and suggesting that an extra locomotive lead the way to clear any obstruction.

Yes, some fiendish rebel plot must be underway. But what lunacy could bring the perpetrators of such a heinous crime to destroy their best hope for magnanimity, fairness, for a future without retribution? They might just rue the act when Vice President Andrew Johnson gets in the White House. What had he said? "Treason is a crime, and a crime must be punished. Treason must be made famous, and traitors impoverished."

He glanced at his reflection in the window and wiped away a tear.

One of the world's greatest men was dying or already dead.

He had been shot by a coward on Good Friday.

When the train finally pulled into Washington at just before eight, church bells were pealing throughout a city that had been celebrating victory for nearly a week. But now they were ringing for a different reason. The suitably leaden sky hung drably over knots of people who were beginning to collect on street corners. The tenor was mixed sorrow, shock, fear and anger. The derringer bullet John Wilkes Booth, the radical Southern actor, had fired into the back of the president's head had finally done its job.

Lincoln was dead.

Andrew Johnson would soon be president and would retain his predecessor's Cabinet—at least for the present.

Charles Dana was waiting when a grim Ulysses S. Grant strode into the War Department. He quickly briefed the general, ending his narrative with, "The bullet lodged behind his left eyeball. By the time he died, the right side of his face had turned purple and the left eye seemed to pop. It's a blessing that he never recovered consciousness."

"What does Stanton want done?" Grant asked, his anger uncharacteristically evident.

"Since he thinks it's possible this is a giant plot, he is charging you with the security of the city. He wants you to use adequate vigilance, and force where necessary, to guard against the large number of rebel parolees and refugees who are in the capital."

Grant nodded. "Then the parole has been broken?"

"I'm not so sure. This may be a minor conspiracy with a handful of fanatics. From what I've been able to deduce, Booth is wildly unbalanced, and no tie-in to the Confederate military has yet been indicated."

"Of course not," Grant bit out. "It's too early." His eye fell on a telegram from Ord, who was commanding in Richmond. Two members of the Confederate legislature wanted permission to visit the president with important communications. It had arrived the night before. Grant tossed the message to Dana. "By lightning, I'll show them! I'll have Ord throw them in Libby Prison. I'll have all rebel officers who have not taken the oath of allegiance arrested."

Dana shrugged. "I wouldn't get too drastic until we know what's going on."

Grant looked up from the message he had begun to scribble to Ord. His expression was stern. "Don't you consider the president's death drastic?"

Ord's alarmed reply stated that the legislators were old and harmless, and that they certainly wouldn't have requested permission to see the president if they'd been involved with the assassination. He also stated that the arrest of paroled officers would include Lee, and could throw the rebellion back into full force. He insisted that paroles had not been violated, and that the conspiracy was not connected to any known rebel leaders.

By nightfall, Grant had stilled his temper and regained his composure. A persuasive note from Dick Ewell had arrived from Fort Warren, where the "eagle with a lisp" was confined with several other rebel generals. It read:

> *You will appreciate, I am sure, the sentiment that prompts me to drop you these lines. Of all the misfortunes that could befall the Southern people, or any Southern man, by far the greatest would be the idea that they could entertain any other than feelings of unqualified abhorrence and indignation for the assassination of the president of the United States. Need I say that we are not assassins, nor the allies of such, be they from the North or South, and that we would be ashamed of our own people were we not assured that they will reprobate this crime.*

Four days later President Johnson, dignitaries from Congress, the Cabinet, and a few senior military officers were seated in the East Room for the funeral service of Abraham Lincoln. Captain Robert Lincoln, alone representing the family, occupied one of the chairs at the foot of the black cloth-draped casket. At the head of the catafalque stood Grant, also alone. Without thinking, he shifted back and forth from parade rest to the position of attention every few minutes. His blank stare acknowledged nothing, as the words rattled on.

The man he considered the greatest person he'd ever known lay sealed in front of him, never again to speak his homespun wisdom, never again to reflect sorrowfully on the massive problems thrust upon his stooped shoulders.

Oh, Lord, as these people spout words they've organized in eulogy, I ask why. Why do You bestow the mantle of greatness, only to turn it so easily into a shroud? The future of an entire divided country had been put in the hands of a man to whom you had provided many gifts. And now You pluck him away like a blade of grass in the wind.

But we aren't supposed to question, are we?

Within two feet of him, inside the silent black coffin, lay the gaunt face with its gentle eyes closed, the big ears and warts unseen; the strength, the compassion, the immeasurable love of country and his people forever silenced . . .

Grant blinked, his eyes close to brimming.

CHAPTER 57

War is at best barbarism . . . Its glory is all moon-
shine. It is always those who have neither fired a
shot nor heard the shrieks and groans of the
wounded who cry aloud for more blood, more venge-
ance, more desolation. War is hell.
—WILLIAM TECUMSEH SHERMAN

This agreement, if approved by the President of the United States, will
produce peace from the Potomac to the Rio Grande . . ."

Grant read on through Sherman's message, a copy of the formal
surrender terms between the redhead and General Joe Johnston down at
Raleigh, North Carolina. But as he read, he grew uneasy—Sherman had
gone too far!

Sherman's terms required *all* Confederate armies to disband and proceed to their state capitals, where arms were to be turned in to *state* arsenals . . . State officers and legislatures, after taking the oath, would be
reinstated . . . There would be immunity for Confederate citizens, so long
as they lived in peace and quiet, and obeyed the laws . . . A general amnesty.

It went far beyond what even he had given to Lee!

Grant turned to Rawlins. "I wonder what's wrong with Sherman. He
can't get into these areas; they're executive decisions."

Rawlins scowled. "Sounds like the scourge of the South has turned
pussycat. Do you think he has a guilty conscience?"

"Huh, you don't know Sherman. He's just being a gentleman at the
end. He wants general reunion as much as we do. I just can't figure out
why he assumed such sweeping authority."

"Maybe success has gone to his head."

"No, not Sherman."

"What are you going to do?"

"Pass this on to Stanton. He'll give it to the president."

The temper of the Cabinet was obvious. Lincoln had been placed in the
ground only two days earlier and this upstart general wanted to make the
war look like a silly little rebellion, easily erasable by a few words and
the signature of a defeated rebel general. They interpreted Sherman's agreement as a sellout. They seethed, angry in their compelling suspicion that a
hard peace was slipping from their grasp.

Grant chewed a cold cigar as he listened to the venom. Stanton was
most bitter. The secretary's eyes were cold as he said, "There's more to

this than meets the eye, gentlemen. I say Sherman's gotten too big for his goddamned britches! He has big plans for himself, that's what. Remember that push for him to run for the presidency after his Atlanta victory? Well, I think this is nothing but some groundwork for the next election!"

"Just a minute, Mr. Secretary," Grant said firmly. "You are maligning one of the most loyal and unpolitical leaders this country has ever produced."

"I say it's treason!" Stanton retorted.

Grant held his ground. "And I, sir, consider such a statement ridiculous. This war isn't even over yet, and you are condemning one of our most valiant generals for compassion."

President Johnson was also angry. His habitual scowl was worse than usual as he snapped in his Tennessee twang, "Well then, General, would you mind telling us just what the son of a bitch had in mind?"

Grant looked at the former tailor, and remembered that the man hadn't even been able to read until taught by his wife. Without a doubt, a man of Sherman's intellect would be considered a threat by the new resident of the White House. He leaned forward, his expression earnest. "Mr. President, there is no doubt that General Sherman has erred. Your statement is correct that he has—by letting the states keep arms—kept the door open for a return to hostilities. But as far as that being his intent, I know the man better. And if you'll pardon my saying so, he disdains politicians, including his own brother. His being interested in the presidency is out of the question."

Grant looked around at the other Cabinet members, coming back to Johnson. "As far as his terms with General Johnston go, he's dead wrong. He assumed too many prerogatives. I would like to take this agreement back to him personally and have it renegotiated."

The man from Tennessee held Grant's gaze for several moments, then cleared his throat. "All right, General, you go back to Sherman and tear this thing up right in front of him. Then you tell Johnston to surrender properly, or else you'll send every one of his traitorous sons of bitches straight to hell. And if he doesn't like that, you can tell him he'll hang from the same damned tree as Davis. Is that clear?"

"Yes, sir, quite clear." Grant sensed at that moment that Andrew Johnson was not going to be the best president the country ever had.

Sitting over coffee and cigars at Sherman's Raleigh headquarters, Grant handed him the letter Lincoln had dictated back in March—the one in which Grant was directed to deal only in military matters, leaving all political surrender matters to the president. Sherman read the short message and shook his head. He said, "If I'd been aware of this, it could have saved a lot of trouble."

Grant shrugged. "I'm sorry, but I had no idea you'd be in a position where it would matter. We all believed Johnston would be finished along with Lee."

"Well, that's water under the bridge. Johnston will understand. Two days ago, I got a bale of Northern newspapers—all spitting violent words about hard peace and revenge. I sent some over to him along with a note voicing my doubts about acceptance of our terms in Washington."

"Acceptance isn't even close. Angry rejection covers it."

"By whom?"

"The whole Cabinet and the president. Particularly Stanton."

"To hell with him. Doesn't he realize it's over? Damn it, Sam, we've got to start putting the pieces back together."

"I know. But you've been out here in the field a long time. The politicians are flexing their muscles now. As a Southerner who was a loyal Unionist, Andrew Johnson is going to make it hard for those who went with the rebellion. And he's surrounded by snapping dogs."

Sherman sipped from his cup. "I never realized how important Lincoln was to the peace."

"You will now."

"What do you want me to do?"

"Inform General Johnston that the truce is over. You are authorized by Washington to accept only the surrender of his army along the precise lines of Lee's capitulation. All other terms of your original memorandum are negated."

"Why don't you do it?"

Grant looked directly into his eyes. "For two reasons. It really is your show, and I'm not giving them the doggone satisfaction of belittling you in such a manner."

Sherman started to say something, but stopped, cornering his emotions. Slowly, he at last replied, "Thank you, Sam."

But it wasn't that easy for Sherman up north. First Stanton released his original memorandum to the press, then Halleck made a degrading statement. And finally, the radicals jumped on him as if he were an enemy general. The New York *Herald* blasted, "Sherman has fatally blundered; his pen has blurred all the triumphs of his sword!" The Chicago *Tribune* called him a proslaver and a Copperhead plotter, accusing him of being starkly insane.

When the Northern newspapers finally reached Raleigh, Sherman exploded. All of his disgust with newspapermen boiled over once more. He would recover, but his cold revulsion for Stanton and Halleck would not cease for the rest of his life.

The Great War between the States was now a matter of bringing in the last of the diehards. On April 26, the limping actor, John Wilkes Booth, was cornered in a tobacco shed south of Fredericksburg by a platoon of New York cavalry. Outlined by blazing firelight in the burning shed, the scion of a famous theater family was shot through the neck, to die the next morning.

In the Southwest, various remnants of the Confederate Army were faced with their own moments of truth. Kirby Smith had a purported forty thousand men in Texas and Louisiana, but in reality his scattered troops were much fewer in number. But before they could call it quits, an officer who had ridden defiantly out of Fort Donelson through three feet of water as a colonel had to make his decision. He was the only man in either army to enter as a private and achieve the rank of lieutenant general. The former slave trader had been wounded four times, had killed thirty men in hand-to-hand combat, and had had twenty-nine horses shot from under him. Going to Mexico was a popular alternative for Confederates, and he had said, "If one road led to hell and the other to Mexico, I would be indifferent which to take." His name was Nathan Bedford Forrest. When he drew what was left of his command up in their last formation in Gainesville on the 9th of May, he told his veterans to accept the favorable surrender and to return peacefully to their homes.

On the same day at a small hamlet in southern Georgia, a detachment of James Wilson's cavalry surprised the camp of Jefferson Davis. Together with his family, the leader of the rebellion was moved to Macon, to be further dispatched to Fortress Monroe. The last vestige of Confederate government had fallen with a treasury of $3,500 in its fiery president's possession.

Also on May 9, Grant forwarded a special letter recommending John Rawlins's promotion to brevet major general. Through an oversight, the chief of staff's name had been left off the first nominations for the honors list. Grant reflected deeply as he worked through the wording. What would have happened to him in this recent war if Rawlins had not been Rawlins? His mother hen. With his Galena friend now deeply engrossed in polishing the final reports, Grant had been free to perform the myriad requirements of a true general in chief. But that was merely a pebble on the long road on which he and Rawlins had at times tripped, at times had bogged down, and at times had been feted . . .

"General Rawlins has served me through the entire war, from the battle of Belmont to the surrender of Lee. No staff officer ever before had it in his power to render as much service . . ."

On May 30, John Bell Hood and two aides would be caught trying to cross the river outside of Natchez. The crippled general would be making his desperate try for Texas where he intended to raise a last-ditch army.

But the final surrender of the war connected directly to the battle of Fort Donelson. At Galveston, Kirby Smith left a man experienced in capitulation to do the job—Lieutenant General Simon Bolivar Buckner.

CHAPTER 58

Grant glanced up at the grandfather clock. Eight-eleven. He'd been daw-dling over breakfast for nearly an hour. Still time for another cup of coffee, though. Then, on to the greatest day of his life—the second day of the Grand Review, the day the great western army would exhibit itself proudly to the capital. In spite of everything, including his many months with the Army of the Potomac, the gallant colors he'd be seeing today would be *his,* his origins and his constituency.

Julia smiled from across the table. "Afraid you're going to miss it, dear?"

"No, just anticipating a bit."

"Sherman will make it just fine."

"Oh, I'm sure of that. He probably kept everyone in last night to make sure there wasn't any more fighting with the Potomac lads."

Julia shrugged as she filled his cup. "I still don't understand what they're so upset about."

"They're Westerners, dear. And their beloved commander has been slandered. Those gallant rowdies from the little towns and farms of the West have fought themselves proud from Belmont to Raleigh, and they don't take kindly to eastern smears."

"But fighting their brother soldiers at this time of great celebration?"

Grant patted her hand. "It's hard to run down such a tightly coiled spring, my dear. They'd just as soon attack the Army of the Potomac in full force as be insulted. But Sherman has them spending their energies on the parade ground."

"I thought you said he doesn't believe in drill."

"For this shindig today, he does. He's had them marching their legs off for three days. And at yesterday's review he looked like an enemy spy. I saw the glint in his eye as he watched Meade's boys. He's got something up his sleeve."

Julia quietly sipped her coffee for a moment before she unsnapped the locket at her wrist. The tiny face of the young man she'd married peered out, a bit faded, but still recognizable. She spoke softly. "Ulys, do you think this young Mexican War hero ever dreamed such a day as this would come?"

Grant hadn't seen that tiny photo since his wedding night so long ago in St. Louis. How vain he'd been to give her such a thing—but it was about all he could afford at the time. "No," he replied. "All I wanted to do was teach math. And I wish I could have. I also wish there wouldn't have been a reason for a parade like this. Then there wouldn't be thousands of needless graves around this country, and there wouldn't be all those ghosts to watch the victors prance. No, my dear, that young man didn't know much, and he didn't ever dream of anything like this."

Julia came around his chair and brushed her lips against his cheek. "Now, don't spoil it, darling. I was just trying to say that I always knew you'd be someplace like this today. My mother was right about the greatness."

Grant stood and took her in his arms. "Greatness, my dear, is spelled *l-u-c-k.* I'm not so doggone sure that I still don't belong back there at Hardscrabble cutting wood. If I'd been a better farmer, that's where I might be. Now, come on, I have to get into the rest of this silly dress uniform and take my sword to the parade."

* * *

In Elihu Washburne's house, two guests were also rolling up their napkins. Charles A. Dana and John Rawlins had begun breakfast with their host at seven. "Well, John," the congressman said, "it's too bad you aren't going to be out there riding at the head of a division or something."

Rawlins shrugged. "Why? That kind of thing wasn't for me."

"According to Grant you could have been a great commander."

"He's prejudiced."

"He has a right to be," Dana interjected. "He couldn't have gotten the job done without you."

"Huh, I'm not so sure. As I look back, I wonder if I wasn't too much of an alarmist."

"None of it hurt, did it?"

"I don't know. He and I haven't been as close in the last few months."

"Do I detect a bit of pique?" Washburn asked.

"No, just fact. The general hasn't needed me as much. Nor any of us, for that matter."

Washburne nodded. "I guess we can be thankful that we were able to be a part of it. I certainly had no idea he'd reach these heights when you talked me into his nomination for brigadier back in 'sixty-two."

"What do you think he'll do now?" Dana asked.

"His goddamnedest to put it back together."

"That won't be easy, with Johnson and Stanton thirsting for blood."

"No, it won't," Rawlins said, "But he'll sure try."

Dana turned to Washburne. "Do you think you can talk him into running in 'sixty-eight?"

The congressman smiled. "Oh, I think we can convince him—if it's a matter of duty."

Rawlins agreed. "But he won't campaign."

"He won't have to."

"What about you, John?" Dana asked. "What are your plans?"

"I'm not sure. Just try to keep on living, I guess. This damned cough of mine never seems to let up. I had dinner with Grenville Dodge last night, and he invited me to come out West to see if the dry climate will do any good. I might just take him up on it one of these days."

"But for today, you're just going to watch your proud Army of the Tennessee strut its stuff. Right?"

"Absolutely right!"

Two hundred thousand blue-clad soldiers were just part of the assorted mass of people who had descended on Washington for the huge celebration and final look at the Grand Army of the Republic. Festive celebrants had been arriving for over a week from as far away as Vermont and Minnesota. Hotel rooms were filled beyond capacity; fortunately, the balmy late May weather invited outdoor sleeping. Just getting fed was a problem for the hordes of celebrating tourists, who were also placing a heavy drain on city whiskey barrels.

President Johnson had finally declared the war officially over. Down came the black crepe of grief that had marked the city for so long. Up went the red, white, and blue bunting, hanging from every conceivable place. The United States had come out of mourning and four years of debilitating war with all the zest it could muster. And she was having a party.

From sunrise to sunset the day before, national flags had waved at full mast from every flagpole and balcony in the city. Hasty grandstands had been erected along much of Pennsylvania Avenue to hold just a portion of the hordes of spectators who had begun vying for position at midnight. The previous day's parade, accompanied by dozens of bands and the singing of thousands, had been a masterful show. Major General George Meade, out of the public eye since a battle with the press had banished him from print, had ridden at the head of his proud Army of the Potomac. Row after row of glittering, smartly turned-out troops had followed their general to the reviewing stand.

But even then, Meade was not to be granted his due. With Sheridan out in Texas on a special mission, the seven miles of cavalry neared the White House without its colorful leader. Suddenly a twenty-five-year-old major general of one month lost control of his "spooked" horse and stole the show. George Armstrong Custer, with long yellow curls flying, managed to bring his magnificent mount under control just past the presidential reviewing stand.

Grant had watched with pleasure as the battle streamers of the Army of the Potomac, so voluminous that they were unrecognizable, were carried by in the hands of grizzled veterans—some of whom had fought from Bull Run to Appomattox, and were still no more than twenty-one years old.

Yes, it had been quite a show.

But today was the finale, the day of the West!

At three minues before nine, Sherman sat on his favorite bay on a small rise, waiting to join the head of his column. Personally, he was ready. Every touch of metal on his finely tailored dress uniform had been polished to a high luster; his shiny boots reflected each dancing touch of light. The gold color of his general's sash and the trimming on his bright saddle blanket accentuated the predominant dark blues and chestnut browns. The white stock at his throat matched his spotless gloves and the nose blaze and one hoof of his beautiful mount. The round-crowned, medium-brimmed hat which he favored topped off his close-cropped, thinning red hair and beard. Only the memory of Meade's fine show of the day before tweaked at his composure . . . that and the knowledge that his major detractors awaited on the reviewing stand.

He'd been jealous of the fine appearance of Meade's troops the day before, no doubt about it. But why should his proud army try to be what it wasn't? By God, they'd fought from one end of the country to the other, hadn't they? His quartermaster had found a number of new uniforms, but a large portion of his boys were still in the worn, faded rags they'd fought in . . . not much better off than the lads they'd defeated.

Shortly before turning in the night before, he'd made his decision. No mincing, awkward steps for *this* army. They'd, by God, march with their heads up and eyes fifteen feet to the front—swinging along in the lope that had brought them from one victory to another. Long hair, tatters and all!

Pride swelled in him as he glanced over the massed column. The wave of humanity and horseflesh simmering in the bright morning sunlight was coiled for its final effort. Never again would these brave men be together. Never again would the brotherhood of the West be one. He nodded to Howard, who would ride with him. The one-armed Bible thumper had proved to be his best. Yet Logan would ride in Howard's place at the head of the Army of the Tennessee; that much Black Jack deserved after being passed over for its command way back at Atlanta. And his old XV Corps would lead the entire column.

As the spring tightened, a dozen drums began to roll. Regimental colors sprang to attention as the huge body collected itself, and the crash of the howitzer finally signaled the beginning of the end.

Sherman smiled at Howard and urged the bay forward to the rousing strains of "The Battle Hymn of the Republic." In moments he was in place, heading for Pennsylvania Avenue and the waiting throngs of admirers. The entry onto the avenue looked like a gate into a human sea. For a fleeting second he thought of himself as Moses parting the waters. He chuckled at the ridiculous metaphor as the first cheers greeted him. He removed his hat, but rode erectly, facing forward. From the corner of his eye, he detected signs that read, HAIL CHAMPIONS OF DONELSON; HAIL WINNERS AT SHILOH; HAIL CONQUERORS OF VICKSBURG. Other names dotted the huge crowd: Chattanooga, Atlanta, Savannah, Charleston, Corinth. *Hail!*

Hail to Sherman!

Joyous and tearful women held their babies aloft to see. Kerchiefs and scarves waved in the bright, cool air. The cheers continued, as did the singing. "John Brown's body lies amoldering in the grave" was the most repetitious.

Hail! Even his Kentucky thoroughbred, Lexington, seemed to know as he tossed his head and arched his neck.

Oh, how he wanted to turn and check his column. Were those lean ploughboys and woodsmen, those tough Chicago lads and river roustabouts, were they staying straight in line, not gawking? Was the crowd jeering at the high-stepping Negroes with their pigs and goats on leash? After all, they were a part of the ragamuffin legion that had cut the swath across Georgia and broken the heart of the enemy—they belonged in this review too!

But he couldn't look. As soon as the slope in front of the Treasury Building was rounded, the reviewing stand would slide into view. And there, Sam Grant, touching elbows with those who had called him traitor, would be waiting . . .

Grant, hearing but not listening to the light banter between President John-son and Secretary Stanton, turned to see if Ellen Sherman was with Julia. But the high silk hats of all those dignitaries who could buy a place on the reviewing stand obscured his view. He turned as the loud cheer from the Treasury Building announced the arrival of the Army of the West. Sher-man's red head, proud in the sun, topped the rise. He felt his throat tighten and wondered if tears would betray him.

The Army of the Tennessee! A kaleidoscope of memories flashed before him: spurring his horse up the gangplank at Belmont, a gallant old warrior named Smith telling him quietly that Donelson would be taken . . . the nightmare at Shiloh, the frustration of Vicksburg, the miracle of Missionary Ridge . . . Sherman talking him out of quitting, the intense Rawlins ever at his side . . . the brilliant engineer McPherson, the blue-clad corpses and the other faceless ones along the way . . .

He saw Sherman replace his hat and reach for his sword. Cheers began to rise from the reviewing stand, cheers of gratitude and adulation. Grant came to attention. The pitch rose, as a thousand voices joined in. Sherman's gleaming sword snapped into its salute as his head turned. Abruptly, Grant's right hand rose in the most precise salute he had ever rendered. Never had he felt such pride. The lean general on the gleaming, high-stepping bay personified it all.

Then, as Sherman swung out of the line of march to join the reviewing party, Grant's eyes settled on the limp sleeve of Howard, then Logan, with the long black hair and intense eyes . . . and finally on the long-stepping, springy XV Corps. A wide grin broke over Grant's face as the boys of the Fifteenth, without turning their heads or breaking their steely stare to the front, removed their hats with their free hands and broke forth in a lusty cheer!

That was what Sherman had had up his sleeve!

Grant turned to greet the redhead, who was shaking hands with the president. Then the warm grip was his. He looked into the bright smile and said, "Well done, Sherman, well done!"

Sherman nodded. "Just a bunch of country boys, Sam, trying out the city."

Stanton's outstretched hand was next, but Sherman's smile froze in-stantly. With a short, disdainful glance, Sherman walked past the secretary of war and shook the hand of the next Cabinet member. The timing was perfect and would be widely reported. Grant felt a surge of approval, then turned back to watch more of his Army of the Tennessee. From behind, he heard a voice say, "They march like the lords of the world."

Another smile touched Grant's lips.

They are.

PART THREE

CHAPTER 59

O ne war is over, the other has begun. The first was known by many terms, such as the War Between the States, the War of the Rebellion, the Civil War—even the War of Northern Aggression, as some Southerners referred to it. The second can be called the War of Vengeance." This statement appeared in *Army* magazine the day after the Grand Review.

Grant summarized it otherwise to the one-armed Otis Howard as the general sat in his office at the War Department on the 28th of May: "I'd say we fought over two opposing economic systems, and the outcome might be described as the captains of industry over the lords of the manor—or more simply, the factory empire over the plantation paradise."

The handsome Howard nodded his head. "I'd say, sir, that you've made an apt appraisal. And the victors, by hook or by crook, want not just their ounce of blood, but their pound of flesh."

"Correct. But it isn't just the captains, but those politicians whose strings those captains pull who will demand the most Southern blood. But that's the problem at the top level. Your problem, General, will involve everyone from politician to military commander, from defeated legislator and civil official, shopkeeper and farmer, to the coloreds themselves—"

"Excuse me, sir," said Porter, interrupting from the doorway, "but General Eaton is here."

The former regimental chaplain saluted and warmly shook Grant's hand, then was introduced to Howard. Grant said, "I sent for you because you are probably the most experienced man in the country when it comes to the liberated Negro. As head of the new Freedman's Bureau, General Howard will need your advice and help."

He'd known how Lincoln had desired that the religious and caring Howard be given this important job, and had been pleased when President Johnson had honored that wish by appointing him. He'd also wondered if John Eaton hadn't felt a twinge of disappointment at not getting the position himself. He'd had Rawlins check it out with the clergyman, and had been told that Eaton, without rancor, would do whatever was necessary to meet the huge problem.

After talking around the matter for a few minutes, Eaton said, "Sure, this new bureau has responsibility, but I see it also as an *opportunity*." His eyes brightened. "How many men get a chance to be instrumental in helping four million persons rise out of the constraints of slavery to enter a free society? I tell you, we're *lucky!*"

"I agree," Howard replied. "I believe God has charged us with a huge responsibility, but unless we do it wisely and fairly, He will chasten us."

"Yes," Eaton said. "The bureau must first see the true needs, then act vigorously."

"What do you see as the basic needs?" Grant asked.

Eaton's brow furrowed. "Education. I don't mean formal education at the outset, but they need to be taught how to master the simple needs of survival as free people . . . how to be employed, how to handle money, how to plan ahead, how to assume responsibility. Oh, school is a part of it, but mainly for the children. And rights. The Negro must have equal rights with the white man."

"You've been working with them in the South," Howard said. "Do you think this is possible in the rebel states—now?"

"I don't think it will be immediate, but most responsible whites down there will be fair. We may have to wach them closely at first. The legislative process has many loopholes." He looked at Howard. "As you know, several religious organizations and aid societies have been involved in this work. They are fired with crusading zeal that we must channel, because that's where many of our teachers—our missionaries, so to speak—are going to come from. How is this to be handled?"

"It's an army operation all the way," Howard replied. "I plan on having a sort of general staff, with an adjutant, an inspector general, a finance officer, commissary, medical officer, quartermaster, and so on. I also plan to appoint assistant commissioners in different areas. These will be senior army officers and they will have their own departments."

"Yes," Eaton said. "As we did during the war, we'll have to feed and clothe them for a time; give them medical care. And your inspector general will probably have his hands full with all of the cheating that will go on. I can tell you right now that getting fair wages for these people will be difficult—particularly with money being short. Even if they're paid in goods, they'll be victimized."

"Yes," Grant interjected, "and we may have to keep an eye on some of our own people. I can see where a charlatan might take advantage."

Both of his visitors chimed in with, "Yes, sir."

They talked on for another forty minutes with the upshot that Howard had learned a great deal, Grant felt confident in him, and Eaton would go to the vital District of Columbia and Maryland as assistant commissioner. That would also keep him in the neighborhood, should his counsel be desired.

The Freedmen's Bureau was ready to face its enormous challenge.

President Andrew Johnson was facing a challenge as well. Although a loyal Unionist throughout the war, he was still a Southerner, and as he grew more acclimated to the White House, his militancy toward the seceded states diminished and the honeymoon between him and the Republican radicals was over. In fact the battle lines were well-drawn. It didn't take him long to start proving that he would never fill Abraham Lincoln's big footsteps, and his opponents were ever ready to cash in on his faux pas. He issued a weighty proclamation that ignored suffrage for the Negro, and, because he regarded the wealthy men of the South with suspicion, he excluded from his general amnesty those men who owned property worth a minimum of $20,000. The suffrage matter, in particular, was just the ammunition Johnson's radical enemies needed and bitter invectives began to assail him.

Conversely Ulysses S. Grant was, hands down, the most popular man in the country. He was the darling of Northern newspapers, praised daily for his self-restraint, simplicity, and lack of personal ambition. It seemed that the very taciturnity that had marked his life was the trait that made him most attractive to the American public. Grateful citizens heaped gifts upon him. Horses, swords, boxes of fine cigars, honorary degrees, and less significant items such as photographs and poetry cascaded in; but the house at 2009 Chestnut Street in Philadelphia was the most valuable of these tributes.

Presented by the Union League Club to Julia, the small mansion was completely furnished with elegant furniture, a fine piano, a beautifully bound Bible—even an excellent bust of Grant that rested on a richly carved pedestal. The house with its rococo styling was too ostentatious for Grant's taste, but he said nothing and commuted from it to Washington for a period—when he wasn't traveling with his family around the North. There they were greeted by all kinds of public receptions, from parades to eager citizens simply gathered along the road on the slim chance that they might get to shake the general's hand. At one stop, when the crowd begged Grant to give a speech, little Jesse, now seven, implored his papa to do as he was asked. With a laugh, a member of the crowd shouted, "Then *you* give us a speech, boy!"

Before anyone could stop him, Jesse launched bravely into "The Boy Stood on the Burning Deck."

And the crowd loved it!

In June the Grants went to New York City to be part of a rally at Cooper Union in support of the president. Even in the morning, a vast crowd had gathered to meet them as they arrived at the Astor House. The general received visitors for two hours, shaking hands so many times that his right hand grew red and swollen. That afternoon at a dinner, several boring speakers paraded to the lectern before it was Grant's turn. Then he spoke in his normal, quiet manner, making the statement that was growing famous: "I rise only to say I don't intend to say anything. Thank you for your kind words and hearty welcome."

Robust applause followed.

But he did break the pattern that evening. At Cooper Union, a local politician was in the middle of a sentence when a chant that grew quickly in intensity shut him out. "Grant—Grant—Grant—Grant—Grant" announced the general's arrival. On stage, General Black Jack Logan, who was scheduled to speak later, grinned broadly. Only because of urgent requests to say something did Grant finally accede. He murmured, "I want to thank you for inviting me here tonight. It gives me pleasure."

Cheers echoed through the Union as he returned to his seat.

Sitting there, he recalled that he hadn't said anything favorable about President Johnson. But he did note that his reception was pleasing. Yes, he actually liked it, enjoyed being celebrated by the people . . .

A rain squall had just passed, leaving the air moist and fresh as Grant stood on the promontory, the point of ground above the Plain that looked north over the wide bend in the Hudson River. It had been twenty-two years since he had last stood in this spot. His graduation was a clear memory—that time when he had admitted to himself for the first time that he felt pride in belonging to the brotherhood of West Point. He'd been twenty-one years old. He took in a deep breath and watched a small steamer chugging upriver, dark smoke puffing out of her single stack. Further away, a tiny boat was looking about for the light and capricious wind, its sail white against the dark green of the water. The proud hills on each side of the river still watched serenely. It was so green, so overwhelming, so utterly still.

"It's beautiful, darling," Julia said softly from his elbow. "Different from all those other rivers we've seen."

"One forgets," he replied.

"I would have come here often, I think, had I been your girl then. Could you have spent much time with me?"

"No. Cadets were always busy."

She took his arm. "We could have stolen the time."

Grant looked back at the river. "I've often recalled this scene."

"What else?"

"We're going there next—the riding hall. That's where young Fred is meeting us."

"Yes, where you had your greatest triumphs. My brother wrote glowingly about what a magnificent rider you were. I believe that was when I first became interested in you. I pictured you as a strong, gallant young man on a mighty steed. Yes, and always jumping over an obstacle."

The roar of the cadets came back to him as he was once more in the high, long hall. He trotted York back for another jump. The hall was packed; it was his moment, his and York's. And Sergeant Herschberger's. He could even smell the place—sawdust and tanbark. How the big, cantankerous sorrel had glistened. He had tied the record, then asked for the bar to be raised. He could see the pride in the old dragoon's eyes.

And away they flew . . .

* * *

The telegram had read, "From the oldest general to the ablest." It had moved him—quite an accolade from a distinguished man who was "a year older than the American Constitution." He had never forgotten seeing those two magnificent officers at the parade back when he was a raw plebe. C. F. Smith and this fanciful older man they called "Old Fuss and Feathers." He'd thought they were the two most splendid officers in the world. And now he'd been invited to the Cozzens Hotel to see the one who had survived.

Lieutenant General Winfield Scott greeted him warmly. "It's my pleasure, General Grant. Do come in and have a spot of tea with me, or something stronger, if you wish."

"Tea will be fine, sir," Grant replied. Why did he feel insecure in the presence of this great man? It was as if he were an impostor wearing these three stars in front of a *real* lieutenant general!

The white-haired Scott's voice had a slight quaver in it, but his eyes were bright. He said, "I live here at West Point because of its fine army traditions. Couldn't go back to Virginia. You know I was born there, of course. In fact, I'm the only regular army officer—non-West Pointer—from Virginia who didn't run back to fight for the Confederacy."

Grant took the proffered chair. "I didn't know that, sir."

"Yes, and I sent Robert E. Lee up here as superintendent in 'fifty-two. I read something about a parole for him, involving you. What's that about?"

"There are those who want a full pound of flesh, General. Butler came down from Massachusetts to tell the president that Confederate generals were not immune from civil process. Then a grand jury in Norfolk indicted Lee for treason, and he appealed to me. I told him to apply for a pardon, which he sent to me. I took it to the president, who thought Lee and company could be tried, but I explained that the terms of the surrender precluded such, unless they violated parole."

"And that was the end of that."

"So far, sir."

The hero of the War of 1812 thanked the waiter as he brought fresh tea. "I see they've been talking about you as president, General. What's the story on that?"

"Well, it doesn't mean anything. I'm perfectly content in my present position."

Scott cackled. "I've heard that story before. They started talking me up for the presidency as early as 'thirty-nine. Then I ran on the Whig ticket in 'fifty-two. Got soundly thrashed by Pierce. I'm not so sure we generals are worldly enough in politics for such offices. Maybe too naive."

They talked on, mostly about the war. The portly Scott was particularly interested in Vicksburg. Then he asked, "What about Halleck? I heard rumors that he undermined you at times."

Grant shook his head. "I have no evidence of such. Since there's no need of having two chiefs of staff now, I'm going to give him command of the Division of the Pacific."

"And Sherman?"

"Command of the Department of Missouri."

"Sheridan?"

"He's got the Military Division of the Gulf, where he's providing moral and material support to Juarez and his liberal forces against the French-imposed government of Maximilian in Mexico."

"Yes, I did read about that. Is that Johnson's idea?"

Grant sipped his tea. "Not exactly. I don't think the French have any business down there. But there isn't anything official about what Sheridan's doing. He's just got a good-sized army for Maximilian to think about."

"He's some fighter, isn't he?"

"The best, General. I think if I told him to take *Europe,* he'd do it."

Scott smiled, and after a pause asked, "What about troops in the South?"

"I think we have a big enough problem with Reconstruction without rubbing blue uniforms into those folks. I'm going to try and keep it to the minimum. One thing I won't do is send colored troops down there. I'm afraid that would be too much, at least for some time." Grant gave him a brief rundown on the Freedman's Bureau.

Finally, after over an hour, Scott sighed. "An old man gets tired, General. I've most enjoyed your discourse, and I want you to know that I'm right here if you need anything."

Grant thanked him, shook his hand, and departed.

Winfield Scott would die in a year.

At an earlier time, when asked what he would do after the war, Grant had replied, "Why, I think I'll run for mayor of Galena and put in a sidewalk." When the Grants arrived in a special railroad car in August, it seemed the whole town had turned out to welcome him. He had lived in the town less than a year, but the populace was eager to claim him as their own. Stretching across Main Street in front of the De Soto House was a huge sign that shouted, GENERAL, HERE IS YOUR SIDEWALK.

Their gift was another house, not as elegant as the one in Philadelphia, but completely furnished and ready for occupancy should the Grants desire to return to what the Galenians liked to refer to as "their home."

Following a short stop in Ohio, where Grant spent some time with the quiet Hannah and the still more than opinionated Jesse, it was back to work in Washington. But living in Philadelphia was simply too impractical. After moving into a rented house in Georgetown Heights, they found a fine four-story house to buy at 205 I Street near New Jersey Avenue. The price was an attractive $30,000 that was favorably financed. To make it more appealing, the committee that had purchased the Philadelphia house for the Grants shipped all of its furniture and draperies to their new home. And to top it all off, these fine Pennsylvanians also found good renters for their gift house. Julia was ecstatic because now she had a most acceptable place to entertain in a manner befitting the general in chief.

With the acquisition of real estate and the honors of a grateful nation behind him, it was time for Grant to face his next step—his role in the peacetime conflicts of the newly reunited United States.

CHAPTER 60

G rant's immense popularity was not lost on the men seeking power, whether they were New York financiers or the radical Republicans. A man did not have to be too astute to see that the general was vastly more popular than the less than competent president, or that Ulysses S. Grant could well be the next president of the United States. In fact, possibly the only man who didn't see him in the White House was Grant himself. In the spring of 1866, Dick Taylor, the son of "Old Rough and Ready" and Jefferson Davis's onetime brother-in-law, came north on a visit to Washington. It was to Taylor over a quiet supper that Grant said, "These months in Washington have made politics and politicians all the more distasteful to me. I wish that I could lock myself up in my office and simply confine my duties to the actual running of the army."

A week after this, John Rawlins spirited Grant off for an afternoon ride near the old George Washington estate at Mount Vernon. They took a steamer down the Potomac, rode their horses down the gangplank, and trotted off into the profusion of the late Virginia spring. Rawlins had eschewed an immediate escort, although Sergeant Major Bolding rode quietly a few paces to the rear. Topping a rise where a lane led off the highway, they rode on to an open bluff overlooking the broad river. There they stopped, Rawlins sitting easily on his black gelding, while Grant lit a cigar. Putting his lighter away, Grant said, "I'm glad you talked me into this little jaunt, Rawlins. Cincinnati needed a workout and it was good for me to get out of the city."

"I had to talk to you totally alone, General."

Grant looked out at the dark green river as a boat blasted its whistle. "I figured that."

"I want you to take stock."

"Of what?"

"Of who you are and where you are."

"And that is?"

Rawlins coughed into his handkerchief and cleared his throat. "You are possibly the most popular, sought-after, *naive* man in America. The president wants everyone to think you are fully aligned with him, the radical Republicans are doing their goddamnedest to make it look like you agree with them, those rich men in New York are still falling all over themselves trying to figure out what to give you next, and even the Southerners are saying something nice about you once in a while."

Grant removed his hat and brushed off a big bug. "I think you worry too easily," he replied.

Rawlins frowned. "No, I don't. You've been plied with one gift after another. Several of those gentlemen in New York gave you that fine horse, the fifty so-called solid men in Boston gave you the seventy-five-thousand-dollar library. This was followed with another gift of one hundred thousand dollars from New York to pay off your mortgage. Do you honestly think all of these offerings are strictly because they just wish you well?"

"That's all the good it will do them."

"I know that. You're possibly the most honest man in Washington. But you are too damned *gullible*! Remember when we first came here in 'sixty-four? I told you I was worried then, and now I'm *more* worried. You simply have no idea of the power you hold in your hands."

"Well, I don't want it."

"You may mean that now, but you have a chink in your armor, General."

"And what's that?"

"You *like* being popular. That makes you accessible."

"No one can buy me."

Rawlins tugged at his fierce black beard. "I know. But I once heard Lincoln say, 'There's a funny thing about being president. Once a man starts getting it in his head, the strangest things start happening. His mouth keeps on denying that he wants any part of it, but that head of his starts getting more and more familiar with Pennsylvania Avenue.' "

Grant shook his head and clamped down on the cigar. "Lincoln wasn't talking about me."

Rawlins leaned over and put his hand on Grant's shoulder. "You are my finest friend, Ulys. I give thanks to God every night for letting me be close to you, but I fear for you. There are men out there who would sell an ounce of your body, a drop of your blood, the very ash from your cigar . . . given half the chance."

Grant smiled. "Thanks for the warning, but as I said, I think you worry too easily. Besides, how can they take advantage of me when you're around?"

"I'm not that close anymore."

"I'm only a whistle away."

"Just be careful and store this little lecture away, will you, please?"

Grant nodded. "I will."

Elihu Washburne smiled as he handed Grant a cup of coffee. They were in the congressman's parlor on a Sunday afternoon in late July. John Rawlins sat off to the side beaming like a cat with feathers around his mouth. "General," Washburne said, "I have some wonderful news for you. I know you've known this has been afoot for some time, but I have the proud opportunity to tell you that it will soon be official—in two days, as a matter of fact. By what may well be the last act of the first session of the Thirty-ninth Congress, you are to be promoted to the rank of general of the army."

Grant's expression didn't change.

"Not since George Washington has an officer held this exalted rank, not even Scott. It is but one more endorsement by the people for your remarkable feats in the war. To most, it is also one more acknowledgment that you are the savior of the Union."

"Which you are!" Rawlins said, raising his coffee cup. "If we were drinking men, this would be a glass. But the meaning is the same—congratulations, General. Now, we'll have to have a *four-star* shoulder board made!"[3]

Grant had, naturally, heard about the bill creating the rank, but hadn't expected it to pass. Why should it? He could do the job with three stars, or even with two. It was the designation of general in chief that counted. Still, a man would have to be crazy not to be pleased by the honor. He held up his coffee cup.

"Hear, hear!" Washburne said over his raised cup. "To the general of the army!"

"To the general of the army!" Rawlins echoed.

Grant nodded his head. It was yet another honor for the family. And Julia in particular would be most pleased. With emoluments and salary, he would be earning some $20,000 per year—enough to readily enable them to live and entertain on the scale required of the general in chief.

Yes, it was a nice thing. He said, "I know both of your Machiavellian hands were in on this, even though that man in Massachusetts started it. I want to thank you."

His two friends brought their cups up again. Washburne said, "To the best investment we ever made for our country—General of the Army Ulysses S. Grant."

Rawlins added, "Hear, hear!"

The tug-of-postwar between Johnson and the radicals continued after the 1866 election and on into the following year when an equally uncooperative 40th Congress was at loggerheads with the president. And it wasn't just the Congress, his own Cabinet was in the act in the person of the conniving Ewin Stanton. Finally, Johnson would brook no more insubordination in his own house; he fired Stanton. Later, *Harper's Weekly* tried to put the whole Reconstruction picture into context:

> *Ah, Reconstruction—the means by which the defeated South will rebuild itself politically (with a great deal of Northern control). This program has followed a path that would be hard to believe if we had not already had a war over the differences. Let's look at the events—*
>
> *1. A Southerner is in the White House. He understands Southern thinking and doesn't want to cram too much that is indigestible down the throats of Southern political leaders. In essence, he wants to rehabilitate*

those states, and if they repudiate secession, take oaths of loyalty, ratify the constitutional amendment abolishing slavery, their congressmen and senators can be reseated in the Congress. Yet even he doesn't completely trust their leaders.

2. Congress is controlled by the Republicans, many of whom are radical in their approach to the victor getting the spoils (i.e., the merchant prince structure of the North and the high tariffs that protect it). The view of the radicals is that seceded states committed suicide and cannot be restored as states, nor have a voice in the federal government until that government says so. They have been at extreme odds with the president since the end of the war.

3. Thus we have the age-old dilemma—who runs the country, the president or the Congress?

4. And what about the Negro? The radicals want enfranchisement for the former slaves, and disenfranchisement for the whites . . . who will not stand for coloreds ruling them. Suffrage for the Negro is a badly bouncing ball. Several Southern states are adopting "black codes" designed to tie the colored man to a system barely different from slavery. The radicals protest strongly, but the fact remains that few Northern states actually give the Negro equality.

5. And in the middle of it all is the nation's great hero, Ulysses S. Grant, the softspoken man who won the war and the heart of the North. The radicals tug at him, as does the president, both wanting his considerable influence. But he stands above the smoke, unwilling to align himself with either faction.

6. The army's Freedman's Bureau tries to take care of the black man in the South, but has its problems. The president sets up five military districts to be administered by army generals acting roughly as governors. (One of these is George Thomas, the Rock of Chickamauga.) With all of the struggling over the Negro, the country forgets that poor whites in the South need assistance as well. And a new name for a bird of prey has become commonplace: the carpetbagger.

7. Secretary of War Stanton thumbs his nose at the president and Johnson fires him. But Stanton won't leave, citing the newly passed Tenure of Office Act, which precludes a Cabinet member's dismissal without Senate approval. But Congress is out. Johnson declares the office vacant and appoints the popular General Grant, who agrees, after strenuous objection, to fill the post only until the Senate returns and makes a decision. They do, in favor of Stanton, and Grant resigns the interim secretaryship. Johnson flies into a rage, accusing Grant of breaking his word—which finally ruptures his pleasant relationship with the general for good.

8. As 1868 begins to mature, Reconstruction has not been resolved, and another major political event hovers over the horizon: November madness that will probably put a new face in the White House. Will that face, undoubtedly one accustomed to the highest of military honors, be able to solve these ills?

*   *   *

The split between the president and Grant over his giving up the War Department portfolio was not a pretty thing for either of them. Grant stuck to his guns that he had agreed only to an ad interim appointment, and would leave the position at such time as the law prescribed. Like a petulant child, Johnson flailed at him for being untrustworthy. And Grant stumbled, indecisively, at the onslaught.

John Rawlins had been on an extensive trip through the West with Major General Grenville Dodge, who had resigned from the army to become chief engineer with the company building the Union Pacific Railroad. The chief of staff had been granted an extended leave of absence to take care of personal matters and recover his health. It was felt that the dry air of the West would be good for his infected lungs, and for a time he believed this had been true. But soon his flagging strength and persistent cough told him otherwise. At the first word of Grant's problem with Johnson, he rushed back to Washington to lend his experience as a lawyer to the growing turmoil.

"It's an obvious ploy by the president to discredit you," Rawlins said, after listening to what had taken place. He looked tired and thin, but the fire was still in his black eyes as he paced around Grant's desk.

"I should have read the Tenure of Office Act closely," Grant said, frowning. "It specifically forbids my holding that secretaryship once the Senate has acted. For me to do so would bring on a ten-thousand-dollar fine and a possible five-year prison sentence. When I brought this to the president's attention, he told me he would pay the fine and serve my time, if necessary."

"That's pure bullshit!" Rawlins snapped. "Imagine a president of the United States making such a statement! And I'm sure he said it without witnesses. Andrew Johnson is no genius, but he has political cunning. But it doesn't matter now. Is Stanton back?"

"Yes, but Johnson won't accept him."

"This will positively bring on his impeachment."

Grant shook his head. "Why can't he understand it is the will of the people that matters? He constantly insists that it is the chief executive, employing the legality of the Constitution, who prevails."

"Okay, I'll help you with a letter to him. We'll employ a little political and legal muscle, and end this damned farce."

The press had a field day with the quarrel. One pro-radical newspaper, the New York *Tribune,* commented, "In a question of veracity between U.S. Grant and Andrew Johnson, between a soldier whose honor is as untarnished as the sun, and a president who has betrayed every friend, and broken every promise, the country will not hesitate."

Pro-Johnson newspapers characteristically accused Grant of being drunk.

That albatross continued to hang around Grant's neck. A few months earlier Ben Butler, active in Massachusetts politics again, claimed to have set detectives on Grant's trail "to prove that the general was still a drunkard, after fast horses, women and whores."

Sherman, who had been rewarded with the vacated lieutenant generalcy, came into town to render his support to his old friend. The redhead had earlier been offered the secretary of war post by Johnson, and had vehemently turned it down. Following dinner at the Grant house the night after he arrived, cigars were lit as Julia poured coffee. "What's he going to do about the presidency, Mrs. Grant?" Sherman asked lightly.

"I don't know, General. He won't talk about it." She caressed Grant's cheek. "Will you, dear?"

"I feel as Sherman does about politicians, darling."

"And right now, probably stronger," Sherman added. "But you can't keep on ignoring them, Sam. You are the heads-on favorite of anyone and everyone to be the next president. Hell, even the Democrats would run you in a minute."

Grant blew out bluish smoke. "I don't care."

Sherman mentioned his brother John, the senator. "He hopes you turn down the nomination. He says your military accomplishments will not shield you from the partisan abuse you would get in the election. You know it'll be a no-holds-barred contest."

"I know. Say, I saw the best-looking bay mare the other day."

Sherman grinned. "I knew it. The word's around that every time someone brings up your entry into politics, you start talking about horses."

Grant smiled. "That mare just *reeks* of speed."

CHAPTER 61

When Andrew Johnson appointed Lorenzo Thomas, the former army adjutant general, to replace Stanton as another interim secretary of war, the die was finally cast. The House voted to impeach the president. In April, Johnson appointed Major General John M. Schofield, nine years Grant's junior, to the Cabinet post. Schofield, out of respect to his former boss, made the situation easy, but Grant remained as aloof from him as possible.

And another die had been cast . . .

Like it or not, through his confrontation with Johnson, Grant had entered the political arena. He was even talked into accepting a tacit truce with influential Congressman Ben Butler after the former general had decided to jump on Grant's bandwagon and forget their wartime troubles. This was perhaps the most bitter political pill to swallow, but Butler did have the muscle to help him on various vital army programs.

Grant kept totally out of the impassioned impeachment trial, another sign of growing political acuity to his observers. Actually, he was reacting out of natural instinct—it was dirty political linen that was being washed in public, and he had no use for the game. Privately, he told Rawlins, "I'm now convinced that Johnson is an incompetent president who manufactures uses of the Constitution to support his needs. The country will be better off without him in the White House."

Rawlins shrugged. "I'd just as soon see him stay in office. Then we won't have to go through the inauguration of an interim president to muddy the waters for the forthcoming election. In the meantime, Chase isn't gaining any ground in the trial." Chief Justice Salmon P. Chase and his beautiful daughter, Kate, had been actively pursuing the presidential nomination. Kate had distanced herself from Julia in the past eighteen months.

"How do you think the Johnson vote will go?"

"It depends on those renegade Republican senators. Last I heard, over a half dozen of them were ready to support Johnson."

The end of the spectacular trial in mid-May would prove Rawlins right. Johnson escaped impeachment by one vote because seven Republican senators voted in his favor.

But another chapter of stinking government had been written into the history books.

A couple of days later, a zestful "Soldiers and Sailors" convention assembled in Chicago. Three wartime generals—Hawley, the governor of Connecticut; Dan Sickles, who had lost a leg at Gettysburg and was again in Congress; and the darkly handsome Congressman Black Jack Logan—led the impassioned veterans in denouncing the seven deserting senators and President Johnson himself. They had even brought old Jesse Grant in from Covington, a risky ploy to those who knew his fondness for the limelight. But the longwinded old man managed to avoid antagonizing anyone, and, amid rousing cheers, the former warriors nominated Ulysses S. Grant for the presidency of the United States. "If he doesn't want to run on the Republican ticket," shouted one attendee, a former commander of an Indiana regiment, "we'll elect him as an *independent*!"

The next night at shortly after ten, Grant put down the book he was reading and went out into the backyard. The wrought-iron gate was closed and the large lawn smelled most pleasant, having been mowed that day before the early evening shower. Lighting a fresh cigar, he sat on the back steps and looked up at the three-quarter moon through the leaves of a large oak tree. It was a warm May night, quite humid, and he felt a bit of sweat on his brow. He blew out a cloud of smoke and looked around for a familiar constellation. Spotting the red star of Mars, he wondered why it had caught his attention. Could another war be in the offing—perhaps the unfamiliar conflict of the presidency? Yes, the thing he'd dreaded was about to become a reality. And he had to admit he was pleased. He thought a man who was being mentioned in every quarter as the next president of the country would be dishonest if he didn't admit that it pleased him. Lincoln had been right. Once that thing about the presidency got in a man's head, it was hard to get it out.

But he truly didn't want it.

He was the first to admit that he wasn't equipped. He was a quiet Ohio farm boy who had come leagues beyond his station. It had been simply a matter of luck and opportunity. If grand old C. F. Smith had lived, U. S. Grant might have faded into eternity as just another briefly lit major general. Oh, he'd worked hard and had withstood some difficult times—like the Wilderness and Cold Harbor, when all those lads had been killed. And he'd never lost his faith in the victory. But he'd been lucky, and no one knew it any better than he did.

He'd be perfectly content to stay right on in his exalted position. Their fine home was paid for, and they could manage on an income of $20,000, even in Washington. Scott had been general in chief for over twenty years; he could probably stay on even longer. And he knew what he was doing in the army. He'd made a mistake about squabbling with the president, but he'd stayed completely out of the fracus over the impeachment. He could easily tuck himself in behind the battlements of the military and stay out of politics for as long as he wanted. Twenty thousand for life . . . that was far beyond what a mathematics professor at West Point earned. Hard to give up. He was barely forty-six—

"So there you are," Julia said from behind him. Putting her head on his shoulder, she asked, "Thinking about the White House?"

"Uh-huh."

"What are you going to do?"

He shrugged. Duty. Rawlins had said it. The newspapers said it every day. It was his duty to serve as president. The people *wanted* him. "I don't know," he replied, taking her hand. "The convention is about to convene, and I suppose I'll be nominated. And I'll probably be elected. I don't want to be president, but if I'm nominated, I feel it's my duty to go ahead with it. On the positive side, however, if I'm elected, perhaps I can find ways to give the widely separated sections of this country satisfaction. I don't know. It'll be difficult, my dear. What do *you* want?"

"I'm perfectly happy being Mrs. General Grant."

He put his hand to his forehead and sighed. "It's a dilemma."

She kissed his cheek. "I know, and I also know how you are about duty."

He looked back up at the sky, trying to find the red star.

It was still there.

Some eight thousand Republicans gathered at the Crosby Opera House on May 20. The zestful band played "The Battle Hymn of the Republic" as Dan Sickles, wearing his two-star uniform with one pants leg pinned up and striding proudly on his crutches, followed Old Glory into the building.

Group by group, he led the delegates of each state to their seats in the orchestra pit. The flavor of the convention was definitely military, with blue uniforms and regimental colors everywhere, and martial songs filling the air. A radical Methodist bishop opened the proceedings with a prayer and an appeal for Negro justice. Then Governor Hawley, the chairman, took over and the work of forming a platform got under way.

The following day, Black Jack Logan got to his feet and quieted the assembly. "Gentlemen," he said in his clear deep voice, "I need not go to any length to introduce the name of the man I will place on the ballot. We all know of his great feats in the war. But I have a special connection with him, because, you see, when he was a raw colonel with his first regiment, I helped convince his men to reenlist and give him their support. I later proudly served in his eminent western commands as he led the boys in blue to a marvelous victory over the rebels who would tear our great country asunder! I—"

A deafening cheer shook the opera house for the next two minutes. When it died down, Logan grinned, held up his arms and went on, "I speak of none other than the great general who saved our proud Union. *Gentlemen, I nominate General Ulysses S. Grant to be the next president of the United States of America!*"

Grant's army headquarters was in a small two-story house at 17th and F Streets. His office was a large, brightly carpeted room at the front of the upstairs. The general in chief was working at his desk when Edwin M. Stanton, breathing heavily from having hurried up the steps, rushed in waving a telegram. "General," he panted, "you have been nominated by the Republicans for president of the United States!"

Grant's expression didn't change as he looked from Stanton to his secretary, Adam Badeau, and back to Stanton. The former Cabinet member warmly shook his hand. "My congratulations, General. I think they've made a wise decision."

Badeau chimed in with a broad grin and hearty handshake. "You'll make a great president, sir!"

Rawlins heard and rushed into the office, hand outstretched, his eyes brimming. For once the Galenian was at a loss for words. He embraced Grant for a moment and murmured, "I'm so very proud."

Grant quietly thanked them. *Now* the fat was truly in the fire . . . It was somehow exciting, yet strangely quieting . . . out of his hands, finalized. No more soul searching, no more speculation. "Who did they select for vice president?" he asked.

"Schuyler Colfax, on the fifth ballot."

Grant nodded his head. His running mate would be the amiable speaker of the house, who had a reputation for never having lost a friend or made an enemy. His nickname was "Smiler." Hopefully, the man's fourteen years of experience in Congress would be of value to him. He reached for his hat and excused himself. He'd have to go right home and tell Julia.

Little would be remembered of Grant's acceptance speech except its final short sentence, which would never be forgotten. It would make a superb campaign slogan for a populace that was still recovering from the war and its open wounds. It was beautiful in its simplicity, and everyone knew it came from the heart of the man who said it: "Let us have peace."

Salmon Chase switched party allegiance and sought the Democratic nomination. Now alienated from the Republicans, Andrew Johnson also made himself available to that party. Delegates from the South such as Nathan Bedford Forrest mixed with onetime Federal officers when the convention assembled in the ornate new Tammany Hall in New York City in July. But in the end, on the twenty-second ballot, they made a strange decision by nominating a wartime Copperhead to oppose Grant—Horatio Seymour, a former governor of New York. A onetime Union general, Francis Preston Blair, was his running mate.

"Let us have peace."

The next morning Rawlins came to the house on I Street for breakfast. It was a cool morning, gray and forbidding, with a biting wind swirling the leaf-thick tree branches and verdant shrubbery like roiling waves anchored to a grasping green sea. Rawlins coughed as he handed his campaign hat to a servant. After making his way to the dining room where Grant and Julia were reading the morning papers, he gave Mrs. Grant a peck on the cheek. He greeted his boss, sat down, and poured himself a cup of coffee. Julia excused herself, heading for the kitchen to order some eggs for her visitor.

Rawlins and Grant discussed the morning's news and then some pertinent army affairs until, just as the eggs were being served, Grant looked up. "You haven't said anything for several minutes. Something wrong?"

Rawlins's frown deepened. "Yes, I'm worried. I had a bad dream last night."

"You're always having bad dreams."

"No, this one made too much sense not to worry me. It was about you."

"And?"

"You were on trial on the portico of the White House. Robert E. Lee was the judge and all kinds of people were raising their fists and screaming at you angrily. I was your defense counsel and I seemed bolted to the floor. Each time I tried to speak, I was paralyzed and no sounds came out of my mouth. Finally, Ben Butler and John McClernand came, put manacles on you, and dragged you away. Moments later, I saw you hanging, all dressed in black, from a high tree limb."

Grant chuckled. "That *was* a bad dream."

Rawlins shook his head. "I admit it was far-fetched, but I can't get it out of my head. And part of it is possible. Your future worries me."

"You've said that before. The first time was when I came to Washington to be general in chief."

"I know, but this time I'm *really* worried. You will surely be elected, and just as surely, these sharks who call themselves politicians will tear you apart and throw your bloody pieces of flesh into the garbage."

Grant smiled. "I'm not *that* innocent."

"And it won't be just the politicians. You know how many grasping crooks there were around our different army headquarters—well, there'll be tenfold around the presidency. Except they'll be slicker. Remember, I told you to watch those people who showered you with gifts after the war, now they'll come forth and really multiply."

"I'll survive."

"I hope so, General. I'm not going to be around to protect you forever, you know."

Grant patted his hand. "Nonsense. You're my eternal swearer."

Seldom over the years had tears welled in Rawlins's eyes during their many discussions, but now they brimmed. "Just weather the storms, my friend."

Grant had stated that he wouldn't campaign and he didn't. On a western trip, Cump Sherman and he joined Phil Sheridan in Kansas, after which the three generals visited Denver and relaxed for a couple of days in Iowa. Grant then headed for Galena, where he and his family would settle down until the election. Riding along on the train with Badeau, he closed his eyes and recalled the past few days. What a pleasure it had been to be with those two old wartime friends. No pretense, no subterfuge. They had reminisced, refought some battles, and talked about army matters in general. Somehow he knew it might be the last time he would ever be with them in such a relaxed position. If he were elected, his being president would make a difference, no matter how much he cared for them. It had to.

And that was sad.

Colonel Adam Badeau was writing on one of those foldaway tables the compartment provided. Thickset and beefy-faced, the well-educated New Yorker was a skilled writer. At thirty-seven, he was very bright, dependable, gossipy, and a discreet homosexual. Grant was comfortable with him, and Julia liked him. He had been wounded once, and had received a gratuitous brevet to brigadier general at the end of the war. He considered himself quite a student of social behavior, but could be petty at times. He also imbibed rather heavily when away from Grant.

"You now have in Ohio alone thirty-six tanneries, sir."

Grant looked at him quizzically.

"You know, the popular name for Grant clubs, relating to your boyhood."

Grant shook his head. If they only knew how much he hated that memory.

"Also in Ohio, there are twenty-seven Boys in Blue groups, and over two dozen Grant bands. As we guessed, the veterans in the North are strongly behind you. But the news isn't all good. I have a letter from Charles Dana and he says you may lose the popular vote!"

"How is that?"

"He quotes some of the mud-slinging—that you are being called 'the butcher of Cold Harbor, the drunk of Shiloh, the nigger-lover, the puppet of the do-gooders, and the yes-man of the New York money men.' "

Grant shrugged. "Well, we were told it could get dirty."

"He also predicts that you'll lose the South, where you are still disliked, and some of the larger northern states, such as New York and Illinois."

"But Illinois is my adopted home."

"Doesn't matter, sir. It's pegged to go Democratic."

"Hmm." Grant was surprised. He'd been buttered up so much that not winning hadn't entered his head, nor had the possibility that maybe the populace wasn't all that much enthralled by his wartime exploits. A whole different light was now cast over things. Perhaps the whole thing *was* a great mistake. Maybe he should never have let them talk him into it.

No, he'd talked *himself* into it.

"The Negro vote is good and bad, Dana says. Knowing the coloreds are going to vote for you, a lot of whites won't."

Now that he was in the running, he didn't want to lose. Why had they told him the whole country wanted him in the White House if it wasn't true? Over three years in Washington, and he still didn't know much about politics.

"Dana wishes you'd get out and campaign—even a little bit, where it would do the most good."

"I'm not going to. I didn't ask to be nominated, and I won't beg the American public to elect me. It's the way I feel."

The most popular of the opprobrious charges hurled at Grant was that he was the father of a half-Indian girl from Vancouver, Washington. But when it was established that the poor girl had been born less than nine months after his arrival there, the lively story died out. It was more logical to keep his drunkenness in front of the public. A popular Democratic ditty was sung to the tune of "Captain Jinks of the Horse Marines":

> *I am Captain Grant of the Black Marines,*
> *The stupidest man that ever was seen . . .*
> *I smoke my weed and drink my gin,*
> *Paying with the people's tin.*

But the large number of ex-soldiers steadfastly pushed for their former commander as the days flew by and the day of voting drew near.

*   *   *

On election day, Grant went to Washburne's house in Galena early in the evening. A telegraph line had been set up in the congressman's library, where several local acquaintances and leading Republicans, as well as Grant's aides, Badeau and Comstock, had gathered to stay abreast of the results. Cigar smoke hung thickly in the small room as the voting teetered back and forth. As suspected, the popular vote stayed close. Grant appeared unperturbed as many of the men present imbibed from the available whiskey, but he really wanted to have a drink. It was one of those times when the desire was irrationally strong. And, under the circumstances, no one would have blamed him for taking a glass or two. But two things stopped him: going home to Julia smelling of the stuff, or drunk—and the thought of how Rawlins would feel when he heard about it.

As predicted, New York went for Seymour. So did Maryland, Georgia, Illinois, Kentucky, New Jersey, and Louisiana. Oregon would follow suit later. But the electoral votes continued to come his way. At ten-thirty the Galena Lead Mine Band paraded over and began a concert in front of the house. Everyone went out on the front porch to listen. As usual, the music was nothing more than a racket to Grant, but he thanked them for the effort.

Now the electoral votes looked good: 133–67.

Time dragged on with the intermittent clacking of the telegraph sounding its announcements. Something could still go wrong. And that popular vote was still nip and tuck. Once, Grant heard Comstock say, "Thank God for the Negro vote."

In the wee hours of the morning it was all over. The electoral vote gave the election handily to Grant: 214–80. A rousing cheer shook the Washburne house as everyone pumped Grant's hand. Until this moment, it had all seemed like some sort of a play, a game or dream that somehow wasn't real. But now the actuality of it all hit him. He had to leave before it showed.

Julia was dozing under a blanket in the parlor as Grant slipped into the house. The kerosene lamp on the mantel was turned down low and only a bit of red showed in the fire's embers. He tiptoed up to her and leaned down. Her eyes slowly opened as he kissed her cheek. "Oh!" she exclaimed. "You startled me, darling."

He pulled her up into his arms and held her close, saying nothing.

She drew back, looking fearfully into his eyes. "Is it bad? Is—"

He kissed her on the lips, then pulled back and smiled. He spoke softly, "In four months you will move into a white mansion, my dear. It will be much nicer and larger than Hardscrabble, and many of the world's most important people will come to visit you there—"

Her eyes widened.

"—because you will be the first lady of the land."

CHAPTER 62

G eneral," Badeau announced from the doorway to Grant's second-story
office at the army headquarters house, "Mr. Alexander Stewart and his
party are here."

Grant looked over to where Sherman had been writing at the aide's
desk. "You ready to acquire some property, General?" he asked.

Sherman grinned as he got to his feet. "Good a time as any, I suppose."

"Show them in, Badeau."

Since even before the time when Wellington received bountiful gifts
from the citizens of England for his great victory over Napoleon, it had
been customary for a grateful citizenry to shower largess on its heroes.
Often, as in the case of Grant, a leader who had risen to top command was
without funds and property. In such cases, it was not thought unseemly to
raise money to make life easier for that individual and his family. This was
particularly so if that hero was required to live on a much higher and more
expensive level than previously.

Following some pleasantries, Stewart—a wealthy merchant who owned
the largest department store in New York—withdrew a check from his
pocket, cleared his throat and announced, "It gives me great pleasure on
the part of the committee listed on the enclosed letter to present you,
General Grant, with this check for sixty-five thousand dollars for the purchase of your house and its furniture on I Street." Turning, he said, "And
it gives me equal pleasure, General Sherman, to inform you that the deed
to the aforementioned house will be delivered to you within the week. You
will be free to move your family into the dwelling as soon as it is deemed
convenient by the new president."

Grant smiled as Sherman thanked Stewart and the others.

Sherman's appointment as general in chief, and his accompanying pro-
motion to general of the army, would be effective after the inauguration.
Grant shook Sherman's hand warmly and smiled. "I agree on one condition,
Sherman, and that is that you'll invite me over once in a while."

"Agreed." This time Sherman pulled out the cigars and passed them
around.

After tossing and turning in bed for a couple of hours, Grant finally swung
his feet to the floor, found his slippers, and arose. It was a few minutes
after four A.M. on the 4th of March, 1869—the day he would become
president. Glancing at the sleeping Julia as he donned his favorite robe, he
quietly left the bedroom and headed for the large kitchen, where he lit a
kerosene lamp. The cook had banked the fire in the cookstove, so he had

only to stick in some pieces of wood to get a fire going for some coffee. He pulled out a cigar and bit off the end. It was pretty early to start smoking, but it would taste good. Lighting it with a match and blowing a cloud of smoke into the semidarkness, he went to the door that led out to the big yard.

Just as he thought, it was raining. Not heavily, but enough to have dropped quite a bit of water during the night. It would probably be a soggy day, the kind reserved for funerals, not inaugurations. He chuckled to himself. Maybe it was his funeral day.

No, he was ready.

They'd continue to stay here in the place on I Street until renovations were complete in the White House, but he was ready to occupy the executive suite and take command of the country. In these months of being president-elect, he'd grown used to the idea, and had few doubts about handling the job. But everyone kept plaguing him about what he was going to do. For weeks now, they'd been questioning him about who would be in his Cabinet. And he hadn't even told Julia.

There might be some mixup, certainly there would be some quick changes made. For one thing, he'd promised Washburne the secretary of state post the night of the election, but in the interim he'd been strongly advised that his friend lacked the polish to represent the country with foreign rulers. In the end he had given in and recommended that Washburne accept appointment as minister to France, but since he had offered him the state portfolio, he would appoint the congressman to the post for a short period. Washburne had reluctantly agreed.

Grant didn't feel right about it—particularly because of all the congressman had done for him, but there were compromises that had to be made.

The other change was in the secretary of war post. He had decided, due to Rawlins's critical health, that he would give him the army command down in Arizona. There, the dry air might be good for his health. But then he'd learned of his friend's real desire: the war portfolio. So it was arranged that Schofield would continue in the post for a short period, resign, and turn the job over to Rawlins. Actually, this development pleased Grant because a voice he could trust implicitly would be right at his shoulder.

The others he'd selected would be satisfactory. With all of Alexander Stewart's millions, he should make a good secretary of the treasury. That post was most important because of everyone's interest in the national debt and the financial management of the country.

He glanced at the coffee pot.

The army changes had been a bit sticky. There had been little problem in designating Sherman as his successor in command of the army, but awarding the lieutenant general's stars to Sheridan had caused a bitter reaction from both Thomas and Meade, who outranked the feisty cavalryman considerably. Even Halleck had voiced a complaint, but Old Brains hadn't been near the starting gate.

It would all settle down.

The drip, drip, drip from the back porch roof was all he could hear.

*   *   *

The sky was the color of cold lead as the Negro coachman slapped the reins on the rumps of the team of handsome bays. Grant and John Rawlins smiled and waved back at Julia and the kids as they pulled away from the house in the shiny new phaeton. It was 9:25. Several minutes later, they stopped in front of the two-story army headquarters house where Company K of the Fifth Cavalry, Grant's personal honor guard, was drawn up at attention. They went upstairs to Grant's office, where Vice President–elect Schuyler Colfax and Colonel Fred Dent, Grant's brother-in-law and aide, awaited with the rest of Grant's staff. Tea, cigars, and conversation lasted until 10:40, when Grant and Rawlins once more climbed into the well-appointed phaeton and headed for the Capitol. This time they waved cheerily to a throng of Negroes in their Sunday clothes, who had gathered near the open carriage.

The driver turned onto Pennsylvania Avenue and soon pulled up at the gates of the White House. Rawlins addressed the marine guard. "Please tell President Johnson that General Grant would like to offer him a ride to the inauguration."

The guard spoke from the position of attention. "Sir, I have been instructed to tell the general that the president is otherwise detained."

"Very well. Thank you, Sergeant." As they pulled away, Rawlins shook his head. "Well, that takes care of that."

The *New York Times* had reported that President Johnson had written to Grant, suggesting that they ride to the ceremony together. Grant had received no such note and had, therefore, not contacted the outgoing president. He had made a gesture and had been rebuffed. Grant shrugged. It all seemed so petty.

He felt comfortable in the well-tailored black suit, although the yellow kid gloves seemed somehow frivolous. As the twenty-two-gun salute sounded, he smiled at Julia, who, with the children, her father, and other relatives, was in place a few yards away on the east portico. With them was Jesse Grant, all puffed up and ready to talk to anyone willing to listen about how his son was going to lead the country back to the success of Whig leadership.

The cannon salute seemed interminably slow.

The vivid red, white, and blue of the national colors caught his eye.

For some reason the cracked mirror of a cheap San Francisco hotel room flashed back to him. He finished retching and looked up at his pale reflection. His eyes were blood red . . .

He looked into Julia's eyes and saw her slight, reassuring smile.

How many salute rounds had they fired—a dozen?

Rawlins's dark eyes were shining with pride.

He should have done better by Washburne. Who had gotten him that first star and defended him incessantly in the halls of power? Maybe he could make it up to him later.

Little Jesse was as puffed up as his grandfather.

Another old scene came back. It was cold in the tall trees. He spoke softly to the shaggy horse as it pulled the wagon piled high with freshly cut wood down the snow-covered path. He was all hunkered down in a faded old blue army overcoat. A rough two-story house that he'd built himself stood off through the trees . . .

Standing at a casual parade rest beside his mother, young Fred looked handsome in his cadet gray uniform. Nellie, at his side, had never been prettier. He wondered how many beaux she'd find as a president's daughter.

Too bad his mother had decided not to come. Maybe they could have sat quietly somewhere in the White House and enjoyed each other.

As the final round of the salute faded away, a sergeant at arms held out a Bible. He put his hand on it as Chief Justice Salmon Chase stepped forward and began to administer the oath of office.

His own voice sounded strange, hollow, as he repeated the words.

It was all so quick.

The applause began. He had to say a few words, had to tell them that he would always follow the will of the people.

He was the eighteenth president of the United States of America.

Chapter 63

I don't care what Mrs. Lincoln paid for these dreadful curtains," Julia said. "They have to go. Here, I've made drawings of different rooms and have listed the work that has to be done." She dropped a sheaf of papers on Grant's desk in his new office. "The place is a mess," she sniffed. "No wonder the place on I Street will be welcome when this is over."

Grant asked Badeau to leave them alone for a few minutes. "But, darling," he said when the secretary was gone, "we can't go back there. I sold it."

She looked at him with a start. "You what?"

"Alexander Stewart and some other fellows raised some money to buy it for Sherman. I thought it a good idea."

Julia felt a sudden wave of hurt and anger. She loved that house; he couldn't sell it! "But you didn't even ask me," she said.

"It all happened so quickly. Besides, we don't want to rent it, and we can't just board it up for several years."

"Then I have nothing to say about it?"

"I just forgot to mention it."

"Huh!" She remembered that whenever Colonel Dent bought a piece of land, he would buy her mother a nice gift to induce her to sign the deed. Otherwise the deed would be imperfect. Huh! Her tone was icy. "And if I refuse to sign the deed, what will the consequences be?"

Grant shook his head and laughed. "Oh, nothing. I've already accepted the check."

Now she was really seeing red! She stamped her foot. "I won't sign it!"

Grant sighed. "Very well, I'll send a note to both Stewart and Sherman that my *wife* won't *let* me sell the house."

She shook her head. "I don't care what you tell them!" She whirled and was out of his office before he could say anything more.

Having faced a palace revolt with Julia after being in office for less than twenty-four hours, he turned to other matters. Several of his military secretary/aides would be serving on his staff in the White House, although Badeau might be leaving shortly for a diplomatic assignment. Comstock, Babcock, and Porter, all having reverted from their brevet general's rank to that of colonel, had been with him so long that they were almost considered family. Now the thirty-three-year-old Cyrus Babcock said, "Sir, there are rumbles of discontent because you didn't consult the party leaders before you selected your Cabinet members."

Grant looked puzzled. "But they are *my* Cabinet members. They're here to help run this government just like you are."

Babcock looked uncomfortable. "Sir, *we* understand that, but people like Senator Sumner don't. They want a hand in the pie."

Rawlins had been listening from where he was glancing at some papers in the corner of the office. "He's right, General. I haven't said anything because I'll be one of those members, but there's really quite a bit of peevish talk going on around the Congress."

Grant looked from Rawlins to Babcock. "Huh, well, I think that's silly, and I'm not going to worry about it."

It was his first major mistake in office.

That night, facing a wall of silence from Julia as they began dinner, Grant pulled an envelope from his breast pocket and handed it to her.

She looked at it coolly and placed it on the table.

"Don't you want to read it?" he asked pleasantly.

She glanced at it, gave him a steady look, and went back to her salmon.

"You might find it interesting," he said.

Nellie and Jesse were eating with them. All of the other members of the family and guests were elsewhere. Nellie said, "Can I look at it, Papa?"

"You'll have to ask your mother."

"Leave it be," Julia said.

"But, Mama, isn't that impolite?"

Julia gave her daughter an icy look. "You stick to your own business, young lady."

Minutes passed, during which Grant asked Jesse about school. Now and then Julia stole a glance at the envelope, but she neither touched it nor said anything. Finally, Grant said, "I talked to your father this afternoon and he told me about the custom of gift-giving in your family."

Julia looked up. "And?"

"Why don't you look in the envelope?"

"*Mother!*" Nellie said, "for goodness' sake."

"All right," Julia said, and slit the cream-colored wrapper open. Inside was a bank deposit for sixty-five thousand dollars and a check made out to her for one thousand dollars.

She pursed her lips as she looked up at Grant. After a moment, she said, "I suppose it would look pretty bad if I made a scene about this, wouldn't it? I mean, every newspaper in the country would make hay out of President Grant's first bill being rejected."

The Cabinet selections did create a problem, and not just because Grant didn't consult with the party powers. An obscure law from 1784 did Alexander Stewart in as secretary of the treasury. It stated essentially that no person appointed a commissioner of the treasury could be engaged in any trade or commerce. It had been brought out of the dust by an aide to Senator Charles Sumner, a growing thorn in Grant's side.

To Grant, who had developed a deep respect for men with a lot of money, Stewart had been an excellent choice for the treasury portfolio— and not because he had been involved in the Sherman house deal. Grant simply thought that a poor immigrant Irishman who had started from scratch in the retail world and had become one of the richest men in America would be an excellent choice to manage the money of the country in an intelligent, honest fashion.

Grant wrote a note to the Senate, asking those astute gentlemen to make an exception for the ridiculous statute. But the powerful Sumner and Senator Roscoe Conkling, who was no friend of Stewart's, wouldn't hear of it. Grant asked if Stewart might sell his business, but the New Yorker simply couldn't do that. Instead, he sent two documents back to the president. One was his resignation, the other an ingenious alternative in which Stewart would place his vast interests in the hands of an independent committee for as long as he was secretary. But Grant, knowing the latter approach would cause Sumner and cohorts to hold everything up in committee for an interminable period, sadly opted for the resignation.

His replacement was Congressman Charles Boutwell of Massachusetts, the second member of the Cabinet from that state, since Ebenezer Rockwood Hoar had been selected to be attorney general.

The two temporary appointments brought criticism from the *New York Times:*

> *Apparently President Grant thinks he is still a commanding general and that his Cabinet is his staff. Unfortunately that isn't so. A Cabinet officer has vast responsibilities of his own. In several cases, it is rumored*

that General Grant didn't even ask the prospective secretaries if they wanted the job. This gives us cause for concern, as does the short tenure of two secretaryships: war and state. The very short stay of his original appointees makes us wonder if he knows what he is doing. And so does an irate Congress for not being consulted.

He faces some major problems, and if he is to be effective, he must learn that honesty and good intentions alone do not make the wheels of government in Washington work. He may be able to size up generals with the flick of an eye, and he certainly knows what makes soldiers tick, but politicians are another breed.

The first of these problems is Reconstruction of the South. He has stated in his inaugural speech that he desires "security of person, property, and free religious and political opinion in every part of our common country." Does he mean for all unreconstructed rebel leaders and for all Negroes everywhere? Is the current, fumbling policy to continue or will Grant find a truly workable solution?

Next is the monetary problem. Can he resolve the gold vs. greenback controversy for the best of the country? There are many who wish to profit from this situation.

Then comes the Indian problem. With rapid settlement of the West, are we to continue fighting the savage tribes? Or are we to soothe their breast and teach them how to live as domesticated members of our society? Are they part of our common country?

What about our relationship with Britain—will the English ever make restitution for aiding the Confederacy in the past war?

And finally, what about Civil Service reform? Are cushy government jobs to forever remain the rewards of the spoils system, positions to be passed out by any unethical politician with favor to dispense?

You have every right to be naive, Mr. President. You have stated that your concern is for the greatest good for the greatest number. We hope that you will not become lost in the shadows of the power brokers who will have you act otherwise.

Reading the editorial that night in his study, Grant circled each problem as he came to it. He *did* consider the Cabinet posts as senior staff jobs. And he wanted to get that ridiculous Tenure of Office Act repealed, the one that Stanton had used. It just wasn't logical that a commander couldn't fire a subordinate who was incompetent without getting Senate approval.

As far as Reconstruction went, he knew the Freedman's Bureau was essentially a failure because of the roadblocks Southern states threw in its way. There were only three states not yet fully back in the Union, and he was going to work on that. As soon as he could do it, he wanted to pull the army out of the South—at least as an occupation and governmental force. He was confident that a satisfactory solution would be reached in the South. And he truly cared about what happened to the Negro.

The monetary problem. Secretary Boutwell, in accordance with his instructions, would pay off enough of the national debt with gold to keep the gold market stable.

The Indians. War had broken out the year before with the Cheyenne, Sioux, and Arapaho. Sheridan, who was in command, was in accord with Sherman that a good Indian was a dead Indian—an opinion he definitely didn't subscribe to. His peace policy would put into motion an equitable solution that would bring the Indian into the fold as an American citizen— similar to the man whom he would make head of the Indian Bureau. At ten the next morning, he would appoint Ely Parker, his wartime staff officer and the well-educated son of a Seneca chief, as Commissioner of Indian Affairs. The heavy-set brigadier was trustworthy and, of course, would bring special insight to the position.

The problem with Britain wasn't as important as many thought.

And finally, the civil service reform. He was all for it.

The war hadn't been easy, but he'd plugged on, trusting in his own judgment and learning as he went. Since he'd announced to the country that he was merely an administrator of the wishes of the people, he'd, by lightning, learn how to best do that.

It was Rawlins that he was most worried about . . .

It was whispered among the Washington women that the reason Julia Grant liked Julia Kean Fish so much was that the wealthy New Yorker was truly without spite. The well-bred and wealthy Mrs. Fish had paid a call on Mrs. Grant during an 1865 visit to West Point and Julia had liked her instantly. Mrs. Fish was kind and above common gossip. Not once had she been heard mocking Julia's figure, her twitching eye, or her provincialism. The friendship had grown over the years, and now the first lady stepped into pillow politics. As she and her husband were retiring a few nights later, she turned on her side and said softly, "Victor, I know who would be the perfect secretary of state."

Grant replied sleepily, "And who is that, my dear?"

"Hamilton Fish in New York. He is a true aristocrat with scads of money, and you know how much I adore his wife. He's a brilliant man who has served both in the House and the Senate. He's a lawyer, and has also been governor of New York. I know you don't know him very well, but I would love having them here in Washington. She's such a warm, gentle person. And he's so nice, just the type of quiet man who could work with you."

Grant was fully awake now. He pursed his lips. Hamilton Fish. Hmmm. Nice man, kind, unassuming. Very bright. About sixty. Unimpeachable background, if he remembered correctly. Old New York lineage and money. Yes, he might be just the man . . . He'd send him a letter in the morning. He took Julia's hand and kissed it. "Good idea. Now, do you have a solution for my other problems?"

She beamed, coming into his arms. "I'll work on them."

*   *   *

Grant rose from his desk, stepped quickly around it, and extended his hand as Babcock announced his visitor. Shaking hands, he smiled and spoke warmly, "It's a great pleasure to see you, sir."

Robert E. Lee nodded his head slightly in greeting; his tone was cool. "Mr. President."

Grant pointed to a wingback chair and asked his visitor to be seated. He took a chair facing the general as a maid hurried in with a silver tray with coffee and placed it on a low table between them. "I'm so glad you had time to come, General."

Lee regarded the man he'd last seen at the McLean house in Appomattox Courthouse. He had heard that the new president wished to see him, and had thought it would be impolite not to come to the White House. Although he knew the man meant him no malice, the idea of the visit was unappealing to him. Five years earlier, in June of '65, he'd written the letter asking for amnesty and pardon. He had sent it through Grant to President Andrew Johnson, and Grant had replied that he was forwarding it with his "earnest" recommendation for approval. But it had never been granted. He'd heard that Stanton had blocked it, Stanton and possibly other radicals in the Johnson administration. There were plenty of people in the North who had wanted his scalp—still did. Now Grant was president and still nothing had been done about it. Five years. The request was probably filed in a cabinet somewhere, drawing dust. But there was simply no way he would grovel; to ask again would be begging. He shouldn't resent the matter, but he couldn't help himself. "Thank you for seeing me, Mr. President," he murmured.

They casually passed the time of day until Grant said, "I just got a letter from Pete Longstreet yesterday. He's down in New Orleans."

"Yes, I heard that."

"He seems to be doing all right."

"Yes, a number of our senior officers are managing."

"How do you like being a college president, General?"

"It's quiet and challenging."

"Washington College is in Lexington, isn't it?"

"Yes. It's a poor school trying to make ends meet."

"I understand you've built quite a chapel there."

And a vault for my family, Lee wanted to add. Since the Federal government had stolen their proud Arlington for a pittance in unpaid taxes during the war, a proper burial place for the Lees had been a vital requirement. "Yes, you must visit it sometime," he replied quietly.

Grant was still acting most pleasant, almost deferential. "I understand, General, that you came up to Baltimore to coordinate construction of a possible rail line that would go through the Shenandoah Valley to Lexington."

"Yes, that's correct, your excellency."

Grant chuckled. "Seems that you and I have had more to do with tearing up railroads than building them."

Lee just looked frostily into Grant's blue eyes for a few seconds. Nothing about the war was humorous to him. Nothing. He didn't reply.

Grant cleared his throat, hiding whatever slight he might have felt at the unspoken rebuff. "Well, then," he said, getting to his feet after a couple of awkward moments, "I want to thank you for your efforts in trying to weld our proud country back together, sir. And I'm sure your contribution to the molding of young Southern minds is of great value. Please come and see me again at any time."

They shook hands, said good day to each other, and Lee departed.

The white-bearded man stepped out into the sunshine in front of the White House and sighed deeply. This place had once meant so much to him. In a way, it still did.

He frowned.

He would never know that Grant had forgotten about the request, that he was unaware it had never been granted. But it was only moments after he began to make his way down Pennsylvania Avenue that he felt a touch of ire with himself for his boorishness. After all, what had Grant ever done to him . . . except beat him in battle? Yes, that was it—deep down there somewhere was that unconquerable resentment, that chunk of wounded pride. He always prayed for his enemies, but there was that tiny piece of him that resisted graciousness. He usually kept it under lock and key, but today it had slipped out.

He was sorry.

CHAPTER 64

It's the stupidest damned law this country has ever passed. It was designed to hold Johnson in rein, and now you've given in," John Rawlins growled, glaring at Grant. They were alone in Grant's office, as they often were when the secretary of war acted in his usual adversarial manner. Now it was the Tenure of Office Act. The senators had refused Grant's request to repeal it, and Grant—against Rawlins's advice—had agreed to modifications in face of the warning of a party split. He had thought the House would kill it, but that body had failed to do so.

"It won't be a factor in the overall appointment scheme," Grant replied.

"That doesn't matter. To the public, it looks like you backed down from your first fight. The newspapers will have a heyday."

"I can't veto it."

Rawlins shook his head. "It'll go down as the first defeat for the man the country thought was going to be a heroic reform president."

Grant frowned. "There are many more important problems to be solved."

Grant didn't even know about one of them, because the plot hadn't been quite hatched. His sister, Jennie, headed for spinsterhood in her late thirties, had married an opportunistic financier from New York named Abel Rathbone Corbin. Sixty-one years old, Corbin had obviously married her because of her connection to Grant—not a totally bad situation, for she had moved into an interesting life in a nice house in the big city. It wasn't so much his marriage to the president's sister as the role Corbin would play in the forthcoming gold plot that would provide him a place in financial history.

The Corbin house in New York was where Grant first met Jay Gould and his partner on Wall Street, James Fisk, Jr. At thirty-three, Gould was a contradiction—a skinny, delicate man whose hobbies were gardening and history, yet a business shark bold enough to grab control of the Erie Railroad from the powerful Vanderbilts. He was possibly the most brilliant investor in New York. Fisk, a year older and only a step behind in brilliance, was every bit as audacious as his daring partner. A flashy dresser, a reckless gambler, and a man who enjoyed to the hilt the charms of many women, Fisk liked being rich. And he had never been accused of being overly truthful.

Yet because they were friends of Corbin, these opportunistic financiers were accepted as acquaintances of the president and his lady. On June 15, after a stop at West Point, the Grants visited the Corbins in New York. Gould and Fisk were present to escort the visitors to the flagship of Gould's steamer line for a trip past Long Island to Fall River, Massachusetts. There, the Grants would proceed by train to Boston. Aboard the steamer a sumptuous dinner was served, and a collection of more Wall Street men listened keenly for glimpses of the president's thoughts on monetary policy. Following the meal, Julia retired to a cabin to rest, while Grant lit another cigar and settled back to converse with the others.

It wasn't long before it became obvious to him that the others wanted the price of gold to stay up. Since the country had been on a specie, or coin, basis since the war, gold was a commodity that could be purchased like any other. Speculators could buy or sell for future delivery, gambling on the oscillating balance between inflation and deflation. Since the prices of other commodities were related to the swing of gold, the secretary of the treasury would release a few million dollars' worth every now and then to retire outstanding government bonds—in order to stabilize the market. It would obviously be to the advantage of any manipulator to know the government's plans in this regard.

Timing was the name of the game.

But Grant had no suspicions that anything shady was afoot as the stimulating conversation proceeded. In fact, he enjoyed the discussion.

"Do you expect the economy to shrink, Mr. President?" Gould asked after a lengthy discussion about the economics of the North and South.

"I think there is a certain amount of fictitiousness about the prosperity of the country," Grant replied.

"But wouldn't it be better to let Secretary Boutwell increase the supply of money to stimulate the economy?" Fisk asked. "Continued stringency will lead us back toward another civil war."

Grant frowned. "I think that's an exaggeration."

"But," Gould persisted, "if the price of gold is high, it will stimulate the sale of wheat abroad. You know how important it will be to our western farmers to get a good price at harvest time."

"I don't see that we have a serious problem in that area, sir," Grant replied firmly. "Secretary Howell has a firm grip on the currency and gold situation."

Everyone at the table craned forward as Gould asked, "Then you are for the government selling more gold and keeping the money supply down?"

Grant slowly blew out a small cloud of cigar smoke as he studied the young financier's slender face. At length he said, "Retiring the nation's debt is a paramount goal. As you know, we are doing so by buying back bonds at convenient intervals with our gold. If it coincides with market stability, I'm—quite naturally—in favor of it."

"But specifically?" Fisk interjected, obviously trying to pin Grant down.

The sharply dressed financier also received a long look before the president replied. "I have no specific response, except what I've already said—the secretary of the treasury has control of this situation, and he has shown the utmost capability in this area of government finance." Grant looked around the table in the following silence for several moments before saying, "Now, gentlemen, if you don't mind, let's talk about good horses."

As the president and his lady debarked to catch their waiting train, Gould and Fisk stood waving goodbye in the moonlight at the rail of the steamer. "We didn't get much good news out of him tonight," Fisk said quietly.

"No, but this is just the first scene. At least we can get the word around that we're intimate with him."

"What's next?"

"The key is Corbin. He's in for a big piece already. Now we have to get a line into the Treasury Department. All we need is advance warning on when Boutwell is going to dump gold."

"What do you think of Grant?"

"He's smarter and better informed than I thought."

Fisk grinned. "I think we are going to get very rich over this."

Gould nodded, his eyes alight. "*Very* rich."

The "line" into the Treasury Department was a noted general with a brilliant war record. The son of the famous expressman, Daniel Butterfield had begun the war as a first sergeant, but had quickly become a colonel. Getting his first star in the fall of '61, he went as high as corps command, and was wounded a number of times, including at Gettysburg. He had been cited for personal heroism at Gaines Mills, and had written the bugle call taps while at Harrison's Landing with McClellan. Butterfield had stayed on active duty after the war, and was currently commanding the army troops in New York Harbor.

Corbin lobbied to have General Butterfield appointed assistant secretary for the New York subtreasury. This position would give him access to information from Washington about the release of government gold. In spite of his many accomplishments, Daniel Butterfield's greed got the better of him and he succumbed to temptation: he played the market he was sworn to regulate with a margin account supplied by Jay Gould.

Another reason for the conspirators to anticipate that Grant would not influence the price of gold was the rumor, planted by Gould and Fisk, that Abel Corbin was not only carrying an account of over two million in gold for himself, but was also managing gold accounts for a half million for both Horace Porter, Grant's aide—and *Julia Grant!* The rumor even added the supposed fact that Mrs. Grant had already made $27,000.

Even though Grant encountered Gould twice at Corbin's house in the next two months, he paid little attention to the financier's probing questions, and was too preoccupied with other matters to suspect anything. And the man who might have seen through the conspiracy, his mother hen, was in no condition to jar him into alertness . . .

The Grants enjoyed travel in the summer, and they liked Sarasota, New York. On this Sunday, the 5th of September, they were going to go with Senator Roscoe Conkling over to Utica for a visit. And Julia was looking forward most particularly to the trip. The president was in a good mood on this warm, sunny day as he and Porter strolled from the morning church service toward the hotel where he and Julia were staying. Julia hadn't gone to the service with him, claiming she had too much to do for the Utica jaunt. So Porter had been his only companion. "What did you think about the sermon?" Grant asked casually.

"I've always been intrigued by Lazarus, the beggar," his aide replied.

"More so than the Lazarus who was raised from the dead by Jesus?"

"Yes, the idea that a beggar with leprosy can die and sit at the hand of God, while a rich man who denied him succor can go to hell is sort of an interesting extension, or use, of the golden rule. At least in my thinking."

"I prefer the other Lazarus," Grant said. "A Catholic chaplain told me his feast day was Palm Sunday eve. And since that's the night before Lee came to Appomattox, it holds special meaning for me."

Horace Porter smiled. "We can find all kinds of interesting interpretation in the Bible. I—"

The man touched the brim of his hat as he hurried up waving a telegram. "Sir, I have an urgent message for you from General Sherman!"

Porter took the yellow envelope and tore it open. Reading the wire quickly, he turned sadly to Grant and handed it to him.

Grant sucked in a deep breath as he read, "Rawlins quite ill. May not live much longer. W. T. Sherman"

Fear and sadness stabbed at him. The failing Rawlins had been stricken by a severe hemorrhage in Connecticut late in August, but had headed for Washington for a called Cabinet meeting. Even after experiencing another bad hemorrhage in New York, he had continued on to the Capitol and attended the meeting. Now—

Grant looked up at Porter, his concern showing. "I must get back."

"Do you want me to order a special train, General?"

"No, it's Sunday. I'll go on the evening train."

"Very well, sir. I'll arrange it."

Rawlins coughed and spit up more blood from where he was propped up on pillows on a double bed. An army surgeon wiped the scarlet mucus away and tossed the cloth into a waste container by the bed. A window was open, permitting both sunlight and the muggy Washington heat into the room. Rawlins's black eyes seemed dull in the dark circles that surrounded them. His proud black beard, now touched by slivers of gray, hung long and listless below his chin. His emaciated body was skinny, down somewhere below 120 pounds. Seated beside him was Secretary of the Interior Jacob Dolson Cox. Oberlin College graduate, former general, and recent governor of Ohio, Cox was a man of many talents who had been recommended for his post by Sherman. Across the bed sat Ely Parker, his dark face set in its usual stoic expression, but his concern apparent in his eyes. Pacing near the foot of the bed, a cold cigar shoved into his mouth, Cump Sherman scowled and looked intently at the surgeon.

But before he could say anything, Rawlins spoke in a faint voice, a raspy rattle of death. "I'll never forget . . . the first day I came to his headquarters. I didn't even know how to wear a uniform, much less—" He coughed again, a racking heave that ended in another expulsion of red matter. The surgeon, a colonel named Bradley, blotted the tears from his eyes. Rawlins coughed again, cleared his throat, and went on. "He taught me how to be an officer . . . in many ways. Not just how to salute and shoot a revolver, but how to act, how to be worthy of the rank one wore.

"But he taught me much more than that. I've never known a more honest man, or . . . one who could bear up under such intense pressure. And pain. No one knows how much he . . . suffered over our losses. And I was much too hard on him. I didn't know all of his torments." He caught Sherman's eye. "Do you think he'll forgive me?"

Sherman nodded, replying gruffly, "Grant would forgive you if you shot his favorite horse—or even if you shot *him*! He loves you as no other man in the world, John."

Rawlins smiled softly and was quiet for a few minutes. Finally, his eyes widened in concern. He said, "Do you think he could have made it without me?"

Sherman patted his hand. "He'd never have had a chance, my friend."

Once more Rawlins smiled and drifted off. Opening his eyes a couple of minutes later, he looked around anxiously. "What time is it?"

Sherman pulled out his watch. "It's one thirty-five."

"When will he get here?"

"In about ten minutes," Sherman lied softly.

Rawlins went back to sleep.

Grant canceled the trip to Utica, even though it disappointed Julia, and, as he waited during the afternoon, he felt sorry about not ordering the special train. At 4:45 he was even more regretful, for another telegram arrived from Sherman: "Rawlins close to death and asking for you."

The next train was at 5:50, and Senator Conkling joined him and Porter as a dining room was cleared to give them privacy. Grant had little to say as they headed for Albany, where a special train was to meet them. Arriving shortly after seven, they were dismayed to find that the train wasn't waiting. "Why?" Grant asked quietly.

Porter shrugged. "I'll send another telegram."

"Don't bother. Let's see if we can catch a boat downriver to New York City."

Conkling thought that was the best idea, since the next regular train wouldn't be through for seven hours, and now it would take too long to arrange a special.

Grant stood at the bow rail, watching the dark shadows of hills in the dim light of the half-moon. He could see the slight wake of water in the otherwise still Hudson as the steamer puffed along. It seemed agonizingly slow to him. The sound of the engine was all he heard in the otherwise silent world that had belonged to proud Indians before the first white man had seen it. He could picture war canoes being paddled by fiercely painted Iroquois— perhaps moving even faster than this lumbering boat on which he was riding. These eastern tribes, like Parker's Senecas, had long been peaceful and part of the melting pot. Why couldn't the western tribes be the same?

The Hudson was wide here, as it neared West Point. He looked ahead as the steamer began a slight turn to stay in midchannel for the wide bend in the river, seeing the dark, high land mass that held the Academy. He wondered if Rawlins had ever visited there. Yes, surely he had. A secretary of war would visit his military academy, particularly *this* secretary. And Danbury, Connecticut, was so close, the city where Emma and John Rawlins had made their home.

He thought of the lovely Emma Hurlbut back at the Lum mansion in Vicksburg, and how his adjutant general had walked around with stars in his eyes as he fell madly in love with her. How much time had they had— six years? How Rawlins had adored his Emma. He should have them stop the boat so he could dash over to Danbury to ease her pain.

But no, Rawlins needed him in Washington.

The doggone steamer seemed to be barely moving! How would he ever get there on time? He hoped Rawlins wasn't in too much pain.

One memory after another piled up.

He saw his friend back in Galena—the intense, dedicated, impassioned young lawyer who was his neighbor, whose eyes glowed when he listened to a former captain turned leather goods clerk tell stories of the Mexican War. Actually, Rawlins had been good for him even then, when his self-esteem was low. Who would have guessed the profane, truly spiritual ex-farmer, a man totally untrained in the military, would rise to the rank of major general and become secretary of war?

Or for that matter, who would have guessed that Sam Grant would get this far?

No one except maybe Ellen Dent, possibly Julia in her wildest dreams.

And he could never have done it without Rawlins. Never. His friend's connection with Washburne had been important, but it was far more than that. It was the daily help he had rendered at every headquarters, the support only a close friend could provide. His continual war with alcohol had perhaps been too extreme, but who knows—he might well have slipped back into the alcoholic haze of his earlier years if the fanatical Rawlins hadn't watched him like a hawk.

And he'd even lied to this fine man about his drinking.

Lied to him.

That would perhaps be his saddest memory of their friendship.

Would he ever look into those passionate dark eyes again?

He found a short smile, remembering how Rawlins had once apologized for uttering a particularly strong string of oaths. As he had ruefully said at the time, "Every great man ought to have a swearer, General. I'm yours."

A tear slipped down his cheek.

Only thirty-eight years of age.

His best friend . . .

Once more, in Jersey City, a scheduled special train was *not* waiting the next day. Grant, uncharacteristically, upbraided Porter, telling him to see to it that someone involved with the railroads be chastised. Finally arriving in Baltimore, a locomotive with a special car sat waiting with steam up on a siding. Grant looked at his watch. There'd been no further word from Sherman. And the trip had been agonizingly slow. Was Rawlins—

He didn't want to face it.

Sherman and Secretary Cox were waiting as the train pulled into the Washington station. "Yes, he was still alive when we left him," Cump Sherman replied to his first question. "A carriage is waiting."

They hurried outside, and on the way to Rawlins's house Grant just stared out the window. He didn't want any conversation; all that mattered was his friend. He *had* to be in time . . .

He hurried into the bedroom at five-fifteen. Ely Parker got hurriedly to his feet from where he'd been sitting by the window. The figure in bed was covered by a sheet that extended over his face.

Grant couldn't stop the *"No!"* that escaped his lips.

"He died at four-twelve," Parker said softly.

CHAPTER 65

The ravening vultures shall enshroud you with the flapping of their dark wings and devour you.
—HOMER, THE *ILIAD*

Jay Gould looked up from the coffee Jennie Corbin had served him. "I'm worried," he said.

"Why?" Abel Corbin asked. "Your bank should have everything under control."

He was referring to the Tenth National Bank, which Gould's brokers and several other brokerage houses had acquired. That bank was serving as a conduit for the manipulations. Gould shook his head. "That's no problem. It's your brother-in-law I'm worried about. The damned contractionists, who want tight money, are working on Secretary Boutwell to unload some gold. If Grant goes along, we're in deep trouble."

"But he won't. You know how he has talked. He's swallowed that story about foreign purchase of the wheat crop being related to the gold price—hook, line, and sinker."

"Well, I wish I were as sure as you are. I have a lot of money in this." Gould snapped his fingers. "I know what—why don't you write him a letter reemphasizing how good it will be for the nation not to suppress the market by releasing government gold? You know, refresh his memory. What do you think of that?"

Corbin's dark eyes glowed. "I think it's a great idea. Yes, I'll go into detail about the matter. Uh-huh, I'm sure that'll reaffirm his position."

"He's vacationing out in the Pennsylvania hills, isn't he?"

"Right. We'll have to send the letter by messenger."

Gould nodded. "I'll get somebody dependable."

Corbin jumped to his feet. "I'll get right on it."

It was most pleasant in the hills of southwestern Pennsylvania on Sunday, the 19th of September. Fall was lurking, but a stubborn summer was refusing to go quietly, and it was a bright, sunny day. Grant was glad they had come to the little town of Washington to visit Julia's cousin; it was a new escape for him. Thirty miles below Pittsburgh, the remote village didn't even have a telegraph connection—a perfect place to truly get away and hide. And he liked this relatively new game of croquet, which was just beginning to get popular. He'd been told the French had adapted the game from the British, who had called it "pall mall" at the height of its favor in the seventeenth century. He smiled as he swung hard and knocked Porter's ball sixty feet away. He got a certain thrill out of that part of the game. "Okay," he said, "let's see you get it through the wicket from *there!*"

"Excuse me, sir."

Grant turned to see the housemaid standing a few yards away. "Yes?"

"There's a gentleman from New York to see you, sir."

"I'll see to it," Horace Porter said, heading for the house.

"I'll come along. I could stand some lemonade anyway."

The well-dressed man introduced himself politely as W. O. Chapin. He handed over Abel Corbin's carefully composed letter. Leaving Porter to talk to the visitor, Grant went out to the porch to open the envelope. He read through the letter quickly, then, feeling a rush of suspicion, went over it again. Corbin's air of desperation was readily apparent in the wording. *The man was twisting his arm not to sell government gold!* His own brother-in-law. And that meant he was probably in cahoots with Gould and Fisk, and those others, in some kind of a scheme to manipulate the market. They'd been chaffing and guying him all along. And he'd been too busy rubbing shoulders with the big money men to notice. What a fool he was! What a dupe. *Doggone it!*

He collected himself as he lit a cigar. If Corbin was in on it, his own sister probably was too. Doggone it! He went back into the parlor, where Chapin waited expectantly. "Is there any reply, Mr. President?"

Grant shook his head. "No, everything's all right. Thank you for coming."

Chapin excused himself and went on out to his buggy.

Grant strode purposefully into the library, where Julia was writing a short response to the note Chapin had also brought along from Jennie. "Has that man left yet?" she asked.

"Yes," Grant replied grimly. "What did Jennie have to say?"

"Oh, just the usual woman chatter. Wants us to visit again as soon as it's convenient."

"Is that all?"

Julia looked alarmed. "Why? You look worried."

Grant briefly related his suspicions.

She looked upset. "I don't believe it. Not Jennie, not Abel. No, it must be a mistake."

"I wish it were. Now, here's what I want you to add to your letter . . ."

The plot now sped on because of a telegrapher's minor change of wording. Chapin wired the following to Gould in New York: "Letter delivered all right." But it read, "Letter delivered. All right." The manipulators, gathered in the Corbin house, gleefully interpreted the message to mean that the president had agreed with the reasoning in Corbin's letter and would go along as he had previously indicated—to wit, he would *not* sell government gold. They toasted each other with champagne that Jennie quickly ordered opened. Now they could enlarge their buying efforts!

But their exultation would be short-lived.

On the 23rd, the Corbins' mail included the letter from Washington, Pennsylvania. Abel Corbin looked at his frightened wife with alarm as she handed him Julia's letter. Following the usual amenities, it was short and to the point: "Tell your husband that my husband is very much annoyed by your speculations. You must close them as quick as you can." It was signed simply "Sis."

The Corbins stared at each other in anguish. The worst had happened. Jennie burst into tears and buried her face in Abel's chest. "Oh, God, what are we going to do?" she sobbed.

Abel blew out a deep breath. "We have to get out of the market at once. Yes, we'll sell now and then we can tell your brother that we don't hold any speculative gold. Oh Lord, I thought he would see how good it was for the country . . . oh Lord, the president of the United States thinks we are scoundrels. Oh Lord . . ."

Gould looked up from Julia's letter, his thin, dark face set in a frown. "This *is* bad news." He stroked his chin. "The question is, when and how much gold will the government drop on the market?"

Corbin, wide-eyed and nervous, shook his head. "I have no idea."

"The next question is, how do we ease out of the market without starting a panic? We have to be very careful."

"I must get out, Gould. He's my brother-in-law!"

The financier's answer was cold. "You should have thought of that before you got involved."

"You *have* to buy my share, Jay, you must! Then I can tell Ulys that I have no personal interest. If my credibility is renewed, you'll see, he'll listen and hold off. I know he will!"

Gould watched quietly as Corbin fidgeted. He couldn't let Corbin sell out, not let everyone know that Julia Grant wasn't in. That would surely tip the hand and cause the market to collapse. It would be hard enough to ease out his own holdings . . .

"If I'm out," Corbin insisted, "Grant won't let Boutwell sell."

"I can't buy you out," Gould replied. "But I'll tell you what—keep this letter quiet and stay in the market, and I'll give you a hundred thousand dollars."

Jennie Corbin stepped forward from where she'd been eavesdropping. "No, Mr. Gould. We can't deceive Ulys any further."

The financer shrugged. "Think about it."

*   *   *

"Show the secretary in," Grant told Porter that night.

George Boutwell hurried forward, hand outstretched. He had just returned from vacationing at Martha's Vineyard after getting Grant's urgent summons. He quickly took a chair, listening as Grant frankly outlined what he knew about the gold market manipulations in New York. Boutwell replied that he had heard rumors in Massachusetts that something was afoot. He'd also heard gossip that General Butterfield might be involved.

"What is the price of gold now?" Grant asked.

"It was one hundred forty-one an ounce when I left my office."

"What price do you think is safe for the sale of our wheat abroad?"

"One forty-five."

"If it goes higher, we're facing runaway speculation, right?"

"Most certainly."

"You know what happened in 'fifty-seven. I was just a small farmer and it almost wiped me out. We can't let it occur again."

"No, Mr. President. If it goes up any more, we'll have to move."

"I agree. How much?"

"I think three million should do it."

Grant didn't want to take any chances. "I was thinking more along the line of five million."

"I'm sure four will be more than enough."

"All right, but we can't let Butterfield find out." Grant hated the thought that one of his good generals was crooked.

"If we have to sell, I'll do it by wire to New York."

"What about the telegraph operators?"

"They'll have no more than a minute to do anything."

"Very well," Grant said. "Watch it closely and use your own judgment on if and when." A flash of sadness hit him as he thought of Rawlins warning him about things like this. His good friend, he had known . . .

Black Friday!

James Fisk was bragging that he would drive the price of gold to $200 an ounce! The Tenth National Bank had certified checks totalling $18 million during the previous two days for the conspiring brokers, and it was still doing so. Everyone who had access to the Gold Exchange was filled with excitement on the morning of Friday, the 24th of September. Fortunes would be made this great day!

By eleven-thirty, gold had soared: 144, 147, 151, 154—

Wild, unbelievable!

Could it really go to 200? A man could make a killing at 160.

Who could stay out?

Grant, sitting in Boutwell's office in the Treasury Building, watched as the price jumped to $147 an ounce. He looked at the secretary, who nodded to his assistant. The telegram authorizing the four-million-dollar government sale had been written earlier and would be sent immediately.

Grant tugged at his beard. "I hope we're not too late," he said. How could he have let himself be duped like that? Stupid! No matter what happened, he would always feel that part of this was his fault. They'd played with him as if he were a dumb kid who'd just gotten off the farm. Stupid! If he'd just tumbled to what they were doing earlier, Gould and company might not have even tried this audacious scheme. Even with the four-million gold sale, it could be bad . . .

"I'm afraid there'll be some panic," Boutwell said.

"I know."

Sitting in the Gold Room of the Exchange, Gould had watched the frenzied activity for over an hour as gold was bought and sold in a bedlam of wild activity. From his stool, he stolidly watched the price climb slowly, switching his attention back and forth between the big clock and the board. The price went to $161 at 11:53. His magic number was 160, the price where his aides would dump the remainder of his gold. At 11:55 the price began to fall: 159, 158, 157—a direct result of his sales. At 11:58 an aide whispered that the government telegram had arrived.

"How much?" Gould asked.

"Four million."

Gould nodded his head, his dark eyes glinting. "That'll tip it." He gathered up his hat and cane and headed, expressionless, out of the room. He had made millions.

At 12:08 the price of gold reached $140 an ounce.

And panic ruled.

Many investors were ruined; some had made money on the crash. It was unknown how Fisk had fared. The Tenth National Bank failed. Abel Corbin lost heavily and had to sell his fine home in New York so he could survive in New Jersey. Congressman and former general James A. Garfield of Ohio would later chair an investigation of the panic. Democrats on the committee would want to sniff out the rumor that Julia Grant had been involved, but the Republican majority would block their attempt. The sale of government gold had held the damage sufficiently in check for the country to avoid a major collapse.

Black Friday.

Talking to Cump Sherman a few days later, Grant said, "You know, Sherman, I was terribly gullible in this thing. I just don't *understand* enough about the handling of money."

The general in chief clapped him on the back. "That's all right, Sam, you're learning."

Grant shook his head. "I'll *never* get caught wanting in the investment game again."

Chapter 66

After observing President Grant in action, it's un-
derstandable how Caligula made a consul of his
horse.

—A POPULAR ANTI-GRANT REMARK
ATTRIBUTED TO A
PHILADELPHIA NEWSPAPER

Colonel Frederick Dent of St. Louis, formerly of White Haven, had moved into the White House as if he owned it. Or perhaps it was an unspoken message from Julia, who—having never quite gotten over Ulys's selling of the house on I Street without consulting her—was flexing her muscles. Surely the days of her sitting around holding hands with her beloved Victor had grown shorter in number. But the pressures of being the president's wife could do that sort of thing to a woman, even a woman more sophisticated than she. Old Colonel Dent seemed bent on exerting every bit of rascality he could in bringing his outspoken Southern sympathies to the Executive Mansion. He went beyond the role of curmudgeon as he happily taunted Republican guests.

But he wasn't alone. Often on the scene at the White House was Jesse Root Grant, every bit as good, or better, in the role as Colonel Dent. The main difference between the two old knaves was that Jesse loved to play to the office-seekers and the press. He exacted "back-home" patronage from his busy son in the form of post office appointments and painted an important picture of himself. Along with Grant's placing of so many army subordinates in important posts, justifiable criticism grew in intensity. The public didn't know that he still didn't trust politicians, that he was appointing people to positions because he thought he could count on their honesty— rather than if they were fully qualified to be in them.

It wasn't well received that he had tried to appoint Alexander Stewart to the Treasury post—a man who had helped raise the money to buy his I Street house for sixty-five thousand dollars.

Nor did it add to his popularity when he appointed his old friend and former best man, General Pete Longstreet, to the position of surveyor of customs in New Orleans.

One popular quip was that "No president had ever 'got in the family way' so soon after taking office," or that his "gratitude to his family and generous friends was much like Desdemona's love for Othello."

And although he had been personally innocent in the Black Friday affair, its scandal had tainted him and left a scar on his administration. And, of course, the liberal press did what it could to enhance the negative publicity. One reporter who had been a war correspondent at Petersburg wrote, "Grant the general appeared to me far more the commanding person than Grant the president when I saw him standing inside the White House gates one morning, wearing a silk top hat."

It wasn't too long after the Black Friday scandal that trouble began in earnest with Senator Charles Sumner. The self-appointed savior of the country and, more specifically, the Negro, had for some time considered himself the most important man in America. When Grant had not only *not* deferred to him when he took office, had selected someone else for secretary of state, and had actually ignored him in selecting his Cabinet, Sumner had drawn the line in the sand. Eleven years older than Grant, the senator was a handsome and vain man with thick silver hair. He had once been caned in the Senate by a Southern congressman, and, in addition to considering himself the conscience of the Republican party, had been chairman of the Senate foreign relations committee since 1861.

He considered as his private domain the problem of exacting damages from Britain for the Federal losses caused by five ships during the war: the *Florida,* the *Rappahannock,* the *Georgia,* the *Shenandoah,* and the focus of the whole thing, the *Alabama.* English shipyards had built these vessels for the Confederacy, and the craft had wreaked havoc on the wartime blockade, had destroyed Union ships, and in general had disrupted commercial shipping. The United States had been trying vainly for a monetary settlement since the war, but the campaign had gone nowhere. Now, Senator Sumner was torpedoing Secretary of State Hamilton Fish's efforts. Fish had calculated that a sum of $48 million for direct losses would be adequate compensation. If this sum were agreed upon, the two countries could settle up and start rebuilding a peaceful friendship.

But the acerbic Sumner wanted his pound of flesh. He demanded "indirect" damages in an amount that could mean not only long-lasting hostilities, but possibly war with England. His price: 2.5 *billion* dollars! And if Britain weren't willing to cough up that unheard-of amount, she might offer Canada. Fish's hands were tied. And surprisingly, Grant's interest was only lukewarm. But the problem did place him at loggerheads with the arrogant Sumner. And Grant would support his secretary of state to the hilt.

The other major enterprise that arose was Santo Domingo.

Joseph Pulitzer was a part-Jewish Hungarian immigrant who had come to America near the end of the war to serve as a disgruntled rear rank private in a German cavalry regiment under Sheridan. Now, in early May 1870, he was a twenty-three-year-old state legislator from St. Louis. He was also an enterprising follower of the former Union general who was now a Missouri senator, Carl Schurz. But mostly the young Pulitzer was a reporter for the most important German-language newspaper west of New York, the prosperous *Westliche Post* in St. Louis. A tall beanpole, with a big cobnose and bullfrog eyes behind small eyeglasses, the young reporter was also a fiery idealist. Now, as he knocked on the door of General Cump Sherman's hotel suite, he removed his hat and rehearsed his opening.

Moments later an aide ushered him into the elaborate sitting room, where General of the Army Sherman sat working at a table. They shook hands and Pulitzer spoke in his badly accented English. "I thank you, General, for giving a former soldier an interview. The Germans of the West will also appreciate it."

Because he was visiting the city he so liked, and because he thought the German-language newspaper might be of value to his friend, the president, Sherman had agreed to grant the interview. But he was still far from enamored with the press, never would be.

As soon as Pulitzer draped his lanky body over a Queen Anne chair, he began to ask questions about the army and the Indian situation in the western states and territories. Finally he got to the subject most on his mind. "General," he asked, "aren't you a friend of President Grant?"

Cump Sherman brushed back his disheveled red hair, which the young Pulitzer noted was showing bits of gray. "Yes, I am," the general said. "We've known each other a long time."

"Have you had any differences since he became president, sir?"

Sherman lit a cigar and settled back in his chair. "Of course we have. He's a politician now, and I've always had problems with politicians."

"Do you—"

"Hold on," Sherman said with a wave of the hand. "I've always had *more* problems with reporters, so I'd better warn you to be careful with your questions, young man, or I'll have you thrown right out on your ass and blackballed from *any* further army interviews. Do you understand?"

Pulitzer sat a little straighter in his chair. "Yes, sir," he replied. He cleared his throat and went on in his thick accent. "Do you see many differences in Ulysses S. Grant as the president, sir?"

"Yes and no. Yes, he has different problems. No, he's the same honest, straightforward man I knew as a country youth when he entered West Point. You see—and you'd better get this right—the president is a *non*-politician politician now. He is above reproach personally, he has a lofty spirit of patriotism and a high sense of public duty. But he's in a den of snakes."

Sherman glared into the young newspaperman's dark eyes. "This is not for print, Pulitzer. He's just unversed in the guile of politics. He's too damned honest and accessible to self-seekers. He's also totally ignorant in the art of bending other men to his purposes." The general blew out a cloud of cigar smoke. "Now we can go back on the record."

"Would you give me your impression of the Santo Domingo enterprise?"

Sherman frowned. "It's an idea that started with Secretary Seward in the Johnson administration. That potentially rich Caribbean island holds a Negro republic that's in a chronic state of revolution and is always broke. Its current boss, Buenaventura Báez, wants it to be annexed by the United States. The president's concept is to do so because it could easily hold ten million people. It could be very attractive to our country's recently freed slaves. Three or four Negro states could be set up there, easing some of our tension in this area. It would also speed full citizenship for these people and eliminate some of the roadblocks the Southerners have set before them."

"Such as what, General?"

"Come now, Pulitzer, you know about the Black Codes, the separate schools, and all of the other hindrances, such as illiteracy. There's an old joke making the rounds—and this is not for publication. A darky goes up to a Georgia polling place to vote on election day. The official says, 'Can you read?' And the darky says, 'Sure, I can read.' And the official hands him an upside-down Chinese newspaper and says, 'What does this say?' And the darky looks at it a couple of minutes, then says, 'It say they ain't no nigras votin' in Georgia this year.' "

"Do you think the Freedman's Bureau should have been discontinued?"

"No. I think it should have been given more authority. If the army could have run it without political interference, it would have worked." Sherman shrugged. "But it's time for the states, both North and South, to meet the problem squarely."

Pulitzer scribbled a long note before asking, "Back to Santo Domingo, don't you think the president's idea of shuffling Negroes off to live there is avoiding the issue of making them true citizens?"

"Not necessarily. Wouldn't they be better off ruling themselves without restriction?"

The young reporter's frown was dark behind his eyeglasses. "Senator Schurz says it's a Ku Klux Klan plan. Anything to get the Negro out of the way."

Now it was Sherman's turn to frown. "Schurz sees a member of the KKK behind every tree trunk. And, since I've heard that you are one of his disciples, you know that he has split with Grant and is yet another recalcitrant Republican. He's no better than that egotist Sumner. And you aren't paying enough attention, young man. I told you the idea was Seward's in the beginning."

Pulitzer started to retort, caught himself and switched gears. "Isn't President Grant making a *lot* of enemies?"

Sherman blew cigar smoke toward his questioner. After a moment, he said, "*All* presidents make enemies. And particularly those honest ones who can't be bent."

"Since we've been talking about Negroes, what do you think about the current state of Reconstruction? Will it ever be successful?"

"That's a big question, young man. I think it can best be answered this way . . . The Union has been put back together. We had a terribly bloody revolt for four years. There still exists a great deal of hard feelings over it. Reconstruction is difficult and mistakes have been made while we bumbled our way through it. But there isn't any McGuffey's *Reader* to tell us how to do it right. I think the best way to summarize its success is this—we have not resorted to the gallows or the proscription list. We've basically stayed away from the word 'treason,' and the 'conquered province' theory has about died out. Some of the ills the war and Reconstruction have brought about will be slow to be rectified in their entirety. Social change, as in the case of the Negro, does not occur in the sublime or in actuality with the flourish of a pen. I don't think anyone knows how long complete equality will take. In the meantime, we just have to keep filing away on the edges until the word 'Reconstruction' is a memory and the United States of America is one truly united nation."

"When do you think that will be?"

Sherman shrugged. "Soon, I hope. Okay, I think that's enough for your good German readers. Except that you can tell them I think Otto von Bismarck is the greatest statesman in Europe." He grinned. "Don't you?"

Joseph Pulitzer rose to leave. "I suppose so," he murmured, clicking his heels and nodding his head. He was obviously not a happy journalist.

"Mr. President, I want to thank you for seeing me." The speaker was William Welsh, a wealthy Philadelphian who had come to Grant and Secretary of the Interior Jacob Cox shortly after Grant took office, and had proposed that a private board of Indian commissioners could help eliminate widespread graft in Indian affairs. The idea had made sense to both of them and Welsh had chaired the board, commencing in the spring of '69. Wealthy and strong-willed, Welsh was an ardent reformer who saw in every Indian agent a crooked mastermind as bad as Lucifer himself—which many of them were. Of course there were exceptions: dedicated and caring missionary agents, those who were army officers, and here and there a government employee. But Welsh's bitter fight was with the government, and the government was personified in Brigadier General Ely Parker. One would have thought the Philadelphian would have been pleased to have an Indian as commissioner, but he detested the Seneca and wanted no challenge from anyone, let alone an assimilated eastern army officer as spokesman for the Indian cause. Welsh's intentions were good, but he saw the Indian on a high, nobler plane than the average American, not a savage who could be taught the ways of American white man's civilization and become a part of it, as in the case of the commissioner of Indian affairs. He had angrily resigned in protest when Grant had refused to fire Parker, but he was still unofficially the power behind the board.

"How can I help you, Mr. Welsh?" Grant asked from behind his desk. Babcock, pencil and notebook in hand, and Secretary Cox were standing quietly to the side. Ely Parker was away from the city.

Welsh was a stocky man, sure of himself, easily angered when it came to anything that rubbed his mission in life the wrong way. When that happened, his voice was a file on a dull saw. "I question your peace policy, sir. Since your vainglorious Custer killed Black Kettle and over one hundred helpless Cheyenne and Arapaho on the Washita in November 'sixty-eight, there have been several outright slaughters by the army. In January, with your bloodthirsty Sheridan approving, that murderer, Colonel Baker, massacred a whole settlement of Piegans. That, sir, is not a *peace* policy!"

Grant glanced at Secretary Cox before replying. "You know that I abhorred both of those actions. Your board member, Vincent Colyer, has already raked everyone over the coals publicly."

Welsh's jaw jutted as he said, "But that's only part of the problem. As you know, even though I'm no longer on the board, I stay close to its functions. You might say I've become an accountant, or an inspector general, when I examine your expenditures." He looked meaningfully at Cox, then back to Grant. "Your damned commissioner, Parker, is not advertising his contracts properly. I demand his removal!"

Cox interrupted. "Mr. Welsh, there are times when the regulation isn't appropriate."

"Such as?"

"Contractors are infamous for padding. When we find one who provides us with the best product for the money, it may not always be the lowest bid. In that case, we have to make allowances. It isn't crooked."

"Then change the damned law!"

Cox shrugged. "I don't know how we can write it to obviate every scheme by every sharper. We are talking about feeding and caring for a hell of a lot of Indians *every* day."

"Like I said, you can start by getting rid of Parker."

"But he's an honest man," Grant protested. "The congressional committee found him innocent of any misconduct in its hearing. You know that."

"An incompetent!" Welsh blazed back. "I warn you, sir. Our board will pull out all its political stops if that man isn't removed!"

"Sir," the president said patiently, "I don't like threats, but I'll look into the matter again. In the meantime, I appreciate all you do in this difficult area." He got to his feet. "Now, if you'll excuse me, I'm late for another appointment."

As he strode past the rich Philadelphian, he wondered how much of a help John Rawlins would be right now. He probably would have jumped all over Welsh. A pang of sadness struck him. Doggone it, he missed his friend.

And now the end was approaching for Parker. He had to look at the big picture, and if Parker cast a shadow over the administration, even though he was totally innocent, he would have to go.

Another friend from the old days departing . . .

But not right away. That would give meaning to Welsh's threats.

CHAPTER 67

A s Sherman had patiently explained to young Pulitzer, the acquisition of Santo Domingo *was* an important part of Grant's agenda. He felt, without reservation, that the island would be of great value to the country and to the newly freed Negroes. Privately, he approved of American expansion, but to him the specific worth of Santo Domingo far outshadowed that theory. The other major role in this drama was being played by Buenaventura Báez. Báez seemed possessed in his pursuit of a merger with the United States, and understandably it was believed that he had a personal interest in such an annexation. If it took place, the Janus-faced ruler would not only feather his own nest financially, he would forestall any local move to remove him from power. Not only did the mulatto strongman paint a rosy picture of the republic as a mineral-rich land of opportunity for American Negroes, he extolled the values of its Bay of Samana as an American naval base.

A major supporting role was played by Colonel Orville E. Babcock, whom Grant sent down to the republic to coordinate possible annexation proceedings and to get the lay of the land. During his stay, the colonel negotiated a lease for Samana and developed a strong case of Domingan enthusiasm. He was also aware of the need for speed in the annexation process, because there was a strong possibility of British interest.

Orville Babcock, the aide who had played such an active part in the surrender ceremony at Appomattox, had, as much as possible, taken on the role of John Rawlins with Grant. Although he would never approximate the intimacy Rawlins had with the general, he was nevertheless close to him. He had none of the passion or moral drive of the fiery man from Galena, but he was pleasant and understanding, never threatening to his boss, yet capable of espousing Grant's opinions or desires when the need arose. A slender, dark-eyed man of thirty-five, the West Pointer was now enjoying the president's complete trust.

His zeal for the Domingan deal merely added to Grant's confidence in him.

But Congress was lukewarm. The radical zealots, led by Charles Sumner and Carl Schurz, portrayed the annexation idea as a means of shuttling the Negroes off to exile, instead of bringing them immediately into full assimilation within the everyday community.

In typical Grant fashion, the president attacked the problem head-on.

Early on a Sunday evening, President Grant strolled across Lafayette Square to the house of Charles Sumner. Although Washington would buzz over the visit, and the country's newspapers would remark on how Grant had splintered protocol, it was a simple decision for Grant. As much as he disliked the senator, he needed him to get the annexation through the Congress. He calmly walked up the front steps of the two-story red brick house and banged the large brass door knocker.

A haughty butler raised an eyebrow when he answered the door. "The senator is at table, sir."

Grant looked him evenly in the eye, quietly saying, "Please tell him I'm here."

At that moment, Sumner appeared behind his servant and said, "Come in, Mr. President." Even his arrogance seemed to be momentarily eroded by the shock of the unprecedented visit. "I was just eating with some newspaper friends. Will you join us?"

"Thank you," Grant replied, "but I've eaten."

"Some coffee perhaps?"

Grant went inside. "Yes, that will be fine."

The visitors at the dining table were Ben Perley Poole, a correspondent, and John "Dead Duck" Forney, the editor of two radical newspapers. They jumped to their feet as Grant approached the table. As soon as all were seated, the conversation began casually. Before long, Sumner turned it to the problems of one James Ashley, a former governor of the Montana Territory who had been fired by Andrew Johnson. Grant wasn't interested in Ashley; he had come to the senator's house for one thing and didn't want to be deterred from getting it.

The newspapermen remained mostly quiet as the two antagonists sparred.

In response to Sumner's argument that the black man be treated as an equal within the confines of the country, Grant replied, "The forces that defeat equality in the South, such as secret organizations like the Ku Klux Klan and biased state election procedures, may stand in the way of our goal to accomplish this for a long time. On Santo Domingo, black America will be free of those shackles."

The discussion continued until finally the handsome Sumner said, "What do you think, Mr. President, of reinstating Ashley out in Montana?"

Grant tried to look into his opponent's eyes, but all he saw was challenge. The senator was tossing him an obvious trade-off. After a moment, the president said, "I believe I can look favorably on such an appointment. It depends."

"Depends on what, sir?"

"Will you support the annexation?"

Sumner smiled. "Mr. President, I'm an administration man, and whatever you do will always find in me the most careful and candid consideration."

Grant decided the senator meant he'd give him full support, and rose to say goodbye. The visit had been worthwhile.

Julia was in a festive mood. She was wearing a new pale lavender summer frock of light silk, trimmed in an off-white Chantilly lace. Her hat, a wide-brimmed creation of satin and voile, matched the long-skirted dress, as did her lace-trimmed parasol. Julia Fish's yellow gown was somewhat similar, but a bit busier with its lace trim. Julia Grant had a right to be in a gay mood. After so many years of hearing Ulys talk about his graduation at West Point, she was a part of one. Her oldest son was about to throw his cap in the air with a shout of joy and she was going to relish the gesture nearly as much as he would.

A brother and her grand husband had graduated from this great institution and now her firstborn son was about to. It definitely made her a part of West Point tradition and glory. For a moment she thought of how much fun she'd have had if the Dent family had lived nearby. Just as in St. Louis, she'd have been popular, going to all of the balls and picnics. Handsome cadets everywhere. What a romantic time that would have been!

Maybe she would have met her Ulys that way. But no, he didn't dance.

Besides, it was perfect the way it had happened at White Haven.

She looked sideways at Ulys and wondered what was going through his mind as they sat there on the reviewing stand. Was he reliving his own graduation so long ago? Was he—

"Oh, your Fred is so handsome in his uniform," Julia Fish said pleasantly. "He'll be one of the best-looking young officers in the army."

The words warmed her heart. This fine, well-educated woman with impeccable taste was such a good friend. And always so supportive, so gentle, ever capable of brightening a day. And Fred *was* handsome. Much taller than his father. She'd tried to get Sherman to take him as an aide after graduation, but Cump had thought it best for him to serve a time with his regiment. Oh well, at least he was graduating. And in the Fourth Cavalry. It had been close though; he was ranked thirty-seventh academically in his class, and dead last in discipline. But being the son of the general in chief and president had produced its pressures. Certainly. Without a doubt, they had made it particularly hard on him. Like that time the Democrats had criticized his conduct in the hazing of a colored cadet—they were just screaming "nepotism" to get at Ulys. But none of that mattered now; he was graduating!

And it was so nice that the Fishes had been able to come with them. The secretary of state was proving such a stalwart friend to Ulys. He was so knowledgeable, so dependable.

Usually the ceremony was devoid of a speaker other than a member of the board of visitors, but this year General Sherman had changed the routine. The words of the guest, General James Harrison Wilson, broke into her reverie. ". . . My record in the past war illustrates my point. A graduate of this fine institution can meet any challenge. Three years and four months after I stood out there on this Plain waiting to celebrate my graduation, the stars of a brigadier general were pinned on my shoulders. Granted, it was wartime, and opportunities abounded, but my West Point training provided the background and basis for me to prove to General Grant that I could master any need he might have for me . . ."

General Wilson had resigned from the army as a permanent lieutenant colonel just the year before, and was engaged in railroad construction—*not* the Union Pacific—Ulys had told her. He'd been such a valuable general to Ulys during the war. One of the true "boy wonders." Now just listen to him!

She squinted into the sun as she looked back at Fred's company and thought she spotted him in ranks. How could she miss such a handsome young man?

The Santo Domingo annexation had its supporters, including legislators loyal to Grant, those who considered it a wise move, those persons with a personal financial interest in it, and outright speculators. When the treaty reached a committee vote, it was defeated by a vote of 5–3. Its chairman, Charles Sumner, did not support it.

Grant was furious. "The man promised me!" he said more angrily than Babcock had ever heard him speak. "Right there in his own house, he smugly made a deal, telling me he was an administration man."

"I hope this doesn't mean you'll give up on the proposal," Babcock said.

"I won't stop just because of the committee."

"Then I think we'd best get Secretary Fish more strongly behind it. With State pushing it, we'll have a better chance."

Grant nodded. "I'll talk to him today."

But he knew the possibility of passage was dimming.

A short time later, a report from Santo Domingo denounced a number of those involved as corrupt. It mentioned Grant's old friend and roommate, General Rufe Ingalls, as being involved—he had gone along with Babcock on one trip to the island. It also included Babcock.

And now Senator Carl Schurz was demanding blood.

Grant was again infuriated. It seemed that the frustrations of his office were more difficult to deal with than the war. Then he had suffered rebukes with a certain aplomb and without losing his temper. If someone attacked his plans, operations, or one of his subordinates, he ignored it. Even with a McClernand, who was now a circuit judge out in Illinois, he had remained patient. But, he reminded himself, the army was far more insulated than the presidency. Or any political office, for that matter. He should keep that in mind.

But he couldn't do it on this latest attack.

The unsupported charge was that both Ingalls and Babcock had been given land on Santo Domingo that would become highly valuable should the annexation come about. And that reflected directly on the president. In short order, both officers were exonerated, but one more bit of stench was added to Grant's administration.

Once more he thought of Rawlins warning him . . .

The proposal didn't look good. Schurz polled the Senate and the unofficial count showed that nearly half of that august body was against the annexation, that far from the required two-thirds would approve. Hamilton Fish advised Grant to take it easy on the issue, that it was probably doomed. "Don't beat a dead horse," he said gently.

The president grudgingly accepted the advice, but he would never cease to believe that Santo Domingo would have been a valuable acquisition.

* * *

It was shortly after nine A.M. on October 12 when Babcock brought the telegram to Grant. The president was having a late breakfast with his daughter, Nellie—now a lovely fifteen—and his secretary of state, Hamilton Fish. "I'm sorry to interrupt," the colonel said, "but I think you will want to see this."

Grant read quickly:

> General Robert E. Lee died after an illness of two weeks at his home on the grounds of Washington College in Lexington, Virginia. Commanding general of the famed Army of Northern Virginia in the late War of Secession, General Lee was revered by his officers, his men, and the people of the South. His widow, Mary Custis Lee, has announced that his funeral in the Lee Chapel will be conducted by General (Rt. Rev.) William Pendleton.

Grant stared at the message, feeling as if he'd lost a close friend. Yet he hardly knew the man. No, that wasn't true. No commander of a huge army could fight another and not know him. He had known what Lee would do when they faced each other in Virginia; each time he moved south, he was as certain as sunrise that Lee would move with him and be waiting.

The years fell away. It was a still early morning in the valley that held the City of Mexico, shrouded in mist, stretching out below the parapet where he sat on his horse. It was utterly silent. A major rode up, an engineer with dark eyes and a mustache. About forty years old. He was the famed Robert E. Lee, and he shared some brief thoughts with the discontented young quartermaster . . .

It was 1864 and he was seated on his horse, Cincinnati, by the Rapidan, watching the huge Army of the Potomac work its way across the river. He was the new general in chief and he was thinking about the general who awaited his host, the general who had been built into a god. And he had said to himself, "I'm coming, General Lee. And I'm not turning back."

The next time he saw the brilliant man had been on the day that would live forever—Palm Sunday, April 9, 1865. At Appomattox, in the two-story McLean house. Lee had used the square table; he had used the round one, marble tops on both. The great man had been attired in a new dress uniform, he in his shabby, dirty undress. The great general had maintained his strained, yet majestic presence throughout.

A thoroughbred, one of the greatest the country had ever produced.

His eyes filled as he dropped the telegram to the table.

CHAPTER 68

Grant's battle to keep the ship of state above water continued. He found an unwelcome bedfellow in General Ben Butler, who had gained considerable power in the House of Representatives. Although he still privately disliked the man, the president had no choice but to value his support. Also powerful, but sometimes aligned against Grant, was Black Jack Logan. The former corps commander under Sherman was now a junior United States senator and president of the Grand Army of the Republic. He had also been the founder in 1868 of Decoration Day, the May 30th holiday that commemorated the war veterans.

Grant and Hamilton Fish aggressively fought Sumner and company on the *Alabama* claims with Britain. It was in this conflict that Grant showed both his stubborn willingness to do open combat with a senatorial foe, and his statesmanship—although the New York *Tribune* defined it as a "linkage." "If Grant," the paper insisted, "had not been so intent on removing Charles Sumner, he might never have consummated such a remarkable act of statesmanship."

Grant was as relentless as Sumner was outrageous in his charges against the president. When he heard that the senator had said he was drunk when he went to Sumner's house to discuss the Santo Domingo problem, Grant declared war. In the party rift, Senator Roscoe Conkling was one of his ardent supporters against Sumner.

When the smoke cleared in March 1871, and the 42nd Congress was organized, Charles Sumner had been deposed as chairman of the powerful Senate Foreign Relations Committee. For the remaining three years of his life, he would be, in essence, defanged. There were those who said it was this enfeeblement that brought on his death in 1874. The man simply could not live without being the center of gravity in the government.

The "remarkable act of statesmanship" that the *Tribune* had mentioned was actually a combination of astute maneuverings. Grant publicly stated at one point in the proceedings that he was definitely not interested in acquiring Canada as a part of the United States. This statement brought out a huge sigh of relief from the Crown, and opened the doors for even friendlier negotiations. The second step by Hamilton Fish, at Grant's suggestion, was to disregard Sumner's monstrous "indirect" claims. During the presidential election campaign in 1872, an international board of arbitration met in Geneva and agreed that England would pay a sum of $15 million. Since nations had gone to war over much smaller disagreements, this solution, which began a strong friendship between Uncle Sam and John Bull, was truly remarkable.

*   *   *

But as Grant's term of office neared its end, two problems defied resolution. Reconstruction had become such a muddle of politics and racial antagonism that it should have been called Obstruction. The carpetbaggers and scalawags—the native white Southerners who had cooperated with the Federal government, often for their own gain—were by now so firmly entrenched that they couldn't simply be kicked out of power. Add the stubborn retaliation of Southerners in the form of the Black Codes and terrorist organizations such as the Ku Klux Klan, and one side became as bad as the other at times. The KKK had been organized and led by General Nathan Bedford Forrest after the war, but when its acts became too violent and uncontrollable, he had disbanded the movement in 1869. But a new KKK continued its bedsheet intimidation. Grant had issued a proclamation declaring the cross-burning Klan illegal and ordering hundreds of arrests, but the secret klaverns continued to spread their fear.

The other problem that seemed insolvable was Civil Service reform. There was simply too much patronage and favoritism in the system, and Grant himself wasn't innocent in this respect. With his staunchest supporters in Congress against a determined fight to change the system, Grant finally decided that it was the Congress's responsibility. It should be the voice of the people; if the populace wanted reform, its elected officials in the two Houses should effect it. And little was done.

Election time was approaching.

The country had been rapidly retiring its debt, there had been no major recessions, prosperity was in the air, railroads had been extended, the U.S. was at peace, and the pursuit of a second term faced Grant. For now he had decided he *liked* being president; and Julia *liked* being the president's wife. The problem facing him and his radical Republican supporters was the reform wing of the party. The reformers decided to unite with the Democrats on a joint platform and toss out Grant and his radicals. They pledged a softer Reconstruction program, widespread Civil Service reform, and lower tariffs.

It all looked good, and the Democrats bought it—even the hard-to-swallow candidate the dissident Republicans proposed to nominate: Horace Greeley. The influential publisher of the New York *Tribune* had been a persuasive part of America's conscience for forty years. Philosophically, the energetic editor had bounced all over the place. He had denounced monopoly, the railroads, the Mexican War, and was a fierce opponent of slavery. Yet he was also against abolition. Like Grant, he had favored a vigorous prosecution of the war, yet endorsed general amnesty at its end. He irked many Northerners when he signed a bail bond that freed Jefferson Davis. Deciding that Grant's administration was hopelessly corrupt, Greeley easily fit in with the reformers. But a whole generation of Democrats had learned to hate him, and he *looked* funny with his long gray hair hanging down from his bald head.

His chances of defeating even a less popular President Grant were slim. In fact it looked like the coalition had shot itself in the foot.

Then the Crédit Mobilier rocket struck.

Crédit Mobilier of America, named after the French company, was a construction syndicate that had been created by Oakes Ames, his brother Oliver, and other major stockholders of the Union Pacific Railroad in 1864. Crédit Mobilier purchased the remainder of the railroad company's stock, thereby combining the ownership of the two corporations. Then the government got involved, hiring the Union Pacific to complete nearly seven hundred miles of the intercontinental railroad from the Midwest to the Pacific coast. Part of the largess to the Union Pacific was in the form of loans, land grants and subsidies. Union Pacific then awarded the construction contract to Crédit Mobilier itself, which grossly inflated its costs to some $94 million instead of the actual $44 million. Its stockholders' dividends increased 500 percent per year in 1867 and 1868.

But suspicions arose.

The fun began. *Congressman* Oakes Ames hit upon a scheme to stave off a congressional investigation. All he had to do was distribute shares in Crédit Mobilier among his cronies in the House, including its then speaker, who was now the vice president. He even had it figured so they wouldn't have to put up any cash for the stock; they could make long-term purchases and use the dividends and interest to pay for them.

The day the New York *Sun* published the story with banner headlines, Orville Babcock brought the newspaper to Grant's office in the White House. It was a warm September morning, and the windows were wide open. A shaft of sunlight illuminated the carpet, but it was the only sunshine this room would see on this dark morning. The *Sun*'s story on the scandal listed the congressmen who held stock and quoted some of Oakes Ames's letters regarding the dealings. The article stated that $33 million profit was made by those who accepted the bribes. The vice president's name was on top of the list.

Grant blanched while reading the *Sun*. This scandal would be the worst in the country's history, and even though it hadn't occurred during his administration, he most surely would get all the taint from it! He looked up. "Get the attorney general over here at once. We'll have to suspend all of that company's operations immediately. And we'll need a full investigation. Of all the doggone times for this to happen—"

A secretary stuck his head through the door. "Sir," he said, "Vice President Colfax wishes to see you."

Grant frowned at Babcock, then replied, "Send him right in."

Schuyler Colfax wore a worried look as he hurried in. "Mr. President," he said quickly, "I suppose you've seen the *Sun* this morning. Well, I want you to know I did buy some Crédit Mobilier stock, but only a few shares, and I paid cash for them. In no way was I involved in any payoff or bribe by Oakes Ames. My total involvement was about sixty-one dollars."

Grant said nothing as the vice president went on. "I know the embarrassment this will undoubtedly cause you. It's incredibly distasteful to me, although I'm innocent of any wrongdoing. It will probably mean the end of my career. But I must think of the party and you. I ask that you remove me immediately from the ticket for reelection."

Grant blew out a deep breath as he shook his head. "I wonder, Colfax, when this doggone stuff is ever going to end. I'll think about your offer, which is most considerate. I'd keep you on to prove your honesty, but my advisers will probably disagree." He eyed the man who had been second in line for the throne for four years for a few moments, then added, "I'll let you know."

The Crédit Mobilier scandal did taint Grant. And his election team did pick a new vice presidential candidate: Henry Wilson, a onetime shoemaker from Massachusetts who had been an able senator since 1855. One election poster depicted the two candidates in aprons with their sleeves rolled up, dubbing them "the Tanner" and "the Cobbler."

But none of it mattered; Grant had enough popularity among the midwestern farmers, the ex-soldiers, and the Negroes who could vote, to carry the election. He triumphed over Horace Greeley and headed into a second term.

Greeley, whose wife had died a week before Americans went to the polls, died three weeks after the election. His contributions to nineteenth-century America were never fully appreciated. Many hundreds of settlers in the western part of the country would never forget him, though; for Greeley had popularized another man's famous words: "Go West, young man."

Six weeks after the election a full investigation of the Crédit Mobilier abomination was dropped. Cleared were Schuyler Colfax, future president James Garfield, House Speaker James Blaine, and several others. Many political careers were ruined by the disclosures, and a number of judges were impeached or forced to resign. Oakes Ames managed to get his punishment reduced to censure by Congress; he died a few months afterward. And finally, the Union Pacific Railroad was stripped of all its assets except the roadbed and its machinery to pay government loans, leaving it debt-ridden.

The broad result of the scandal was further awakening of the public to widespread political corruption and unethical business practices. Many Americans, who read only the anti-Grant papers during the election campaign would go to their grave believing and convincing others that "that crook, Grant, had his fingers in the French railroad thing right up to his elbows."

CHAPTER 69

1873 was a memorable year in Grant's second administration, mostly because of the bad things that happened. His father, the irrepressible old conniver, died that summer in Covington, Kentucky. Grant stood at his graveside during the service and thought back through his boyhood, then through the later years, remembering how old Jesse Root Grant had bailed him out of trouble when he was destitute in New York—following the binge in San Francisco—and when he gave him the job in the Galena store. He pushed away memories of when the old man had tried to take monetary advantage during the war and later. Choleric old rascal. He guessed he got the temper he'd been showing more and more lately from him.

The funeral brought back memories of another man who had lived in Georgetown, the man who had given him his West Point appointment, the one who might have been president and given U. S. Grant a valuable livelihood as a mathematics professor, enabling him to possibly retire as a lieutenant colonel someday in the future . . . General Tom Hamer, long turned to dust in a Mexican grave.

As he replaced his hat and turned away from the grave, Grant wondered if Hamer, in some way, knew what had happened to his one-time protégé. He'd never thought much about heaven and hell, or an afterlife. He'd certainly been to church enough in his fifty-one years to know what was taught by scripture and dogma. Could Hamer be watching? Was John Rawlins observing from somewhere? Surely Rawlins deserved such a reward, if there was one. Where would his father fit in? His mother, bless her soul?

He would stand by a second gravesite near the end of the year, that of another stubborn old man—eighty-seven-year-old Colonel Frederick Dent, the man who had thought him unworthy of marriage to his favorite daughter. He and Colonel Fred Dent, Jr., along with young Fred, would accompany the body back to St. Louis for burial. That funeral, as well, would bring back many memories. Afterward, Julia's real estate holdings would increase and Grant would think about creating a country gentleman's estate back at White Haven and Hardscrabble. But it would never work out. Some sort of failure seemed to hang like a shroud of fog around that place.

The major calamity of 1873 was the financial collapse that was triggered on September 18 by the failure of Jay Cooke & Company. The banker blamed the ruin on his inability to sell the securities of his Northern Pacific Railway. As on Black Friday, panic reigned on Wall Street, and two days later Grant went to New York with his new secretary of the treasury, William Richardson. They met with conservative bankers in an effort to find the best finger to stick in the dike. In the end, he went back to Washington and listened to Hamilton Fish. He then told Richardson to reissue $26 million worth of greenbacks that had been redeemed. This was a compromise between the easy-money people and the hardliners, and it reduced the pain on Wall Street. But unlike Black Friday, which healed quickly, the illness lingered in the form of a depression that would last for several years and leave the working people of the country in distress.

The hard times that had been avoided since the war settled in on the country and there was only one figurehead on whom to place the blame: the president. One incident they couldn't blame on him was the death of Charles Sumner on March 11, 1874. The sixty-three-year-old senator had left the Republican party to support Greeley in '72, but had come back with hat in hand. Cump Sherman was visiting Grant in his White House office when news of the senator's death was brought in by Babcock. The redhead slowly lit a cigar, blew out the smoke, and said quite calmly, "The old bastard just couldn't stand being relegated to second fiddle. He still thought he was the Paul Revere of the Negro support movement. He really died of sadness over the fact that the government and the country could run without him at the reins."

Grant sighed as he looked out the window into the morning rain. "I suppose that had some effect," he said. "Maybe I was too hard on him."

"Huh!" Sherman snorted. "If you hadn't been, he'd have devoured you and spit out the seeds without an ounce of concern. You'll be remembered, you know, for your settlement of the English problem more than any other feat in your presidency. And if that son of a bitch had had his way, we'd be at war with them right now."

Grant shrugged. "Still, he gave a lot of service to his country."

"And his ego was well rewarded."

Grant didn't believe he would feel so emotional. He, the stone-faced, stolid man who had been accused over and over in the newspapers of being uncaring, the indifferent one, the butcher. What were some of the other words the newspapers used—enigmatic, impassive, imperturbable . . . a stoic? Well, when one's little girl got married, a man was liable to be most anything. He barely heard the minister's words, ". . . *the holy ship of matrimony.*"

Even the newspapers commented on how beautiful Nellie was. She'd been the darling of the White House when she came to live there at age thirteen. The country hadn't had a young girl in its executive mansion in a quarter of a century when she arrived and the people had loved reading about her. Now at eighteen, she was going into another man's arms and leaving. Going off to England. Leaving him. He'd probably remember May 21, 1874, as the day some of the light went out of his life.

She looked like a young queen, or at least a princess, as she stood there in front of him on the dais in the East Room. A bell of fresh white camellias served as a crown for the ceremony. Her long gown with its tiers and ruffles of, well, he didn't know much about fabrics, but it was made of laces and satins and silks and all kinds of delicate white parts. Son Fred, in his dress uniform, was standing up for the groom. The bridesmaids were off to the side, while Julia—also sad in her lovely silk gown—was standing to Nellie's right with Buck and Jesse.

The minister rambled on . . .

Everyone felt that the English bridegroom, Algernon Sartoris—pronounced Sar-tress—was a fine catch for Nellie. She'd fallen in love with him on the ship coming back from her European trip. A handsome and charming young man, Algernon was the grandson of the great actor Charles Kemble, and the son of the bright and talented opera singer Adelaide Kemble Sartoris. Nellie's new mother-in-law had been one of the most popular hostesses in London until the death of Algernon's older brother the year before. Grant was certain his daughter would have a most interesting and agreeable life in England, though he hated the thought of not being able to see her.

But she had promised to visit them in their summer home in Long Branch.

"Do you, Nellie, promise to love, honor, and obey . . ."

Julia tried to hold back the tears. After all, it wasn't as if her daughter were going off to Siberia. Nellie would have a cousin through marriage who was a real *countess,* and White Haven would finally have a titled connection, as it should. It was just too bad her grandmother, Ellen, couldn't be here to see it. Or even her grandfather.

A smile touched her lips. Nellie was so very pretty. And Fred, the best-man lieutenant—could any young man be more handsome? Buck on her left was just as good-looking. A student at Harvard, he was headed toward a career in the law. The sixteen-year-old Jesse on her right, was still the comedian of the family. He'd be the only one left at home in the White House now. And before long, he'd be off to school. She sighed.

Ah, what a frantic, fun-filled time the preparation of the wedding had been! The dressmakers had been so busy. And all the rest of the staff— the chef, the decorator—why, the flowers alone were enough to occupy two people. But that was all right—the country was having a wedding!

Her departure from her usual black velvet, which showed off her shoulders and arms to such advantage, was required. She'd first thought she'd wear a baby blue gown. After all, one old rhyme said, "Green is forsaken, and yellow forlorn, but blue is the prettiest color that's worn."

And of course there was the adage that no bride will be lucky who does not wear "something old and something new, something borrowed and something blue." The fancy blue lace garter on Nellie's right thigh would take care of the latter. But that didn't have anything to do with the mother of the bride. At the last minute, she'd heard that blue was considered unlucky in a wedding in certain parts of England, and, after all, wasn't the groom British? Pale lavender had won out, with lots of lace. And her gown was as pretty as anyone's. Except the bride's, of course.

She glanced at Ulys, attired in his finely tailored black suit. He was staring at the floor, and she knew the sadness had caught up with him. They had always indulged their children, sharing triumph and fun with them, never once using the rod for punishment. In fact, Ulys was probably the most relaxed, indulging father in the world. And now he was losing his little girl.

Pity.

She smiled, once more noticing the appealing scent of the flowers. How she loved life here in the White House.

"*. . . I now pronounce you man and wife.*"

CHAPTER 70

But the mild glance that sly Ulysses lent,
Showed deep regard and smiling government.
—SHAKESPEARE, *THE RAPE OF*
LUCRECE

Joseph Pulitzer was paying his way through law school in New York by working as a reporter for the *Sun*. With his connections in St. Louis, and his continuing affiliation with Senator Carl Schurz, it was only natural that he should discover and write about the Whiskey Ring:

> St. Louis, Mo., March 22, 1875. *"Whiskey Ring." Sounds like a bunch of people sitting in a circle and passing around a jug of liquor. It isn't. It's a group of crooks who cheat the government out of millions of dollars in tax money each year. Distillers and distributors make a practice of bribing tax agents to provide tax stamps in excess of the money paid for them. These same corrupt tax agents also ignore cheating on the measure of whiskey in a bottle. The government loses up to $15 million per year and the public, as usual, gets robbed.*
>
> *There are whiskey rings in the large cities such as Chicago and Milwaukee, where liquor is being distilled. But the one this reporter has inside knowledge of is in St. Louis, where the most active and brazen of the rings operates. It is so corrupt that Secretary of the Treasury Benjamin Bristow has obtained from Congress $125,000 to conduct an investigation. A brilliant St. Louis investigative reporter has been hired to do the spade work.*
>
> *The collector of internal revenue in St. Louis just happens to be a general who is an old friend of President Grant. This general is reported to be the keystone. It is believed that as much as two million dollars in graft may be involved in that whiskey ring alone, and there is a strong rumor that some of it may be reaching the White House.*

Secretary of the Treasury Benjamin Helm Bristow was an honest man. He had been solicitor general—the government's lawyer when cases are presented to the Supreme Court—and had been appointed to his present post in June 1874. He had barely taken office when he encountered evidence that crime involving distillers was rampant within his own department. He soon began the private investigation that led to his obtaining the money from Congress for a formal inquiry into a scandal that was cheating the government out of tax on over fourteen million gallons of whiskey a year.

Now he sat in the president's office as Grant asked him about Pulitzer's article in the *Sun*.

"I don't know where the man got this much information, Mr. President. We've certainly kept quiet about the investigation. However, Pulitzer may know the investigative reporter I've hired in St. Louis, or may have just heard about it nosing around out there. He lived there for a time, you know, and was a protégé of Carl Shurz."

Grant stroked his beard. "No wonder."

"I warned you, you know, of the possibility that General McDonald's skirts may be far from clean."

Grant hoped McDonald wasn't involved. He was so doggone tired of finding crookedness in people who should be honorable. McDonald had done a good job in the war and was a loyal Republican. Upon Sherman's recommendation, he had appointed the man collector for Arkansas and Missouri back in 1870, and had gotten to know him during his visit to White Haven. If McDonald was involved, it would be yet one more black mark on the administration. "I hope this is all a big mistake," Grant replied.

"It may be worse," Bristow said.

"And how's that?"

Bristow inhaled before presenting the very bad news. "There is a strong possibility that Orville Babcock is involved."

Grant's famous inscrutability cracked as he scowled. His secretary and closest friend? Impossible. "Are you sure someone isn't just trying to involve me personally?"

"No, sir. There are mounting indications."

Grant shook his head. "No, I don't believe it. They came after him on the Santo Domingo project, you know. And he was innocent."

Bristow's expression was pained, his voice low. "Yes, I know. But this is different."

Grant looked away. "Well, I won't hear of it without powerful evidence. I'd trust Babcock with everything I own."

As soon as Bristow left, Grant called the skinny, dark-eyed Babcock in, and went straight to the point, "There are going to be accusations that you have been involved in bribes with the whiskey ring in St. Louis. I know they can't be true, but I have to ask you directly. Have you accrued any value from any activity with the whiskey industry?"

"No, General, I haven't," Babcock replied evenly. "I can't imagine how such rumors get started."

"Secretary Bristow says there is evidence."

Babcock frowned, shaking his head. "I wouldn't know what it could be. Is the secretary out to get my head or something?"

"I don't believe so. The information is apparently showing up in St. Louis."

Babcock looked directly into his boss's eyes. "It has to be false."

"Very well. And what about General McDonald out in St. Louis? He is being accused as well."

"As far as I know, McDonald has done nothing wrong."

Grant nodded his head. "All right. We'll weigh it all accordingly."

His aide wouldn't lie to him.

On May 7, Bristow brought news to Grant that he had summoned Mc-Donald to Washington to face irrefutable charges that he was in the eye of the St. Louis storm. "The general broke down and confessed," he told the president. "He is the central figure out there all right."

Grant lit a fresh cigar and blew out the smoke. His eyes were chilly. "I've been told by Babcock that McDonald is okay," he said.

"That's not possible, Mr. President."

"Are you saying that Babcock is lying?"

Bristow's eyes hardened as well. "I told you that McDonald *confessed*."

Grant regarded his treasury secretary calmly. The man had to be disloyal. All of this was reformer activity really aimed at himself. Why couldn't even his own Cabinet be trustworthy? How he needed Rawlins at a time like this. Rawlins would line everything up and straighten it out. That was the good part about an army command—having a good chief of staff.

"The collector of internal revenue in Chicago is also in this up to his knees," Bristow added.

Grant blew out another batch of cigar smoke. If he didn't accept the secretary's statements, the man would resign. Then there would be more stench. "Are you quite certain that McDonald is guilty?"

"Mr. President, he is presently in New York with an estimated one hundred and sixty thousand dollars of misgotten funds ready to flee the country."

Grant sighed. "All right. Arrest both collectors."

"What about Babcock?"

"He has assured me of his innocence and I don't want to hear any more accusations."

Bristow started to say something, then stopped. After a moment, he replied, "Very well, Mr. President." He excused himself and marched stiffly out of the office.

The Grants awaited the birth of their first grandchild at the seaside cottage in Long Branch, New Jersey, during the summer. Nellie was back from England for the occasion, big in the belly. In August, Ben Bristow and Attorney General Edwards Pierrepont came down to the shore from New York with evidence against Babcock. Bristow watched as Pierrepont handed over some telegrams that Babcock had sent to McDonald and another member of the St. Louis ring, warning them to beware of the investigation. The messages were cryptically worded and had been sent in the spring, just after Bristow had alerted Grant. The most damaging was a note to McDonald that read, "We have official information that the enemy weakens. Push things." It was signed "Sylph" and was written in Babcock's hand.

"We believe the meaning of this telegram is that the sender had gotten the investigation stymied," Bristow said.

Grant reread the message. It could mean anything. "I wouldn't take this to court on that assumption. Would you?"

"No, but it's from Babcock to McDonald."

Grant shrugged. "Okay, let no guilty man escape—if it can be avoided."

The United States district attorney in St. Louis felt he had sufficient evidence against Babcock to get him before a grand jury. When confronted, the aide looked over the telegrams and shrugged. Looking the president in the eye, he explained, "This particular 'Sylph' message that seems to have everyone so wrought up is about a bridge project that General McDonald had me look into. I told him that the opposition to the funding was weakening."

"What about these other messages?"

"Same thing. It was sort of a code we were using."

Grant nodded. "Why did you tell me McDonald was innocent of any misconduct in the whiskey ring?"

"I was misinformed, General. He lied to me."

"Very well."

Once more Babcock was off the hook.

As December blew in with an ice storm, Babcock requested a military court of inquiry to clear himself of all charges. He managed to get the court stacked in his favor, down to the judge advocate general—the prosecuting attorney—who was a West Point lawyer who had once performed legal services for him. Grant knew nothing of this part, although he was aware that the three general officers comprising the court would not be prejudiced against his secretary. He directed that findings of the ongoing grand jury in St. Louis be provided to the court of inquiry in Washington. The army court cleared Babcock, but the grand jury brought in a true bill requiring the colonel to stand trial in a civilian court.

Grant was angry, once more feeling that Bristow was conspiring against him. After conducting his own investigation into Babcock's activities, he called the chief justice of the Supreme Court into his office to witness a presidential deposition stating that his aide was innocent.

It was the swing of power that brought in Babcock's acquittal at the end of February. Grant was mostly pleased. Attacked, he had bowed his head and met the enemy head on. And, as in the war, he had won out. But part of him was not pleased, and a touch of guilt bothered him. He had used naked power to protect himself, and to spare his friend, but he had done so deviously—a method that was simply not his. He still believed Babcock, but there was just too much evidence for the man to be *totally* innocent. He'd have to be banished from the White House.

Another friend gone.

Had he been used?

Or had he become the deceitful politician that Cump Sherman so detested?

Was there a word *duplicitous*?

Perhaps this would be the end of graft and thievery in his administration, and his last year in office could be devoted to bettering the country. Perhaps he could even end some of the racial violence in the South without resorting to another conflict.

He knew the odds would be bad for him to end his administration peacefully because the Democrats had a majority in the House, and their sworn goal was to exploit Republican corruption.

Still . . .

CHAPTER 71

And Jove answered, "Set Minerva on to him, for she punishes him more often than any one else does."
—HOMER, *ILIAD*

The enemy guns had just fallen silent over the whiskey ring scandal when, on March 2, Secretary of War William Worth Belknap dropped a bomb on the presidential doorstep. A fleshy two-hundred-pounder, the easygoing former general had tears in his eyes when he came to the White House that evening. He immediately launched into a confession: "Sir, as you know, it costs a lot of money to entertain at Cabinet level in Washington . . ."

Grant felt a tug of fear as the secretary went on.

A Princetonian who claimed Iowa as home, the forty-six-year-old Belknap had fought from Shiloh on during the war, leading a division and finally a corps. He was a lawyer who had been thrice married and had, upon Sherman's urging to Grant, followed Rawlins as secretary of war. In fact, it was his marriages that had brought him to this sad point, he told the president.

He was tearful as he continued, his voice low and broken at times. "As you know, my second wife was Carrie Tomlinson, a fine woman who died in 'seventy from consumption. Without my knowledge, Carrie worked out a scheme whereby a New York friend, Caleb Marsh, entered into a contract with the holder of the Fort Sill trading post in Indian Territory."

Belknap stopped and brushed his eyes with a handkerchief. "The Indian trading posts supposedly make quite a bit of money for their operators."

"Yes," Grant murmured, "the Democrats are pointing that out." He was referring to the investigation a House committee had begun.

"As I said," Belknap went on, steadying himself, "I didn't know about these arrangements. She just suggested to me that the holder of the contract, John Evans, be allowed to continue in that capacity—which, of course, I agreed to. But I later learned that Carrie was to receive some six thousand dollars per year from Marsh, who was being paid by Evans. She received only one payment, because she passed away a month after our poor little boy was born. Her sister, Amanda, took the child to care for, and shortly after, Caleb Marsh came to her and told her that the payments would continue with the child as beneficiary. As you know, Mr. President, I was terribly shaken by Carrie's death . . . and then a few months later our fine little son died . . ."

Again Belknap paused, blotting his eyes and collecting himself. "When Amanda went to Europe, the payments came to me. I don't know what possessed me, sir, but like I said, it costs a lot of money to entertain in this town, and . . . well, you know I married Amanda in 'seventy-two—"

Grant knew very well. The curvacious and beautiful Amanda, or "Puss" as her friends called her, had become a close associate of his wife. Julia liked her and shared activities such as luncheons and charities with the well-groomed woman. In fact, to make the story all the more implausible, the Belknaps attended the same Bible class with the Bristows. And Bristow, as the self-appointed reformer of the conservative Republicans, considered himself the watchdog in the Cabinet. It sounded like some kind of a dime novel. No, it was more like an Edgar Allan Poe story.

"And Amanda is an an expensive woman. You know."

"Yes," Grant replied. Amanda always dressed exquisitely. "All told," he asked, "how much money did you realize from this trading post arrangement?"

The reply was a whisper. "A little over twenty thousand dollars."

"Does the investigating committee know this?"

"I believe so."

Grant frowned. The whole doggone story would hit the front pages everywhere. Another crooked Grant scheme! *When was it going to stop?* This man had been his secretary of war for nearly seven years. Was anyone honorable any more?

"Here is my letter of resignation," Belknap blurted, holding out a sheet of bond paper.

Grant scanned the single line: "I, William Worth Belknap, resign as Secretary of War, effective this date, March 2nd Inst., 1876."

The president nodded, dropped the note on his desk, and reached for his pen. As he wrote, he said, "I'll accept your resignation immediately, with deep regret." Signing his short acceptance, he looked up sadly. This man, his friend, had committed a criminal act. And, incredibly, two of the accomplices had been his wives.

Tears were now streaming down Belknap's cheeks. He reached for Grant's hand. "Mr. President, I can't tell you how sorry I am. It sort of started and couldn't be stopped. I—"

Grant turned away. "Good night, General."

William Tecumseh Sherman strode up the sidewalk to the front of the White House at 8:25 the following morning. Although a touch of moist chill was in the air, the sun was beginning to make steam out of it. A few puffy white clouds hung like cotton balls in the bright sky. Sherman wondered if they would climb later in the day to roiling thunderstorms that would disgorge some more rain. He noted that a couple of pink buds were out, the early birds. He was in town on a visit, since he had made St. Louis his headquarters for some time. He'd sold Grant's former house and had shed himself of conniving and socially expensive Washington with great relief. Scott had set the precedent when he headquartered in New York, and Grant had raised no objection when he requested the move to Missouri. His *Memoirs* had been published the previous year, and while they had served to make him even more unpopular in the South, they had honestly put his views and life on public record. There had been various attempts to get him to run for the presidency, but he had continued to flatly refuse. Seeing what had happened to Grant had only confirmed his ongoing disgust with politicians.

The president was just finishing some fried eggs and well-done bacon when the general in chief was shown into his private dining room. Grant looked up from the Washington *Star*. "Morning, Sherman. Thanks for coming over. You had breakfast?"

"Yes, sir, but I'll take some of your coffee. What's up, as if I didn't know."

Grant tossed the newspaper in front of him. The Belknap story was splashed across its front page. "The biggest news in the world. Our secretary of war is a crook."

Sherman frowned. "I know."

"Did you have any idea?"

"Nope. Although I kinda wondered about all those dresses and jewels his pretty lady wore. What does a Cabinet member make—eight thousand a year?"

"About."

"When did you find out?"

Grant told him about Belknap's confession.

Sherman shook his head. "He's always been an honorable man."

"Not lately. Tell me some more about these Indian trading posts of yours."

"Rumor has it that some of the operators make quite a bit of money."

"These trading posts are under the army. Don't you *know?*"

Sherman's expression hardened. "Some of these sutlerships were in effect when you were general in chief. Evans was one of them."

"I'm aware of that."

"I'll start my own investigation right away. But unless I have full control over the selection of these sutlers—without any influence from the War Department—the goddamned patronage will continue."

"Good. In the meantime, we'd better get ready for the onslaught. The wolves will be howling."

"To hell with them."

"You're not sitting in my seat."

"And I never will be."

"I think you'd better move your headquarters back to Washington."

Sherman sighed. "I suppose so."

Grant handed over a cigar. While each lit up, he said, "And while we're on the subject of Indians, how are things out in the Black Hills?" Gold had been discovered in the sacred domain of the Sioux in Dakota Territory, and the race of human flotsam for the yellow metal was on. During a meeting the past November, Grant had told Sheridan he didn't want the army to actually prohibit the gold miners from going into that area, which had been reserved for the Indians under the Fort Laramie treaty of '68, but to discourage it. It was an impossible situation.

Sherman blew out a cloud of smoke and looked at the cigar appreciatively. "It's trouble. The Sioux keep growling that we are breaking our treaty with them by letting the miners in. And there's a strong chief by the name of Sitting Bull stirring things up. Sheridan thinks we ought to go after them, and so do I. George Custer wants to fight them as well. As you know, he's pleading his case *publicly* in Chicago. He's nothing but trouble."

"I ought to have him shot," Grant growled. "What do you think?"

"Let's give him the Seventh Cavalry again. He'll serve under Terry in the field, and if he acts up, we'll court-martial him again." He smiled at Grant through the smoke hanging over the table. "And *then* we'll shoot him."

Grant nodded his head.

He was truly sorry about having to go back on his word with the Sioux.

In four short months, Grant would be even sorrier.

His son, Buck, now serving as his secretary in Babcock's place, brought the morning newspapers to his bedroom early on the morning of the 5th of July. Buck's voice was excited as he said, "Look, it's Custer!"

Julia looked up in alarm from where she was combing her hair at the vanity. "What about Custer?"

"He and his whole command have been killed at some place called the Little Big Horn!"

Grant quickly read the front-page account in the *Star,* wondering how the newspapers could have such news when the president of the United States didn't even know about it. But there it was—while taking part in an offensive under General Terry, Custer and his Seventh Cavalry had gone into battle against "several thousand savage Indians under Sitting Bull, Crazy

Horse, Gall, and other chiefs. The golden-haired hero of the Civil War and other Indian battles had apparently been surprised and had bravely perished with nearly three hundred of his proud cavalrymen." The engagement already had a romatic name: "Custer's Last Stand."

"How could such a thing happen?" Buck asked anxiously.

"I don't know," Grant replied.

But he could guess.

The Democrats were not about to let the Republican secretary of war off the hook. In spite of the resignation, Congress set up an impeachment trial for Belknap. July was the month of the nation's centennial, and many visitors were on hand to jam the Senate gallery. Having a government bigwig on the hot seat was an attraction few voters who could make it to the capital could pass up. And so much space in the newspapers had been devoted to the defendant's beautiful wife and her ample charms that spectators packed the trial just to get a glimpse of Amanda. The unfolding drama of how a poor general, a mild-mannered Cabinet officer to boot, could be so involved in a sinister plot by a pair of beauteous conniving sisters was the juiciest of Grant's many scandals.

But Amanda disappointed them by not appearing.

The Senate's verdict was reached on August 1. Inasmuch as the defendant was no longer in office, and therefore since that astute body no longer had any jurisdiction over him—regardless of how guilty he might be—Major General W. W. Belknap was acquitted of having committed all crimes as charged.

Once more an adroit action by the president—this time by promptly accepting Belknap's resignation—had saved a once-trusted subordinate's skin.

"Here, darling," Julia said a few days later. "This is the note I sent to all of the Cabinet members' wives." She handed a piece of notepaper to Grant.

He looked up from the report he was reading in their dining room and hastily read it. He blinked, then read it again.

A terrible thing has happened to the poor Belknaps. Please remember that the lovely, fun-loving lady we know as Amanda has suffered a terrible reverse. She is such a warm-hearted person, and I'm sure she is terribly lonesome. Please find it in your heart to call on her at your earliest convenience. Thank you.

Sincerely yours,
Julia Grant

Grant slowly put the note on the table, saying nothing.

Julia smiled brightly. "It's the least I can do. If that doesn't work, I'll go see each wife and beseech her personally."

His voice was soft. "I don't think you should."

"After all, *she* didn't do it."

"It already looks bad."

Julia looked at him askance. "What are you saying?"

"I'm saying that you should wash your hands of the Belknaps for a while."

"Why?"

"Because it could look like we are condoning his crime."

"But he was found innocent."

"Only because I let him resign, which I shouldn't have done."

"Why not? Isn't he your friend?"

He sighed. "That doesn't make it right."

"Friends should stand by friends. And she's my poor, lonesome, ostracized friend."

"And I am the president of the United States, whose administration has been badly damaged by a dishonest Cabinet member."

"And I am the president's wife," Julia blazed. "She will be welcome here at the White House at any time."

He looked up into her angry eyes. They seldom had differences, almost never had anything like this. "And if I forbid it?" he asked.

Her voice was flat. "You sold our house without even asking me. And now, in a few months we'll be leaving here. We could be going back to that fine mansion, but we can't . . . because you sold it. Now, I'm going to do what I can for poor Amanda, and you are not going to have anything to say about it!" She spun on her heel and left the room.

CHAPTER 72

Julia stuck to her guns and did exactly as she had said.

All Grant could do was ride it out, which he did with his usual outward aplomb. But inside, the pain lingered.

It seemed only logical that Grant's term in office should end with a troublesome 1876 presidential election. Enough else had gone wrong in his administration. Scrambling for the Republican nomination were James G. Blaine of Maine, Senator Roscoe Conkling, Senator Oliver Morton, Benjamin Bristow—the discomforting reformer whom Grant had fired from the Cabinet in June—Rutherford Hayes from Ohio, and Grant's old mentor, Elihu Washburne, now back from the European diplomatic wars.

Grant felt he owed support to Washburne, but he was also a friend of Conkling's. In the end, after a friendly chat with Washburne, he elected to stay out of it, and endorsed no one. Governor Hayes, yet another wartime major general from the Buckeye State, won the nomination. He was opposed by Democrat Samuel J. Tilden, the governor of New York who had gained fame in fighting the infamous "Boss Tweed" Tammany Hall political machine in New York City.

The national election was more than troublesome. Had it not been for Grant's calm use of troops to show strength, and his overall coolness, another civil war might well have begun. It all started when Tilden, who pulled a popular-vote majority of about 250,000, appeared to have lost by a hair in three supposedly solid Democratic Southern states: South Carolina, Florida, and Louisiana. All at once the *New York Times* discovered that these states may not have actually gone to Tilden. Pencil was hastily put to paper and it was determined that if Hayes had indeed won in these states, he would win the election by *one* electoral vote!

The mad scramble to get the "right" votes tabulated was on. And partisan party loyalty had nothing to do with accurate eyesight or arithmetic. Grant, not wanting to be a part of the possible scandal, yet in no way desiring to have either anarchy or a country without a president, supported a special commission to supervise the vote counting.

By special legislation, a fifteen-member electoral commission was organized with House and Senate members and Supreme Court justices. There were seven Democrats and eight Republicans. The scrutiny of the count started in the beginning of February and ended on March 2, two days before Grant's term was to expire.

The final results: Hayes 185, Tilden 184.

It was possible that the Republicans had *stolen* the election! Immediately Rutherford Hayes was tagged with the nickname "Old Eight to Seven." But the country's still-lingering trust in Grant was such that no major disorder resulted.

It was finally time for the citizens to say goodbye to a man they had never stopped admiring, regardless of what had happened around him. The powerful congressman and former general from Ohio, James Garfield—who would later live briefly in the White House—said, "I am again impressed with the belief that when his presidential term is ended, General Grant will regain his place as one of the foremost of Americans. His power of staying, his imperturbability, has been of incalculable value to the nation, and will be prized more and more as his career recedes."

Against Grant's suggestion that they quietly leave the White House early, Julia Grant gave a memorable inaugural day luncheon for the new president and his family. That over, it was time for a tearful goodbye to the servants before departing for the Fishes' house, where they would stay for a couple of weeks until Nellie had her baby. As they entered the carrriage in front of the mansion, Grant tugged his high silk hat lower over his eyes. Looking at his wife, he felt her sadness. She had truly enjoyed being the mistress of the White House, the president's lady. He knew it was taking all the spirit Julia could muster to hold back her tears.

His heart was heavy as well. In spite of all the problems and the mistakes that he had made, he had truly enjoyed being president of the United States of America, he truly had. Lincoln had been right about that. "When a man gets a hankering . . ."

The driver spoke to the quartet of horses, and the open landau began to roll. Grant held Julia's hand tightly as she stared stiffly ahead. He glanced back once at the stately mansion and drew in a deep breath.

It was over.

CHAPTER 73

How dull it is to pause, to make an end,
To rust unburnish'd, not to shine in use!
—TENNYSON, *ULYSSES*

Everyone knows that an ex-president isn't overwhelmed with things to do when he finishes his term of office. Everything is an anticlimax. And the Grants didn't actually have a home. They'd outgrown Galena; after the capital and New York, White Haven would be backwoods. They had no place or enterprise in Washington. Their children were all married and capable of taking care of themselves. Old Hannah Grant was living comfortably with her daughter, Mary Corbin. So why not take a trip, travel, see some of the world? Most Americans want to experience merry old England, why not the Grants? Their daughter lived there, and so did a lot of other interesting people.

It was decided, and the means found, to take an extended trip that might lead to who knew where? But first things first, and that was Britain. The simple trip quickly became involved as the plans became more intricate. Financing had to be arranged, and lodging—which rich Americans with English residences and wealthy Britishers alike scrambled to provide. A New York *Herald* reporter, John Russell Young, would remain glued to Grant's shadow, and would later write a book about what was becoming more of a grand expedition than a vacation. Certainly, it was only logical that some of the publisher's money would be used for expenses along the way.

The Grants actually did England up royally. They were entertained by Queen Victoria in Windsor Castle, by the Prince of Wales, by Wellington's son, and by dozens of lesser lights. But it was in Newcastle-upon-Tyne that Grant was most appreciated. Thousands of common workers turned out to greet and cheer America's most famous common man. It was said that the hurrahs fairly shook the old Cathedral of St. Nicholas the day he visited.

Paris, Naples, Pompeii, and other parts of the Mediterranean extended the tour. One of the most notable visits was with the great German leader

Bismarck, with whom Grant had a memorable conversation on war, and in whose palace Julia was truly treated like a queen.

The Grants, having nothing better to do, continued on to India, Burma, Siam, Saigon, Singapore, China, and Japan—where the emperor, who had only recently become even slightly accessible to the world, shook Grant's hand in the imperial palace. By the time their ship docked at San Francisco, the Grants had spent two years on their grand trip around the world. And they had enjoyed it immensely. What else, considering the adulation they'd received wherever they stopped?

They had been, in essence, the finest traveling ambassadorial team in the history of the United States. The raw power and promise of a sprawling young nation—only a hundred years old—had been brought to far-off courts by an ex-president with simple moral values and an uncomplicated personality. But he represented more: he had commanded in victory the most powerful army the world had ever known.

So the pleasure of the enjoyable journey had meaning.

But finally it was time to stop playing.

They stopped in Galena and settled down for six weeks. It was during this period that a man came into Grant's life who would have vital impact on it. It was at a huge reunion of the Army of the Tennessee when the celebrating veterans met in Chicago in November 1879. The man had never been in the army, had in fact been briefly in Confederate gray. But he was a proud, important American—a writer, world renowned for his humor and his depiction of jumping frogs and freckle-faced boys on the Mississippi. Known as Mark Twain, the one-time riverboat pilot was the forty-five-year-old Samuel Langhorne Clemens, a fascinated admirer of the former commanding general. A late reunion dinner speaker at the Palmer House, Clemens regaled the veterans with a story about Grant as a baby in his crib—and also brought a broad smile to Grant's face. Afterward, the humorist invited Grant to visit him at his home in Hartford.

"You aren't going to let them talk you into running again, are you, Sam?" Cump Sherman asked as he stood by the window of his Washington office.

"I don't know," Grant replied, lighting a fresh cigar. Still "visiting around," he and Julia were spending a few days in the capital in February.

It was two days after Sherman's sixtieth birthday and he was just as Theodore Lyman, one of Meade's staff officers, had once described him: "the quintessence of Yankeedom—tall, spare, sinewy; a very homely man, with a regular nest of wrinkles in his face, which play and twist as he eagerly talks on each subject." Now he was scowling as he turned back. "Goddamn it, Sam, you spent eight years there and all it brought you was grief. Those crooked bastard politicians almost ate your guts out. And you made your share of mistakes, God knows."

Grant nodded, blowing out the smoke. "I most certainly did."

"Then why even think about more punishment?"

"Julia wants to go back."

"To hell with Julia. She's not the one who will have to deal with all those pressures. We're not talking about just a nice place to live and have tea parties, you know."

"There are some things I left undone."

Sherman snorted. "Like what—letting someone rob the damned treasury?"

"That's a little severe, Sherman."

"It's a severe business."

"I don't know. I guess I can't stop them from running me. I don't have to campaign, you know."

"I'd sure as hell let them know that right from the start."

Grant nodded his head. "As usual, you make a lot of sense."

The ex-president didn't campaign for the nomination, not actively, although he would gladly have accepted it. Julia tried to act as his campaign manager, so much did she want to return to the White House, but he called her off and they waited out the decision of the Republican powers. Senator John Sherman, Cump's brother, was one of the nominees, but with little chance of getting the nod. It didn't matter. After Grant's strong early showing, James A. Garfield from Ohio was nominated, with New Yorker Chester Arthur as his running mate.

Garfield won the election by a scant ten thousand votes, but would be shot by a jealous office-seeker just four months after taking office. Chester Arthur assumed the presidency in August when Garfield succumbed. And Grant had to turn back to the land of his first war to find a job.

There were two reasons why Grant couldn't watch a bullfight while in Mexico—one, he didn't like to see any animal tortured or hurt; two, the gory finale reminded him of his father's slaughterhouse in the tannery. Otherwise, he very much liked visiting Mexico, where he had been feted as warmly as on his world tour. And the idea of being president of the Mexican Southern Railroad was interesting. His friend, Matías Romero, the former Mexican envoy, had dreamed of a railroad that would connect the southern state of Oaxaca to Mexico City, and then to the United States. And he saw in Grant the great man whose name and participation could make it possible. The bald-headed Romero, as Benito Juárez's man, had been his country's only representative in Washington during the war and afterward because in those days Maximilian, whom the United States didn't recognize, sat on the Mexican throne. Romero had gone on to a cabinet post after Maximilian was shot.

The railroad presidency was highly appealing to Grant. He couldn't take just any position, yet he needed to be busy. Most importantly, he needed to make *money*. With all of his success, one thing continued to elude him—money. Millionaires had stood before him, hat in hand. They had revered him, had given him many gifts; some had used him. But *all* had been able to make money, the one vital commodity that he needed. He had needed it after getting married while in the army; he had performed the most menial of labor for it after getting out; and now he was still on tenuous financial ground—at least for an ex-president. He had a small income from interest, and investments from the subscription money that had been raised in earlier years provided an annual income of about $6,000, but that wasn't nearly enough.

Many of his friends had money, *real* money.

All he wanted to do was have the opportunity to make it.

And railroad presidents made it.

He opened an office on Wall Street and was given the presidency of an additional company, one that was trying to get a canal built across the Panamanian Isthmus. But even though several of the big money men in New York were interested in the Mexican Southern Railroad, including good old Jay Gould of Black Friday fame, nothing serious in the way of capital was found for the project.

"I suppose I ought to have some pride about such matters," Grant said.

"Why?" Hamilton Fish asked. "These people have scads of money, and you do not. And you've given mightily of yourself in the service of your country. They have nothing to gain by giving you the money for this house except pleasure. Would you deny them that?"

"I still feel that a man my age shouldn't be getting expensive gifts."

"Poppycock!"

"There'll still be a considerable mortgage on the place."

"General," the former secretary of state said with a warm smile, "you don't have to justify anything to me. I've come just to see your new residence. Now, if you don't mind, sir, would you please get on with showing it to me?"

The address was 3 East 66th Street, an excellent neighborhood. Just off Fifth Avenue and close to Central Park, it had four substantial floors above a basement that housed the kitchen and servant's quarters. With ample bedrooms for their often visiting children and grandchildren, it held two excellent parlors and a dining room more than adequate for Julia's entertaining. In fact, she had been the one who had selected the house after much shopping around. Grant mentioned all of this as he led Fish from room to room. "Julia will stay busy for months putting things in their proper place," he explained. "She has a formal plan and it's a good thing. In addition to all of our other mementos, we accumulated quite a collection of fine souvenirs and superb gifts during our tour."

Fish looked around the master bedroom, nodding approvingly. "I think you've done very well in this selection, General. You should have many years of happiness here."

The New Yorker couldn't have been more wrong.

Strangely, the opportunity for Grant to make big money was provided by his middle son, Buck. The boy had borrowed $100,000 from his banker father-in-law, Jerome Chaffee, to set up a partnership in a Wall Street brokerage firm in 1881. His partner was Ferdinand Ward, a rising young force in the New York investment field. The son of a Baptist preacher, Ward was married to the daughter of the cashier of the Marine Bank, and had built a reputation for shrewdness in the marketplace.

Buck, chubby and popular, had married Fannie Chaffee in 1880. Her father was president of the First National Bank of Denver and had become one of Colorado's first senators when the territory achieved statehood. In the two years since forming Grant & Ward, Buck's investments had grown to a substantial sum and it looked as if he was well on the road to riches. One day he took his father to lunch in a fashionable financial district restaurant. As Grant's usual well-done steak was served, Buck said, "How would you like to come into business with Ward and me, Papa? I know the railroad isn't bringing in the money you expected, and we're making so much money that we can't keep up with it. If you would be willing to invest, we could take you in as a full partner, and in no time you could be coining a fortune!"

Grant stopped in midbite. "I don't know anything about the stock market, son."

"Do you know how much I've made in two years?"

"No."

"Three hundred thousand dollars, and that includes the start-up period when we were finding our first clients."

"How do you make the money?"

"Easy. Clients, or investors, buy securities through our firm and leave them with the company as collateral for loans with which we buy more securities for them. We, in turn, borrow against this collateral to invest for the company's own account."

"Is that legal?"

"Perfectly so. It's done by all the investment houses."

Grant rubbed his beard. "Well, you're a lawyer. I guess you ought to know." He ate another piece of meat, chewing slowly. Finally he said, "Three hundred thousand in two years, huh?"

Buck nodded, smiling. "And the firm's established now. Imagine what it'll be like with your name on the letterhead, Papa!"

He told Julia about Buck's proposal that night at dinner. She listened carefully, nodding her head and smiling.

Her eyes were bright as she asked, "Three hundred thousand dollars?"

"That's what he told me."

"He wouldn't lie."

"Of course not."

"What would you have to do, darling? You don't know much about the brokerage business."

"Buck told me I wouldn't have to do much of anything. Ward is the genius, and between the two of them, they know just what they're doing."

She put her fork down. "Oh, Ulys, it sounds like a wonderful opportunity to me."

"It may be what we've always been waiting for."

She smiled again. "And just think, it's coming from our own son. He's so good-hearted."

"Yes, that makes it all the more agreeable."

"He's such a bright boy."

"Maybe all of that education is paying off."

"I'm so proud of him."

Grant got up from his chair and went around the corner of the table to her place. Leaning down, he kissed her soundly on the mouth and said, "Very well, Mrs. Grant, we'll join our smart and wealthy young son in business."

She leaned her head against his side. "I won't be able to sleep tonight."

As Ward explained it, the more cash Grant invested initially, the more quickly he would accrue a large return. He decided to round up everything that was negotiable and invest it, a sum of about $100,000. Soon Ward brought in another partner, James D. Fish—no relative of Hamilton. Fish had the added distinction of being president of the Marine Bank. And Buck had been right, they seldom asked much of him. It was everything Grant had always wanted. Why, if everything went well, he should be worth over a million dollars in a rather short time. Security, yes, all the security he'd ever want. Oh, he knew a lot of people were investing with Grant & Ward because they trusted in his name, but that was all right. If, by so doing, they made money, then he was serving them well. And, as Buck had said, the money was pouring in so fast they couldn't keep up with it.

Late in the spring of 1884, the company was rated at $15 million!

CHAPTER 74

At shortly after two o'clock on the afternoon of May 4, a servant told Grant that Mr. Ferdinand Ward was calling. It was a warm, quiet Sunday and Grant had been reading. Joining his visitor in the parlor, Grant greeted him pleasantly. "What brings you clear up here from Brooklyn Heights?" he asked.

Ward looked worried. His necktie was slightly askew and perspiration dotted his brow. He went directly to the point. "We've suffered a reversal at the company, General, and unless we can patch up the hole, we may be in for a difficult time of it."

Grant looked into the younger man's worried eyes and felt a stab of fear. His legs felt suddenly weak. "What do you mean?" he asked quietly.

"Some investments have taken a turn for the worse, and unless we get an infusion of money, I won't be able to cover the day loans tomorrow morning."

"I don't understand. Isn't everything collateralized?"

Ward blew out a deep breath as he sat on the edge of a wingback chair. "Yes, but you have to understand hypothecation in investments. I don't know if I've ever explained it fully to you, but hypothecation is the pledging of collateral for a loan without handing it over . . . as we do. But to make *more* money, we needed to borrow more money faster. Therefore, I have *re*hypothecated a number of securities—borrowed twice against the same securities. And now the loans are due and I can't make them good."

Now it was Grant's turn to sit down. He felt a flush, a shortness of breath. His voice was hardly more than a whisper. "Isn't that illegal?"

"In a sense, yes. But as long as everything is sailing along, it does no harm."

"Can anything be done?"

"Yes. If I can raise one hundred and fifty thousand dollars by tomorrow we might be able to hold it together."

Grant shook his head. "Everything I had is in the company."

"Can you raise the money somewhere?"

Grant blew out a deep breath. "Did you say we *might* be able to hold it together?"

Ward nodded his head, regaining his assurance. "I'm certain we can, sir. If the banks can see the support of someone who is very wealthy, they'll carry the company until we can pay back the loans."

Grant stared at the young man. Who? Who had enough money? Whom could he approach for such a favor? Faces flickered before him. *Vanderbilt.* William Henry Vanderbilt might be the best chance for the money. If the railroad baron would loan him the money . . . He nodded his head as he got to his feet. "I'll see what I can do," he said. "Wait here until I return."

William Henry Vanderbilt was the son of Commodore Cornelius Vanderbilt, who had made a fortune in shipping before moving into railroads. The older Vanderbilt, a noted philanthropist, had become one of America's richest men before dying seven years earlier. His son had assumed control of the New York Central and other railroads. The younger Vanderbilt was a year older than Grant and a well-wishing supporter. He received the former president warmly in his study.

Pleasantries were exchanged and coffee was served.

And suddenly it was time for Grant to broach the difficult subject. It was terribly difficult for him as he looked into Vanderbilt's patient, curious gaze. Another face flashed before him: Simon Bolivar Buckner—it was 1854 in this same city, and he was a down-at-the-heels resigned captain living off a loan from the other captain while he waited for money to arrive from old Jesse. The manager of the Astor House wanted to throw him out for being unable to pay his bill, he had no money for Julia, and he was in debt. Another scene danced before him—when he asked his father for a position after failing at White Haven . . .

He felt like a huge rock was smashing into his chest. Failure, failure, no matter how high he'd flown, the bottom line was failure. His sister's money, that of all those people who had invested in the good name of Grant. Oh, how could it have happened?

"Mr. Vanderbilt," he began quietly, "a terrible thing has happened at Grant and Ward. I have to have been exceedingly remiss in not being aware, in not knowing . . ." He went on, explaining the problem as best he could, and in the end, William Vanderbilt softly asked, "How much do you think you'll need, General?"

Grant sighed. "I think one hundred and fifty thousand."

Vanderbilt reached for a sheet of paper and dipped his pen in the desk's inkwell. "I'll make it a note to you personally, sir."

Moments later, the railroad baron smiled as he handed the paper to Grant. "I hope this serves the purpose, sir."

It didn't. The banks refused to bail Grant & Ward out, and not only was Grant suddenly broke, but Vanderbilt's money was gone as well. The firm went down, dragging with it some other investment companies and the Marine Bank. The Mexican Southern Railroad, never much of a success, was finished. To the men of Wall Street, rehypothecation was not only ethically wrong, but a criminal offense. Ferdinand Ward skipped the country. The country buzzed with the scandal. Black Friday was revived. Was Grant the biggest crook of them all? The New York *World* asked on its front page: "Is Grant Guilty?"

Not only hundreds of innocent investors but other members of his own family had been hurt. Guilt all but consumed Grant, but his resilience somehow permitted him to stand pat and remain silent. The man who had been under so many kinds of fire in his life maintained his dignity in this, the worst of all degradations . . . outwardly.

And, as if the nation were reluctant to lose its greatest hero, the people closed ranks behind him. Ulysses S. Grant had been wronged. The hero of Donelson, Vicksburg, Chattanooga—the general who had saved the Union and had been president of the United States of America—had once again been the victim of dishonest men. A man couldn't trust anyone anymore.

And the people were right.

But the man in question couldn't accept such blamelessness. He was the goat. He had been stupid, a supposedly intelligent man with strong scruples who had allowed himself to be a pawn in a game that a dozen friends could have warned him about had he only asked them. But, oh no, he had been too busy being the big entrepreneur, and who would tell an ex-president he didn't know what he was doing?

Grant agonized terribly in his despair.

Grant stood in front of the store window and looked at the bottles. A display consisting of bourbon quarts greeted him. Old Fitzgerald. On sale. His look turned into a stare. Yes, why not? Why not drink himself into a better frame of mind. He'd barely slept for a week, tossing in bed, pacing the floor, unable to read. He'd even tried to pray, but his remorse was too deep, and he didn't believe in asking the Lord for help when he was a victim of his own stupidity. Some whiskey might help . . .

He'd been good. Oh, he'd had a glass of wine here and there over the years, a brandy now and then. But no more of those oblivion sieges such as the one he'd pulled before Vicksburg fell . . . the time on the boat to Sartaria when he'd really let Rawlins down. If he had a hundred dollars for every time he'd been reported drunk, he could almost pay off the Grant & Ward debacle.

Old Fitzgerald . . . it sounded like a good old bourbon with a bite.

Rawlins would understand. So would Julia.

He needed *something* to wash away the mortification.

He went inside and bought two bottles.

He went to the guest bedroom they called the Belmont Room on the third floor. There were no house guests and Julia had retired early with a head-ache. He had a pocketful of cigars and both bottles of bourbon in a paper sack. He'd had the butler put a tray, complete with a glass and a pitcher of water, in the room a short time earlier. The oil lamp on the nightstand was turned down low; he left it that way. Slowly he took one of the bottles from the sack and extracted the cork. Pouring carefully, he filled the glass nearly full of the amber liquid, held it up to the light, and tasted it. Brrrrr. He shook his head as the warmth spread in his mouth and throat.

He took a full, big drink. A pleasant burn.

Biting the end off a cigar, he stuck it in his mouth and used the old wartime silver lighter to get it going. Blowing out the smoke, he went to the window and sipped some more of the whiskey. A couple of carriages were moving down Fifth Avenue, their lamps dull glows in the night air, gliding along like big ants with tiny lightning bugs attached. The people in them probably didn't have a care in the world, certainly hadn't been taken for everything because of ignorant negligence. Nor had those people been the cause of so many others losing life savings.

He drained the glass and looked back down at the moving rigs.

Feeling better, he went back to the table and poured another glassful of Old Fitzgerald. He could already feel the warmth from the first. He'd drink this one more slowly, let it brush away the dark ghosts one by one.

Too bad he didn't have someone to share this with . . . oh well, he had plenty of memories. Too bad so many of them were unpleasant. *Rehypothecation*—doggone term. Why hadn't he questioned?

He took another big sip. What was the difference? It was done, and he hadn't stolen anything, he hadn't *stolen* a solitary penny. No, he had to think about something pleasant. The grand review after the war, yes, now *that* was pleasant . . . yes, when Sherman had snubbed Stanton. And the whole country was at their feet.

He smiled. That was good old William Tecumseh Sherman, all right. Good old Buckeye friend. They'd probably make him president some of these days, maybe on the next go-around. No, Sherman was too smart to be president. If he'd only listened to his old friend, he would have stayed out of the doggone White House and this debacle wouldn't have happened. That's right!

He drained the glass and went back to the bottle.

Uh-huh, nothing was all bad.

Not really.

The chirping of the birds outside the open window awoke him. He looked up from where he was draped across the bed on his stomach. The sunlight streaming into the room hurt his eyes. He blinked, turned his head. His mouth was a sour ball of cotton. Legs, in a skirt. Someone sitting in a chair. In the shadow. Ohhhh, his head. He closed his eyes, opened them again.

The legs moved, recrossed.

"Are you all right?" It was Julia. Her voice sounded strange. He looked at her. She wasn't smiling.

He pulled himself up to a sitting position. "I don't know," he replied. His head gave him a jolt of pain.

"You drank a whole bottle," she said quietly.

She went to the washstand, dipped a towel in the bowl and wrung it out. Coming to the bed, she wiped his face. "Did you solve anything?" she asked.

"I don't know."

Her voice was soothing. "You had it coming."

"Did I?"

"Certainly, darling. Some of the steam had to blow out somewhere."

"Huh?"

"Come now, we have to get you cleaned up. Looks like you got sick on yourself."

He smelled as sour as he tasted. Drawing in a deep breath and blowing it out, he got to his feet. His head was *terrible*! He unbuttoned the two remaining buttons that held his shirt together and pulled off the soiled garment. Julia took his elbow and helped him to the basin. "Rinse off," she said, "and we'll get you down to the bathroom. A half-hour in a good hot tub will make a new man out of you."

"Thanks." Wasn't she going to ask him if this was the start of him drinking again, or something like that? Well, it wasn't—he *couldn't!*

"Some coffee and breakfast will help too."

His voice sounded strange as he said, "I love you, darling."

She brushed away the tear that escaped from her eye and found a smile.

CHAPTER 75

Adam Badeau had been recalled by President James Garfield as consul-general to Britain. Since that time, the onetime brigadier and secretary to Grant had been busy writing. His most famous work was the three-volume *Military History of Ulysses S. Grant,* which had been published two years earlier. Now, stopping by the Grant house on East 66th Street two days after Grant's one-night drunk, he was his usual effusive, friendly self. That is, he was friendly except when gossiping, and then he could be quite sharp-fanged about his targets. A bit plumper and redder in the face than when he had lived at the White House, the fifty-three-year-old Badeau still thrived on what was happening in the social world. His heavy drinking was sporadic, and he hadn't had a steady male mate since leaving England. Besides, it was public attention and the illusion of power that fed his most demanding needs. Now, sitting in the parlor and sipping tea, he had a case to plead.

"Robert Johnson, the associate editor of *Century* magazine, has asked me to talk you into writing those articles he and you talked about some time back."

Grant shrugged. "I told him—I'm not a writer. Besides, everyone and his brother has written a memoir about the war."

"But that's wrong, General. I've seen the orders you used to write. They were totally clear, uncluttered. Besides, what Johnson wants is basically some battle reports. You've already written them. All you would have to do is pull them out and rewrite them in a casual manner with your personal sense of what happened."

"I don't know."

"They'll pay you very well."

Grant stroked his beard. "I could certainly use the money."

"Why don't you let me tell Johnson to get in touch with you again?"

"I guess we could talk about it."

The article "Shiloh" reached the *Century* office on July 1. Everyone there was excited about it, and the recommended changes were minimal. No one could believe the clarity in the writing. It was scheduled for publication in February 1885. After Grant worked throughout July on the next article,

"Vicksburg," Robert Johnson came to see him at the cottage in the lovely little village of Long Branch on the Jersey shore. Strolling along the beach, just out of range of the white-foamed breakers, Johnson got to the point of his visit. "General, we at *Century* are thinking about a series of articles just like you are writing by various generals, which we might call 'Battles and Leaders of the Civil War.' You know, get Sherman and Sheridan to write some, Meade, Hancock, maybe even some Confederate commanders. We would like to have some more pieces by you."

Grant nodded. They were paying him $500 each for the articles—not enough to pay back Vanderbilt or any of the other debts, but enough to live on for a little while.

"You know, sir, that your writing is of excellent quality."

"Thank you."

"In fact, and this is mostly what I came down here to talk about, we hope you will consider writing a whole book. It could be your memoirs of the war, or, preferably, of your life."

Grant didn't reply, just glanced offshore where a large sailboat was tacking along close to the wind, its sails billowing white against a darkening sky.

"We think such a book could do very well, due to your everlasting popularity. A preliminary estimate indicates that it would sell from two hundred thousand to three hundred thousand copies. With a standard royalty of ten percent, this should bring you from twenty to thirty thousand dollars."

As in the case of the articles, Grant thought, not a princely sum. But one had to consider where else that much money could be raised. Certainly, no one was going to invest heavily in his investment advice. "I'll think about it," he replied.

It was a few days later, while eating dinner, that Grant bit into a peach and got a very sour taste. He put the fruit down and spit the part he'd bitten off into his plate. "Sorry," he said to Julia, with a wry face. "That was the sourest doggone peach I've ever encountered." His throat still stung.

Julia picked up a second peach and bit into it. "This one is nice and sweet," she said, and handed it to him.

This bite was just as bad, bitterly sour. Spitting it out, he shook his head. "Must be something stuck down there in my throat," he said.

Dinner was finished uneventfully, and the pain subsided completely. But the next day, as he took a break from polishing the Vicksburg article, he kicked back on a beach chair and took a sip of lemonade. Again, he got a strong sour taste that hurt his throat. He decided to just lay off the tart stuff for a while.

A week later, he noticed a slight tickle in his throat like the beginning of an old-fashioned cold. But it too went away after a couple of days. His old army surgeon from the Cairo days, Dr. Joe Brinton, dropped in to see him at the cottage about a week later. Grant mentioned his throat discomfort in the course of the conversation, and Brinton used a teaspoon to look inside his mouth and throat. "All I can see is a touch of redness," he said. "But I'd see a throat specialist just to be on the safe side."

"It might be just a cold—right, Doctor?" Grant asked.

Brinton nodded. "Could be."

Grant went to work on the third article, "Chattanooga," but the throat affliction continued. Now the minor irritation was accompanied by a troublesome dryness that came and went in intensity. He mentioned it to his friend and neighbor, publisher George Childs, who said, "General, my friend Doctor Da Costa, from Philadelphia, is one of the most eminent physicians in the country. He's coming out for a short visit soon, and I'll ask him to have a look at you, if you wish."

Grant agreed, and a few days later he was examined by Dr. Da Costa. The physician frowned through his eyeglasses as he finished the checkup. "It could be a number of things, General," he said quietly. "But rather than guess and perhaps needlessly alarm you, I think you ought to see your family physician and get a complete workup."

"I can't," Grant replied. "He's in Europe."

"Well," Da Costa said, "I recommend you see him as soon as he returns, or see someone else. If you wish, I can refer you to a number of excellent doctors."

"I may take advantage of your offer."

The physician reached for a prescription pad and began to scribble. "In the meantime, here is something that will relieve the discomfort."

The medicine did diminish the symptoms for a period of time, but they were eventually back with an added dimension—Grant began to have some trouble swallowing food that he failed to chew well. His favorite meat— well-done steak—was one, crisp bacon another, apples, anything hard or coarse in texture were difficult to get down without discomfort. He developed some congestion. But he was busy and thought he should wait for Dr. Barker to return from his trip. He decided to ignore the problem and pour himself deeper into the work. The weeks flew by in the research and writing of the Chattanooga article. He was particularly careful about how he described his slightly strained relationships with Thomas and Hooker just before that battle. He wanted to be factual, but there was no need to unnecessarily criticize anyone.

It was during this period that he decided he would definitely write the book of memoirs. He found that he enjoyed writing, particularly the research, the going back over the old reports and maps, examining records and photographs. But it was more; he *liked* the writing, its challenge, and the reward of seeing a memory clearly expressed in words. And his recall was excellent. Young Fred—a colonel now, owing to the fact that he was the former president's son—was helping him. And Badeau was doing some minor editing.

Suddenly it was October, and the winds blowing off the ocean onto the bluffs of the Long Branch shore turned cold and threatening. It was time to pack up all of the maps and other research materials and head for upper Manhattan. Dr. Fordyce Barker saw him on the 17th, examined him thoroughly, and set up an appointment for him to see Dr. John H. Douglas, New York's leading throat specialist.

Grant, who had in July been some thirty pounds overweight and still gimpy from a fall the previous December, was now losing a few pounds every couple of weeks. He had celebrated his sixty-second birthday on April 22. Now, moving stiffly on his cane, he presented his card to Dr. Douglas's nurse. She jumped to her feet, exclaiming, "Oh, Mr. President, I'm so pleased to meet you. I'll tell Doctor you're here. He's one of your greatest admirers!"

Douglas, who had a full gray beard that reached six inches below his chin and a head of thick gray-white hair, had served on the U.S. Sanitary Commission during the war. He had met Grant shortly after the battle of Donelson and still considered the occasion one of the most important moments of his life. He smiled as he shook hands and introduced himself. Following some pleasantries, he questioned Grant extensively and began a thorough examination.

As he was doing so, Grant sat in what might have been one of the most complete vacuums he'd ever known. It seemed at this moment that nothing else in the world mattered—it was all still, in limbo. It was him and the doctor, alone, with the judgment hanging in the balance. He knew what his affliction might be, he'd already used the dreaded word . . .

Cancer.

But until he was told for sure, he would hope otherwise. It was like hearing the whine of a loud incoming artillery shell and wondering where it would hit. He kept his eyes closed as Douglas had him say "Ahhhhh" and "Eeeeee," and probed around his throat. He gagged twice, and the doctor apologized each time. Yes, surely it was something else . . .

Had to be.

Cancer killed people.

No, it was something else.

The doctor sure was taking a long time.

At last Dr. Douglas turned the mirror away from the lamps. After another couple of moments of that terrible silence, the doctor cleared his throat. It was time for the verdict. He watched the doctor's eyes, not breathing . . .

"General, your soft palate is inflamed, slightly dark in color, somewhat scaly." Douglas paused, cleared his throat again.

Grant asked quietly, "Is it cancer?" His voice sounded hollow.

"The tongue is somewhat rigid at the base of the right side. General, the disease is serious, epithelial in character, and sometimes capable of being cured."

"What does epithelial mean?"

"That unwanted tissue or cells are lining the soft palate."

The terrible silence. *He had it.* He blinked. There it was. He drew in a deep breath, let it out. He had it. After a moment, he said, "You said it was sometimes capable of being cured. Do you mean surgery?"

"No. That's out of the question now. It's too late."

"Then how can it be cured?"

Douglas looked him directly in the eye. "Sometimes nature works its own wonders. Sometimes there are recoveries that are beyond medical science. We don't understand them. They just happen."

Grant went home, knowing the truth, but not wanting to fully admit it. Douglas's words lingered in his mind: ". . . *beyond medical science.*" Julia met him at the door, dread in her eyes. "What did he say?" she asked softly.

"He said I have a complaint with a cancerous tendency."

"What does that mean?"

His faithful colored valet, Harrison Tyrell, took his hat and listened fearfully from a few feet away.

He wanted to lie to her, tell her nothing was definite. But he couldn't. They'd shared too much over the years for him to do so. "It means that I have a growth over my soft palate."

She wasn't to be put off. "Is it cancer?"

"It has that tendency, but Dr. Douglas said it is sometimes capable of being cured."

Julia just stared, holding his eyes. Harrison Tyrell shook his head and murmured, "Oh, Lordy."

"I want to talk to him," Julia said.

"I'm going back to see him tomorrow. I'll arrange an appointment for you."

She took his hand, frowning, fighting the tears. "Ulys," she said, "you do have it, don't you?"

He took her in his arms. "Yes, my darling, I'm afraid I do."

"The disease will take a long course," John Douglas said, looking from Julia to Fred, and back to Grant. "There will probably be several degrees of pain. As you know, we all have different thresholds, so it will be up to your own perception, General. But I must warn you that it can get severe. You may also suffer from varying levels of depression and despair."

"Can I help with that part?" Julia asked.

"Of course, Mrs. Grant. You can be vital in that area." Dr. Douglas held up some bottles. "I'm going to give you some different medicines— one for prophylaxis, another for relieving the congestion, and one for removing odors from the ulcerated surfaces. We'll work together all the way on this, but I want you to carry out my orders assiduously."

"What can I do, Doctor?" Fred asked.

"Just be part of the team, young man."

"Anything in particular I should do?" Grant asked.

Dr. Douglas pointed to the cigar Grant was about to light. "I don't think that smoke will do your condition any good. I'd recommend you quit those things."

"But they're one of my few pleasures."

"Well, try smoking a fewer number each day."

Grant shook his head, found a short smile. "I suppose you want me to quit drinking too."

Douglas had learned in getting Grant's medical history that the general's reputation as a drunk hadn't been justified since '54. He chuckled. "Let's just say you shouldn't get drunk before eight in the morning."

They all laughed, but it was a nervous reaction.

Grant awakened at shortly after two the next morning, and had trouble getting back to sleep. He got up quietly, put on his robe, and went to his work area—a large square table in the front room of the second floor. Filing cabinets and boxes of reports added a certain amount of clutter around the busy tabletop. He carried an oil lamp as he limped to the nearby window and looked out at the cold October drizzle. Putting the lamp on the table, he reached into a convenient cigar box and pulled out a Havana. It smelled good. He was about to light it when he remembered what Dr. Douglas had said.

Shaking his head, he picked up a lighter and lit it anyway. He blew out a cloud of smoke and returned to the window. It was pretty dreary outside, quite dark, reminded him of that wet night at Shiloh, for some reason. He took another drag on the cigar. It would be difficult to quit them. But then, everything was going to be difficult from now on. He'd done a lot of thinking in the past thirty-six hours and he thought he had a handle on his future. He was a sick man and would probably die from the disease. He couldn't duck that, no matter what.

This wasn't the heat of battle, where he could lead a charmed life and escape shot and shell. No, it was a different battlefield. In effect, he had already been hit. It was just a matter of how long it would take for the wound to take over. Oh, sure—the doctor had told him that "sometimes nature worked its own wonders," but he couldn't count on that. As far as he was concerned, that was like drawing an inside straight flush—and who ever made one of those?

Since he was relating to poker, he'd just have to play each hand as it was dealt . . .

He took another long pull on the cigar.

One thing was certain. He was still a financial failure. Broke. When he was gone, Julia would have nothing. The lady who had ridden all the way to the White House with him would be a pauper, a ward of her children or society.

The thought wrenched at his gut.

He thought of her in Japan, curtsying to the emperor in the forbidden imperial palace, of her smiling in conversation with Queen Victoria . . . of the fuss that Bismarck made over her, of her many successful entertainments as the wife of the president of the United States. No, not for a single moment could he consider leaving her penniless!

The memoirs might not bring in a fortune, but whatever the book might earn would be all he could leave to her . . .

He turned back to the table and saw his tablet, the sharpened pencils. And he knew.

He would not let this thing kill him until he finished the book!

CHAPTER 76

There is not one of his subjects but has forgotten Ulysses, who ruled them as though he were their father. There he is, lying in great pain . . .
—HOMER, THE *ODYSSEY*

D r. Douglas had been right about the pain—now definitely centered in his mouth, it came and it went. But mostly it lingered. The congestion diminished in the ensuing weeks, but at times, the specter of what lay ahead brought gloom to Grant. But even on the darkest days, he worked. The pain from an abscessed tooth was severe, but its removal brought quick relief. On Thanksgiving Day he quit smoking for good, shaking his head as he handed his last partial box of cigars to Harrison Tyrell. "Give these to some poor man on the street, Harrison," he said. "Make it an old soldier, someone who was in the war, if you can. Tell him who sent them, and wish him well."

It would be too much to ask that the valet find a veteran from Donelson. That was where it had all started—the cigar thing. They had run that picture of him in the papers with a cigar, and he'd been inundated with the things for years to come. And he'd enjoyed them immensely. But now Dr. Douglas thought they might have had something to do with the cancer.

There was no mincing of words with Grant now. To his intimates, he simply had cancer. And it wasn't cancer of the throat or the tongue. It was, according to Douglas, of the mouth. Not that it mattered.

One day an interesting visitor came to the house on 66th Street. He had bushy eyebrows, a walrus mustache, and an unruly head of graying hair. "Sir," said Samuel Clemens, better known to his literary audience as Mark

Twain, "I would like to talk to you about the memoirs I've heard you're writing."

Grant hadn't seen the peppery author since the Chicago reunion of the Army of the Tennessee following his return from the grand tour of the world, but he had laughed often at Clemens's usually brilliant writings about the world's absurdities. "Have a seat, Mr. Clemens," he said pointing to the only comfortable chair in the vicinity of his working table. "Pardon the mess."

"I know all about such messes, General."

They passed the time of day as Tyrell served coffee. Sipping, Grant said, "All right, what is it you wish to know about my memoirs?"

"Who's going to publish them, General?"

"I'm not exactly sure, although I believe *Century* magazine is under the impression that they are."

"And how much have they offered you, sir?"

Grant fished around among the many papers on his desk and produced *Century*'s offer. Clemens read it quickly and snorted. "Ha! Strike out that ten percent royalty and write in twenty percent. No, make it *seventy-five!*"

Grant chuckled. "They'll never pay anything like that."

Clemens's eyes lit up as he pounded the table with his fist. "By God, sir, they are *thieves!* All publishers are thieves, but what these scoundrels are offering is an outrage to a colossus such as you."

"But seventy-five percent—Mr. Clemens, such a demand would make a robber out of me."

The author sighed and shook his head. "General, if you think you would be robbing this publisher, it's because you aren't knowledgeable enough about this business. If you ever perpetrated a crime like this, you would be rewarded with *two* halos when you get to heaven!"

"All right, what publisher would be willing to pay such terms?"

"The American Publishing Company of my home town of Hartford."

"How can you prove this?"

"Give me six hours, General. Three for my dispatch to get there, and three hours for their jubilant acceptance to return by the same electric gravel train. If you need it any quicker, I'll walk up to Hartford and fetch it!"

Grant chuckled again. "Then go to it, sir."

It took more than six hours, but Samuel Clemens was back the next afternoon with the answer: the American Publishing Company had rejected the offer. "Damn fools," he said, "I was fully expecting to hand them your fine book and make that den of reptiles rich. But you know what, General? They've been robbing me blind for years and building theological factories out of the proceeds. I've had a grudge against those thieves for a long time, and now's my chance to get even."

Grant waited as Clemens closed his eyes dramatically for a moment.

"General Grant," he said, frowning, "I am busy establishing my own publishing house, Charles L. Webster and Company. That's where I'm publishing my new book *The Adventures of Huckleberry Finn*. Tell you what I'll do, General—I'll give you a ten thousand dollar advance and maybe we can work out this seventy-five percent royalty I mentioned. I'll even take all the *costs* out of my twenty-five percent!"

Grant laughed. "What kind of a profit can you make out of a deal like that?"

Clemens's merry eyes danced. "I'll make a hundred thousand dollars in six months!"

Grant sobered, coughed, and waited for the pain to subside. He now regarded his visitor steadily. "I have one primary thing on my mind, Mr. Clemens. This book must make enough money for Mrs. Grant to be independent financially. To this end, I've sworn that no matter what, I'll finish the work."

Clemens looked into his troubled eyes and nodded. "General, I assure you that your wishes will be met. I'll guarantee that this will be an immensely successful book."

Working hard in December, even though he saw Douglas nearly every other day, Grant finished the Mexican War portion of his manuscript just before Christmas. Except for the Civil War battle elements already finished as articles for the *Century,* he had decided to work chronologically, starting with a brief portion about his childhood. Even he was amazed at how clearly those years came back to him.

But a new problem arose—Badeau started acting moodily and bickering with Fred, who was doing a good job in assisting with the research. The former staff officer began to take on airs about the writing, intimating that his part was indispensable, when in reality it was minor. And now, with the far more famous Mark Twain popping into the house periodically, Badeau became jealous of him as well.

On a visit to Douglas's office in mid-February Grant caught cold, not at all a pleasant turn. The doctor, warning that his resistance wasn't strong enough to continue exposing himself in public, decided to start treating him at home. It was at this time that he brought more bad news. "The ulcers in your throat are acting up again, General. I want to snip out a bit of tissue and give it to Dr. George Elliott. He's a noted microscopist."

"What are you looking for?"

"We want to see what's in the tissue, that's all."

Grant looked at him gravely. "I thought you said the cancer was in the mouth."

"It is. We just want to look further."

On the 19th, Doctors Douglas and Barker were joined by two other specialists in the Grant home. Each made a thorough examination of his mouth and throat. When they finished, they went to the other parlor room to hold a conference. While Grant waited for the verdict, they discussed what should be done.

When the deliberation was finished it was agreed that the method of treatment currently being employed was correct; that the tissue sample from the throat had proved malignant; that regardless of the danger, surgery could not be successfully performed and would only cause great distress, at best, to the patient; and that the cancer was sure to end fatally.

"However," Douglas cautioned the others, "as I have told the general, there is always that unknown that's beyond us. And he's a fighter."

Barker nodded. "Still, I don't think we should tell him about our findings until we have to."

They all agreed.

Returning to Grant, Dr. Douglas said, "We have decided that you are doing remarkably well, General."

"What about the microscopic finding from my throat?" Grant asked.

"Inconclusive." Douglas smiled. "Just keep up the good work."

Grant noticed the evasiveness of the answer, but partly out of relief, and partly because he didn't want to hear anything else, he didn't pursue the matter.

The doctors held out for ten days, then had to disclose part of the truth. And the newspapers pounced on the information. The *New York Times* ran headlines such as GRANT SLOWLY DYING FROM CANCER, GRANT SINKING INTO THE GRAVE, and GEN. GRANT'S FRIENDS GIVE UP HOPE.

The public was fully alerted and deeply concerned.

Julia tried to keep the newspapers from him, but Grant usually found them. He had been reviled so many times in the press that he accepted their stories as just another way to sell papers. No one truly knew his condition any better than he did. He did have cancer, though he always referred to it as his "throat condition" and unless one of those miracles that Douglas had obliquely referred to came along, he *was* going to die. *When* was the question, and he hoped, by lightning, to have something to say about that!

The persistent Samuel Clemens, even though he had spoken to Dr. Douglas and knew Grant's true condition, wanted the memoirs more than ever and finally won out. *Century* had refused to match the Webster contract terms, as had Scribner's—who had been represented by no less a negotiator than Andrew Carnegie.

Julia, by now, had finished working out arrangements with William Vanderbilt to forgive the $150,000 Grant had borrowed at the time of the Grant & Ward crash. Part of the deal was that she would leave in his custody the many fine and intriguing gifts the Grants had accrued on their world tour. Thus these valued items were safe from creditors and would be kept together to give to the people of the country following the demise of the general. No longer would the shadow of bankruptcy hang like a dark vulture over their house.

And Samuel Clemens's $10,000 advance on the book gave them some slack.

While Grant's health continued to fail, his financial status improved a little more. On the last day of the current session of Congress, March 4, a bill was passed that had been introduced by none other than former Confederate general and now congressman Joseph E. Johnston. Grant was placed on the army retired list as a full general to receive a pension. Clemens was present when the telegram arrived.

Grant read it and turned away, hiding his emotion.

Julia gaily kissed his cheek. "Isn't that wonderful, darling?"

"They finally realized they owe you something, General," Clemens added. "Damn fools. They could've done it long before this."

Grant turned back, swallowing hard and waiting for the pain to pass. "The fact that they did it is all that matters," he said. He smiled at Julia. "Now we can afford for you to go out and buy a fresh loaf of bread, dear."

A few days later, Badeau flared into an argument with Fred, whom he had been picking away at over meaningless items. And a couple of days after this, he had an argument with Julia. This was the last straw. Grant called him into the work parlor. "What's going on with you, Adam?" he asked sternly.

The portly man's red face flushed even brighter in anger. "If you're referring to my difficulties with your family, General," he replied huffily, "I don't think we need them meddling in the book. The writing is difficult enough, what with your not listening to me."

Grant raised an eyebrow. "I thought it was coming along quite well. Volume one is finished and Clemens likes it. What is it that I'm not listening to?"

"Everything. Everyone forgets that I'm the professional writer here."

Grant nodded, waiting for more. Finally he said, "Nellie is coming to visit in a couple of weeks. She'll need the bedroom you're using. Perhaps this is a good time for you to arrange for other lodgings."

"What does *that* mean?"

"Just what I said."

"Very well, I'll be out as soon as I make other arrangements."

Grant caught his sleeve. "Adam, try to be patient. There is a lot of pressure around here—what with my throat condition and the book."

Badeau scowled. "I know a dismissal when I hear it."

Grant shook his head. "It isn't that at all."

Badeau whirled and stomped out.

On March 26, Grant worked with the lawyers on a long and involved deposition for the trial of James Fish, the former president of the Marine

Bank and former partner in Grant & Ward. At the end of the long day, he felt exceedingly tired. By the 28th, another top specialist, Dr. George F. Shrady, had been called into the case. He agreed with Douglas and Barker that Grant was sinking fast. At this time a sanctimonious Methodist minister, one John Newman, had ingratiated himself with Julia and Grant's sister Mary. He now presented himself as the anointed savior of Grant's soul and insisted that he be baptized. For some reason, Hannah had failed to have this rite performed when Grant was young, and now Reverend Newman wanted to cash in on the publicity.

Quite weak and in a lot of pain, Grant posed no opposition.

Shortly after the ceremony, while Newman was praying loudly, Dr. Shrady injected brandy into Grant's bloodstream—a rather common practice.

Within hours, there was a decided turn for the better in Grant's condition. Reverend Newman told the press that it was positively due to his prayers and the baptism. Later, Dr. Shrady casually noted that he attributed the result to the brandy.

When Grant heard this, he shrugged and said, "That's the first time anyone ever said liquor did me some good."

The coughing and vomiting that had become prevalent began to diminish and Grant did become much better. One medical expert speculated that Grant had "bled into his tumor, killing many cancer cells—resulting in a shrinking of the mass on the soft palate." Dr. Douglas refused to comment on this novel assumption.

Grant was greatly pleased at the diminished pain and his improvement. The little corner of hope he had never lost now enlarged. He went back to work on the second volume of the memoirs with a new vigor. He received friends, dined with the family, went for drives. After a family conference, it was decided that the public deserved to know his day-to-day condition, so the doctors were authorized to issue bulletins to the wire services. But now his condition was less newsworthy.

On April 19, the New York *World* printed a column that Grant simply could not ignore. It stated, ". . . another false idea of Gen. Grant is given out by some of his friends, and that is that he is a writer. He is not a writer. He does not compose easily. Writing for him is a labor. The work upon his new book about which so much has been said is the work of Gen. Adam Badeau . . ."

Samuel Clemens exploded. "A libel suit should be instituted at once against those bastards!"

But Grant remained cool, writing a letter to Clemens's publishing company specifically for release to the press. In essence it stated simply, "The composition is entirely my own."

He didn't know whether it was a bad dream or what. But he sat up shaking in bed. He was sticky, but not hot. Actually, rather cold. And terribly unnerved. As frightened as he'd ever been in his life. He took several deep breaths, trying to relax, but nothing changed. *He was scared and he didn't know why!* It was all over him, like a black, inky blanket. He looked at his shaking hand in the dim light and stuck it under his armpit to make it still. Swinging his legs out of bed, he reached for his cane and got unsteadily to his feet. He looked around the room warily. *What was it?*

He could call Harrison, or Julia.

No, not yet. He had to figure it out.

The kerosene lamp was burning dimly. He turned it up, brightening the room. That should be better. But it wasn't. *Something was bearing down on him like a nightmare.* He could feel his heart beating like a tom-tom. He was finished, that was it! His hands were still shaking. Terrible fear. He wanted to crawl under the bed, cry out. Death was coming for sure. He grabbed his throat. The horrible cancer was enveloping him, crawling all over his throat and mouth, going down into his chest.

There was nothing left for him!

He had never known such apprehension, such disquiet. He looked at the bed. He could cover his head with a pillow. That was it—get back in bed and cover up, quit shaking.

In moments, he was under the pillow, but it didn't do any good. He blew out some deep breaths, over and over. And finally it started to lessen. He tried to think of something pleasant, but nothing seemed pleasant. The night he was elected, that was it! Going up the steps to the house in Galena to tell his beaming Julia that she was to be the president's lady!

Yes, what a fine moment!

Gradually the fear receded. He removed the pillow and sat up, then slowly got to his feet. He was glad he hadn't called her. How silly this, this *thing* had been . . . just a bad dream. Still, there had been no place to turn . . .

Maybe he needed some—what could he call it?

He wouldn't actually describe it as religious help. He wasn't that religious. He'd put up with that Newman thing, the baptism, to keep Julia happy. But it really hadn't been too meaningful to him. Maybe he could call it spiritual . . .

Yes, spiritual—getting closer to God.

But if he hadn't tried when he was well, how could he have the right now?

Maybe Eaton could help him.

"I'm sorry it took me so long to get here, sir," Reverend John Eaton said as he was ushered into Grant's working parlor. "I had to take care of some vital details and then I couldn't get a train until early this morning." The former manager of the "contrabands" had gone on from his job with the Freedman's Bureau to serving on the West Point board of visitors, then as U.S. commissioner of education. Now he was president of little Marietta

College in southern Ohio. The fifty-six-year-old former minister was balding, with a short gray beard and some heavy lines around his eyes—probably from too many years of caring about people, his host thought.

Grant shook his hand warmly and asked him to sit. "Can you stay a few days, General?" he asked.

"No, my wife is ill and I have to return tomorrow."

"Very well. I need to talk to you, as my wire stated."

He called Harrison, who took Eaton's bag, and told the valet that under no circumstances were they to be disturbed after he served the minister some tea.

They chatted for a few minutes, catching up, before Grant settled into the reason for the summons. "There's a good chance I may be dying," he said.

Eaton nodded. "I read about it."

Grant told him about the anxious time he'd experienced. The preacher listened carefully as his former boss gradually headed toward his bottom line. Finally, Grant asked, "Have you ever been overwhelmed, with no place to turn for help?"

Eaton's reply was soft. "Not since God came into my life."

Grant looked away, came back to his eyes. "But you are a minister. You're always close to God."

A smile touched the preacher's lips. "Not always. Sometimes we men of the cloth slip away. We get too involved in ourselves, too material, too vain. But that doesn't matter. We can always turn to Him in time of need." He paused a moment. "So can you. Everyone can."

Grant's gaze suddenly grew intense. "I don't think I've earned the right."

"You always have the right. It doesn't have to be earned. I can quote dozens of passages from the Scriptures that prove it. One from Psalms is, 'God is our refuge and strength, a very present help in trouble.' Another is, 'Call upon me in the day of trouble: I will deliver thee.' Neither one says you must *earn* the right to ask."

Grant frowned. "I wish I could believe that."

"You can. Try it. The next time you're faced with fear, ask God for help."

"I think I'd feel awkward about it."

"He doesn't care. Try it."

Grant nodded his head.

They talked on, until Grant suddenly grew weary. His voice was about gone for the day anyway. They agreed to talk some more before Eaton left for his train the next morning.

Later, in bed, Grant closed his eyes and prayed: "Father, this may be the first time I've ever really tried to reach You. I think all that went before was kind of going through the motions. Now, I want to try to be worthy of You, if You'll accept me. I was told You would. All I'm asking right now is that You give me the strength to withstand whatever it is that I must, and that you let me turn to You when I feel fearful. Also that You let me finish my book so that Julia will be taken care of when I pass on. Thank you, Father."

He felt some peace as he closed his eyes. If only he could believe Eaton . . .

Fortunately, his panic attack from a couple of nights earlier was the only one he ever experienced. And for this, among other things, he prayed his thanks to the Lord every day. But he never spoke of it, not even to Julia.

On April 27, his sixty-third birthday, Grant awoke to a big hug from Julia. Drawing open the bedroom drapes, she smiled and said, "The world wishes you a happy birthday, darling." Outside the sun was shining and a bird was singing on a budding branch. There was other noise. He hobbled to the window and was surprised to see that the street had been filled with flags and bunting. Hundreds of people were already filing past. Shaking his head, he said, "I never fail to wonder when they do something like this."

Julia put her arm around him. "They'll never quit loving you, Ulys."

Telegraph boys arrived all day long with birthday messages from around the country, and cards kept coming in by the basketful. Grant spent most of the day in the company of several friends. Hamilton Fish was there, and George Child from Philadelphia. Roscoe Conkling, the former senator who had turned down a Supreme Court appointment from President Arthur, dropped in—he had long since lived down the scandal of his love affair with Kate Chase Sprague a dozen years earlier. Others. Cump Sherman stayed after everyone else was gone. He refused to light up a cigar, but helped himself to the bottle of Napoleon brandy that Fish had brought. They were in Grant's work parlor. "Sure you won't have a glass?" Sherman asked.

"I suppose one won't hurt me," Grant replied. "Dr. Shrady injects it into me now and then. And it *is* my birthday, maybe the last one I'll ever have."

"Why are you talking like that?"

Grant shrugged as he poured a half glass. "You know I've always been pragmatic."

"But you're on the mend."

Grant sipped. "I still have a throat condition."

Sherman switched the subject. "I think your memoirs are going to be exceptional, possibly the most definitive account of the war."

"I want very much to finish them. I use yours, you know, to refresh my memory. They are very well-written."

Sherman grinned. "What is this, a mutual admiration meeting?" He had retired in February 1884 after the many years in the army's top job, and had been succeeded by Little Phil Sheridan. The Republicans had practically foamed at the mouth to have Sherman run for the presidency, but before the 1884 nomination could be forced on him, he had made the famous statement, "If nominated, I will not accept. If elected, I will not serve."

They talked on, naturally about the war, and Grant shared one more glass of brandy with his old friend. He wasn't even tempted to have a third. Finally Sherman said, "You know I live in St Louis again. The other day, knowing I was coming here to see you, I dropped by that saloon where we met all those years ago when you were hauling wood and I didn't know what the hell I was going to do. Uh-huh, it was still there and open. And I went inside and ordered a whiskey. The bartender looked at me funny when I held the glass up and said, 'To the best damned general the United States Army has ever known.' I downed the drink and headed for the door, filled with warm memories of you."

Grant patted his arm. "He probably thought you were talking about a man named Sherman."

A few minutes later, as Sherman walked down the front steps and turned to wave, Grant was struck by a sudden feeling that he would never see the loquacious redhead again.

He turned sadly, and quietly closed the door.

Adam Badeau entered the parlor with a grim look. Holding out an envelope, he said, "I was afraid Fred might intercept this and so I brought it myself."

Grant adjusted his reading eyeglasses. He read:

My Dear General,

For some time now I've been accepting copy from Fred or a stenographer instead of direct from you. This forces me to piece the fragments together. I see now that Mark Twain's subscriptions could well reach 300,000. Thus, my book will be stamped out—as will my proud reputation as your historian. As you become more ill and unable to complete the work, no one will be fit except myself to finish it. For this I want to be reimbursed by $1,000 per month and 10% of the entire profits.

Adam Badeau
Brig. Gen.

Grant looked up, feeling the flush rise in his cheeks. This was preposterous! He looked sternly in Badeau's eyes. At last he said, "I think, sir, that your demands are illogical."

"That is your prerogative, sir!" Badeau spat out. He turned and quickly left.

Three days later, Grant's cough was worse. And the pain intensified in his throat. But he simply reminded himself that it wouldn't deter him from his goal. Dipping a pen in the inkwell, he began a firm letter to Badeau. He didn't like having to write it, but the man had to be straightened out:

> *I'm sorry that you feel as you do about the Memoirs. I believe they will enhance your book, not supplant it. Relative to your finishing my book, you are over 100 pages behind me in editing now. Therefore I do not believe it would ever be done by you in case of my death while $1,000 per month was coming in. Besides, I believe your petulance and arrogance would create a rupture between you and my family that would be irreversible. Regarding the 10% of the profits, I find the idea preposterous.*
>
> *I do not want a book bearing my name to go before the world that is not fully entitled to the credit of my authorship. I may fail, but I will not put myself in any such position.*
>
> *Therefore, you and I must give up all association as far as the preparation of any literary work goes that is to bear my signature.*
>
> *Otherwise, I hope our normally pleasant and friendly relations will continue.*

He began to guard the working hours like jewels, sometimes dictating thousands of words a day. In one two-day period Grant dictated a full fifty-one pages of manuscript to his son, Fred. But his voice was about gone. The pain had reached the point where every word felt as if it had marched through a column of razor blades. He had to return to the more laborious method of writing by pencil. Sometimes he was simply too weak to do any work at all. Samuel Clemens visited often, cheering his favorite author on. Grant's regular physician, Dr. Barker, headed off to Europe again, but the general was left in the able hands of Dr. Douglas and Dr. Shrady. A swelling developed behind Grant's ear, but it subsided. He was also able to eat solid food off and on.

"The strange thing about this cancer," Dr. Shrady said, "is that the patient can be at death's door one minute, and looking well-recovered the next."

On the 26th of May a messenger summoned Clemens to 66th Street. Grant sat in silhouette by the window as the valet ushered him into the work parlor. The humorist waited a moment, then cleared his throat. Grant turned, murmuring in a raspy tone, "Thanks for coming." He pointed to an envelope. "There it is, the last of it. I finished last night."

"That's remarkable, General. I don't know how you did it."

"It's done, but it isn't done. I'm afraid it's about two hundred pages too long. I've got some more work to do on it."

Clemens shook his head. "At one time we were worried that it would be four hundred pages too short! You're truly remarkable, sir."

"We'll see."

"I've already told the press that I think your work will compare favorably to Caesar's *Commentaries,* particularly in its clarity, directness, simplicity, manifest truthfulness, its fairness to friend and foe alike, frankness and soldierly avoidance of flowery speech."

438

Grant found a smile. "That's quite a mouthful."

"Aren't you proud?"

"Somewhat. But there are still many plums and spices to be added. I'd prefer that you wait on the typesetting of the second volume until I finish them."

"We can do that. We'll get the prospectus, with extensive quotations, out shortly. Our canvassers will spread them around the country and overseas. Our target for publication of volume one is December first." Clemens grinned. "We're going to sell a *hell* of a lot of books, General!"

Grant nodded again. Yes, he was proud of getting it done. Now he had to stay well enough to polish it off.

CHAPTER 77

Yes, I want to move General Grant out of the sticky heat of New York City for the summer," Dr. Douglas replied.

"As you know," Joseph Drexel said, "Mount McGregor is being developed as a summer and fall vacation resort. A handsome new hotel, the Balmoral, is being constructed there, and lots for nice cottages are being sold."

"I've been told the air is keen and bracing there."

"Yes, it's at an altitude of about fifteen hundred feet."

Douglas nodded. "That mountain air might be just the ticket for him."

"I have recently purchased the old McGregor Hotel and had it moved to an excellent site. It's to be my cottage. It's in Queen Anne style, two stories with about a dozen rooms. A wide veranda surrounds three sides. It isn't luxurious, but quite comfortable. The general could use a pleasant downstairs corner bedroom and wouldn't have to climb stairs. To ensure coolness, all meals would be cooked in the Balmoral and carried to the cottage. There's plenty of room for the general's family and staff. Any overflow can stay at the hotel at my cost."

Dr. Douglas nodded his head. "It sounds perfect."

Joseph W. Drexel did not know Grant as well as his brother Anthony did. Anthony had a cottage on the Long Branch shore that was quite close to the Grants' former summer residence, and he was also an acquaintance of George Childs, Grant's publisher friend. After the Civil War, Joseph Drexel, of the prosperous Philadelphia banking family, had moved his business to New York. There he had formed a partnership with J. Pierpont Morgan. Although still president of the New York banking firm, he was now dedicating most of his time to philanthropic pursuits. One of his interests was the New York Cancer Hospital, of which he was treasurer. Having heard of Dr. Douglas's need for a cool place for Grant to stay, he had readily made his offer. "General Grant may have the premises at any time, Doctor."

Douglas nodded. "I'm sure he'll be most appreciative."

"How is he, Doctor—or is it out of order for me to ask?"

"He's suffering, Mr. Drexel. He doesn't complain, but that nasty fall he took a while back is bothering him. He has neuralgia, and of course his cancer would render a lesser man incapacitated. The pain is intense. But he still works on that book of his. Mostly, he can barely whisper, so he writes away with pencil and tablet."

"Do you think he'll get it finished?"

Douglas shook his head. "I don't know how he's lasted this long."

"Heroic, isn't it?"

"His greatest hour, I believe."

At first, Dr. Douglas had thought the June air too chilly for Grant atop Mount McGregor, but the miserable heat of the city prompted him to expedite the move. William Vanderbilt provided the train—a locomotive, an extra car for the press, and his luxurious private car. Grant's private entourage included Julia, Nellie, Fred and his wife Ida, Dr. Douglas, Grant's nurse Henry McQueeney, Harrison Tyrell, his valet, and Julia's maid.

As the train chugged out of Grand Central Station on the morning of June 16, Grant looked out the window. Only a few of the hurrying faces looked up for a moment in brief curiosity; most were caught up in their own world. Would this be the last time he'd experience a departure from this huge, teeming city? He'd asked himself the same question when he looked back at the house on 66th Street. He'd agonized a great deal in that structure, but it had held some pleasurable moments as well. He'd found he could write there, a great value in itself.

He'd looked out of a lot of train windows, he thought. Done a lot of thinking doing so. It was impossible, in his condition, not to think that an experience of any kind might be his last. There was no way around it . . . his last time writing at the table in his parlor, the last time he might see this or that person, thing, or place. One just *thought* that way when cancer was the uninvited guest. Or invader. That was a better word for a soldier to use when talking about an enemy. And this was the most formidable enemy he'd ever encountered. He felt the way Lee must have felt in the last days before Appomattox. There was a *chance* he could win out, but a very slim out. Yes, he still believed he might beat it—with that intangible of Douglas's. But he was really drawing to that inside straight flush now.

Still—

The afternoon sunshine flooded through the window, causing him to blink as he reached up to feel the growth on his neck. He could still talk with difficulty part of the time, but swallowing anything that wasn't soft was now out of the question. Douglas had said the ulceration on the back of the throat and the side of his tongue was active, caused most probably by the heat.

He was much thinner, and had trouble moving his bowels—the result of the morphine on his colon, Dr. Shrady said. His face was drawn, a bit haggard.

But he was a long way from giving up.

Still had all that work to do on the second volume.

"There it is, darling!"

Grant jerked his head up at Julia's words. "What?"

She pointed, smiling, at the window. "Your favorite school."

He turned. There, in its tall green trees, the United States Military Academy looked back at him from its heights. He felt a stirring as he looked at the tops of the buildings. Mid-June—the Animals of the new class would be reporting in about now, not aware of how their world was going to turn upside down. He remembered how small he'd been, not wanting to be there, and having two left feet . . . an awkward new name . . . a big bully pushing him in ranks, and socking the fellow . . . roasting turkey in the room . . . sweating out demerits . . . a big, powerful horse named York . . . the flag coming down at Retreat.

He could hear the bugle calls now.

Julia squeezed his hand. "Memories?"

He nodded his head.

Good memories.

A sick old man didn't have any other kind.

They arrived at Saratoga Springs shortly before two o'clock. He got down from Vanderbilt's plush car and made it with his cane to the nearby special car on the Mount McGregor narrow-gauge track. A rousing cheer went up from the assembled crowd that included a large contingent of Grand Army of the Republic veterans in some semblance of uniform. There had been cheers from well-wishers at each station stop on the way up, but this one was the most meaningful to him. After making it up the steps of the car, he turned, smiled, and tipped his silk top hat. Now, that's a tonic! he told himself.

Joseph Drexel and some more newspapermen greeted him warmly. As soon as everyone was seated, the little engine began its troublesome climb up the curving, steep rails in a smoke-belching, side-to-side pitching adventure that finally dragged its cargo into the mountaintop platform that served as its home station.

This time when Grant laboriously climbed down, a grizzled man with a bushy gray mustache, wearing a fresh blue uniform with sergeant major's stripes, stepped forward and saluted. "Sir, they was gonna have some fella from the Albany G.A.R. guard you, but I told them they wasn't no one doin' it but me. I'm gonna be guarding your door as long as you're in our mountains." It was the retired old dragoon, Bolding.

Grant nodded, returning the salute with his cane, smiling and whispering, "Thank you, Sergeant Major."

Soon after beginning the short trip up the hill, Drexel pointed to a house that had been freshly painted in gold with brown trim. It had a wide porch and was set in a green collage of richly foliaged maples, oaks, and pines. "It's rather modest," its owner said.

"It'll do just fine," Grant replied.

Grant's bedroom contained a mahogany suite and several pieces of wickerwork furniture. But the bed would be of little use, since he had been sleeping in a sitting position on two facing leather chairs for some time now. He coughed less that way. An adjoining room was Julia's bedroom; another was for his nurse and valet. Dr. Douglas, who had elected to be with Grant during his stay on Mount McGregor, would occupy two of the upstairs rooms with his family. Nellie would have another, and Fred and Ida still another. Bolding had pitched a tent out back.

Grant had Harrison Tyrell, whom he called by his first name, help dress him after freshening up. Then it was back out to the porch to sit and enjoy the air. There was something about being the object of so much public attention again that was heady, even invigorating. The trip had tired him, but he felt better than usual. He decided to just sit here and take in the natural beauty as he waved to the large numbers of well-wishers who began to arrive.

When Julia came out to hold his hand, he smiled and said, "Sure is good to be back in the human race."

She kissed his cheek. "I think seeing how much the people care for you is as good an elixir as this clean air, darling."

He nodded as he tipped his hat to a group of young ladies who cheered him from the bottom of the front steps. "Maybe."

One thing was certain; it was better to be out here tipping his hat than hidden away as a pathetic patient in some dark room.

Far better.

Wrapped up in a muffler and often an overcoat, and wearing his traditional silk top hat, Grant continued to enjoy his daily piazza sojourns. And the public kept flocking to the Mount McGregor cottage, where Bolding stood guard at the steps. But the attention and the crisp air could be only so much of a tonic; Grant's condition worsened, although he still had a few good hours on occasional days—that was when he worked. Once, on a particularly warm day, he came outside to his now usual corner of the porch to work on the galley proofs. When one particularly persistent photographer caught his attention, he allowed the man to come up and take his picture.

It was just a few minutes later that a voice from the past said to Bolding, "Tell the general that General Simon Bolivar Buckner would like a few words with him."

When the guard relayed the message, Grant put down his pencil and tablet, adjusted his eyeglasses and peered down to the bottom of the steps. "Is that really you, Buckner?" he said in his loudest whisper.

The well-dressed man nodded back.

Grant managed to get to his feet with help from Harrison and walked stiffly forward. "Come here, sir."

Buckner was quickly up the steps and warmly shaking his onetime friend's hand. "I hear you're loafing up here in the hills," he said gruffly, putting his other hand on Grant's arm.

Grant nodded, whispering, "Beats working." He looked into his visitor's eyes. At sixty-two, Buckner cut an impressive figure. After spending some time in New Orleans following the war, he had reclaimed valuable real estate holdings in Chicago that he had wisely put in his Yankee brother-in-law's name—and eventually sold them for a fortune. Following a stint as editor of the Louisville *Courier,* he had devoted his time to business interests there.

"I started to send a wire, but I wanted to surprise you."

"I don't get many surprises these days."

The catch-up pleasantries continued as Grant went back to his chair and Harrison pulled up a seat for Buckner. When Grant asked him about his entry into politics, the Kentuckian replied, "This is not for publication, but I may run for governor in the next election."

"As a Democrat, I assume."

"Naturally."

Grant scribbled "Pity," and smiled.

Quietly Buckner switched the subject. "I don't wish to offend you, Sam, but I would be more than happy to help you out financially, if you have any need."

Grant patted his hand, replying, "Again? No, but a thousand thanks."

At length, Dr. Douglas came out and, after meeting the former Confederate general, said, "General Grant, I don't want you to overdo it now."

Grant wrote on his pad, "I won't. Need some privacy now."

The doctor said, "All right," and went back inside.

After a few moments, Grant wrote, "I've long felt badly about Donelson."

Buckner again touched his arm. "So have I."

"Perhaps I was hasty."

"No, Sam, I was the one who was hasty. And boorish."

"It seemed the only way at the time."

"In retrospect, I'd have demanded unconditional surrender myself."

They looked into each other's eyes and both nodded. Once more, they shook hands. At the top of the steps, Buckner turned and slowly raised his hand in a proper salute.

As the July days mounted, Grant continued to plug away at his revisions. When Samuel Clemens insisted that the work was ready, Grant said, "There are still anecdotes that might hurt someone."

"But you can't keep working like this. Dr. Douglas is already threatening to bar me from the cottage."

"I'm almost finished."

The next day Fred brought in the dedication page, which read, *These volumes are dedicated to the American soldier and sailor.* "Father," he said, "I want to talk to you about this dedication. I think it should read to the *Union* soldier and sailor. That's who you led to victory. They are the ones who fought for you."

Grant shook his head and scribbled on his tablet, "No. This work is for those we fought against as well as those we fought with."

As if on cue, a messenger from the Boston *Globe* brought a very special letter to the cottage that afternoon. Grant adjusted his eyeglasses and read it slowly:

> *Dear Sir—Your request in behalf of a Boston journalist for me to prepare a criticism of General Grant's military career cannot be complied with for the following reasons:*
>
> *1. General Grant is dying.*
>
> *2. Though he invaded our country, it was with an open hand, and, as far as I know, he abetted neither arson nor pillage, and has since the war, I believe, showed no malignity to Confederates either of the military or civil service.*
>
> *Therefore, instead of seeking to disturb the quiet of his closing hours, I would, if it were within my power, contribute to the peace of his mind and the comfort of his body.*
>
> *Jefferson Davis*

It hurt to swallow, but seeing such warm words from the former president of the Confederacy moved him considerably. Once more, he wished he could have been more effective in the settlement of the South in that first decade after the war. At least some of its leaders knew he'd tried.

Cocaine and morphine, with intermittent brandy injections, were his constant companions. Plenty of each were his only means of coping with the pain now. He dozed often, and was usually awake most of the night. On one of his good days a letter arrived late in the afternoon from John Eaton:

> *I read that your days may be limited, sir, and I wish to bring some ease to your possible trepidation. It isn't my ease, but God's, and it comes from Psalms again. You know about the 23rd. But read the first 18 verses of the 139th. It is about how the Lord knows you, how He made you, and how no matter where you go, He is with you. And then read the 27th, 4th verse, which says, 'One thing have I asked of the Lord, that will I seek after; that I may dwell in the house of the Lord all the days of my*

life . . .' Sir, if you believe in a life hereafter, it means that you will be
with Him forever, that your life will extend forever. Therefore, you are
merely preparing to go on a new and great adventure.

Grant had Harrison bring him the Bible and asked him to locate the 139th
Psalm, then leave the room. He adjusted his round, black-rimmed spectacles
and began to read. Eaton was right, the verses did give him comfort. He
read them again and nodded his head. God must have made him and was
with him, had always been. So why wouldn't He be now, and in what lay
ahead? Made sense.

He leafed back to the 27th Psalm. Yes, if there was life after death—
and he didn't know that there wasn't—he might be with the Lord "all the
days of my life." It, too, made sense and was comforting.

". . . preparing to go on a new and great adventure?"

It was possible.

At least that was one way to look at it.

What was the hinge for all of this? He'd often been able to cut through
the haze and see the bottom line . . .

Wasn't it a matter of belief?

If he truly believed in God, then this was all possible.

He was merely leaving this body behind.

If he believed.

That night at bedtime Grant read and reread the Psalms, including David's
encouraging 23rd. He glanced at a warm note from Rufe Ingalls and drifted
back to a pier at Fort Vancouver, Washington, in 1852. "No, I don't drink
anymore," he was telling his former roommate. What a bad time that West
Coast assignment had been for him. His failure and the waste on whiskey,
the drunken spree in San Francisco, that horrible day at the pay table at
Fort Humboldt. Buchanan confining him to quarters . . . Old Buck had
fought in several of the early battles of the war and had been promoted to
brigadier in late '62, only to lose his star because of some factionalism that
caused the Senate to deny his confirmation. Did well in Reconstruction.
He wondered what Old Buck must have thought about serving in an army
commanded by General in Chief Grant.

There was a recent letter from Senator Black Jack Logan, who had lost
his bid for the vice presidency in the previous year's election. Another from
Little Phil Sheridan, now getting white-haired and fat as general of the army.
One from that worthless Butler, now governor of Massachusetts. There
was even an encouraging note from Lew Wallace, his tardy division commander at Shiloh, who had written his big novel *Ben Hur* while he was
governor of New Mexico.

He thought some more about those two terrible days at Shiloh, and
the bleakness of the months to come . . . uncomfortable days under Halleck,
when he thought of quitting. Old Brains had died in '72. Let history write

the man's epitaph. Another early nemesis, Frémont, had recently gone out of office as governor of Arizona, but had been convicted for railroad fraud in absentia by the French.

There was a card from Oliver Otis Howard. The religious general who had left his superintendency of West Point to command the Department of the Platte wrote, "God is there for you, sir. Only believe."

Bolding had quietly handed him a note the day before that read, "If you want me to watch over you in the Great Beyond, Genrl, my rifle is loaded."

He picked up a note from Pete Longstreet and glanced at it. His old friend had been president of an insurance company in New Orleans. A Republican, he then had served as minister to Turkey, and had attained some Southern disfavor after the war—something to do with being the cause of the rebel defeat at Gettysburg and criticism of Lee. Thinking of Old Pete brought back memories of a St. Louis wedding on a rainy night . . . with his lovely Julia all dressed in white, coming radiantly down the candlelit staircase.

He thought of General Tom Hamer, buried all these years in Mexico—how had he faced *his* death? Quite well, he would imagine . . .

A warm note from General Joe Johnston brought on some recollection of other rebel leaders in the war . . . The Little Frenchman, Beauregard, had been a railroad president and was now running some kind of a state lottery in Louisiana. The contentious Braxton Bragg had been state engineer for Alabama, but had died in Texas in '76. Pemberton, the loser at Vicksburg, had gone back to farming in Virginia, and had died in '81 in Pennsylvania. John Bell Hood had fathered eleven children and had died suddenly of yellow fever—imagine a fiery one-legged, one-armed leader who could be strapped into a saddle to fight . . . imagine him being felled in such a manner!

He picked up the letter from a rebel soldier he'd never met. Fellow named Arnold from a place called Rockbridge Baths, Virginia: "Dear General, I have watched your movements from the hour you gave me my horse and sword and told me to go home and 'assist in making a crop.' And now, dear Genl in this hour of your tribulation I weep that so brave, so magnanimous a soul must suffer as you do . . . May the God who overlooked you in battle and who has brought you this far give you the grace to meet whatever He has in store for you. And may He restore you to health & friends is the fervent prayer of one who at 15 years of age entered the lists against you and accepted the magnanimous terms you accorded us at Appomattox."

He wiped the moistness from his eyes.

Enough reminiscing. He could dwell on the good times with Cump Sherman all night. And Rawlins. His swearer. If there was a heaven and John Rawlins hadn't profaned his way out of it by now, he was surely there.

If there was a heaven, or some place in which to go on—maybe the cavalry's Fiddler's Green—and *if* he were to arrive there, he might even run into Rawlins. As good a friend as any man might have. He had even broken faith with the man about his drinking, and had been forgiven without a word.

What if there had been no Rawlins?

He sighed.

After a couple of minutes, he reached for his pad and pencil and wrote:

Dear Dr. Douglas: Thanks to you and whatever Power there may be, I have been given the time I wanted to work on my book so the authorship will be clearly mine. I worked hastily on the first part, but I did it all over again from the crossing of the Rapidan in June of '64 to Appomattox. And since then I have added 50 pages. There is nothing more I should do to it now, and therefore I am not likely to be more ready to go than at this moment.

He then turned to the last pages he had corrected. Yes, he had done it. Oh, he could keep changing them, but they were done. Fred could read the page proofs of the second volume when they were ready. The book might not bring in all the money Clemens was predicting, but there would be enough for Julia to live comfortably.

It was done.

Three nights later, Grant was quite weak. Alone in his room at shortly after midnight, he was wide awake in spite of the brandy and morphine injections. Fred had brought a bed down from the hotel and had talked him into forgoing the leather chairs. The pain had subsided for a while, and he knew he could do it. He'd hidden the cigar in the back of the drawer in the writing table. It would be a little stale, and he could never smoke it in the old way, but he was doggone sure going to have one final taste. He managed to swing his feet over the side of the bed and get shakily to his feet. Three steps would do it, then he could rest and make the three steps back.

There it was, waiting. His final cigar. He bit off the end and put it in his mouth. The match struck on the first scratch, and the flame was in front of his face. The cigar, a simple but clear memory of many battles. How many thousand artillery shells had exploded while he had a cigar in his mouth?

He drew in, held the smoke in his mouth for several moments, then blew it out. Tasted bitter and made him want to cough, but it was worth it. Just doing it was worth it. He looked at it, watching a little stream of smoke swirl upward. He'd had a lot of failures with a cigar in his mouth, particularly those in the White House and on Wall Street, but he'd also had several without one.

But he'd somehow stayed alive to finish the book.

Now, maybe he could put his demons to rest.

He'd done as well as he could.

Would history understand that?

He hoped so.

There wasn't any more he could do.

He dropped the cigar in a water glass, heard the hiss, and started to lie back. But the door opened. "Are you awake, Ulys?" Julia asked softly.

He whispered, "Yes."

"May I come in?"

She came to the bed and stopped. "Is that cigar smoke I smell?" she asked.

He shook his head, but smiled.

She gently put her arm around him and held his head to her breast. "That's all right. What have you been doing?"

"Purging my last ghosts."

"Are you comfortable? Can I get you another pillow?"

He shook his head again and put his arms around her. With all his feeble strength, he held her tight. It was another pretty summer day at White Haven and they were young and in love. They were racing along on their horses beside the bubbling stream. The trees were full and green, the bushes bright with blossoms. Only a few soft clouds dotted the warm, blue sky. She was ahead and turned to smile at him. "C'mon, laggard!" she shouted over her shoulder.

He grinned and touched the spurs to his horse's flanks.

They had a long ride ahead.

Even so did Ulysses cover himself up with leaves, and Minerva shed a sweet sleep upon his eyes, closed his eyelids, and made him lose all memory of his sorrows.

—HOMER, THE ODYSSEY